Cold War Europe

0 Miles 100 200 300

0 Kilometers 200 300

SWEDEN

Baltic
Sea

Moscow ★

20°E

Elbe R.

Berlin ★

EAST
ERMANY

POLAND

UNION OF
SOVIET SOCIALIST
REPUBLICS

50°N

Nuremberg

CZECHOSLOVAKIA

Carpathian Mountains

Munich

Danube R.

Vienna ★

HUNGARY

Alps AUSTRIA

Börzsöny Mtns.

★Budapest

TRANSYLVANIA

Sighişoara

Lake Bled

Julian Alps

Ljubljana

SLOVENIA

Zagreb

ROMANIA

Danube R.

Ploieşti

Venice

BOSNIA AND
HERCEGOVINA

CROATIA

Belgrade ★

Târgovişte

Lake Snagov

Arges R.

Bucharest ★

Black Sea

orence

Sarajevo

SERBIA

WALLACHIA

Danube R.

BULGARIA

Montepulciano

Split

YUGOSLAVIA

Sofia
★

Balkan Mountains

Assisi

UMBRIA

MONTENEGRO

Dubrovnik

Plovdiv

Rila

Haskovo

Bosphorus

ome ★

Adriatic Sea

ALBANIA

MACEDONIA

Rila Mtns.

Bachkovo

Chepelarska R.

Edirne

Rhodope Mtns.

Istanbul
(Constantinople)

ITALY

Naples

Sea of Marmara

40°N

yrrhenian
Sea

GREECE

TURKEY

Aegean Sea

SICILY

Athens ★

Mediterranean Sea

CRETE

Knossos

20°E

30°E

The
Historian

A Novel

Elizabeth Kostova

LITTLE, BROWN AND COMPANY

LARGE PRINT

Little, Brown and Company
Time Warner Book Group
1271 Avenue of the Americas, New York, NY 10020
Visit our Web site at www.twbookmark.com

First Large Print Edition: June 2005

The Large Print Edition published in accord with the standards of the N.A.V.H.

Library of Congress Cataloging-in-Publication Data
Kostova, Elizabeth.
    The historian : a novel / Elizabeth Kostova. — 1st ed.
        p.   cm.
    ISBN 0-316-01177-0 / ISBN 0-316-05886-6 (large print)
    1. Vampires — Fiction.   I. Title.

PS3611.O74927H57 2005
813'.6 — dc22   2004022563

10 9 8 7 6 5 4 3 2 1

Q-FF

Printed in the United States of America

For my father,
who first told me
some of these stories

A Note to the Reader

THE STORY THAT FOLLOWS is one I never intended to commit to paper. Recently, however, a shock of sorts has prompted me to look back over the most troubling episodes of my life and of the lives of the several people I loved best. This is the story of how as a girl of sixteen I went in search of my father and his past, and of how he went in search of his beloved mentor and his mentor's own history, and of how we all found ourselves on one of the darkest pathways into history. It is the story of who survived that search and who did not, and why. As a historian, I have learned that, in fact, not everyone who reaches back into history can survive it. And it is not only reaching back that endangers us; sometimes history itself reaches inexorably forward for us with its shadowy claw.

In the thirty-six years since these events transpired, my life has been relatively quiet. I have devoted my time to research and uneventful travel, to my students and friends, to the writing of books of a historical and mainly impersonal nature, and to the affairs of the university in which I have ultimately taken shelter. In reviewing the past, I've been fortunate in having access to most of the personal documents in question, because they have been in my possession for many years. Where I felt it appropriate, I've stitched them together to make a continuous narrative, which I have occasionally had to supplement from my own reminiscences. Although I have presented my father's first stories to me as they were told aloud, I've also drawn heavily on his letters, some of which duplicated his oral accounts.

In addition to reproducing these sources almost in their entirety, I've tried every possible avenue of recollection and research, sometimes revisiting a place in order to brighten the faded areas of my memory. One of the greatest pleasures of this undertaking has been the interviews — in some cases, the correspondences — I have conducted with the few remaining scholars who were involved in the events related here. Their memories have provided an invaluable supplement to my other sources. My text has also benefited from consultations with younger scholars in several fields.

A Note to the Reader

There is a final resource to which I've resorted when necessary — the imagination. I have done this with judicious care, imagining for my reader only what I already know is very likely, and even then only when an informed speculation can set these documents into their proper context. Where I have been unable to explain events or motives, I have left them unexplained, out of respect for their hidden realities. The more distant history within this story I have researched as carefully as I would any academic text. The glimpses of religious and territorial conflict between an Islamic East and a Judeo-Christian West will be painfully familiar to a modern reader.

It would be difficult for me to adequately thank all those who have helped me with this project, but I would like to name at least a few. My profound gratitude goes to the following, among many others: Dr. Radu Georgescu of the University of Bucharest's Archaeological Museum, Dr. Ivanka Lazarova of the Bulgarian Academy of Sciences, Dr. Petar Stoichev of the University of Michigan, the tireless staff of the British Library, the librarians at the Rutherford Literary Museum and Library of Philadelphia, Fa-

A Note to the Reader

ther Vasil of Zographou Monastery on Mount Athos, and Dr. Turgut Bora of Istanbul University.

My great hope in making this story public is that it may find at least one reader who will understand it for what it actually is: a cri de coeur. To you, perceptive reader, I bequeath my history.

Oxford, England
January 15, 2008

Part One

How these papers have been placed in sequence will be made manifest in the reading of them. All needless matters have been eliminated, so that a history almost at variance with the possibilities of later-day belief may stand forth as simple fact. There is throughout no statement of past things wherein memory may err, for all the records chosen are exactly contemporary, given from the stand-points and within the range of knowledge of those who made them.

— Bram Stoker, *Dracula,* 1897

Chapter 1

IN 1972 I WAS SIXTEEN — young, my father said, to be traveling with him on his diplomatic missions. He preferred to know that I was sitting attentively in class at the International School of Amsterdam; in those days his foundation was based in Amsterdam, and it had been my home for so long that I had nearly forgotten our early life in the United States. It seems peculiar to me now that I should have been so obedient well into my teens, while the rest of my generation was experimenting with drugs and protesting the imperialist war in Vietnam, but I had been raised in a world so sheltered that it makes my adult life in academia look positively adventurous. To begin with, I was motherless, and the care that my father took of me had been deepened by a double sense of responsibility, so that he protected me more completely than he might have otherwise. My mother had died when I was a baby, before my father founded the Center for Peace and Democracy. My father never spoke of her and turned quietly away if I asked questions;

3

I understood very young that this was a topic too painful for him to discuss. Instead, he took excellent care of me himself and provided me with a series of governesses and housekeepers — money was not an object with him where my upbringing was concerned, although we lived simply enough from day to day.

The latest of these housekeepers was Mrs. Clay, who took care of our narrow seventeenth-century town house on the Raamgracht, a canal in the heart of the old city. Mrs. Clay let me in after school every day and was a surrogate parent when my father traveled, which was often. She was English, older than my mother would have been, skilled with a feather duster and clumsy with teenagers; sometimes, looking at her too-compassionate, long-toothed face over the dining table, I felt she must be thinking of my mother and I hated her for it. When my father was away, the handsome house echoed. No one could help me with my algebra, no one admired my new coat or told me to come here and give him a hug, or expressed shock over how tall I had grown. When my father returned from some name on the European map that hung on the wall in our dining room, he smelled like other

4

times and places, spicy and tired. We took our vacations in Paris or Rome, diligently studying the landmarks my father thought I should see, but I longed for those other places he disappeared to, those strange old places I had never been.

While he was gone, I went back and forth to school, dropping my books on the polished hall table with a bang. Neither Mrs. Clay nor my father let me go out in the evenings, except to the occasional carefully approved movie with carefully approved friends, and — to my retrospective astonishment — I never flouted these rules. I preferred solitude anyway; it was the medium in which I had been raised, in which I swam comfortably. I excelled at my studies but not in my social life. Girls my age terrified me, especially the tough-talking, chain-smoking sophisticates of our diplomatic circle — around them I always felt that my dress was too long, or too short, or that I should have been wearing something else entirely. Boys mystified me, although I dreamed vaguely of men. In fact, I was happiest alone in my father's library, a large, fine room on the first floor of our house.

My father's library had probably once been a

sitting room, but he sat down only to read, and he considered a large library more important than a large living room. He had long since given me free run of his collection. During his absences, I spent hours doing my homework at the mahogany desk or browsing the shelves that lined every wall. I understood later that my father had either half forgotten what was on one of the top shelves or — more likely — assumed I would never be able to reach it; late one night I took down not only a translation of the *Kama Sutra* but also a much older volume and an envelope of yellowing papers.

I can't say even now what made me pull them down. But the image I saw at the center of the book, the smell of age that rose from it, and my discovery that the papers were personal letters all caught my attention forcibly. I knew I shouldn't examine my father's private papers, or anyone's, and I was also afraid that Mrs. Clay might suddenly come in to dust the dustless desk — that must have been what made me look over my shoulder at the door. But I couldn't help reading the first paragraph of the topmost letter, holding it for a couple of minutes as I stood near the shelves.

The Historian

December 12, 1930
Trinity College, Oxford

My dear and unfortunate successor:

It is with regret that I imagine you, whoever you are, reading the account I must put down here. The regret is partly for myself — because I will surely be at least in trouble, maybe dead, or perhaps worse, if this is in your hands. But my regret is also for you, my yet-unknown friend, because only by someone who needs such vile information will this letter someday be read. If you are not my successor in some other sense, you will soon be my heir — and I feel sorrow at bequeathing to another human being my own, perhaps unbelievable, experience of evil. Why I myself inherited it I don't know, but I hope to discover that fact, eventually — perhaps in the course of writing to you or perhaps in the course of further events.

At this point, my sense of guilt — and something else, too — made me put the letter hastily back in its envelope, but I thought about it all that day and all the next. When my father returned from his latest trip, I looked for an opportunity to ask him about the letters and the strange book. I waited for him to be free, for us

7

to be alone, but he was very busy in those days, and something about what I had found made me hesitate to approach him. Finally I asked him to take me on his next trip. It was the first time I had kept a secret from him and the first time I had ever insisted on anything.

Reluctantly, my father agreed. He talked with my teachers and with Mrs. Clay, and reminded me that there would be ample time for my homework while he was in meetings. I wasn't surprised; for a diplomat's child there was always waiting to be done. I packed my navy suitcase, taking my schoolbooks and too many pairs of clean kneesocks. Instead of leaving the house for school that morning, I departed with my father, walking silently and gladly beside him toward the station. A train carried us to Vienna; my father hated planes, which he said took the travel out of traveling. There we spent one short night in a hotel. Another train took us through the Alps, past all the white-and-blue heights of our map at home. Outside a dusty yellow station, my father started up our rented car, and I held my breath until we turned in at the gates of a city he had described to me so many times that I could already see it in my dreams.

Autumn comes early to the foot of the Slovenian Alps. Even before September, the abundant harvests are followed by a sudden, poignant rain that lasts for days and brings down leaves in the lanes of the villages. Now, in my fifties, I find myself wandering that direction every few years, reliving my first glimpse of the Slovenian countryside. This is old country. Every autumn mellows it a little more, *in aeternum*, each beginning with the same three colors: a green landscape, two or three yellow leaves falling through a gray afternoon. I suppose the Romans — who left their walls here and their gargantuan arenas to the west, on the coast — saw the same autumn and gave the same shiver. When my father's car swung through the gates of the oldest of Julian cities, I hugged myself. For the first time, I had been struck by the excitement of the traveler who looks history in her subtle face.

Because this city is where my story starts, I'll call it Emona, its Roman name, to shield it a little from the sort of tourist who follows doom around with a guidebook. Emona was built on Bronze Age pilings along a river now lined with art-nouveau architecture. During the next day or two, we would walk past the mayor's mansion, past seventeenth-century town houses trimmed with silver fleurs-de-lis, past the solid golden back of a great market building, its steps leading down to the surface of the water from heavily barred old doors. For centuries, river cargo had been hoisted up at that place to feed the town. And where primitive huts had once proliferated on the shore, sycamores — the European plane tree — now grew to an immense girth above the river walls and dropped curls of bark into the current.

Near the market, the city's main square spread out under the heavy sky. Emona, like her sisters to the south, showed flourishes of a chameleon past: Viennese Deco along the skyline, great red churches from the Renaissance of its Slavic-speaking Catholics, hunched brown medieval chapels with the British Isles in their features. (Saint Patrick sent missionaries to this region, bringing the new creed full circle, back to its Mediterranean origins, so that the city claims one of the oldest Christian histories in Europe.) Here and there an Ottoman element flared in doorways or in a pointed window frame. Next to the market grounds, one little Austrian church sounded its bells for the evening mass. Men and women in blue cotton work coats were moving toward home at the end of the socialist workday, holding umbrellas over their packages. As my father and I drove into the heart of Emona, we crossed the river on a fine old bridge, guarded at each end by green-skinned bronze dragons.

"There's the castle," my father said, slowing at the edge of the square and pointing up through a wash of rain. "I know you'll want to see that."

I did want to. I stretched and craned until I caught sight of the castle through sodden tree branches — moth-eaten brown towers on a steep hill at the town's center.

"Fourteenth century," my father mused. "Or thirteenth? I'm not good with these medieval ruins, not down to the exact century. But we'll look in the guidebook."

"Can we walk up there and explore it?"

"We can find out about it after my meetings tomorrow. Those towers don't look as if they'd hold a bird up safely, but you never know."

He pulled the car into a parking space near the town hall and helped me out of the passenger side, gallantly, his hand bony in its leather glove. "It's a little early to check in at the hotel. Would you like some hot tea? Or we could get a snack at that *gastronomia*. It's raining harder," he added doubtfully, looking at my wool jacket and skirt. I quickly got out the hooded water-proof cape he'd brought me from England the year before. The train trip from Vienna had taken nearly a day and I was hungry again, in spite of our lunch in the dining car.

But it was not the *gastronomia,* with its red and blue interior lights gleaming through one dingy window, its waitresses in their navy plat-form sandals — doubtless — and its sullen picture of Comrade Tito, that snared us. As we picked our way through the wet crowd, my father suddenly darted forward. "Here!" I followed at a run, my hood flapping, almost blinding me. He had found the entrance to an art-nouveau teahouse, a great scrolled window with storks wading across it, bronze doors in the form of a hundred water-lily stems. The doors closed heavily be-hind us and the rain faded to a mist, mere steam on the windows, seen through those silver birds as a blur of water. "Amazing this survived the last thirty years." My father was peeling off his London Fog. "Socialism's not always so kind to its treasures."

At a table near the window we drank tea with lemon, scalding through the thick cups, and ate our way through sardines on buttered white bread and even a few slices of *torta.* "We'd better stop there," my father said. I had lately come to dislike the way he blew on his tea over and over to cool it, and to dread the inevitable moment when he said we should stop eating, stop doing whatever was enjoyable, save room for dinner. Looking at him in his neat tweed jacket and turtleneck, I felt he had denied himself every adventure in life except diplomacy, which consumed him. He would have been happier living a little, I thought; with him, everything was so serious.

But I was silent, because I knew he hated my criticism, and I had something to ask. I had to let him finish his tea first, so I leaned back in my chair, just far enough so that my father couldn't tell me to please not slump. Through the silver-mottled window I could see a wet city, gloomy in the deepening afternoon, and people passing in a rush through horizontal rain. The teahouse, which should have been filled with ladies in long straight gowns of ivory gauze, or gentlemen in pointed beards and velvet coat collars, was empty.

"I hadn't realized how much the driving had worn me out." My father set his cup down and pointed to the castle, just visible through the rain. "That's the direction we came from, the other

13

side of that hill. We'll be able to see the Alps from the top."

I remembered the white-shouldered mountains and felt they breathed over this town. We were alone together on their far side, now. I hesitated, took a breath. "Would you tell me a story?" Stories were one of the comforts my father had always offered his motherless child; some of them he drew from his own pleasant childhood in Boston, and some from his more exotic travels. Some he invented for me on the spot, but I'd recently grown tired of those, finding them less astonishing than I'd once thought.

"A story about the Alps?"

"No." I felt an inexplicable surge of fear. "I found something I wanted to ask you about."

He turned and looked mildly at me, graying eyebrows raised above his gray eyes.

"It was in your library," I said. "I'm sorry — I was poking around and I found some papers and a book. I didn't look — much — at the papers. I thought —"

"A book?" Still he was mild, checking his cup for a last drop of tea, only half listening.

"They looked — the book was very old, with a dragon printed in the middle."

14

He sat forward, sat very still, then shivered visibly. This strange gesture alerted me at once. If a story came, it wouldn't be like any story he'd ever told me. He glanced at me, under his eyebrows, and I was surprised to see how drawn and sad he looked.

"Are you angry?" I was looking into my cup now, too.

"No, darling." He sighed deeply, a sound almost grief stricken. The small blond waitress refilled our cups and left us alone again, and still he had a hard time getting started.

Chapter 2

YOU ALREADY KNOW, my father said, that before you were born I was a professor at an American university. Before that, I studied for many years to become a professor. At first I thought I would study literature. Then, however, I realized I loved true stories even better than imaginary ones. All the literary stories I read led me into some kind of — exploration — of history. So finally I gave myself up to it. And I'm very pleased that history interests you, too.

One spring night when I was still a graduate student, I was in my carrel at the university library, sitting alone very late among rows and rows of books. Looking up from my work, I suddenly realized that someone had left a book whose spine I had never seen before among my own textbooks, which sat on a shelf above my desk. The spine of this new book showed an elegant little dragon, green on pale leather.

I didn't remember ever having seen the book there or anywhere else, so I took it down and looked through it without really thinking. The binding was soft, faded leather, and the pages inside appeared to be quite old. It opened easily to the very center. Across those two pages I saw a great woodcut of a dragon with spread wings and a long looped tail, a beast unfurled and raging, claws outstretched. In the dragon's claws hung a banner on which ran a single word in Gothic lettering: DRAKULYA.

I recognized the word at once and thought of Bram Stoker's novel, which I hadn't yet read, and of those childhood nights at the movie theater in my neighborhood, Bela Lugosi hovering over some starlet's white neck. But the spelling of the word was odd and the book clearly very old. Besides, I was a scholar and deeply interested in European history, and after staring at it for a few seconds, I remembered something I'd read. The name actually came from the Latin root for *dragon* or *devil,* the honorary title of Vlad Ţepeş — the "Impaler" — of Wallachia, a feudal lord in the Carpathians who tormented his subjects and prisoners of war in unbelievably cruel ways. I was studying trade in seventeenth-century Amsterdam, so I didn't see any reason for a book on this subject to be tucked in among mine, and I decided it must have been left there accidentally, perhaps by someone who was working on the history of Central Europe, or on feudal symbols.

I flipped through the rest of the pages — when you handle books all day long, every new one is a friend and a temptation. To my further surprise, the rest of it — all those fine old ivory-colored leaves — was completely blank. There wasn't even a title page, and certainly no information about where or when the book had been printed, no maps or endpapers or other illustrations. It showed no imprint of the university library, no card or stamp or label.

After gazing at the book for a few more minutes, I set it on my desk and went down to the card catalog on the first floor. There was indeed a subject card for "Vlad III ('Ţepeş') of Wallachia, 1431–1476 — *See also Wallachia, Transylvania, and Dracula.*" I thought I should check a map first; I quickly discovered that Wallachia and Transylvania were two ancient regions in what was now Romania. Transylvania looked more mountainous, with Wallachia bordering it on the southwest. In the stacks I found what seemed to be the library's only primary source on the subject, a strange little English translation from the 1890s of some pamphlets about "Drakula." The original pamphlets had been printed in Nuremberg in the 1470s and '80s. The mention of

Nuremberg gave me a chill; only a few years earlier, I had followed closely the trials there of Nazi leaders. I'd been too young by one year to serve in the war before it ended, and I had studied its aftermath with all the fervor of the excluded. The volume of pamphlets had a frontispiece, a crude woodcut of a man's head and shoulders, a bullnecked man with hooded dark eyes, a long mustache, and a hat with a feather in it. The image was surprisingly lively, given the primitive medium.

I knew I should be getting on with my work, but I couldn't help reading the beginning of one of the pamphlets. It was a list of some of Dracula's crimes against his own people, and against some other groups, too. I could repeat what it said, from memory, but I think I won't — it was extremely disturbing. I shut the little volume with a snap and went back to my carrel. The seventeenth century consumed my attention until nearly midnight. I left the strange book lying closed on my desk, hoping its owner would find it there the next day, and then I went home to bed.

In the morning I had to attend a lecture. I was tired from my long night, but after class I drank two cups of coffee and went back up to my research. The antique book was still there, lying open now to that great swirling dragon. After my short sleep and jarring lunch of coffee, it gave me a turn, as old novels used to say. I looked at the book again, more carefully. The central image was clearly a woodcut, perhaps a medieval design, a fine sample of bookmaking. I thought it might be valuable in a cold-cash way, and maybe also of personal value to some scholar, since it obviously wasn't a library book.

But in that mood I didn't like the look of it. I shut the book a little impatiently and sat down to write about merchants' guilds until late afternoon. On my way out of the library, I stopped at the front desk and handed the volume to one of the librarians, who promised to put it in the lost-and-found cabinet.

The next morning at eight o'clock, when I hauled myself up to my carrel to work on my chapter some more, the book was on my desk again, open to its single, cruel illustration. I felt some annoyance — probably the librarian had misunderstood me. I put the thing quickly away on my shelves and came and went all day without letting myself look at it again. In the late afternoon I had a meeting with my adviser, and as I swept up my papers, I pulled out the strange book and added it to the pile. This was an impulse; I didn't intend to keep it, but Professor Rossi enjoyed historical mysteries, and I thought it might entertain him. He might be able to identify it, too, with his vast knowledge of European history.

I had the habit of meeting Rossi as he finished his afternoon lecture, and I liked to sneak into the hall before it ended, to watch him in action. This semester he was giving a course on the ancient Mediterranean, and I had caught the end of several lectures, each brilliant and dramatic, each imbued with his great gift for oratory. Now I crept to a seat at the back in time to hear him concluding a discussion of Sir Arthur Evans's restoration of the Minoan palace in Crete. The hall was dim, a vast Gothic auditorium that held five hundred undergraduates. The hush, too, would have suited a cathedral. Not a soul stirred; all eyes were fixed on the trim figure at the front.

Rossi was alone on a lit stage. Sometimes he wandered back and forth, exploring ideas aloud as if ruminating to himself in the privacy of his study. Sometimes he stopped suddenly, fixing his students with an intense stare, an eloquent gesture, an astonishing declaration. He ignored the podium, scorned microphones, and never used notes, although occasionally he showed slides, rapping the huge screen with a pole to make his point. Sometimes he got so excited that he raised both arms and ran partway across the stage. There was a legend that he'd once fallen off the front in his rapture over the flowering of Greek democracy and had scrambled up again without missing a beat of his lecture. I'd never dared to ask him if this was true.

Today he was in a pensive mood, pacing up and down with his hands behind his back. "Sir Arthur Evans, please remember, restored the palace of King Minos at Knossos partly according to what he found there and partly according to his own imagination, his vision of what Minoan civilization had been." He gazed into the vault above us. "The records were sparse and he was dealing mainly with mysteries. Instead of adhering to limited accuracy, he used his imagination to create a palace style breathtakingly whole — and flawed. Was he wrong to do this?"

Here he paused, looking almost wistfully out over the sea of tousled heads, cowlicks, buzz cuts, the purposely shabby blazers and earnest young male faces (remember, this was an era when only boys attended such a university as undergraduates, although you, dear daughter, will probably be able to enroll wherever you want to). Five hundred pairs of eyes gazed back at him. "I shall leave you to ponder that question." Rossi smiled, turned abruptly, and left the limelight.

There was an intake of breath; the students began to talk and laugh, to collect their belongings. Rossi usually went to sit on the edge of the stage after the lecture, and some of his more avid disciples hurried forward to ask him questions. These he answered with seriousness and good humor until the last student had trailed away, and then I went over to greet him.

"Paul, my friend! Let's go put our feet up and speak Dutch." He clapped me affectionately on the shoulder and we walked out together.

Rossi's office always amused me because it defied the convention of the mad professorial study: books sat neatly on the shelves, a very modern little coffee burner by the window fed his habit, plants that never lacked water adorned his desk, and he himself was always trimly dressed in tweed trousers and an immaculate shirt and tie. His face was of a crisp English mold, sharp-featured and intensely blue-eyed; he'd told me once that from his father, a Tuscan immigrant to Sussex, he'd acquired only a love of good food. To look into Rossi's face was to see a world as definite and orderly as the changing of the guards at Buckingham Palace.

His mind was another thing altogether. Even after forty years of strict self-apprenticeship, it boiled over with remnants of the past, simmered with the unsolved. His encyclopedic production had long since won him accolades in a publishing world much wider than the academic press. As soon as he finished one work, he turned to another, often an abrupt change of direction. As a result, students from a myriad of disciplines sought him out, and I was considered lucky to have acquired his advisership. He was also the kindest, warmest friend I'd ever had.

"Well," he said, turning on his coffeepot and waving me to a chair. "How's the opus coming along?"

I filled him in on several weeks' work, and we had a short argument about trade between Utrecht and Amsterdam in the early seventeenth century. He served up his fine coffee in porcelain cups and we both stretched back, he behind the big desk. The room was permeated with the pleasant gloom that still came in at that hour, later each evening now that spring was deepening. Then I remembered my antique offering.

"I've brought you a curiosity, Ross. Someone's left a rather morbid object in my carrel by mistake and after two days I didn't mind borrowing it for you to take a look at."

"Hand it over." He set down the delicate cup and reached out to take my book. "Good binding. This leather might even be some kind of heavy vellum. And an embossed spine." Something about the spine of the book brought a frown to his usually clear face.

"Open it," I suggested. I couldn't understand the flickering throb my heart gave as I waited for him to repeat my own experience with the nearly blank book. It opened under his practiced hands to its exact center. I couldn't see what he saw, behind his desk, but I saw him see it. His face was suddenly grave — a still face, and not one I knew. He turned through the other leaves, front and back, as I had, but the gravity didn't become surprise. "Yes, empty." He laid it open on his desk. "All blank."

"Isn't it an odd thing?" My coffee was growing cold in my hand.

"And quite old. But not blank because it is unfinished. Just terribly blank, to make the ornament in the center stand out."

"Yes. Yes, it's as if the creature in the middle

25

has eaten up everything else around it." I'd begun flippantly, but I finished slowly.

Rossi seemed unable to drag his eyes from that central image spread before him. At last he shut the book firmly and stirred his coffee without sipping it. "Where did you get this?"

"Well, as I said, someone left it in my carrel by accident, two days ago. I guess I should have taken it to Rare Books immediately, but I honestly think it's someone's personal possession, so I didn't."

"Oh, it is," Rossi said, looking narrowly at me. "It is someone's personal possession."

"So you know whose?"

"Yes. It's yours."

"No, I mean that I simply found it in my —" The expression on his face stopped me. He looked ten years older, by some trick of the light from the dusky window. "What do you mean, it's mine?"

Rossi rose slowly and went to a corner of his study behind the desk, climbing two steps of the library stool to bring down a little dark volume. He stood looking at it for a minute, as if unwilling to put it in my hands. Then he passed it across. "What do you think of this?"

The book was small, covered in ancient-looking brown velvet like an old prayer missal or Book of Days, with nothing on the spine or front to give it an identity. It had a bronze-colored clasp that slipped apart with a little pressure. The book itself fell open to the middle. There, spread across the center, was my — I say *my* — dragon, this time overflowing the edges of the pages, claws outstretched, savage beak open to show its fangs, with the same bannered word in the same Gothic script.

"Of course," Rossi was saying, "I've had time, and I've had this identified. It's a Central European design, printed about 1512 — so you see it could very well have been set with movable-type text throughout, if there had been any text."

I flipped slowly through the delicate leaves. No titles on the first pages — no, I knew it already. "What a strange coincidence."

"It's been stained by salt water on the back, perhaps from a trip on the Black Sea. Not even the Smithsonian could tell me what it's seen in the course of its travels. You see, I actually took the trouble of getting a chemical analysis. It cost me three hundred dollars to learn that this thing sat in an environment heavily laden with stone dust at some point, probably prior to 1700. I also went all the way to Istanbul to try to learn more about its origins. But the strangest thing is the way I acquired this book." He stretched out a hand and I gladly gave the volume back, old and fragile as it was.

"Did you buy it somewhere?"

"I found it in my desk when I was a graduate student."

A shiver went over me. "Your desk?"

"My library carrel. We had them, too. The custom goes back to seventh-century monasteries, you know."

"Where did you — where did it come from? A gift?"

"Maybe." Rossi smiled strangely. He seemed to be controlling some difficult emotion. "Like another cup?"

"I will, after all," I said, dry throated.

"My efforts to find its owner failed, and the library couldn't identify it. Even the British Museum Library had never seen it before and offered me a considerable sum for it."

"But you didn't want to sell."

"No. I like a puzzle, as you know. So does every scholar worth his salt. It's the reward of the business, to look history in the eye and say, 'I know who you are. You can't fool me.'"

"So what is it? Do you think this larger copy was made by the same printer at the same time?"

His fingers drummed the windowsill. "I haven't thought much about it in years, actually, or I've tried not to, although I always sort of — feel it, there, over my shoulder." He gestured up toward the dark crevice among the book's fellows. "That top shelf is my row of failures. And things I'd rather not think about."

"Well, maybe now that I've turned up a mate for it, you can fit the pieces in place better. They can't be unrelated."

"They can't be unrelated." It was a hollow echo, even if it came through the swish of fresh coffee.

Impatience, and a slightly fevered feeling I often had in those days from lack of sleep and mental overexertion, made me hurry him on. "And your research? Not just the chemical analysis. You said you tried to learn more — ?"

"I tried to learn more." He sat down again and spread small, practical-looking hands on either side of his coffee cup. "I'm afraid I owe you more than a story," he said quietly. "Maybe I owe you a sort of apology — you'll see why — although I would never consciously wish such a legacy on any student of mine. Not on most of my students, anyway." He smiled, affectionately, but sadly, I thought. "You've heard of Vlad Ţepeş — the Impaler?"

"Yes, Dracula. A feudal lord in the Carpathians, otherwise known as Bela Lugosi."

"That's the one — or one of them. They were an ancient family before their most unpleasant member came to power. Did you look him up on your way out of the library? Yes? A bad sign. When my book appeared so oddly, I looked up the word itself, that afternoon — the name, as well as *Transylvania, Wallachia,* and the *Carpathians.* Instant obsession."

I wondered if this might be a veiled compliment — Rossi liked his students working at a high pitch — but I let it pass, afraid to interrupt his story with extraneous comment.

"So, the Carpathians. That's always been a mystical spot for historians. One of Occam's students traveled there — by donkey, I suppose — and produced out of his experiences a funny little thing called *Philosophie of the Aweful.* Of course, the basic story of Dracula has been hashed over many times and doesn't yield much to exploration. There's the Wallachian prince, a fifteenth-century ruler, hated by the Ottoman Empire and his own people — both. Really among the nastiest of all medieval European tyrants. It's estimated that he slaughtered at least twenty thousand of his fellow Wallachians and Transylvanians over the years. *Dracula* means *son of Dracul* — son of the dragon, more or less. His father had been inducted into the Order of the Dragon by Holy Roman Emperor Sigismund — it was an organization for the defense of the Empire against the Ottoman Turks. Actually, there is evidence that Dracula's father gave Dracula over to the Turks when he was a boy as hostage in a political bargain, and that Dracula acquired some of his taste for cruelty from observing Ottoman torture methods."

Rossi shook his head. "Anyway, Vlad's killed in a battle against the Turks, or perhaps just by accident by his own soldiers, and buried in a monastery on an island in Lake Snagov, now in the possession of our friend socialist Romania. His memory becomes legend, passed down through generations of superstitious peasants. At the end of the nineteenth century, a disturbed and melodramatic author — Abraham Stoker — gets hold of the name *Dracula* and fastens it on a creature of his own invention, a vampire.

Vlad Ţepeş was horrifyingly cruel, but he wasn't a vampire, of course. And you won't find any mention of Vlad in Stoker's book, although his version of Dracula talks about his family's great past as Turk-fighters." Rossi sighed. "Stoker assembled some useful lore about vampire legends — about Transylvania, too, without ever going there — actually, Vlad Dracula ruled Wallachia, which borders Transylvania. In the twentieth century, Hollywood takes over and the myth lives on, resurrected. That's where my flippancy stops, by the way."

Rossi set his cup aside and folded his hands together. For a moment, he seemed unable to continue. "I can joke about the legend, which has been monstrously commercialized, but not about what my research turned up. In fact, I felt unable to publish it, partly because of the presence of that legend. I thought the very subject matter wouldn't be taken seriously. But there was another reason, too."

This brought me to a mental standstill. Rossi left no stone unpublished; it was part of his productivity, his lavish genius. He sternly instructed his students to do the same, to waste nothing.

"What I found in Istanbul was too serious not to be taken seriously. Perhaps I was wrong in my decision to keep this information — as I can honestly call it — to myself, but each of us has his own superstitions. Mine happen to be an historian's. I was afraid."

I stared and he gave a sigh, as if reluctant to go on. "You see, Vlad Dracula had always been studied in the great archives of Central and Eastern Europe or, ultimately, in his home region. But he began his career as a Turk-killer, and I discovered that no one had ever looked in the Ottoman world for material on the Dracula legend. That was what took me to Istanbul, a secret detour from my research on the early Greek economies. Oh, I published all the Greek stuff, with a vengeance."

For a moment he was silent, turning his gaze toward the window. "And I suppose I should just tell you, straight out, what I discovered in the Istanbul collection and tried not to think about afterward. After all, you've inherited one of these nice books." He put his hand gravely on the stack of two. "If I don't tell you all this myself, you will probably simply retrace my steps, maybe at some added risk." He smiled a little grimly at the top of the desk. "I could save you a great deal of grant writing, anyway."

I couldn't bring the dry chuckle out of my

throat. What on earth was he driving at? It occurred to me that perhaps I'd underestimated some peculiar sense of humor in my mentor. Maybe this was an elaborate practical joke — he'd had two versions of the menacing old book in his library and had planted one in my stall, knowing I'd bring it to him, and I'd obliged, like a fool. But in the ordinary lamplight from his desk he was suddenly gray, unshaven at the end of the day, with dark hollows draining the color and humor from his eyes. I leaned forward. "What are you trying to tell me?"

"Dracula —" He paused. "Dracula — Vlad Ţepeş — is still alive."

"Good Lord," my father said suddenly, looking at his watch. "Why didn't you tell me? It's almost seven o'clock."

I put my cold hands inside my navy jacket. "I didn't know," I said. "But please don't stop the story. Please don't stop there." My father's face looked momentarily unreal to me; I'd never before considered the possibility that he might be — I didn't know what to call it. Mentally unbalanced? Had he lost his balance for a few minutes, in the telling of this story?

"It's late for such a long tale." My father picked

up his teacup and put it down again. I noticed that his hands were shaking.

"Please go on," I said.

He was ignoring me. "Anyway, I don't know whether I've scared you or simply bored you. You probably wanted a good straightforward tale of dragons."

"There was a dragon," I said. I wanted, too, to believe he had made the story up. "Two dragons. Will you at least tell me more tomorrow?"

My father rubbed his arms, as if to warm himself, and I saw that for now he was fiercely unwilling to talk about it further. His face was dark, closed. "Let's go get some dinner. We can leave our luggage at Hotel Turist first."

"All right," I said.

"They're going to throw us out in a minute, anyway, if we don't leave." I could see the light-haired waitress leaning against the bar; she didn't seem to care whether we stayed or went. My father got out his wallet, smoothed flat some of those big faded bills, always with a miner or farmworker smiling heroically off the back, and put them in the pewter tray. We worked our way around wrought-iron chairs and tables and went out the steamy door.

Night had come down hard — a cold, foggy,

wet, East European night, and the street was almost deserted. "Keep your hat on," my father said, as he always did. Before we stepped out under the rain-washed sycamores, he suddenly stopped, held me back behind his outstretched hand, protectively, as if a car had gone rushing past us. But there was no car, and the street dripped quiet and rustic under its yellow lights. My father looked sharply left and right. I thought I saw no one, although my long-eaved hood partly blocked my sight. He stood listening, his face averted, body stock-still.

Then he let his breath out heavily and we walked on, talking about what to order for dinner at the Turist when we got there.

There would be no more discussions of Dracula on that journey. I was soon to learn the pattern of my father's fear: he could tell me this story only in short bursts, reeling it out not for dramatic effect but to preserve something — his strength? His sanity?

Chapter 3

AT HOME IN AMSTERDAM, my father was unusually silent and busy, and I waited uneasily for opportunities to ask him about Professor Rossi. Mrs. Clay ate dinner with us every night in the dark-paneled dining room, serving us from the sideboard but otherwise joining in as a member of the family, and I felt instinctively that my father would not want to tell more of his story in her presence. If I sought him in his library, he asked me quickly about my day or wanted to see my homework. I checked his library shelves in secret soon after our return from Emona, but the book and papers had already vanished from their high place; I had no idea where he'd put them. If it was Mrs. Clay's night out, he suggested that we go to a movie ourselves, or he took me for coffee and pastries at the noisy shop across the canal. I might have said he was avoiding me, except that sometimes when I sat near him, reading, watching for an opening to ask questions, he would reach out and stroke my hair with an abstracted sadness in

37

his face. At those moments, I was the one who could not bring up the story.

When my father went south again, he took me with him. He would have only one meeting, and an informal one at that, almost not worth the long trip, but he wanted me to see the scenery, he said. This time we rode the train far beyond Emona and then settled for taking a bus to our destination. My father preferred local transportation whenever he could use it. Now, when I travel, I often think of him and bypass the rental car for the metro. "You'll see — Ragusa is no place for cars," he said as we clung to the metal bar behind the bus driver's seat. "Always sit up front and you're less likely to be sick." I squeezed the bar until my knuckles were white; we seemed to be airborne among the towering piles of pale-gray rock that served as mountains in this new region. "Good God," my father said after one horrible leap across a hairpin turn. The other passengers looked completely at ease. Across the aisle an old woman in black sat crocheting, her face framed by the fringe of her shawl, which danced as the bus jolted. "Watch carefully," my father said. "You're going to see one of the greatest sights of this coast."

I gazed diligently out the window, wishing he

didn't find it necessary to give me so many instructions, but taking in everything I could of the rock-piled mountains and the stone villages that crowned them. Just before sunset I was rewarded by the sight of a woman standing at the edge of the road, perhaps waiting for a bus going in the opposite direction. She was tall, dressed in long, heavy skirts and a tight vest, her head crowned by a fabulous headdress like an organdy butterfly. She stood alone among the rocks, touched by late sun, a basket on the ground beside her. I would have thought she was a statue, except that she turned her magnificent head as we passed. Her face was a pale oval, too far away for me to see any expression. When I described her to my father, he said she must have been wearing the native dress of this part of Dalmatia. "A big bonnet, with wings on each side? I've seen pictures of that. You could say she's a sort of ghost — she probably lives in a very small village. I suppose most of the young people here wear blue jeans now."

I kept my face glued to the window. No more ghosts appeared, but I didn't miss a single view of the miracle that did: Ragusa, far below us, an ivory city with a molten, sunlit sea breaking around its walls, roofs redder than the evening sky inside their tremendous medieval enclosure. The city sat on a large round peninsula, and its walls looked impenetrable to sea storm and invasion, a giant wading off the Adriatic coast. At the same time, seen from the great height of the road, it had a miniature appearance, like something carved by hand and set down out of scale at the base of the mountains.

Ragusa's main street, when we reached it a couple of hours later, was marble underfoot, highly polished by centuries of shoe soles and reflecting splashes of light from the surrounding shops and palaces so that it gleamed like the surface of a great canal. At the harbor end of the street, safe in the city's old heart, we collapsed on café chairs, and I turned my face straight into the wind, which smelled of crashing surf and — strange to me in that late season — of ripe oranges. The sea and sky were almost dark. Fishing boats danced on a sheet of wilder water at the far reaches of the harbor; the wind brought me sea sounds, sea scents, and a new mildness. "Yes, the South," my father said with satisfaction, pulling up a glass of whiskey and a plate of sardines on toast. "Say you put your boat in right here and had a clear night to travel. You could steer by the stars from here directly to Venice, or to the Albanian coast, or into the Aegean."

"How long would it take to sail to Venice?" I stirred my tea, and the breeze pulled the steam out to sea.

"Oh, a week or more, I suppose, in a medieval ship." He smiled at me, relaxed for the moment. "Marco Polo was born on this coast, and the Venetians invaded frequently. We're actually sitting in a kind of gateway to the world, you could say."

"When did you come here before?" I was only beginning to believe in my father's previous life, his existence before me.

"I've been here several times. Maybe four or five. The first was years ago, when I was still a student. My adviser recommended I visit Ragusa from Italy, just to see this wonder, while I was studying — I told you I studied Italian in Florence one summer."

"You mean Professor Rossi."

"Yes." My father looked sharply at me, then into his whiskey.

There was a little silence, filled by the café awning, which flapped above us on that unseasonably warm breeze. From inside the bar and restaurant came a blur of tourists' voices, clinking china, saxophone and piano. From beyond came the slop of boats in the dark harbor. At last my father spoke. "I should tell you a little more about him." He didn't look at me, still, but I thought his voice had a fine crack in it.

"I'd like that," I said cautiously.

He sipped his whiskey. "You're stubborn about stories, aren't you?"

You are the stubborn one, I longed to say, but I held my tongue; I wanted the story more than I did the quarrel.

My father sighed. "All right. I'll tell you more about him tomorrow, in the daylight, when I'm not so tired and we have a little time to walk the walls." He pointed with his glass to those gray-white, luminous battlements above the hotel. "That'll be a better time for stories. Especially that story."

By midmorning we were seated a hundred feet above the surf, which crashed and foamed white around the city's giant roots. The November sky was brilliant as a summer day. My father put on his sunglasses, checked his watch, folded away the brochure about the rusty-roofed architecture below, let a group of German tourists drift past us out of earshot. I looked out to sea, beyond a forested island, to the fading blue horizon. From that direction the Venetian ships had come, bringing war or trade, their red and gold banners restless under the same glittering arc of sky. Waiting for my father to speak, I felt a stirring of apprehension far from scholarly. Perhaps those ships I imagined on the horizon were not simply part of a colorful pageant. Why was it so difficult for my father to begin?

Chapter 4

AS I'VE TOLD YOU, my father said, clearing his throat once or twice, Professor Rossi was a fine scholar and a true friend. I wouldn't want you to think anything different of him. I know that what I made the mistake, perhaps, of telling you earlier makes him sound — crazy. You remember that he'd described to me something terribly difficult to believe. And I was deeply shocked, and filled with doubt about him, although I saw sincerity and acceptance in his face. When he finished speaking he glanced at me with those keen eyes.

"What on earth do you mean?" I must have been stammering.

"I repeat," Rossi said emphatically, "I discovered in Istanbul that Dracula lives among us today. Or did then, at least."

I stared at him.

"I know you must think I'm insane," he said, relenting visibly. "And I grant you that anyone who pokes around in history long enough may well go mad." He sighed. "In Istanbul there is a little-known repository of materials, founded by

Sultan Mehmed II, who took the city from the Byzantines in 1453. This archive is mostly odds and ends collected later by the Turks as they were gradually beaten back from the edges of their empire. But it also contains documents from the late fifteenth century, and among them I found some maps that purported to give directions to the Unholy Tomb of a Turk-slayer, who I thought might be Vlad Dracula. There were three maps, actually, graduated in scale to show the same region in greater and greater detail. There was nothing on these maps that I recognized or could tie to any area I knew of. They were labeled mainly in Arabic, and they dated from the late fifteenth century, according to the archive's librarians." He tapped the strange little volume that I told you resembled my own find so closely. "The information in the center of the third map was in a very old Slavic dialect. Only a scholar with multiple linguistic resources at his command could have made head or tail of them. I did my best, but it was uncertain work."

At this point, Rossi shook his head, as if still regretting his limits. "The effort I poured into this discovery drew me unreasonably far from my official summer research on the ancient trade of Crete. But I was beyond the reach of reason, I think, sitting in that hot, sticky library in Istanbul. I remember I could see the minarets of the Hagia Sophia through the grimy windows. I worked there, with those clues to the Turkish view of Vlad's kingdom resting on the desk in front of me, toiling over my dictionaries, taking copious notes, and copying the maps by hand.

"To make a long research story short, there came an afternoon when I found myself closing in on the carefully marked spot of the Unholy Tomb, on the third and most puzzling map. You remember that Vlad Ţepeş is supposed to have been buried at the island monastery on Lake Snagov, in Romania. This map, like the others, didn't show any lake with an island in it — although it did show a river running through the area, widening in the middle. I had translated everything around the borders already, with the help of a professor of Arabic and Ottoman language at Istanbul University — cryptic proverbs about the nature of evil, many of them from the Qur'an. Here and there on the map, nestled among roughly sketched mountains, was some writing that at first glance appeared to be place-names in a Slavic dialect but that translated as riddles, probably a code for real locations: the Valley of Eight Oaks, Pig-Stealing Village, and so forth — strange peasant names that meant nothing to me.

"Well, in the center of the map, above the site of the Unholy Tomb, wherever it was supposed to be located, was a rough sketch of a dragon, wearing a castle as a sort of crown on its head. The dragon looked nothing like the one in my — our — old books, but I conjectured it must have come down to the Turks with the legend of Dracula. Below the dragon someone had inked tiny words, which I thought at first were Arabic, like the proverbs in the map's borders. Looking at them through a magnifying glass, I suddenly realized that these markings were actually Greek, and I translated aloud before I had thought about courtesy — although of course the library room was empty except for myself and occasionally a bored librarian who came in and out, apparently to make sure I didn't steal anything. At this moment I was completely alone. The infinitesimal letters danced under my eyes as I sounded them out: 'In this spot, he is housed in evil. Reader, unbury him with a word.'

"At that moment, I heard a door slam in the downstairs foyer. Heavy footsteps came up the stairwell. I was still occupied with a flash of thought, however: the magnifying glass had just told me that this map, unlike the first two more general ones, had been labeled by three different people, in their three different languages. The handwritings as well as the languages were dissimilar. So were the colors of the old, old inks. Then I had a sudden vision — you know, that intuition that a scholar can almost trust when it's backed by weeks of careful work.

"It seemed to me that the map had originally consisted of this central sketch, and the mountains that surrounded it, with the Greek command in the center. It had probably only later been labeled in that Slavic dialect to identify the places it referred to — in code, at least. Then it had somehow fallen into Ottoman hands and been surrounded by Qur'anic material, which appeared to house or imprison that ominous message at the center, or to encircle it with talismans against the dark. If this were true, who, knowing Greek, had marked the map first, perhaps even drawn it? I knew that Greek was used by Byzantine scholars of Dracula's time, not by most scholars in the Ottoman world.

"Before I could write down even a note on this theory, which might involve tests beyond my own powers, the door on the other side of the stacks flew open, and a tall, well-built man came in, hurrying wildly past the books and stopping on the other side of the table where I worked. He had the air of a conscious intruder, and I felt sure he wasn't one of the librarians. I also felt for some reason that I should rise to my feet, but out of a certain pride I couldn't bring myself to; it might have seemed deferential, when the interruption had been sudden and rather rude.

"We looked each other in the face, and I was more startled than ever. The man was distinctly out of place in that esoteric setting, handsome and well-groomed in a swarthy Turkish or South Slavic way, with a drooping, heavy mustache and tailored dark clothes like a Western business-man's. His eyes met mine belligerently, and their long lashes looked somehow disgusting in that stern face. His skin was sallow but beautifully unblemished, and his lips very red. 'Sir,' he said in a low, hostile voice, almost a growl of Turk-accented English. 'I do not think you have proper permissions for this.'

"'For what?' My academic hackles rose at once.

"'For this work of research. You are involved in material the Turkish government considers private Turkish archive. May I see your papers, please?'

"'Who are you?' I asked with equal coolness. 'May I see yours?'

"He pulled a wallet out of his interior jacket pocket, slapped it open on the table in front of me, and snapped it shut again. I had just time to see an ivory card with a jumble of Turkish titles on it. The man's hand was unpleasantly waxen and long-nailed, with a ridge of dark hair on the back. 'Ministry of Cultural Resources,' he said coldly. 'I understand you do not have actual exchange arrangement with Turkish government to examine these materials. Is this true?'

"'It most certainly is not.' I produced for him a letter from the National Library, stating that I was to be permitted research rights in any of its divisions in Istanbul.

"'Not good enough,' he said, tossing it down on my papers. 'Maybe you will need to come with me.'

"'Where?' I stood up, feeling safer on my feet now, but hoping he would not take my rising as compliance.

"'To police, if necessary.'

"'This is outrageous.' When in bureaucratic doubt, I had learned, raise your voice. 'I am a doctoral candidate at Oxford University and a citizen of the United Kingdom. I registered with the university here the day I arrived and received this letter as proof of my status. I will not be questioned by the police — or by you.'

"'I see.' He smiled in a way that curled my stomach into a knot. I had read a little about Turkish prisons and their occasionally Western inmates, and my situation struck me as precarious, although I didn't understand what kind of trouble I could possibly be in. I hoped one of the shuffling librarians had heard me and would come in to quiet us down. Then I realized that they would certainly have been responsible for admitting this character, with his intimidating business card, into my presence. Perhaps he was actually someone important. He leaned forward. 'Let me see what you are doing here. Move, please.'

"I stepped aside, reluctantly, and he bent over my work, slapping shut my dictionaries to read their covers, still with that disquieting smile. He was a massive presence across the table, and I noticed he had an odd smell, like a cologne used not quite successfully to cover something disagreeable. At last he picked up the map I had been working over, his hands suddenly gentle, handling it almost tenderly. He looked at it as if he didn't need to examine it long to know what it was, although I thought that must be a bluff. 'This is your archival material, yes?'

"'Yes,' I said angrily.

"'This is very valuable possession of Turkish state. I do not believe that you will be needing it for foreign purposes. And this piece of paper, this little map, brings you whole way from your English university to Istanbul?'

"I considered retorting that I had other business as well, to throw him off my scholar's track, but realized at once that this might invite further questioning. 'Yes, in a nutshell.'

"'Nutshell?' he said, more mildly. 'Well, I think you will find this temporarily confiscated. What a shame for foreign researcher.'

"I boiled, standing there, so close to my solution, and felt thankful that I hadn't brought with me that morning any of my own careful copies of old maps of the Carpathians, which I'd meant to start comparing to this map the next day. They were hidden in my suitcase at the hotel. 'You have absolutely no right to confiscate material I've already been given permission to work on,' I said, gritting my teeth. 'I will certainly take this up with the National Library immediately. And with the British embassy. Anyway, what possible objection can you have to my studying these documents? They are obscure pieces of me-dieval history. They have nothing to do with the interests of the Turkish government, I'm sure.'

"The bureaucrat stood looking away from me, as if the spires of Hagia Sophia presented an in-teresting new angle he'd never had occasion to see before. 'It is for your own good,' he said dis-passionately. 'Much better to let someone else work on that. Some other time.' He remained quite still there, head turned toward the window, almost as if he wanted me to follow his gaze to something. I had a childish feeling that I shouldn't, because it might be a trick, so I looked at him, in-stead, waiting. And then I saw, as if he meant the greasy daylight to fall on it, his neck above his expensive shirt collar. On the side of it, in the deepest flesh of a muscular throat, were two brown-scabbed puncture marks, not fresh but not fully healed, as if he had been stabbed by twin thorns, or mutilated at knifepoint.

"I stepped back, away from the table, thinking I'd lost my mind with all my morbid readings, that I'd actually come unhinged. But the daylight was quite ordinary, the man in his dark wool suit per-fectly real, down to the smell of unwash and perspiration and something else under his cologne. Nothing disappeared or changed. I couldn't drag my eyes from those two half-healed little wounds. After a few seconds he turned back from the absorbing view, as if satisfied with what he had seen — or what I had — and smiled again. 'For your own good, Professor.'

"I stood there wordlessly while he left the room with the map rolled up in his hand, and listened to his steps dying away on the stairs. A few minutes later one of the elderly librarians came in, a man with bushy gray hair, carrying two old folios, which he began to put away on a low shelf. 'Excuse me,' I said to him, my voice almost stuck in my throat. 'Excuse me, but this is perfectly outrageous.' He looked up at me, puzzled. 'Who was that man? That bureaucrat?'

"'Bureaucrat?' The librarian faltered over my word.

"'I must have an official letter from you at once about my right to work in this archive.'

"'But you have all the right to work here,' he said soothingly. 'I have registered you here myself.'

"'I know, I know. So you must catch him and make him return the map.'

"'Catch who?'

"'The man from the Ministry of — the man who just came up here. Didn't you let him in?'

"He looked at me curiously from under his gray thatch. 'Someone came in now? No one has come in for the last three hours. I am down at the entrance myself. Unfortunately we have few who do research here.'

"'The man —' I said, and stopped. I saw myself, suddenly, a crazy gesturing foreigner. 'He took my map. I mean the archive's map.'

"'Map, Herr Professor?'

"'I was working on a map. I signed it out this morning, at the desk.'

"'Not that map?' He pointed to my worktable. In the middle of it lay an ordinary road map of the Balkans that I had never seen in my life. It certainly hadn't been there five minutes before. The librarian was putting away his second folio.

"'Never mind.' I gathered my books as quickly as I could and left the library. In the busy, traffic-filled street there was no sign of the bureaucrat, although several men of his build and height in similar suits hurried past me carrying briefcases. When I reached the room where I was staying, I found that my belongings had been moved, owing to some practical problems with the room. My first sketches of the old maps, as well as the completed notes I hadn't needed that day, were gone. My suitcase had been perfectly repacked. The hotel staff said they knew nothing about it. I lay awake all night listening to every sound outside. The next morning I gathered up my un-washed clothes and my dictionaries and took the boat back to Greece."

Professor Rossi folded his hands again and looked at me, as if waiting patiently for my dis-belief. But I was suddenly shaken by belief, not doubt. "You went back to Greece?"

"Yes, and I spent the rest of the summer ig-noring the memory of my adventure in Istanbul, although I couldn't ignore its implications."

"You left because you were — frightened?"

"Terrified."

"But later you did all that research — or had it done — on your strange book?"

"Yes, mainly the chemical analysis at the Smithsonian. But when it was inconclusive — and under some other influences — I dropped the whole thing and put the book on my shelf. Up there, eventually." He nodded to the highest roost in his cage. "It's odd — I think about these events occasionally, and I seem to remember them very clearly sometimes and then only in fragments at other times. I suppose familiarity erodes even the most awful memories, though. And there are certainly periods — years at a time — when I don't want to think about this at all."

"But do you really believe — this man with the wounds on his neck —"

"What would you have thought, if he'd been standing in front of you and you'd known yourself to be sane?" He stood leaning against the shelves, and for a moment his tone was fierce.

I took a last sip of cold coffee; it was very bitter, the dregs. "And you never tried again to figure out what the map meant, or where it had come from?"

"Never." He seemed to pause for a moment. "No. One of the few pieces of research I'm sure I'll never finish. I have a theory, however, that this ghastly trail of scholarship, like so many less awful ones, is merely something one person makes a little progress on, then another, each contributing a bit in his own lifetime. Perhaps three such people, centuries ago, did just that in drawing up those maps and adding to them, although I admit that all those talismanic sayings from the Qur'an probably didn't further anyone's knowledge about the whereabouts of Vlad

Ţepeş's real tomb. And of course it could all be nonsense. He could perfectly well have been buried in his island monastery, as reported by Romanian tradition, and stayed there peacefully like a good soul — which he wasn't."

"But you don't think so."

Again he hesitated. "Scholarship must go on. For good or for evil, but inevitably, in every field."

"Did you ever go to Snagov to see for yourself, somehow?"

He shook his head. "No. I gave up the search."

I put down my icy cup, watching his face. "But you kept some information," I guessed slowly.

He reached up among the books on his top shelf again, pulling down a sealed brown envelope. "Of course. Who destroys any research completely? I copied from memory what I could of the three maps and saved my other notes, the ones I had with me that day in the archive."

He laid the unopened packet on his desk, between us, and touched it with a tenderness that didn't seem to me to match his horror of its contents. Maybe it was that disjunction, or the deepening of the spring evening into night outside, that made me even more nervous. "Don't you think this might be a dangerous sort of legacy?"

"I wish to God I could say no. But perhaps dangerous only in a psychological sense. Life's better, sounder, when we don't brood unnecessarily on horrors. As you know, human history is full of evil deeds, and maybe we ought to think of them with tears, not fascination. It's been so many years that I can't even be certain of my memories of Istanbul anymore, and I've never cared to go back there. Besides, I have the feeling I took away with me all I could have needed to know."

"To go further, you mean?"

"Yes."

"But you still don't know who could have concocted a map that showed where this tomb is? Or was?"

"No."

I put my hand out toward the brown envelope. "Don't I need a rosary to go with this, or something, some charm?"

"I'm sure you carry your own goodness, moral sense, whatever you want to call it, with you — I like to think most of us are capable of that, anyway. I wouldn't go around with garlic in my pocket, no."

"But with some strong mental antidote."

"Yes. I've tried to." His face was deeply sad, almost grim. "Perhaps I've been wrong not to make use of those ancient superstitions, but I'm a rationalist, I suppose, and I'll stick to that."

I closed my fingers over the package.

"Here's your book. It's an interesting one and I wish you luck in identifying its source." He handed me my vellum-covered volume, and I thought the sorrow in his face belied the lightness of his words. "Come two weeks from now and we'll get back to trade in Utrecht."

I must have blinked; even my dissertation sounded unreal to me. "Yes, all right."

Rossi cleared away the coffee cups and I packed my briefcase, stiff fingered.

"One last thing," he said gravely, as I turned back to him.

"Yes?"

"We won't talk about this again."

"You don't want to know how I get on?" It left me aghast, lonely.

"You could put it that way. I don't want to know. Unless, of course, you find yourself in trouble." He took my hand in his usual affectionate grip. His face wore a look of actual grief that was new to me, and then he seemed to make himself smile.

"All right," I said.

"Two weeks from now," he called almost cheerfully as I went out. "Bring me a finished chapter, or else."

My father stopped. To my astonished embarrassment, I saw that there were tears in his eyes. That gleam of emotion would have halted my questions even if he hadn't spoken. "You see, writing a dissertation's the really grisly thing," he said lightly. "Anyway, we probably shouldn't have gotten into all this. It's such a convoluted old story, and obviously everything turned out fine, because here I am, not even a ghostly professor anymore, and here you are." He blinked; he was recovering. "That's a happy ending, as endings go."

"But maybe there's a lot in between," I managed to say. The sun reached only through my skin, not to my bones, which had picked up some cold breeze coming off the sea. We stretched and turned this way and that to look at the town below. The latest group of milling tourists had wandered past us along the wall and were standing in a distant alcove, pointing out the islands or posing for one another's cameras. I glanced at my father, but he was gazing out to sea. Behind the other tourists, and already far ahead of us, was a man I hadn't noticed before, walking slowly but inexorably out of reach, tall and broad shouldered in a dark wool suit. We had seen other tall men in dark suits in that city, but for some reason I couldn't stop staring after this one.

Chapter 5

BECAUSE I FELT such constraint with my father, I decided to do a little exploring by myself, and one day after school I went alone to the university library. My Dutch was reasonably good, I had studied French and German for years now, and the university had a vast collection in English. The librarians were courteous; it took me only a couple of shy conversations to find the material I was looking for: the text of the Nuremberg pamphlets about Dracula that my father had mentioned. The library did not own one of the original pamphlets — they were very rare, the elderly librarian in their medieval collection explained to me, but he found the text in a compendium of medieval German documents, translated into English. "Will that be what you need, my dear?" he said, with a smile. He had one of those very fair, clear faces you see sometimes among the Dutch — a direct, blue gaze, hair that seemed to have grown paler instead of going gray. My father's parents, in Boston, had died when I was a little girl, and I thought that I would have liked a grandfather of this model.

"I'm Johan Binnerts," he added. "You may call for me whenever you need more help."

I said it was exactly what I needed, *dank u,* and he patted my shoulder before going quietly away. I reread the first section from my notebook in the empty room:

In the Year of Our Lord 1456 Drakula did many terrible and curious things. When he was appointed Lord in Wallachia, he had all the young boys burned who came to his land to learn the language, four hundred of them. He had a large family impaled and many of his people buried naked up to the navel and shot at. Some he had roasted and then flayed.

There was a footnote, too, at the bottom of the first page. The typeface of the note was so fine that I almost missed it. Looking more closely, I realized it was a commentary on the word *impaled.* Vlad Ţepeş, it claimed, had learned this form of torture from the Ottomans. Impalement of the sort he practiced involved the penetration of the body with a sharpened wooden stake, usually through the anus or genitals upward, so that the stake sometimes emerged through the mouth and sometimes through the head.

I tried for a minute not to see these words;

then I tried for several minutes to forget them, with the book shut.

The thing that most haunted me that day, however, as I closed my notebook and put my coat on to go home, was not my ghostly image of Dracula, or the description of impalement, but the fact that these things had — apparently — actually occurred. If I listened too closely, I thought, I would hear the screams of the boys, of the "large family" dying together. For all his attention to my historical education, my father had neglected to tell me this: history's terrible moments were real. I understand now, decades later, that he could never have told me. Only history itself can convince you of such a truth. And once you've seen that truth — really seen it — you can't look away.

When I reached home that night, I felt a kind of devilish strength, and I confronted my father. He was reading in his library while Mrs. Clay rattled the dinner dishes in the kitchen. I went into the library, closed the door behind me, and stood in front of his chair. He was holding one of his beloved volumes of Henry James, a sure sign of stress. I stood without speaking until he looked up. "Hello, there," he said, finding his bookmark with a smile. "Algebra homework?" His eyes were anxious already.

"I want you to finish the story," I said.

He was silent, tapping his fingers on the arm of the chair.

"Why won't you tell me more?" It was the first time I had ever felt myself a menace to him. He looked at the book he had just closed. I knew that I was being cruel to him in a way I could not understand, but I had begun my bloody work, so I would have to finish. "You don't want me to know things."

He looked up at me, finally. His face was inscrutably sad, deeply furrowed in the light from his lamp. "No, I don't."

"I know more than you think," I said, although I felt that was a childish stab; I wouldn't have wanted to tell him what I knew, if he'd asked me.

He folded his hands under his chin. "I know you do," he said. "And because you know anything at all I will have to tell you everything."

I stared at him, surprised. "Then just tell me," I said fiercely.

He looked down again. "I will tell you, and I'll tell you as soon as I can. But not all at once." Suddenly he burst out, "I can't bear it all at once! Be patient with me."

But the look he gave me was pleading, not accusing. I went to him and put my arm around his bowed head.

March would be chill and blustery in Tuscany, but my father thought a short trip in the countryside there was in order after four days of talks — I always knew his occupation as "talks" — in Milan. This time, I didn't have to ask him to take me along. "Florence is wonderful, especially off-season," he said one morning as we drove south from Milan. "I'd like you to see it one of these days. You'll have to learn a little more about its history and paintings first, to really get a kick out of it. But the Tuscan countryside's the real thing. It rests your eyes and excites them at the same time — you'll see."

I nodded, settling into the passenger seat of the rented Fiat. My father's love of freedom was contagious, and I liked the way he loosened his shirt collar and tie when we headed off for a new place. He was setting the Fiat to a hum on the smooth northern highway. "Anyway, I've been promising Massimo and Giulia for years that we'd come. They'd never forgive my passing this close without a visit." He leaned back and stretched his legs. "They're a little strange — *eccentric* is the way to put it, I guess, but very kind. Are you game?"

"I said I was," I pointed out. I preferred staying alone with my father to visiting strangers, whose presence always brought out my native shyness, but he seemed eager to see his old friends. In any case, the vibration of the Fiat was lulling me to sleep; I was tired from the train trip. A spell had come over me that morning, the alarmingly belated trickle of blood my doctor was always worrying about and for which Mrs. Clay had awkwardly supplied my suitcase with a mass of cotton pads. My first glimpse of this change had brought tears of surprise to my eyes in the train lavatory, as if someone had wounded me; the smudge on my sensible cotton underpants looked like the thumbprint of a murderer. I'd said nothing about it to my father. River valleys and village-piled distant hills became a hazy panorama past the car window, then blurred. I was still sleepy at lunch, which we ate in a town made up of cafés and dark bars, the street cats curling and uncurling around the doorways.

But when we pulled upward with the twilight toward one of twenty towering hill towns, stacking themselves around us like the subjects of a fresco, I found myself wide awake. The windy, cloud-swept evening showed cracks of sunset on the horizon — toward the Mediterranean, my father said, toward Gibraltar and other places we might go someday. Above us was a town built on stilts of stone, its streets nearly vertical and its alleys terraced with narrow stone steps. My father guided the little car here and there, once past a trattoria doorway that streamed light onto the damp cobbles. Then he steered cautiously down the other side of the hill. "It's in here, if I'm remembering correctly." He turned between dark guardian cypresses into a rutted lane. "Villa Montefollinoco, at Monteperduto. Monteperduto's the town. Remember?"

I remembered. We'd looked at the map over breakfast, my father tracing with one finger past his coffee cup: "Siena, here. That's your focal point. That's in Tuscany. Then we cross just into Umbria. Here's Montepulciano, a famous old place, and on this next hill is our town, Monteperduto." The names ran together in my head, but *monte* meant *mountain* and we were among mountains for a large dollhouse, small painted mountains like children of the Alps, which I'd traveled through twice now.

• • •

In the impending darkness, the villa looked small, a low-slung farmhouse made of fieldstone, with cypress and olive trees clustered around its reddish roofs and a couple of leaning stone posts to mark a front walk. Light glowed in the windows on the first floor, and I found myself suddenly hungry, tired, filled with a young crankiness I would have to hide in front of our hosts. My father took our bags from the trunk of the car and I followed him up the walk. "Even the bell's still here," he said, satisfied, pulling on a short rope by the entryway and smoothing his hair back in the gloom.

The man who answered came out like a tornado, hugging my father, slapping him hard on the back, kissing him soundly on both cheeks, bending over a little too far to shake my hand. His own hand was enormous and warm and he put it on my shoulder to lead me in with him. In the front hall, which was low beamed and full of ancient furniture, he bellowed like a farm animal. "Giulia! Giulia! Quickly! The big arrival! Come here!" His English was ferocious and sure, strong, loud.

The smiling tall woman who came in pleased me at once. Her hair was gray but it gleamed silver, pinned back from a long face. She smiled at

70

me first and didn't bend over to meet me. Her hand was warm, like her husband's, and she kissed my father on each cheek, shaking her head through a gentle stream of Italian. "And you," she said to me in English, "must have your own room, a good one, okay?"

"Okay," I agreed, liking the sound of that and hoping it would be safely near my father's and would have a view of the surrounding valley from which we'd climbed so precipitously.

After dinner in the flagstoned dining room, all the grown-ups leaned back and sighed. "Giulia," my father said, "you become a greater cook every year. One of the great cooks of Italy."

"Nonsense, Paolo." Her English breathed Oxford and Cambridge. "You always talk nonsense."

"Maybe it's the Chianti. Let me look at that bottle."

"Let me fill your glass again," Massimo interjected. "And what are you studying, lovely daughter?"

"We study all subjects at my school," I said primly.

"She likes history, I think," my father told them. "She's a good sightseer, too."

"History?" Massimo filled Giulia's glass again, and then his own, with wine the color of garnets, or dark blood. "Like you and me, Paolo. We gave your father this name," he explained to me, aside, "because I can't stand those boring Anglo names you all have. Sorry, I just can't. Paolo, my friend, you know I could have dropped dead when they told me you gave up your life in the academy to *parley-vous* all over the world. So he likes to talk more than he likes to read, I said to myself. A great scholar lost to the world, that's your father." He gave me half a glass of wine without asking my father and poured some water into it from the jug on the table. I felt fond of him now.

"Now you're talking nonsense," my father said contentedly. "I like to travel, that's what I like."

"Ah." Massimo shook his head. "And you, Signor Professor, once said you'd be the greatest of them all. Not that your foundation isn't a wonderful success, I know."

"We need peace and diplomatic enlightenment, not more research on tiny questions no one else cares about," my father countered, smiling. Giulia lit a lantern on the sideboard, turning off the electric light. She brought the lantern to the table and began to cut up a *torta* I'd been trying not to stare at earlier. Its surface gleamed like obsidian under the knife.

"In history, there are no tiny questions." Massimo winked at me. "Besides, even the great Rossi said you were his best student. And the rest of us could hardly please the fellow."

"Rossi!"

It was out of my mouth before I could stop myself. My father glanced uneasily at me over his cake.

"So you know the legends of your father's academic successes, young lady?" Massimo filled his mouth hugely with chocolate.

My father gave me another glance. "I've told her a few stories about those days," he said. I didn't miss the undercurrent of warning in his voice. A moment later, however, I thought it might have been directed at Massimo, not me, since Massimo's next comment shot a chill through me before my father quashed it with a quick shift to politics.

"Poor Rossi," Massimo said. "Tragic, wonderful man. Strange to think anyone one has known personally can just — *poof* — disappear."

The next morning we sat on the sun-washed piazza at the town's summit, jackets firmly buttoned and brochures in hand, watching two boys who should, like me, have been at school.

They shrieked and punted their soccer ball back and forth in front of the church, and I waited patiently. I had been waiting all morning, through the tour of dark little chapels "with elements of Brunelleschi," according to the vague and bored guide, and the Palazzo Pubblico, with its reception chamber that had served for centuries as a town granary. My father sighed and gave me one of two Oranginas in dainty bottles. "You're going to ask me something," he said a little glumly.

"No, I just want to know about Professor Rossi." I put my straw into the neck of the bottle.

"I thought so. Massimo was tactless to bring that up."

I dreaded the answer, but I had to ask. "Did Professor Rossi die? Is that what Massimo meant when he said *disappear?*"

My father looked across the sun-filled square to the cafés and butcher shops on the other side. "Yes. No. Well, it was a very sad thing. Do you really want to hear about that?"

I nodded. My father glanced around, quickly. We were sitting on a stone bench that projected from one of the fine old palazzi, alone except for the fleet-footed boys on the square. "All right," he said at last.

Chapter 6

YOU SEE, my father said, that night when Rossi gave me the package of papers, I left him smiling at his office door, and as I turned away I was seized by the feeling that I should detain him, or turn back to talk with him a little longer. I knew it was merely the result of our strange conversation, the strangest of my life, and I buried it at once. Two other graduate students in our department came by, deep in conversation, greeting Rossi before he shut his door and walking briskly down the stairs behind me. Their animated talk gave me the sensation that life was going on around us as usual, but I still felt uneasy. My book, ornamented with the dragon, was a burning presence in my briefcase, and now Rossi had added this sealed packet of notes. I wondered if I should look through them later that night, sitting alone at the desk in my tiny apartment. I was exhausted; I felt I couldn't face whatever they held.

I suspected, also, that daylight, morning, would bring a return of confidence and reason. Perhaps I wouldn't even believe Rossi's story by the time

I awoke, although I also felt sure it would haunt me whether I actually believed it or not. And how, I asked myself — outside now, passing under Rossi's windows and glancing up involuntarily to where his lamp still shone — how could I not believe my adviser on any point related to his own scholarship? Wouldn't that call into question all the work we had done together? I thought of the first chapters of my dissertation, sitting in piles of neatly edited typescript on my desk at home, and shuddered. If I didn't believe Rossi's story, could we go on working together? Would I have to assume he was mad?

Maybe it was because Rossi was on my mind as I passed under his windows that I became acutely aware of his lamp still shining there. In any case, I was actually stepping into the puddles of light thrown from them onto the street, heading toward my own neighborhood, when they — the pools of light — went out quite literally under my feet. It happened in a fraction of a second, but a thrill of horror washed over me, head to foot. One moment I was lost in thought, stepping into the pool of brightness his light threw on the pavement, and the next moment I was frozen to the spot. I had realized two strange things almost simultaneously. One was that I had never seen this light on the pavement there, between the Gothic classroom buildings, although I'd walked up the street perhaps a thousand times. I had never seen it before because it had never been visible there before. It was visible now because all the streetlights had suddenly gone off. I was alone on the street, my last footstep the only sound lingering there. And except for those broken patches of light from the study where we'd sat talking ten minutes earlier, the street was dark.

My second realization, if it actually came second, swooped over me like a paralysis as I halted. I say *swooped* because that was how it came over my sight, not into my reason or instinct. At that moment, as I froze in its path, the warm light from my mentor's window went out. Maybe you think this sounds ordinary: office hours finish, and the last professor to leave the building turns off his lamps, darkening a street on which the streetlights have momentarily failed. But the effect was nothing like this. I had no sense of an ordinary desk lamp's being switched out in a window. Instead it was as if something raced over the window behind me, blotting out the source of light. Then the street was utterly dark.

For a moment I stopped breathing. Terrified and clumsy, I turned, saw the darkened windows, all but invisible above the dark street, and on impulse ran toward them. The door through which I'd made my exit was firmly bolted. No other lights showed in the building's facade. At this hour, the door was probably set to lock behind anyone who walked out — surely that was normal. I was standing there, hesitating, on the verge of running around to the other doors, when the streetlights came on again, and I felt suddenly abashed. There was no sign of the two students who'd walked out behind me; they must, I thought, have gone off in a different direction.

But now another group of students was strolling past, laughing; the street was no longer deserted. What if Rossi came out in a minute, as he certainly would after having switched off his light and locked his office door behind him, and found me waiting here? He had said he didn't want to discuss further what we'd been discussing. How could I explain my irrational fears to him, there on the doorstep, when he'd drawn a curtain over the subject — over all morbid subjects, perhaps? Embarrassed, I turned away before he could catch up with me and hurried home. There, I left the envelope in my briefcase, unopened, and slept — although restlessly — through the night.

The next two days were busy, and I didn't let myself look at Rossi's papers; in fact, I put all esoterica resolutely out of my mind. It took me by surprise, therefore, when a colleague from my department stopped me in the library late on the afternoon of the second day. "Have you heard about Rossi?" he demanded, grabbing my arm and wheeling me around as I hurried past. "Paolo, wait!" Yes, you're guessing correctly — it was Massimo. He was big and loud even as a graduate student, louder than he is now, maybe. I gripped his arm.

"Rossi? What? What about him?"

"He's gone. He's disappeared. The police are searching his office."

I ran all the way to the building, which now looked ordinary, hazy inside with late-afternoon sun and crowded with students leaving their classrooms. On the second floor, in front of Rossi's office, a city policeman was talking with the department chairman and several men I'd never seen before. As I arrived, two men in dark jackets were leaving the professor's study, closing the door firmly behind them and heading toward the stairs and classrooms. I pushed my way through and spoke to the policeman. "Where's Professor Rossi? What's happened to him?"

"Do you know him?" asked the policeman, looking up from his notepad.

"I'm his advisee. I was here two nights ago. Who says he's disappeared?"

The department chairman came forward and shook my hand. "Do you know anything about this? His housekeeper phoned at noon to say he hadn't come home last night or the night before — he didn't ring for dinner or breakfast. She says he's never done that before. He missed a meeting at the department this afternoon without phoning first, which he's never done before, either. A student stopped by to say his office was locked when they'd agreed on an appointment during office hours and that Rossi had never shown up. He missed his lecture today, and finally I had the door opened."

"Was he in there?" I tried not to gasp for breath.

"No."

I pushed blindly away from them toward Rossi's door, but the policeman held me back by one arm. "Not so fast," he said. "You say you were here two nights ago?"

"Yes."

"When did you last see him?"

"About eight-thirty."

"Did you see anyone else around here then?"

I thought. "Yes, just two students in the department — Bertrand and Elias, I think, going out at the same time. They left when I did."

"Good. Check that," the policeman said to one of the men. "Did you notice anything out of the ordinary in Professor Rossi's behavior?"

What could I say? Yes, actually — he told me that vampires are real, that Count Dracula walks among us, that I might have inherited a curse through his own research, and then I saw his light blotted out as if by a giant —

"No," I said. "We had a meeting about my dissertation and sat talking until about eight-thirty."

"Did you leave together?"

"No. I left first. He walked me to the door and then went back into his office."

"Did you see anything or anyone suspicious around the building as you left? Hear anything?"

I hesitated again. "No, nothing. Well, there was a brief blackout on the street. The streetlights went off."

"Yes, that's been reported. But you didn't hear anything or see anything out of the usual?"

"No."

"So far you're the last person to see Professor Rossi," the policeman insisted. "Think hard. When you were with him, did he do or say anything strange? Any talk of depression, suicide, anything like that? Or any talk of going away, going on a trip, say?"

"No, nothing like that," I said honestly. The policeman gave me a hard look.

"I need your name and address." He wrote down everything and turned to the chairman. "You can vouch for this young man?"

"He's certainly who he says he is."

"All right," the policeman told me. "I want you to come in here with me and tell me if you see anything unusual. Especially anything different from two nights ago. Don't touch anything. Frankly, most of these cases turn out to be something predictable, family emergency or a little breakdown — he'll probably be back in a day or two. I've seen it a million times. But with blood on the desk we're not taking any chances."

Blood on the desk? My legs were weakening under me, but I made myself walk in slowly after the policeman. The room looked as it had on dozens of other occasions when I'd seen it in daylight: neat, pleasant, the furniture in precise attitudes of invitation, books and papers in exact stacks on the tables and the desktop. I stepped closer. Across the desk, on Rossi's tan blotting paper, lay a dark reservoir, long since spread and soaked and still. The policeman put a steadying hand on my shoulder. "Not a big enough loss of blood to be a cause of death in itself," he said. "Maybe a bad nosebleed, or some kind of hemorrhage. Did Professor Rossi ever have a nosebleed when you were with him? Did he seem ill that night?"

"No," I said. "I never saw him — bleed — and he never talked about his health to me." I realized suddenly, with appalling clarity, that I'd just spoken of our conversations in past tense, as if they were ended forever. My throat closed with emotion when I thought of Rossi standing cheerfully at the office door, seeing me off. Had he cut himself somehow — on purpose, even? — in a moment of instability, and then hurried out of the room, locking the door behind him? I tried to imagine him raving in a park, perhaps cold and hungry, or boarding a bus to some randomly chosen destination. None of it fit. Rossi was a solid structure, as cool and sane as anyone I'd ever met.

"Look around very carefully." The policeman released my shoulder. He was watching me hard, and I sensed the chairman and the others hovering in the doorway behind us. It dawned on me that until proven otherwise I would be among the suspects if Rossi had been murdered. But Bertrand and Elias would speak up for me, as I could for them. I stared at everything in the room, trying to see through it. It was an exercise in frustration; everything was real, normal, solid, and Rossi was utterly gone from it.

"No," I said finally. "I don't see anything different."

"All right." The policeman turned me toward the windows. "Look up, then."

On the white plaster ceiling over the desk, high above us, a dark smear about five inches long drifted sideways, as if pointing toward something outside. "This appears to be blood, too. Don't worry; it may or may not be Professor Rossi's. That ceiling's too high for a person to reach it easily, even with a step stool. We'll have everything tested. Now think hard. Did Rossi mention a bird getting in that night? Or did you hear any sounds as you left, maybe like something getting in? Was the window open, do you remember?"

"No," I said. "He didn't mention anything like

that. And the windows were shut, I'm sure." I couldn't take my eyes off the stain; I felt if I stared hard enough I might read something in its horrible and hieroglyphic shape.

"We've had birds in this building several times," the chairman contributed behind us. "Pigeons. They get in through the skylights once in a while."

"That's a possibility," the policeman said. "Although we haven't found any droppings, it's certainly a possibility."

"Or bats," the chairman said. "What about bats? These old buildings probably have all kinds of things living in them."

"Well, that's another possibility, especially if Rossi tried to hit something with a broom or umbrella and wounded it in the process," suggested a professor in the doorway.

"Did you see anything like a bat in here, ever, or a bird?" the policeman asked me again.

It took me a few seconds to form the simple word and get it past my dry lips. "No," I said, but I could hardly make sense of his question. My eyes had finally caught the inner end of the dark stain and what it seemed to trail away from. On the top shelf of Rossi's bookcase, in his row of "failures," a book was missing. Where he had re-placed his mysterious book two nights before, one narrow black crevice now gaped among the spines.

My colleagues were leading me out again, pat-ting my back and telling me not to worry; I must have looked white as a piece of typing paper. I turned to the policeman, who was shutting and locking the door behind us. "Is there any chance Professor Rossi is already in a hospital some-where, if he cut himself, or if someone injured him?"

The officer shook his head. "We've got a line to the hospitals, and we've done a first check. No sign of him. Why? Do you think he might have injured himself? I thought you said he didn't seem suicidal or depressed."

"Oh, he didn't." I took a deep breath and felt my feet under me again. The ceiling was too high for him to have smeared his wrist on, any-way — that was a grim consolation.

"Well, folks, we'll be on our way." He turned to the department chairman, and they went off in low-voiced conference. The crowd around the office door was beginning to disperse, and I moved away ahead of them. I needed above all a quiet place to sit down.

The Historian

•   •   •

My favorite bench in the nave of the old university library was still being warmed by the last sun of a spring afternoon. Around me three or four students read or talked in low voices, and I felt the familiar calm of that scholar's haven soak through my bones. The great hall of the library was pierced by colored windows, some of which looked into its reading rooms and cloisterlike corridors and courtyards, so that I could see people moving around inside or outside, or studying at big oak tables. It was the end of an ordinary day; soon the sun would desert the stone tablets under my feet and plunge the world into twilight — marking a full forty-eight hours since I'd sat talking with my mentor. For now, scholarship and activity prevailed here, pushing back the verges of darkness.

I should tell you that usually when I studied in those days I liked to be completely alone, undisturbed, in monastic silence. I've already described the study carrels I often worked in, on the upper floors of the library stacks, where I had my own niche and where I'd found that weird book that had changed my life and thoughts almost overnight. Two days ago at this time I'd been studying there, busy and unafraid, about to sweep up my books on the Netherlands and hurry toward a pleasant conference with my mentor. I'd thought of nothing but what Heller and Herbert had written the year before on Utrecht's economic history and how I might refute it in an article, perhaps an article filched efficiently from one of my own dissertation chapters.

In fact, if I had imagined any part of the past at all, then, I had been picturing those innocent, slightly grasping Nederlanders debating their guilds' little problems, or standing, arms akimbo, in doorways above the canals, watching some new crate of goods as it was hauled up to the top floor of their houses-cum-warehouses. If I had had any visions of the past, I had seen only their rose-tinted, sea-freshened faces, beetling brows, capable hands, heard the creaking of their fine ships, smelled the spice and tar and sewage of the wharf and rejoiced in the sturdy ingenuity of their buying and bartering.

But history, it seemed, could be something entirely different, a splash of blood whose agony didn't fade overnight, or over centuries. And today my studies were to be of a new sort — novel to me, but not to Rossi and not to many others who had picked their way through the same dark underbrush. I wanted to begin this new kind of research in the cheerful murmur and clang of the main hall, not in the silent stacks, with their occasional wearily treading footsteps on distant stairs. I wanted to open the next phase of my life as a historian there under the unsuspecting eyes of young anthropologists, graying librarians, eighteen-year-olds thinking of their squash games or new white shoes, of smiling undergraduates and harmlessly lunatic professors emeritus — all the traffic of the university evening. I looked once more around the teeming hall, the rapidly withdrawing patches of sunlight, the brisk business of the doors at the main entrance swinging open and shut on bronze hinges. Then I picked up my shabby briefcase, unsnapped the top, and drew out a thickly full dark envelope, labeled in Rossi's handwriting. It said, merely: SAVE FOR NEXT ONE.

Next one? I hadn't looked closely at it two nights before. Had he meant to save the information enclosed for the next time he attempted this project, this dark fortress? Or was I myself the "next one"? Was this a proof of his madness?

Inside the open envelope I saw a pile of papers of different weights and sizes, many dingy and delicate with age, some of them onionskin covered with dense rows of typing. A great deal of material. I would have to spread it out, I decided. I went to the nearest honey-colored table by the card catalog. There were still plenty of people around, all friendly strangers, but I looked superstitiously over one shoulder before drawing out the documents and arranging them on the table.

I had handled some of Sir Thomas More's manuscripts two years before, and some of the elder Albrecht's letters from Amsterdam, and more recently had helped to catalog a set of Flemish account books from the 1680s. I knew, as a historian, that the order of any archival find is an important part of its lesson. Digging out a pencil and paper, I made a list of the order of the items as I withdrew them. The first, the topmost, of Rossi's documents proved to be the onion-skin sheets. They had been covered by the neatest possible typing, more or less in the form of letters. I kept them carefully together without letting myself look closely.

The second item was a map, hand drawn with awkward neatness. This was already fading, and the marks and place-names showed up poorly on a thick foreign-feeling notebook paper obviously torn from some old tablet. Two similar maps followed it. After these came three pages of scattered handwritten notes, in ink and quite legible at first glance. I set these together, too. Next was a printed brochure inviting tourists to "Romantic Roumania," in English, that looked from its Deco embellishments like a product of the 1920s or '30s. Next, two receipts for a hotel and for meals taken there. Istanbul, in fact. Then a large old road map of the Balkans, untidily printed in two colors. The last item was a little ivory envelope, sealed and unlabeled. I set it aside, heroically, without touching the flap.

That was it. I turned the big brown envelope upside down, even shook it, so that not so much as a dead fly could go unnoticed. While I was doing this I suddenly (and for the first time) had a sensation that would accompany me through all the ensuing efforts required of me: I felt Rossi's presence, his pride in my thoroughness, something like his spirit living and speaking to me through the careful methods he himself had taught me. I knew he worked swiftly, as a researcher, but also that he abused nothing and neglected nothing — not a single document, not an archive, however far from home it was located, and certainly not an idea, however unfashionable it might be among his colleagues.

His disappearance, and — I thought wildly — his very need of me, had suddenly made us almost equals. I had the sense, also, that he had been promising me this outcome, this equality, all along, and waiting for the time when I would earn it.

I now had every dry-smelling item spread on the table in front of me. I began with the letters, those long dense epistles typed on onionskin with few mistakes and few corrections. There was one copy of each, and they seemed to be in chronological order already. Each was carefully dated, all from December 1930, more than twenty years before. Each was headed TRINITY COLLEGE, OXFORD, without any further address. I glanced through the first letter. It told the story of his discovery of the mysterious book, and of his initial research at Oxford. The letter was signed, "Yours in grief, Bartholomew Rossi." And it began — I held the onionskin carefully even when my hand started to shake a little — it began affectionately: "My dear and unfortunate successor —"

My father suddenly stopped, and the trembling of his voice made me turn tactfully away before he could force himself to say anything more. By unspoken consent, we gathered our jackets and strolled across the famous little piazza, pretending the facade of the church still held some interest for us.

Chapter 7

MY FATHER DID NOT LEAVE Amsterdam again for several weeks, and during that time I felt that he shadowed me in a new way. I came home from school a little later than usual one day and found Mrs. Clay on the phone with him. She put me on at once. "Where have you been?" my father asked. He was calling from his office at the Center for Peace and Democracy. "I phoned twice and Mrs. Clay hadn't seen you. You've put her in a big pother."

He was the one in a pother, I could tell, although he kept his voice level. "I was reading at a new coffee shop near school," I said.

"All right," my father said. "Why don't you just call Mrs. Clay or me if you're going to be late, that's all."

I didn't like to agree, but I said I would call. My father came home early for dinner that night and read aloud to me from *Great Expectations*. Then he got out some of our photograph albums and we looked through them together: Paris, London, Boston, my first roller skates, my graduation from third grade, Paris, London, Rome. It was always just me, standing in front of the Pantheon or the gates of Père Lachaise, because my father took the pictures and there were only two of us. At nine o'clock he checked all the doors and windows and let me go to bed.

The next time I was going to be late, I did call Mrs. Clay. I explained to her that some of my classmates and I were going to do our homework together over tea. She said that was fine. I hung up and went by myself to the university library. Johan Binnerts, the librarian in the medieval collection in Amsterdam, was getting used to the sight of me, I thought; at least he smiled gravely whenever I stopped by with a new question, and he always asked how my history essays were coming along. Mr. Binnerts found for me a passage in a nineteenth-century text that I was particularly pleased to have, and I spent some time making notes from it. I have a copy of the text now, in my study at Oxford — I found the book again a few years ago in a bookshop: Lord Gelling's *History of Central Europe*. I have a sentimental attachment to it, after all these years, although I never open it without a bleak feeling, too. I remember very well the sight of my own hand, smooth and young, copying down passages in my school notebook:

In addition to displaying great cruelty, Vlad Dracula possessed great valor. His daring was such that in 1462 he crossed the Danube and carried out a night raid on horseback in the very encampment of Sultan Mehmed II and his army, which had assembled there to attack Wallachia. In this raid Dracula killed several thousand Turkish soldiers, and the Sultan barely escaped with his life before the Ottoman guard forced the Wallachians into a retreat.

A similar quantity of material might be dredged up in connection with the name of any great feudal lord of his era in Europe — more than this, in many cases, and much more, in a few. The extraordinary thing about the information available on Dracula is its longevity — that is to say, his refusal to die as an historical presence, the persistence of his legend. The few sources available in England refer directly or obliquely to other sources whose diversity would make any historian profoundly curious. He seems to have been notorious in Europe even during his own life-

time — a great accomplishment in days when Europe was a vast and by our standards disjointed world whose governments were connected by horse messenger and river freight, and when horrifying cruelty was not an unusual characteristic among the nobility. Dracula's notoriety did not end with his mysterious death and strange burial in 1476, but seems to have continued almost unabated until it faded into the brightness of the Enlightenment in the West.

The entry on Dracula ended there. I'd had enough history to puzzle over for one day, but I wandered into the English literature division and was glad to find that the library owned a copy of Bram Stoker's *Dracula*. In fact, it would take me quite a few visits to read it. I didn't know if I was allowed to check out books there, but even if I had been, I wouldn't have wanted to bring it home, where I would have the difficult choice of hiding it or leaving it carefully out in the open. Instead, I read *Dracula* sitting in a slippery chair by a library window. If I peered outside, I could see one of my favorite canals, the Singel, with its flower market, and people buying snacks of herring from a little stand. It was a wonderfully secluded spot, and the back of a bookshelf sheltered me from the other readers in the room.

There, in that chair, I gradually allowed Stoker's alternating Gothic horror and cozy Victorian love stories to engulf me. What I wanted from the book, I didn't quite know; according to my father, Professor Rossi had thought it mainly useless as a source of information about the real Dracula. The courtly, repulsive Count Dracula of the novel was a compelling figure, I thought, even if he didn't have much in common with Vlad Ţepeş. But Rossi himself had been convinced that Dracula had become one of the undead, in life — in the course of history. I wondered if a novel could have the power to make something so strange happen in actuality. After all, Rossi had made his discovery well after the publication of *Dracula*. Vlad Dracula, on the other hand, had been a force for evil almost four hundred years before Stoker's birth. It was very perplexing.

And hadn't Professor Rossi also said that Stoker had turned up lots of sound information about vampire lore? I had never even seen a vampire movie — my father did not like horror of any sort — and the conventions of the story were new to me. According to Stoker, a vampire could attack his victims only between sunset and sunrise. The vampire lived indefinitely, feasting on the blood of mortals and thereby converting them to his own undead state. He could take the form of bat or wolf or mist; he could be repelled by the use of garlic blossoms or a crucifix; he could be destroyed if you drove a stake through his heart and filled his mouth with garlic while he slept in his coffin during the daylight. A silver bullet through the heart could also destroy him.

None of this would have frightened me, in itself; it all seemed too remote, too superstitious, quaint. But there was one aspect of the story that haunted me after each session, after I'd put the book back on its shelf, carefully noting the page number where I'd left off. It was a thought that followed me down the steps of the library and across the canal bridges, until I reached our door. The Dracula of Stoker's imagination had a favorite sort of victim: young women.

My father was longing more than ever, he said, for the South in spring; he wanted me to see its beauties, too. My vacation was coming soon, anyway, and his meetings in Paris would detain him only a few days. I had learned not to press him, either for travel or for stories; when he was ready, the next would come, but never, never when we were at home. I believe that he didn't want to bring that dark presence directly into our house.

We took the train to Paris and later a car south into the Cévennes. In the mornings I worked on two or three essays in my increasingly lucid French, to mail back to school. I still have one of these; even now, decades later, unfolding it returns to me that feeling of the untranslatable heart of France in May, the smell of grass that was not grass but *l'herbe,* edibly fresh, as if all French vegetation were fantastically culinary, the ingredients of a salad or something to stir into cheese.

At farms along the road we stopped to buy picnics better than any restaurant could have made for us: boxes of new strawberries that gave off a red glow in the sun and seemed to need no washing; cylinders of goat cheese weighty as barbells and encrusted with a rough gray mold, as if they'd been rolled across a cellar floor. My father drank dark red wine, unlabeled and costing only centimes, which he recorked after each meal, carrying with it a small glass wrapped carefully in a napkin. For dessert we ravaged whole loaves of newly baked bread from the last town, inserting squares of dark chocolate into them. My stomach ached with pleasure and my father said ruefully that he'd have to diet again when we returned to our ordinary lives.

That road led us through the Southeast and then, a blurred day or two later, up into cooler mountains. "Les Pyrénées-Orientales," my father told me, unfolding the road map across one of our picnics. "I've been wanting to come back down here for years." I traced our route with my finger and found we were surprisingly close to Spain. This thought — and the beautiful word *Orientales* — jolted me. We were approaching the edges of my known world, and for the first time I realized that someday I might go farther and farther out of it. My father wanted to see a particular monastery, he said. "I think we can reach the town at its foot by tonight and walk up there tomorrow."

"Is it high up?" I asked.

"It's about halfway up the mountains, which protected it from all sorts of invaders. It was built just at the year 1000. Incredible — this little place carved into a rock, difficult for even the most enthusiastic pilgrims to reach. But you'll like the town below it just as much. It's an old spa town. It's really charming." My father smiled when he said this, but he was restless, folding the map too quickly. I felt that he would soon tell me another story; perhaps this time I wouldn't need to ask.

I did like Les Bains, when we drove into it that afternoon. It was a large sand-colored rock village spread over one small peak. The great Pyrénées hung above it, shadowing all but its broadest lower streets, which stretched toward river valleys and the dry flat farms below. Dusty plane trees, cropped square around a series of dusty piazzas, provided no shade whatsoever for the strolling townspeople and the tables where old women sold crocheted tablecloths and bottles of lavender extract. From there we could look up to the predictable stone church, haunted by swallows, at the town's summit, and see the church tower floating in an enormous shadow of mountains, a long peak of gloom that would stretch down this side of the village street by street as the sun set.

We dined heartily on a soup something like gazpacho, and then on veal cutlets, in the first-floor restaurant of one of the town's nineteenth-century hotels. The restaurant manager put one foot on the brass rail of the bar next to our table and asked idly, yet courteously, about our travels. He was a homely man, dressed in immaculate black, with a narrow face and sharply olive complexion. He spoke staccato French, flavored by some spice I hadn't encountered before, and I understood far less of it than my father did. My father translated.

"Ah, of course — our monastery," began the maître d', in answer to my father's question. "You know that Saint-Matthieu draws eight thousand visitors every summer? Yes, it really does. But they are all so nice, quiet, lots of foreign Christian people who go up on foot, it's a real pilgrimage still. They make their own beds in the mornings, and we hardly notice them come and go. Of course, many other people come for *les bains*. You will take the waters, no?"

My father replied that we had to turn north again after just two nights here and that we planned to spend all of the next day at the monastery.

"You know there are a lot of legends in this place, some remarkable ones, and all true," the maître d' said, smiling, which made his narrow face suddenly handsome. "The young lady understands? She might be interested to know them."

"Je comprends, merci," I said politely.

"Bon. I shall tell you one. You don't mind? Please, eat your cutlet — it's best very hot." At that moment, the restaurant door swung open, and a smiling old couple who could only have been residents came in and chose a table. *"Bon soir, buenas tardes,"* our manager said in one breath. I looked a question at my father, and he laughed.

"Yes, we are very mixed up here," the manager said, laughing too. "We are *la salade,* all the different cultures. My grandfather spoke very good Spanish — perfect Spanish — and he fought in their civil war when he was already an old man. We love all our languages here. No bombs for us, no terrorists, like les Basques. *We* are not criminals." He looked around indignantly, as if someone had contradicted him.

"Explain to you later," my father said under his breath.

"So, I will tell you a story. I am proud to say they call me the historian of our town. Eat. Our monastery was founded in the year 1000, you know already. Actually, the year 999, because the monks who chose this spot were preparing for the Apocalypse to come, you know, in the millennium. They were climbing in these mountains looking for a place for their church. Then one of them had a vision in his sleep that Saint Matthieu stepped down from heaven to place a white rose on the peak above them. The next day they climbed up there and consecrated the mountain with their prayers. Very pretty — you will love it. But that is not the great legend. That is only the founding of the abbey church.

"So, when the monastery and its little church were just a century old, one of the most pious monks, who taught the younger ones, died mysteriously in middle age. He was called Miguel de Cuxa. They mourned him terribly, and he was buried in their crypt. You know, that is the crypt we are famous for, because it is the oldest Romanesque architecture in Europe. Yes!" He tapped the bar crisply with long, squared-off fingers. "Yes! Some people say this honor goes to Saint-Pierre, outside Perpignan, but they are just lying for the tourist trade.

"In any case, this great scholar was buried in the crypt, and soon after that a curse came over the monastery. Several monks died of a strange plague. They were found dead one by one in the cloisters — the cloisters are beautiful, you will love them. They are the most beautiful in Europe. So, the dead monks were found white as ghosts, as if they had no blood in their veins. Everyone suspected poisons.

"Finally one young monk — he was the favorite student of the monk who had died — he went down into the crypt and dug up his teacher, against the wishes of the abbot, who was very frightened. And they found the teacher alive, but not really alive, if you know what I mean. A living death. He was rising at night to take the lives of his fellow monks. In order to send the poor man's soul up to the right place, they brought holy water from a shrine in the mountains and got a very sharp stake —" He made a dramatic shape in the air, so I would understand the sharpness of the object. I had been fixed on him and his strange French, putting his story together in my mind with the greatest effort of concentration. My father had stopped translating for me, and at that moment his fork clinked against his plate. When I looked up, I suddenly saw that he was as white as the tablecloth, staring at our new friend.

"Could we —" He cleared his throat and wiped his mouth with his napkin once or twice. "Could we have coffee?"

"But you have not had the *salade*." Our host looked distressed. "It is exceptional. And then we have *poires belles-Hélène* this evening, and some nice cheese, also a *gâteau* for the young lady."

"Certainly, certainly," my father said hurriedly. "Let's have all those things, yes."

The lowest of the dusty squares was full of thrumming loudspeaker music when we emerged; some kind of local show was in progress in the form of ten or twelve children in costumes that reminded me of *Carmen*. The small girls quivered in place, rustling their yellow taffeta flounces from hip to ankles, their heads swaying gracefully under lace mantillas. The little boys stamped and knelt, or circled the girls disdainfully. Each boy was dressed in a short black jacket and tight trousers and carried a velvet hat. We could hear the music flaring up now and then, accompanied by a sound like the crack of whips, which grew louder as we came close. A few other tourists were standing around watching the dancers, and a row of parents and grandparents sat on folding chairs by the empty fountain, applauding whenever the music or the boys' stamping reached a crescendo.

We lingered only a few minutes before turning onto the road upward, the one that led so clearly out of the square to the church at the top. My father said nothing about the rapidly sinking sun, but I felt our pace was set by the day's sudden death, and I wasn't surprised when all the light in that wild country plunged away from it suddenly. The rim of the blue-black Pyrénées on the horizon stood out starkly as we climbed. Then it melted into blue-black sky. The view from the foot of the church wall was enormous — not dizzying like the views we'd caught in those Italian towns I still dreamed about, but vast: plains and hills gathering themselves into foothills, and foothills rearing up into dark peaks that blocked out whole portions of the distant world. Just below us the town's lights were coming on, people were walking up the streets or along alleys, talking and laughing, and a smell like the scent of carnations came from the narrow walled gardens. Swallows flew in and out of the church tower, wheeling as if outlining something invisible with filaments of air. I noticed one that cartwheeled drunkenly among the rest, weightless and awkward instead of swift, and realized it was a single bat, just visible against the faltering light.

My father sighed, leaning against the wall, and put one foot up on a block of stone — a hitch-

ing post, something to climb onto a donkey
from? He wondered this aloud, for my benefit.
Whatever it was, it had seen centuries of this
view, the countless similar sunsets, the relatively
recent change from candle glow to electric
lights in the high-walled streets and cafés. My father looked relaxed again, propped there after a
fine meal and a stroll in the absolutely clear air,
but it seemed to me that he was relaxed on purpose. I hadn't dared to ask him about his strange
reaction to the story the restaurant maître d' had
told us, but it had opened up to me a sense that
there might be stories more horrifying to my father even than the one he'd begun telling me.
This time, I didn't have to ask him to go on with
our story; it was as if he preferred it, for now, to
something worse.

Chapter 8

December 13, 1930
Trinity College, Oxford
My dear and unfortunate successor:

I take some comfort today in the fact that this date is dedicated in the church calendar to Lucia, saint of light, a holy presence carted home by Viking traders from southern Italy. What could offer better protection against the forces of darkness — internal, external, eternal — than light and warmth, as one approaches the shortest, coldest day of the year? And I am still here, after another sleepless night. Would you be less puzzled if I told you that I now slumber with a wreath of garlic under my pillow, or that I keep a little gold crucifix on a chain around my atheist neck? I don't, of course, but I will leave you to imagine those forms of protection, if you like; they have their intellectual, their psychological, equivalents. To these latter, at least, I cling night and day.

To resume my account of my research: yes, I changed my travel plans last summer to include Istanbul, and I changed them under the influence of one small piece of parchment. I had examined every source I could find at Oxford and in London that might pertain to the Drakulya of my mysterious blank book. I had taken a sheaf of notes on the subject, which you, unquiet reader of the future, will find with these letters. I have expanded them a little since then, as you shall hear later, and I hope they will protect as well as guide you.

I had every intention of dropping this pointless research, this chase after a random sign in a randomly discovered book, on the eve of my departure for Greece. I knew perfectly well that I had taken it up as a challenge dealt me by fate, in whom, after all, I didn't even believe, and that I was probably pursuing the elusive and evil word Drakulya back into history out of a sort of scholarly bravado, to prove I could find the historical traces of anything, anything at all. In fact, I had so nearly lapsed into a chastened frame of mind, packing my clean shirts and my weather-beaten sun hat, that I almost forsook the whole thing, that last afternoon.

But, as usual, I had prepared too diligently for my travels, I was ahead of myself, I had a little time before my last sleep and the morn-

ing train. Either I could go down to the Golden Wolf to order a pint of stout and see if my good friend Hedges was there or — here I made an unfortunate detour, in spite of myself — I could stop one last time in the Rare Book Room, which would be open until nine. There was a file I had intended to try there (although I doubted it would bring anything to light), an entry under Ottoman that had struck me as pertaining to precisely the period of Vlad Dracula's life, since the documents listed in it were, I'd noticed, mainly from the mid- to late fifteenth century.

Of course, I reasoned with myself, I couldn't go hunting through every source from that period for all of Europe and Asia; it would take years — lifetimes — and I didn't foresee getting even an article out of this bloody goose chase. But I turned my feet away from the cheering pub — a mistake that has been the downfall of many a poor scholar — and towards Rare Books.

The boxed file, which I found without difficulty, contained four or five flattened short scrolls of Ottoman workmanship, all part of an eighteenth-century gift to the University. Each scroll was covered with Arabic calligra-

phy. An English description at the front of the file assured me that this was no treasure trove, as far as I was concerned. (I referred immediately to the English because my Arabic is depressingly rudimentary, as I'm afraid it will probably remain. One has time for only a handful of the great languages unless one gives up everything else in favor of linguistics.) Three of the scrolls were inventories of taxes levied on the peoples of Anatolia by Sultan Mehmed II. The last of them listed taxes collected from the cities of Sarajevo and Skopje, a little closer to home, if home for me just now was Dracula's abode in Wallachia, but still a distant part of empire from his, in that day and time. I reassembled them with a sigh and considered the short but satisfying visit I might still pay to the Golden Wolf. As I gathered the parchments to return them to their cardboard file, however, a bit of writing on the back of that last one caught my eye.

It was a short list, a casual graffito, an ancient doodle on the reverse of Sarajevo and Skopje's official paperwork for the sultan. I read it curiously. It appeared to be a record of expenses — the objects purchased had been noted down on the left and the cost, in an un-

specified currency, noted neatly down on the right. "Five young mountain lions for his Gloriousness the Sultan, 45," I read with interest. "Two golden belts with precious stones for the Sultan, 290. Two hundred sheepskins for the Sultan, 89." And then the final entry, which made the hair rise along my arm as I held that aging parchment up: "Maps and military records from the Order of the Dragon, 12."

How, you ask, could I take all this in at a glance, when my knowledge of Arabic is as crude as I've already confessed? My quick-minded reader, you are staying awake for me, following my lucubrations with care, and I bless you for it. This scrawl, this mediaeval memorandum, was written out in Latin. Below it, a faintly scratched date seared the thing into my brain: 1490.

In 1490, I recalled, the Order of the Dragon lay in ruins, crushed by Ottoman might; Vlad Dracula was fourteen years' dead and buried, according to legend, in the monastery at Lake Snagov. The Order's maps, records, secrets — whatever this elusive phrase referred to — had been bought cheap, very cheap, compared to the bejewelled belts and the loads of stinking sheep wool. Perhaps they'd been thrown into this merchant's purchase at the last minute, as a curiosity, a sample of the bureaucracy of conquest to flatter and amuse an erudite sultan whose father or grandfather had expressed grudging admiration for the barbaric Order of the Dragon that harassed him at the edge of the Empire. Was my merchant a Balkan traveller, Latin writing, speaking some Slav or Latinate dialect? Certainly he was highly educated, since he could write at all, perhaps a Jewish merchant with three or four languages at his command. Whoever he was, I blessed his dust for jotting down those expenses. If he had sent off the caravan of spoils without incident, and if it had reached the sultan safely, and if — least likely of all — it had survived in the sultan's treasure-house of jewels, beaten copper, Byzantine glass, barbarous church relics, works of Persian poetry, books of cabala, atlases, astronomical charts —

I went to the desk, where the librarian was checking through a drawer. "Excuse me," I said. "Do you have a listing of historical archives by country? Archives in — in Turkey, for example?"

"I know what you're looking for, sir. There is such a listing, for universities and museums, although it's by no means complete. We don't

have it here — the central library desk can show it to you. They open tomorrow at nine o'clock in the morning."

My train to London, I remembered, didn't leave until 10:14. It would take only ten minutes or so to glance through the possibilities. And if Sultan Mehmed II's name, or the names of his immediate successors, appeared among any of the possibilities — well, I hadn't wanted to see Rhodes so very badly after all.

Yours in profoundest grief,
Bartholomew Rossi

Time seemed to have stopped in the high-vaulted library hall, despite the activity all around me. I had read one whole letter, but there were at least four more in the pile beneath it. I noticed, looking up, that a blue depth had opened behind the upper windows: twilight. I would have to walk home in it alone, I thought like a frightened child. Again I felt the urge to rush to Rossi's office door and knock briskly on it. Surely I'd find him sitting there turning over pages of manuscript in the pool of yellow light on his desk. I was perplexed, all over again, the way one is after a friend's death, by the unreality of the situation, the impossibility it presented to the mind. In fact, I was as much puzzled as I was afraid, and my bewilderment increased my fear because I couldn't recognize my usual self in that state.

As I pondered this, I glanced down at the neat piles of papers on my table. I had taken up a great deal of the surface with this spread. As a consequence, probably, no one had tried to sit down opposite me or to occupy any of the other chairs at the table. I was just wondering if I should gather up all of this work and walk home to continue there later when a young woman approached and seated herself at one end of the table. I saw, looking around, that the surrounding catalog tables were full to capacity and strewn with other people's books, type-scripts, card-catalog drawers, and notepads. She had no other place to sit, I realized, but I felt suddenly protective of Rossi's documents; I dreaded the involuntary glance of a stranger's eye on them. Did they look obviously mad? Or did I?

I was just about to gather the papers together, carefully, preserving their original order, and pack them away, just about to make those slow and polite movements with which you try falsely to assure the other person who has just sat down apologetically at the cafeteria table that you really were leaving anyway — when I suddenly noticed the book the young woman had propped up in front of her. She was already flipping through the center section of it, a notebook and pen lying ready at her elbow. I glanced from the book's title to her face, in astonishment, and then at the other book she had set down nearby. Then I looked back at her face.

It was a young face but already aging very slightly and handsomely, with the light crinkling of skin I recognized around my own eyes in the mirror every morning, a barely veiled fatigue, so I knew she must be a graduate student. It was also an elegant, angular face that wouldn't have been out of place in a medieval altar painting, saved from a pinched look by the delicate widening of cheekbones. Her complexion was pale but could have turned olive after a week in the sun. Her lashes were lowered toward the book, her firm mouth and spreading eyebrows somehow made alert by whatever her eyes followed on the page. Her dark, almost sooty hair sprang away from her forehead with more vigor than was fashionable in those tightly groomed days. The title of her reading, in this place of myriad inquiry — I looked again, again astonished — was *The Carpathians*. Under her dark-sweatered elbow rested Bram Stoker's *Dracula*.

At that moment, the young woman glanced up and met my gaze, and I realized I'd been staring directly at her, which must have been offensive. In fact, the dark, deep stare I got back — although her eyes also had a curious amber in their depths, like honey — was extremely hostile. I wasn't what people still called then a ladies' man; in fact I was something of a recluse. But I knew enough to feel ashamed, and I hurried to explain. Later I realized that her hostility was the defense of the striking-looking woman who is stared at again and again. "Excuse me," I said quickly. "I couldn't help noticing your books — I mean, what you're reading."

She stared unhelpfully back at me, keeping her book open in front of her, and raised the dark sweep of her eyebrows.

"You see, I'm actually studying the same subject," I persisted. Her eyebrows rose a little higher, but I indicated the papers in front of me. "No, really. I've just been reading about —" I looked at the piles of Rossi's documents in front of me and stopped abruptly. The contemptuous slant of her eyelids made my face grow warm.

"Dracula?" she said sarcastically. "Those appear to be primary sources you have got there." She had a rich accent I couldn't place, and her voice was soft, but library soft, as if it could spring into real strength when uncoiled.

I tried a different tactic. "Are you reading those for fun? I mean, for enjoyment? Or are you doing research?"

"Fun?" She kept the book open, still, maybe to discourage me with every possible weapon.

"Well, that's an unusual topic, and if you've also gotten out a work on the Carpathians, you must be deeply interested in your subject." I hadn't spoken so quickly since the orals for my master's degree. "I was just about to check that book out myself. Both of them, in fact."

"Really," she said. "And why is that?"

"Well," I hazarded, "I've got these letters here, from — from an unusual historical source — and they mention Dracula. They're about Dracula."

A faint interest dawned inside her gaze, as if the amber light had won out and was turned reluctantly on me. She slumped slightly in her chair, relaxed into something like masculine ease, without taking her hands off her book. It struck me that this was a gesture I had seen a hundred times before, this slackening of tension that accompanied thought, this settling into a conversation. Where had I seen it?

"What are those letters, exactly?" she asked, in her quiet foreign voice. I thought with regret that I should have introduced myself and my credentials before getting into any of this. For some reason, I felt I couldn't start over at this point — couldn't suddenly put out my hand to shake hers and tell her what department I was in, and so on. It also occurred to me that I'd never seen her before, so she certainly wasn't in history, unless she was new, a transfer from some other university. And should I lie to protect Rossi? I decided, at random, not to. I simply left his name out of the equation.

"I'm working with someone who's — having some problems, and he wrote these letters more than twenty years ago. He gave them to me thinking I might be able to help him out of his current — situation — which has to do with — he studies, I mean he was studying —"

"I see," she said with cold politeness. She stood up and started collecting her books, deliberately and without haste. Now she was picking up her briefcase. Standing, she looked as tall as I'd imagined her, a little sinewy, with broad shoulders.

"Why are you studying Dracula?" I asked in desperation.

"Well, I must say it is not any of your business," she told me shortly, turning away, "but I am planning a future trip, although I do not know when I will take it."

"To the Carpathians?" I felt suddenly rattled by the whole conversation.

"No." She flung that last word back at me, disdainfully. And then, as if she couldn't help herself, but so contemptuously that I didn't dare follow her: "To Istanbul."

"Good Lord," my father prayed suddenly against the twittering sky. The last swallows were homing in above us, the town with its diminished lights settling heavily into the valley. "We shouldn't be sitting around here with a hike ahead of us tomorrow. Pilgrims are supposed to turn in early, I'm sure. With the coming of dark, or something like that."

I shifted my legs; one foot had fallen asleep under me and the stones of the churchyard wall felt suddenly sharp, impossibly uncomfortable, especially with the thought of bed looming ahead of me. I would have pins and needles on the stumbling walk downhill to the hotel. I felt a boiling irritation, too, far sharper than the sensations in my feet. My father had stopped his story too soon, again.

"Look," my father said, pointing straight out from our perch. "I think that must be Saint-Matthieu."

I followed his gesture to the dark, massed mountains and saw, halfway up, a small, steady light. No other light appeared close to it; no other habitation seemed anywhere near it. It was like a single spark on immense folds of black cloth, high up but not close to the highest peaks — it hung between the town and the night sky. "Yes, that's just where the monastery must be, I think," my father said again. "And we'll have a real climb tomorrow, even if we go by the road."

As we set off along moonless streets, I felt that sadness that comes with dropping down from a height, leaving anything lofty. Before we turned the corner of the old bell tower, I glanced back once, to pin that tiny spot of light in my memory. There it was again, gleaming above a house wall tumbled over with dark bougainvillea. Standing still for a moment, I looked hard at it. Then, just once, the light winked.

Chapter 9

December 14, 1930
Trinity College, Oxford

My dear and unfortunate successor:

I shall conclude my account as rapidly as possible, since you must draw from it vital information if we are both to — ah, to survive, at least, and to survive in a state of goodness and mercy. There is survival and survival, the historian learns to his grief. The very worst impulses of humankind can survive generations, centuries, even millennia. And the best of our individual efforts can die with us at the end of a single lifetime.

But to proceed: on my journey from England to Greece, I experienced some of the smoothest travelling I have ever known. The director of the museum in Crete was actually at the dock to welcome me, and he invited me to return later in the summer, to attend the opening of a Minoan tomb. In addition, two American classicists whom I had wanted for years to meet were staying at my pension. They urged me to inquire about a faculty position that had just become available at their university — exactly the thing for someone with my background — and heaped my work with compliments. I had easy access to every collection I approached, including some private ones. In the afternoons, when the museums shut down and the town took its siesta, I sat on my lovely vine-shaded balcony, fleshing out my notes, and in the process derived ideas for several other works to be attempted at some later date. Under these idyllic circumstances I considered dropping entirely what now seemed to me to be a morbid fancy, the pursuit of that peculiar word, Drakulya. I had brought the antique book with me, not wanting to be parted from it, but I had not opened it for a week now. All in all, I felt free of its spell. But something — an historian's passion for thoroughness, or maybe sheer love of the chase — compelled me to stick to my plans and go on to Istanbul for a few days. And now I must tell you of my singular adventure in an archive there. This is perhaps the first of several events I shall describe that may inspire your disbelief. Only read to the end, I beg you.

In obedience to this plea, my father said, I read every word. That letter told me again about Rossi's chilling experience among the documents of Sultan Mehmed II's collection — his finding there a map labeled in three languages that seemed to indicate the whereabouts of Vlad the Impaler's tomb, the map's theft by a sinister bureaucrat, and the two tiny, blistered wounds on the bureaucrat's neck.

In the telling of this story, his writing style lost some of the compactness and control I had noticed in the earlier two letters, stretching thin and harried and blossoming with small errors, as if he had typed it in great agitation. And despite my own uneasiness (for it was now night, I had returned to my apartment, and I was reading alone there, with the door bolted and the curtains superstitiously drawn), I noticed the language he used in unfolding those events; it followed closely what he'd said to me only two nights before. It was as if the story had bitten so deeply into his mind, nearly a quarter-century earlier, that it needed only to be read off to a new listener.

There were three letters left, and I went on to the next one eagerly.

The Historian

December 15, 1930
Trinity College, Oxford

My dear and unfortunate successor:

From the moment the ugly official snatched away that map, my luck failed. On my return to my rooms, I found that the hotel manager had moved my belongings to a smaller and rather dirtier chamber because one corner of the ceiling had fallen in, in my own room. During this process, some of my papers had disappeared, and a pair of gold cuff-links of which I was extremely fond had also vanished.

Sitting in my cramped new quarters, I tried at once to resurrect my notes on Vlad Dracula's history — and the maps I had seen in the archives — from memory. Then I hurried away from that place back into Greece, where I attempted to resume my studies on Crete, since I now had extra time at my disposal.

The boat trip to Crete was horrendous, the sea being very high and rough. A hot, crazing wind, like France's infamous mistral, *blew down over the island without cease. My previous rooms were occupied and I found only the most pitiful lodgings, dark and musty. My American colleagues had departed. The kindly director of the museum had fallen ill and no one seemed to remember his having invited me to the opening of a tomb. I tried to go on with my writing about Crete but searched my notes in vain for inspiration. My nervousness was hardly appeased by the primitive superstitions I encountered even among townspeople, superstitions I hadn't noticed on previous trips, although they are so widespread in Greece that I must have come across them before. In Greek tradition, as in many others, the source of the vampire, the* vrykolakas, *is any corpse not properly buried, or slow to decompose, not to mention anybody accidentally buried alive. The old men in Crete's* tavernas *seemed much more inclined to tell me their two hundred and ten vampire stories than they were to explain where I might find other shards of pottery like that one, or what ancient shipwrecks their grandfathers had dived into and plundered. One evening I let a stranger buy me a round of a local speciality called, whimsically, amnesia, with the result that I was sick all the next day.*

Nothing, in fact, went well with me until after I reached England, which I did in a terrible rainy gale that caused me the most gruesome seasickness I have ever experienced.

I note down these circumstances in case they have some bearing on other aspects of my case. At the very least, they will explain to you my state of mind when I arrived in Oxford: I was exhausted, dejected, fearful. In my mirror I looked pale and thin. Whenever I cut myself shaving, which I did frequently in my nervous clumsiness, I winced, remembering those half-congealed little wounds on the Turkish bureaucrat's neck and doubting more and more the sanity of my own recollection. Sometimes I had the sense, which haunted me almost to madness, of some purpose unfulfilled, some intention whose form I could not reconstruct. I was lonely and full of longing. In a word, my nerves were in a state I'd never known before.

Of course, I attempted to carry on as usual, saying nothing of these matters to anyone and preparing for the upcoming term with my usual care. I wrote to the American classicists I'd met in Greece, intimating that I would be interested in at least a brief appointment in the States, if they could help me acquire one. I was nearly done with my degree, I felt more and more the need to start afresh, and I thought the change would do me good. I also completed two short articles on the juncture of archaeological and literary evidence in the study of Crete's pottery production. With effort, I brought my natural self-discipline to bear on each day, and each day calmed me further.

For the first month after my return, I tried not only to stifle all memory of my unpleasant journey but also to avoid any renewal of my interest in the odd little book in my luggage, or in the research it had precipitated. However, my confidence reasserting itself and my curiosity growing again — perversely — within me, I picked up the volume one evening and reassembled my notes from England and Istanbul. The consequence — and from then on I did view it as a consequence — was immediate, terrifying, and tragic.

I must pause here, brave reader; I cannot bring myself to write more, for the moment. I beg you not to desist in these readings but to pursue them further, as I will try to, myself, tomorrow.

Yours in profoundest grief,
Bartholomew Rossi

Chapter 10

AS AN ADULT, I have often known that peculiar legacy time brings to the traveler: the longing to seek out a place a second time, to find deliberately what we stumbled on once before, to recapture the feeling of discovery. Sometimes we search out again even a place that was not remarkable in itself — we look for it simply because we remember it. If we do find it, of course, everything is different. The rough-hewn door is still there, but it's much smaller; the day is cloudy instead of brilliant; it's spring instead of autumn; we're alone instead of with three friends. Or, worse, with three friends instead of alone.

The very young traveler knows little of this phenomenon, but before I knew it in myself, I saw it in my father, at Saint-Matthieu-des-Pyrénées-Orientales. I sensed in him, rather than read clearly, the mystery of repetition, already knowing he had been there years before. And, oddly, this place drew him into abstraction in a way no other we'd visited had done. He had been to the region of Emona once before our visit, and to Ragusa several times. He had visited Massimo and Giulia's stone villa for other happy suppers, in other years. But at Saint-Matthieu I sensed that he had actually longed for this place, thought it through over and over for some reason I could not excavate, relived it without telling anyone. He did not tell me now, except to recognize aloud the curve of the road before it finally ran up against the abbey wall, and to know, later, which door opened into sanctuary, cloister, or — finally — crypt. This memory for detail was nothing new to me; I had seen him reach for the right door in famous old churches before, or take the correct turn to the ancient refectory, or stop to buy tickets at the right guardhouse in the right shady gravel drive, or recall, even, where he had previously had the finest cup of coffee.

The difference at Saint-Matthieu was a difference of alertness, an almost cursory scanning of walls and cloistered walkways. Instead of seeming to say to himself, "Ah, there's that fine tympanum above the doors; I *thought* I remembered it was on this side," my father appeared to be checking off views he could already have described with his eyes closed. It came over me gradually, even before we had finished climbing the steep, cypress-shaded grounds to the main entrance, that what he remembered here were not architectural details, but events.

A monk in a long brown habit stood by the wooden doors, quietly handing brochures to the tourists. "As I told you, it's a working monastery still," my father was saying in an ordinary voice. He had put on his sunglasses, although the monastery wall threw a deep shade over us. "They keep the crowds down to a dull roar by letting everyone in for only a few hours a day." He smiled at the man as we approached, then stretched his hand out for a pamphlet. "*Merci beaucoup* — we'll take just one," he was saying in his courteous French. But this time, with the intuitive accuracy the young turn on their parents, I knew even more surely that he had not merely seen this place before, camera in hand. He hadn't just "done" it properly, even if he knew all its art-historical coordinates from his guidebook. Instead, something, I felt sure, had happened to him here.

My second impression was as fleeting as my first, but sharper: when he opened the pamphlet and put one foot on the stone threshold, bending his head too casually to the words instead of to the beasts in relief overhead (which would normally have caught his eye), I saw that he hadn't lost some old emotion for the sanctuary we were about to enter. That emotion, I realized without breathing between my intuition and the thought that followed it — that emotion was either grief or fear, or some terrible blend of the two.

Saint-Matthieu-des-Pyrénées-Orientales sits at a height of four thousand feet above sea level — and the sea is not as distant as this walled-in landscape with its wheeling eagles would have you believe. Red-roofed and precariously high at the summit, the monastery seems to have grown directly out of a single pinnacle of mountain rock, which is true, in a way, since the earliest incarnation of its church was hewed straight down into the rock itself in the year 1000. The main entrance to the abbey is a later expression of the Romanesque, influenced by the art of the Muslims who fought over the centuries to take the peak: a squared-off stone portal crowned by geometric, Islamic borders and two grimacing, groaning Christian monsters in bas-relief, creatures that might be lions, bears, bats, or griffins — impossible animals whose lineage could be anything.

Inside lies the tiny abbey church of Saint-Matthieu and its wonderfully delicate cloister, hedged in by rosebushes even at that tremendous altitude, surrounded by twisted single columns of red marble so fragile in appearance that they could have been corkscrewed into shape by an artistic Samson. Sunlight splashes onto the flagstones of the open courtyard, and blue sky arches suddenly overhead.

But the thing that caught my attention as soon as we entered was the sound of trickling water, unexpected and lovely in that high, dry place and yet as natural as the sound of a mountain stream. It came from the cloister fountain, around which the monks had once paced their meditations: a six-sided red marble basin, decorated on its flat exterior with chiseled relief that showed a miniature cloister, a reflection of the real one around us. The fountain's great basin stood on six columns of red marble (and one central support through which the springwater rose, I think). Around its exterior, six spigots burbled water into a pool below. It made an enchanting music.

When I went to the outside edge of the cloisters and sat down on a low wall there, I could look out over a drop of several thousand feet and see thin mountain waterfalls, white against the vertical blue forest. Already perched on a peak, we were surrounded by the looming, un-scalable walls of the highest Pyrénées-Orientales. At this distance, the waterfalls plunged down-ward in silence, or appeared as mere mist, while the living fountain behind me trickled and dripped audibly without pause.

"The cloistered life," my father murmured, set-tling down next to me on the wall. His face was strange, and he put one arm around my shoul-ders, something he rarely did. "It looks peaceful, but it's very hard. And wicked, sometimes, too." We sat gazing across that gulf, which was so deep that morning light hadn't yet reached the chasm below. Something hung and glinted in the air beneath us, and I realized even before my father pointed to it what it was: a bird of prey, hunting slowly along the pinnacle walls, sus-pended like a drifting flake of copper.

"Built higher than the eagles," my father mused. "You know, the eagle is a very old Chris-tian symbol, the symbol of Saint John. Matthew — Saint Matthieu — is the angel, and Luke is the ox, and Saint Mark of course is the winged lion. You see that lion all over the Adriatic, because he was Venice's patron saint. He holds a book in his paws — if the book is open, that statue or re-lief was carved at a moment when Venice was at peace. Closed, it means Venice was at war. We saw him at Ragusa — remember? — with his book closed, over one of the gates. And now we've seen the eagle, too, guarding this place. Well, it needs its guards." He frowned, stood up, and swung away. It struck me that he regretted, almost to tears, our visit here. "Shall we take a tour?"

It was not until we were descending the steps to the crypt that I saw again in my father that indescribable attitude of fear. We had finished our attentive pacing through cloisters, chapels, nave, wind-worn kitchen buildings. The crypt was the last item on our self-guided tour, dessert for the morbid, as my father said in some churches. At a yawning stairwell he seemed to go forward a little too deliberately, keeping me behind him without even raising an arm as we stepped down into the hold of the rock. A stunningly cold breath reached up for us from the earthy dark. The other tourists had moved on, finished with this attraction, and left us there alone.

"This was the nave of the first church," my father explained again, unnecessarily, in his thoroughly ordinary voice. "When the abbey grew stronger and they could continue building, they simply burst into the open air up there and built a new church on top of the old." Candles interrupted the darkness from stone sconces on the heavy pillars. A cross had been cut into the wall of the apse; it hovered, like a shadow, above the stone altar, or sarcophagus — it was hard to tell which — that stood in the apse's curve. Along the sides of the crypt lay two or three other sarcophagi, small and primitive, unmarked. My father drew a long breath, looking around that great cold hole in the rock. "The resting place of the founding abbot and of several later abbots. And that completes our tour. All right. Let's go get some lunch."

I paused on the way out. The urge to ask my father what he knew about Saint-Matthieu, what he remembered, even, came over me in a wave, almost a panic. But his back, broad in a black linen jacket, said as clearly as spoken words, "Wait. Everything in its time." I looked quickly toward that sarcophagus at the far end of the ancient basilica. Its form was crude, stolid in the unflickering light. Whatever it hid was part of the past, and guessing would not unbury it.

And I knew something else already, without having to guess. The story that I would hear over lunch on the monastic terrace, a tactful drop below the monks' quarters, might turn out to be about someplace very distant from this one, but like our visit here, it would certainly be another step toward that fear I had begun to see brooding in my father. Why had he not wanted to tell me about Rossi's disappearance until Massimo had blundered into it? Why had he choked, white, when the maître d' of the restaurant had told us a legend about the living dead? Whatever haunted my father's memory was brought out for him vividly by this place, which should have been more sacred than horrible and yet was horrible to him, so much so that his shoulders were squared against it. I would have to work, as Rossi had, to collect my own clues. I was becoming wise in the way of the story.

Chapter 11

ON MY NEXT VISIT to the library in Amsterdam, I found that Mr. Binnerts had actually looked some things up for me during my absence. When I went into the reading room straight from school, my book bag still on my back, he glanced up with a smile. "So it's you," he said in his nice English. "My young historian. I have something for you, for your project." I followed him to his desk and he took out a book. "This is not such an old book," he told me. "But it has some very old stories in it. They are not very happy reading, my dear, but maybe they will help you write your paper." Mr. Binnerts settled me at a table, and I looked gratefully at his retreating sweater. It touched me to be trusted with something terrible.

The book was called *Tales from the Carpathians,* a dingy nineteenth-century tome published privately by an English collector named Robert Digby. Digby's preface outlined his wanderings among wild mountains and wilder languages, although he had also gone to German and Russian sources for some of his work. His tales had a wild sound, too, and the prose was romantic enough, but examining them long afterward, I found his versions of them compared favorably to those of later collectors and translators. There were two tales about "Prince Dracula," and I read them eagerly. The first recounted how Dracula liked to feast out of doors among the corpses of his impaled subjects. One day, I learned, a servant complained openly in front of Dracula about the terrible smell, whereupon the prince ordered his men to impale the servant above the others, so the smell would not offend the dying servant's nose. Digby presented another version of this, in which Dracula shouted for a stake three times the length of the stakes on which the others had been impaled.

The second story was equally gruesome. It described how Sultan Mehmed II had once sent two ambassadors to Dracula. When the ambassadors came before him, they did not remove their turbans. Dracula demanded to know why they were dishonoring him in this way, and they replied that they were simply acting in accordance with their own customs. "Then I shall help you to strengthen your customs," replied the prince, and he had their turbans nailed to their heads.

I copied Digby's versions of these two little tales into my notebook. When Mr. Binnerts came back to see how I was getting along, I asked him if we might look for some sources on Dracula by his contemporaries, if there were any. "Certainly," he said, nodding gravely. He was going off his desk then, but he would look around for something as soon as he had time. Perhaps after that — he shook his head, smiling — perhaps after that I would find some pleasanter topic, such as medieval architecture. I promised — smiling, too — that I would think about it.

There is no place on earth more exuberant than Venice on a breezy, hot, cloudless day. The boats rock and swell in the Lagoon as if launching themselves, crewless, on adventure; the ornate facades brighten in the sunlight; the water smells fresh, for once. The whole city puffs up like a sail, a boat dancing unmoored, ready to float off. The waves at the edge of the Piazza di San Marco become raucous in the wake of the speedboats, producing a festive but vulgar music like the clash of cymbals. In Amsterdam, Venice of the North, this jubilant weather would have made the city sparkle with renewed purpose. Here, it ended by showing cracks in the perfection — a weedy fountain in one back square, for example, whose water should have been on full spray and instead made a rusty dribble over the lip of the basin. Saint Mark's horses pranced shabbily in the glittering light. The columns of the doge's palace looked disagreeably unwashed.

I commented on this air of dilapidated celebration, and my father laughed. "You've got an eye for atmosphere," he said. "Venice is famous for her stage show, and she doesn't mind if she gets a little run-down, as long as the world pours in here to worship her." He gestured around the outdoor café — our favorite place after Florian's — at the perspiring tourists, their hats and pastel shirts flapping in the breeze off the water. "Wait till evening and you won't be disappointed. A stage set needs a softer kind of light than this. You'll be surprised by the transformation."

For now, sipping my orangeade, I was too comfortable to move, anyway; waiting for a pleasant surprise suited my aims exactly. It was the last hot spell of summer before autumn blew in. With autumn would come more school and, if I was lucky, a little peripatetic studying with my father as he roamed a map of negotiation, compromise, and bitter bargains. This fall he would be in Eastern Europe again, and I was already lobbying to be taken along.

My father drained his beer and flipped through a guidebook. "Yes." He pounced suddenly. "Here's San Marco. You know, Venice was a rival of the Byzantine world for centuries, and a great sea power, too. In fact, Venice stole some remarkable things from Byzantium, including those carousel animals up there." I looked out from under our awning at Saint Mark's, where the coppery horses seemed to be dragging the weight of the dripping leaden domes behind them. The whole basilica looked molten in this light — garishly bright and hot, an inferno of treasure. "Anyway," said my father, "San Marco was designed partly in imitation of Santa Sophia, in Istanbul."

"Istanbul?" I said slyly, dredging my glass for ice. "You mean it looks like the Hagia Sophia?"

"Well, of course the Hagia Sophia was overrun by the Ottoman Empire, so you see those minarets guarding the outside, and inside there are huge shields bearing Muslim holy texts. You really *see* East and West collide in there. But then there are the great domes on the top, distinctly Christian and Byzantine, like San Marco's."

"And they look like these?" I pointed across the piazza.

"Yes, very much like these, but grander. The scale of the place is overwhelming. It takes your breath away."

"Oh," I said. "Could I get another drink, please?"

My father glared at me suddenly, but it was too late. Now I knew that he had been to Istanbul himself.

Chapter 12

December 16, 1930
Trinity College, Oxford
My dear and unfortunate successor:

At this point, my history has almost caught up with me, or I with it, and I must narrate events that will bring my story up to the present. There, I hope, it will stop, since I can hardly bear the thought that the future may contain more of these horrors.

As I have related, I eventually picked up my strange book again, like a man compelled by an addiction. I told myself before I did it that my life had returned to normal, that my experience in Istanbul had been odd but was surely explicable and had taken on exaggerated proportions in my travel-wearied brain. So I literally picked the book up again, and I feel I should tell you about that moment in the most literal terms.

It was a rainy evening in October, only two months ago. Term had begun, and I sat in pleasant solitude in my rooms, whiling away an hour after supper. I was waiting for my *friend Hedges, a don only ten years older than myself of whom I was extremely fond. He was an awkward and eminently good-natured person, whose apologetic shrugs and kind, shy smile disguised a wit so keen that I often felt thankful he turned it on eighteenth-century literature and not on his colleagues. Except for his shyness, he could have been at home among Addison, Swift, and Pope, gathering in some London coffeehouse. He had only a few friends, had never so much as looked directly at a woman not related to him, and fostered no dreams that reached beyond the Oxford countryside, where he liked to walk, leaning over a fence now and then to watch the cows chewing. His gentleness was visible in the shape of his big head, his meaty hands, and his soft brown eyes, so that he seemed rather bovine himself, or badgerlike, until that clever sarcasm of his suddenly stung the air. I loved to hear about his work, which he discussed in a modest but enthusiastic way, and he never failed to urge me on in my own pursuits. His name was — well, you could find it in any library, with a little poking around, since he brought several of England's literary geniuses back to life for the lay reader. But I will call him Hedges, a* nom de guerre *of my own devising, to give him in this narrative the privacy and decency that were his in life.*

This particular evening Hedges was to drop by my rooms with drafts of the two articles I had squeezed out of my work at Crete. He had read and corrected them for me, at my request; although he couldn't comment on the accuracy or inaccuracy of my descriptions of trade in the ancient Mediterranean, he wrote like an angel, the sort of angel whose precision would indeed have allowed him to dance on the head of a pin, and he often suggested polish for my style. I anticipated half an hour's friendly critique, then sherry and that gratifying moment when a true friend stretches his legs at your fireside and asks you how you've been. I wouldn't tell him the truth about my rattled and still-healing nerves, of course, but we might discuss anything and everything else.

While I waited I poked up the fire, added another log, set out two glasses, and surveyed my desk. My study also served me for a sitting room, and I made sure it was kept as orderly and comfortable as the solidity of its nineteenth-century furnishings demanded. I had completed a great deal of work that afternoon, supped off a plate brought up to me at six o'clock, and then cleared the last of my papers. Dark was coming in early already, and with it arrived a gloomy, slanting rain. I find this the most appealing kind of autumn evening, not the most dismal, so I felt only a faint shiver of premonition when my hand, searching for ten minutes' reading, fell casually on the antique volume I had been avoiding. I'd left it tucked among less disturbing items on a shelf above my desk. Now I sat down there, feeling with lurking pleasure the suede-soft old cover fitting into my hand again, and opened the book.

Immediately I became aware of something very strange. A smell rose from its pages that was not merely the delicate scent of aging paper and cracked vellum. It was a reek of decay, a terrible, sickening odor, a smell of old meat or corrupted flesh. I had never noticed it before, and I leaned closer, sniffing, unbelieving, then shut the book. I reopened it after a moment, and again stomach-turning fumes rose from its pages. The little volume seemed alive in my hands, yet it smelled of death.

This unsettling malodor brought back to me all the nervous fear of my return trip from the Continent, and I stilled my feelings only with a concerted effort. Old books rotted, that was fact, and I had travelled with this one through rain and storm. The smell could surely be explained thus. Maybe I would take it to the Rare Book Room again and get some advice on having it cleaned, or fumigated, whatever was required.

If I had not been studiously avoiding my reaction to this unpleasant presence, I would've dropped the thing, put it away again. But now, for the first time in many weeks, I made myself turn to that extraordinary central image, the wide-winged dragon snarling over his banner. Suddenly, with jarring accuracy, I saw something afresh and comprehended it for the first time. I have never been gifted with great sharpness in my visual understanding of the world, but some flicker of heightened senses showed me the outline of the whole dragon, his spread wings and looped tail. In a spasm of curiosity I rummaged through the package of notes I had brought back from Istanbul, which had lain ignored in my desk drawer. Fumbling, I found the page I wanted; torn from my own notebook, it showed a sketch I had made in the archives in Istanbul, a copy of the first of the maps I'd found there.

The Historian

You will remember that there were three of those maps, graduated in scale to show the same unnamed region in greater and greater detail. That region, even sketched in my inartistic if careful hand, had a most definite shape. It looked for all the world like a symmetrically winged beast. A long river wound away from it to the southwest, curling back as the dragon's tail did. I studied the woodcut, my heart fluttering strangely. The dragon's tail was barbed, tipped with an arrow that pointed — here I almost gasped aloud, forgetting all the intervening weeks of recovery from my former obsession — towards the spot that corresponded on my map to the site of the Unholy Tomb.

The visual resemblance between the two images was too striking to be coincidence. How had I not noticed, in the archive, that the region represented on those maps had exactly the brooding, spread-winged shape of my dragon, as if he cast his shadow over it from above? The woodcut I had puzzled over so deeply before my trip must hold a definite meaning, a message. It was designed to threaten and intimidate, to commemorate power. But for the persistent, it might be a clue; its tail pointed to the tomb as surely as any finger points to the self: this is me. I am here. And who was there, in that central point, that Unholy Tomb? The dragon held up his answer in cruelly sharpened talons: DRAKULYA.

I tasted an acrid tension, like my own blood, at the back of my throat. I knew I must hold myself back from these conclusions, as my training warned me, but I felt a conviction deeper than reason. None of the maps showed Lake Snagov, where Vlad Ţepeş was supposed to have been buried. Surely this meant Ţepeş — Dracula — rested somewhere else, someplace not even legend had recorded reliably. But where was his tomb, then? I grated out the question aloud, in spite of myself. And why had its location been kept a secret?

As I sat there trying to fit these pieces together, I heard the familiar sound of footsteps along the college hall — Hedges's shuffling, endearing walk — and I thought distractedly that I must hide these materials, go to the door, pour out sherry, rearrange myself for convivial talk. I had half risen, gathering papers, when I suddenly heard the silence. It was like an error in music, a note held one beat too long, so that it arrested the listener in a way no definite chord could have done. The famil-

iar, good-natured steps had stopped outside my door, but Hedges hadn't knocked, as he usually did. My heart echoed that perceptibly skipped beat. Over the rustling of my papers and the spat of rain on the gutter above my window, now darkened, I heard a hum — the sound of my blood rising in my ears. I dropped the book, hurried to the outer door of my rooms, unlocked it, and pulled it open.

Hedges was there, but he lay sprawled on the polished floor, his head thrown backwards and his body twisted sideways, as if a great force had hurled him down. I realized with a thrill of nausea that I hadn't heard him cry out or fall. His eyes were open, staring hard past me. For an endless second I thought he was dead. Then his head moved and he groaned. I crouched beside him. "Hedges!"

He moaned again and blinked rapidly.

"Can you hear me?" I gasped, almost sobbing with relief because he was alive. At that moment his head rolled convulsively, revealing a bloody gash in the side of his neck. It wasn't large, but it looked deep, as if a dog had leapt up and torn at the flesh, and it was bleeding profusely down his collar and onto the floor by his shoulder. "Help!" I shouted. I doubt anyone had so vio-

*lently broken the hush of that oak-panelled hall
in the centuries since it was built. And I didn't
know if it was any use; this was the night when
most of the fellows dined with the college master.
Then a door flew open at the far end and Professor Jeremy Forester's valet came running, a
nice chap named Ronald Egg who has since left
the house. He seemed to take everything in at
once, his eyes bulging, and then he knelt to tie
his handkerchief over the wound on Hedges's
neck.*

*"Here," he said to me. "We've got to get him
sitting up, sir, elevate that cut, if he has no
other injuries." He felt carefully up and down
Hedges's rigid body, and when my friend
didn't protest, we propped him against the
wall. I supported him on my shoulder, where
he leaned heavily, his eyes closing. "I'm going
for the doctor," Ronald said and vanished
down the hallway. I kept a finger on Hedges's
pulse; his head lolled next to me but his heart-
beat seemed steady. I couldn't help trying to
call him back to consciousness. "What happened, Hedges? Did someone strike you? Can
you hear me? Hedges?"*

*He opened his eyes and looked at me. His
head listed to one side and half his face looked*

slack, bluish, but he spoke intelligibly. "He said to tell you . . ."

"What? Who?"

"He said to tell you he will brook no trespasses."

Hedges's head fell back against the wall, that big, fine head that sheltered one of England's best minds. The skin crawled on my arms as I held him. "Who, Hedges? Who said that to you? Did he hurt you? Did you see him?"

Saliva bubbled at the corner of his mouth and his hands worked by his sides.

"Brook no trespasses," he gurgled.

"Lie still now," I urged. "Don't talk. The doctor will be here in a few minutes. Try to relax and breathe."

"Dear me," Hedges murmured. "Pope and the alliterative. Sweet nymph. For argument."

I stared at him, my stomach tightening. "Hedges?"

"'The Rape of the Lock,'" Hedges said politely. "Without a doubt."

The university doctor who admitted him to the hospital told me Hedges had suffered a stroke along with his wound. "Brought on by the shock. That gash on his neck," he added outside Hedges's room. "It looks as if it was made by something sharp, most likely sharp teeth, an animal. You don't keep a dog?"

"Of course not. They aren't permitted in college chambers."

The doctor shook his head. "Very odd. I believe he was attacked by some animal on his way to your room, and the shock brought on a stroke that was perhaps waiting to occur. He's pretty well off his head, for now, although he can form coherent words. There will be an investigation, I'm afraid, because of the wound, but it seems to me we'll find someone's nasty watchdog at the bottom of this. Try to think out what walk he would've taken to your digs."

The investigation turned up nothing satisfactory, but neither was I indicted, since the police could find no motive and no evidence for my having hurt Hedges myself. Hedges was incapable of testifying, and they finally recorded the incident as "self-injury," which seemed to me an avoidable blight on his reputation. One day during a visit to his rest home, I quietly asked Hedges to think about these words: "I will brook no trespasses."

He turned incurious eyes on me, touching with idle, puffy fingers the red wound on his neck. "If so, Boswell," he said pleasantly, almost *humorously. "If not, begone." A few days later he was dead, of a second stroke suffered during the night. No external injuries to the body were reported by the rest home. When the college master came to tell me, I swore to myself that I would work tirelessly to avenge Hedges's death, if I could only figure out how.*

I do not have the heart to record in detail the pain of the service held for him in our chapel at Trinity, the stifled sobs of his old father when the boys' choir began their beautifully set psalms to comfort the living, the anger I felt towards the impotent Eucharist on its tray. Hedges was buried in his own village in Dorset, and I have visited the grave alone, on a mild November day. The stone says REQUIESCAT IN PACE, *which would have been my exact choice, too, had the decision been mine. To my infinite relief, it is the quietest of country churchyards, and the parson speaks as mildly of Hedges's interment as he might of any local honor. I heard no tales of an English* vrykolakas *at the pub on the high street, even when I dropped the broadest, blandest hints. After all, Hedges was attacked only once, not the several times Stoker describes as necessary to infect a living person with the contagion of the undead. I believe he was sacrificed as a mere warning — to me. And to you, as well, unfortunate reader?*

> *Yours in profoundest grief,*
> *Bartholomew Rossi*

My father stirred the ice in his glass, as if to steady his hand and give himself something to do. Afternoon heat was relaxing into a calm Venetian evening, making the shadows of tourists and buildings stretch long across the piazza. A mass of pigeons started up off the paving stones, frightened by something, and wheeled overhead, enormous in flight. The chill from all those cold drinks had finally reached me, seeped into my bones. Someone laughed, far away, and I could hear seagulls crying above the pigeons. As we sat there a young man in a white shirt and blue jeans came loping up to speak with us. He had a canvas bag slung over one shoulder and his shirt was spotted with colors. "Buy a painting, signore?" he said, smiling at my father. "You and the signorina are the stars of my painting today."

"No, no, *grazie*," my father replied automatically. The squares and alleys were full of these art-student figures. This was the third scene of Venezia we'd been offered that day; my father hardly glanced at the picture. The young man, still smiling and perhaps unwilling to leave us without at least a compliment for his work, held it up for me to see, and I nodded sympathetically, glancing at it. A second later he was bobbing away in search of other tourists, and I sat frozen, watching him go.

The painting he had shown me was a richly hued watercolor. It depicted our café, and the edge of Florian's, a bright and unprovoking impression of the afternoon. The artist must have been stationed somewhere behind me, I thought, but fairly close to the café; he had caught a splotch of color that I recognized as the back of my red straw hat, with my father in blurry tan and blue just beyond. It was an elegant, casual piece of work, the image of summer indolence, something a tourist might well want to keep as the souvenir of an unblemished Adriatic day. But my glance at it had shown me a lone figure sitting beyond my father, a broad-shouldered, dark-headed figure, a crisp black silhouette among the cheerful colors of awning and tablecloths. That table, I recalled clearly, had been vacant all afternoon.

Chapter 13

OUR NEXT TRIP took us east again, beyond the Julian Alps. The little town of Kostanjevica, "place of the chestnut tree," was indeed full of chestnuts at this time of year, some already underfoot, so that if you set your shoe down wrong on the cobbled streets you slid precariously on a sharp burr. In front of the mayor's house, originally built to shelter an Austro-Hungarian bureaucrat, the nuts in their wicked-looking shells lay everywhere, a swarm of tiny porcupines.

My father and I walked slowly along, enjoying the end of a warm autumnal day — in the local dialect, this was called gypsy summer, a woman in a shop had told us — and I reflected on the differences between the Western world, a few hundred kilometers away, and this Eastern one, just a little south of Emona. Here everything in the stores looked like everything else, and the shop clerks, too, seemed to me exactly like one another, in royal blue work coats and flowered scarves, their gold or stainless steel teeth glinting at us over the half-empty counter. We had bought an enormous chocolate bar to supplement our picnic of sliced salami, brown bread, and cheese, and my father carried bottles of my favorite Naranča, an orange drink that reminded me already of Ragusa, Emona, Venezia.

The last meeting in Zagreb had ended the day before while I put the finishing flourish to my history homework. My father wanted me to study German now, too, and I was eager to, not because of his insistence but despite it; I would begin that tomorrow, out of a book from the foreign-language store in Amsterdam. I had a new short green dress and yellow kneesocks, my father was smiling over some unintelligible spoof that had passed between one diplomat and another that morning, and the Naranča bottles clinked together in our net bag. Ahead of us lay a low stone bridge, spanning the River Kostan. I hurried there for my first look, which I wanted to enjoy in private, without even my father beside me.

The river curved out of sight close to the bridge, and in its curve huddled a diminutive castle, a villa-sized Slav château with swans paddling below its walls and grooming themselves on the bank. As I watched, a woman in a blue coat opened an upstairs window, pushing it outward, making its latticed glass wink in the sun, and shook her dust mop. Below the bridge, young willows crowded together and swallows flew in and out of the mud bluffs at their roots. In the castle park, I saw a stone bench (not too close to the swans, whom I feared even now, in my teens) with chestnut trees leaning over it and the castle walls throwing a soothing shade on it. My father's clean suit would be safe there, and he might sit longer than he'd intended and talk in spite of himself.

All the time I was looking through these letters in my apartment, my father said, wiping the traces of salami from his hands with a cotton handkerchief, something outside the whole tragic problem of Rossi's disappearance kept nagging at the back of my mind. When I put down the letter recounting his friend Hedges's gruesome accident, I felt too ill for a few moments to think clearly. I had stumbled into a world of sickness, a netherworld of the familiar academic one I'd known for many years, a subtext of the ordinary narrative of history I'd always taken for granted. In my historian's experience, the dead stayed respectably dead, the Middle Ages held real horrors, not supernatural ones, Dracula was a colorful East European legend resurrected by the movies of my childhood, and 1930 was three years before Hitler assumed dictatorial powers in Germany, a terror that surely precluded all other possibilities.

So I felt sick, for a second, and corrupted, angry with my vanished mentor for having bequeathed me these nasty illusions. Then the regretful, gentle tone of his letters worked on me again, and I was filled with compunction for my disloyalty. Rossi depended on me — on me alone; if I refused to suspend disbelief because of some pedantic principle, I would surely never see him again.

And something else nagged at me. As my brain cleared a little, I realized it was my memory of the young woman at the library, whom I'd met only a couple of hours before, although it already seemed to me days. I remembered the extraordinary light in her eyes as she had listened to my explanation of Rossi's letters, the masculine drawing together of her eyebrows in concentration. Why had she been reading about Dracula, at my table of all tables, that evening of all evenings, at my very elbow? Why had she mentioned Istanbul? I was rattled enough by what I had read in Rossi's letters to suspend my disbelief further, to reject the notion of coincidence in favor of something stronger. And why not? If I accepted one supernatural occurrence, I should certainly accept others; it was only logical.

I sighed and picked up Rossi's last letter. After this I would need only to review the other materials that had been hidden in that innocuous envelope and then I was on my own. Whatever the girl's appearance meant — and it probably meant nothing out of the ordinary, didn't it? — I did not have time yet to find out who she was or why we shared this interest in the occult. It was odd for me to think of myself as someone interested in the occult; I wasn't, in the slightest, when you got right down to it. I was interested in finding Rossi.

The last letter, unlike the others, was handwritten — on lined notebook paper, in a dark ink. I unfolded it.

August 19, 1931

My dear and unfortunate successor:

Well, I cannot pretend you may not be out there for me still, somewhere, waiting to save me if my life one day collapses. And because I have a further bit of information to add to everything you have already (presumably) perused, I feel I should fill this bitter vial up to the brim. "A little learning is a dangerous thing," my friend Hedges would have quoted. But he is gone, and gone as surely by my hand as if I had opened my study door, struck the blow myself, and then shouted for assistance. I didn't do that, of course. If you have consented to read this far, you do not doubt my word.

But I finally doubted my own strength, a few months ago, and I did so for reasons connected with Hedges's enraging and terrible end. I fled his graveside for America — almost literally; my appointment had become reality and I was already packing my boxes at the time I took a day out in Dorset to see where he rested in peace. After I departed for America, disappointing a few in Oxford and saddening my parents greatly, I'm afraid, I found myself in a new and brighter world, where the term (I have been appointed for three and will fight for more) begins earlier, and the students have an open and practical outlook unknown at Oxford. And even after all this I could not bring myself to drop entirely my acquaintance with the undead. As a consequence, apparently, he — It — could not bring himself to drop his acquaintance with me.

You will remember that on the night Hedges

was attacked, I had unexpectedly discovered the meaning of the central woodcut in my sinister book and verified to myself that the Unholy Tomb on the maps I'd found in Istanbul must be the tomb of Vlad Dracula. I had spoken my remaining question aloud — where was his tomb, then? — as I had spoken aloud in the archive in Istanbul, conjuring up this second time some terrible presence, which wreaked its warning to me on my dear friend's life. Perhaps only an abnormal ego would pit itself against natural forces — unnatural, in this case — but I swear to you that this punishment angered me beyond terror, for a time, and made me vow to ferret out the last clues and, if my strength held, to pursue my pursuer to his lair. This bizarre thought became as ordinary to me as the desire to publish my next article, or to earn a permanent place at the cheerful new university that was claiming my jaded heart.

After I had settled into the routine of academic duties, and prepared to return briefly to England at the end of term to see my parents and to turn the pages of my doctoral thesis over to that kind London press where I was increasingly well looked after, I set out once more on the scent of Vlad Dracula, the historical or the supernatural, whichever he might prove to be. It seemed to me that my next task was to learn more about my strange old book: whence it had come, who had designed it, how old it was. I gave it up (reluctantly, I admit) to the laboratories of the Smithsonian. They shook their heads there over the specificity of my questions and hinted that the consultation of powers beyond their own means would cost me more. But I was stubborn, and I didn't think that a farthing of my inheritance from my grandfather, or my meagre savings from Oxford, should go to clothe or feed or entertain me while Hedges lay unavenged (but, thank God, at peace) in a churchyard that ought not to have seen his coffin for another fifty years. I was no longer afraid of consequences, since the worst I could have imagined had already befallen me; in this sense, at least, the forces of darkness had miscalculated.

But it was not the brutality of what occurred next that changed my mind and brought home to me the full meaning of fear. It was the brilliance of it.

My book was being handled at the Smithsonian by a bibliophilic little person named

167

Howard Martin, a kind if rather taciturn man who had taken my cause to heart as thoroughly as if he'd known my whole story. (No — on second thought, if he had known my whole story, he would perhaps have shown me the door on my first visit.) But he apparently saw only my passion for history, sympathized, and did his best for me. His best was very good, very thorough, and he assimilated what the laboratories sent him with a care that would have graced Oxford better than it did those rather bureaucratic museum offices in Washington. I was impressed, and further impressed by his knowledge of European bookmaking in the centuries just before and after Gutenberg.

When he had apparently done everything he could for me, he wrote to me that I could have the results, such as they were, and that he would hand the book to me in person, as I had first handed it to him, if I didn't wish it to be shipped north. I made the train trip down, doing a little sightseeing the next morning and then appearing at his office door ten minutes before the appointed time. My heart was thudding and my mouth had gone dry; I itched both to have my hands on my book again and to know what he had learned about its origins.

Mr. Martin opened the door and ushered me in with a little smile. "So glad you could come down," he said in the flat American twang that had become for me the most welcoming speech in the world.

When we were seated in his manuscript-filled office, I found myself facing him and was immediately shocked by the change in his appearance. I had seen him briefly a few months before and remembered his face, and nothing in his neat and professional correspondence with me had implied illness. Now he was drawn and pale, haggard in a way that caused his skin to look grey-yellow, his lips unnaturally crimson. He had lost a great deal of weight, so that his outdated suit hung limply from his thin shoulders. He sat hunched slightly forwards, as if some pain or weakness made it impossible for him to stand up straight. He seemed drained of life.

I tried to tell myself that I had merely been in a hurry during my first visit and that my acquaintance with the man by post had made me more observant this time, or more com-

passionate in my observations, but I couldn't shake the feeling of having seen him decay with the lapse of a short time. I assured myself that he might have some unfortunate and degenerative disease, a rapidly advancing cancer of some sort. Of course, politeness precluded any mention of his appearance.

"Now, Dr. Rossi," he said, in the American way. "I don't believe you realize what a valuable little item you've had here all along."

"Valuable?" He could not possibly know its value to me, I thought, not with all the chemical analyses in the world. It was my key to revenge.

"Yes. It's a rare example of Central European mediaeval printing, a very interesting and unusual thing, and I'm pretty well satisfied now that it was probably printed about 1512, perhaps in Buda or perhaps in Wallachia. That date would place it safely after the Corvinus Saint Luke but before the Hungarian New Testament of 1520, which would probably have had an influence on such a work if it had already existed." He shifted in his creaking chair. "It's even possible that the woodcut in your book actually influenced the New Testament of 1520, which has a similar illustration, a winged Satan. But there's no way to prove that. Any-

way, it would be a funny influence, wouldn't it? I mean, to see part of the Bible decorated with illustrations anything like this diabolical one."

"Diabolical?" I relished the sound of the condemnation on someone else's lips.

"Sure. You filled me in on the Dracula legend, but do you think I stopped there?"

Mr. Martin's tone was so flat and bright, so American, that it took me a moment to react. Never had I heard that sinister depth in a voice so perfectly ordinary. I stared at him, puzzled, but the tone was gone and his face smooth. He was looking through a pile of papers he had taken out of a folder.

"Here are the results of our tests," he said. "I've made clean copies of them for you, along with my write-up, and I think you'll find them interesting. They don't say much more than I've just told you — oh, there are two interesting additional facts. It appears from the chemical analysis that this book was stored, probably for a long time, in an atmosphere heavily laden with stone dust, and that that occurred before 1700. Also, the back section of it was stained at some point with salt water — perhaps from exposure to an ocean voyage. I suppose it could

have been the Black Sea, if our guesses about production location are correct, but there are a lot of other possibilities, of course. I'm afraid we haven't set you farther on your quest than that — didn't you say you're writing a history of mediaeval Europe?"

He looked up and gave me his casual, good-natured smile, weird in that wasted face, and I perceived simultaneously two things that made my marrow go cold as I sat there.

The first was that I had never told him anything about writing a history of mediaeval Europe; I had said I wanted information on my volume to help me complete a bibliography of materials related to the life of Vlad the Impaler, known in legend as Dracula. Howard Martin was as precise a man, in his curatorial way, as I was in my scholarly one, and he would never unknowingly have committed such an error. His memory had previously struck me as nearly photographic in its capacity for detail, something I notice and appreciate heartily whenever I meet it in other people.

The second thing I perceived at this moment was that, perhaps due to whatever illness he was suffering — the poor man, I almost made myself say, internally — his lips had a decayed,

flaccid look when he smiled and his upper ca-
nine teeth were bared and somehow promi-
nent in a way that gave his whole face an
unpleasant appearance. I remembered all too
well the bureaucrat in Istanbul, although there
was nothing wrong with Howard Martin's
neck, as far as I could see. I had just quelled my
tremor and taken book and notes from his
hand when he spoke up again.

"That map, by the way, is remarkable."

"Map?" I froze. Only one map I knew of —
three, actually, in graduated scale — had any-
thing to do with my present intentions, and I
was sure I had never so much as mentioned
their existence to this stranger.

"Did you sketch it yourself? It's not old, obvi-
ously, but I wouldn't have put you down as an
artist. And certainly not a morbid type, any-
way, if you don't mind my saying that."

I stared at him, unable to decipher his words
and afraid to give something away by asking
what he meant. Had I left one of my sketches
in the book? How utterly stupid, if I had. But I
was sure I'd checked the book carefully for
loose leaves before handing it over to him.

"Well, I tucked it back in the book, so it's
there," he said comfortingly. "Now, Dr. Rossi, I

can show you down to our accounting department if you'd like, or I can arrange for you to be billed at home." He opened the door for me and smiled his professional grimace again. I had the presence of mind not to hunt through the volume in my hand then and there, and I saw in the light of the corridor that I must have imagined Martin's peculiar smile, and perhaps even his illness; he was normal-skinned, just a little stooped from decades of work among the leaves of the past, nothing more. He stood by the door with one hand thrust out in a hearty Washingtonian good-bye, and I shook it, muttering that I should like the bill sent to my university address.

I made my way warily out of sight of his door, then out of that hall and finally away from the great red castle that housed all his labours and those of his colleagues. Out in the fresh air of the Mall, I strolled across the bright green grass to a bench and sat down, trying both to appear and to feel unconcerned.

The volume fell open in my hand, with its usual sinister obligingness, and I looked in vain for a loose sheet of something to surprise me there. Only turning back through the pages did I find it — a very fine tracing on carbon *paper, as if someone had had the third and most intimate of my secret maps actually in front of him, and had copied all its mysterious lineaments for me. The place-names in Slavic dialect were exactly those I knew from my own map — Pig-Stealing Village, Valley of Eight Oaks. In fact, this sketch was unfamiliar to me in only one particular. Below the appellation of the Unholy Tomb, there was some neat Latin lettering in an ink that seemed to match that of the other titles. Over the apparent location of the tomb, arched around it as if to prove its absolute association with that spot, I read the words* BARTOLOMEO ROSSI.*

Reader, judge me a coward if you must, but I desisted from that moment. I am a young professor and I live in Cambridge, Massachusetts, where I lecture, dine out with my new friends, and write home to my aging parents every week. I don't wear garlic, or crucifixes, or cross myself at the sound of a step in the hall. I have a better protection than that — I have stopped digging at that dreadful crossroads of history. Something must be satisfied to see me quiet, because I have been untroubled by further tragedy.

Now, if you yourself had to choose your sanity, your remembered life, over true instability, which would you select, as the proper way for a scholar to live out his days? Hedges would not, I know, have required of me a headlong plunge into darkness. And yet, if you are reading this at all, it means that harm has finally come to me. You must choose, too. I have given you every shard of knowledge that I possess, where these horrors are concerned. Knowing my story, can you refuse me succor?

Yours in grief, Bartholomew Rossi

The shadows beneath the trees had lengthened to yawning proportions, and my father kicked at a chestnut burr under his good shoes. I had the sudden sense that if he had been a cruder man, he would have spat on the ground at this moment, to expel some appalling taste. Instead, he seemed to swallow hard and gather himself to smile. "Lord! What've we been talking about? How grim we seem to be this afternoon." He tried to smile, but he also threw me a glance that spoke of worry, as if some shadow might come down over me, me in particular, and remove me without warning from the scene.

I uncurled my cold hand from the edge of the bench and made the effort to be lighthearted now, too. When had it become effort? I wondered, but it was too late. I was doing his work for him, distracting him as he had once tried to distract me. I took refuge in a slight petulance — not too much or he would suspect it. "I have to say I'm hungry again, for real food."

He smiled a little more naturally, and his good shoes thumped on the ground as he gave me a gallant hand off the bench and set about packing our bag with empty Naranća bottles and the other relics of our picnic. I gathered up my share with a will, relieved now because this meant he would stride away with me toward town instead of turning to linger over our view of the castle's facade. I had turned once already, near the end of the story, and seen that upper window, where a dark and stately shape had replaced the housecleaning old woman. I talked, rapidly, of anything else that came into my head. As long as my father didn't see it, too, there could be no confrontation. We might both be safe.

Chapter 14

I HAD STAYED AWAY from the university library for some time, partly because I'd been feeling strangely nervous about my research there, and partly because I had the sense that Mrs. Clay was suspicious about my absences after school. I had always called her, as I'd promised to, but something increasingly shy in her voice on the phone had made me picture her holding uncomfortable discussions with my father. I couldn't imagine her knowing enough about vice to guess anything specific, but my father might have embarrassing surmises of his own — pot? Boys? And he looked so anxiously at me sometimes, already, that I was unwilling to trouble him further.

Finally, however, the temptation was too great, and I decided in spite of my uneasiness to go back to the library. This time I feigned an evening movie with a dull girl from my class — I knew that Johan Binnerts worked in the medieval section on Wednesday nights and that my father was at a meeting at the Center — and I went out in my new coat before Mrs. Clay could say much.

The Historian

It was odd, going to the library at night, especially since I found the main hall as full as ever of weary-looking university students. The medieval reading room was empty, however. I made my way quietly to Mr. Binnerts's desk and found him turning through a pile of new books — nothing that would interest me, he reported with his sweet smile, since I liked only horrible things. But he did have a volume set aside for me — why hadn't I come in sooner for it? I apologized weakly and he chuckled. "I was afraid something must have happened to you, or that you had taken my advice and found a nicer topic for a young lady. But you have got me interested, too, so I looked this up for you."

I took the book gratefully, and Mr. Binnerts said he was going into his workroom and would be back soon to see if I needed anything. He had shown me the workroom once, a little stall with windows, at the back of the reading room, where the librarians repaired wonderful old books and glued cards into new ones. The reading room was quieter than ever when he had gone, but I eagerly opened the volume he'd given me.

It was a remarkable find, I thought then, although I know now what a basic source it is for fifteenth-century Byzantine history — a translation of Michael Doukas's *Istoria Turco-Bizantina*. Doukas has quite a bit to say about the conflict between Vlad Dracula and Mehmed II, and it was at that table that I first read the famous description of the sight that met Mehmed's eyes when he invaded Wallachia in 1462 and made his way to Târgoviste, Dracula's deserted capital. Outside the city, Doukas asserted, Mehmed was greeted by "thousands and thousands of stakes bearing dead people instead of fruit." At the center of this garden of death was Dracula's pièce de résistance: Mehmed's favorite general, Hamza, impaled among the others in his "thin garment of purple."

I remembered Sultan Mehmed's archive, the one Rossi had gone to Istanbul to explore. The prince of Wallachia had been a thorn in the sultan's side — that was clear. I thought it would be a good idea for me to read something about Mehmed; perhaps there were sources about him that explained his relationship with Dracula. I didn't know where to start, but Mr. Binnerts had said he would return soon to check on me.

I had turned, impatiently, with the idea of going to see where he was, when I heard a noise from the back of the room. It was a kind of thump, more a vibration through the floor than an actual sound, like the feel of a bird hitting a polished window in full flight. Something made me start up in the direction of the impact, whatever it was, and I found myself dashing into the work-room at the back of the hall. I could not see Mr. Binnerts through the windows, which was for one moment a reassurance, but when I opened the wooden door, there was a leg on the floor, a gray-trousered leg attached to a twisted body, the blue sweater askew on the wrenched torso, the pale-gray hair matted with blood, the face — mercifully half hidden — crushed, a bit of it still on the corner of the desk. A book had apparently just fallen from Mr. Binnerts's grasp; it lay sprawled, like him. On the wall above the desk, there was a smear of blood with a large, fine handprint in it, like a child's finger painting. I tried so hard not to make a sound that my scream, when it came, seemed to belong to someone else.

I spent a couple of nights at the hospital — my father insisted, and the attending doctor was an old friend. My father was gentle and grave, sitting on the edge of the bed, or standing by the window with his arms crossed as the police officer questioned me for the third time. I had seen no one come into the library room. I had been reading quietly at the table. I had heard a thump. I had not known the librarian personally, but I had been fond of him. The officer assured my father that I was not under suspicion; I was simply the closest thing they had to a witness. But I had witnessed nothing, nobody had come into the reading room — I was certain about that — and Mr. Binnerts had not cried out. There had been no wounds to any other part of the body; someone had simply dashed the poor man's brain out against the corner of the desk. It would have taken prodigious strength.

The officer shook his head, perplexed. The handprint on the wall had not been made by the librarian himself; there hadn't been blood on his hands. Besides, the print did not match his, and it was a strange print, the whorls of the fingers unusually worn. It would have been easy to match — the officer waxed talkative with my father — except that they'd never recorded one like it. A bad case. Amsterdam was not the city he had grown up in — now people threw bicycles into the canals, and what about that terrible incident last year with the prostitute who — my father stopped him with a look.

When the officer was gone, my father sat on the edge of my bed again and asked me for the first time what I'd been doing in the library. I explained that I'd been studying, that I'd liked to go there after school to do my homework because the reading room was quiet and comfortable. I was afraid he might be on the verge of asking me why I had chosen the medieval section, but to my relief he lapsed into silence.

I did not tell him that in the eruption of the library after my scream, I had instinctively shoved into my bag the volume Mr. Binnerts had been holding when he died. The police had searched my bag, of course, when they'd entered the room, but they had said nothing about the book — and why would they have noticed it at all? There had been no blood on it. It was a nineteenth-century French volume on Romanian churches and it had fallen open to a page on the church at Lake Snagov, endowed with magnificence by Vlad III of Wallachia. His grave was traditionally located there, in front of the altar, according to a little text below a plan of the apse. The author noted, however, that villagers near Snagov had their own stories. What stories? I wondered, but there was nothing more on that particular church. The sketch of the apse showed nothing unusual, either.

Sitting gingerly on the edge of my hospital bed, my father shook his head. "I want you to study at home from now on," he said quietly. I wished he hadn't said it; I would never have entered that library again anyway. "Mrs. Clay can sleep in your room for a while if you feel upset, and we can see the doctor again, whenever you want to. Just let me know." I nodded, although I thought I would almost rather be alone with the description of the church at Snagov than with Mrs. Clay. I pondered the idea of dropping the volume into our canal — the fate of the bicycles the policeman had mentioned — but I knew that I would want eventually to reopen it, in daylight, to read it again. I might want to do this not only for my own sake but also for that of grandfatherly Mr. Binnerts, who now lay somewhere in a city morgue.

A few weeks later, my father said he thought it would be good for my nerves to take a trip, and I knew that he meant it would be better for him not to leave me at home. "The French," he explained, wanted to confer with representatives from his foundation before beginning talks in

Eastern Europe that winter, and we were going to meet them one last time. It would be the best possible moment on the Mediterranean coast, too, after the hordes of tourists left but before the landscape began to look barren. We examined the map carefully and were pleased that the French had foregone their usual choice of a meeting in Paris and settled on the privacy of a resort near the Spanish border — close to the little gem of Collioure, my father gloated, and perhaps something like it. Just inland were Les Bains and Saint-Matthieu-des-Pyrénées-Orientales, I pointed out, but when I mentioned them my father's face clouded and he began to hunt along the coast for other interesting names.

Breakfast on the terrace at Le Corbeau, where we stayed, was so good in the fresh morning air that I lingered there after my father had joined the other dark-suited men in the conference hall, taking out my books reluctantly and looking up often at the aquamarine water a few hundred yards away. I was on my second cup of that bitter Continental *chocolat*, made bearable with a cube of sugar and a pile of fresh rolls. The sunlight on the faces of the old houses looked eternal in the dry Mediterranean climate with its preternaturally clear light, as if no storm had ever dared to approach these inlets. From where I sat I could see a couple of early sailboats out on the edge of the marvelously colored sea and a family of small children going with their mother and their pails and their (to me) unusual French bathing suits down to the sand beach below the hotel. The bay curved around us to the right, in the form of jagged hills. One of these was topped by a rotting fortress the same color as the rocks and sere grasses, olive trees climbing ineffectively toward it, the delicately blue morning sky stretched behind it.

I felt a sudden twinge of unbelonging, of envy for those unbearably complacent children with their mother. I had no mother and no normal life. I wasn't sure what I meant by *normal life,* but as I flipped through my biology book looking for the beginning of the third chapter, I thought vaguely it might mean living in one place, with a mother and father who were there every evening at dinnertime, a household in which travel meant the occasional beach vacation, not an endlessly nomadic existence. I felt sure, glaring at the children as they settled onto the sand with their shovels, that these creatures were never threatened by the grimness of history, either.

Then, looking down on their glossy heads, I realized that they were indeed threatened; they were simply unaware of it. We were all vulnerable. I shivered and glanced at my watch. In another four hours, my father and I would have lunch on this terrace. Then I would study again, and after five o'clock we would take a walk toward the eroded fortress that ornamented the near horizon — from which, my father said, you could see the little sea-bathed church on the other side, at Collioure. In the course of this day I would learn more algebra, some German verbs, read a chapter on the War of the Roses, and then — what? Up on the dry cliff, I would listen to my father's next story. He would tell it unwillingly, looking down at the sandy soil or drumming his fingers on rock quarried centuries ago, lost in his own fear. And it would be up to me to study it again, to piece it all together. A child shrieked below me and I started, spilling my cocoa.

Chapter 15

WHEN I FINISHED READING the last of Rossi's letters, my father said, I felt a new desolation, as if he had vanished a second time. But by now I was convinced that his disappearance had nothing to do with a bus trip to Hartford or a family illness in Florida (or London), as the police had tried to postulate. I put these thoughts out of my mind and set myself to looking through his other papers. Read first, absorb everything. Then build a chronology and begin — but slowly — to draw conclusions. I wondered if Rossi had had any premonition that in training me he might have been ensuring his own survival. It was like a gruesome final exam — although I devoutly hoped it would not be final for either of us. I wouldn't make a plan until I had read everything, I told myself, but already I had an inkling of what I would probably have to do. I opened the faded packet again.

The next three items were maps, as Rossi had promised, each drawn by hand and none of them looking older than the letters. Of course: these would be his own versions of the maps he had seen in the archive in Istanbul, copied from memory after his adventures there. On the first that came to hand, I saw a great region of mountains, which were drawn in as little triangular notches. They formed two long east-west crescents across the page and clustered densely on the west side as well. A broad river looped along the northern edge of the map. No cities were visible, although three or four little Xs among the western mountains might have marked towns. No place-names appeared on this map, but Rossi — it was the penmanship of that last letter — had written around the borders: "Those who do not believe and die while they are unbelievers, on them falls the curse of Allah, of angels, and of men (The Qur'an)," and several similar passages. I wondered if the river I saw here could be the one that had seemed to him symbolized by the dragon's tail in his book. But no; in that case he'd been referring to the largest-scale map, which must be among these. I cursed the circumstances — all of them — that prevented my seeing and holding the originals; in spite of Rossi's fine memory and neat hand, there must surely be omissions or discrepancies between original and copy.

The next map seemed to focus more closely

on the western mountain region shown in the first. Again, I saw here and there Xs, marked in the same relation to one another as on the first map. A smaller river appeared, curling through the mountains. Again, no place-names. Rossi had noted across the top of this map: "(Same Qur'anic mottoes, repeated)." Well, he had been just as careful in those days as the Rossi I knew. But these maps, so far, were too simple, too crude an outline, to suggest any specific region I'd ever seen or studied. Frustration rose in me like a fever, and I swallowed it down with difficulty, forcing myself to concentrate.

The third map was more enlightening, although I wasn't sure exactly what it could tell me, at this point. Its general outline was indeed the fierce silhouette I knew from my dragon book and Rossi's, although without Rossi's discovery of the fact, I might not have noticed that at once. This map showed the same kind of triangular mountains. They were very tall now, forming heavy north-south ridges, a river looping through them and opening out into a reservoir of some sort. Why couldn't this be Lake Snagov, in Romania, as the legends of Dracula's burial suggested? But, as Rossi had noted, there was no island in the broadened part of the river, and it didn't look like a lake, anyway. The Xs appeared again, this time labeled in tiny Cyrillic letters. I assumed these were the villages Rossi had mentioned.

Among these scattered village names I saw a square, marked by Rossi: "(Arabic) The Unholy Tomb of One Who Kills Turks." Above this box was a rather nicely drawn little dragon, a castle crowning its head, and under it I read more Greek letters, and Rossi's English translation: "In this spot, he is housed in evil. Reader, unbury him with a word." The lines were unbelievably compelling, like an incantation, and I had opened my mouth to intone them aloud when I stopped and closed my lips tightly. They made a sort of poetry in my head, nevertheless, which danced there infernally for a couple of seconds.

I set the three maps aside. It was terrifying to see them there, exactly as Rossi had described them, and stranger yet to see not the originals but these copies in his own hand. What was to prove to me, ultimately, that he hadn't made the whole thing up, drawing these very maps as a prank? I had no primary sources in this matter, apart from his letters. I drummed my fingers on the desktop. The clock in my study seemed to be ticking unusually loudly tonight, and the urban

half darkness seemed too still behind my venetian blinds. I hadn't eaten in hours and my legs
ached, but I couldn't stop now. I glanced briefly
at the road map of the Balkans, but there was
nothing unusual on it, apparently — no handwritten marks, for example. The brochure on
Romania also yielded nothing striking, apart
from the weird English in which it was printed:
"Avail yourselves of our lush and appalling countryside," for example. The only items that remained to be examined were the notes in Rossi's
hand and that small sealed envelope I'd noticed
on first turning through the papers. I had meant
to leave the envelope for last, because it was
sealed, but I couldn't wait longer. I found my letter opener among the papers on my desk, carefully broke the seal, and drew out a sheet of
notepaper.

It was the third map again, with its dragon
shape, curling river, towering caricature mountain peaks. It had been copied in black ink, like
Rossi's version, but the hand was slightly different — a good facsimile but somehow cramped,
archaic, a little ornate, when you looked at it
closely. I should have been prepared by Rossi's
letter for the sight of the one difference from
the first version of the map, but it still hit me like

a physical blow: over the boxlike tomb site and its guardian dragon curved the words BARTOLOMEO ROSSI.

I fought down assumptions, fears, and conclusions, and willed myself to set the paper aside and read the pages of Rossi's notes. The first two he had apparently made in the archives at Oxford and the British Museum Library, and they told me nothing he had not already. There was a brief outline of Vlad Dracula's life and exploits, and a listing of some literary and historical documents in which Dracula had been mentioned over the centuries. Another page followed these, on a different notepaper, and this was marked and dated from his trip to Istanbul. "Reconstituted from memory," said his swift yet careful handwriting, and I realized they must be the notes he had thrown onto paper after his experience in the archive, when he'd sketched the maps from memory before leaving for Greece.

These notes listed the Istanbul library's holdings of documents from Sultan Mehmed II's time — at least whatever had struck Rossi as pertaining to his own research — the three maps, scrolls of accounts from the Carpathian wars against the Ottomans, and ledgers of goods traded among Ottoman merchants at the edge of that region. None of this seemed to me very enlightening; but I wondered at what point, exactly, Rossi's labors had been interrupted by the ominous-looking bureaucrat. Could the scrolls of accounts and ledgers of trade he mentioned here contain clues to Vlad Ţepeş's demise or burial? Had Rossi actually looked through them himself, or had he merely had time to list the possibilities in that archive before being scared away from it?

There was one last item on the list from the archive, and this one took me by surprise, so that I lingered over it for a few minutes. "Bibliography, Order of the Dragon (partial scroll form)." What surprised me about this jotting and made me hesitate over it was the fact that it was so uninformative. Usually Rossi's notes were thorough, self-explanatory; that, he liked to say, was the point of note taking. Was this bibliography he mentioned so hurriedly a list the library had put together to record all the material they housed that pertained to the Order of the Dragon? If so, why would it be in "partial scroll form"? It must be something ancient itself, I thought — perhaps one of the library's holdings from the time of the Order of the Dragon. But why had Rossi not explained further, on this otherwise mute sheet of notebook paper? Had the bibliography, whatever it was, proven irrelevant to his search?

These musings over a far-away archive, which Rossi had looked through so long ago, hardly seemed a direct path to his disappearance, and I dropped the page in disgust, tired suddenly of the trivia of research. I craved answers. With the exception of whatever lay in the scrolls of accounts, in the ledgers, and in that old bibliography, Rossi had been surprisingly thorough in sharing with me his discoveries. But that was like him, that conciseness; besides, he'd had the luxury, if it could be called that, of explaining himself in many pages of letters. And yet I knew little, except what I must probably attempt to do next. The envelope was completely, depressingly empty now, and I hadn't learned much more from the last documents it had contained than I'd learned from his letters. I realized also that I must act as fast as possible. I had often stayed up all night before, and in the next hour I might be able to assemble for myself what Rossi had told me about the previous threats on his life, as he saw them.

I stood, my joints creaking, and went to my dismal little kitchen to boil some bouillon for soup.

As I reached for a clean pot, I realized that my cat had not come in for his supper, a meal I shared with him. He was a stray, and I suspected that our arrangement was not wholly monogamous. But around supper time he was usually there at my narrow kitchen window, peering in from the fire escape to let me know he wanted his can of tuna or, when I'd splurged on him, his dish of sardines. I had come to love the moment when he jumped down into my lifeless apartment, stretching and crying in an extravagance of affection. He often stayed a while after eating, sleeping on the end of the sofa or watching me iron my shirts. Sometimes I thought I saw an expression of tenderness in his perfectly round yellow eyes, although it might also have been pity. He was powerful and sinewy, with a soft black-and-white coat. I called him Rembrandt. Thinking of him, I lifted the edge of the blind, pushed up the window, and called him, waiting for the thud of feline feet on the windowsill. I could hear only distant night traffic from the center of the city. I lowered my head and looked out.

His shape filled the space, grotesquely, as if he had rolled there in play and then gone limp. I drew it into the kitchen with gentle, fearful hands, immediately aware of the broken spine and weirdly flopping head. Rembrandt's eyes were open wider than I'd ever seen them in life, his lips drawn back in a snarl of fear and his front paws splayed and thorny. I knew at once he could not have fallen there, so precisely, onto the narrow windowsill. It would take a large and strong grip to kill such a creature — I touched his soft coat, rage welling under my terror — and the perpetrator would have been scratched and perhaps bitten fiercely. But my friend was incontrovertibly dead. I had set him softly down on the kitchen floor, my lungs filling with a smoky hate, before I realized that under my hands his body was still warm.

I whirled around, closed and latched the window, then thought frantically of my next move. How could I protect myself? The windows were all locked, and the door was double bolted. But what did I know about horrors from the past? Did they leak into rooms like mist, under the doors? Or shatter windows and burst directly into one's presence? I looked around for a weapon. I didn't own a gun — but guns never prevailed against Bela Lugosi, in the vampire movies, unless the hero was equipped with a special silver bullet. What had Rossi advised? "I wouldn't go around with garlic in my pocket, no." And something else, too: "I'm sure you carry your own goodness, moral sense, whatever you want to call it, with you — I like to think most of us are capable of that, anyway."

I found a clean towel in one of the kitchen drawers and gently wrapped my friend's body in it, laying him out in the front hall. I would have to bury him tomorrow, if tomorrow were going to come around the way it usually did. I would inter him in the backyard of the apartment house — deeply, where dogs couldn't get at him. It was hard for me to imagine eating now, but I made my cup of soup and cut a slice of bread to go with it.

Then I sat down at the desk again and cleared away Rossi's papers, putting them neatly back in the envelope. I set my mysterious dragon book on top of that, taking care not to let it fall open. On top of these I placed my copy of Hermann's classic *Golden Age of Amsterdam*, which had long been one of my favorite books. I opened my dissertation notes across the center of the desk and propped up in front of me a pamphlet on merchants' guilds in Utrecht, a reproduction from the library that I had yet to peruse. I laid my watch beside me and saw with a thrill of superstition that it showed a quarter to twelve. Tomorrow, I told myself, I would go to the library and swiftly do any reading I could find there that might equip me for the coming days. It couldn't hurt to know more about silver stakes, garlic flowers, and crucifixes, if those were the peasant remedies prescribed against the undead for so many centuries. That would show a faith in tradition, at least. For now I had only Rossi's advice, but Rossi had never failed me where it was in his power to help. I picked up my pen and bent my head over the pamphlet.

Never had I found it so difficult to concentrate. Every nerve in my body seemed alert to the presence outside, if it was a presence, as if my mind rather than my ears might be able to hear it brushing up against the windows. With an effort, I planted myself firmly in Amsterdam, 1690. I wrote a sentence, then another. Four minutes to midnight. "Look for some anecdotes about Dutch sailors' lives," I noted on my papers. I thought of the merchants, banding together in their already ancient guilds to squeeze the best they could from their lives and their wares, acting day by day on their rather simple sense of duty, using some of their surplus to build hospitals for the poor. Two minutes to midnight. I wrote down the name of the pamphlet's author, to look up again later. "Explore the significance for merchants of the city's printing presses," I noted.

The minute hand on my watch jumped suddenly, and I jumped with it. It showed just shy of twelve o'clock. The printing presses might be extremely significant, I realized, forcing myself not to look behind me as I sat there, especially if the guilds had controlled some of them. Could they actually have purchased control of some of them, bought up ownership? Did the printers have their own guild? How did ideas about freedom of the press among Dutch intellectuals in that setting relate to the ownership of the presses? I grew interested for a moment, in spite of myself, and tried to remember what I'd read about early publishing in Amsterdam and Utrecht. Suddenly I felt a great stillness in the air, then a snapping of tension. I glanced at my watch. Three minutes after midnight. I was breathing normally and my pen moved freely across the page.

Whatever stalked me wasn't quite as clever as I'd feared, I thought, careful not to pause in my work. Apparently, the undead took some appearances at face value, and I appeared to have heeded Rembrandt's warning and settled down to my usual task. I wouldn't be able to hide my real actions for long, but for tonight my own appearance was the only protection I had. I moved the lamp closer and settled into the seventeenth century for another hour, to deepen the impression of retreat into work. As I pretended to write, I reasoned with myself. The final threat to Rossi, in 1931, had been his own name on the location of Vlad the Impaler's tomb. Rossi hadn't been found lying dead over his desk two days ago, as I might be soon if I weren't careful. He hadn't been discovered wounded in the hallway, like Hedges. He had been abducted. He might be lying dead somewhere else, of course, but until I knew that for certain, I had to hope he was alive. Beginning tomorrow, I would have to try to find the tomb myself.

Seated on that old French fortress, my father was staring out to sea, rather as he'd looked across the gap of mountain air at Saint-Matthieu, watching the eagle bank and wheel. "Let's go back to the hotel," he said finally. "The days are getting shorter already, have you noticed? I don't want to be caught up here after sunset."

In my impatience, I dared a direct question. "Caught?"

He glanced at me seriously, as if considering the relative risks of the answers he could give.

"The path is really steep," he said at last. "I wouldn't want to have to find my way back through those trees in the dark. Would you?" He could be daring, too, I saw.

I looked down into the olive groves, gray-white now instead of peach and silver. Each tree was twisted, straining up toward the ruins of a fortress that had once guarded it — or its ancestors, anyway — from Saracen torches. "No," I answered, "I wouldn't."

Chapter 16

IT WAS EARLY DECEMBER, we were on the road again, and the lassitude of our summer trips to the Mediterranean seemed far behind us. The high Adriatic wind was combing my hair again and I liked the feel of it, its awkward roughness; it was as if a beast with heavy paws clambered over everything in the harbor, making flags snap sharply in front of the modern hotel and straining the topmost branches of the plane trees along the promenade. "What?" I shouted. My father again said something unintelligible, pointing at the top story of the emperor's palace. We both craned back to look.

Diocletian's elegant stronghold towered over us in the morning sunlight, and I almost fell over backward trying to see the upper edge of it. Many of the spaces between its beautiful columns had been filled in — often by people dividing up the building for apartments, my father had explained earlier — so that a patchwork of stone, much of it Roman-hewn marble plundered from other structures, shone across the whole strange facade. Here and there water or earthquake had broken long cracks in it. Tenacious little plants, even some trees, hung out of the fissures. The wind whipped up the broad collars of sailors strolling along the quay in twos and threes, their faces brass colored against white uniforms and their crew-cut dark hair shining like wire brushes. I followed my father around the edge of the building, over fallen black walnuts and the litter from sycamore trees, to the monument-lined square behind it, which smelled of urine. Just in front of us rose a fantastic tower, open to the winds and decorated like a piece of pastry, a tall thin wedding cake. It was quieter back here and we could stop shouting.

"I've always wanted to see this," my father said in his normal voice. "Would you like to climb to the top?"

I led the way, taking the iron steps with gusto. In the open-air market near the quay, which I glimpsed from time to time through a marble frame, the trees had turned gold-brown, so that the cypresses along the water looked more black than green against them. As we rose I could see the water of the harbor navy blue beneath us, the small white shapes of the sailors on leave roaming among the outdoor cafés. Distant curving land, beyond our big hotel, pointed like an arrow to the interior region of the Slavic-speaking world, where my father would soon be drawn into the flood of détente spreading across it.

Just under the roof of the tower, we stood catching our breath. Only an iron platform suspended us above the drop to earth; from there we could see all the way to the ground through a spiderweb of plaited iron steps, which we'd just climbed. The world around us stretched out beyond stone-framed openings, each possibly low enough to let an unwary tourist topple nine stories to the paved courtyard below. We chose a bench in the center instead, looking out toward the water, and sat so quietly that a swift came in, its wings arched against the blustering sea wind, and disappeared under the eaves. It had something bright in its beak, something that caught the glint of the sun as it flew in off the water.

I woke early, my father said, the morning after I'd finished reading through Rossi's papers. I've never been so glad to see sunshine as I was that morning. My first and very sad business was to bury Rembrandt. After that, I had no trouble arriving at the library just when the doors were opening. I wanted this whole day to ready myself for the next night, the next onslaught of darkness. For many years, night had been friendly to me, the cocoon of quiet in which I read and wrote. Now it was a threat, an inevitable danger just hours away. I might also be setting out on a journey soon, with all the preparations that would entail. It would be a little easier, I thought ruefully, if I just knew where I'd be going.

The main hall of the library was very still except for the echoing steps of librarians going about their business; few students got here this early, and I would have peace and quiet for at least half an hour. I went into the maze of the card catalog, opened my notebook, and began pulling out the drawers I needed. There were several listings for the Carpathians, one on Transylvanian folklore. One book on vampires — legends from the Egyptian tradition. I wondered how much vampires had in common around the world. Were Egyptian vampires anything like East European vampires? It was a study for an archaeologist, not for me, but I copied down the call number of the book on Egyptian tradition anyway.

Then I looked up Dracula. Subjects and titles

were mixed together in the catalog; between "Drab-Ali the Great" and "Dragons, Asia," there would be at least one entry: the title card for Bram Stoker's *Dracula,* which I had seen the dark-haired young woman reading here the day before. Perhaps the library even had two copies of such a classic. I needed it right away; Rossi had said it was the distillation of Stoker's research on vampire lore, and it might contain suggestions for protection I could use myself. I hunted backward and forward. There was not a single entry under "Dracula" — nothing, nothing whatsoever. I hadn't expected the legend to be a major topic of scholarship, but surely that one book would be listed somewhere.

Then I caught sight of what actually lay between "Drab-Ali" and "Dragons." A little shard of twisted paper at the bottom of the drawer showed clearly that at least one card had been wrenched out. I hurried to the "St" drawer. No entries for "Stoker" appeared there — only further signs of a hasty theft. I sat down hard on the nearest wooden stool. This was too strange. Why would anyone have ripped out these particular cards?

The dark-haired girl had checked out the

book last, I knew that. Had she wanted to re-move the evidence of what she had checked out? But if she'd wanted to steal or hide the copy, why had she been reading it publicly, in the middle of the library? Someone else must have pulled the cards out, perhaps somebody — but why? — who didn't want anyone looking up the book here. Whoever it was had done it hurriedly, neglecting to remove traces of the job. I thought it through again. The card catalog was sacrosanct here; any student who even left a drawer out on the tables and was caught in this error got a sharp lecture from the clerks or librarians. Any violation of the catalog would have to be accomplished quickly, that was cer-tain, at some odd moment when no one was around or looking in that direction. If the young woman hadn't committed this crime herself, then maybe she didn't know that someone else didn't want that book checked out. And she probably still had it in her possession. I almost ran to the main desk.

This library, built in the highest of high Gothic-revival styles about the time Rossi was finishing his studies at Oxford (where he was surrounded by the real thing, of course), had al-ways appealed to me as both beautiful and comical. To reach the main desk, I had to hurry up a long cathedral nave. The circulation desk stood where the altar would have in a real cathedral, under a mural of Our Lady — of Knowledge, presumably — in sky blue robes, her arms full of heavenly tomes. Checking out a book there had all the sanctity of taking communion. Today this seemed to me the most cynical of jokes, and I ignored Our Lady's bland, unhelpful face as I addressed the librarian, trying not to seem ruffled myself.

"I'm looking for a book that's not on the shelves at the moment," I began, "and I wonder if it's actually checked out right now, or on its way back."

The librarian, a short, unsmiling woman of sixty, glanced up from her work. "The title, please," she said.

"*Dracula,* by Bram Stoker."

"Just a minute, please; I'll see if it's in." She thumbed through a little box, her face expressionless. "I'm sorry. It's currently checked out."

"Oh, what a shame," I said heartily. "When will it be coming back?"

"In three weeks. It was checked out yesterday."

"I'm afraid I simply can't wait that long. You

see I'm *teaching a course* . . ." These were usually the magic words.

"You are welcome to put it on reserve, if you
like," the librarian said coldly. She turned her
coiffed gray head away from me, as if she wanted
to get back to her work.

"Maybe one of my students has checked it out,
to read ahead for the course. If you'd just let me
have his name, I'll get in touch with him myself."

She looked narrowly at me. "We don't usually
do that," she said.

"This is an unusual situation," I confided. "I'll
be frank with you. I really must use one section
of that book to prepare my exam for them,
and — well, I loaned my own copy to a student
and he's unable to find it now. It was my mistake, but you know how these things go, with
students. I should have known better."

Her face softened and she looked almost sympathetic. "It's terrible, isn't it?" she said, nodding.
"We lose a stack of books every term, I'm sure.
Well, let me see if I can get the name for you, but
don't spread around that I did this, all right?"

She turned away to root in a cabinet behind
her, and I stood reflecting on the duplicity I had
suddenly discovered in my own nature. When
had I learned to lie so fluently? It gave me a feel-

ing of uneasy pleasure. While I was standing there, I realized that another librarian behind the big altar had moved closer and was watching me. He was a thin middle-aged man I'd often seen there, only slightly taller than his colleague and shabbily dressed in a tweed jacket and stained tie. Perhaps because I'd noticed him before, I was unexpectedly struck by a change in his appearance. His face looked sallow and wasted, perhaps even seriously ill. "Can I help you?" he said suddenly, as if he suspected I might steal something from the desk if I weren't attended to at once.

"Oh, no, thank you." I waved at the lady librarian's back. "I'm being helped already."

"I see." He stepped aside as she returned with a slip of paper and put it in front of me. At that moment I didn't know where to look — the paper swam under my eyes. For as the second librarian turned aside, he leaned over to examine some books that had obviously been returned to the desk and were waiting to be dealt with. And as he bent myopically toward them, his neck was exposed for a moment above the threadbare shirt collar, and I saw on it two scabbed, grimy-looking wounds, with a little dried blood making an ugly lacework on the skin just below them. Then he straightened and turned away again, holding his books.

"Is this what you wanted?" the lady librarian was asking me. I looked down at the paper she pushed toward me. "You see, it's the slip for Bram Stoker, *Dracula.* We have just one copy."

The grubby male librarian suddenly dropped a book on the floor, and the sound of it reverberated with a bang through the high nave. He straightened and looked directly at me, and I have never seen — or until that moment had never seen — a human gaze so full of hatred and wariness. "That's what you wanted, right?" the lady was insisting.

"Oh, no," I said, thinking fast, catching hold of myself. "You must have misunderstood me. I'm looking for Gibbon's *Decline and Fall of the Roman Empire.* I told you, I'm teaching a course on it and we've got to have extra copies."

She frowned heavily. "But I thought —"

I hated to sacrifice her feelings, even in that unpleasant moment, when she'd unbent so far toward me. "That's all right," I said. "Maybe I didn't look carefully enough. I'll go back and check the catalog again."

As soon as I said the word *catalog,* however, I knew I'd overused my new fluency. The tall librarian's eyes narrowed further and he moved his head slightly, like an animal following the motions of its prey. "Thanks very much," I murmured politely and walked off, feeling those sharp eyes boring into my back all the way down the great aisle. I made a show of going back to the catalog for a minute, then closed my briefcase and went purposefully out the front door, through which the faithful were already flocking for their morning study. Outside, I found a bench in the brightest possible sunlight, my back against one of those neo-Gothic walls, where I could safely see everyone around me coming and going. I needed five minutes to sit and think — reflection, Rossi always taught, should be well-timed rather than time-consuming.

It was all too much to digest quickly, however. In that dazed moment I had taken in not only my glimpse of the librarian's wounded neck but also the name of the library patron who had beaten me to *Dracula*. Her name was Helen Rossi.

The wind was cold and increasingly strong. My father paused here and drew from his camera bag two waterproof jackets, one for each of us. He kept them rolled up tightly to fit with his photographic equipment, canvas hat, and a little first-aid kit. Without speaking, we put them over our blazers, and he continued.

Sitting there in the late-spring sunshine, watching the university stir and wake to its usual activities, I felt a sudden envy of all those ordinary-looking students and faculty striding here and there. They thought that tomorrow's exam was a serious challenge, or that department politics constituted high drama, I reflected bitterly. Not one of them could have understood my predicament, or helped me out of it. I felt the loneliness, suddenly, of standing outside my institution, my universe, a worker bee expelled from the hive. And this state of things, I realized with surprise, had come about in forty-eight hours.

I had to think clearly now, and fast. First, I had observed what Rossi himself had reported: someone outside the immediate threat to Rossi — in this case the someone was a half-washed, eccentric-looking librarian — had been bitten in the neck. Let us presume, I told myself, almost laughing at the preposterousness of the things I was starting to believe, let us presume that our librarian was bitten by a vampire, and quite recently. Rossi had been swept out of his office — with bloodshed,

I reminded myself — only two nights earlier. Dracula, if he were at large, seemed to have a predilection not only for the best of the academic world (here I remembered poor Hedges) but also for librarians, archivists. No — I sat up straight, suddenly seeing the pattern — he had a predilection for those who handled archives that had something to do with his legend. First there had been the bureaucrat who had snatched the map from Rossi in Istanbul. The Smithsonian researcher, too, I thought, recalling Rossi's last letter. And, of course, threatened all along, there was Rossi himself, who had a copy of "one of these nice books" and had examined other possibly relevant documents. And then this librarian, although I had no proof yet that the fellow had handled any Dracula documents. And finally — me?

I picked up my briefcase and hurried to a public phone booth near the student commons. "University information, please." No one had followed me here, as far as I could see, but I closed the door and through it kept a sharp eye on the passersby. "Do you have a listing for a Miss Helen Rossi? Yes, graduate student," I hazarded.

The university operator was laconic; I could hear her shuffling slowly through papers. "We have an H. Rossi listed in the women's graduate dormitory," she said.

"That's it. Thank you so much." I scribbled the number down and dialed again. A matron answered, her voice sharp and protective. "Miss Rossi? Yes? Who's calling, please?"

Oh, God. I hadn't thought ahead to this. "Her brother," I said quickly. "She told me she'd be at this number."

I could hear footsteps leaving the phone, a sharper stride returning, the rustle of a hand taking the receiver. "Thank you, Miss Lewis," said a distant voice, as if in dismissal. Then she spoke into my ear and I heard the low, strong tone I remembered from the library. "I do not have a brother," she said. It sounded like a warning, not a mere statement of fact. "Who is this?"

My father rubbed his hands together in the chill wind, making the sleeves of his jacket crinkle like tissue paper. Helen, I thought, although I did not dare repeat the name aloud. It was a name I had always liked; it evoked for me something valiant and beautiful, like the Pre-Raphaelite frontispiece showing Helen of Troy in my *Children's Book of the Iliad,* which I had owned at home in the United States. Above all, it had been my mother's name, and she was a topic my father never discussed.

I looked hard at him, but he was already speaking again. "Hot tea in one of those cafés down there," he said. "That's what I need. How about you?" I noticed for the first time that his face — the handsome, tactful face of a diplomat — was marred by heavy shadows, which ringed his eyes and gave his nose a pinched look at the base, as if he never slept enough. He rose and stretched, and then we looked out at each of the giddily framed views a last time. My father held me back a little as if he feared I would fall.

Chapter 17

ATHENS MADE MY FATHER nervous and tired; I could see that plainly after only a day there. For my part, I found it exhilarating: I liked the combined senses of decay and vitality, the suffocating, exhaust-spewing traffic that whirled around its squares and parks and outcroppings of ancient monuments, the Botanic Gardens with a lion caged in the middle, the soaring Acropolis with frivolous-looking restaurant awnings fluttering around its base. My father promised we would climb up for a view as soon as he had time. It was February of 1974, the first time in nearly three months he'd traveled anywhere, and he'd brought me reluctantly, because he disliked the Greek military presence on the streets. I intended to make the most of every moment.

Meanwhile, I worked diligently in my hotel room, keeping an eye on the temple-crowned heights out my one window as if they might take wing after twenty-five hundred years and fly off without my ever having explored them. I could see the roads, paths, alleys that wound upward toward the base of the Parthenon. It would be a long, slow walk — we were in hot country again, and summer began early here — among white-washed houses and stuccoed lemonade shops, a path that broke out into ancient marketplaces and temple grounds from time to time, then cut back through the tile-roofed neighborhoods. I could see some of this labyrinth from the dingy window. We would rise from one view to another, looking out on what the residents of the Acropolis neighborhood saw from their front doors every day. I could imagine from here the vistas of ruins, looming municipal buildings, semitropical parks, winding streets, gold-tipped or red-tiled churches that stood out in the evening light like colored rocks scattered on a gray beach.

Farther away, we would see the distant ridges of apartment buildings, newer hotels than this one, a sprawl of suburbs through which we'd traveled by train the day before. Beyond that, I couldn't guess; it was too distant to imagine. My father would wipe his face with his handker-chief. And I would know, stealing a glance at him, that when we reached the summit he would show me not only the ancient ruins there but also another glimpse of his own past.

• • •

The diner I'd chosen, my father said, was far enough from campus to make me feel out of range of that creepy librarian (who was surely required to stay on the job but probably took a lunch break somewhere) and yet close enough to be a reasonable request, not the assignation in some lonely spot that an ax murderer might make with a woman he hardly knew. I'm not sure I'd actually expected her to be late, hesitating about my motives, but Helen was there before me, so that when I pushed in through the diner door, I saw her unwinding her blue silk scarf in a far corner and taking off her white gloves — remember that this was still an era of impractical, charming accoutrements for even the most hard-boiled of female academics. Her hair was rolled back almost smoothly and pinned away from her face, so that when she turned to regard me, I had a sense of being stared at even more enormously than I had been at the library table the day before.

"Good morning," she said in a cold voice. "I have ordered you some coffee, since you sounded so fatigued on the phone."

This struck me as presumptuous — how would

she know my fatigued voice from my well-rested one, and what if my coffee were already cold? But I introduced myself by name this time, and shook hands with her, trying to hide my uneasiness. I wanted to ask her immediately about her own last name, but I thought I'd better wait for the right opportunity. Her hand was smooth and dry, cool in mine, as if she still wore her gloves. I pulled out a chair opposite her and sat down, wishing I'd put on a clean shirt even for the occasion of hunting vampires. Her mannish white blouse, severe under a black jacket, looked immaculate.

"Why did I think I would be hearing from you again?" Her tone was close to insulting.

"I know you find this strange." I sat up straight and tried to look her in the eye, wondering if I could ask her all the questions I wanted to before she stood up and walked off again. "I'm sorry. It's not a practical joke and I'm not trying to bother you or disrupt your work."

She nodded, humoring me. Watching her face, it struck me that her general outline — certainly her voice — was ugly as well as elegant, and I took heart from this, as if the revelation made her human. "I discovered something odd this morning," I began, with fresh confidence. "That's why I called you out of the blue. Have you still got that copy of *Dracula* from the library?"

She was quick, but I was quicker, since I'd been waiting for the flinch, the drop in color under her already pale face. "Yes," she said warily. "Whose business is it what another person checks out from the library?"

I ignored this bait. "Did you tear out all the cards in the card catalog pertaining to that book?"

This time her reaction was genuine and undisguised. "Did I what?"

"This morning I went to the card catalog to look for some information on — on the subject we both seem to be studying. I found that all the cards for Dracula and Stoker had been wrenched out of the drawer."

Her face had tightened and she was staring at me, the ugliness very close to the surface now, her eyes too bright. But at that moment, for the first time since Massimo had shouted to me that Rossi had disappeared, I felt an infinitesimal lightening of burdens, a shifting of the weight of loneliness. She hadn't laughed at my melodrama, as she could have called it, or frowned, puzzled. Most importantly, there was no cunning in her look, nothing to indicate that I was talking with an enemy. Her face registered only one emotion, as far as she allowed it: a delicate, flickering fear.

"The cards were there yesterday morning," she said slowly, as if laying down a weapon and preparing to talk. "I looked up *Dracula* first, and there was an entry for it, only one copy. Then I wondered if they had other works by Stoker, and I looked him up, too. There were a few entries under his name, including one for *Dracula*."

The diner's indifferent waiter was setting coffee on the table, and Helen drew hers toward her without looking at it. I thought with sudden fierce longing of Rossi, pouring out far finer coffee than this for himself and me — his exquisite hospitality. Oh, I had other questions for this strange young woman.

"Someone obviously doesn't want you — me — anybody — checking out that book," I observed. I kept my voice quiet, watching her.

"That's the most ridiculous thing I have ever heard," she said sharply, putting sugar in her cup and stirring it. But she looked unconvinced by her own words, and I pressed on.

"Do you still have the book?"

"Yes." Her spoon fell with an annoyed clatter. "It is in my book bag." She glanced down, and I noticed beside her the briefcase I'd seen her carrying the day before.

"Miss Rossi," I said. "I beg your pardon, and I'm afraid I'm going to sound like a maniac, but it's my personal belief that there may be some danger to you in possessing this book, which someone else clearly doesn't want you to have."

"What makes you think that?" she countered, not meeting my eye now. "Who do you think would not want me to have that book?" A slight flush had spread over her cheekbones again, and she looked guiltily down into her cup; that was the only way to describe it — she looked downright guilty. I wondered with horror if she might not be in league with the vampire: Dracula's bride, I thought, aghast, the Sunday matinees coming back to me in rapid frames. That smoky dark hair would fit, the rich, unidentifiable accent, the lips like blackberry stain on the pale skin, the elegant black-and-white garb. I put this idea firmly out of my mind; it was fantasy and it fit too well with my jittery mood.

"Do you actually know someone who wouldn't want you to have that book?"

"Yes, as a matter of fact. But that is certainly none of your business." She glared at me and went back to her coffee. "Why were you hunting for the book, anyway? If you wanted my phone number, why did you not simply ask me for it, without going through all this rigmarole?"

This time I felt my own face redden. Talking with this woman was like sitting still for a series of slaps, delivered arhythmically so you couldn't know when the next one was coming. "I had no intention of asking for your phone number until I realized those cards had been torn out of the catalog and thought you should know about it," I said, stiffly. "I needed that book very badly myself. So I went to the library to see if they had a second copy I might be able to use."

"And they didn't," she said fiercely, "so you had the perfect excuse to call me looking for it. If you wanted my library book, why didn't you just put it on reserve?"

"I need it now," I retorted. Her tone was beginning to exasperate me. We might both be in serious trouble, and she was quibbling about this meeting as if it were a bid for a date, which it wasn't. I reminded myself that she couldn't know what dire straits I was in. Then it occurred to me that if I told her the whole story, she might not merely think I was insane. But it might also put her in greater danger. I sighed aloud, without meaning to.

"Are you trying to intimidate me out of my library book?" Her tone was a little softened now, and I caught the amusement that made her strong mouth twitch. "I believe you are."

"No, I'm not. But I would like to know who you think might not want you checking out this book." I set down my cup and looked across at her.

She moved her shoulders restlessly under the lightweight wool of her jacket. I could see one longish hair clinging to the lapel, her own dark hair, but glinting with copper lights against the black fabric. She appeared to be making up her mind to say something. "Who are you?" she asked suddenly.

I took the question at academic face value. "I'm a graduate student here, in history."

"History?" It was a quick, almost angry interjection.

"I'm writing my dissertation on Dutch trade in the seventeenth century."

"Oh." She was silent for a moment. "I am an anthropologist," she said finally. "But I am also very much interested in history. I study the customs and traditions of the Balkans and Central Europe, especially of my native" — her voice dropped a little, but sadly, not secretively — "my native Romania."

It was my turn to flinch. Really, this was all more and more peculiar. "Is that why you wanted to read *Dracula?*" I asked.

Her smile surprised me — white, even, her teeth a little small for such a strong face, the eyes shining. Then she tightened her lips again. "I suppose you could say that."

"You're not answering my questions," I pointed out.

"Why should I?" She shrugged. "You are a total stranger and you want to take my library book."

"You may be in danger, Miss Rossi. I'm not trying to threaten you, but I'm perfectly serious."

Her eyes narrowed on mine. "You are hiding something, too," she said. "I will tell you if you tell me."

I had never seen, met, or spoken with a woman like this. She was combative without being in the least flirtatious. I had the sensation that her words were a pool of cold water, into which I now plunged without stopping to count the consequences.

"All right. You answer my question first," I said, borrowing her tone. "Who do you think might not want you to have that book in your possession?"

"Professor Bartholomew Rossi," she said, her voice sarcastic, grating. "You're in history. Maybe you've heard of him?"

I sat there dumbfounded. "Professor Rossi? What — what do you mean?"

"I have answered your question," she said, straightening up and adjusting her jacket and piling her gloves one on the other again, as if finished with a task. I wondered fleetingly if she were enjoying the effect her words had on me, seeing me stammer over them. "Now tell me what you mean by all this drama about danger from a book."

"Miss Rossi," I said. "Please. I will tell you. Whatever I can. But please explain to me your relation to Professor Bartholomew Rossi."

She bent down, opened her book bag, and took out a leather case. "Do you mind if I smoke?" For the second time, I saw in her that masculine ease, which seemed to come over her when she put aside her defensively ladylike gestures. "Would you like one?"

I shook my head; I hated cigarettes, although I would almost have accepted one from that spare, smooth hand. She inhaled without any flourish, smoking dexterously. "I do not know why I am telling a stranger this," she said reflectively. "I guess the loneliness of this place is affecting me. I have hardly spoken with anyone in two months, except about work. And you do not strike me as a gossiping type, although God knows my department is full of them." I could hear her accent welling up fully under the words, which she spoke with a soft rancor. "But if you'll keep your promise . . ." The hard look came over her again; she straightened, cigarette jutting defiantly from one hand. "My relationship to the famous Professor Rossi is very simple. Or it should be. He is my father. He met my mother while he was in Romania looking for Dracula."

My coffee splashed across the table, over my lap, down the front of my shirt — which hadn't been perfectly clean, anyway — and spattered her cheek. She wiped it off with one hand, staring at me.

"Good God, I'm sorry. I'm sorry." I tried to clean up, using both our napkins.

"So this really shocks you," she said, without moving. "You must know him, then."

"I do," I said. "He's my adviser. But he never told me about Romania, and he — he never told me he had a family."

"He doesn't." The coldness in her voice cut through me. "I have never met him, you see, although I guess it is only a matter of time now." She leaned back in the little chair and hunched her shoulders, crudely, as if defying me to come closer. "I have seen him once, from a distance, at a lecture — imagine, seeing your father for the first time at a distance like that."

I had made a soggy heap of napkins and now I pushed everything aside, heap, coffee cup, spoon. "Why?"

"It's a very odd story," she said. She looked at me, but not as if she were lost in thought. She seemed instead to be gauging my reactions. "All right. It's a love 'em and leave 'em story." This sounded strange in her accent, although I wasn't moved to smile. "Maybe that's not so odd. He met my mother in her village, enjoyed her company for a while, and left her after a few weeks with an address in England. After he had gone, my mother discovered she was pregnant, and then her sister, who lived in Hungary, helped her flee to Budapest before I was born."

"He never told me he'd been to Romania." I was croaking, not speaking.

"Not surprising." She smoked bitterly. "My mother wrote him from Hungary, to the address he'd left her, and told him about their baby. He wrote her back saying he had no idea who she was or how she'd found his name, and that he'd never been to Romania. Can you imagine anything so cruel?" Her eyes bored into me, huge and starkly black now.

"What year were you born?" It didn't occur to me to apologize before asking the lady this question; she was so unlike anyone I'd ever encountered that the usual rules didn't seem to apply.

"In 1931," she said flatly. "My mother took me to Romania for a few days once, before I even knew about Dracula, but even then she would not go back to Transylvania."

"My God." I whispered it to the Formica tabletop. "My God. I thought he'd told me everything, but he didn't tell me that."

"He told you — what?" she asked sharply.

"Why haven't you met him? Doesn't he know you're here?"

She looked at me strangely but answered without demurring. "It's a game, I guess you could say. Just a fancy of mine." She paused. "I was not doing so badly in the university in Budapest. In fact, they considered me a genius." She announced this almost modestly. Her English

231

was phenomenally good, I realized for the first time — supernaturally good. Maybe she *was* a genius.

"My mother did not finish grade school, if you can believe it, although she got some more education later in life, but I was attending the university by the time I was sixteen. Of course, my mother told me my paternal heritage, and we do know Professor Rossi's outstanding books even in the murky depths of the East Bloc — Minoan civilization, Mediterranean religious cults, the age of Rembrandt. Because he wrote sympathetically on British socialism, our government allows the distribution of his works. I studied English throughout high school — would you like to know why? So I could read the amazing Dr. Rossi's work in the original. It wasn't exactly hard to find out where he was, either, you know; I used to stare at the university name on the jackets of his books and vow to go there one day. I thought things through. I made all the right connections, politically — I started by pretending I wanted to study the glorious labor revolution in England. And when the time came, I had my pick of scholarships. We have been enjoying some freedom in Hungary these days, although everyone wonders how long the Soviets will tolerate that. Speaking of impalers. In any case, I went to London first, for six months, and then got my fellowship to come here, four months ago."

She blew out a curl of gray smoke, thinking, but her eyes never left mine. It occurred to me that Helen Rossi was likelier to run into persecution by the communist governments she referred to with such cynicism than by Dracula. Perhaps she had actually defected to the West. I made a mental note to ask her about this later. Later? And what had become of her mother? And had she made all of this up, in Hungary, in order to attach herself to the reputation of a famous Western academic?

She was following her own train of thought. "Isn't it a pretty picture? The long-lost daughter turns out to be a great credit, finds her father, happy reunion." The bitterness in her smile turned my stomach. "But that is not quite what I had in mind. I have come here to let him hear about me, as if by accident — my publications, my lectures. We will see if he can hide from his past then, ignore me as he ignored my mother. And about this Dracula thing — " She pointed her cigarette at me. "My mother, bless her simple soul for thinking of it, told me something about that."

"Told you what?" I asked faintly.

"Told me about Rossi's special research on the subject. I had not known about it, not until last summer, just before I left for London. That is how they met; he was asking around in the village about vampire lore, and she had heard something about local vampires from her father and his cronies — not that a man alone should have been addressing a young girl in public, you understand, in that culture. But I suppose he did not know any better. Historian, you know — not an anthropologist. He was in Romania looking for information on Vlad the Impaler, our own dear Count Dracula. And don't you think it's strange" — she leaned forward suddenly, bringing her face closer to mine than it had been yet, but ferociously, not in appeal — "don't you think it is downright weird that he has not published a thing on the subject? Not one thing, as you surely know. Why? I asked myself. Why should the famous explorer of historical territories — and women, apparently, since who knows how many other genius daughters he has out there — why should he not have published anything out of this very unusual research?"

"Why?" I asked, not moving.

"I'll tell you. Because he is saving it up for a grand finale. It is his secret, his passion. Why else would a scholar remain silent? But he has a surprise coming to him." Her lovely smile was a grin this time, and I didn't like it. "You would not believe how much ground I have covered in a year, since I learned about this little interest of his. I have not contacted Professor Rossi, but I have been careful to make my expertise known in my department. What a shame it will be for him when someone else publishes the definitive work on the subject first — someone with his own name, too. It is beautiful. You see, I even took his name, once I arrived here — an academic nom de plume, you might say. Besides, in the East Bloc, we do not like other people stealing our heritage and commenting on it; they usually misunderstand it."

I must have groaned out loud, because she paused momentarily and frowned at me. "By the end of this summer, I will know more than anyone in the world about the legend of Dracula. You can have your old book, by the way." She opened the bag again and thumped it horribly, publicly, on the table between us. "I was simply checking something in it yesterday and I did not have time to go home for my own copy. You see, I do not even need it. It is only literature, in any case, and I know the whole damn thing almost by heart."

My father looked around him like a man in a dream. We'd been standing on the Acropolis in silence for a quarter of an hour now, our feet planted on that crest of ancient civilization. I was awed by the muscular columns above us, and surprised to find that the most distant view on the horizon was of mountains, long dry ridges that hung darkly over the city at this sunset hour. But as we started back down, and he came out of his reverie to ask how I liked the great panorama, it took me a minute to collect my thoughts and answer. I had been thinking about the night before.

I'd gone into his room a little later than usual so that he could look through my algebra homework, and I found him writing, mulling over the day's paperwork, as he often did in the evening. That night he sat very still with his head bent above the desk, drooping toward some documents, not upright and paging through them with his usual efficiency. I couldn't tell from the doorway whether he was intently scanning something he'd just written, almost without seeing it, or simply trying not to doze. His form cast a great shadow on the undecorated hotel-room wall, the figure of a man slumped dully over another, darker desk. If I hadn't known his fatigue, and the familiar shape of his shoulders sloping above the page, I might for a second — not knowing him — have said he was dead.

Chapter 18

TRIUMPHAL, CLEAR WEATHER, the days enormous as a mountain sky, followed us with spring into Slovenia. When I asked if we'd have time to see Emona again — I connected it already with an earlier era in my life, one with a different flavor altogether, and with a beginning, and as I've said before one tries to revisit such places — my father said hurriedly that we'd be far too busy, staying at a great lake north of Emona for his conference and then rushing back to Amsterdam before I fell behind in school. Which I never did, but the possibility worried my father.

Lake Bled, when we arrived, was no disappointment. It had poured into an alpine valley at the end of one of the Ice Ages and provided early nomads there with a resting place — in thatched houses out on the water. Now it lay like a sapphire in the hands of the Alps, its surface burnished with whitecaps in the late-afternoon breeze. From one steep edge rose a cliff higher than the rest, and on this, one of Slovenia's great castles roosted, restored by the tourist bureau in unusually good taste. Its crenellations looked down on an island, where a specimen of those modest red-roofed churches of the Austrian type floated like a duck, and boats went out to the island every few hours. The hotel, as usual, was steel and glass, socialist tourism model number five, and we escaped it on the second day for a walk around the lower part of the lake. I told my father I didn't think I could wait another twenty-four hours without seeing the castle that dominated the distant view at every meal, and he chuckled. "If you must, we'll go," he said. The new détente was even more promising than his team had hoped, and some of the lines on his forehead had relaxed since our arrival here.

So on the morning of the third day, leaving a diplomatic rehash of what had been rehashed the day before, we took a little bus around the lake, riding nearly to the level of the castle, and then dismounted to walk to the summit. The castle was made of brown stones like discolored bone, joined neatly together after some long state of dilapidation. When we came through the first passageway to a chamber of state (I suppose it was), I gasped: through a leaded window the surface of the lake shone a thousand feet below, stretching white in the sunlight. The castle seemed to be clinging to the edge of the precipice with only its toes dug in for support. The yellow-and-red church on the island below, the cheerful boat docking just then among tiny beds of red-and-yellow flowers, the great blue sky, had all served centuries of tourists, I thought.

But this castle, with its rocks worn smooth since the twelfth century, its tepees of battle-axes, spears, and hatchets in every corner, threatening to crash down if touched — this was the essence of the lake. Those early lake dwellers, moving skyward from their thatched, flammable huts, had ultimately chosen to perch here with the eagles, ruled over by one feudal lord. Even restored so deftly, the place breathed an ancient life. I turned from the dazzling window to the next room and saw, in a coffin of glass and wood, the skeleton of one small woman, dead long before the advent of Christianity, her bronze cloak ornament resting on her crumbling breastbone, green-bronze rings sliding off the bones of her fingers. When I bent over the case to look down at her, she smiled at me suddenly out of eye-sockets deep as twin pits.

On the castle terrace, tea came in white porce-lain pots, an elegant concession to the tourist trade. It was strong and good, and the paper-wrapped cubes of sugar were not stale, for once. My father was clenching his hands together on the iron table; the knuckles showed white. I stared at the lake instead, then poured him another cup. "Thank you," my father said. There was a distant pain in his eyes. I noticed again how worn and thin he looked these days; should he be seeing a doctor? "Look, darling," he said, turning away a little so that I could see only his profile against that terrific drop of cliff and sparkling water. He paused. "Would you consider writing them down?"

"The stories?" I asked. My heart contracted, sped up its count in my chest.

"Yes."

"Why?" I countered finally. It was an adult question, with no hedge of childhood wiles around it. He looked at me, and I thought that behind all their fatigue his eyes were full of goodness and sorrow.

"Because if you don't, I might have to," he said. Then he turned to his tea, and I saw that he wouldn't speak about it again.

That night, in the grim little hotel room next to his, I began to write down everything he had told me. He had always said I had an excellent memory — too good a memory, was the way he sometimes put it.

My father told me at breakfast the next morning that he wanted to sit still for two or three days. It was hard for me to picture him actually sitting still, but I could see dark rings under his eyes and I liked the idea of his having a rest. I couldn't help feeling that something had happened to him, that he was burdened by some silent new anxiety. But he told me only that he was longing again for the Adriatic beaches. We took an express train south through stations whose names were posted in both Latin and Cyrillic letters, then through stations whose names were posted in Cyrillic only. My father taught me the new alphabet, and I amused myself trying to sound out the station signs, each of which looked to me like code words that could open a secret door.

I explained this to my father and he smiled a little, leaning back in our train compartment with a book propped on his briefcase. His gaze wandered frequently from his work to the window, where we could see young men riding little tractors with plows behind, sometimes a horse pulling a cartload of something, old women in their kitchen gardens bending, scraping, weeding. We were moving south again and the land mellowed to gold and green as we hurried through it, then rose up into rocky gray mountains, then dropped on our left to a shimmering sea. My father sighed deeply, but with satisfaction, not the fatigued little gasp he gave more and more often these days.

In a busy market town we left the train and my father rented a car to drive us along the folded complexities of the coastal road. We both craned to see the water on one side — it stretched to a horizon full of late-afternoon haze — and on the other side the skeletal ruins of Ottoman fortresses that climbed steeply toward the sky. "The Turks held this land for a long, long time," my father mused. "Their invasions involved all kinds of cruelty, but they ruled rather tolerantly, as empires go, once they'd conquered — and efficiently, too, for hundreds of years. This is pretty barren land, but it gave them control of the sea. They needed these ports and bays."

The town where we parked was right on the sea; the little harbor there was lined with fishing boats knocking against one another in a translucent surf. My father wanted to stay on a nearby island, and he engaged a boat with a wave to its owner, an old man with a black beret on the back of his head. The air was warm, even this late in the afternoon, and the spray that reached my fingertips was fresh but not cold. I leaned out of the bow, feeling like a figurehead. "Careful," my father said, gathering the back of my sweater in his hand.

The boatman was steering us close to an island port now, an old village with an elegant stone church. He slung a rope around a stump of pier and offered me one gnarled hand up out of the boat. My father paid him with some of those colorful socialist bills, and he touched his beret. As he was clambering back to his seat, he turned. "Your girl?" he shouted in English. "Daughter?"

"Yes," my father said, looking surprised.

"I bless her," the man said simply and carved a cross in the air near me.

My father found us rooms that looked back at the mainland, and then we ate our dinner at an outdoor restaurant near the docks. Twilight was coming down slowly, and I noticed the first stars visible above the sea. A breeze, cooler now than it had been in the afternoon, brought me the scents I had already grown to love: cypress and lavender, rosemary, thyme. "Why do good smells get stronger when it's dark?" I asked my father. It was something I genuinely wondered, but it served also to postpone our discussing anything else. I needed time to recover somewhere where there were lights and people talking, needed at least to look away from that aged trembling in my father's hands.

"Do they?" he asked absently, but it brought me relief. I grasped his hand to stop its shaking, and he closed it, still absently, over mine. He was too young to grow old. On the mainland, the silhouettes of mountains danced almost into the water, looming over the beaches, looming almost over our island. When civil war broke out in those coastal mountains almost twenty years later, I closed my eyes and remembered them, astonished. I couldn't imagine that their slopes housed enough people to fight a war. They had seemed utterly pristine when I saw them, devoid of human habitation, the home of empty ruins, guarding only the monastery on the sea.

Chapter 19

AFTER HELEN ROSSI slammed the book *Dracula* — which she obviously thought was our bone of contention — onto the diner table between us, I half expected everyone in the place to rise and run, or someone to cry, "Aha!" and come over to kill us. Of course, nothing at all happened, and she sat there looking at me with the same expression of bitter pleasure. Could this woman, I asked myself slowly, with her legacy of resentment and her scholarly vendetta against Rossi, have injured him herself, caused his disappearance?

"Miss Rossi," I said as calmly as I could, taking the book off the table and putting it facedown beside my briefcase, "your story is extraordinary and I have to say it'll take me some time to digest all this. But I must tell you something very important." I drew in a deep breath, then another. "I know Professor Rossi quite well. He has been my adviser for two years now and we've spent hours together, talking and working. I'm sure if you — when you — meet him you will find him a far better and kinder person than you can imagine at this point —" She made a movement as if to speak, but I rushed on. "The thing is — the thing is — I take it from the way you talked about him that you don't realize Professor Rossi — your father — has disappeared."

She stared at me, and I couldn't detect any guile in her face, only confusion. So this news was a surprise. The pain over my heart lessened a little. "What do you mean?" she demanded.

"I mean — three nights ago I was talking with him as usual, and by the next day he had vanished. The police are looking for him now. He apparently disappeared from his office, and was maybe even injured there, because they found blood on his desk." I recounted briefly the events of that evening, beginning with my bringing him my strange little book, but said nothing about the story Rossi had told me.

She looked at me, her face twisted with perplexity. "Is this some kind of trick you are playing on me?"

"No, not in the least. It really isn't. I've hardly been able to eat or sleep since it happened."

"Don't the police have any idea where he is?"

"None, as far as I can tell."

Her look was suddenly shrewd. "Do you?"

I hesitated. "Possibly. It's a long story, and it seems to be getting longer by the hour."

"Wait." She looked hard at me. "When you were reading those letters in the library yesterday, you said they had to do with a problem some professor was having. Did you mean Rossi?"

"Yes."

"What problem was he having? Is he having?"

"I don't want to involve you in unpleasantness or danger by telling you even what little I know."

"You promised to answer my questions after I answered yours." If she'd had blue eyes instead of dark ones, her face would have been the twin of Rossi's at that moment. I imagined I could see a resemblance now, an uncanny molding of Rossi's English crispness into the strong, dark frame of Romania, although it could merely have been the effect of her assertion that she was his daughter. But how could she be his daughter if he had stoutly denied having been in Romania? He had said, at least, that he'd never been to Snagov. On the other hand, he had left that brochure on Romania among his papers. Now she was glaring at me, too, something Rossi had never done. "It is too late to tell me I shouldn't ask questions. What did those letters have to do with his disappearance?"

"I'm not sure yet. But I may need the help of

an expert. I don't know what discoveries you've made in the course of your research —" Again, I received her wary, heavy-lidded look. "I'm convinced that before he vanished Rossi believed he was in personal danger."

She seemed to be trying to take all of this in, this news of a father she had known for so long only as a symbol of challenge. "Personal danger? From what?"

I took the plunge. Rossi had asked me not to share his insane story with my colleagues. I hadn't done that, but now, unexpectedly, I had available to me the possibility of assistance from an expert. This woman might know already what it would take me many months to learn; she might be right, even, in thinking she knew more than Rossi himself. Rossi always emphasized the importance of seeking expert help — well, I would do that now. Forgive me, I prayed to the forces of good, if this endangers her. Besides, it had a peculiar kind of logic. If she was actually his daughter, she might have the greatest right of all to know his story. "What does Dracula mean to you?"

"Mean to me?" She frowned. "As a concept? My revenge, I suppose. Eternal bitterness."

"Yes, I understand that. But does Dracula mean anything more to you?"

"What do you mean?" I couldn't tell whether she was being evasive or simply honest.

"Rossi," I said, still hesitating, "your father, was — is — convinced that Dracula still walks the earth." She stared at me. "What do you make of that?" I asked. "Does it seem insane to you?" I waited for her to laugh, or stand up and leave as she had in the library.

"It's funny," Helen Rossi answered slowly. "Normally I'd say that was peasant legend — superstition about the memory of a bloody tyrant. But the strange thing is that my mother is absolutely convinced of the same thing."

"Your mother?"

"Yes. I told you, she is a peasant by birth. She has a right to these superstitions, although she is probably less convinced of them than her parents were. But why an eminent Western scholar?" She was an anthropologist, all right, despite her bitter quest. The detachment of her quick intelligence from personal questions was astonishing to me.

"Miss Rossi," I said, making up my mind suddenly. "I somehow don't have the smallest doubt that you like to examine things for yourself. Why don't you read Rossi's letters? I'm giving you my frankest warning that everyone who has handled his papers on this topic has been subjected to some kind of threat, as far as I can tell. But if you aren't afraid, read them for yourself. It'll save us the time of my trying to persuade you that his story is true, which I firmly believe it is."

"Save us time?" she echoed contemptuously. "What are you planning for my time?"

I was too desperate to be stung. "You'll read these letters with a better-educated eye, in this case, than mine."

She seemed to be thinking over this proposal, her chin in her fist. "All right," she said finally. "You have got me in a vulnerable spot. Of course I cannot resist the temptation to learn more about Father Rossi, especially if it puts me ahead of his research. But if he seems to me merely insane, I warn you that you will not get much sympathy from me. That would be just my luck, for him to be shut away in an institution before I have my fair chance to torture him." Her smile was not a smile.

"Fine." I ignored the last remark and the ugly grimace, forcing myself not to glance at her canine teeth, which I could already see plainly weren't longer than normal. Before we concluded our transaction, however, I had to lie on one point. "I'm sorry to say I don't have the letters with me. I was afraid to carry them around today." Actually, I'd been thoroughly afraid to leave them in my apartment, and they were hidden in my briefcase. But I'd be damned — literally, maybe — if I pulled them out in the middle of the diner. I had no idea who might be there, watching us — the creepy librarian's little friends, for example? I had another reason, too, which I had to test even if my heart sank under its unpleasantness. I had to be sure Helen Rossi, whoever she was, was not in league with — well, wasn't it just possible that the enemy of her enemy was already her friend? "I'll have to go home and get them. And I'll have to ask you to read them in my presence; they're fragile and very precious to me."

"All right," she said coolly. "Can we meet tomorrow afternoon?"

"That's too late. I'd like you to see them immediately. I'm sorry. I know it sounds odd, but you'll understand my sense of urgency once you've read them."

She shrugged. "If it will not take too long."

"It won't. Can you meet me at — at Saint Mary's Church?" This test, at least, I could perform with Rossi's own thoroughness. Helen

Rossi looked unflinchingly at me, her hard, ironic face unchanged. "That's on Elm Street, two blocks from —"

"I know where it is," she said, gathering her gloves and putting them on very neatly. She re-wound the blue scarf, which shimmered around her throat like lapis lazuli. "What time?"

"Give me thirty minutes to get the papers from my apartment and meet you there."

"At the church. All right. I will stop by the library for an article I need today. Please be on time — I have a lot to do." Her black-coated back was lean and strong, moving out the diner door. I realized too late that she had somehow paid the bill for our coffee.

Chapter 20

SAINT MARY'S CHURCH, my father said, was a homely little piece of Victoriana that lingered at the edge of the old section of campus. I'd passed it hundreds of times without ever going in, but it seemed to me now that a Catholic church was the right companion for all these horrors. Didn't Catholicism deal with blood and resurrected flesh on a daily basis? Wasn't it expert in superstition? I somehow doubted that the hospitable plain Protestant chapels that dotted the university could be much help; they didn't look qualified to wrestle with the undead. I felt sure those big square Puritan churches on the town green would be helpless in the face of a European vampire. A little witch burning was more in their line — something limited to the neighbors. Of course, I would be at Saint Mary's long before my reluctant guest. Would she even show up? That was half the exam.

Saint Mary's was indeed open, fortunately, and its dark paneled interior smelled of wax and dusty upholstery. Two old ladies in hats sprigged with fake flowers were arranging real ones on the carved altar up front. I stepped in rather awkwardly and settled myself in a back pew, where I could see the doors without being seen at once by anyone who entered. It was a long wait, but the quiet interior and the ladies' hushed conversation soothed me a little. I began to feel tired for the first time, after my late night. At last the front door swung open again on its ninety-year-old hinges, and Helen Rossi stood hesitating for a moment, looked behind her, and then stepped in.

Sunlight from the side windows threw turquoise and mauve on her clothes as she stood there. I saw her glance around the carpeted entrance. Seeing no one, she moved forward. I watched for any kind of cringing, for an evil shriveling of skin or color in her firm face — anything, I didn't know what, that might show an allergy to Dracula's ancient enemy, the church. Perhaps a boxy Victorian relic wouldn't ward off the forces of darkness anyway, I thought doubtfully. But this building apparently had some power of its own for Helen Rossi, because after a moment she moved through the radiant colors of the window toward the wall font. With a sense of shame for my voyeurism, I saw her remove her gloves and dip one hand into the basin, then touch her forehead. The gesture was tender; her face from where I sat had a grave look. Well, I was doing it for Rossi. And now I knew absolutely that Helen Rossi was not a *vrykolakas*, however hard and sometimes sinister her appearance.

She came into the nave and then drew back a little, seeing me get to my feet. "Did you bring the letters?" she whispered, her eyes fixing me accusingly. "I have to return to my department by one o'clock." She glanced around again.

"What's wrong?" I asked quickly, my arms prickling with instinctive nervousness. I seemed to have developed some sort of morbid sixth sense over the last two days. "Are you afraid of something?"

"No," she said, still whispering. She clenched her gloves together in one hand so that they looked like a flower against her dark suit. "I simply wondered — did someone else come in just now?"

"No." I glanced around, too. The church was pleasantly empty except for the altar-guild ladies.

"Someone was following me," she said in the same low voice. Her face, framed by the roll of heavy dark hair, wore an odd expression, mixed suspicion and bravado. For the first time, I wondered what it had cost her to learn her own species of courage. "I think he was following me. A small, thin man in shabby clothes — tweed jacket, green tie."

"Are you sure? Where did you see him?"

"In the card catalog," she said softly. "I went to check your story about the missing cards. I simply was not sure I believed it." She spoke matter-of-factly, without apology. "I saw him there, and the next thing I knew he was following me, but at a distance, on Elm Street. Do you know him?"

"Yes," I said dismally. "He's a librarian."

"A librarian?" She seemed to wait for more, but I couldn't bring myself to tell her about the wound I'd seen on the man's neck. It was too incredible, too strange; hearing that, she would certainly give me up as a mental case.

"He seems suspicious of my movements. You absolutely must stay out of his way," I said. "I'll tell you more about him later. Come, sit down and be comfortable. Here are the letters."

I made room for her in one of the velvet-cushioned pews and opened my briefcase. Immediately her face was intent; she lifted out the package with careful hands and removed the letters almost as reverently as I had the day before. I could only wonder what kind of sensation this must be for her, to see on some of them the handwriting of the alleged father she had known only as a source of anger. I looked at it over her shoulder. Yes, it was a firm, kind, upright hand. Perhaps it had already made him seem faintly human to his daughter. Then I thought I should stop watching, and I got to my feet. "I'll just wander around here and give you whatever time you need. If there's anything I can explain or help you with —"

She nodded absently, eyes fixed on the first letter, and I walked away. I could see she would handle my precious papers with care, and that she was already reading Rossi's lines with great swiftness. For the next half hour I examined the carved altar, the paintings in the chapel, the tasseled hangings at the pulpit, the marble figure of the exhausted mother and her squirming baby. One of the paintings in particular caught my attention: a ghoulish Pre-Raphaelite Lazarus, tottering out of the tomb into the arms of his sisters, his ankles gray-green and his grave clothes dingy. The face, faded after a century of smoke and incense, looked bitter and weary, as if gratitude were the last thing he felt on being called back from his rest. The Christ who stood impatiently at the tomb's entrance, holding up his hand, had a countenance of pure evil, greedy and burning. I blinked, turned away. My lack of sleep was clearly poisoning my thoughts.

"I'm done," Helen Rossi said behind me. Her voice was low, and she looked pale and tired. "You were right," she said. "There is no mention of his affair with my mother, or even of his traveling to Romania. You were telling the truth about that. I cannot understand it. This must have been during the same period, surely the same trip to the Continent, because I was born nine months after that."

"I'm sorry." Her dark face hadn't asked for pity, but I felt it. "I wish I had some clues for you here, but you see how it is. I can't explain it, either."

"At least we believe each other, don't we?" She looked directly at me.

I was surprised to discover I could feel pleasure in the midst of all this grief and apprehension. "We do?"

"Yes. I don't know if something called Dracula exists, or what it is, but I believe you when you say Rossi — my father — felt himself in danger. He clearly felt it many years ago, so why not a return of his fears when he saw your little book, an uncomfortable coincidence and reminder of the past?"

"And what do you make of his disappearance?"

She shook her head. "It could have been a mental breakdown, of course. But I understand what you mean, now. His letters have the mark of" — she hesitated — "a logical and fearless mind, just like his other works. Besides, you can tell a great deal from a historian's books. I know his very well. They are the efforts of stable, clear thought."

I led her back to the letters and my briefcase; it made me nervous to leave them alone for even a few minutes. She had put everything neatly back in the envelope — in its original order, I had no doubt. We sat down on the pew together, almost companionably.

"Let's just say there might be some supernatural force involved in his disappearance," I ventured. "I can't believe I'm saying this, but for the sake of argument. What would you advise doing next?"

"Well," she said slowly. Her profile was sharp and thoughtful, close to me in the dim light. "I cannot see that this will help you very much in a modern investigation, but if you were to obey the dictates of Dracula lore, you would have to assume that Rossi has been assaulted and removed by a vampire, who would either kill him or — more likely — pollute him with the curse of the undead. Three attacks that mingle your blood with that of Dracula or one of his disciples make you a vampire eternally, you know. If he has been bitten once already, you will have to find him as soon as possible."

"But why would Dracula appear here, of all places? And why abduct Rossi? Why not just strike him and corrupt him, without making the change noticeable to anyone?"

"I don't know," she said, shaking her head. "It is unusual behavior, according to the folklore. Rossi must be — I mean, if this were all a supernatural occurrence — he must be of special interest to Vlad Dracula. Perhaps even a threat to him somehow."

"And do you believe my finding this little book and bringing it to Rossi had something to do with his disappearance?"

"Logic tells me that it is an absurd idea. But —" She folded her gloves carefully in her black-skirted lap. "I wonder if there's not another source of information we're overlooking." Her mouth drooped. Silently, I thanked her for that *we*.

"What's that?"

She sighed and unfolded the gloves. "My mother."

"Your mother? But what would she know about —" I had only begun my string of questions when a shift in light and the breath of a draft made me turn. From where we sat, we could see the church doors without being seen from them — the vantage point from which I'd chosen to watch Helen's entrance. Now a hand inserted itself between the doors, then a bony, pointed face. The strange-looking librarian was peering into the church.

I can't describe to you the feeling I had in that quiet church when the librarian's face appeared between the doors. I had the sudden image of a sharp-nosed animal, something stealthy and sniffing, a weasel or a rat. Beside me, Helen was frozen, staring at the door. Any moment now he would be catching our scent. But we had a second or two left, I calculated, and I gathered the briefcase and stack of papers silently in one arm, grasped Helen with the other — there was no time to ask for her permission — and drew her from the end of the pew into the side aisle. A door was open there, leading into a small chamber beyond, and we slipped in. I closed it quietly. There was no way to lock it from the inside, I noted with a pang, although it had a big iron-lined keyhole.

It was darker in this little room than in the nave. There was a baptismal font in the middle, a cushioned bench or two along the walls. Helen and I looked silently at each other. I couldn't read her expression, except that it seemed to hold as much alertness and defiance as fear. Without words or gestures, we moved cautiously behind the font, and Helen put a hand on it to steady herself. After another minute, I couldn't stay still any longer; I handed her the papers and went back to the keyhole. Looking carefully through it, I could see the librarian moving past a column. He did resemble a weasel, his pointed face thrust forward, glancing around at all the pews. He turned in my direction, and I drew back a little. He seemed to study the door to our hiding place, and even took a step or two toward it, then stepped away again. Suddenly a lavender sweater moved into my field of view. It was one of the altar ladies. I could hear her voice, muffled. "Can I help you?" she said kindly.

"Well, I'm looking for someone." The librarian

had a sharp, whistling voice, too loud for a sanctuary. "I — did you see a young lady come in here, in a black suit? Dark hair?"

"Why, yes." The kind woman looked around, too. "There was someone by that description here a little while ago. She was with a young man, sitting in the back pews. But she's certainly not here now."

The weasel swiveled this way and that. "Couldn't she be hiding in one of those rooms?" He wasn't subtle, that was clear.

"Hiding?" The lavender lady turned our way, too. "I'm sure there's no one hiding in our church. Wouldn't you like me to call the priest? Do you need some help?"

The librarian backed away. "Oh, no, no," he said. "I must have made a mistake."

"Would you like some of our literature?"

"Oh, no." He backed down the aisle. "No, thank you." I saw him peer around again, and then he passed out of my range of vision. There was a heavy click, a thump — the front door closing behind him. I gave Helen a nod and she sighed noiseless relief, but we waited a few more minutes there, glancing at each other over the font. Helen looked down first, her brow furrowed. I knew she must be wondering how on earth she'd gotten into such a situation and what it really meant. The top of her hair was glossy, ebony — she was hatless again today.

"He's looking for you," I said in a low voice.

"Maybe he is looking for you." She indicated the envelope I held.

"I have a strange idea," I said slowly. "Maybe he knows where Rossi is."

She frowned again. "None of this makes much sense anyway, so why not?" she muttered.

"I can't let you go back to the library. Or your rooms. He'll be looking for you in both places."

"Let me?" she echoed ominously.

"Miss Rossi, please. Do you want to be the next disappearance?"

She was silent. "So how do you plan to protect me?" Her voice held a mocking note, and I thought of her strange childhood, her original flight to Hungary in her mother's womb, the political savvy that had allowed her to travel to the other side of the world for academic revenge. If her story were all true, of course.

"I have an idea," I said slowly. "I know this is going to sound — undignified, but I would feel better if you would humor me about it. We can take some — charms — with us from the church here —" She raised her eyebrows. "We'll

find something — candles or crucifixes or something — and buy some garlic on the way home —
I mean to my apartment —" The eyebrows went
up further. "I mean, if you would consent to accompany me — and you could — I may have to
leave for a trip tomorrow, but you could —"

"Sleep on the sofa?" She had her gloves on
again and now she folded her arms. I felt myself
flushing.

"I can't let you go back to your rooms knowing you might be pursued — or to the library, of
course. And we have more to discuss, I think. I'd
like to know what you think your mother —"

"We can discuss that right here, right now,"
she said — coldly, I thought. "As for the librarian,
I doubt he would be able to follow me to my
room, unless —" Did she have a sort of dimple
on one side of her stern chin, or was that sarcasm? "Unless he can turn himself into a bat already. You see, our matron doesn't allow vampires
in our rooms. Or men, for that matter. Besides,
I'm hoping he will follow me back to the library."

"Hoping?" I was startled.

"I knew he wouldn't talk with us here, not in
the church. He is probably waiting outside for
us. I have a bone to pick with him" — that ex-

traordinary English again — "because he is trying to interfere with my library privileges, and
you believe he has information for you about
my — Professor Rossi. Why not let him follow
me? We can discuss my mother on the way." I
must have looked more than doubtful, because
she suddenly laughed, her teeth white and even.
"He is not going to jump on you in broad daylight, Paul."

Chapter 21

THERE WAS NO SIGN of the librarian outside the church. We strolled toward the library — my heart was thumping hard, although Helen looked cool — with twin crucifixes from the church vestibule in our pockets ("Take one, leave a quarter"). To my disappointment, Helen did not mention her mother. I had the sense that she was merely cooperating temporarily with my madness, that she was going to vanish once we reached the library, but she surprised me again. "He is back there," she said quietly about two blocks from the church. "I saw him when we turned the corner. Do not look behind you." I stifled an exclamation and we walked on. "I am going to go into the upper stacks in the library," she said. "How about the seventh floor? That is the first really quiet area. Do not go up there with me. He is more likely to follow me if I'm alone than to follow you — you are stronger."

"You are absolutely not going to do that," I murmured. "Getting information about Rossi is my problem."

"Getting information about Rossi is precisely my problem," she muttered back. "Please do not think that I am doing you a favor, Mr. Dutch Merchants."

I glanced sidelong at her. I was getting used to her harsh humor, I realized, and something about the curve of her cheek next to that long straight nose looked almost playful, amused. "All right. But I'll be right behind him, and if you get into trouble I'll be up there in a split second to help you."

At the library doors we parted with a show of cordiality. "Good luck with your research, Mr. Dutch," Helen said, shaking my hand in her gloved one.

"And you with yours, Miss —"

"Shh," she said and walked off. I retreated into the card-catalog stands and pulled out a drawer at random to make myself look busy: "*Ben-Hur* to Benedictine." With my head bent over it, I could still see the circulation desk; Helen was getting a permission slip to enter the stacks, her form tall and slim in the black coat, her back turned decisively on the long nave of the library. Then I saw the librarian creeping along the other side of the nave, keeping close to the other half of the card catalog. He had reached "H" by the time Helen moved toward the door of the stacks. I knew that door intimately, went through it almost daily, and never before had it yawned with meaning for me as it did now. It stayed propped open during the day, but a guard nearby checked entrance slips. In a moment, Helen's dark figure had vanished up the iron stairs. The librarian lingered for a minute at "G," then groped for something in his jacket pocket — he must have special library identification, I realized — flashed a card, and disappeared.

I hurried to the circulation desk. "I'd like to use the stacks, please," I said to the woman on duty. I'd never seen her before — she was very slow — and it seemed to me her round little hands fumbled for an eternity with the yellow slips before she could give me one. At last I made it through the doorway and put a cautious foot on the stairway, looking up. On each floor you could see up one level through the metal steps, but no farther. No sign of the librarian above me, no sound.

I crept to the second floor, past economics and sociology. The third was deserted, too, except for a couple of students at their carrels. On the fourth floor I began to feel really worried. It was too quiet. I should never have let Helen use herself as bait on this mission. I suddenly remembered Rossi's story about his friend Hedges, and it made me quicken my pace. The fifth floor — archaeology and anthropology — was full of students, undergraduates attending some kind of study group, comparing notes sotto voce. Their presence relieved me somewhat; nothing heinous could be going on just two floors above that. On the sixth floor I could hear footsteps above me, and on the seventh — history — I paused, unsure how to enter the stacks without giving my presence away.

At least I knew this floor well; it was my kingdom, and I could have told you the placement of every carrel and chair, every row of oversize books. At first, history seemed as still as the other floors, but after a moment I picked up muffled conversation from a corner of the stacks. I crept toward it, past Babylon and Assyria, treading as quietly as I could. Then I caught Helen's voice. I was sure it was Helen's, and then an unpleasant scraping voice that must be the librarian's. My heart turned over. They were in the medieval section — I knew it well, now — and I got close enough to hear their words, although I couldn't risk looking around the end of the next stack. They seemed to be on the other side of the shelves to my right. "Is that correct?" Helen was asking in a hostile tone.

The scraping little voice came again. "You have no right poking around in those books, young lady."

"Those books? University property? Who are you to confiscate university library books?"

The librarian's voice was angry and wheedling at the same time. "You don't need to fool around with such books. They aren't nice books for a young lady to be reading. Just turn them in today and nothing more will be said."

"Why do you want them so badly?" Helen's voice was firm and clear. "Does it have something to do with Professor Rossi, perhaps?"

Cowering behind English feudalism, I wasn't sure whether to cringe or to cheer aloud. Whatever Helen thought of all this, she was at least intrigued. Apparently she did not consider me crazy. And she was willing to help me, if only to gather information about Rossi for her own ends.

"Professor — who? I don't know what you mean," the librarian snapped.

"Do you know where he is?" Helen asked sharply.

"Young lady, I have no idea what you're talking about. But I need you to return those books, for which the library has other plans, or there will certainly be consequences for your academic career."

"My career?" Helen scoffed. "I cannot possibly return those books just now. I have important work to do with them."

"Then I will have to force you to return them. Where are they?" I heard a step, as if Helen had moved away. I was on the verge of swinging around the end of the stack and bringing a folio of Cistercian abbeys down on the nasty little weasel when Helen suddenly played a new card.

"I'll tell you what," she said. "If you can tell me something about Professor Rossi, maybe I could share with you a little —" She paused. "A little map I saw recently."

My stomach dropped all seven stories at once. The map? What was Helen thinking? Why was she giving away such a vital piece of information? That map might be our most dangerous possession, if Rossi's analysis of its meaning were true, and our most important one. My most dangerous possession, I corrected myself. Was Helen double-crossing me? I saw it in a flash: she wanted to use the map to get to Rossi first, complete his research, use me to learn all he had learned and passed on to me, publish, expose him — I didn't have time for more than a fleeting revelation because the next moment the librarian let out a roar. "The map! You have Rossi's map! I'll kill you for that map!" A gasp from Helen, then a cry and a thump. "Put that down!" screamed the librarian.

My feet didn't touch the ground until I was on top of him. His little head hit the floor with a thump that rattled my brains, too. Helen crouched next to me. She was very white but looked calm. She was holding up her twenty-five-cent silver crucifix from the church, keeping it trained on him as he fought and spat under me. The librarian was frail, and for a few minutes I could more or less pin him down — lucky for me, since I'd spent the last three years turning through brittle Dutch documents, not lifting weights. He flailed in my grasp, and I brought my knee down on his legs. "Rossi!" he shrieked. "It's not fair! I should have gone instead — it was my turn! Give me the map! I waited so long — I did twenty years of research for this!" He began to sob, a pitiful, ugly sound. As his head jerked back and forth, I saw the double wound near the edge of his collar, two scabby thorn holes. I kept my hands as far away from it as I could.

"Where's Rossi?" I growled. "Tell us this instant where he is — did you hurt him?" Helen held the little cross closer and he turned his face away, writhing under my knees. It was astounding to me, even at that moment, to see the effect of that symbol on the creature. Was this Hollywood, superstition, or history? I wondered how he'd been able to walk into the church — but there he had stayed far from the altar and chapels, I remembered, and had shrunk away even from the altar-guild lady.

"I didn't touch him! I don't know anything about it!"

"Oh, yes, you do." Helen bent closer. Her expression was fierce, but she was very white, and I noticed now that she held her free hand tightly over her neck.

"Helen!"

I must have gasped aloud, but she waved me away, glaring at the librarian. "Where is Rossi? What was it you waited years for?" He shrank back. "I'm going to put this on your face now," Helen said, lowering the crucifix.

"No!" he screamed. "I'll tell you. Rossi didn't want to go. I wanted to. It wasn't fair. He took

Rossi instead of me! He took him by force —
I would have gone willingly to serve him, to
help him, to catalog —" He suddenly clamped
his mouth shut.

"What?" I thumped his head slightly on the
floor for good measure. "Who took Rossi? Are
you keeping him somewhere?"

Helen held the cross right over his nose, and
he began to sob again. "My master," he whim-
pered. Helen, next to me, drew a long breath and
sat back on her heels, as if recoiling involuntarily from his words.

"Who is your master?" I dug my knee into his
leg. "Where did he take Rossi?"

His eyes blazed. It was a shocking sight — the
contortion, the normal human features hieroglyphic with terrible meaning. "Where I should
have been allowed to go! To the tomb!"

Maybe my grip had weakened, or maybe his
confession made him suddenly strong — probably
from terror for himself, I realized afterward. In
any case, he suddenly freed one hand, swung
around like a scorpion, and bent my wrist backward where it held down his shoulder. The pain
was unbearably sharp, and I jerked my arm back
in fury. He was gone before I could understand
what had happened, and I took off after him

down the stairs, clattering past the undergraduate seminar and the quiet realms of knowledge below. But I was hampered by my briefcase, which I still clutched in one hand. Even in that first moment of pursuit, I realized fleetingly, I hadn't wanted to drop it. Or throw it to Helen. She had told him about the map. She was a traitor. And he had bitten her, if only for a moment. Wouldn't she be tainted herself now?

For the first and last time I ran through the hushed nave of the library instead of walking, only half seeing the astonished faces that turned toward me as I flew along. There was no sign of the librarian. He could have escaped into any backstage region, I realized with despair, any cataloging dungeon or broom closet for librarians only. I thrust open the heavy front door, an opening cut in the great double Gothic-style doors to the hall, which were never fully opened. Then I stopped short on the steps. The afternoon light blinded me as if I, too, had been living in an underworld, a cave of bats and rodents. On the street in front of the library, several cars had stopped. Traffic was at a halt, in fact, and a girl in a waitress uniform was crying on the sidewalk, pointing at something. Someone was shouting, and a couple of men knelt by the front tire of one of the stopped cars. The weaselly librarian's legs stuck out from under the car, twisted at an impossible angle. One of his arms was flung over his head. He lay facedown on the pavement in a little blood, asleep forever.

Chapter 22

MY FATHER WAS RELUCTANT to take me to Oxford. He would be there six days, he said, a long time for me to miss school again. I was surprised that he was willing to leave me at home; he hadn't done that even once since I'd found the dragon book. Was he planning to leave me with particular precautions? I pointed out that our trip along the Yugoslav coast had taken almost two weeks, without any sign of detriment to my schoolwork. He said education should always come first. I pointed out that he had always postulated travel as the best education, and that May was the pleasantest month for travel. I produced my latest report card, which gleamed with high grades, and a history paper on which my rather pompous instructor had written, "You show extraordinary insight into the nature of historical research, especially for one of your years," a comment I had memorized and often repeated to myself as a mantra before I slept.

My father wavered visibly, setting his knife and fork down in a way I knew meant a pause in our dinner in the old Dutch dining room, not a decisive end to the first course. He said his work would prevent him from showing me around properly this time and he didn't want to spoil my first impressions of Oxford by keeping me cooped up somewhere. I said I preferred being cooped up in Oxford to being cooped up at home with Mrs. Clay — at this point we dropped our voices, although she was having her evening off. Besides, I was old enough, I said, to wander around by myself. He said he just didn't know if it was a good idea for me to go, since these talks promised to be rather — tense. It might not be quite — but he couldn't go on and I knew why. Just as I could not use my real argument for going to Oxford, he could not use his for wanting to prevent me from going. I could not tell him aloud that I couldn't bear to let him, with his dark-circled eyes and the fatigued stoop of shoulder and head, out of my sight now. And he could not counter aloud that he might not be safe in Oxford and that, therefore, I might not be safe with him. He was silent for a minute or two, and then he asked me very gently what we were having for dessert, and I brought in Mrs. Clay's dreary rice pudding with currants, which she always left as a compensation for going out to the movies at the British Centre without us.

• • •

I had imagined Oxford hushed and green, a kind of outdoor cathedral where dons in medieval dress paraded around, each with a single student at his side, lecturing on history, literature, obscure theology. The reality was shockingly lively: beeping motorcycles, little cars darting here and there and narrowly missing students as they crossed the streets, a crowd of tourists photographing a cross on the sidewalk where a couple of bishops had been burned at the stake four hundred years earlier, before sidewalks. The dons and students alike wore disappointingly modern dress, mostly wool sweaters, with dark flannel trousers for the mentor and blue jeans for the disciple. I thought with regret that in Rossi's time, a good forty years before we stepped off our bus onto Broad Street, Oxford must at least have dressed with a little more dignity.

Then I caught sight of the first college I ever saw there, towering over its walled enclosure in the morning light, and looming near it the perfect shape of the Radcliffe Camera, which I took at first for a small observatory. Behind that rose the spires of a great brown church, and along the street ran a wall that looked so old even the lichens on it seemed antique. I couldn't imagine how we would have appeared to whoever had walked these streets when that wall was young — I in my short red dress and crocheted white stockings and my book bag, my father in his navy jacket and gray slacks, his black turtleneck and tweed hat, each of us lugging a small suitcase. "Here we are," my father pronounced, and to my delight we turned in at a gate in the lichened wall. It was locked, and we waited there until a student held the wrought-iron bars open for us.

At Oxford my father was to speak at a conference on political relations between the United States and Eastern Europe, now in the full flower of a thaw. Because the university was hosting the conference, we were invited to stay in private rooms in the house of one of the college masters. The masters, my father explained, were benevolent dictators who looked after the students who lived in each college. As we made our way through the dark, low entryway and into the blazing sunlight of the college quadrangle, I realized for the first time that soon I, too, would go to college, and I crossed my fingers on my book-bag handle and breathed a wish that I would then find myself in a haven like this one.

Around us lay softly worn flagstones, inter-

rupted here and there by heavy shade trees —
serious, melancholy old trees with the occasional
bench underneath. A little rectangle of perfect
grass and a narrow pool of water lay at the feet
of the college's main building. It was one of Oxford's oldest, endowed by Edward III in the thirteenth century, its newest additions shaped by
Elizabethan architects. Even that patch of carefully clipped grass looked venerable; certainly I
never saw anyone step on it.

We skirted the grass and water and made our
way to the porter's office just inside, and from
there to a suite of rooms adjoining the master's
house. These rooms must have been part of the
original design of the college, although it was
hard to tell what they had originally been used
for; they were very low-ceilinged, with dark pan-
eling and tiny leaded windows. My father's bedroom had blue draperies. Mine, to my infinite
satisfaction, had a high chintz canopy bed.

We unpacked a little, washed our travelers'
faces in a pale-yellow basin in our shared bathroom, and went to meet Master James, who was
expecting us in his office at the other end of the
building. He turned out to be a hearty, kind-
spoken man with graying hair and a knobby scar

on one cheekbone. I liked his warm handshake and the expression of his large, rather protuberant hazel eyes. He seemed to find nothing strange about my accompanying my father to the conference and went so far as to suggest that I tour the college with his student assistant that afternoon. His assistant, he said, was an obliging and very knowledgeable young gentleman. My father said I could certainly do that; he himself would be busy with meetings then, and why shouldn't I see the treasures of the place while I was there?

I turned up eagerly at three o'clock, my new beret in one hand and a notebook in the other, since my father had suggested I might get notes for a school paper out of the tour. My guide was a pale-haired, gangly undergraduate, whom Master James introduced as Stephen Barley. I liked Stephen's fine, blue-veined hands and heavy fisherman's sweater — "jumpah," he called it when I admired it aloud. It gave me a feeling of temporary acceptance into that elite community to stroll across the quad at his side. It also gave me my first faint quaver of sexual belonging, the elusive feeling that if I slipped my hand into his as we walked along, a door would fall open somewhere in the long wall of reality as I knew it, never to be closed again. I've explained that I had led an extremely sheltered life — so sheltered, I see now, that even at nearly eighteen I hadn't realized how close its confines were. The quiver of rebellion I felt walking beside a handsome university student came to me like a strain of music from an alien culture. But I clutched my notebook and my childhood more tightly and asked him why the courtyard was mainly stone instead of grass. He smiled down at me. "Well, I don't know. No one's asked that before."

He took me into the dining hall, a high-ceilinged, Tudor-beamed barn full of wooden tables, and showed me where a young Earl of Rochester had cut something rude into a bench while dining there. The hall was lined with leaded windows, each ornamented in the center with an ancient scene of good works: Thomas à Becket kneeling at a deathbed, a priest in a long gown ladling out soup for a line of the cowering poor, a medieval doctor bandaging someone's leg. Above the Rochester bench was a scene I couldn't figure out, a man with a cross around his neck and a stick in one hand bending over what looked like a bundle of black rags. "Oh, that's a curiosity indeed," Stephen Barley told me. "We're very proud of that. You see, this man is a don from the early years of the college, driving a silver stake through the heart of a vampire."

I stared at him, speechless for a moment. "Were there vampires in Oxford in those days?" I asked finally.

"I don't know about that," he admitted, smiling. "But there's a tradition that the early scholars of the college helped protect the countryside around here from vampires. Actually, they collected quite a bit of lore on vampires, quaint stuff, and you can still see it in the Radcliffe Camera, across the way. The legend says that the early dons wouldn't even have books about the occult housed in the college, so they were put in various other places and finally ended up there."

I suddenly remembered Rossi and wondered if he'd seen some of this old collection. "Is there any way of finding out the names of students from the past — I mean — maybe — fifty years ago — in this college? Graduate students?"

"Of course." My companion looked quizzically at me across the wooden bench. "I can ask the master for you, if you like."

"Oh, no." I felt myself blushing, the curse of my youth. "It's nothing important. But I would — could I see the vampire lore?"

"You like scary stuff, eh?" He looked amused. "It's not much to look at, you know — just some old folios and a lot of leather books. But all right. We'll go and see the college library now — you can't miss that — and then I'll take you up to the Camera."

The library was, of course, one of the gems of the university. Since that innocent day, I have seen most of those colleges and known some of them intimately, wandered through their libraries and chapels and dining halls, lectured in their seminar rooms and taken tea in their parlors. I can safely say there is nothing to equal that first college library I saw, except perhaps Magdalen College Chapel, with its divine ornamentation. We first went into a reading room surrounded by stained glass like a tall terrarium, in which the students, rare captive plants, sat around tables whose antiquity was almost as great as that of the college itself. Strange lamps hung from the ceiling, and enormous globes from the era of Henry VIII stood on pedestals in the corners. Stephen Barley pointed out the many volumes of the original *Oxford English Dictionary* lining the shelves of one wall; others were filled with atlases from a long sweep of centuries, others with ancient peerages and works of English history, still others with Latin and Greek textbooks from every era of the college's existence. In the center of the room stood a giant encyclopedia on a carved baroque stand, and near the entrance to the next room rested a glass case in which I could see a stark-looking old book that Stephen told me was a Gutenberg Bible. Above us, a round skylight like the oculus of a Byzantine church admitted long tapers of sunlight. Flights of pigeons wheeled overhead. The dusty sunshine touched the faces of students reading and turning pages at the tables, brushed their heavy jumpers and serious faces. It was a paradise of learning, and I prayed for eventual admission.

The next room was a vast hall hung with balconies, winding staircases, a high clerestory of old glass. Every available wall was lined with books, top to bottom, stone floor to vaulted ceiling. I saw acres of finely tooled leather bindings, swaths of portfolios, masses of little dark red nineteenth-century volumes. What, I wondered, could be in all those books? Would I understand anything in them? My fingers itched to take a few off the shelves, but I didn't dare touch even a binding. I wasn't sure if this was a library or a museum. I must have been gazing around with naked emotion on my face, because I suddenly caught my guide smiling at me, amused. "Not bad, eh? You must be a bookworm yourself. Come on, then — you've seen the best of it, and we'll go up to the Camera."

The bright day and the noisy, speeding cars were more jarring than ever after the hush of the library. I had them to thank, however, for a sudden gift: as we hurried across the traffic, Stephen took my hand, pulling me along to safety. He might have been someone's peremptory big brother, I thought, but the touch of that dry, warm palm sent a tingling signal into mine, which glowed there after he'd dropped my hand. I felt sure, stealing glances at his cheerful, unchanged profile, that the message had registered in only one direction. But it was enough, for me, to have received it.

The Radcliffe Camera, as every Anglophile knows, is one of the great charms of English architecture, beautiful and odd, a huge barrel of books. One edge of it stands almost in the street, but with a large lawn around the rest of the building. We made our way in very quietly, although a talkative tour group filled the center of the glorious round interior. Stephen pointed out various aspects of the building's design, studied in every course on English architecture, written up in every guidebook. It was a lovely and moving place, and I kept looking around thinking what a strange repository this was for evil lore. At last he led me toward a staircase, and we climbed up to the balcony. "Over here." He motioned toward a doorway in the wall, cut, as it were, into a sheer cliff face of books. "There's a little reading room in there. I've been up here just once, but I think that's where they keep the vampire collection."

The dim room was indeed tiny, and hushed, too, set far back from the voices of tourists below. August volumes crowded the shelves, their bindings caramel colored and brittle as old bone. Among them, a human skull in a little gilded glass case attested to the collection's morbid nature. The chamber was so small, in fact, that there was just space in the center for one reading desk, which we almost stumbled against as we stepped in. That meant that we were suddenly face-to-face with the scholar who sat there turning over the leaves of a folio and making rapid notes on a pad of paper. He was a pale, rather gaunt man. His eyes were dark hollows, startled and urgent but also full of absorption as he glanced up from his work. It was my father.

Chapter 23

IN THE CONFUSION of ambulances, police cars, and spectators that accompanied the dead librarian's removal from the street in front of the university library, I stood frozen for a minute. It was horrible, unthinkable, that even the most unpleasant man's life should have ended so suddenly there, but my next concern was for Helen. A crowd was gathering fast, and I pushed here and there looking for her. I was infinitely relieved when she found me first, tapping me on the shoulder from behind with her gloved hand. She looked pale but composed. She had wrapped her scarf tightly around her throat, and the sight of it on her smooth neck made me shiver. "I waited a few minutes and then followed you down the stairs," she said under the noise of the crowd. "I want to thank you for coming to my assistance. This man was a brute. You were truly brave."

I was surprised to find how kind her face could look, after all. "Actually, you were the brave one. And he hurt you," I said in a low voice. I tried not to gesture publicly at her neck. "Did he — ?"

"Yes," she said quietly. Instinctively, we'd drawn close together, so that no one else could hear our conversation. "When he flew at me up there, he bit me on the throat." For a minute her lips seemed to tremble, as if she might cry. "He did not draw much blood — there was no time. And it hurts very little."

"But you — " I was stammering, unbelieving.

"I do not think there will be any infection," she said. "It bled very little and I have closed it up as well as I can."

"Should we go to the hospital?" I regretted it as soon as I'd said it, only partly because of the withering look she gave me. "Or can we treat it somehow?" I think I was half imagining we could remove the venom, as with a snakebite. The pain in her face suddenly made my heart twist within me. Then I remembered her betrayal of the secret of the map. "But why did you —"

"I know what you are wondering," she interrupted hurriedly, her accent thickening. "But I could not think of any other bait for the creature, and I wanted to see his reaction. I would not have given him the map or any more information. I promise you that."

I studied her suspiciously. Her face was serious, her mouth drawn down into a grim curve. "No?"

"I give you my word," she said simply. "Besides" — her sarcastic smile reversed the grimace — "I'm not necessarily in the habit of sharing what I can use for myself, are you?"

I had to let that pass, but something in her face did calm my fears. "His reaction was extremely interesting, wasn't it?"

She nodded. "He said he should have been allowed to go to the tomb, and that Rossi was taken there by someone. It is very strange, but he did seem to know something about the whereabouts of my — your adviser. I cannot believe in this Drakulya business, exactly, but perhaps some weird occult group has kidnapped Professor Rossi, something of that sort."

It was my turn to nod, although I was obviously closer to believing than she was.

"What will you do now?" she asked, with curious detachment.

I hadn't quite planned my answer before it came out. "Go to Istanbul. I'm convinced there's at least one document there that Rossi never had the chance to examine, and that it might contain information about a tomb, perhaps Dracula's tomb at Lake Snagov."

She laughed. "Why not take a little vacation to my lovely native Romania? You could go to Dracula's castle with a silver stake in your hand, or visit him yourself at Snagov. I've heard it is a pretty place for a picnic."

"Look," I said irritably. "I know this is all very peculiar, but I absolutely must follow any trace I can of Rossi's disappearance. And you know perfectly well an American citizen can't just penetrate the Iron Curtain to look for someone." My loyalty must have shamed her a little, because she did not answer. "I do want to ask you something. You said as we were leaving the church that your mother might have some information about Rossi's hunt for Dracula. What did you mean by that?"

"I simply meant that when they met, he told her he was in Romania to study the legend of Dracula, and that she herself believes in the legend. Maybe she knows more about his research there than I have ever heard from her — I'm not sure. She does not talk easily about this, and I have been pursuing this little interest of the dear old paterfamilias through scholarly channels, not in the bosom of the family. I should have asked her more about her own experience."

"An odd oversight for an anthropologist," I retorted crankily. Now that I believed again that she was on my side, I felt all the annoyance of relief. Her face lit up with amusement.

"Touché, Sherlock. I'll ask her all about it next time I see her."

"When will that be?"

"In a couple of years, I suppose. My precious visa doesn't allow me to bounce easily back and forth between East and West."

"Don't you ever call or write her?"

She stared. "Oh, the West is such an innocent place," she said finally. "Do you think she has a telephone? Do you think my letters are not opened and read every time?"

I was silent, chastened.

"What is this document you are so eager to look for, Sherlock?" she asked. "Is it that bibliography, something about the Order of the Dragon? I saw that on the last list in his papers. It was the only thing he did not describe fully. Is that what you want to find?"

She'd guessed right, naturally. I was getting an uncanny sense of her intellectual powers, and I thought a little wistfully of the conversations we might have had under better circumstances. On the other hand, I didn't completely like her guessing so much. "Why do you want to know?" I countered. "For your research?"

"Of course," she said sternly. "Will you get in touch with me again when you come back?"

I felt suddenly very weary. "Come back? I have no idea what I'm getting into, let alone when I'll be back. Maybe I'll be struck down by the vampire myself when I get wherever it is I'm going."

I had meant to utter this ironically, but the unreality of the whole situation dawned on me again as I spoke; here I was, standing on the sidewalk in front of the library as I had hundreds of times before, except that this time I was talking about vampires — as if I believed in them — with a Romanian anthropologist, and we were watching ambulance drivers and police officers swarm across a death scene in which I had been involved, at least indirectly. I tried not to see them at their grisly work. It occurred to me that I ought to leave the quad soon, but without visible haste. I couldn't afford to be taken in by the police at this point, not even for a few hours' questioning. I had a great deal to do, and it had to be done immediately — I would need a visa to Turkey, which I might be able to obtain in New York, and a plane ticket, and I would need to leave safely at home a copy of all the information I had already. I was not teaching this term, thank goodness, but I'd have to present some kind of alibi to my department and give my parents some explanation to keep them from worrying.

I turned to Helen. "Miss Rossi," I said. "If you will keep this business to yourself, I promise to get in touch with you as soon as I come back. Is there anything else you can tell me? Can you think of a way I could reach your mother before I go?"

"I cannot reach her myself, except by letter," she said flatly. "Besides, she speaks no English. When I go home in two years I will ask her about these matters myself."

I sighed. Two years was too late, unimaginably so. I was feeling a sort of anxiety already at being separated from this strange companion of a few days — hours, really — the only person besides myself who knew anything about the nature of Rossi's disappearance. After this I would be on my own in a country I had barely ever thought about. It had to be done, however. I extended my hand. "Miss Rossi, thank you for putting up with a harmless lunatic for a couple of days. If I come back safely I will certainly let you know — I mean, maybe — if I bring your father back safely —"

She made a vague gesture with her gloved hand, as if her interest could not possibly lie with Rossi's safe return, but then she put the hand in mine and we shook on it, cordially. I had the sense that her firm grasp was my last contact with the world I knew. "Good-bye," she said. "I wish you the best possible luck with your research." She turned away in the crowd — the ambulance drivers were shutting the doors. I turned away, too, and started down the steps and across the quadrangle. A hundred feet from the library, I stopped and looked back, hoping to glimpse her dark-suited figure among the ambulance watchers. To my surprise, she was hurrying toward me, already almost on my heels. She reached me quickly, and I saw that her face had picked up a ruby flush over the cheekbones. Her expression was urgent. "I have been thinking," she said, and then stopped. She seemed to take a deep breath. "This concerns my life more than any other thing." Her gaze was direct, challenging. "I am not quite sure how to do it, but I think I will come with you."

Chapter 24

MY FATHER HAD some pleasant excuses for being in the Oxford vampire collection instead of at his meeting. The meeting had been canceled, he said, shaking Stephen Barley's hand with his customary warmth. My father said he'd wandered up here to an old haunt — there he stopped, almost biting his lip, and tried again. He'd been looking for some peace and quiet (that I could easily believe). His gratitude for Stephen's presence, for Stephen's tall, blooming good health, his woolly sweatered wholesomeness, was palpable. After all, what could my father have said to me, if I'd surprised him there by myself? How could he have explained, or even casually closed, the folio under his hand? He did it now, but too late; I had already seen a chapter title stark on thick ivory paper: *"Vampires de Provence et des Pyrénées."*

I slept poorly that night in the canopied chintz bed at the college master's house, waking from strange dreams every few hours. Once I saw light under the door in the bathroom between my room and my father's, which reassured me. Sometimes, though, the sense of his not being asleep, of quiet activity in the room next door, dragged me suddenly from my rest. Near dawn, when a slate-colored haze was starting to show through the net curtains, I woke for the last time.

This time it was the silence that awakened me. Everything was too still: the faint outlines of trees in the courtyard (I peered around the edge of the curtains), the huge armoire next to my bed, and above all my father's room next door. It was not that I expected him to be up at this hour; if anything, he would still be sleeping — maybe snoring a little if he was lying on his back — trying to erase the cares of the day before, postponing the grueling schedule of lectures and seminars and debate that lay ahead of him. During our trips, he usually gave my door a genial tap after I'd already gotten up myself, an invitation to hurry out to meet him for a walk before breakfast.

This morning the silence oppressed me for no good reason, and I climbed down from my big bed and dressed and slung a towel over my shoulder. I would wash in the bathroom basin and listen a bit for my father's nocturnal breathing while I was at it. I knocked gently at the bathroom door to be sure he wasn't inside. The silence was even deeper once I was there in front of the mirror, drying my face. I put an ear to his door. He was certainly sleeping soundly. I knew it would be heartless to interrupt his hard-won rest, but panic had begun to creep up my legs and arms. I tapped lightly. There was no stir inside. We had for years left each other's privacy intact, but now, in that gray morning light from the bathroom window, I turned the door handle.

Inside my father's bedroom the heavy drapes were still drawn, so that it took me a few seconds to register the dim outline of furniture and pictures. The quiet made the skin quiver along the back of my neck. I took a step toward the bed, spoke to him. But up close the bed lay smooth and neat, dark in the dark room. The room was empty. I let out my indrawn breath. He had gone outside, gone walking alone, probably, needing solitude and time for reflection. But something made me switch on the light by the bed, to look around more carefully. In the circle of brightness lay a note addressed to me, and on the note rested two objects that took me by surprise: a small silver crucifix on a sturdy chain and a head of fresh garlic. The stark reality of these items made my stomach turn over even before I read my father's words.

My dear daughter:

I am terribly sorry to surprise you like this, but I've been called away on some new business and didn't want to disturb you during the night. I'll be gone just a few days, I hope. I've arranged with Master James to get you safely home in the company of our young friend Stephen Barley. He has been excused from classes for two days and will see you to Amsterdam this evening. I wanted Mrs. Clay to come for you, but her sister is ailing and she has gone to Liverpool again. She'll try to join you at home tonight. In any case, you will be well cared for and I trust you will look after yourself sensibly. Don't worry about my absence. It's a confidential matter, but I'll be home as quickly as possible and will explain then. In the meantime, I ask you from the bottom of my heart to wear the crucifix at all times, and to carry some of the garlic in each of your pockets. You know I have never been one to press either religion or superstition on you, and I remain a firm unbeliever in either. But we must deal with evil on its own terms, as far as possible, and you already know the domain of those terms. I beg you from a father's heart not to disregard my wishes on this point.

It was signed with affectionate warmth, but I could see that he had written it hastily. My heart was pounding. I quickly fastened the chain around my neck and divided the garlic to put in the pockets of my dress. It was like my father, I thought, looking around the empty room, to make the bed so neatly in the middle of a silent hurry to leave the college. But why this haste? Whatever his errand was, it could not be a simple diplomatic mission, or he would have told me as much. He'd often had to respond to professional emergencies; I had known him to leave with little warning to attend a crisis on the other side of Europe, but he always told me where he was going. This time, my racing heart told me, he hadn't departed on business. Besides, he was supposed to be here in Oxford this week, giving lectures and attending meetings. He was not one to break an obligation lightly.

No. His disappearance must have some connection with the strain he'd been showing lately — I realized now that I'd feared something like this all along. Then there was that scene yesterday in the Radcliffe Camera, my father deep in — what had he been reading, exactly? And where, oh where, had he gone? Where, without me? For the first time in all the years I remembered, all the years in which my father had sheltered me from the loneliness of life with no mother, no siblings, no home country, all the years of his being both father and mother — for the first time, I felt like an orphan.

The master was very kind when I appeared with my suitcase packed and my raincoat over my arm. I explained to him that I was fully ready to travel by myself. I assured him I was grateful for his offer of a student to see me home — across the whole Channel — and that I would never forget his kindness. I felt a twinge at that, a small but distinct twang of disappointment — how pleasant it could have been to travel for a day with Stephen Barley smiling at me from the opposite train seat! But it had to be said. I would be safely home within hours, I repeated, pressing down my sudden mental picture of a red marble basin filled with melodic water, afraid this kindly smiling man might divine it in me, might see it on my face, even. I would be safely home soon and could call him if he needed extra reassurance. And then, of course, I added with still greater duplicity, my father would be home in a few days himself.

Master James was certain I was capable of traveling alone; I looked like an independent lass, to be sure. It was just that he couldn't — he turned an even gentler smile on me — he simply couldn't go back on his word to my father, an old friend. I was my father's most priceless treasure, and he couldn't ship me off without proper protection. It wouldn't be for my sake, exactly, I must realize that, but for my father's — we had to indulge him a bit. Stephen Barley materialized before I could argue more, or even fully register the idea that the master was my father's old friend when I'd believed they'd met just two days ago. But I had no time for this irregularity; Stephen was standing there looking like my old friend, in his turn, his own jacket and bag in hand, and I couldn't be completely sorry to see him. I regretted the detour it would cost me, but not as thoroughly as I should have. It was impossible for me not to welcome his practical grin, or his "Got me out of a little work, you did!"

Master James was more sober. "You're on the

job yet, my lad," he told him. "I want a call from Amsterdam as soon as you're there, and I want to talk with the housekeeper. Here's money for your tickets and some meals, and you'll bring me back your receipts." His hazel eyes twinkled then. "That's not to say you can't get a little Dutch chocolate for yourself at the station. Fetch me a bar, too. It's not as good as Belgian, but it'll do. Off with you now, and use your head." Next he gave me a grave handshake and his card. "Good-bye, my dear. Come again and see us when you're thinking of university for yourself."

Outside the office, Stephen grabbed my bag for me. "Let's go, then. We've tickets for the ten-thirty, but we might as well get a head start."

The master and my father had taken care of every detail, I noted, and I wondered what extra chains I'd have to slip at home. I had other business for now, however. "Stephen?" I began.

"Oh, call me Barley." He laughed. "Everyone else calls me that, and I'm so used to it now that it gives me the creeps to hear my real name."

"All right." His smile was just as contagious to-day — easily as contagious. "Barley, I — could I ask you a favor before we leave?" He nodded. "I'd just like to go into the Camera one more time. It was so beautiful, I — and I'd like to see the vampire collection. I didn't really get to look at it."

He groaned. "I could tell you like grisly stuff. Seems to run in your family."

"I know." I felt myself flushing.

"All right. Let's take a quick look again, but then we've got to run. Master James will put a stake through *my* heart if we miss the train."

The Camera was quiet this morning, nearly empty, and we hurried up a polished staircase to the macabre niche where we'd surprised my father the day before. I swallowed a threat of tears as we entered the tiny room; hours ago, my father had been sitting here, that strangely distant look veiling his eyes, and now I didn't even know where he was.

I remembered where he'd shelved the book, though, replaced it so casually as we talked. It would be below the case with the skull, to the left. I ran a finger along the edge of the shelf. Barley stood near me (it was impossible for us not to stand close together in that tiny space, and I wished he would wander out to the balcony instead), watching with frank curiosity. Where the book should have been was a gap like a missing tooth. I froze: surely my father would never, ever steal a book, so who could have taken it? But a second later I recognized the volume a hand's length away. Someone had certainly moved it since I'd been there last. Had my father returned for a second look? Or had someone else taken it off the shelf? I glanced suspiciously at the skull in the glass case, but it gave back a bland, anatomical gaze. Then I lifted the book down, very carefully — there was the tall, bone-colored binding with a black silk ribbon protruding from the top. I laid it on the table and found the title page: *Vampires du Moyen Age,* Baron de Hejduke, Bucarest, 1886.

"What do you want with this morbid rubbish?" Barley was gazing over my shoulder.

"School paper," I mumbled. The book was divided into chapters, as I remembered: *"Vampires de la Toscane," "Vampires de la Normandie,"* and so on. I found the right one at last: *"Vampires de Provence et des Pyrénées."* Oh, Lord, was my French up to this? Barley was starting to look at his watch. I ran a quick finger above the page, careful not to touch the magnificent type or ivory paper. *"Vampires dans les villages de Provence —"* What had my father been looking for here? He'd been poring over this first page of the chapter. *"'Il y a aussi une legende . . .'"* I leaned closer.

Since that moment, I have known many times what I first experienced then. Until then, my forays into written French had been purely utilitarian, the completion of almost mathematical exercises. When I comprehended a new phrase it was merely a bridge to the next exercise. Never before had I known the sudden quiver of understanding that travels from word to brain to heart, the way a new language can move, coil, swim into life under the eyes, the almost savage leap of comprehension, the instantaneous, joyful release of meaning, the way the words shed their printed bodies in a flash of heat and light. Since then I have known this moment of truth with other companions: German, Russian, Latin, Greek, and — for a brief hour — Sanskrit.

But that first time held the revelation of all the others. *"Il y a aussi une legende,"* I breathed, and Barley suddenly bent to follow the words. What he translated aloud, however, I had already taken in with a mental gasp: "'There is also a legend that Dracula, noblest and most dangerous of all vampires, attained his power not in the region of Wallachia but through a heresy in the monastery of Saint-Matthieu-des-Pyrénées-Orientales, a Benedictine house founded in the year 1000 of Our Lord.' What is this, anyway?" Barley said.

"School paper," I repeated, but our eyes met strangely over the book, and he looked as if he were seeing me for the first time. "Is your French very good?" I asked humbly.

"Of course." He smiled and bent over the page again. "'Dracula is said to visit the monastery every sixteen years to pay tribute to his origins and to renew the influences that have allowed him to live in death.'"

"Go on, please." I gripped the edge of the table.

"Certainly," he said. "'The calculations done by Brother Pierre de Provence in the early seventeenth century indicate that Dracula visits Saint-Matthieu in the half-moon of the month of May.'"

"What is the moon now?" I gasped, but Barley didn't know either. There was no further mention of Saint-Matthieu; the remaining pages paraphrased a document from a church in Perpignan about disturbances among sheep and goats in the region in 1428; it wasn't clear whether the cleric-author blamed vampires or sheep rustlers for these problems. "Odd stuff," Barley commented. "Is this what your family reads for fun? Do you want to hear about vampires in Cyprus?"

Nothing else in the book looked relevant to my purposes, and when Barley glanced at his watch again, I turned sadly away from the enticing walls of volumes.

"Well, that was cheerful," Barley said on the way down the staircase. "You're an unusual girl, aren't you?" I couldn't tell how he meant this, but I hoped it was a compliment.

On the train, Barley entertained me with chat about his fellow students, a pageant of madcaps and scapegoats, then carried my bag onto shipboard for me above the oily gray water of the Channel. It was a bright, chill day and we settled into the vinyl seats inside, sheltered from the wind. "I don't sleep much during term," Barley informed me, and promptly dozed off with his coat rolled into a ball under one shoulder.

It was just as well for me that he slept for a couple of hours, because I had a lot to ponder, matters of a practical nature as well as a scholarly one. My immediate problem was not a question of links among historical events but of Mrs. Clay. She would be waiting all too solidly in the front hall of our house in Amsterdam, full of smothering concern for my father and me. Her presence would keep me housebound at least overnight, and if I didn't appear after school the next day, she would be on my trail like a pack of wolves, probably with half the police force of Amsterdam to keep her company. Also, there was Barley. I glanced at his sleeping face across from me; he was snoring discreetly against his jacket. Barley would be headed off to the ferry again as I left for school tomorrow, and I would have to be careful not to intercept him on the way.

Mrs. Clay was indeed home when we arrived. Barley stood with me on the doorstep while I searched for my keys; he was craning admiringly at the old mercantile houses and gleaming canals — "Excellent! And all those Rembrandt faces in the streets!" When Mrs. Clay suddenly opened the door and drew me inside, he almost didn't make it in after me. I was relieved to see his good manners take over. While the two of them disappeared into the kitchen to call Master James, I hurried upstairs, calling back that I wanted to wash my face. In fact — the thought made my heart beat with guilty rapidity — I intended to sack my father's citadel at once. I would figure out later how to deal with Mrs. Clay and Barley. Now I had to find what I felt sure must be hidden there.

Our town house, built in 1620, had three bedrooms on the second floor, narrow dark-beamed rooms that my father adored because, he said, they seemed to him still full of the hardworking and simple people who had first lived in them. His room was the largest of these, an admirable period display of Dutch furniture. He had mixed the spartan furnishings with an Ottoman carpet and bed hangings, a minor sketch by van Gogh, and twelve copper pans from a French farmhouse — these made a gallery on one wall and picked up glints of light from the canal below. I realize now what a remarkable room this was, not only for its display of eclectic tastes but also for its monastic simplicity. It did not contain a single book; those had all been relegated to the library downstairs. No clothing ever hung over the back of the seventeenth-century chair; no newspaper ever profaned the looming desk. There was no telephone and not even a clock — my father woke naturally in the early hours every morning. It was pure living space, a chamber in which to sleep, wake, and perhaps pray — although whether any prayer still occurred there I couldn't guess — as it had been when it was new. I loved the room but seldom entered it.

Now I went in as quietly as a burglar, shut the door, and opened his desk. It was a terrible feeling, like breaking the seal of a coffin, but I pressed forward, pulling everything out of the pigeonholes, rooting through the drawers but replacing each item with care as I went along — the letters from his friends, his fine pens, his monogrammed notepaper. At last my hand closed on a sealed package. I undid it shamelessly and saw a few lines inside, addressed to me and admonishing me to read the enclosed letters only in the case of my father's unexpected demise or long-term disappearance. Hadn't I seen him writing, night after night, something that he covered with one arm when I drew near? I seized the package greedily, closed the desk, and took my find to my own room, listening hard for Mrs. Clay's foot on the stairs.

The packet was full of letters, each neatly folded into an envelope and addressed to me at our home, as if he had thought he might have to mail them to me one at a time from some other location. I kept them in order — oh, I had learned things without knowing it — and carefully opened the first. It was dated six months earlier and it seemed to begin not with mere words but with a cry from the heart. "My dear daughter" — his handwriting trembled under my eyes — "If you are reading this, forgive me. I have gone to look for your mother."

Part Two

What sort of place had I come to, and among what kind of people? What sort of grim adventure was it on which I had embarked? . . . I began to rub my eyes and pinch myself to see if I were awake. It all seemed like a horrible nightmare to me, and I expected that I should suddenly awake, and find myself at home, with the dawn struggling in through the windows, as I had now and again felt in the morning after a day of overwork. But my flesh answered the pinching test, and my eyes were not to be deceived. I was indeed awake and among the Carpathians. All I could do now was to be patient, and to wait the coming of the morning.

— Bram Stoker, *Dracula,* 1897

Chapter 25

THE TRAIN STATION in Amsterdam was a familiar sight to me — I'd passed through it dozens of times. But I had never been there alone before. I had never traveled anywhere alone, and as I sat on a bench waiting for the morning express to Paris, I felt a quickening of my pulses that was not entirely trepidation for my father — a rising of sap that was simply the first moment of complete freedom I had ever known. Mrs. Clay, doing the breakfast dishes at home, thought I was on my way to school. Barley, safely packed off to the ferry wharf, also thought I was on my way to school. I regretted deceiving kind, boring Mrs. Clay and I regretted even more parting from Barley, who had kissed my hand with sudden gallantry on the front step and given me one of his chocolate bars, although I'd reminded him that I could buy Dutch treats anytime I wanted. I thought I might write him a letter when all this trouble had ended — but that far ahead, I could not see.

For now, the Amsterdam morning sparkled, gleamed, shifted around me. Even this morning I found something comforting in the walk along canals from our house to the station, the scent of bread baking and the humid smell of the canals, the not-quite-elegant, busy cleanliness of everything. On a bench at the station, I reviewed my packing: change of clothes, my father's letters, bread, cheese, foil packages of juice from the kitchen. I had raided the plentiful kitchen cash, too — if I was going to do one bad thing, I was going to do twenty — to supplement what was in my purse. That would tip Mrs. Clay off all too quickly, but there was no help for it — I couldn't linger until the banks opened to get money out of my childishly small savings account. I had a warm sweater and a rain jacket, my passport, a book for the long train rides, and my French pocket dictionary.

I had stolen something else. From our parlor I had taken a silver knife that sat in the curio cabinet among souvenirs of my father's far-flung first diplomatic missions, the journeys that had constituted his early attempts to establish his foundation. I had been too young to accompany him, and he'd left me in the United States with various relatives. The knife was of a sinister sharpness and had an ornately embossed handle. It rested in a sheath, also highly decorated. It was the only weapon I'd ever seen in our household — my father disliked guns, and his collector's taste did not run to swords or battle-axes. I had no idea how to protect myself with the little blade, but I felt more secure knowing it was in my purse.

The station was crowded by the time the express pulled up. I felt then, as I do now, that there is no joy like the arrival of a train, no matter how disturbing your situation — particularly a European train, and particularly a European train that will carry you south. During that period of my life, in the final quarter of the twentieth century, I heard the whistle of some of the last steam locomotives to cross the Alps on a regular run. I boarded now, clutching my school-bag, almost smiling. I had hours ahead of me, and I was going to need them, not to read my book but to peruse again those precious letters from my father. I believed I'd picked my destination correctly, but I needed to ruminate on why it was correct.

I found a quiet compartment and drew the curtains shut along the aisle next to my seat, hoping no one would follow me in there. After a moment a middle-aged woman in a blue coat and hat came in anyway, but she smiled at me and settled down with a pile of Dutch magazines. In my comfortable corner, watching the old city and then the little green suburbs trundle past, I unfolded again the first of my father's letters. I knew its opening lines by heart already, the shocking shapes of the words, the startling place and date, the urgent, firm handwriting.

"My dear daughter:

"If you are reading this, forgive me. I have gone to look for your mother. For many years I have believed she was dead, and now I am not certain about that. This uncertainty is almost worse than grief, as you may someday understand; it tortures my heart night and day. I have never told you much about her, and that has been a weakness in me, I know, but our story was too painful for me to relate to you easily. I'd always intended to tell you more as you grew older and could understand it better without being terribly frightened — although, as far as that goes, it has frightened me so much, so unendingly, that this has been the poorest of my excuses to myself about the matter.

"During the last few months, I have tried to compensate for my weakness by telling you little by little what I could about my own past, and

I intended to bring your mother gradually into the story, although she entered my life rather suddenly. Now I fear I may not manage to tell you all you should know of your heritage before I am either silenced — literally unable to inform you myself — or fall prey again to my own silences.

"I have described to you some of my life as a graduate student before your birth and have told you a little about the odd circumstance of my adviser's disappearance after his revelations to me. I have told you also how I met a young woman named Helen who had as great an interest as mine in finding Professor Rossi, perhaps a greater one. At every quiet opportunity I have tried to advance this story for you, but now I feel I should begin to write down the rest of it, commit it securely to paper. If you must read it now instead of listening to me unfold it for you on some rocky hilltop or quiet piazza, in some sheltered harbor or at some comfortable café table, then the fault is mine for not telling it quickly enough or sooner.

"As I write this I am looking out over the lights of an old harbor — and you sleep undisturbed and innocent in the next room. I am tired after the day's work, and tired at the thought of beginning this long narrative — a sad duty, an unfortunate precaution. I feel I have some weeks, possibly months, in which I will certainly be able to continue my tale in person, so I will not retrace all the ground I have already covered for you during our strolls in so many countries. Past that stretch of time — weeks or months — I am less certain. These letters are my insurance against your solitude. In the worst case, you will inherit my house, my money, my furniture and books, but I can easily believe that you will treasure these documents in my hand more than any of the other items, because they will contain your own story, your history.

"Why have I not told you all the facts of this history at a blow, to get it over with, to inform you fully? The answer lies, again, in my own weakness, but also in the fact that an abbreviated version would be exactly that — a blow. I can't possibly wish you such pain, even if it would be a mere fraction of my own. Furthermore, you might not fully believe it if I told it at a blow, just as I could not believe my adviser Rossi's story fully without pacing the length of his own reminiscences. And, finally, what story can be reduced in actuality to its factual elements? Therefore, I relate my story one step at a time. I must hazard a guess, too, at how much I will have managed to tell you already if these letters come into your hands."

My father's guess had not been quite accurate, and he had picked up the story a beat or two beyond what I already knew. I might never hear his response to Helen Rossi's astounding resolution to go with him on his search, I thought sadly, or the interesting details of their journey from New England to Istanbul. How, I wondered, had they managed to perform all the necessary paperwork, to clear the hurdles of political estrangement, the visas, the customs? Had my father told his parents, kind and reasonable Bostonians, some fib about his sudden plan to travel? Had he and Helen gone to New York immediately, as he'd planned to? And had they slept in the same hotel room? My adolescent mind could not solve this riddle any more than it could avoid pondering it. I had to content myself at last with a picture of the two of them as characters in some movie of their youth, Helen stretched out discreetly under the covers of the double bed, my father miserably asleep in a wing chair with his shoes — but nothing else — off, and the lights of Times Square blinking a sordid invitation just outside the window.

"Six days after Rossi's disappearance, we flew to Istanbul from Idlewild Airport on a foggy weeknight, changing planes in Frankfurt. Our second plane touched down the next morning, and we were herded out with all the other tourists. I had been to Western Europe twice by then, but those jaunts now seemed to me excursions to a completely different planet from this one — Turkey, which in 1954 was even more a world apart than it is today. One minute I was huddled in my uncomfortable airplane seat, wiping my face with a hot washcloth, and the next we were standing outside on an equally hot tarmac, with unfamiliar smells blowing over us, and dust, and the fluttering scarf of an Arab in line ahead of us — that scarf kept getting into my mouth. Helen was actually laughing next to me, watching my amazement at all this. She had brushed her hair and put on lipstick in the airplane and looked remarkably fresh after our cramped night. She wore the little scarf on her neck; I still had not seen what lay under it and wouldn't have dared to ask her to remove it. 'Welcome to the big world, Yankee,' she said, smiling. It was a real smile this time, not her customary grimace.

"My amazement increased during the taxi ride to town. I don't know exactly what I had expected of Istanbul — nothing, maybe, since I had had so little time to anticipate the journey — but the beauty of this city knocked the wind out of me. It had an *Arabian Nights* quality that no number of honking cars or businessmen in Western suits could dissolve. The first city here, Constantinople, the capital of Byzantium and the first capital of Christian Rome, must have been splendid beyond belief, I thought — a marriage of Roman wealth and early Christian mysticism. By the time we found some rooms in the old quarter of Sultanahmet, I had received a dizzying glimpse of dozens of mosques and minarets, bazaars hung with fine textiles, even a flash of the many-domed, four-horned Hagia Sophia billowing above the peninsula.

"Helen had never been here either, and she studied everything with quiet concentration, turning to me only once during the cab ride to remark how strange it was for her to see the wellspring — I believe that was her word — of the Ottoman Empire, which had left so many traces on her native country. This was to become a theme of our days there — her brief, pungent remarks on all that was already familiar to her: Turkish place-names, a cucumber salad consumed in an outdoor restaurant, the pointed arch of a window frame. This had a peculiar effect on me, too, a sort of doubling of my experience, so that I seemed to be seeing Istanbul and Romania at the same time, and as the question gradually arose between us of whether we would have to go into Romania itself, I had a sense of being led there by the artifacts of the past as I saw them through Helen's eyes. But I digress — this is a later episode of my story.

"Our landlady's front hall was cool after the glare and dust of the street. I sank gratefully into a chair in the entrance there, letting Helen reserve two rooms in her excellent but weirdly accented French. The landlady — an Armenian woman who was fond of travelers and had apparently learned their languages — didn't know the name of Rossi's hotel, either. Perhaps it had vanished years before.

"Helen liked to run things, I mused, so why not allow her the satisfaction? It was unspoken but firmly agreed between us that I would later pay the bill. I had withdrawn all of my sparse savings from the bank at home; Rossi deserved every effort I could make, even if I failed. I would simply have to go home bankrupt if it came to that. I knew that Helen, a foreign student, probably had less than nothing, lived on nothing. I had already noticed that she seemed to own just two suits, which she varied with a selection of sternly tailored blouses. 'Yes, we'll take the two separate rooms side by side,' she told the Armenian lady, a fine-featured old woman. 'My brother — *mon frère — ronfle terriblement.*'

"*'Ronfle?'* I asked from the lounge.

"'Snores,' she said tartly. 'You do snore, you know. I didn't get a blink of sleep in New York.'

"'Wink,' I corrected.

"'Fine,' she said. 'Just keep your door shut, *s'il te plaît.*'

"With or without snoring, we had to sleep off the exhaustion of travel before we could do anything else. Helen wanted to hunt down the archive at once, but I insisted on rest and a meal. So it was late afternoon before we began our first prowl of those labyrinthine streets, with their glimpses of colorful gardens and courtyards.

"Rossi had not named the archive in his letters, and in our conversation he had called it only 'a little-known repository of materials, founded by Sultan Mehmed II.' His letter about his research in Istanbul added that it was attached to a seventeenth-century mosque. Beyond this, we knew that he'd been able to see the Hagia Sophia from a window there, that the archive had more than one floor, and that it had a door communicating directly with the street on the first floor. I had tried cautiously to find information on such an archive at the university library at home just before our departure, but without success. I wondered at Rossi's not giving the name of the archive in his letters; it wasn't like him to leave out that detail, but perhaps he hadn't wanted to remember it. I had all his papers with me in my briefcase, including his list of the documents he'd found there, with that strangely incomplete line at the end: 'Bibliography, Order of the Dragon.' Looking through an entire city, a maze of minarets and domes, for the source of that cryptic line in Rossi's handwriting was a daunting prospect, to say the least.

"The only thing we could do was to turn our feet toward our one landmark, the Hagia Sophia, originally the great Byzantine Church of Saint Sophia. And once we drew near it, it was impossible for us not to enter. The gates were open and the huge sanctuary pulled us in among the other tourists as if we rode a wave into a cavern. For fourteen hundred years, I reflected, pilgrims had been drawn into it, just as we were now. Inside, I walked slowly to the center and craned my head back to see that vast, divine space with its famous whirling domes and arches, its celestial light pouring in, the round shields covered with Arabic calligraphy in the upper corners, mosque overlaying church, church overlaying the ruins of the ancient world. It arched far, far above us, replicating the Byzantine cosmos. I could hardly believe I was there. I was stunned by it.

"Looking back at that moment, I understand that I had lived in books so long, in my narrow university setting, that I had become compressed by them internally. Suddenly, in this echoing house of Byzantium — one of the wonders of history — my spirit leaped out of its confines. I knew in that instant that, whatever happened, I could never go back to my old constraints. I wanted to follow life upward, to expand with it outward, the way this enormous interior swelled upward and outward. My heart swelled with it, as it never had during all my wanderings among the Dutch merchants.

"I glanced at Helen and saw that she was equally moved, her head tipped back like mine so that her dark curls fell over the collar of her blouse, her usually guarded and cynical face full of a pale transcendence. I reached out, impulsively, and took her hand. She grasped mine hard, with that firm, almost bony grip I knew already from her handshake. In another woman, this might have been a gesture of submission or coquetry, a romantic acquiescence; in Helen it was as simple and fierce a gesture as her gaze or the aloofness of her posture. After a moment she seemed to recall herself; she dropped my hand, but without embarrassment, and we wandered around the church together admiring the fine pulpit, the glinting Byzantine marble. It took me a mighty effort to remember that we could return to Hagia Sophia at any time during our stay in Istanbul, and that our first business in this city was to find the archive. Helen apparently had the same thought, for she moved toward the entrance when I did, and we made our way through the crowds and into the street again.

"'The archive could be quite far away,' she observed. 'Saint Sophia is so large that you could see it from almost any building in this part of the city, I think, or even on the other side of the Bosphorus.'

"'I know. We've got to find some other clue.

The letters said that the archive was attached to a small mosque from the seventeenth century.'

"'The city is filled with mosques.'

"'True.' I flipped through my hastily purchased guidebook. 'Let's start with this — the Great Mosque of the Sultans. Mehmed II and his court might have worshipped there sometimes — it was built in the late fifteenth century, and that would be a logical neighborhood for his library to end up in, don't you think?'

"Helen thought it was worth a try, and we set off on foot. Along the way, I dipped into the guidebook again. 'Listen to this. It says that *Istanbul* is a Byzantine word that meant *the city*. You see, even the Ottomans couldn't demolish Constantinople, only rename it — with a Byzantine name, at that. It says here that the Byzantine Empire lasted from 333 to 1453. Imagine — what a long, long afternoon of power.'

"Helen nodded. 'It is not possible to think about this part of the world without Byzantium,' she said gravely. 'And, you know, in Romania you see glimpses of it everywhere — in every church, in the frescoes, the monasteries, even in the people's faces, I think. In some ways, it is closer to your eyes there than it is here, with all of this Ottoman — sediment — on top.' Her face clouded. 'The conquest of Constantinople in 1453 by Mehmed II was one of the greatest tragedies in history. He broke down these walls with his cannonballs and then he sent his armies in to pillage and murder for three days. The soldiers raped young girls and boys on the altars of the churches, even in Saint Sophia. They stole the icons and all the other holy treasures to melt down the gold, and they threw the relics of the saints in the streets for the dogs to chew. Before that, this was the most beautiful city in history.' Her hand closed in a fist at her waist.

"I was silent. The city was still beautiful, with its delicate, rich colors and its exquisite domes and minarets, whatever atrocities had occurred here long ago. I was beginning to understand why an evil moment five hundred years ago was so real to Helen, but what did this really have to do with our lives in the present? It struck me suddenly that perhaps I had come a long way for nothing, to this magical place with this complicated woman, looking for an Englishman who might be on a bus trip to New York. I swallowed the thought and tried instead to tease her a little. 'How is it that you know so much about history? I thought you were an anthropologist.'

"'I am,' she said gravely. 'But you cannot study cultures without a knowledge of their history.'

"'Then why didn't you simply become a historian? You could still have studied culture, it seems to me.'

"'Perhaps.' She looked forbidding now, and would not meet my eye. 'But I wanted a field that my father had not already made his own.'

"The Great Mosque was still open in the golden evening light, to tourists as well as to the faithful. I tried my mediocre German on the guard at the entrance, an olive-skinned, curly headed boy — what had those Byzantines looked like? — but he said there was no library within, no archive, nothing of the sort, and he had never heard of one nearby. We asked if he had any suggestions.

"We could try the university, he mused. As for small mosques, there were hundreds of them.

"'It's too late to go to the university today,' Helen told me. She was studying the guidebook. 'Tomorrow we can visit there and ask someone for information about archives that date from Mehmed's time. I think that will be the most efficient way. Let's go see the old walls of Constantinople. We can walk to one section of them from here.'

"I followed her through the streets as she traced our way for us, the guidebook in her gloved hand, her small black purse over her arm. Bicycles darted past us, Ottoman robes mingled with Western dress, foreign cars and horse carts wove around one another. Everywhere I looked I saw men in dark vests and small crocheted caps, women in brightly printed blouses with ballooning trousers underneath, their heads wound in scarves. They carried shopping bags and baskets, cloth bundles, chickens in crates, bread, flowers. The streets were overflowing with life — as they had been, I thought, for sixteen hundred years. Along these streets the Roman Christian emperors had been carried by their entourages, flanked by priests, moving from palace to church to take the Holy Sacrament. They had been strong rulers, great patrons of the arts, engineers, theologians. And nasty, too, some of them — prone to cutting up their courtiers and blinding family members, in the tradition of Rome proper. This was where the original byzantine politics had played themselves out. Perhaps it wasn't such an odd place for a vampire or two, after all.

"Helen had stopped in front of a towering, partly ruined stone compound. Shops huddled at its base and fig trees dug their roots into its flank; a cloudless sky was fading to copper above the battlements. 'Look what remains of the walls of Constantinople,' she said quietly. 'You can see how enormous they were when they were intact. The book says the sea came to their feet in those days, so the emperor could embark by boat from the palace. And over there, that wall was part of the Hippodrome.'

"We stood gazing until I realized that I'd again forgotten Rossi for a whole ten minutes. 'Let's look for some dinner,' I said abruptly. 'It's already past seven and we'll need to turn in early tonight. I'm determined to find the archive tomorrow.' Helen nodded and we walked quite companionably back up through the heart of the old city.

"Near our pension we discovered a restaurant decorated inside with brass vases and fine tiles, with a table in the arched front window, an opening without glass where we could sit and watch people walking past on the street outside. As we waited for our dinner, I was struck for the first time by a phenomenon of this Eastern world that had escaped my notice until then: everyone who hurried by was not actually hurrying but simply walking along. What looked like a hurry here would have been a casual saunter on the sidewalks of New York or Washington. I pointed this out to Helen, and she laughed cynically. 'When there is not much money to be made, no one goes rushing around for it,' she said.

"The waiter brought us chunks of bread, a dish of smooth yogurt studded with slices of cucumber, and a strong fragrant tea in glass vases. We ate heartily after the fatigue of the day and had just moved on to roasted chicken on wooden skewers when a man with a silver mustache and a mane of silver hair, wearing a neat gray suit, entered the restaurant and glanced around. He settled at a table near us and put a book down by his plate. He ordered his meal in quiet Turkish, then seemed to take in our pleasure in our dinner and leaned toward us with a friendly smile. 'You like our native food, I see,' he said in accented but excellent English.

"'We certainly do,' I answered, surprised. 'It's excellent.'

"'Let me see,' he continued, turning a handsome, mild face on me. 'You are not from England. America?'

"'Yes,' I said. Helen was silent, cutting up her chicken and eyeing our companion warily.

"'Ah, yes. How very nice. You are sightseeing in our beautiful city?'

"'Yes, exactly,' I concurred, wishing Helen would at least look friendly; hostility might appear suspicious somehow.

"'Welcome to Istanbul,' he said with a very pleasant smile, raising his glass beaker to toast us. I returned the compliment and he beamed. 'Forgive the question from a stranger, but what do you love best here in your visit?'

"'Well, it would be hard to choose.' I liked his face; it was impossible not to answer him truthfully. 'I'm most struck by the feeling of East and West blending in one city.'

"'A wise observation, young man,' he said soberly, patting his mustache with a big white napkin. 'That blend is our treasure and our curse. I have colleagues who have spent a lifetime studying Istanbul, and they say they will never have time to explore all of it, although they are living here always. It is an amazing place.'

"'What is your profession?' I asked curiously, although I had the sense from Helen's stillness that she would step on my foot under the table in another minute.

"'I am a professor at Istanbul University,' he said in the same dignified tone.

"'Oh, how extremely lucky!' I exclaimed. 'We are —' Just then Helen's foot came down on mine. She wore pumps, like every woman in that era, and the heel was rather sharp. 'We are very glad to meet you,' I finished. 'What do you teach?'

"'My speciality is Shakespeare,' said our new friend, helping himself carefully to the salad in front of him. 'I teach English literature to the most advanced of our graduate students. They are valiant students, I must tell you.'

"'How wonderful,' I managed to say. 'I am a graduate student myself, but in history, in the United States.'

"'A very fine field,' he said gravely. 'You will find much to interest you in Istanbul. What is the name of your university?'

"I told him, while Helen sawed grimly away at her dinner.

"'An excellent university. I have heard of it,' observed the professor. He sipped from his vase and tapped the book by his plate. 'I say!' he exclaimed finally. 'Why don't you come to see our university while you are in Istanbul? It is a venerable institution also, and I would be pleased to show you and your lovely wife around.'

"I registered a faint snort from Helen and hurried to cover for her. 'My sister — my sister.'

"'Oh, I beg your pardon.' The Shakespeare scholar bowed to Helen over the table. 'I am Dr. Turgut Bora, at your service.' We introduced ourselves — or I introduced us, because Helen kept obstinately silent. I could tell she didn't like my using my real name, so I quickly gave hers as Smith, a piece of dull-wittedness that drew an even deeper frown from her. We shook hands all around, and there was nothing for us to do but to invite him to join us at our table.

"He protested politely, but only for a moment, and then sat down with us, bringing along his salad and his glass vase, which he immediately raised on high. 'A toast to you and welcome to our fair city,' he intoned. 'Cheerio!' Even Helen smiled slightly, although she still said nothing. 'You must forgive my lack of discretion,' Turgut told her apologetically, as if sensing her wariness. 'It is very rare that I have the opportunity to practice my English with native speakers.' He had not yet noticed that she wasn't a native speaker — although he might never notice that in Helen, I thought, because she might never utter a word to him.

"'How did you come to specialize in Shakespeare?' I asked him as we began to eat our dinners again.

"'Ah!' Turgut said softly. 'That is a strange story. My mother was a very unusual woman — brilliant — a great lover of languages, as well as a diminutive engineer' — *Distinguished?* I wondered — 'and she studied at the University of Rome, where she met my father. He, the delectable man, was a scholar of the Italian Renaissance, with a particular lust for —'

"At this very interesting point, we were suddenly interrupted by the appearance of a young woman peering in the arched window from the street. Although I'd never seen one, except in pictures, I took her for a Gypsy; she was dark skinned and sharp featured, dressed in tatty bright colors, black hair raggedly cut around penetrating dark eyes. She could have been fifteen or forty; it was impossible to read age on her thin face. In her arms she carried bunches of red and yellow flowers, which she apparently wanted us to buy. She thrust some of them at me over the table and began a shrill chant I couldn't understand. Helen looked disgusted and Turgut annoyed, but the woman was insistent. I was just getting out my wallet with the idea of presenting Helen — in jest, of course — with a Turkish bouquet, when the Gypsy suddenly wheeled on her, pointing and hissing. Turgut started and Helen, usually fearless, shrank back.

"This seemed to bring Turgut to life; he half stood and with a scowl of indignation began to berate the Gypsy. It was not difficult to understand his tone and gestures, which invited her in no uncertain terms to take herself off. She glared at all of us and withdrew as suddenly as she'd appeared, vanishing among the other pedestrians. Turgut sat down again, looking wide-eyed at Helen, and after a moment he rummaged in his jacket pocket and drew out a small object, which he placed next to her plate. It was a flat blue stone about an inch long, set with white and paler blue, like a crude eye. Helen blanched when she saw it and reached as if by instinct to touch it with her forefinger.

"'What on earth is going on here?' I couldn't help feeling the fretfulness of the culturally excluded.

"'What did she say?' Helen spoke to Turgut for the first time. 'Was she speaking Turkish or the Gypsy language? I could not understand her.'

"Our new friend hesitated, as if he did not want to repeat the woman's words. 'Turkish,' he murmured. 'Maybe it is not the better part of valor that I tell you. It is very rude what she said. And strange.' He was looking at Helen with interest but also with something like a flicker of fear, I thought, in his genial eyes. 'She used a word I will not translate,' he explained slowly. 'And then she said, "Get out of here, Romanian daughter of wolves. You and your friend bring the curse of the vampire to our city."'

"Helen was white to the lips, and I fought the impulse to take her hand. 'It's a coincidence,' I told her soothingly, at which she glared; I was saying too much in front of the professor.

"Turgut looked from me to Helen and back. 'This is very odd indeed, gentle companions,' he said. 'I think we must talk further without ado.'"

I had almost dozed in my train seat, despite the extreme interest my father's story held for me; reading all this the first time, during the night, had kept me up late, and I was weary. A feeling of unreality settled over me in the sunny compartment, and I turned to look out the window at the orderly Dutch farmlands slipping by. As we approached and departed from each town, the train clicked past a series of small vegetable gardens, growing green again under a cloudy sky, the rear gardens of thousands of people minding their own business, the backs of their houses turned toward the railway. The fields were wonderfully green, a green that begins, in Holland, in early spring and lasts almost until the snow falls again, fed by the moisture of air and land and by the water that glints in every direction you look. We had already left behind a broad region of canals and bridges and were out among cows in their neatly delineated pastures. A dignified old couple on bicycles rolled along on a road next to us, swallowed the next minute by more pastures. Soon we'd be in Belgium, which I knew from experience one could miss entirely on this trip in the course of a short nap.

I held the letters in my lap tightly, but my eyelids were beginning to droop. The pleasant-faced woman in the seat opposite was already dozing off, magazine in hand. My eyes had closed for just a second when the door to our compartment flew open. An exasperated voice broke in and a lanky figure inserted itself between me and my daydream. "Well, of all the nerve! I thought so. I've been searching every carriage for you." It was Barley, mopping his forehead and scowling at me.

Chapter 26

BARLEY WAS ANGRY. I couldn't blame him, but this was a most inconvenient turn of events for me, and I was a little mad, too. It made me all the angrier that my first twinge of annoyance was followed by a secret swelling of relief; I hadn't realized before seeing him how thoroughly alone I'd felt on that train, headed toward the unknown, headed perhaps toward the larger loneliness of being unable to find my father or even toward the galactic loneliness of losing him forever. Barley had been a stranger to me only a few days before, and now his face was my vision of familiarity.

At this moment, however, it was still scowling. "Where in bloody hell do you think you're going? You've given me a pretty chase — what are you up to, anyhow?"

I evaded the last question for now. "I didn't mean to worry you, Barley. I thought you'd gone on the ferry and would never know."

"Yes, and hurry back to Master James, tell him you were safe in Amsterdam and then get word that you'd vanished. Oh, I would have been in

344

his good graces then." He plunked himself down next to me, folded his arms, and crossed his long legs. He had his little suitcase with him, and the front of his straw-colored hair stood on end. "What's got into you?"

"Why were you spying on me?" I countered.

"The ferry was delayed this morning for repairs." It seemed he couldn't help smiling a little now. "I was hungry as a horse, so I went back a few streets to get some rolls and tea, and then I thought I saw you slipping out the other direction, way up the street, but I wasn't at all sure. I thought I might be imagining things, you know, so I stayed and bought my breakfast. And then my conscience smote me, because if it was you I was in big trouble. So I hurried this way and saw the station, and then you boarded the train and I thought I was going to have heart failure." He glared at me again. "You've been quite a bother this morning. I had to run around and get a ticket — and I almost didn't have enough guilders for it, too — and hunt through the whole train for you. And now it's been moving so long we can't get off right away." His narrow bright eyes strayed to the window and then to the pile of envelopes in my lap. "Would you mind explaining why you're on the Paris express instead of at school?"

What could I do? "I'm sorry, Barley," I said humbly. "I didn't mean to involve you in this for a minute. I really thought you were on your way a long time ago and could go back to Master James with a clean conscience. I wasn't trying to be any trouble to you."

"Yes?" He was clearly waiting for more enlightenment. "So you just had a little hankering for Paris instead of history class?"

"Well," I began, stalling for time. "My father sent me a telegram saying he was fine and I should join him there for a few days."

Barley was silent for a moment. "Sorry, but that doesn't explain everything. If you'd got a telegram it would probably have come last night and I'd have heard about it. And was there any question of your father's not being 'fine'? I thought he was just away on business. What's all that you're reading?"

"It's a long story," I said slowly, "and I know you already think I'm strange —"

"You're awfully strange," Barley put in crossly. "But you'd better tell me what you're up to. You'll have just time before we get off in Brussels and take the next train back to Amsterdam."

"No!" I hadn't meant to cry out like that. The

lady across from us stirred in her gentle sleep, and I dropped my voice. "I have to go on to Paris. I'm fine. You can get off there, if you want, and then get back to London by tonight."

"'Get off there,' eh? Does that mean you won't be getting off there? Where else does this train go?"

"No, it does stop in Paris —"

He had folded his arms and was waiting again. He was worse than my father. Maybe he was worse than Professor Rossi had been. I had a brief vision of Barley standing at the head of a classroom, arms folded, eyes scanning his hapless students, his voice sharp: "And what finally leads Milton to his terrible conclusion about Satan's fall? Or hasn't *anybody* done the reading?"

I swallowed. "It's a long story." I said it again, more humbly.

"We have time," said Barley.

"Helen and Turgut and I looked at one another around our little restaurant table, and I sensed a signal of kinship passing among us. Perhaps to delay for a moment, Helen picked up the round blue stone Turgut had put next to her plate and held it out to me. 'This is an ancient symbol,' she said. 'It is a talisman against the Evil Eye.' I took it, felt its heavy smoothness, warm from her hand, and set it down again.

"Turgut was not to be distracted, however. 'Madam, you are Romanian?' She was silent. 'If this is true, you must be careful here.' He lowered his voice a little. 'The police might be rather interested in you. Our country is not on friendly terms with Romania.'

"'I know,' she said coldly.

"'But how did the Gypsy woman know this?' Turgut frowned. 'You did not speak to her.'

"'I do not know.' Helen gave a helpless shrug.

"Turgut shook his head. 'Some people say the Gypsies have the talent of special vision. I have never believed this, but —' He broke off and patted his mustache with his napkin. 'How strange that she talked of vampires.'

"'Is it?' Helen countered. 'She must have been a crazy woman. Gypsies are all mad.'

"'Perhaps, perhaps.' Turgut was silent. 'However, it is very strange to me, the way she spoke, because that is my other speciality.'

"'Gypsies?' I asked.

"'No, good sir — vampires.' Helen and I stared at him, carefully not meeting each other's eyes. 'Shakespeare is my life's work, but the legend of the vampire is my hobby. We have an ancient tradition here of vampires.'

"'Is that — ah — a Turkish tradition?' I asked in astonishment.

"'Oh, the legend goes back at least to Egypt, dear colleagues. But here in Istanbul — to begin with, there is a story that the most bloodthirsty of the emperors of Byzantium were vampires, that some of them understood the Christian communion as an invitation to quaff the blood of mortals. But I do not believe this. I believe it appeared later.'

"'Well —' I didn't want to reveal too keen an interest, more for fear that Helen would jab my foot under the table again than from any conviction that Turgut was aligned with the powers of darkness. But she was staring at him, too. 'What about the legend of Dracula? Have you heard of that?'

"'Heard of that?' snorted Turgut. His dark eyes shone, and he twisted his napkin into a knot. 'You know that Dracula was a real person, a figure of history? A countryman of yours, actually, madam —' He bowed to Helen. 'He was a lord, a *voivoda,* in the western Carpathians in the fifteenth century. Not an admirable person, you know.'

"Helen and I were nodding — we couldn't help it. I couldn't, at least, and she seemed too intent now on Turgut's words to stop herself. She had leaned forward a little, listening, and her eyes shone with the same rich darkness as his. Color had blossomed under her usual pallor. It was one of those many moments, I observed, even in the midst of my excitement, when beauty suddenly filled her rather harsh countenance, lighting it from within.

"'Well —' Turgut seemed to be warming to his subject. 'I do not mean to bore you, but I have a theory that Dracula is a very important figure in the history of Istanbul. It is known that when he was a boy, he was held captive by Sultan Mehmed II in Gallipoli and then farther east in Anatolia — his own father gave him to the father of Mehmed, Sultan Murad II, as ransom for a treaty, from 1442 to 1448, six long years. Dracula's father was not a gentleman, either.' Turgut chuckled. 'The soldiers who guarded the boy Dracula were masters in the art of torture, and he must have learned too much when he watched them. But, my good sirs' — he seemed to have forgotten Helen's gender for the moment, in his collegial fervor — 'I have my own theory that he left his mark on them, too.'

"'What on earth do you mean?' My breath was coming short.

"'From about that time, there is a record of vampirism in Istanbul. It is my notion — and it is still unpublished, alack, and I cannot prove it — that his first victims were among the Ottomans, maybe the guards who became his friends. He left behind him contamination in our empire, I propose, and then it must have been carried into Constantinople with the Conqueror.'

"We stared at him, speechless. It occurred to me that, according to legend, only the dead became vampires. Did this mean that Vlad Dracula had actually been killed in Asia Minor and become undead then, as a very young man, or that he'd simply had a taste for unholy libations very early in his life and had inspired it in others? I filed this away to ask Turgut in case I ever knew him well enough. 'Oh, this is my eccentric hobby, you know.' Turgut lapsed into a genial smile again. 'Well, excuse me for climbing up onto my soap dish. My wife says I am intolerable.' He toasted us with a subtle, courtly gesture before sipping from his little vase again. 'But, by heaven, I have proof of one thing! I have proof that the sultans feared him as a vampire!' He gestured toward the ceiling.

"'Proof?' I echoed.

"'Yes! I discovered it some few years ago. The sultan was so much interested in Vlad Dracula that he collected some of his documents and possessions here after Dracula died in Wallachia. Dracula killed many Turkish soldiers in his own country, and our sultan hated him for this, but that was not why he founded this archive. No! The sultan even wrote a letter to the pasha of Wallachia in 1478 asking him for any writings he knew of about Vlad Dracula. Why? Because — he said — he was creating a library that would fight the evil that Dracula had spread in his city after his death. You see — why would the sultan still fear Dracula when Dracula was dead, if he did not believe Dracula could return? I have found a copy of the letter the pasha wrote to him in response.' He thumped a fist on the table and smiled at us. 'I have even found the library he created to fight evil.'

"Helen and I sat motionless. The coincidence was almost unbearably strange. Finally I ventured a question. 'Professor, was this collection by any chance created by Sultan Mehmed II?'

"This time he stared at us. 'By my boots, you are a fine historian indeed. You are interested in this period in our history?'

"'Ah — very much so,' I said. 'And we would be — I'd be very much interested in seeing this archive you found.'

"'Of course,' he said. 'With great pleasure. I will show you. My wife will be astounded that anyone wants to see.' He chuckled. 'But, alack, the beautiful building in which it was once housed has been torn down to make way for an office of the Ministry of Roads — oh, eight years ago. It was a lovely little building near the Blue Mosque. Such a shame.'

"I felt the blood draining from my face. So that was why we had had such difficulty locating Rossi's archive. 'But the documents —?'

"'Do not worry, kind sir. I myself ensured them to become part of the National Library. Even if no one else adores them as I do, they must be preserved.' Something dark crossed his face for the first time since he had scolded the Gypsy woman. 'There is still evil to fight in our city, as there is everywhere.' He looked from one of us to the other. 'If you like old curiosities, I will most joyfully take you there tomorrow. It is closed this evening, of course. I know well the librarian who can allow you to peruse the collection.'

"'Thank you very much.' I didn't dare look at

Helen. 'And how — how did you come to be interested in this unusual topic?'

"'Oh, it is a long story,' Turgut countered seriously. 'I cannot be allowed to bore you so much.'

"'We're not bored at all,' I insisted.

"'You are very kind.' He sat silent for some minutes, polishing his fork between thumb and forefinger. Outside our brick alcove, honking cars dodged bicycles in the crowded streets and pedestrians came and went like characters across a stage — women in flowing patterned skirts, scarves, and dangling gold earrings, or black dresses and reddish hair, men in Western suits and ties and white shirts. The breath of a mild, salty air reached us there at our table, and I imagined ships from all over Eurasia bringing their bounty to the heart of an empire — first Christian, then Muslim — and docking at a city whose walls stretched down into the very sea. Vlad Dracula's forested stronghold, with its barbaric rituals of violence, seemed far indeed from this ancient, cosmopolitan world. No wonder he had hated the Turks, and they him, I thought. And yet the Turks of Istanbul, with their crafts of gold and brass and silk, their bazaars and bookshops and myriad houses of worship, must have had much more in common with the Christian

Byzantines they had conquered here than did
Vlad, defying them from his frontier. Viewed
from this center of culture, he looked like a
backwoods thug, a provincial ogre, a medieval
redneck. I remembered the picture I'd seen of
him in an encyclopedia at home — that woodcut of an elegant, mustached face framed by
courtly dress. It was a paradox.

"I was lost in this image when Turgut spoke
again. 'Tell me, my fellows, what makes you to be
interested in this topic of Dracula?' He had turned
the table on us, with a gentlemanly — or suspicious? — smile.

"I glanced at Helen. 'Well, I'm studying the fifteenth century in Europe as background for my
dissertation,' I said, and was immediately punished for my lack of candor by a sense that this
lie might already be true. God knew when I'd be
working on my dissertation again, I thought, and
the last thing I needed was a broader topic. 'And
you,' I pressed again. 'How did you jump from
Shakespeare to vampires?'

"Turgut smiled — sadly, it seemed to me, and
his quiet honesty punished me further. 'Ah, it is a
very strange thing, a long time ago. You see, I
was working on my second book about Shakespeare — the tragedies. I sat to work every day

in a little — how do you say? — niche in our English room at the university. Then one day I found a book I never saw there before.' He turned to me with that sad smile again. My blood had already run cold in every extremity. 'This book was like no other, an empty book, very old, with a dragon in the middle and a word — DRAKULYA. I had never heard about Dracula before. But the picture was very strange and strong. And then I thought, I must know what this is. So I tried to learn everything.'

"Helen had frozen across from me, but now she stirred, as if with eagerness. 'Everything?' she echoed softly."

Barley and I had almost reached Brussels. It had taken me a long time — although it seemed like a few minutes — to tell Barley as simply and clearly as I could what my father had related of his experiences in graduate school. Barley stared past me out the window at the little Belgian houses and gardens, which looked sad under a curtain of clouds. We could see the occasional shaft of sunlight picking out a church spire or an old industrial chimney as we drew close to Brussels. The Dutch woman snored quietly, her magazine on the floor by her feet.

I was about to embark on a description of my father's recent restlessness, his unhealthy pallor and strange behavior, when Barley suddenly turned to face me. "This is awfully peculiar," he said. "I don't know why I should believe this wild tale, but I do. I want to, anyway." It struck me that I'd never before seen him look serious — only humorous or, briefly, annoyed. His eyes, blue as chips of sky, narrowed further. "The funny thing is that it all reminds me of something."

"What?" I was almost faint with relief at his apparent acceptance of my story.

"Well, that's the odd thing. I can't think what. Something to do with Master James. But what was it?"

Chapter 27

BARLEY SAT MUSING in our train compartment, chin in his long-fingered hands, trying in vain to remember something about Master James. Finally he looked at me, and I was struck by the beauty of his narrow, rosy face when it was serious. Without that unnerving jollity, it could have been the face of an angel, or maybe a monk in a Northumbrian cloister. I perceived these comparisons dimly; they bloomed for me only later.

"Well," he said at last, "as I see it, there are two possibilities. Either you're daft, in which case I have to stick with you and get you back home safely, or you're not daft, in which case you're headed for a lot of trouble and I have to stick with you anyway. I'm supposed to be in lecture tomorrow, but I'll figure out what to do about that." He sighed and glanced at me, leaned back against the seat again. "I have this idea Paris is not going to be your terminal destination. Could you enlighten me about where you're going after that?"

"If Professor Bora had given us each a slap across the face at that pleasant restaurant table in Istanbul, it would not have been more stunning than what he'd told us about his 'eccentric hobby.' It was a salutary slap, however; we were wide-awake now. My jet lag was gone, and with it my feeling of hopelessness about finding more information about Dracula's tomb. We had come to the right place. Perhaps — here my heart lurched, and not with mere hope — perhaps Dracula's tomb was in Turkey itself.

"This had never really occurred to me before, but now I thought it might make sense. After all, Rossi had been severely admonished here by one of Dracula's henchmen. Could the undead have been guarding not only an archive but also a grave? Could the strong presence of vampires to which Turgut had referred just now be a legacy of Dracula's continuing occupation of this city? I ran over what I knew already about Vlad the Impaler's career and legend. If he had been imprisoned here in his youth, couldn't he have returned after his death to this site of his early education in torture? He might have had a sort of nostalgia for the place, like people who retire to the town where they grew up. And if Stoker's novel was to be trusted for its chronicling of a vampire's habits, the fiend could certainly leave one place for another, making his grave wherever he liked; in the story, he had traveled in his coffin to England. Why couldn't he have come to Istanbul somehow, moving by night after his demise as a mortal into the very heart of the empire whose armies had brought about his death? It would have been a fitting revenge on the Ottomans, after all.

"But I couldn't ask Turgut any of these questions yet. We had just met the man, and I was still wondering whether we could trust him. He seemed genuine, and yet his turning up at our table with his 'hobby' was almost too strange to be countenanced. He was talking to Helen now, and she, at last, was talking to him. 'No, dear madam, I do not actually know "everything" about Dracula's history. In truth, my knowledge is far from ravishing. But I suspect that he had a great influence on our city, for evil, and that keeps me searching. And you, my friends?' He glanced keenly from Helen to me. 'You seem a portion interested in my topic yourselves. What is your dissertation about, exactly, young man?'

"'Dutch mercantilism in the seventeenth century,' I said lamely. It sounded lame to me, in any case, and I was beginning to wonder if it had always been a rather bland endeavor. Dutch merchants, after all, did not prowl the centuries attacking people and stealing their immortal souls.

"'Ah.' I thought Turgut looked puzzled. 'Well,' he said finally, 'if you are interested also in the history of Istanbul, you can come with me to-morrow morning to see Sultan Mehmed's collec-tion. He was a splendid old tyrant — he collected many interesting things, in addition to my fa-vorite documents. I must get home to my wife now, as she will be in a state of dissolution, I am so late.' He smiled, as if her state was more pleas-ant to anticipate than otherwise. 'She will cer-tainly wish you to come dine with us tomorrow, too, as I wish you to.' I pondered this for a mo-ment; Turkish wives must be as submissive, still, as the harems of legend. Or did he just mean that his wife was as hospitable as he? I waited for Helen to snort, but she sat quiet, watching both of us. 'So, my friends —'Turgut was gather-ing himself to leave. He drew a little money out of nowhere — I thought — and slid it under the edge of his plate. Then he toasted us a last time and downed the remainder of his tea. 'Adieu un-til the morrow.'

"'Where shall we meet you?' I asked.

"'Oh, I will come here to fetch you. Let us say exactly here at ten o'clock in the morning?

Good. I wish you a merry evening.' He bowed and was gone. After a minute I realized that he had barely eaten dinner, had paid our bill as well as his own, and had left us the talisman against the Evil Eye, which shone at the center of the white tablecloth.

"I slept that night like the dead, as they say, after the exhaustion of travel and sightseeing. When the sounds of the city woke me, it was already six-thirty. My small room was dim. In the first moment of consciousness, I looked around at the whitewashed walls, the simple, somehow foreign furniture, and the gleam of the mirror above the washstand, and I felt a weird confusion. I thought of Rossi's sojourn here in Istanbul, his tenure in that other pension — where had it been? — where his bags had been ransacked and his sketches of the precious maps removed, and I seemed to remember it as if I had been there myself, or was living the scene now. After a minute I realized that all was peaceful and orderly in the room; my suitcase lay undisturbed on the top of the bureau, and — more importantly — my briefcase with all its precious contents sat untouched next to the bed, where I could stretch out a hand and feel it. Even in my sleep I had been somehow aware of that ancient, silent book resting inside it.

"Now I could hear Helen in the hall bathroom, running water and moving around. After a moment, I realized this might constitute eavesdropping on her, and I felt ashamed. To cover my feeling, I got up quickly, ran water into the washstand in my room, and began to splash my face and arms. In the mirror, my face — and how young I looked even to myself in those days, my dear daughter, I cannot possibly convey to you — was the same as usual. My eyes were rather bleary after all this travel, but alert. I polished my hair with a little of the ubiquitous oil of the epoch, combed it back flat and shiny, and dressed in my rumpled trousers and jacket, with a clean, if wrinkled, shirt and tie. As I straightened my tie in the mirror, I heard the sounds in the bathroom cease, and after a few moments I got out my shaving kit and forced myself to knock briskly at the door. When there was no answer, I went in. Helen's scent, a rather harsh and cheap-smelling cologne, perhaps one she had brought from home, lingered in the tiny chamber. I had almost grown to like it.

"Breakfast in the restaurant was strong

coffee — very strong — in a copper pot with a long handle, served with bread, salty cheese, and olives and accompanied by a newspaper we couldn't read. Helen ate and drank in silence and I sat musing, sniffing the cigarette smoke that drifted across our table from the waiter's corner. The place was empty this morning apart from some sunlight that crept in through the arched windows, but the bustle of morning traffic just outside filled it with pleasant sounds and with glimpses of people passing by dressed for work, or carrying baskets of market produce. We had instinctively sought a table as far from the windows as possible.

"'The professor won't be here for another two hours,' Helen observed, loading her second cup of coffee with sugar and stirring vigorously. 'What shall we do?'

"'I was thinking we might walk back to Hagia Sophia,' I said. 'I want to see the place again.'

"'Why not?' she murmured. 'I do not mind being the tourist while we are here.' She looked rested, and I noticed that she had put on a clean pale-blue blouse with her black suit, the first color I had seen her wear, an exception to her black-and-white garb. As usual, she wore the little scarf over the place in her neck where the librarian had bitten her. Her face was ironic and wary, but I had the sense — with no particular proof — that she was getting used to my presence across the table, almost to the point of relaxing some of her ferocity.

"The streets were filled with people and cars by the time we took ourselves out, and we wandered among them through the heart of the old city and into one of the bazaars. Every aisle was full of shoppers — old women in black who stood fingering rainbows of fine textiles; young women in rich colors, their heads covered, bargaining for fruits I had never seen before or examining trays of gold jewelry; old men with crocheted caps on their white hair or balding pates, reading newspapers or bending over to examine a selection of carved wooden pipes. Some of them carried prayer beads in their hands. Everywhere I looked I saw handsome, shrewd, strong-featured, olive-skinned faces, gesturing hands, pointing fingers, flashing smiles that sometimes showed a glimpse of gold teeth. All around us I heard the clamor of emphatic, confident, haggling voices, sometimes a laugh.

"Helen wore her bemused, upside-down smile, looking about her at these strangers as if they pleased her, but as if she thought she understood them all too well. To me the scene was delightful, but I, too, felt a wariness, a sensation that I could have dated in myself as less than a week old, a feeling I had these days in any public place. It was a sense of searching the crowd, of glancing over my shoulder, of scanning faces for good or ill intent — and perhaps also of being watched. It was an unpleasant feeling, a harsh note in the harmony of all those lively conversations around us, and I wondered not for the first time if it was partly the contagion of Helen's cynical attitude toward the human race. I wondered, too, if that attitude in her was intrinsic or simply the result of her life in a police state.

"Whatever its roots, I felt my own paranoia as an affront to my former self. A week ago I'd been a normal American graduate student, content in my discontent with my work, enjoying deep down a sense of the prosperity and moral high ground of my culture even while I pretended to question it and everything else. The Cold War was real to me now, in the person of Helen and her disillusioned stance, and an older cold war made itself felt in my very veins. I thought of Rossi, strolling these streets in the summer of 1930 before his adventure in the archive had sent him pell-mell out of Istanbul, and he was real to me, too — not only Rossi as I knew him but also the young Rossi of his letters.

"Helen tapped my arm as we walked and nodded in the direction of a couple of old men at a little wooden table tucked away near a booth. 'Look — there's your theory of leisure in person,' she said. 'It's nine in the morning and they are already playing chess. It is strange that they are not playing *tabla* — that is the favorite game, in this part of the world. But I believe this is chess, instead.' Sure enough, the two men were just setting up their pieces on a worn-looking wooden board. Black was arrayed against ivory, knights and rooks guarded their lieges, pawns faced one another in battle formation — the same arrangement of war the world over, I mused, stopping to watch. 'Do you know about chess?' Helen asked.

"'Of course,' I said a little indignantly. 'I used to play it with my father.'

"'Ah.' The sound was acerbic, and I remembered too late that she had had no such childhood lessons, and that she played her own kind of chess with her father — with her image of him, in any case. But she seemed to be caught up in historical reflections. 'It's not Western, you know — it's an ancient game from India — *shahmat* in

Persian. *Checkmate,* I think you say in English. *Shah* is the word for *king.* A battle of kings.'

"I watched the two men beginning their game, their gnarled fingers selecting the first warriors. Jokes flashed between them — probably they were old friends. I could have stood there all day, watching, but Helen moved restlessly away, and I followed her. As we went by, the men seemed to notice us for the first time, glancing up quizzically for a moment. We must look like foreigners, I realized, although Helen's face blended beautifully with the countenances around us. I wondered how long their game would take — all morning, maybe — and which of them would win this time.

"The booth near them was just opening up. It was really a shed, wedged under a venerable fig tree at the edge of the bazaar. A young man in a white shirt and dark trousers was pulling vigorously at the stall's doors and curtains, setting up tables outside and laying out his wares — books. Books stood in stacks on the wooden counters, tumbled out of crates on the floor, and lined the shelves inside.

"I went forward eagerly, and the young owner nodded a greeting and smiled, as if he recognized a bibliophile whatever his national cut. Helen followed more slowly, and we stood turning through volumes in perhaps a dozen languages. Many of them were in Arabic, or in the modern Turkish language; some were in Greek or Cyrillic alphabets, others in English, French, German, Italian. I found a Hebrew tome and a whole shelf of Latin classics. Most were cheaply printed and shoddily bound, their cloth covers already shabby with handling. There were new paperbacks with lurid scenes on the covers, and a few volumes that looked very old, especially some of the works in Arabic. 'The Byzantines loved books, too,' Helen murmured, leafing through what looked like a set of German poetry. 'Perhaps they bought books on this very spot.'

"The young man had finished his preparations for the day, and he came over to greet us. 'Speak German? English?'

"'English,' I said quickly, since Helen did not answer.

"'I have books in English,' he told me with a pleasant smile. 'No problem.' His face was thin and expressive, with large greenish eyes and a long nose. 'Also newspaper from London, New York.' I thanked him and asked if he carried old books. 'Yes, very old.' He handed me a nineteenth-century edition of *Much Ado About Nothing* — cheap looking, bound in worn cloth. I wondered what library this had drifted from and how it had made its journey — from bourgeois Manchester, say — to this crossroads of the ancient world. I flipped through the pages, to be polite, and handed it back. 'Not enough old?' he asked, smiling.

"Helen had been peering over my shoulder, and now she looked pointedly at her watch. We hadn't even reached Hagia Sophia, after all. 'Yes, we've got to be going,' I said.

"The young bookseller gave us a courteous bow, volume in hand. I stared at him for a second, troubled by something that bordered on recognition, but he had turned away and was helping a new customer, an old man who could have been a triplet to the chess players. Helen nudged my elbow, and we left the shop and went more purposefully around the edge of the bazaar and back toward our pension.

"The little restaurant was empty when we entered, but a few minutes later Turgut appeared in the doorway, nodding and smiling, and asked us how we had slept. He was wearing an olive wool suit this morning, despite the gathering heat, and seemed full of suppressed excitement. His curly dark hair was slicked back, his shoes shone with polish, and he moved quickly to usher us out of the restaurant. I noticed again that he was a person of great energy, and I felt relief at having such a guide. Excitement was rising in me, too. Rossi's papers rested securely in my briefcase, and perhaps the next few hours would bring me a step closer to his whereabouts. Soon, at least, I might be able to compare his copies of the documents with the originals he had examined so many years before.

"As we followed Turgut through the streets, he explained to us that Sultan Mehmed's archive was not housed in the main building of the National Library, although it was still under state protection. It was now in a library annex that had once been a *mendrese,* a traditional Islamic school. Ataturk had closed these schools in his secularization of the country, and this one currently contained the National Library's rare and antique books on the history of the Empire. We would find Sultan Mehmed's collection among others from the centuries of Ottoman expansion.

"The annex to the library proved to be an exquisite little building. We entered it from the street through brass-studded wooden doors. The windows were covered with a tracery of marble; sunlight filtered through them in fine geometric shapes, decorating the floor of the dim entryway with fallen stars and octagons. Turgut showed us where to sign the register, which lay on a counter at the entrance (Helen put down an illegible scrawl, I noticed), and signed it himself with a flourish.

"Then we proceeded into the collection's one room, a large, hushed space under a dome set with green-and-white mosaic. Polished tables ran the length of it, and three or four researchers already sat working there. The walls were lined not only with books but also with wooden drawers and boxes, and delicate brass lamp shades fitted with electric lighting hung from the ceiling. The librarian, a slender man of fifty with a string of prayer beads on his wrist, left his work and came over to shake both of Turgut's hands in his. They spoke for a minute — on Turgut's side of the conversation I caught the name of our university at home — and then the librarian addressed us in Turkish, smiling and bowing. 'This is Mr. Erozan. He welcomes you to the collection,' Turgut told us with a look of satisfaction. 'He would like to be of assassination to you.' I recoiled, in spite of myself, and Helen smirked. 'He will set forth for you immediately Sultan Mehmed's documents from the Order of the Dragon. But first, we must sit in comfort here and wait for him.'

"We settled at one of the tables, carefully distant from the few other researchers. They eyed us with transitory curiosity and then returned to their work. After a moment, Mr. Erozan came back carrying a large wooden box with a lock on the front and Arabic lettering carved into the top. 'What does that say?' I asked the professor.

"'Ah.' He touched the top of the box with his fingertips. 'It says, "Here is evil" — hmm — "here is evil contained — housed. Lock it with the keys of holy Qur'an."' My heart made a jump; the phrases were strikingly similar to what Rossi had reported reading in the margins of the mysterious map and had spoken aloud in the old archives where it had once been stored. He'd made no mention of this box in his letters, but perhaps he'd never seen it, if a librarian had brought him just the documents. Or perhaps they had been placed in the box sometime after Rossi's sojourn here.

"'How old is the box itself?' I asked Turgut.

"He shook his head. 'I don't know, and neither

does my friend here. Because it is of wood, I do not think it is very likely to be as old as the time of Mehmed. My friend told me once' — he beamed in Mr. Erozan's direction, and the man beamed back without comprehension — 'that these documents were put in the box in 1930, to keep them safe. He knows that because he discussed it with the previous librarian. He is most meticulous, my friend.'

"In 1930! Helen and I looked at each other. Probably by the time Rossi had penned his letters — December 1930 — to whoever might later receive them, the documents he had examined had already been put into this box for safekeeping. An ordinary wooden receptacle might have kept out mice and damp, but what had prompted the librarian of that era to lock the documents of the Order of the Dragon inside a box ornamented with a sacred warning?

"Turgut's friend had produced a ring of keys and was fitting one to the lock. I almost laughed, remembering our modern card catalog at home, the accessibility of thousands of rare books in the university library system. I had never imagined myself doing research that required an old key. It clicked in the lock. 'Here we are,' Turgut murmured, and the librarian withdrew. Turgut smiled at each of us — rather sadly, I thought — and lifted the lid."

In the train, Barley had just finished reading my father's first two letters for himself. It gave me a pang to see them lying open in his hands, but I knew Barley would trust my father's authoritative voice, whereas he might only half believe my weaker one. "Have you been to Paris before?" I asked him, partly to cover my emotion.

"I suppose I have," Barley said indignantly. "I studied there for a year before I went to university. My mother wanted me to know French better." I longed to ask about his mother and why she required this delectable accomplishment in her son, and also what it was like to have a mother, but Barley was deep in the letter again. "Your father must be a very good lecturer," he mused. "This is a lot more entertaining than what we get at Oxford."

This opened up another realm for me. Were lectures at Oxford ever dull? Was that possible? Barley was full of things I wanted to know, a messenger from a world so large I could not begin to imagine it. I was interrupted this time by a conductor hurrying down the aisle past our door. "Bruxelles!" he called. The train was slowing already, and a few minutes later we were looking out the window into the Brussels station; the customs officers were boarding. Outside, people were rushing for their trains and pigeons were hunting for morsels from the platform.

Perhaps because I was secretly fond of pigeons, I was gazing hard enough into the crowd to suddenly notice one figure that was not moving at all. A woman, tall and dressed in a long black coat, stood quietly on the platform. She had a black scarf tied over her hair, framing a white face. She was a little too far away for me to see her features clearly, but I caught a flash of dark eyes and an almost unnaturally red mouth — bright lipstick, maybe. There was something odd about the silhouette of her clothes; amid the miniskirts and hideous block-heeled boots of the day, she wore narrow black pumps.

But what caught my attention about her first, and held it for a moment before our train began to move again, was her attitude of alertness. She was scanning our train, up and down. I drew back from the window instinctively, and Barley looked a question at me. The woman apparently hadn't seen us, although she took a hovering step in our direction. Then she seemed to change her mind and turned to scan another train, which had just pulled in on the opposite side of the platform. Something about her stern, straight back kept me staring until we began to move out of the station again, and then she disappeared among the throngs of people there, as if she had never existed.

Chapter 28

I HAD DOZED off this time, instead of Barley. When I woke, I found myself wedged against him, my head lolling on the shoulder of his navy sweater. He was staring out the window, my father's letters stored neatly again in their envelopes on his lap, his legs crossed, his face — not so far above mine — turned to the passing scenery of what I knew must by now be the French countryside. I opened my eyes to a view of his bony chin. When I looked down I could see Barley's hands clasped loosely together over the letters. I noticed for the first time that he bit his nails, as I always did myself. I closed my eyes again, feigning continued sleep, because the warmth of his shoulder was so comforting. Then I was afraid he wouldn't like my leaning against him, or that I had drooled on his sweater in my doltish slumber, and I sat quickly upright. Barley turned to look at me, his eyes full of faraway thoughts, or perhaps just full of the land beyond the window, no longer flat but rolling, a modest French farm country. After a minute he smiled.

• • •

"As the lid went up on Sultan Mehmed's box of secrets, a smell I knew well drifted out of it. It was the scent of very old documents, of parchment or vellum, of dust and centuries, of pages time had long since begun to defile. It was the smell, too, of the small blank book with the dragon in the middle, my book. I had never dared put my nose directly into it, as I secretly had with some of the other old volumes I'd handled — I feared, I think, that there might be a repulsive edge to its perfume or, worse, a power in the scent, an evil drug I didn't want to inhale.

"Turgut was gently lifting documents from the box. Each was wrapped in yellowing tissue paper, and the items varied in shape and size. He spread them carefully on the table before us. 'I will show you these papers myself and tell you what I know of them,' he said. 'Then perhaps you would like to sit and brood on them, don't you think?' Yes, perhaps we would — I nodded, and he unwrapped a scroll and unwound it delicately under our gaze. It was parchment attached to fine wooden spindles, very different from the large flat pages and bound ledgers I was used to in my research on Rembrandt's world. The edges of the parchment were decorated in a colorful border of geometric patterns, gilt and deep blue and crimson. The handwritten text, to my disappointment, was in Arabic lettering. I'm not sure what I had expected; this document had come from the heart of an empire that spoke the Ottoman language and wrote it down in Arabic letters, resorting to Greek only to bully the Byzantines, or Latin to storm the gates of Vienna.

"Turgut read my face and hurried to explain. 'This, my friends, is a ledger of the expenses of a war with the Order of the Dragon. It was written in a town on the southern side of the Danube by a bureaucrat who was spending the sultan's money there — it is a report of business, in other words. Dracula's father, Vlad Dracul, cost the Ottoman Empire a great deal of money in the mid-fifteenth century, you see. This bureaucrat commissioned armor and — how do you say? — scimitars for three hundred men to guard the border of the western Carpathians so that the local people would not revolt, and he bought horses for them, also. Here' — he pointed a long finger at the bottom of the scroll — 'it says that Vlad Dracul was an expense and a — a rotten nuisance and had cost them more money than the pasha wanted to spend. The pasha is very sorry and miserable, and he wishes a long life to the Incomparable One in the name of Allah.'

"Helen and I glanced at each other, and I thought I read in her eyes something of the awe I felt myself. This corner of history was as real as the tiled floor under our feet or the wooden tabletop under our fingers. The people to whom it had happened had actually lived and breathed and felt and thought and then died, as we did — as we would. I looked away, unable to watch the flicker of emotion on her strong face.

"Turgut had rolled up the scroll again and was opening a second package, which contained two more scrolls. 'Here is a letter from the pasha of Wallachia in which he promises to send Sultan Mehmed any documents he can find about the Order of the Dragon. And this is an account of trading along the Danube in 1461, not far from where the Order of the Dragon had control. The boundaries of this area were not stalwart, you understand — they were continually changing. Here it lists the silks, spices, and horses the pasha requests to trade for wool from the shepherds of his domain.' The next two scrolls proved to be similar accounts. Then Turgut unrolled a smaller package, which contained a flat sketch on parchment. 'A map,' he said. I made an involuntary move for my briefcase, which held Rossi's sketches and notes, but Helen shook her head almost imperceptibly. I understood her meaning — we did not know Turgut well enough to spread all our secrets in front of him. Not yet, I amended mentally; after all, he had apparently opened all his own resources to us.

"'I have never been able to understand what this map is, my fellows,' Turgut told us. There was regret in his voice, and he stroked his mustache with a thoughtful hand. I looked closely at the parchment and saw with a thrill a neat, if faded, version of the first map Rossi had copied, the long crescents of mountains, the curving river north of them. 'It does not resemble any region I have studied myself, and there is no way to know the — how do you say? — scale of the map, you know?' He set it aside. 'Here is another map, which appears to be a closer view of the area in the first.' I knew it was — I had seen all this already, and my excitement climbed. 'I believe these are the mountains shown in the west on the first map, no?' He sighed. 'But there is no further information, and you see it is not much labeled, except for some lines from the Qur'an and this strange motto — I translated it carefully, once — that says something like "Here he is housed with evil. Reader, with your words dig him up."'

"I had put out a startled hand to stop him, but Turgut had spoken too quickly and caught me off guard. 'No!' I cried, but too late, so that Turgut stared at me in astonishment. Helen looked from one of us to the other, and Mr. Erozan turned from his work on the other side of the hall and stared at me, too. 'Excuse me,' I whispered. 'I'm just excited by seeing these documents. They're so — interesting.'

"'Oh, I am glad you find them interesting.' Turgut almost beamed through his gravity. 'And these words do sound a wit strange. They give one a — you know? — a turn.'

"At that moment there was a step in the hall. I looked around nervously, half expecting to see Dracula himself, whatever he looked like, but it was only a small man in a white cap and shaggy gray beard. Mr. Erozan went to the door to greet him, and we turned back to our documents. Turgut drew from the box another parchment. 'This is the last document in here,' he said. 'I have never been able to make sense of it. It is listed in the library catalog as a bibliography of the Order of the Dragon.'

"My heart lurched, and I saw the color rise in Helen's face. 'A bibliography?'

"'Yes, my friend.' Turgut spread it gently on the table before us. It looked very old and quite brittle, written in Greek in a fine hand. The top curved raggedly, as if it had once been part of a longer scroll, and the bottom edge was clearly torn off. There were no ornaments of any sort on the manuscript, just the finely penned words in rows. I sighed. I had never studied Greek, although I doubted anything but complete mastery would have helped me with such a document, anyway.

"As if divining my problem, Turgut took a notebook from his briefcase. 'I have had this translated by a scholar of Byzantium from our university. He has a ravishing knowledge of their language and documents. This is a list of works of literature, although many of them I have never found mentioned in any other example.' He opened his notebook and smoothed out a page. It was covered in neat Turkish script. This time Helen sighed. Turgut slapped his forehead. 'Oh, a million pardons,' he said. 'Here, I shall translate for you as we go along, all right? "Herodotus, *The Treatment of Prisoners of War.* Pheseus, *On Reason and Torture.* Origen, *Treatise on First Principles.* Euthymius the Elder, *The Fate of the Damned.* Gubent of Ghent, *Treatise on Nature.* St. Thomas Aquinas, *Sisyphus.*" You see, it is quite a strange selection, and some of the books on it are very rare. My friend who is a Byzantine scholar told me, for example, that it would be a miracle if a previously unknown version of this treatise by the early Christian philosopher Origen had survived somewhere — most of Origen's work was destroyed because he was accused of heresy.'

"'What heresy?' Helen looked interested. 'I am sure I have read about him somewhere.'

"'He was accused of arguing in this treatise that it is a matter of Christian logic that even Satan will be saved and resurrected,' Turgut explained. 'Shall I go on with the list?'

"'If you wouldn't mind,' I said, 'could you write the titles down for us in English, just as you are reading them?'

"'With pleasure.' Turgut sat down with his notebook and drew out a pen.

"'What do you make of this?' I asked Helen. Her face said more plainly than any words, *We came all this way for a jumbled list of books?* 'I know it makes no sense yet,' I told her in a low voice, 'but let's see what it leads to.'

"'Now, then, my friends, let me read you the next few titles.' Turgut was writing cheerfully away. 'Almost all of them are connected with torture or murder or something else unpleasant, you can see. "Erasmus, *Fortunes of an Assassin.* Henricus Curtius, *The Cannibals.* Giorgio of Padua, *The Damned.*"'

"'No dates for these works are listed with them?' I asked, bending over the documents.

"Turgut sighed. 'No. And I have never been able to find other references to some of these titles, but of those I have located, there is none written later than 1600.'

"'And yet that is later than the lifetime of Vlad Dracula,' Helen commented. I looked at her in surprise; I hadn't thought of that. It was a simple point, but quite true and very puzzling.

"'Yes, dear madam,' Turgut said, looking up at her. 'The most recent of these works was written more than a hundred years after his death and after the death of Sultan Mehmed, as well. Alas, I have been unable to find any information about how or when this bibliography became part of Sultan Mehmed's collection. Someone must have added it later, perhaps long after the collection came to Istanbul.'

"'But before 1930,' I mused.

"Turgut looked at me sharply. 'That is the date when this collection was put under lock and key,' he said. 'What makes you say that, Professor?'

"I felt myself reddening, both because I had said far too much, so much that Helen was turning away from me in despair at my idiocy, and because I was not yet a professor. I was silent a minute; I have always hated to lie, and I try, my dear daughter, never to do so if I can possibly avoid it.

"Turgut was studying me, and I felt — uncomfortably — that before this moment I had never fully registered the extreme keenness of his dark eyes with their genial crow's-feet. I took a deep breath. I would have it out with Helen later. I had trusted Turgut all along, and he might well help us more if he knew more. To stall for another moment, however, I looked down at the list of documents he was translating for us, then glanced at the Turkish translation from which he was working. I couldn't meet his eyes. Exactly how much of what we knew should I tell him? If I related the full extent of my knowledge of Rossi's experiences here, would he discredit our seriousness and sanity? It was precisely because I'd lowered my eyes in indecision that I suddenly saw something strange. My hand flew out toward the original Greek document, the bibliography of the Order of the Dragon. Not all of it was in Greek, after all. I could clearly read the name at the bottom of the list: *Bartolomeo Rossi.* It was followed by a phrase in Latin.

"'Good God!' My exclamation had ruffled the silent researchers all over the room, I realized too late. Mr. Erozan, still talking with the man in the cap and long beard, turned quizzically toward us.

"Turgut took alarm at once, and Helen moved swiftly closer. 'What is it?' Turgut put out a hand toward the document. I was still staring; it was easy enough for him to follow my gaze. Then he jumped to his feet, breathing out what could have been an echo of my own agitation, so clear an echo that it brought me a strange comfort in the midst of all that other strangeness: 'My God! Professor Rossi!'

"The three of us looked at one another, and for a moment nobody spoke. Finally I tried. 'Do you,' I said to Turgut in a low voice, 'know that name?'

"Turgut looked from me to Helen. 'Do you?' he said at last."

Barley's smile was kind. "You must have been tired or you wouldn't have slept so hard. I'm tired myself, just thinking what a mess you're in.

What would anyone say if you told them about all this — anyone else, I mean? That lady there, for example." He nodded at our drowsy companion, who hadn't gotten off at Brussels and apparently meant to nap all the way to Paris. "Or a policeman. No one would think you were anything but crazed." He sighed. "And you really intended to travel to the south of France by yourself? I wish you'd tell me the exact location, instead of making me guess it, so I could wire Mrs. Clay and get you in the biggest possible trouble."

It was my turn to smile. We'd been over this ground a couple of times already.

"You're awfully stubborn," Barley groaned. "I never would have thought one little girl could be so much trouble — namely the trouble I'd be in with Master James if I left you in the middle of nowhere in France, you know." That almost made the tears start up behind my eyes, but his next words dried them before they had time to form. "At least we'll have time for lunch before we have to catch our next train. The Gare du Nord has the most delicious sandwiches and we can use up my francs." It was the choice of pronoun that warmed my heart.

Chapter 29

TO STEP OFF even a modern train into that great arena of travel, the Gare du Nord, with its soaring framework of old iron and glass, its hoopskirted, light-filled beauty, is to step directly into Paris. Barley and I descended from the train, bags in hand, and stood for a couple of minutes drinking it all in. At least, that is what I was doing, although I had been there many times by then, passing through on my travels with my father. The *gare* echoed with the sounds of trains braking, people talking, footsteps, whistles, the rush of pigeon wings, the clink of coins. An old man in a black beret passed us with a young woman on his arm. She had beautifully coiffed red hair and wore pink lipstick, and I imagined for a moment trading places with her. Oh, to look like that, to be Parisian, to be grown-up and have high-heeled boots and real breasts and an elegant, aging artist at your side! Then it occurred to me that he might be her father, and I felt very lonely.

I turned to Barley, who had apparently been drinking in the smells rather than the sights.

"God, I'm hungry," he grumbled. "If we're here, let's at least eat something good." He darted off toward a corner of the station as if he knew the way by heart; it turned out, in fact, that he knew not only the way but the mustard and the selection of finely sliced ham by heart, and soon we were eating two large sandwiches in white paper, Barley not even bothering to sit down on the bench I found.

I was hungry, too, but mostly I was worried about what to do next. Now that we were off the train, Barley could go to any public phone in sight and find a way to call Mrs. Clay or Master James or perhaps an army of gendarmes to take me back to Amsterdam in handcuffs. I looked warily up at him, but his face was mostly obscured by the sandwich. When he emerged from it to drink a little orange soda, I said, "Barley, I'd like you to do me a favor."

"Now what?"

"Please don't make any phone calls. I mean, please, Barley, don't betray me. I'm going south from here, no matter what. You can see I can't go home without knowing where my father is and what's happening to him, can't you?"

He sipped gravely. "I can see that."

"Please, Barley."

"What do you take me for?"

"I don't know," I said, bewildered. "I thought you were angry about my running away and might still feel you had to report me."

"Just think," said Barley. "If I were really up-standing, I could be on my way back to tomorrow's lectures — and a good sound scolding from James — right now, with you in tow. Instead, here I am, forced by gallantry — and curiosity — to accompany a lady to the south of France at the drop of a hat. You think I'd miss out on that?"

"I don't know," I repeated, but more gratefully.

"We'd better ask about the next train to Perpignan," Barley said, folding up his sandwich paper decisively.

"How did you know?" I said, astonished.

"Oh, you think you're so mysterious." Barley was looking exasperated again. "Didn't I translate all that business in the vampire collection for you? Where could you be going if not to that monastery in the Pyrénées-Orientales? Don't I know my map of France? Come on, don't start scowling. It makes your face so much less piquant." And we went to the *bureau de change* arm in arm, after all.

• • •

"When Turgut uttered Rossi's name in that unmistakable tone of familiarity, I had the sudden sense of a world shifting, of bits of color and shape knocked out of place into a vision of intricate absurdity. It was as if I'd been watching a familiar movie and suddenly a character who had never been part of it before had strolled onto the screen, joining the action seamlessly but without explanation.

"'Do you know Professor Rossi?' Turgut repeated in the same tone.

"I was still speechless, but Helen had apparently made a decision. 'Professor Rossi is Paul's adviser in the history department of our university.'

"'But that is incredible,' Turgut said slowly.

"'You knew of him?' I asked.

"'I have never met him,' Turgut said. 'But I heard of him in a most unusual way. Please, this is a story I must tell you, I think. Sit down, my fellows.' He gestured hospitably, even in the midst of his amazement. Helen and I had leaped to our feet, but now we settled near him. 'There is something here too extraordinary — ' He broke off, and then seemed to force himself to explain to us. 'Years ago, when I became enamored of this archive, I asked the librarian for all possible information about it. He told me that in his memory no one else had ever examined it, but that he thought his ancestor — I mean, the librarian before him — knew something about it. I went to see the old librarian.'

"'Is he alive now?' I gasped.

"'Oh, no, my friend. I am sorry. He was terribly old then, and he died a year after I talked with him, I believe. But his memory was excellent, and he told me that he had locked up the collection because he had a bad feeling about it. He said a foreign professor had looked at it once and then become very — how do you say? — upset and almost crazy, and run out of the building suddenly. The old librarian said that a few days after this happened, he was sitting alone in the library one day with some work, and he looked up and suddenly noticed a large man examining the same documents. No one had come in, and the door to the street was locked because it was evening, after the public hours for the library. He could not understand how the man had got in. He thought perhaps he had not locked the door after all, and had not heard the man come up the stairs, although this hardly seemed possible. Then he told me' — Turgut

leaned forward and lowered his voice further —
'he told me that when he went close to the man
to ask him what he was doing, the man looked
up and — you see — there was a little bit of blood
dripping from the corner of his mouth.'

"I felt a wave of revulsion, and Helen raised
her shoulders as if to ward off a shudder. 'The
old librarian did not want to tell me about it, at
first. I believe he was afraid I would think he was
losing his mind. He told me the sight made him
feel faint, and when he looked again the man
was gone. But the documents were still scattered on the table, and the next day he bought
this holy box in the antiques market and put the
documents into it. He kept them locked up, and
he said no one troubled them again while he
was librarian here. He never saw the strange
man again.'

"'And what about Rossi?' I demanded.

"'Well, you see, I was determined to trace
every little path of this story, so I asked him for
the foreign researcher's name, but he could not
remember anything except that he thought it
was Italian. He told me to look in the register for
1930, if I wanted to, and my friend here allowed
me to do so. I found Professor Rossi's name, after
some searching, and discovered he was from En-

gland, from Oxford. Then I wrote him a letter in Oxford.'

"'Did he reply?' Helen was almost glaring at Turgut.

"'Yes, but he was no longer at Oxford. He had gone to an American university — yours, although I didn't connect the name when we first talked — and the letter found him there after a long time, and then he wrote back. He told me that he was sorry but he did not know anything about the archive to which I referred and could not help me. I will show you the letter at my apartment when you come for dinner with me. It arrived shortly before the war.'

"'This is very strange,' I muttered. 'I just can't understand it.'

"'Well, this is not the strangest thing,' Turgut said urgently. He turned to the parchment on the table, the bibliography, and his finger traced Rossi's name at the bottom. Looking at it, I noticed again the words after the name. They were Latin, I was sure, although my Latin, dating back to my first two years of college, had never been impressive and was now rusty, to boot.

"'What does that say? Do you read Latin?'

"To my relief, Turgut nodded. 'It says, "Bartolomeo Rossi, 'The Spirit — the Ghost — in the Amphora.'"'

"My thoughts whirled. 'But I know that phrase. I think — I'm sure that's the title of an article he's been working on this spring.' I stopped. 'Was working on. He showed it to me about a month ago. It's about Greek tragedy and the objects the Greek theaters sometimes used as props onstage.' Helen was looking intently at me. 'It's — I'm sure that's his current work.'

"'What is very, very strange,' Turgut said, and now I heard the actual current of fear in his voice, 'is that I have looked at this list many times, and I have never seen this entry on it. Someone has added Rossi's name.'

"I stared at him in amazement. 'Find out who,' I gasped. 'We must find out who has been tampering with these documents. When were you last here?'

"'About three weeks ago,' Turgut said grimly. 'Wait, please, I will first go ask Mr. Erozan. Do not move.' But as he got up, the attentive librarian saw him and came to meet him. They exchanged a few quick words.

"'What does he say?' I asked.

"'Why did he not think to tell me this before?'

Turgut groaned. 'A man came in yesterday and looked through this box.' He questioned his friend further, and Mr. Erozan gestured at the door. 'It was that man,' Turgut said, pointing, too. 'He says it was the man who came in a little while ago, to whom he was talking.'

"We all turned, aghast, and the librarian gestured again, but it was too late. The little man in the white cap and gray beard was gone."

Barley was hunting through his wallet. "Well, we're going to have to change everything I have," he said glumly. "I've got the money from Master James, and a few pounds more from my allowance."

"I brought some," I said. "From Amsterdam, I mean. I'll buy the train tickets south, and I think I can pay for our meals and lodging, at least for a few days." I was wondering, privately, if I would actually be able to pay for Barley's appetite. It was strange that someone so skinny could eat so much. I was still skinny, too, but I couldn't imagine putting away two sandwiches at the rate Barley had just employed. I thought this concern with money was the nagging weight on my mind until we were actually at the exchange counter, and a young woman in a navy blazer was looking us over. Barley spoke with her about the exchange rates, and after a minute she picked up the phone, turning away to talk into the receiver. "Why's she doing that?" I whispered nervously to Barley.

He glanced at me in surprise. "She's checking the rates, for some reason," he said. "I don't know. What did you think?"

I couldn't explain. Perhaps it was just the contagion of my father's letters, but everything looked suspicious to me now. It was as if we were being followed by eyes I could not see.

"Turgut, who seemed to have more presence of mind than I did, hurried to the door and disappeared into the little foyer. He was back a second later, shaking his head. 'He is gone,' he told us heavily. 'I saw no signal of him in the street. He vanished into the throngs.'

"Mr. Erozan seemed to be apologizing, and Turgut spoke with him for a few seconds. Then he turned to us again. 'Do you have any reason to think you have been pursued here, in your research?'

"'Pursued?' I had every reason to think so, but by whom, exactly, I had no idea.

"Turgut looked sharply at me, and I remembered the appearance of the Gypsy at our table the night before. 'My friend the librarian says this man wanted to see the documents we have been examining, and he was angry when he found they were already being used. He says the man spoke Turkish but with an accent, and he thinks he is a foreigner. That is why I ask if someone is following you here. My fellows, let us go out of here, but keep a close watch. I am telling my friend to guard the documents and take notes of this man or anyone else who comes to look at them. He will try to find out who he is if he returns. Perhaps if we leave he will return sooner.'

"'But the maps!' It worried me to leave these precious items in their box. Besides, what had we learned? We had not even begun to solve the puzzle of the three maps, even as we had stood there looking at their miraculous reality on the library table.

"Turgut turned to Mr. Erozan again, and a smile, a signal of mutual understanding, seemed to pass between them. 'Do not worry, Professor,' Turgut told me. 'I have made copies of all these things in my own hand, and the copies are safely in my apartment. Besides, my friend will not permit anything to happen to the originals. You can believe me.'

"I wanted to. Helen was looking searchingly at both our new acquaintances, and I wondered what she made of all this. 'All right,' I said.

"'Come, my fellows.' Turgut began to put away the documents, handling them with a tenderness I could not have equaled myself. 'It seems to me we have much to discuss in private. I will take you to my apartment and we will talk there. I can also show you there some other materials on this topic I have collected. Let us not speak of these matters in the street. We will depart as visibly as possible and' — he nodded at the librarian — 'we will leave our finest general in the breach.' Mr. Erozan shook hands with each of us, locked the box with great care, and carried it away, disappearing with it among the bookshelves at the back of the hall. I watched until he was completely out of sight, and then I sighed out loud in spite of myself. I couldn't shake the feeling that Rossi's fate was still hidden in that box — almost, God forbid, that Rossi himself was entombed there — and that we had been unable to rescue him from it.

"Then we left the building, standing conspicuously on the steps for a few minutes, pretending to converse. My nerves felt shattered and Helen looked pale, but Turgut was composed. 'If he is loitering around here somewhere,' he said in a low voice, 'the little sneak will know we are departing.' He offered his arm to Helen, who took it with less reluctance than I would have predicted, and we set off together through the crowded streets. It was lunchtime, and the smells of roasting meat and baking bread rose everywhere around us, mingling with a dank smell that could have been coal smoke or diesel fuel, a smell I still remember sometimes without warning, and one that means for me the edge of the Eastern world. Whatever came next, I thought, it would be another riddle, as this whole place — I looked around me at the faces of the Turkish crowds, the slender spires of minarets on the horizon of every street, the ancient domes among the fig trees, the shops full of mysterious goods — was a riddle. The greatest riddle of all pulled at my heart again and made it ache: Where was Rossi? Was he here, in this city, or far away? Alive or dead, or something in between?"

Chapter 30

AT 4:02, Barley and I boarded the southern express to Perpignan. Barley swung his bag up the steep steps and reached out a hand to pull me up after him. There were fewer passengers on this train, and the compartment we found stayed empty even after the train pulled out. I was getting tired; if I'd been at home at this hour, Mrs. Clay would have been settling me at the kitchen table with a glass of milk and a slice of yellow cake. For a second I almost missed her annoying ministrations. Barley sat down next to me, although he had four other seats to choose from, and I tucked my hand under his sweatered arm. "I ought to study," he said, but he didn't open his book right away; there was too much to see as we picked up speed through the city. I thought of all the times I'd been here with my father — climbing Montmartre, or gazing in at the depressed camel in the Jardin des Plantes. It seemed now like a city I'd never seen before.

Watching Barley moving his lips over Milton made me sleepy, and when he said he wanted to go to the dining car for tea, I shook my head, drowsing. "You're a wreck," he told me, smiling. "You stay here and sleep, then, and I'll take my book. We can always go back for dinner when you get hungry."

My eyes closed almost as soon as he left the car, and when I opened them again I found I was curled up on the empty seat like a child, with my long cotton skirt pulled over my ankles. Someone was sitting on the opposite bench reading a newspaper, and it was not Barley. I sat up quickly. The man was reading *Le Monde,* and the spread of the paper hid the rest of him — I couldn't see anything of his upper body or face. A black leather briefcase rested on the seat next to him.

For a split second I imagined it was my father, and a wave of gratitude and confusion went through me. Then I saw the man's shoes, which were also black leather and very shiny, the toes perforated with elegant patterns, the leather laces ending in black tassels. The man's legs were crossed, and he wore immaculate black suit trousers and fine black silk socks. Those were not my father's shoes; in fact, there was something wrong with those shoes, or with the feet they contained, although I couldn't understand what made me feel this. I thought that a strange man shouldn't have come in while I was sleeping — there was something unpleasant about that, too, and I hoped he had not been watching me sleep. I wondered in my discomfort if I might be able to get up and open the door to the compartment without his noticing me. Suddenly I saw that he had drawn the curtains to the aisle. No one walking through the train could see us. Or had Barley drawn them before leaving, to let me sleep?

I snuck a glance at my watch. It was almost five o'clock. Outside, a tremendous landscape rolled by; we were entering the South. The man behind the newspaper was so still that I began to tremble in spite of myself. After a while I realized what was frightening me. I had been awake for many long minutes by now, but during all the time I had been watching and listening, he had not turned a single page of his newspaper.

"Turgut's apartment was located in another part of Istanbul, on the Sea of Marmara, and we took a ferry there from the busy port called Eminönü. Helen stood at the rail, watching the seagulls that followed the boat, and looking back at the tremendous silhouette of the old city. I went to stand next to her, and Turgut pointed out spires and domes for us, his voice booming above the rumble of the engines. His neighborhood, we discovered when we disembarked, was more modern than what we'd seen before, but *modern* in this case meant nineteenth century. As we walked along increasingly quiet streets, heading away from the ferry landing, I saw a second Istanbul, new to me: stately, drooping trees, fine stone and wooden houses, apartment buildings that could have been lifted from a Parisian neighborhood, neat sidewalks, pots of flowers, ornamented cornices. Here and there the old Islamic empire erupted in the form of a ruined arch or an isolated mosque, a Turkish house with an overhanging second story. But on Turgut's street, the West had made a genteel and thorough sweep. Later I saw its counterparts in other cities — Prague and Sofia, Budapest and Moscow, Belgrade and Beirut. That borrowed elegance had been borrowed all over the East.

"'Please to enter.' Turgut stopped in front of a row of old houses, ushered us up the double front stair, and checked inside a little mailbox — apparently empty — that carried the name PROFESOR BORA. He opened the door and stepped aside. 'Please, welcome to my abode, where everything is yours. I am sorry that my wife is out — she teaches at the nursery school.'

"We came first into a hall with a polished wooden floor and walls, where we followed Turgut in taking off our shoes and putting on the embroidered slippers he gave us. Then he showed us into a sitting room, and Helen sounded a low note of admiration, which I could not help echoing. The room was filled with a pleasant greenish light, mixed with soft pink and yellow. I realized after a moment that this was sunlight filtering through a blend of trees outside two large windows with hazy curtains of an old white lace. The room was lined with extraordinary furniture, very low, carved of dark wood, and cushioned in rich fabrics. Around three walls ran a bench heaped with lace-covered pillows. Above this, the whitewashed walls were lined with prints and paintings of Istanbul, a portrait of an old man in a fez and one of a younger man in a black suit, a framed parchment covered with fine Arabic calligraphy. There were fading sepia photographs of the city and cabinets lined with brass coffee services. The corners were filled with colorfully glazed vases brimming with roses. Underfoot lay deep rugs in crimson, rose, and soft green. In the very center of the room, a great round tray on legs stood empty, highly polished, as if waiting for the next meal.

"'It is very beautiful,' Helen said, turning to our host, and I remembered how lovely she could look when sincerity relaxed the hard lines around her mouth and eyes. 'It is like the *Arabian Nights*.'

"Turgut laughed and waved off the compliment with a large hand, but he was clearly pleased. 'That is my wife,' he said. 'She loves our old arts and crafts, and her family passed down to her many fine things. Perhaps there is even a little something from Sultan Mehmed's empire here.' He smiled at me. 'I do not make the coffee as well as she does — that is what she tells me — but I will give you my best effort.' He settled us on the low furniture, close together, and I thought with contentment about all those time-honored objects signifying comfort: cushion, divan, and — after all — ottoman.

"Turgut's best effort turned out to be lunch, which he brought in from a small kitchen across the hall, refusing our earnest offers of help. How he had rustled up a meal in such a short time eluded my imagination — it must have been waiting for him there. He brought in trays of sauces and salads, a bowl of melon, a stew of meat and vegetables, skewers of chicken, the ubiquitous cucumber-and-yogurt mixture, coffee, and an avalanche of sweets rolled in almonds and honey. We ate heartily, and Turgut urged food on us until we were groaning. 'Well,' he said, 'I cannot let my wife think I have starved you.' All this was followed by a glass of water with something white and sweet sitting on a plate next to it. 'Attar of roses,' Helen said, tasting it. 'Very nice. They have this in Romania, too.' She dropped a little of the white paste into her glass and drank it, and I followed suit. I wasn't sure what the water might do to my digestion later, but it was not the moment for such worries.

"When we were nearly bursting, we leaned back against the low divans — I now understood their use, recovery after a large meal — and Turgut looked at us with satisfaction. 'You are sure you have had enough?' Helen laughed and I moaned a little, but Turgut refilled our glasses and coffee cups anyway. 'Very good. Now, let us talk of the things we have not yet been able to discuss. First of all, I am astounded to think that you know Professor Rossi, too, but I do not yet understand your connection. He is your adviser, young man?' And he sat down on an ottoman, leaning toward us with an expectant air.

"I glanced at Helen and she nodded slightly. I wondered if the attar of roses had softened her suspicions. 'Well, Professor Bora, I'm afraid we have not been completely open with you up to this point,' I confessed. 'But, you see, we are on a peculiar mission and we have not known whom to trust.'

"'I see.' He smiled. 'Perhaps you are wiser than you know.'

"That gave me pause, but Helen nodded again, and I continued. 'Professor Rossi is of special interest to us, too, not only because he is my adviser but because of some information he communicated to us — to me — and because he has — well, he has disappeared.'

"Turgut's gaze was piercing. 'Disappeared, my friend?'

"'Yes.' Haltingly, I told him about my bond with Rossi, my work with him on my dissertation, and the strange book I'd found in my library carrel. When I began to describe the book, Turgut started up in his seat and struck his hands together but said nothing, only listening more intently. I went on to relate how I'd brought the book to Rossi, and the story he'd told me about finding a book of his own. Three books, I thought, pausing for breath. We knew of three of these strange books, now — a magic number. But exactly how were they related to one another, as they must be? I reported what Rossi had told me about his research in Istanbul — here Turgut shook his head as if baffled — and his discovery in the archive that the dragon image matched the outlines of the old maps.

"I told Turgut how Rossi had vanished, and about the grotesque shadow I had seen pass over his office window the evening he had disappeared, and how I'd begun the search for him on my own, at first only half believing his story. Here I paused again, this time to see what Helen would say, because I didn't want to reveal her story without her permission. She stirred and looked quietly at me from the depths of the divan, and then to my surprise she picked up the tale herself and related to Turgut everything she had already told me, speaking in her low, sometimes harsh voice — the tale of her birth, her personal vendetta against Rossi, the intensity of her research on Dracula's history, and her intention to search for his legend eventually in this very city. Turgut's eyebrows rose to the edge of his pomaded hair. Her words, her deep, clear articulation, the obvious magnificence of her mind, and perhaps also the flush in her cheeks above the pale blue collar all brought an answering hue of admiration to his face — or so I thought, and for the first time since we'd met Turgut, I felt a twinge of hostility toward him.

"When Helen had rounded out the story, we all sat in silence for a moment. The green sunlight filtering into that beautiful room seemed to deepen around us, and a sense of further unreality crept over me. At last Turgut spoke. 'Your experience is most remarkable, and I am grateful that you tell me it. And I am sorry to hear your family's sad story, Miss Rossi. I still wish I knew why Professor Rossi was compelled to write to me that he did not know about our archive here, which seems a lie, does it not? But it is terrible, the disappearance of such a fine scholar. Professor Rossi was punished for something — or he is being punished right now, as we sit here.'

"The languorous feeling cleared from my head in an instant, as if a cold breeze had swept it away. 'But what makes you so certain of this? And how on earth can we find him, if this is true?'

"'I am a rationalist, like you,' Turgut said quietly, 'but I believe by my instinct what you say Professor Rossi told you that evening. And we have proof of his words in what the old librarian of the archive told me — that a foreign researcher was frightened away there — and in my finding Professor Rossi's name in the registry. Not to

mention the appearance of a fiend with blood —'
He stopped. 'And now there is this dreadful aber-
ration, his name — the name of his article —
added somehow to the bibliography in the
archive. It confounds me, that addition! You have
done the right thing, my colleagues, to come to
Istanbul. If Professor Rossi is here, we will find
him. I have long wondered, myself, if Dracula's
tomb could be here in Istanbul. It seems to me
that if someone has placed Rossi's name very recently in that bibliography, then there is a good
chance Rossi himself is here. And you believe
that Rossi will be found at Dracula's place of burial. I will devote myself entirely to your service in
this matter. I feel — responsible to you in this.'

"'Now I have a question for you.' Helen narrowed her eyes at both of us. 'Professor Bora,
how did you come to be in our restaurant last
night? It seems to me too much of a coincidence
that you appeared when we had just arrived in
Istanbul, looking for the archive you have been
so much interested in all these years.'

"Turgut had risen, and now he took a small
brass box from a side table and opened it, offering us cigarettes. I refused, but Helen took one
and let Turgut light it for her. He lit one for himself, too, and sat down again, and they regarded

each other, so that for a moment I felt subtly excluded. The tobacco had a delicate scent and was obviously very fine; I wondered if this was the Turkish luxury so famous in the United States. Turgut exhaled gently and Helen kicked off her slippers and drew her legs up under her, as if used to lounging on Eastern cushions. This was a side of her I hadn't seen before, this easy grace under the spell of hospitality.

"At last Turgut spoke. 'How did I come to meet you in the restaurant? I have asked myself this question several times, because I do not have an answer to it, either. But I can tell you in all honesty, my friends, that I did not know who you were or what you were doing in Istanbul when I sat down near your table. In fact, I often go to that place because it is my favorite in the old quarter, and I take a walk there sometimes between my classes. That day I went in almost without thinking about it, and when I saw no one but two strangers there, I felt lonely and did not want to sit by myself in the corner. My wife says I am a hopeless case of friend making.'

"He smiled and tapped the ash from his cigarette into a copper plate, which he pushed toward Helen. 'But that is not such a bad habit, is it? In any case, when I saw your interest in my archive, I was surprised and moved, and now that I hear your more-than-remarkable story, I feel that somehow I am to be your assistance here in Istanbul. After all, why did *you* come to *my* favorite restaurant? Why did I go in there with my book for dinner? I see you are suspicious, madam, but I have no answer for you, except to say that the coincidence gives me hope. "There are more things in heaven and earth —"' He looked reflectively at both of us, and his face was open and sincere, and more than a little sad.

"Helen blew a cloud of Turkish smoke into the hazy sunlight. 'All right, then,' she said. 'We shall hope. And now, what shall we do with our hope? We have seen the originals of the maps, and we have seen the bibliography of the Order of the Dragon, which Paul wanted so much to look at. But where does that put us?'

"'Come with me,' Turgut said abruptly. He rose to his feet, and the last languor of the afternoon vanished. Helen stubbed out her cigarette and rose, too, her sleeve brushing my hand. I followed. 'Please come into my study for a moment.' Turgut opened a door among the folds of antique wool and silk and stood politely aside."

Chapter 31

I SAT VERY, very still on my seat in the train, staring at the newspaper of the man who sat opposite me. I felt I should move around a little, act natural, or I might actually draw his attention, but he was so perfectly still that I began to imagine I had not even heard him breathe, and to find it difficult to breathe myself. After a moment my worst fear was realized: he spoke without lowering the newspaper. His voice was exactly like his shoes and perfectly tailored pants; he spoke to me in English with an accent I couldn't place, although it had a flavor of French — or was I getting it mixed up with the headlines that danced on the outside of *Le Monde,* scrambling themselves under my agonized gaze? Terrible things were happening in Cambodia, in Algeria, in places I had never heard of, and my French had improved too much this year. But the man was speaking from behind the print, without moving his paper a millimeter. My skin tingled as I listened, because I couldn't believe what I was hearing. His voice was quiet, cultivated. It asked a single question: "Where is your father, my dear?"

I tore myself from my seat and jumped toward the door; I heard his newspaper fall behind me, but all my concentration was on the latch. It was not locked. I got it open in a moment of transcendent fear. I slipped out without turning around and ran in the direction Barley had taken to the dining car. There were other people dotted mercifully here and there in the compartments, their curtains open, their books and newspapers and picnic baskets balanced beside them, their faces turning curiously toward me as I sped past. I couldn't stop even to listen for footsteps behind me. I remembered suddenly that I'd left our valises in the compartment, on the overhead rack. Would he take those? Search them? My purse was on my arm; I had fallen asleep with it slipped over my wrist, as I always wore it in public.

Barley was in the dining car, at the far end, with his book open on a wide table. He had ordered tea and several other things, and it took him a moment to glance up from his little kingdom and register my presence. I must have looked wild, because he pulled me into the booth at once. "What is it?"

I put my face against his neck, struggling not to cry. "I woke up and there was a man in our compartment, reading the paper, and I couldn't see his face."

Barley put a hand in my hair. "A man with a newspaper? What are you so upset about?"

"He didn't let me see his face at all," I whispered, turning to look at the entrance to the dining car. There was no one there, no dark-suited figure entering to search it. "But he spoke to me behind the paper."

"Yes?" Barley seemed to have discovered that he liked my curls.

"He asked me where my father was."

"What?" Barley sat upright. "Are you sure?"

"Yes, in English." I sat up, too. "I ran, and I don't think he followed, but he's on the train. I had to leave our bags there."

Barley bit his lip; I half expected to see blood well up against his white skin. Then he signaled to the waiter, stood, conferred with him for a moment, and fished in his pockets for a large tip, which he left by his teacup. "Our next stop is Boulois," he said. "It's in sixteen minutes."

"What about our bags?"

"You've got your purse and I have my wallet." Barley suddenly stopped and stared at me. "The letters —"

"They're in my purse," I said quickly.

"Thank God. We might have to leave the rest of the luggage, but it doesn't matter." Barley took my hand, and we went through the end of the dining car — into the kitchen, to my surprise. The waiter hurried behind us, ushering us into a little niche near the refrigerators. Barley pointed; there was a door next to it. There we stood for sixteen minutes, I clutching my purse. It seemed only natural that we should stand holding each other tight, in that small space, like two refugees. Suddenly I remembered my father's gift and put my hand up to it: the crucifix hung against my throat in what I knew was plain sight. No wonder that newspaper had never been lowered.

At last the train began to slow, the brakes shuddered and squealed, and we stopped. The waiter pushed a lever and the door near us opened. He gave Barley a conspiratorial grin; he probably thought this was a comedy of the heart, my irate father chasing us through the train, something of that sort. "Step off the train but stay right next to it," Barley advised me in a low voice, and we inched together onto the pavement. There was a broad stucco station there, under silvery trees, and the air was warm and sweet. "Do you see him?"

I peered down the train until finally I saw

someone far along the line among the disembarking passengers — a tall, broad-shouldered
figure in black, with something wrong about his
entirety, a shadowy quality that made my stomach lurch. He wore a low, dark hat now, so that I
couldn't see his face. He held a dark briefcase
and a roll of white, perhaps the newspaper.
"That's him." I tried not to point, and Barley
drew me rapidly back on the steps.

"Stay out of sight. I'll watch where he goes.
He's looking up and down." Barley peered out
while I cowered resolutely back, my heart pounding. He kept a hard grip on my arm. "All right —
he's walking the other way. No, he's coming
back. He's looking in the windows. I think he's
going to get on the train again. God, he's a cool
one — checking his watch. He's stepping up. Now
he's getting off again and coming this way. Get
ready — we're going to go back in and run the
length of the train if we have to. Are you ready?"

At that moment, the fans whirred, the train
gave a heave, and Barley swore. "Jesus, he's getting back on. I think he just realized we didn't
really get off." Suddenly Barley jerked me off the
steps and onto the platform. Next to us the train
heaved again and started up. Several of the passengers had put the windows down and leaned

out to smoke or gaze around. Among them, several cars away, I saw a dark head turned in our direction, a man with his shoulders squared — he was full, I thought, of a cold fury. Then the train was picking up speed, pulling around a curve. I turned to Barley, and we glared at each other. Except for a few villagers sitting in the little rural station, we were alone in the middle of a French nowhere.

Chapter 32

"IF I HAD EXPECTED Turgut's study to be another Oriental dream, the haven of an Ottoman scholar, I had guessed wrong. The room into which he ushered us was much smaller than the large one we had just left, but high-ceilinged like it, and daylight from two windows showed the furnishings plainly. Two walls were lined top to bottom with books. Black velvet curtains hung to the floor beside each window, and a tapestry of horses and hounds riding to the chase gave a feeling of medieval splendor to the room. Piles of English reference books lay on a table in the center of the study; an immense set of Shakespeare took up its own curious cabinet near the desk.

"But the first impression I had of Turgut's study was not one of the preeminence of English literature; I had instead the immediate sense of a darker presence, an obsession that had gradually overcome the milder influence of the English works he wrote about. This presence leaped out at me suddenly as a face, a face that was everywhere, meeting my gaze with arrogance from a print behind the desk, from a stand on the table, from an odd piece of embroidery on one wall, from the cover of a portfolio, from a sketch near the window. It was the same face in every case, caught in different poses and different media, but always the same gaunt-cheeked, mustached, medieval visage.

"Turgut was watching me. 'Ah, you know who this is,' he said grimly. 'I have collected him in many forms, as you can see.' We stood side by side looking at the framed print on the wall behind the desk. It was a reproduction of a woodcut like the one I'd seen at home, but the face was fully frontal, so that the ink-dark eyes seemed to bore into ours.

"'Where did you find all these different images?' I asked.

"'Anywhere I could.' Turgut gestured toward the folio on the table. 'Sometimes I had them sketched from old books, and sometimes I found them in antique shops, or at auctions. It is extraordinary how many pictures of his face still float loose in our city, once you are watching out for them. I felt that if I could gather them all, I might be able to read the secret of my strange empty book in his eyes.' He sighed. 'But these woodcuts are so crude, so — black and white. I could not be satisfied with them, and finally I asked a friend of mine who is an artist to blend them all into one for me.'

"He led us to a niche by one window, where short curtains, also black velvet, were drawn closed over something. I felt a kind of dread even before he put his hand up to pull the cord, and when the cleverly made drapery parted under his grasp, my heart seemed to turn over. The velvet opened to reveal a life-size and radiantly lifelike painting in oils, the head and shoulders of a young, thick-necked, virile man. His hair was long; heavy black curls tumbled around his shoulders. The face was handsome and cruel in the extreme, with luminously pale skin, unnaturally bright green eyes, a long straight nose with flaring nostrils. His red lips were curved and sensual under a drooping dark mustache, but also tightly compressed as if to control a twitching of the chin. He had sharp cheekbones and heavy black eyebrows below a peaked cap of dark green velvet, with a brown-and-white feather threaded into the front. It was a face full of life but completely devoid of compassion, brimming with strength and alertness but without stability of character. The eyes were the most unnerving feature of the painting; they fixed us with a penetration almost alive in its intensity, and after a second I looked away for relief. Helen, standing next to me, moved a little closer to my shoulder, more as if to offer solidarity than to comfort herself.

"'My friend is a very fine artist,' Turgut said softly. 'You can see why I keep this painting behind a curtain. I do not like to look at it while I work.' He might have said instead that he didn't like the painting to look at him, I thought. 'This is an idea of how Vlad Dracula appeared around 1456, when he began his longest rule of Wallachia. He was twenty-five years old and well-educated by the standard of his culture, and he was a very good horseman. In the next twenty years, he killed perhaps fifteen thousand of his own people — sometimes for political reasons, often for the pleasure of watching them die.'

"Turgut closed the curtain, and I was glad to see those terrible bright eyes extinguished. 'I have some other curiosities here to show you,' he said, indicating a wooden cabinet on the wall. 'This is a seal from the Order of the Dragon, which I found in an antiques market down near the old city port. And this is a dagger, made of silver, that comes from the early Ottoman era of Istanbul. It is my belief that it was used to hunt vampires, because there are words on the sheath that indicate something like this. These chains and spikes' — he showed us another cabinet — 'were instruments of torture, I'm afraid, maybe from Wallachia itself. And here, my fellows, is a prize.' From the edge of his desk he took a beautifully inlaid wooden box and unhooked the clasp. Inside, among folds of rusty black satin, lay several sharp tools that looked like surgical instruments, as well as a tiny silver pistol and a silver knife.

"'What is that?' Helen reached a tentative hand toward the box, then drew it back.

"'It is an authentic vampire-hunting kit, one hundred years old,' Turgut reported proudly. 'I believe it to be from Bucharest. A friend of mine who is a collector of antiques found it for me several years ago. There were many of these — they were sold to travelers in Eastern Europe in the eighteenth and nineteenth centuries. It originally had garlic in it, here in this space, but I hang mine up.' He pointed, and I saw with a new chill the long braids of dried garlic on either side of the doorway, facing his desk. It occurred to me, as it had with Rossi only a week earlier, that perhaps Professor Bora was not merely thorough but also mad.

"Years later I understood better this first reaction in myself, the wariness I felt when I saw Turgut's study, which might have been a room in Dracula's castle, a medieval closet complete with instruments of torture. It is a fact that we historians are interested in what is partly a reflection of ourselves, perhaps a part of ourselves we would rather not examine except through the medium of scholarship; it is also true that as we steep ourselves in our interests, they become more and more a part of us. Visiting an American university — not mine — several years after this, I was introduced to one of the first of the great American historians of Nazi Germany. He lived in a comfortable house at the edge of the campus, where he collected not only books on his topic but also the official china of the Third Reich. His dogs, two enormous German shepherds, patrolled the front yard day and night. Over drinks with other faculty members in his living room, he told me in no uncertain terms how he despised Hitler's crimes and wanted to expose them in the greatest possible detail to the civilized world. I left the party early, walking carefully past those big dogs, unable to shake my revulsion.

"'Maybe you think this is too much,' Turgut said

a little apologetically, as if he had caught sight of my expression. He was still pointing at the garlic. 'It is just that I do not like to sit here surrounded by these evil thoughts of the past without pro-tections, you know? And now, let me show you what I have brought you in here to see.'

"He invited us to sit down on some rickety chairs upholstered in damask. The back of mine seemed to be inlaid with a piece of — was it bone? I didn't lean against it. Turgut pulled a heavy file from one of the bookcases. Out of it he took hand-drawn copies of the docu-ments we had been examining in the archives — sketches similar to Rossi's except that these had been made with greater care — and then drew out a letter, which he handed to me. It was typed on university letterhead and signed by Rossi — there could be no doubt of the signature, I thought; its coiling B and R were perfectly famil-iar to me. And Rossi had certainly been teaching in the United States by the time it had been penned. The few lines of the letter ran as Turgut had described; he, Rossi, knew nothing about Sultan Mehmed's archive. He was sorry to disap-point and hoped Professor Bora's work would prosper. It was truly a puzzling letter.

"Next Turgut brought out a small book bound

in ancient leather. It was difficult for me not to reach for it at once, but I waited in a fever of self-control while Turgut gently opened it and showed us first the blank leaves in front and back and then the woodcut in the center — that already familiar outline, the crowned dragon with its wickedly spread wings, its claws holding the banner with that one, threatening word. I opened my briefcase, which I had brought in with me, and took out my own book. Turgut put the two volumes side by side on the desk. Each of us compared his treasure with the other's evil gift, and we saw together that the two dragons were the same, his filling the pages to their edges, the image darker, mine more faded, but the same, the same. There was even a similar smudge near the tip of the dragon's tail, as if the woodcut had had a rough place there that had smeared the ink a little with each printing. Helen brooded over them, silently.

"'It is remarkable,' Turgut breathed at last. 'I never dreamed of such a day, when I would see a second book like this.'

"'And hear of a third,' I reminded him. 'This is the third book like this I've seen with my own eyes, remember. The woodcut in Rossi's was the same, too.'

"He nodded. 'And what, my fellows, can this mean?' But he was already spreading his copies of the maps next to our books and comparing with a large finger the outlines of dragons and river and mountains. 'Amazing,' he murmured. 'To think I never saw this myself. It is indeed similar. A dragon that is a map. But a map of what?' His eyes gleamed.

"'That is what Rossi was trying to figure out in the archives here,' I said with a sigh. 'If only he had taken more steps, later, to find out its significance.'

"'Perhaps he did.' Helen's voice was thoughtful, and I turned to her to ask what she meant. At that moment, the door between the weird braids of garlic swung further open and we both jumped. Instead of some horrible apparition, however, a small, smiling lady in a green dress stood in the doorway. It was Turgut's wife, and we all rose to meet her.

"'Good afternoon, my dear.' Turgut drew her quickly in. 'These are my friends, the professors from the United States, as I told you.'

"He made gallant introductions all around, and Mrs. Bora shook our hands with an affable smile. She was exactly half Turgut's size, with long-lashed green eyes, a delicately hooked nose, and a swirl of reddish curls. 'I am very sorry I do not meet you here before.' Her English was slowly and carefully pronounced. 'Probably my husband does not give you any food, no?'

"We protested that we had been beautifully fed, but she shook her head. 'Mr. Bora is never giving our guests the good dinner. I will — scold him!' She shook a tiny fist at her husband, who looked pleased.

"'I am dreadfully frightened of my wife,' he told us complacently. 'She is as fierce as an Amazon.' Helen, who towered over Mrs. Bora, smiled at both of them; they were indeed irresistible.

"'And now,' Mrs. Bora said, 'he bores you with his terrible collections. I am sorry.' Within minutes we were settled on the rich divans again, and Mrs. Bora was pouring coffee. I saw that she was quite beautiful, in a birdlike, delicate way, a woman of quiet manners, perhaps forty years old. Her English was limited, but she deployed it with graceful good humor, as if her husband frequently dragged home English-speaking visitors. Her dress was simple and elegant and her gestures exquisite. I imagined the nursery-school children she taught clustering around her — they must surely come up to her chin, I thought. I wondered if she and Turgut had children of their own; there were no photographs of children in the room, or any other evidence of them, and I did not like to ask.

"'Did my husband give you a good tour of our city?' Mrs. Bora was asking Helen.

"'Yes, some of it,' Helen answered. 'I'm afraid we have taken a lot of his time today.'

"'No — it is I who have taken much of yours.' Turgut sipped his coffee with obvious pleasure. 'But we still have a great deal of work to do. My dear' — to his wife — 'we are going to look for a missing professor, so I shall be busy for a few days.'

"'A missing professor?' Mrs. Bora smiled calmly at him. 'All right. But we must eat dinner first. I hope that you will eat dinner?' She turned to us.

"The thought of more food was impossible, and I was careful not to meet Helen's eye. Helen, however, seemed to find all this normal. 'Thank you, Mrs. Bora. You are very kind, but we should return to our hotel, I think, because we have an appointment there at five o'clock.'

"We did? This was perplexing, but I played along. 'That's right. Some other Americans are coming for a drink. But we hope to see you both again right away.'

"Turgut nodded. 'I shall immediately look through everything in my library here that might be of help to us. We must think about the possibility that Dracula's tomb is in Istanbul — whether these maps perhaps refer to an area of the city. I have a few old books about the city here, and friends who have fine collections about Istanbul. I will search everything for you tonight.'

"'Dracula.' Mrs. Bora shook her head. 'I like Shakespeare better than Dracula. A more healthier interest. Also' — she gave us a mischievous glance — 'Shakespeare pays our bills.'

"They saw us out with great ceremony, and Turgut made us promise to meet him at our pension the next morning at nine o'clock. He would bring new information, if he could, and we would visit the archive again to see if there were any developments there. In the meantime, he warned, we should exercise the greatest caution, watching everywhere for signs of pursuit or other danger. Turgut wanted to accompany us all the way back to our lodgings, but we assured him that we could take the ferry back by ourselves — it left in twenty minutes, he said. The Boras showed us out the front door of the building and stood together on the steps, hand in hand, calling out good-byes. I glanced back once or twice as we made our way along the street's tunnel of figs and lindens. 'That's a happy marriage, I think,' I commented to Helen, and was immediately sorry, because she gave her characteristic snort.

"'Come on, Yankee,' she said. 'We have some new business to attend to.'

"Normally I would have smiled at her epithet for me, but this time something made me turn and look at her with a deep shudder. There was another thought that belonged to this strange afternoon visit, one I had suppressed until the last possible moment. Looking at Helen as she turned to me with her level gaze, I was unavoidably struck by the similarity between her strong yet fine features and that luminous, appalling image behind Turgut's curtain."

Chapter 33

WHEN THE PERPIGNAN EXPRESS had disappeared completely beyond the silvery trees and village roofs, Barley shook himself. "Well, he's on that train, and we're not."

"Yes," I said, "and he knows exactly where we are."

"Not for very long." Barley marched over to the ticket window — where one old man seemed to be falling asleep on his feet — but soon came back looking chastened. "The next train to Perpignan isn't until tomorrow morning," he reported. "And there's no bus service to a major town until tomorrow afternoon. There's only one boarding room at a farm about half a kilometer outside the village. We can sleep there and walk back for the morning train."

Either I could get angry or I was going to cry. "Barley, I can't wait till tomorrow morning to take a train to Perpignan! We'll lose too much time."

"Well, there's nothing else," Barley told me irritably. "I asked about cabs, cars, farm trucks, donkey carts, hitchhiking — what else do you want me to do?"

We walked through the village in silence. It was late afternoon, a sleepy, warm day, and everyone we saw in doorways or gardens seemed half stupefied, as if he or she had fallen under a spell. The farmhouse, when we reached it, had a handpainted sign outside and a sale table with eggs, cheese, and wine. The woman who came out — wiping her hands on her proverbial apron — looked unsurprised to see us. When Barley introduced me as his sister, she smiled pleasantly and didn't ask questions, even though we had no luggage with us. Barley asked if she had room for two and she said, *"Oui, oui,"* on the inbreath, as if she were talking to herself. The farmyard was hard-packed dirt, with a few flowers, scratching hens, and a row of plastic buckets under the eaves, and the stone barns and house huddled around it in a friendly, haphazard way. We could have our dinner in the garden behind the house, the farmwife explained, and our room would be next to the garden, in the oldest part of the building.

We followed our hostess silently through the low-beamed farm kitchen and into a little wing where the cooking help might once have slept. The bedroom was fitted up with two little beds on opposite walls, I was relieved to see, and a great wooden clothes chest. The washroom next door had a painted toilet and sink. Everything was immaculately clean, the curtains starchy, the ancient needlework on one wall bleached with sunlight. I went into the bathroom and splashed my face with cold water while Barley paid the woman.

When I came out, Barley suggested a walk; it would be an hour before she could have our dinner ready. I didn't like to leave the sheltering arms of the farmyard at first, but outside the lane was cool under spreading trees, and we walked by the ruins of what must have been a very fine house. Barley pulled himself over the fence and I followed. The stones had tumbled down, making a map of the original walls, and one remaining dilapidated tower gave the place a look of past grandeur. There was some hay in the half-open barn, as if that building was still used for storage. A great beam had fallen in among the stalls.

Barley sat down in the ruins and looked at me. "Well, I see you're furious," he said provokingly. "You don't mind my saving you from immediate danger, but not if it's going to inconvenience you afterward."

His nastiness took my breath away for a moment. "How dare you," I said finally, and walked away among the stones. I heard Barley get up and follow me.

"Would you have wanted to stay on that train?" he asked in a slightly more civil voice.

"Of course not." I kept my face turned from him. "But you know as well as I do that my father may already be at Saint-Matthieu."

"But Dracula, or whoever he is, isn't there yet."

"He's a day ahead of us now," I retorted, looking across the fields. The village church showed above a distant row of poplars; it was all as serene as a painting, missing only the goats or cows.

"In the first place," Barley said (and I hated him for his didactic tone), "we don't know who that was on the train. Maybe it wasn't the villain himself. He has his minions, according to your father's letters, right?"

"Even worse," I said. "If that was one of his minions, then maybe he's at Saint-Matthieu already himself."

"Or," said Barley, but he stopped. I knew he had been about to say, "Or perhaps he's here, with us."

"We did indicate exactly where we were getting off," I said, to save him the trouble.

"Who's being nasty now?" Barley came up behind me and put one rather awkward arm around my shoulders, and I realized that he had at least been speaking as if he believed my father's story. The tears that had been struggling to stay under my lids spilled over and rolled down my face. "Come, now," said Barley. When I put my head on his shoulder, his shirt was warm from sun and perspiration. After a moment I pulled away, and we went back to our silent dinner in the farmhouse garden.

"Helen wouldn't say more during our journey back to the pension, so I contented myself with watching the passersby for any signs of hostility, looking around and behind us from time to time to see if we were being followed by anyone. By the time we reached our rooms again, my mind had reverted to our frustrating lack of information about how to search for Rossi. How was a list of books, some of them apparently not even extant, going to help us?

"'Come to my room,' Helen said unceremoniously as soon as we'd reached the pension. 'We need to talk in private.' Her lack of maidenly scruple would have amused me at another moment, but just now her face was so grimly determined that I could only wonder what she had in mind. Nothing could have been less seductive, anyway, than her expression at that moment. In her room, the bed was neatly made and her few belongings apparently stowed out of sight. She sat down on the window seat and gestured to a chair. 'Look,' she said, pulling off her gloves and taking off her hat, 'I've been thinking about something. It seems to me we have reached a real barrier to finding Rossi.'

"I nodded glumly. 'That's just what I've been puzzling over for the last half hour. But maybe Turgut will turn up some information for us among his friends.'

"She shook her head. 'It is a wild duck chase.'

"'Goose,' I said, but without enthusiasm.

"'Goose chase,' she amended. 'I have been thinking that we are neglecting a very important source of information.'

"I stared at her. 'What's that?'

"'My mother,' she said flatly. 'You were right when you asked me about her, while we were still in the United States. I have been thinking about her all day. She knew Professor Rossi long before you did, and I never truly asked her about him after she first told me he was my father. I don't know why not, except that it was clearly a painful subject for her. Also' — she sighed — 'my mother is a simple person. I did not think she could add to my knowledge of Rossi's work. Even when she told me last year that Rossi believed in Dracula's existence, I did not press her much — I know how superstitious she is. But now I wonder if she knows anything that might help us find him.'

"Hope had leaped up in me with her first words. 'But how can we talk with her? I thought you said she had no phone.'

"'She doesn't.'

"'Then — what?'

"Helen pressed her gloves together and slapped them smartly against her knee. 'We will have to go see her in person. She lives in a small town outside Budapest.'

"'What?' Now it was my turn to be irritable. 'Oh, very simple. We just hop a train with your Hungarian passport and my — oops — American passport, and drop by to chat with one of your relatives about Dracula.'

"Unexpectedly, Helen smiled. 'There is no reason to be so bad tempered, Paul,' she said. 'We have a proverb in Hungarian: "If a thing is impossible, it can be done."'

"I had to laugh. 'All right,' I said. 'What's your plan? I've noticed you always have one.'

"'Yes, I have.' She smoothed out her gloves. 'Actually, I am hoping my aunt will have a plan.'

"'Your aunt?'

"Helen glanced out the window, toward the mellowed stucco of the old houses across the street. It was nearly evening, and the Mediterranean light I had already come to love was deepening to gold on every surface of the city outside. 'My aunt has worked in the Hungarian Ministry of the Interior since 1948, and she is a rather important lady. I got my scholarships because of her. In my country, you do not accomplish anything without an aunt or an uncle. She is my mother's older sister, and she and her husband helped my mother flee from Romania to Hungary, where she — my aunt — was already living, just before I was born. We are very close, my aunt and I, and she will do whatever I ask her. Unlike my mother, she has a telephone, and I think I will call her.'

"'You mean, she could bring your mother to the phone somehow to talk with us?'

"Helen groaned. 'Oh, Lord, do you think that we can talk with them on the phone about anything private or controversial?'

"'I'm sorry,' I said.

"'No. We will go there in person. My aunt will arrange it. That way we can talk face-to-face with my mother. Besides' — something gentler crept into her voice — 'they will be so glad to see me. It is not very far from here, and I have not seen them for two years.'

"'Well,' I said, 'I'm willing to try almost anything for Rossi, although it's hard for me to imagine just waltzing into communist Hungary.'

"'Ah,' said Helen. 'Then it will be even harder for you to imagine waltzing, as you say, into communist Romania?'

"This time I was silent for a moment. 'I know,' I said at last. 'I've been thinking about it, too. If Dracula's tomb turns out not to be in Istanbul, where else could it be?'

"We sat for a minute, each of us lost in thought and impossibly far from the other, and then Helen stirred. 'I will see if the landlady can let us call from downstairs,' she said. 'My aunt will be home from work soon, and I would like to talk with her immediately.'

"'May I come with you?' I inquired. 'After all, this concerns me, too.'

"'Certainly.' Helen pulled on her gloves, and we went down to corner the landlady in her parlor. It took us ten minutes to explain our intentions, but the production of a few extra Turkish liras, with the promise of payment in full for the phone call, smoothed the way. Helen sat on a chair in the parlor and dialed through a maze of numbers. At last I saw her face brighten. 'It's ringing.' She smiled at me, her beautiful, frank smile. 'My aunt is going to hate this,' she said. Then her face changed again, to alertness. 'Éva?' she said. 'Elena!'

"Listening carefully, I realized that she must be speaking Hungarian; I knew at least that Romanian was a Romance language, so I thought I might have understood a few words. But what Helen was speaking sounded like the galloping of horses, a Finno-Ugric stampede that I could not arrest with my ear for even a second. I wondered if she ever spoke Romanian with her family, or if perhaps that part of their lives had died long before, under the pressure to assimilate. Her tones rose and fell, interrupted sometimes by a smile and sometimes by a small frown. Her aunt Éva, on the other end, seemed to have a great deal to say, and sometimes Helen listened deeply, then broke in with those strange syllabic hoofbeats again.

"Helen seemed to have forgotten my presence, but she suddenly raised her glance to me again and gave a wry little smile and a triumphant nod, as if the outcome of her conversation was favorable. She smiled into the receiver and hung up. Immediately our concierge was upon us, apparently worried about her phone bill, and I quickly counted out the agreed-upon amount, added a little, and deposited it in her outstretched hands. Helen was already on her way back to her room, beckoning to me to follow; I thought her secrecy unnecessary, but what did I know, after all?

"'Quick, Helen,' I groaned, settling into the armchair again. 'The suspense is killing me.'

"'It's good news,' she said calmly. 'I knew my aunt would try to help in the end.'

"'What on earth did you tell her?'

"She grinned. 'Well, there's only so much I could say on the telephone, and I had to be quite formal about it. But I told her I am in Istanbul on academic research with a colleague

445

and that we need five days in Budapest to conclude our research. I explained that you are an
American professor and that we are writing a
joint article.'

"'On what?' I asked with some apprehension.

"'On labor relations in Europe under the Ottoman occupation.'

"'Not bad. But I don't know a thing about that.'

"'It's all right.' Helen brushed some lint from
the knee of her neat black skirt. 'I'll tell you a little about it.'

"'You do take after your father.' Her casual erudition had reminded me suddenly of Rossi, and
the comment was out of my mouth before I'd
thought about it. I glanced quickly at her, afraid I
had somehow offended. It struck me that this
was the first time I'd found myself thinking of
her quite naturally as Rossi's daughter, as if at
some point unknown even to myself I'd accepted
the idea.

"Helen surprised me by looking sad. 'It is a
good argument for genetics over environment'
was all she said. 'Anyway, Éva sounded annoyed,
especially when I told her that you are an American. I knew she would be, because she always
thinks I am impulsive and that I take too many

risks. Of course, I do. And, of course, she needed to sound annoyed at first, to make it all right on the telephone.'

"'To make it all right?'

"'She has to think of her job and status. But she said she would fix something up for us, and I'm supposed to call her again tomorrow night. So that is that. She is very clever, my aunt, so I have no doubt she will find a way. We will get some round-trip tickets to Budapest from Istanbul, maybe the airplane, when we hear more.'

"I sighed inwardly, thinking of the probable expense and wondering how long my funds would hold out in this chase, but I said only, 'It seems to me she'll have to be a miracle worker to get me into Hungary and keep us out of trouble along the way.'

"Helen laughed. 'She *is* a miracle worker. That is why I am not at home working in the cultural center in my mother's village.'

"We went downstairs again and, as if by mutual consent, drifted out to the street. 'There's not much to do just now,' I mused. 'We've got to wait until tomorrow for results from Turgut and your aunt. I have to say that I find all this waiting difficult. What shall we do, in the meantime?'

"Helen thought a minute, standing in the deepening gold light of the street. She had her gloves and hat firmly on again, but the low rays of sunlight picked out a little red in her black hair. 'I would like to see more of this city,' she said finally. 'After all, I may never come here again. Shall we go back to Hagia Sophia? We could walk around that area a little before dinner.'

"'Yes, I'd like that too.' We did not speak again during our walk to the great building, but as we drew near it and I saw its domes and minarets filling the streetscape again, I felt our silence deepen, as if we were walking closer together. I wondered whether Helen felt it, too, and whether it was the spell of the enormous church reaching out to us in our smallness. I was still pondering what Turgut had told us the day before — his belief that Dracula had somehow left a curse of vampirism in the great city. 'Helen,' I said, although I was half loath to break the quiet between us. 'Don't you think he could have been buried here — here in Istanbul? That would explain Sultan Mehmed's anxiety about him after his death, wouldn't it?'

"'He? Ah, yes.' She nodded, as if approving my not speaking that name in the street. 'That is an interesting idea, but wouldn't Mehmed have known about it, and wouldn't Turgut have found some evidence of it? I cannot believe such a thing could have been hidden here for centuries.'

"'It's also hard to believe that Mehmed would have permitted one of his enemies to be buried in Istanbul, if he'd known about it.'

"She appeared to brood on this. We had almost reached the great entrance to Hagia Sophia.

"'Helen,' I said slowly.

"'Yes?' We stopped among the people, the tourists and the pilgrims flocking in through the vast gate. I moved close to her so that I could speak very quietly, almost in her ear.

"'If there's some chance that the tomb is here, it could mean Rossi is here, too.'

"She turned and looked into my face. Her eyes were lustrous, and there were fine lines of age and worry between her dark eyebrows. 'But of course, Paul.'

"'I read in the guidebook that Istanbul has underground ruins, too — catacombs, cisterns, that kind of thing — like Rome. We have at least a day before we leave — maybe we could talk with Turgut about it.'

"'That is not such a bad idea,' Helen said softly.

'The palace of the Byzantine emperors must have had an underground area.' She almost smiled, but her hand went up to the scarf at her neck, as if something troubled her there. 'In any case, whatever is left of the palace must be full of evil spirits — emperors who blinded their cousins and that kind of thing. Exactly the right company.'

"Because we were reading so closely the thoughts written on each other's faces, and contemplating together the strange, vast hunt they might lead to, I failed at first to look hard at the figure that seemed suddenly to be looking hard at me. Besides, it was no tall and menacing specter but rather a small, slight man, ordinary among those crowds, hovering about twenty feet away against the wall of the church.

"Then, in an instant of shock, I recognized the little scholar with the shaggy gray beard, crocheted white cap, and drab shirt and pants who had come into the archive that morning. But the next second brought a much greater shock. The man had made the mistake of gazing at me so intently that I could suddenly see him head-on through the crowd. Then he was gone, disappearing like a spirit among the cheerful tourists. I dashed forward, almost knocking Helen over, but it was no use. The man had vanished; he had seen me see him. His face, between the awkward beard and new cap, had been indisputably a face from my university at home. I'd last looked at it just before it was covered by a sheet. It was the face of the dead librarian."

Chapter 34

I HAVE SEVERAL photographs of my father from the period just before he left the United States to search for Rossi, although when I first saw those images during my childhood, I knew nothing about what they preceded. One of them, which I had framed a few years ago and which now hangs above my writing desk, is a black-and-white image from an era when black and white was being edged out by the color snapshot. It shows my father as I never knew him. He looks directly into the camera, his chin raised a little as if he's about to respond to something the photographer is saying. Who the photographer was I will never know; I forgot to ask my father if he remembered. It couldn't have been Helen, but perhaps it was some other friend, some fellow graduate student. In 1952 — only the date is recorded in my father's hand on the back of the photo — he had been a graduate student for a year and had already begun his research on the Dutch merchants.

In the photograph my father seems to be posing next to a university building, judging by the

Gothic stonework in the background. He has one foot jauntily up on a bench, his arm slung over it, hand dangling gracefully near his knee. He wears a white or light colored dress shirt and a tie of diagonal stripes, dark creased trousers, shiny shoes. He has the same build I remember from his later life — average height, average shoulders, a trimness that was pleasant but not remarkable and that he never lost in middle age. His deep-set eyes are gray in the photo but were dark blue in life. With those sunken eyes and bushy eyebrows, the prominent cheekbones, thick nose, and wide thick lips parted in a smile, he has a rather simian look — a look of animal intelligence. If the photograph were color, his slicked-down hair would be bronze in the sunlight; I know about that color only because he described it to me once. When I knew him, from as early as I could remember, his hair was white.

"That night, in Istanbul, I took the full measure of a sleepless night. For one thing, the horror of that moment when I first saw a dead face alive and tried to comprehend what I had seen — that moment alone would have kept me awake. For another thing, knowing that the dead librarian had seen me and then disappeared made me feel the terrible vulnerability of the papers in my briefcase. He knew that Helen and I possessed a copy of the map. Had he appeared in Istanbul because he was following us, or had he somehow figured out that the original of this map was here? Or, if he hadn't deciphered this on his own, was he privy to some source of knowledge I did not know about? He had looked at the documents in Sultan Mehmed's collection at least once. Had he seen the original maps there and copied them? I couldn't answer these riddles, and I certainly couldn't risk dozing, when I thought of the creature's lust for our copy of the map, the way he had leaped on Helen to strangle her for it in the library stacks at home. The fact that he had bitten Helen there, had perhaps acquired a taste for her, made me even more nervous.

"If all this had not been enough to keep me wide-eyed that night while the hours passed more and more quietly, there was the sleeping face not far from my own — but not so close, either. I had insisted that Helen sleep in my bed while I sat up in the shabby armchair. If my eyelids drooped once or twice, a glance at that strong, grave face sent a wave of anxiety through me, bracing as cold water. Helen had wanted to stay in her own room — what, after all, would the concierge think, if she found out about this arrangement? — but I had pressed her until she agreed, if irritably, to rest under my watchful eye. I had seen too many movies, or read too many novels, to doubt that a lady left alone for a few hours at night might be the fiend's next intended victim. Helen was tired enough to sleep, as I could see from the deepening shadows under her eyes, and I had the faintest sense that she was frightened, too. That whiff of fear from her scared me more than another woman's sobs of terror would have and sent a subtle caffeine through my veins. Perhaps, too, something in the languor and softness of her usually haughtily erect form, her diurnal broad-shouldered definiteness, kept my own eyes open. She lay on her side, one hand under my pillow, her curls darker than ever against its whiteness.

"I could not bring myself to read or write. Certainly I had no desire to open my briefcase, which in any case I had pushed under the bed where Helen slept. But the hours wore on, and there was no mysterious scratching in the corridor, no snuffling through the keyhole, no smoke pouring silently in under the door, no beating of wings at the window. Finally a little grayness pervaded the dim room, and Helen sighed as if sensing the coming day. Then a hand span of sunlight made its way through the shutters, and she stirred. I took my jacket, slid the briefcase out from under the bed as quietly as I could, and went tactfully away to wait for her in the entrance downstairs.

"It was not yet six o'clock, but a smell of strong coffee came from somewhere in the house, and to my surprise I found Turgut sitting on one of the embroidered chairs, a black portfolio across his lap. He looked amazingly fresh and wide-awake, and when I entered he jumped up to shake my hand. 'Good morning, my friend. Thank the gods I have found you immediately.'

"'I'm thankful to them, too, that you're here,' I responded, sinking into a chair near him. 'But what on earth brings you so early?'

"'Ah, I could not stay away when I have news for you.'

"'I have news for you, too,' I said grimly. 'You go first, Dr. Bora.'

"'Turgut,' he corrected me absently. 'Look here.' He began to undo the string on the portfolio. 'As I promised you, I went through my papers last night. I have made copies of the material in the archives, as you have seen, and I have also collected many different accounts of events in Istanbul during the period of Vlad's life and directly after his death.'

"He sighed. 'Some of these papers mention mysterious occurrences in the city, deaths, rumors of vampirism. I have also collected any information I could from books that might tell me about the Order of the Dragon in Wallachia. But nowhere last night could I find anything new. Then I called my friend Selim Aksoy. He is not at the university — he is a shopkeeper — but he is a very learned man. He knows more about books than anyone in Istanbul, and especially about all books that tell the history and legends of our city. He is a very gracious person, and he gave me much of the evening to look through his own library with me. I asked him to seek for me any trace of a burial of someone from Wallachia here in Istanbul in the late fifteenth century, or any clue that there might be a tomb here somehow connected with Wallachia, Transylvania, or the Order of the Dragon. I also showed him — not for the first time — my copies of the maps, and my dragon book, and I explained to him your theory that those images represent a location, the location of the Impaler's tomb.

"'Together we turned through many, many

pages about the history of Istanbul, and looked at old prints, and at the notebooks in which he copies so many things he finds in libraries and museums. He is most industrious, is Selim Aksoy. He has no wife, no family, no other interests. The story of Istanbul eats him up. We worked late into the night, because his personal library is so large that even he has never dived to the bottom of it and could not tell me what we might discover. At last we found a strange thing — a letter — reprinted in a volume of correspondence between the ministers of the sultan's court and many outposts of the Empire in the fifteenth and sixteenth centuries. Selim Aksoy told me that he bought this book from a bookseller in Ankara. It was printed in the nineteenth century, compiled by one of our own historians from Istanbul who was interested in all the records of that period. Selim told me he has never seen another copy of this book.'

"I waited patiently, sensing the importance of all this background, noting Turgut's thoroughness. For a literary scholar, he made a damned good historian.

"'No, Selim does not know this book from any other edition, but he believes the documents reproduced in it are not — how do you say? — forgeries, because he has seen one of these letters in the original, in the same collection we visited yesterday. He is also very adoring of that archive, you know, and I often meet him there.' He smiled. 'Well, in this book, when our eyes were almost closing with fatigue, and the dawn was about to arrive, we found a letter that may have some importance for your search. The collector who printed it believed it to be from the late fifteenth century. I have translated it for you here.'

"Turgut pulled a sheet of notebook paper from his portfolio. 'The earlier letter to which this letter refers is not in the book, alas. God knows it is probably not in existence anywhere, or my friend Selim would have found it long ago.'

"He cleared his throat and read aloud. '"To the most honored Rumeli Kadiasker —"' He paused. 'That was the chief military judge for the Balkans, you know.' I didn't know, but he nodded and went on. '"Honored One, I have now carried out the further investigation you requested. Some of the monks have been most cooperative for the sum we agreed upon, and I have examined the grave myself. What they reported to me originally is true. They have no further explanation to offer me, only repetitions of their terror. I recommend a new investigation of this matter in Istanbul. I have left two guards in Snagov to watch for any suspicious activity. Curiously, there have been no reports of the plague here. I remain yours in the name of Allah."'

"'And the signature?' I asked. My heart was beating hard; even after my sleepless night, I was wide-awake.

"'There is no signature. Selim thinks that perhaps it was torn off the original, either accidentally or to protect the privacy of the man who wrote the letter.'

"'Or perhaps it was unsigned to begin with, for secrecy,' I suggested. 'And there are no other letters in the book that refer to this matter?'

"'None. No previous letters, no subsequent letters. It is a fragment, but the Rumeli Kadiasker was very important, so this must have been a serious matter. We searched long and hard after this in my friend's other books and papers and found nothing that is relating to it. He told me he has never seen this word *Snagov* in any other accounts of the history of Istanbul that he can remember. He read these letters once a few years ago — it was my telling him where Dracula is supposed to have been buried by his followers that made him notice it while we were looking through the papers. So perhaps he has indeed seen it elsewhere and cannot remember.'

"'My God,' I said, thinking not of the subtle probabilities of Mr. Aksoy's having seen the word elsewhere but rather of the tantalizing nature of this link between Istanbul, all around us, and faraway Romania.

"'Yes.' Turgut smiled as cheerfully as if we'd been discussing a menu for breakfast. 'The public inspectors for the Balkans were very worried about something here in Istanbul, so worried that they sent someone to the grave of Dracula in Snagov.'

"'But, goddammit, what did they find?' I pounded my fist on the arm of my chair. 'What had the priests there reported? And why were they terrified?'

"'Exactly my perplexity,' Turgut assured me. 'If Vlad Dracula was resting peacefully there, why were they worried about him hundreds of kilometers away, in Istanbul? And if Vlad's tomb is indeed in Snagov and always was, why do the maps not match that region?'

"I could only respect the precision of his questions. 'There is another thing,' I said. 'Do you think there is indeed the possibility that Dracula was buried here in Istanbul? Would that explain Meh-med's worry about him after his death, and the presence of vampirism here from that era on?'

"Turgut clasped his hands in front of him and put one large finger on his chin. 'That is an important question. We will need help with it, and perhaps my friend Selim is the person to help us.'

"For a moment we sat looking silently at each other in the dim hall of the pension, with the smell of coffee drifting across us, new friends united by an old cause. Then Turgut roused himself. 'Clearly we must search more, further. Selim says he will lead us to the archive as soon as you can be ready. He knows sources there from fifteenth-century Istanbul that I have not much looked at myself because they lie far afield of my own interests in Dracula. We shall look at them together. No doubt Mr. Erozan will be happy to bring out all these materials for us before the public hours if I call him. He lives close to the archive and can open it for us before Selim must go to work himself. But where is Miss Rossi? Has she risen from her chambers yet?'

"This speech prompted a confused rush of thought in my brain, so that I didn't know which problem to address first. The mention of Turgut's librarian friend reminded me suddenly again of my librarian enemy, whom I had nearly forgotten in my excitement about the letter. Now I faced the peculiar task of straining Turgut's credulity by reporting the visitation of a dead man, although surely his belief in historical vampires might be extended to contemporary ones. But his question about Helen reminded me that I had left her alone for an unpardonably long time. I'd wanted to give her privacy as she awoke, and had fully expected her to follow me downstairs as soon as possible. Why hadn't she reappeared by now? Turgut was still talking. 'So Selim — he never sleeps, you know — went for his morning coffee, because he did not wish to surprise you right away — ah, here he is!'

"The bell at the pension door rang and a slender man stepped in, pulling the door shut behind him. I think I had expected an august presence, an aging man in a business suit, but Selim Aksoy was young and slight, dressed in loose-fitting and rather shabby dark trousers and a white shirt. He hurried toward us with an eager, intense look on his face that was not quite a smile. It wasn't until I was shaking his bony hand that I recognized the green eyes and long thin nose. I had seen his face before, and up close. It took me another second to place him, until I had the sudden memory of a slender hand passing me a volume of Shakespeare. He was the bookseller from the little shop in the bazaar.

"'But we've already met!' I exclaimed, and he was exclaiming something similar at the same moment, in what I took to be an amalgamation of Turkish and English. Turgut looked from one to the other of us, clearly perplexed, and when I explained, he laughed, then shook his head as if in wonder. 'Coincidences' was all he said.

"'Are you ready to go?' Mr. Aksoy waved aside Turgut's offer of a seat in the parlor.

"'Not quite,' I said. 'If you don't mind, I will see where Miss Rossi is and when she can join us.'

"Turgut nodded a little too guilelessly.

"I ran into Helen on the stairs — literally, for I suddenly found myself taking the steps three at a time. She grabbed the railing to keep herself from toppling down the staircase. 'Ouch!' she said crossly. 'What in the name of heaven are you doing?' She was rubbing her elbow, and I was trying not to keep feeling the brush of her black suit and firm shoulder against my arm.

"'Looking for you,' I said. 'I'm sorry — are you

hurt? I just got a little worried because I'd left you alone up there so long.'

"'I'm fine,' she told me more mildly. 'I've had some ideas. How long before Professor Bora arrives?'

"'He's here already,' I reported, 'and he brought a friend.'

"Helen recognized the young bookseller, too, and they talked, haltingly, while Turgut dialed up Mr. Erozan and shouted into the receiver. 'There has been a rainstorm,' he explained when he returned to us. 'The lines get a little furry in this part of town when it rains. My friend can meet us at once at the archive. He sounded sick, actually, maybe with a cold, but he said he'd come right away. Do you want coffee, madam? And I will buy you some sesame rolls on the way.' He kissed Helen's hand, to my displeasure, and we all hurried out.

"I was hoping to keep Turgut back as we walked so that I could tell him privately about the appearance of the vicious librarian from home; I didn't think I could explain this in front of a stranger, particularly one Turgut had described as having little real sympathy for vampire hunts. Turgut was deep in conversation with Helen before we'd walked a block, however, and I had the double misery of watching her bestow her rare smile on him and of knowing I was keeping back information I ought to give him at once. Mr. Aksoy walked next to me, casting a glance at me now and then, but for the most part he seemed so lost in his own thoughts that I didn't feel I should interrupt him with observations on the beauty of the morning streets.

"We found the outer door to the library unlocked — Turgut said with a smile that he'd known his friend would be prompt — and went quietly in, Turgut ushering Helen gallantly before him. The little entrance hall, with its fine mosaics and the registration book lying open and ready for the day's visitors, was deserted. Turgut held the inner door for Helen, and she had gone well into the hushed, dim hall of the library before I heard her intake of breath and saw her stop so suddenly that our friend almost tripped behind her. Something made the hair on the back of my neck rise even before I could tell what was happening, and then something quite different made me push rudely past the professor to Helen's side.

"The librarian waiting for us stood motionless in the middle of the room, his face turned, as if eagerly, toward our arrival. He was not, however, the friendly figure we'd expected, nor was he already bringing out the box we'd hoped to examine again, or some pile of dusty manuscripts on Istanbul's history. His face was pale, as if drained of life — exactly as if drained of life. This was not Turgut's librarian friend but ours, alert and bright-eyed, his lips unnaturally red and his hungry gaze burning in our direction. At the moment his eyes lit on me, my hand gave a throb where he had bent it back so hard in the library stacks. He was famished for something. Even if I'd had the tranquillity of mind in which to conjecture about that hunger — whether it was a thirst for knowledge or for something else — I would not have had time to form the thought. Before I could so much as step between Helen and the ghoulish figure, she pulled a pistol from her jacket pocket and shot him."

Chapter 35

"LATER, I KNEW Helen in a great range of situations, including those we call ordinary life, and she never stopped surprising me. Often what astonished me in her were the quick associations her mind made between one fact and another, associations that usually resulted in an insight I would have been slow to reach myself. She dazzled me, too, with the wonderful breadth of her learning. Helen was full of these surprises, and I grew to consider them my daily fare, a pleasant addiction I developed to her ability to catch me off guard. But she never startled me more than at that moment in Istanbul, when she suddenly shot the librarian.

"I had no time for astonishment, however, because he stumbled sideways and hurled a book toward us, just missing my head. It hit a table somewhere to my left, and I heard it fall to the floor. Helen fired again, stepping forward and aiming with a steadiness that took my breath away. Then the oddness of the creature's reaction struck me. I'd never seen anyone shot before except in the movies, but there, alas, I had seen a thousand Indians die at gunpoint by the time I was eleven, and later every sort of crook, bank robber, and villain, including hosts of Nazis created expressly for shooting by an enthusiastic wartime Hollywood. The strange thing about this shooting, this real one, was that although a dark stain appeared on the librarian's clothes somewhere below his sternum, he did not clutch the spot with an agonized hand. The second shot grazed his shoulder; he was already running, and then he bolted into the stacks at the rear of the hall.

"'A door!' Turgut shouted behind me. 'There is a door there!' And we all ran after him, tripping on chairs and darting among the tables. Selim Aksoy, slight and fleet as an antelope, reached the shelves first and disappeared among them. We heard a scuffle and a crash, then indeed the slamming of a door, and found Mr. Aksoy stumbling up out of a drift of fragile Ottoman manuscripts with a purple lump on the side of his face. Turgut ran for the door and I ran after, but it was shut tightly. When we got it open, we discovered only an alley, deserted apart from a pile of wooden boxes. We searched the labyrinthine neighborhood at a trot, but there was no sign of the creature or his flight. Turgut collared a few pedestrians, but no one had seen our man.

"Reluctantly, we returned to the archive through the back door and found Helen holding her handkerchief to Mr. Aksoy's cheekbone. The gun was nowhere in sight, and the manuscripts were neatly stacked on the shelf again. She looked up when we came in. 'He fainted for a minute,' she said softly, 'but he is all right now.'

"Turgut knelt by his friend. 'My dear Selim, what a bump you have.'

"Selim Aksoy smiled wanly. 'I am in good care,' he said.

"'I can see that,' Turgut agreed. 'Madam, I congratulate you for trying. But it is useless to attempt to kill a dead man.'

"'How did you know?' I gasped.

"'Oh, I know,' he said grimly. 'I know the look of that face. It is the expression of the undead. There is no other face like that. I have seen it before.'

"'It was a silver bullet, of course.' Helen held the handkerchief more firmly on Mr. Aksoy's cheek and eased his head back against her shoulder. 'But, as you saw, he moved, and I missed his heart. I know I took a great risk' — she looked deeply at me for a moment, but I couldn't read her thoughts — 'but you could see for your-selves that I was right in my calculation. A mor-tal man would have been seriously wounded by such shots.' She sighed and adjusted the hand-kerchief.

"I looked from one to the other in bewilder-ment. 'Have you been carrying around that gun all the time?' I asked Helen.

"'Oh, yes.' She pulled Aksoy's arm over her shoulder. 'Here, help me get him up.' Together we lifted him — he was light as a child — and stead-ied him on his feet. He smiled and nodded, shrug-ging off our assistance. 'Yes, I always carry my pistol when I feel any sort of — uneasiness. And it is not so difficult to acquire a silver bullet or two.'

"'That is true.' Turgut nodded.

"'But where did you learn to shoot like that?' I was still stunned by that moment when Helen had drawn and aimed so quickly.

"Helen laughed. 'In my country, our education is deep as well as narrow,' she said. 'I received an award for my shooting in our youth brigade when I was sixteen. I am glad to find I have not forgotten how.'

"Suddenly Turgut gave a cry and struck his forehead. 'My friend!' We all stared. 'My friend — Erozan! I am forgetting him.'

"It took us only a second to grasp his meaning. Selim Aksoy, who seemed recovered now, was the first to hurry into the stacks where he'd received his injury, and the rest of us scattered quickly around the long room, searching under tables and behind chairs. For a few minutes the hunt was fruitless. Then we heard Selim calling us, and we all rushed to his side. He was kneeling in the stacks, at the foot of a high shelf laden with all kinds of boxes, bags, and rolled-up scrolls. The box that housed the papers of the Order of the Dragon lay on the floor beside him, its ornate lid open and some of its contents scattered nearby.

"Among these relics, Mr. Erozan was stretched out on his back, white and still, his head lolling to one side. Turgut knelt and put his ear to the man's chest. 'Thank God,' he said after a moment. 'He is breathing.' Then, examining him more closely, he pointed to his friend's neck. Deep in the loose, pale flesh just above the shirt collar, there was a ragged wound. Helen knelt beside Turgut. We were all silent for a moment. Even after Rossi's description of the bureaucrat who had confronted him many years before, even after Helen's injury in the library at home, I found it hard to believe what I was seeing. The man's face was terribly pale, almost gray, and his breathing came in shallow, short gasps, barely audible until you listened carefully.

"'He has been polluted,' Helen said quietly. 'And I think he has lost quite a bit of blood.'

"'A curse on this day!' Turgut's face was anguished, and he pressed his friend's hand in his two big ones.

"Helen was the first to rally. 'Let us think sensibly. This is perhaps only the first time he has been attacked.' She turned to Turgut. 'You didn't see any sign of this in him when we were here yesterday?'

"He shook his head. 'He was quite normal.'

"'Well, then.' She reached into her jacket pocket, and I recoiled for an instant, thinking she was about to pull out the pistol again. Instead she drew forth a head of garlic and placed it on the librarian's chest. Turgut smiled in spite of the grimness of the whole scene and drew a head of garlic from his own pocket, placing it with hers. I couldn't imagine where she'd gotten it — perhaps on our stroll through the souk, when I'd been absorbed in other sights? 'I see great minds think the same,' Helen told him. Then she took out a paper packet and unwrapped it, revealing a tiny silver crucifix. I recognized it as the one she'd purchased at the Catholic church near our university, the one she had used to intimidate the evil librarian when he'd attacked her in the history section of the library stacks.

"This time Turgut stopped her with a gentle hand. 'No, no,' he said. 'We have our own superstitions here.' From somewhere inside his jacket he took a string of wooden beads, such as I'd seen in the hands of men on the streets of Istanbul. This one ended in a carved medallion with Arabic lettering on its face. He touched the medallion gently to Mr. Erozan's lips, and the librarian's face gave a grimace, as of involuntary disgust, twitching and curling. It was an awful sight, but a momentary one, and then the man's eyes opened and he frowned. Turgut bent over him, speaking softly in Turkish and touching his forehead, then giving the wounded man a sip of something from a little flask he conjured out of his jacket.

"After a minute, Mr. Erozan sat up and looked around, groping at his neck as if it hurt. When his fingers found the little wound with its trickle of drying blood, he buried his face in his hands, sobbing, a heartrending sound.

"Turgut put an arm around his shoulders, and

Helen placed a hand on the librarian's arm. I found myself reflecting that this was the second time in an hour that I had seen her tending with gentle touch to an afflicted being. Turgut began to question the man in Turkish, and after a few minutes he sat back on his heels and looked at the rest of us. 'Mr. Erozan says the stranger came to his apartment very early this morning, while it was still dark, and threatened to kill him unless he opened the library for him. The vampire was with him when I called him this morning, but he dared not tell me about his presence. When the strange man heard who had called, he said they must go at once to the archive. Mr. Erozan was afraid to disobey, and when they arrived here the man made him open the box. As soon as it sprang open, the devil leaped on him, held him on the ground — my friend says he was incredibly strong — and put his teeth in Mr. Erozan's neck. That is all he remembers.' Turgut shook his head sadly. Mr. Erozan suddenly grasped Turgut's arm and seemed to be imploring something of him in a flood of Turkish.

"For a moment Turgut was silent, and then he took his friend's hands in his, pressed the prayer beads into them, and gave him a quiet answer.

'He told me that he understands he can be bitten only twice more by this devil before becoming one himself. He asks me if this thing should come to pass to kill him with my own hands.' Turgut turned away, and I thought I saw a glistening of tears in his eyes.

"'It will not come to that.' Helen's face was hard. 'We are going to find the source of this plague.' I didn't know whether she meant the evil librarian or Dracula himself, but when I saw the set of her jaw I could almost believe in our eventual success in vanquishing both. I had noted that look on her face once before, and the sight of it took me back to the table of the diner at home, where we'd first talked about her parentage. Then she had been vowing to find her disloyal father and unmask him to the academic world. Was I imagining it, I wondered, or had her mission shifted at some moment that she herself hadn't noticed?

"Selim Aksoy had been hovering behind us, and now he spoke to Turgut again. Turgut nodded. 'Mr. Aksoy has reminded me of the work we have come here to do, and he is right. Other researchers will begin to arrive soon, and we must either lock the archive or open it to the public.

He offers to desert his shop today and serve as librarian here. But first we must clean up these documents and see what damage has been done to them, and above all we must find a safe place for my friend to rest. Also, Mr. Aksoy would like to show us something in the archives before other people are present.'

"I began at once to gather up the scattered documents, and my worst fears were immediately confirmed. 'The original maps are gone,' I reported gloomily. We searched the stacks, but the maps of that strange region that looked like a long-tailed dragon had vanished. We could only conclude that the vampire had hidden them on his person even before we'd arrived. It was a dreary thought. We had copies, of course, in both Rossi's hand and Turgut's, but the originals represented to me a key to Rossi's whereabouts, a closer link than any other I'd handled so far.

"In addition to the discouragement of losing this treasure, there came to me the thought that the evil librarian might unlock its secrets before we did. If Rossi was at Dracula's tomb, wherever it lay, the evil librarian now had a fair chance of beating us there. I felt more than ever the twin urgency and impossibility of finding my beloved adviser. At least — it came to me again, strangely — Helen was now solidly on my side.

"Turgut and Selim had been conferring beside the sick man, and now they turned to ask him a question, it seemed, for he tried to raise himself and pointed feebly to the back of the stacks. Selim vanished, returning after a few minutes with a small book. It was bound in red leather, rather worn, with a gold inscription in Arabic on the front. He set it on a nearby table and searched through it for some time before beckoning to Turgut, who was folding his jacket to make a pillow for his friend's head. The man seemed a little more comfortable now. It was on the tip of my tongue to suggest we call an ambulance, but I felt Turgut must know what he was doing. He had risen to join Selim, and they conferred earnestly for a few minutes while Helen and I avoided each other's eyes, both of us hoping for some discovery, and both fearing further disappointment. Finally, Turgut called us over.

"'This is what Selim Aksoy wished to show us here this morning,' he said gravely. 'I do not know, in truth, whether it has any bearing on our search. However, I will read it to you. This is a volume compiled in the early nineteenth century by some editors whose names I have not seen before, historians of Istanbul. They collected here all the accounts they could find of life in Istanbul in the first years of our city — that is, beginning in 1453, when Sultan Mehmed took the city for his own and proclaimed it the capital of his empire.'

"He pointed to a page of beautiful Arabic, and I thought for the hundredth time how terrible it was that human languages and even alphabets were separated from one another by this frustrating Babel of differences, so that when I glanced at a page of Ottoman printing, my comprehension was immediately caught in a bramble of symbols as impenetrable to me as a hedge of magic briars. 'This is a passage that Mr. Aksoy remembered from one of his researches here. The author is unknown, and it is an account of some events in the year 1477 — yes, my friends, the year after Vlad Dracula was killed in battle in Wallachia. Here it tells how in that year there were cases of the plague in Istanbul, a plague that caused the imams to bury some of the corpses with stakes through their hearts. Then it tells about the entrance into the city of a party of monks from the Carpathians — this is what made Mr. Aksoy remember the volume — in a wagon pulled by mules. The monks begged for asylum in a monastery in Istanbul and resided there for nine days and nine nights. That is the whole account, and the connections within it are very unclear — it says nothing more about the monks or what became of them. It was this word *Carpathian* that my friend Selim wished us to know about here.'

"Selim Aksoy nodded emphatically, but I could not help sighing. The passage had a weird resonance; it gave me a feeling of unquiet without shedding any light on our problems. The year 1477 — that was indeed strange, but it could have been a coincidence. Curiosity prompted me to ask Turgut a question, however. 'If the city was already under the rule of the Ottomans, why was there a monastery for the monks to be lodged in?'

"'A good question, my friend,' Turgut observed soberly. 'But I must tell you there were a number of churches and monasteries in Istanbul from the very beginning of the Ottoman rule. The sultan was most gracious in his permissions to them.'

"Helen shook her head. 'After he had allowed his army to destroy most of the churches in the city, or had taken them for mosques.'

"'It is true that when Sultan Mehmed conquered the city, he allowed his troops to pillage it for three days,' Turgut admitted. 'But he would not have done this if the city had surrendered to him instead of resisting — in fact, he offered them a completely peaceful settlement. It is also written that when he entered Constantinople and saw the damage his soldiers had done — the buildings they had defaced, the churches they had defiled, and the citizens they had slain — he wept for the beautiful city. From this time he allowed a number of churches to function and gave many advantages to the Byzantine inhabitants.'

"'He also enslaved more than fifty thousand of them,' Helen put in dryly. 'Don't forget about that.'

"Turgut gave her an admiring smile. 'Madam, you are too much for me. But I meant only to demonstrate that our sultans were not monsters. Once they had conquered an area, they were often rather lenient, for those times. It was just the conquering that was not so delightfully done.' He pointed to the far wall of the archive. 'There is His Gloriousness Mehmed himself, if you would like to greet him.' I went to look, although Helen stood stubbornly where she was. The framed reproduction — apparently a cheap copy of a watercolor — showed a solid, seated man in a white-and-red turban. He was fair skinned and delicately bearded, with calligraphic eyebrows and hazel eyes. He held a single rose up to his great hooked nose, sniffing it and gazing off into the distance. He looked to me more like a Sufi mystic than a ruthless conqueror.

"'It's a rather surprising image,' I said.

"'Yes. He was a devoted patron of the arts and architecture, and he built many lovely buildings here.' Turgut tapped his chin with a large finger. 'Well, my friends, what do you think of this account Selim Aksoy has discovered?'

"'It's interesting,' I said politely, 'but I can't see how it helps us find the tomb.'

"'I can't see that either,' Turgut admitted. 'However, I note a certain similarity here between this passage and the fragment of a letter I read to you this morning. The disturbances in the tomb at Snagov, whatever they were, occurred in the same year — 1477. We know already that that is the year after Vlad Dracula died, and that it was a group of monks who were so concerned about something at Snagov. Couldn't these have been the same monks, or some group connected with Snagov?'

"'Possibly,' I admitted, 'but that is conjecture. This account says only that the monks were from the Carpathians. The Carpathians must have been full of monasteries in that era. How could we be sure they were from the monastery at Snagov? Helen, what do you think?'

"I must have caught her by surprise, because I found she was looking directly at me with a kind of wistfulness I had never seen in her face before. The impression vanished immediately, however, and I thought I might have imagined it, or that perhaps she was remembering her mother and our imminent trip to Hungary. Wherever her thoughts had been, she rallied at once. 'Yes, there were many monasteries in the Carpathians. Paul is right — we cannot connect the two groups without more information.'

"I thought Turgut looked disappointed, and he began to say something, but just then we were interrupted by a wheezing gasp. It was Mr. Erozan, still resting on Turgut's jacket on the floor. 'He's fainted!' Turgut cried. 'Here we are chatting like magpies — ' He held the garlic to his friend's nose again, and the man spluttered and revived a little. 'Quick, we must take him home. Professor, madam, help me. We will call a taxicab and carry him to my apartment. My wife and I can care for him there. Selim will stay here with the archive — it must open very soon.' He gave Aksoy a few rapid orders in Turkish.

"Then Turgut and I lifted the pale, weak man from the floor, propped him between us, and carried him carefully through the back door. Helen followed with Turgut's jacket, we passed through the alley, and a moment later we were out in the morning sunlight. When it struck Mr. Erozan's face, he cringed, shrank against my shoulder, and held one hand up to his eyes as if warding off a blow."

Chapter 36

THE NIGHT I spent in that farmhouse in Boulois, with Barley on the other side of the room, was one of the most wakeful I had ever known. We settled down at nine or so, since there wasn't much to do there except listen to the chickens and watch the light fade over the sagging barns. To my amazement, there was no electricity on the farm — "Didn't you notice the lack of wires?" asked Barley — and the farmwife left us a lantern and two candles before wishing us a good night. By their light the shadows of the polished old furniture grew tall and loomed over us, and the needlework on the wall fluttered softly.

After a few yawns, Barley lay down in his clothes on one bed and promptly went to sleep. I didn't dare follow suit, but I was also afraid to leave the candles burning all night. Finally I blew them out, leaving only the lantern lit, which deepened the shadows all around me terribly and made the dark outside our one window press in from the farmyard. Vines rustled against the pane, trees seemed to lean closer, and a soft noise that could have been owls or doves came eerily to me as I lay curled in my bed. Barley seemed very far away; earlier, I had been glad for those thoroughly separate beds, so that there could be no awkwardness about sleeping arrangements, but now I wished we'd been forced to sleep back-to-back.

After I'd lain there long enough to feel frozen in one position, I saw a mellow light gradually creep onto the floorboards from the window. The moon was rising, and with it I felt a certain lightening of my terror, as if an old friend had come to keep me company. I tried not to think of my father; on any other trip it might have been him lying in that other bed in his dignified pajamas, his book abandoned beside him. He would have been the first to notice this old farmhouse, would have known that the central part of it reached back to the days of Aquitaine, would have bought three bottles of wine from the pleasant hostess and discussed her vineyard with her.

Lying there, I wondered in spite of myself what I would do if my father did not survive his trip to Saint-Matthieu. I couldn't possibly return to Amsterdam, I thought, to rattle around in our house alone with Mrs. Clay; that would only make my heartbreak worse. In the European system, I had two years still until I would go to university somewhere. But who would take me in before that? Barley would return to his old life; I couldn't expect him to worry further about me. Master James crossed my mind, with his deep, sad smile and the kind lines around his eyes. Then I thought of Giulia and Massimo, in their Umbrian villa. I saw Massimo pouring wine for me — "And what are you studying, lovely daughter?" — and Giulia saying I must have the best room. They had no children; they loved my father. If my world came undone, I would go to them.

I blew out the lantern, braver now, and tiptoed over to peer outside. I could just see the moon, halved in a sky full of torn clouds. Across it sailed a shape I knew too well — no, it was just for a moment, and it was only a cloud, wasn't it? The spread wings, the curling tail? It dissolved at once, but I went to Barley's bed instead, and lay shivering for hours against his oblivious back.

"The business of transporting Mr. Erozan and settling him in Turgut's Oriental parlor — where he lay pale but composed on one of the long divans — took much of the morning. We were still there when Mrs. Bora returned at noon from her school. She came in briskly, carrying a bag of produce in each little gloved hand. She was wearing a yellow dress and flowered hat today, so that she looked like a miniature daffodil. Her smile was fresh and sweet, too, even when she saw us all in her living room standing around a prostrate man. Nothing her husband did seemed to surprise her, I thought; perhaps that was one of the keys to a successful union.

"Turgut explained the situation to her in Turkish, and her cheerful expression was replaced first by obvious skepticism and then by a blossoming horror when he gently showed her the wound in her newest guest's throat. She gave Helen and me a look of mute dismay, as if this was for her the initial wave of an evil knowledge. Then she took the librarian's hand, which I knew from a moment before was not only white but cold. She held it briefly, wiped her eyes, and went quickly across to the kitchen, where we heard the distant rattle of her pots and pans. Whatever else happened, the afflicted man would have a good meal. Turgut prevailed upon us to stay for it, and Helen, to my surprise, followed Mrs. Bora to help.

"When we had made sure Mr. Erozan was resting comfortably, Turgut took me into his eerie study for a few minutes. To my relief, the curtains over the portrait were firmly closed. We sat there a while discussing the situation. 'Do you think it's safe for you and your wife to house this man here?' I couldn't help asking it.

"'I will arrange every precaution. If he is better in a day or two, I will find a place for him to stay, with someone to watch him.' Turgut had drawn up a chair for me and settled himself behind his desk. It was almost, I thought, like being with Rossi again in his university office, except that Rossi's office was so determinedly cheerful, with its burgeoning plants and simmering coffee, and this one was so eccentrically somber. 'I do not expect any further attack here, but if there is one, our American friend will face a formidable defense.' Looking at his solid bulk behind the desk, I could easily believe him.

"'I'm sorry,' I said. 'We seem to have brought you a lot of trouble, Professor, right down to importing this menace to your door.' I outlined for him briefly our encounters with the corrupted librarian, including my sighting of him in front of the Hagia Sophia the night before.

"'Extraordinary,' Turgut said. His eyes were alight with a grim interest, and he drummed his fingertips on the top of his desk.

"'I have a question for you, too,' I confessed. 'You said in the archive this morning that you'd seen a face like his before. What did you mean by that?'

"'Ah.' My erudite friend folded his hands on his desk. 'Yes, I will tell you about this. It has been many years since, but I remember it vividly. In fact, it happened a few days after I received the letter from Professor Rossi explaining to me that he knew nothing about the archive here. I had been at the collection in the late afternoon, after my classes — this was when it was housed in the old library buildings, before it was moved to its present location. I remember I was doing some research for an article on a lost work of Shakespeare, *The King of Tashkani,* which some believe was set in a fictional version of Istanbul. Perhaps you have heard of it?'

"I shook my head.

"'It is quoted in the work of several English historians. From them we know that in the original play, an evil ghost called Dracole appears to the monarch of a beautiful old city that he — the monarch — has taken by force. The ghost says he was once the monarch's enemy but that he now comes to congratulate him on his bloodthirstiness. Then he urges the monarch to drink deeply of the blood of the city's inhabitants, who are now the monarch's minions. It is a chilling passage. Some say it is not even Shakespeare, but I' — he slapped a confident hand on the edge of his desk — 'I believe that the diction, if quoted accurately, can only be Shakespeare's, and that the city is Istanbul, renamed with the pseudo-Turkic title Tashkani.' He leaned forward. 'I also believe that the tyrant to whom the spirit appears was none other than Sultan Mehmed II, conqueror of Constantinople.'

"Chills crawled on the back of my neck. 'What do you think the significance of this could be — where Dracula's career is concerned, I mean?'

"'Well, my friend, it is very interesting to me that the legend of Vlad Dracula penetrated even to Protestant England by — let us say — 1590, so powerful it was. Furthermore, if Tashkani was indeed Istanbul, it shows how real a presence Dracula was here in Mehmed's day. Mehmed entered the city in 1453. That was only five years after the young Dracula returned to Wallachia from his imprisonment in Asia Minor, and there is no certain evidence he ever returned to our region in his lifetime, although some scholars think he paid tribute to the sultan in person. I do not think that can be proved. I have a theory that he left a legacy of vampirism here, if not during his life then after his death. But' — he sighed — 'the line between literature and history is often a wobbling one, and I am not an historian.'

"'You are a fine historian indeed,' I said humbly. 'I am overwhelmed by how many historical leads you have followed, and with such success.'

"'You are kind, my young friend. In any case, one evening I was working on my article for this theory — it was never published, alas, because the editors of the journal to which I submitted it proclaimed that it was too superstitious in content — I was working well into the evening, and after about three hours at the archive I went to a restaurant across the street to have a little *börek*. You have had *börek?*'

"'Not yet,' I admitted.

"'You must try it as soon as possible — it is one of our delectable national specialities. So I went to this restaurant. It was already dark outside because this was in winter. I sat down at a table, and while I waited I took Professor Rossi's letter out of my papers and reread it. As I mentioned, I had had it in my possession only a few days, and I was most perplexed by it. The waiter brought my meal, and I happened to see his face as he put down the dishes. His eyes were lowered, but it seemed to me that he suddenly noticed the letter I was reading, with Rossi's name at the top. He glanced sharply at it once or twice, then appeared to erase all expression from his face, but I noticed that he stepped behind me to put another dish down on the table, and seemed to look at the letter again from over my shoulder.

"'I could not explain this behavior, and it gave me a most uncomfortable feeling, so I quietly folded the letter up and prepared to eat my supper. He went away without speaking, and I could not help watching him as he moved around the restaurant. He was a big, broad-shouldered, heavy man with dark hair swept back from his face and large dark eyes. He would have been handsome if he had not looked — how do you say? — rather sinister. He seemed to ignore me throughout an hour, even after I'd finished my meal. I took out a book to read for a few minutes, and then he suddenly came to the table again and set a steaming cup of tea in front of me. I had ordered no tea, and I was surprised. I thought it might be a sort of gift, or a mistake. "Your tea," he said as he put it down. "I made sure that it is very hot."

"'Then he looked me right in the eyes, and I cannot explain how terrifying his face was to me. It was pale, almost yellow, in complexion, as if he had — how to say? — decayed inside. His eyes were dark and bright, almost like the eyes of an animal, under big eyebrows. His mouth was like red wax, and his teeth were very white and long — they looked oddly healthy in a sick face. He smiled as he bent over with the tea, and I could smell his strange odor, which made me feel sick and faint. You may laugh, my friend, but it was a little like an odor that I have always found pleasant under other circumstances — the smell of old books. You know that smell — it is parchment and leather, and — something else?'

"I knew, and I did not feel like laughing.

"'He was gone a second later, moving without any hurry back toward the restaurant kitchen, and I was left there with a feeling that he had meant to show me something — his face, perhaps. He had wanted me to look carefully at him, and yet there was nothing specific I could name that would justify my terror.' Turgut looked pale himself now, as he sat back in his medieval chair. 'To settle my nerves, I put some sugar into my tea from a bowl on the table, picked up my spoon, and stirred it. I had every intention of calming myself with the hot drink, but then something very — very peculiar happened.'

"His voice trailed off as if he almost regretted having begun the story. I knew that feeling all too well, and nodded to encourage him. 'Please, continue.'

"'It sounds strange to say it now, but I am speaking truthfully. The steam rose up from the cup — you know how steam swirls when you stir something hot? — and when I stirred my tea, the steam rose up in the form of a tiny dragon, swirling above my cup. It hovered there for a few seconds before vanishing. I saw it very clearly with my own eyes. You can imagine how I felt, for a moment not trusting myself, and then I quickly gathered my papers, paid, and went out.'

"My mouth was dry. 'And did you ever see that waiter again?'

"'Never. I did not go back to the restaurant for some weeks, and then curiosity came over me, and I went in again after dark, but there was no sign of him. I even asked one of the other waiters about him, and that waiter said the man had worked there only a short while, and he did not know his last name. The man's first name, he said, was Akmar. I never saw any other sign of him.'

"'And did you think his face showed that he was — 'I trailed off.

"'I was terrified by it. That is all I could have told you at that time. When I saw the face of the librarian you have — as you say — imported, I felt I knew it already. It is not simply the look of death. There is something in the expression —' He turned uneasily and glanced toward the curtained niche where the portrait hung. 'One thing that bludgeons me about your story, the information that you have just given me, is that this American librarian has progressed further toward his spiritual doom since you first saw him.'

"'What do you mean?'

"'When he attacked Miss Rossi in your library at home, you were able to knock him down. But my friend from the archive, whom he assaulted this morning, says he was very strong, and my friend is not so much slighter than you. The fiend also was already able to draw considerable blood from my friend, alas. And yet this vampire was out in the daylight when we saw him, so he cannot be yet completely corrupted. I conjecture the creature was drained of life a second time either at your university or here in Istanbul, and if he has connections here he will receive his third evil benediction soon and become forever undead.'

"'Yes,' I said. 'There is nothing we can do about the American librarian without being able to find him, so you will have to guard your friend here very carefully.'

"'I shall,' Turgut said with grim emphasis. He fell silent for a moment, and then turned to his bookcase again. Without a word he pulled from his collection a large album with Latin letters across the front. 'Romanian,' he told me. 'This is a collection of images from churches in Transylvania and Wallachia, by an art historian who died only recently. He reproduced many images from churches that were later destroyed in the war, I am sorry to say. So this book is very precious.' He put the volume into my hand. 'Why don't you turn to page twenty-five?'

"I did. There I found a spread across two pages — a colored engraving of a mural. The church that had once housed it was displayed in a little black-and-white photograph, inset: an elegant building with twisted bell towers. But it was the larger picture that caught my attention. To the left loomed a ferocious dragon in flight, its tail looped not once but twice, its golden eye rolling maniacally, its mouth spewing flame. It seemed about to swoop down to attack the figure on the right, a cowering man in chain mail and striped turban. The man crouched in fear, his curved scimitar in one hand and a round shield in the other. At first I thought he was standing in a field of strange plants, but when I looked carefully I saw that the objects around his knees were people, a tiny forest of them, and that each was writhing, impaled upon a stake. Some were turbaned, like the giant in their midst, but others were dressed in some sort of peasant garb. Still others wore flowing brocades and tall fur hats. There were blond heads and dark; noblemen with long brown mustaches; and even a few priests or monks in black robes and tall hats. There were women with dangling braids, naked boys, infants. There was even an animal or two. All were in agony.

"Turgut was watching me. 'This church was endowed by Dracula during his second reign,' he said quietly.

"I stood gazing at the picture for a moment longer. Then I could bear no more and I shut the book. Turgut took it from my hand and put it away. When he turned to me, his look was fierce.

'And now, my friend, how do you intend to find Professor Rossi?'

"The blunt question went into me like a blade. 'I'm still trying to piece all this information together,' I admitted slowly, 'and even with your generous work last night — and Mr. Aksoy's — I don't feel we know much. Perhaps Vlad Dracula put in some kind of appearance in Istanbul after his death, but how can we find out if he was buried here, or still is? That remains a mystery to me. As far as our next move goes, I can only tell you that we are going to Budapest for a few days.'

"'Budapest?' I could almost see the conjectures racing across his broad face.

"'Yes. You remember Helen told you the story of her mother and Professor — her father. Helen feels strongly that her mother might have information for us that Helen's never drawn out of her, so we're going to talk with her mother in person. Helen's aunt is someone important in the government and will arrange it, we hope.'

"'Ah.' He almost smiled. 'Thank the gods for friends in high places. When will you leave?'

"'Perhaps tomorrow or the day after. We'll stay five or six days, I think, and then come back here.'

"'Very well. And you must carry this with

you.' Turgut stood up suddenly and took from a cabinet the little vampire-hunting kit he had shown us the day before. He set it squarely in front of me.

"'But that is one of your treasures,' I objected. 'Anyway, they might not let it through customs.'

"'Oh, you must never show it at customs. You must hide it with the greatest care. Check your suitcase to see if you can put it in the lining somewhere, or better yet let Miss Rossi carry it. They will not search a woman's luggage as thoroughly.' He nodded encouragement. 'But I will not feel easy in my heart unless you take it. While you are in Budapest, I will be looking through many old books to try to help you, but you will be hunting a monster. For now, keep it in your briefcase — it is very thin and light.' I took the wooden box without another word and fitted it in next to my dragon book. 'And while you are interviewing Helen's mother, I will be digging around here for every possible hint of a tomb. I have not given up on the idea yet.' He narrowed his eyes. 'It would explain very much about the plagues that have cursed our city since that period we have been speaking of. If we could not only explain them but end them —'

"At that moment the door to his study opened

and Mrs. Bora put in her head to call us to lunch. It was as delicious a meal as the one we'd eaten there the day before, but a much more somber one. Helen was quiet and looked tired, Mrs. Bora handed around the dishes with silent grace, and Mr. Erozan, although he sat up for a while to join us, was unable to eat much. Mrs. Bora made him drink a quantity of red wine, however, and eat some meat, which seemed to restore him somewhat. Even Turgut was subdued and seemed melancholy. Helen and I took our leave as soon as we politely could.

"Turgut saw us out of the building and shook our hands with all his usual warmth, urging us to call him when we knew our travel plans and promising us unabated hospitality on our return. Then he nodded to me and patted my briefcase, and I realized he was referring silently to the kit inside. I nodded in response and made a little gesture to Helen to tell her I'd explain later. Turgut waved until we could no longer see him under the lindens and poplars, and when he was out of sight, Helen put her arm wearily through mine. The air smelled of lilacs, and for a minute, on that dignified gray street, walking through patches of dusty sunlight, I could have believed we were on vacation in Paris."

Chapter 37

"HELEN WAS INDEED tired, and I reluctantly left her to nap at the pension. I didn't like her being alone there, but she pointed out that broad daylight was probably protection enough. Even if the evil librarian knew our whereabouts, he was not likely to enter locked rooms at midday, and she had her little crucifix with her. We had several hours before Helen could call her aunt again, and there was nothing we could do to arrange our trip until we received her instructions. I put my briefcase into Helen's care and forced myself to leave the premises, feeling I would go stir-crazy if I stayed there pretending to read or trying to think.

"It seemed a good opportunity to see something else in Istanbul, so I made my way toward the mazelike, domed Topkapı Palace complex, commissioned by Sultan Mehmed as the new seat of his conquest. It had drawn me both from a distance and in my guidebook since our first afternoon in the city. The Topkapı covers a large area on the headland of Istanbul and is guarded on three sides by water: the Bosphorus, the

Golden Horn, and the Marmara. I suspected that if I missed it, I would be missing the essence of Istanbul's Ottoman history. Perhaps I was strolling far afield from Rossi once again, but I reflected that Rossi himself would have done the same with a few hours of enforced idleness.

"I was disappointed to learn, as I wandered the parks, courtyards, and pavilions where the heart of the Empire had pulsed for hundreds of years, that little from Mehmed's time was on exhibit there — little apart from some ornaments from his treasury and some of his swords, nicked and scarred from prodigious use. I think I had hoped more than anything to catch another glimpse of the sultan whose army had battled Vlad Dracula's, and whose police courts had been concerned about the security of his alleged tomb in Snagov. It was rather, I thought — remembering the old men's game in the bazaar — like trying to determine the position of your opponent's shah in *shahmat* by knowing only the position of your own.

"There was plenty in the palace to keep my thoughts busy, however. According to what Helen had told me the day before, this was a world in which more than five thousand servants with titles such as Great Turban-Winder had once served the will of the sultan; where eunuchs guarded the virtue of his enormous harem in what amounted to an ornate prison; where Sultan Süleyman the Magnificent, reigning in the mid-sixteenth century, had consolidated the Empire, codified its laws, and made Istanbul as glorious a metropolis as it had been under the Byzantine emperors. Like them, the sultan traveled out into his city once a week to worship at Hagia Sophia — but on Friday, the Muslim holy day, not Sunday. It was a world of rigid protocol and sumptuous dining, of marvelous textiles and sensuously beautiful tile work, of viziers in green and chamberlains in red, of fantastically colored boots and towering turbans.

"I had been particularly struck by Helen's description of the Janissaries, a crack corps of guards selected from the ranks of captured boys from all over the Empire. I knew I had read about them before, these boys born Christian in places like Serbia and Wallachia and raised in Islam, trained in hatred of the very peoples they sprang from and unleashed on those peoples when they reached manhood, like falcons to the kill. I had seen images of the Janissaries somewhere, in fact, perhaps in a book of paintings. Thinking about their expressionless young faces, massed to protect the sultan, I felt the chill of the palace buildings deepen around me.

"It occurred to me, as I moved from room to room, that the young Vlad Dracula would have made an excellent Janissary. The Empire had missed an opportunity there, a chance to harness a little more cruelty to its enormous force. They would have had to catch him quite young, I thought, perhaps to have kept him in Asia Minor instead of returning him to his father. He had been too independent after that, a renegade, loyal to no one but himself, as quick to execute his own followers as he was to kill his Turkish enemies. Like Stalin — I surprised myself with this mental leap as I gazed out at the glint of the Bosphorus. Stalin had died the year before, and new tales of his atrocities had leaked into the Western press. I remembered one report about an apparently loyal general whom Stalin had accused just before the war of wanting to overthrow him. The general had been removed from his apartment in the middle of the night and hung upside down from the beams of a busy railway station outside Moscow for several days until he died. The passengers getting on and off the trains had all seen him, but no one had dared to glance twice in his direction.

Much later, the people in that neighborhood had not been able to agree on whether or not this had even happened.

"That sort of disturbing thought followed me from room to marvelous room throughout the palace; everywhere I sensed something sinister or perilous, which could simply have been the overwhelming evidence of the sultan's supreme power, a power not so much concealed as revealed by the narrow corridors, twisting passages, barred windows, cloistered gardens. At last, seeking a little relief from the mingled sensuality and imprisonment, the elegance and the oppression, I wandered back outside to the sunlit trees of the outer court.

"Out there, however, I met the most alarming ghosts of all, for my guidebook located there the executioner's block and explained in generous detail the sultan's custom of beheading officials and anyone else with whom he disagreed. Their heads were displayed on the spikes of the sultan's gates, a stern example to the populace. The sultan and the renegade from Wallachia were a pleasant match, I thought, turning away in disgust. A stroll in the surrounding park restored my nerves, and the low, red gleam of sun on the waters, turning a passing ship to black silhou-

ette, reminded me that the afternoon was waning
and that I ought to go back to Helen and perhaps
to some news from her aunt.

"Helen was waiting in the lobby with an English newspaper when I arrived. 'How was your
walk?' she asked, looking up.

"'Gruesome,' I said. 'I went to the Topkapı
Palace.'

"'Ah.' She closed the newspaper. 'I am sorry I
missed that.'

"'Don't be. How are things out in the big
world?'

"She traced the headlines with a finger. 'Gruesome. But I have good news for you.'

"'You spoke to your aunt?' I deposited myself
in one of the sagging chairs near her.

"'Yes, and she has been extraordinary, as always. I'm sure she is going to scold me when we
arrive, but that does not matter. The important
thing is that she has found a conference for us to
attend.'

"'A conference?'

"'Yes. It's magnificent, actually. There is an international conference of historians meeting in
Budapest this week. We will attend as visiting
scholars, and she has arranged our visas so that
we can get them here.' She smiled. 'My aunt has

a friend who is a historian at the University of Budapest, apparently.'

"'What is the topic of the conference?' I asked apprehensively.

"'European Labor Issues to 1600.'

"'A sprawling subject. And I suppose we are to attend in our capacity as Ottoman specialists?'

"'Exactly, my dear Watson.'

"I sighed. 'Good thing I popped into the Top-kapı, then.'

"Helen smiled at me, but whether a little maliciously or simply from confidence in my powers of disguise, I couldn't tell. 'The conference begins on Friday, so we have only two days to get there. Over the weekend we will attend lectures, and you will give one. On Sunday part of the day is free for the scholars to explore historic Budapest, and we will slip out to explore my mother.'

"'I will do what?' I could not help glaring at her, but she smoothed a curl around her ear and met my gaze with an even more innocent smile.

"'Oh, a lecture. You will give a lecture. That is our way to get in.'

"'A lecture on what, pray?'

"'On the Ottoman presence in Transylvania and Wallachia, I think. My aunt has kindly had it added to the program by now. It won't have to be a long lecture, because of course the Ottomans never managed to fully conquer Transylvania. I thought that would be a good topic for you because we both know so much about Vlad already, and he was instrumental in keeping them out, in his time.'

"'That's good of you,' I snorted. 'You mean *you* know so much about him. Are you telling me I have to stand up in front of an international gathering of scholars and talk about Dracula? Please recall for a moment that my dissertation is on Dutch merchant guilds and I haven't even finished it. Why can't you give the lecture?'

"'That would be ridiculous,' Helen said, folding her hands on the newspaper. 'I am — how do you put it in English? — the old hat. Everyone at the university knows me already and has already been bored several times by my work. Having an American will add a little extra éclat to the scene, and they will all be grateful to me for bringing you, even at the last minute. Having an American will make them feel less embarrassed about the shabby university hostel and the canned peas they will serve everyone at the big dinner on the last night. I will help you write the lecture — or write it for you, if you are going to be so unpleasant — and you can deliver it on Saturday. I think my aunt said around one o'clock.'

"I groaned. She was the most impossible person I had ever met. It occurred to me that my presence there with her might be more of a political liability than she was admitting, too. 'Well, what do the Ottomans in Wallachia or Transylvania have to do with European labor issues?'

"'Oh, we will find a way to put in some labor issues. That is the beauty of the solid Marxist education you did not have the privilege of receiving. Believe me, you can find labor issues in any topic if you look hard enough. Besides, the Ottoman Empire was a great economic power, and Vlad disrupted their trade routes and access to natural resources in the Danube region. Do not worry — it will be a fascinating lecture.'

"'Jesus,' I said finally.

"'No.' She shook her head. 'No Jesus, please. Just labor relations.'

"Then I couldn't help laughing and also couldn't help silently admiring the gleam in her dark eyes. 'I just hope no one at home ever gets wind of this. I can imagine what my dissertation committee would have to say. On the other hand, I think Rossi might have enjoyed the whole thing.' I began to laugh again, picturing the corresponding gleam of mischief in Rossi's bright blue glance, then stopped. The thought of Rossi was becoming so sore a spot in my heart that I could hardly bear it; here I was on the other side of the world from the office where he'd last been seen, and I had every reason to believe I would never see him alive again, perhaps never know what had become of him. *Never* stretched long and desolate before me for a second, and then I pushed the thought aside. We were going to Hungary to speak with a woman who had purportedly known him — known him intimately — long before I'd ever met him, when he was in the throes of his quest for Dracula. It was a lead we could not afford to ignore. If I had to give a charlatan's lecture to get there, I would do even that.

"Helen had been watching me in silence, and I felt, not for the first time, her uncanny ability to read my thoughts. She confirmed my sense of this after a moment by saying, 'It is worth it, is it not?'

"'Yes.' I looked away.

"'Very good,' she said softly. 'And I am pleased that you will meet my aunt, who is wonderful, and my mother, who is wonderful, too, but in a different way, and that they will meet you.'

"I looked quickly at her — the gentleness of her tone had made my heart suddenly contract — but her face had reverted to its usual guarded irony. 'When do we leave, then?' I asked.

"'We will pick up our visas tomorrow morning and fly the next day, if everything goes well with our tickets. My aunt told me that we must go to the Hungarian consulate before it opens tomorrow and ring the front bell — about seven-thirty in the morning. We can go straight from there to a travel agent to order plane tickets. If there are no seats, we will have to take the train, which would be a very long trip.' She shook her head, but my sudden vision of a roaring, clattering Balkan train, wending its way from one ancient capital to another, made me hope for a moment that the airline was thoroughly overbooked, despite the time we might lose.

"'Am I correct in imagining that you take after this aunt of yours, rather than after your mother?' Maybe it was simply the mental adventure by train that made me smile at Helen.

"She hesitated only a second. 'Correct again, Watson. I am very much like my aunt, thank goodness. But you will like my mother best — most people do. And now, may I invite you to dine with me at our favorite establishment, and to work on your lecture over dinner?'

"'Certainly,' I agreed, 'as long as there are no Gypsies around.' I offered her my arm with careful exaggeration, and she traded her newspaper for the support. It was strange, I reflected, as we went out into the golden evening of the Byzantine streets, that even in the weirdest circumstances, the most troubling episodes of one's life, the greatest divides from home and familiarity, there were these moments of undeniable joy."

On a sunny morning in Boulois, Barley and I boarded the early train for Perpignan.

Chapter 38

"THE FRIDAY PLANE to Budapest from Istanbul was far from full, and when we had settled in among the black-suited Turkish businessmen, the gray-jacketed Magyar bureaucrats talking in clumps, the old women in blue coats and head shawls — were they going to cleaning jobs in Budapest, or had their daughters married Hungarian diplomats? — I had only a short flight in which to regret the train trip we might have taken.

"That trip, with its tracks carved through mountain walls, its expanses of forest and cliff, river and feudal town, would have to wait for my later career, as you know, and I have taken it twice since then. There is something vastly mysterious for me about the shift one sees, along that route, from the Islamic world to the Christian, from the Ottoman to the Austro-Hungarian, from the Muslim to the Catholic and Protestant. It is a gradation of towns, of architecture, of gradually receding minarets blended with the advancing church domes, of the very look of forest and riverbank, so that little by little you begin to believe you can read in nature itself the saturation of history. Does the shoulder of a Turkish hillside really look so different from the slope of a Magyar meadow? Of course not, and yet the difference is as impossible to erase from the eye as the history that informs it is from the mind. Later, traveling this route, I would also see it alternately as benign and bathed in blood — this is the other trick of historical sight, to be unrelentingly torn between good and evil, peace and war. Whether I was imagining an Ottoman incursion across the Danube or the earlier sweep of the Huns toward it from the East, I was always plagued by conflicting images: a severed head brought into the encampment with cries of triumph and hatred, and then an old woman — maybe the greatest of grandmothers of those wrinkled faces I saw on the plane — dressing her grandson in warmer clothes, with a pinch on his smooth Turkic cheek and a deft hand making sure her stew of wild game didn't burn.

"These visions lay in the future for me, however, and during our plane trip, I regretted the panorama below without knowing what it was, or what thoughts it might later provoke in me. Helen, a more experienced and less excitable traveler, used the opportunity to sleep curled in her seat. We had been up late at the restaurant table in Istanbul two nights in a row, working on my lecture for the conference in Budapest. I had to admit to a greater knowledge of Vlad's battles with the Turks than I'd previously enjoyed — or not enjoyed — although that wasn't saying much. I hoped no one would ask any questions following my delivery of all this half-learned material. It was remarkable, though, what Helen had stored in her brain, and I marveled again that her self-education about Dracula had been fueled by so elusive a hope as showing up a father she could barely claim. When her head lolled in sleep onto my shoulder, I let it rest there, trying not to breathe in the scent — Hungarian shampoo? — of her curls. She was tired; I sat meticulously still while she slept.

"My first impression of Budapest, taken in through the windows of our taxi from the airport, was of a vast nobility. Helen had explained to me that we would be staying in a hotel near the university on the east side of the Danube, in Pest, but she had apparently asked our driver to take us along the Danube before dropping us off. One minute we were traversing dignified eighteenth- and nineteenth-century streets, enlivened here and there by a burst of art-nouveau fantasy or a tremendous old tree. The next minute we were in sight of the Danube. It was enormous — I hadn't been prepared for its grandeur — with three great bridges spanning it. On our side of the river rose the incredible neo-Gothic spires and dome of the Parliament Buildings, and on the opposite side rose the immense tree-cushioned flanks of the royal palace and the spires of medieval churches. In the midst of everything was that expanse of the river, gray-green, its surface finely scaled by wind and glinting with sunlight. A huge blue sky arched over the domes and monuments and churches, and touched the water with shifting colors.

"I had expected to be intrigued by Budapest, and to admire it; I had not expected to be awed. It had absorbed a panoply of invaders and allies, beginning with the Romans and ending with the Austrians — or the Soviets, I thought, remembering Helen's bitter comments — and yet it was different from all of them. It was neither quite Western, nor Eastern like Istanbul, nor, for all its Gothic architecture, northern European. I stared out the confining taxi window at a splendor wholly individual. Helen was staring, too, and after a moment she turned to me. Some of my excitement must have registered on my face, because she burst out laughing. 'I see you like our little town,' she said, and I heard under her sarcasm a keen pride. Then she added in a low voice, 'Dracula is one of our own here — did you know? In 1462 he was imprisoned by King Matthias Corvinus about twenty miles from Buda because he had threatened Hungary's interests in Transylvania. Corvinus apparently treated him more like a houseguest than a prisoner and even gave him a wife from the Hungarian royal family, although no one knows exactly who she was — Dracula's second wife. Dracula showed his gratitude by converting to the Catholic faith, and they were allowed to live in Pest for a while. And as soon as he was released from Hungary —'

"'I think I can imagine,' I said. 'He went right back to Wallachia and took over the throne as soon as possible and renounced his conversion.'

"'That is basically correct,' she admitted. 'You are getting a feel for our friend. He wanted more than anything to take and keep the Wallachian throne.'

"Too soon the taxi was looping back into the old section of Pest, away from the river, but here there were more wonders for me to gawk at, which I did without shame: balconied coffee-houses that imitated the glories of Egypt or Assyria, walking streets crowded with energetic shoppers and forested with iron street lanterns, mosaics and sculptures, angels and saints in marble and bronze, kings and emperors, violinists in white tunics playing on a street corner. 'Here we are,' Helen said suddenly. 'This is the university section, and there is the university library.' I craned to get a look at a fine classical building of yellow stone. 'We will go in there when we have the chance — in fact I want to look at something there. And here is our hotel, just off Magyar *utca* — Magyar Street, to you. I must find you a map somehow so you don't get lost.'

"The driver hauled out our bags in front of an elegant, patrician facade of gray stone, and I gave my hand to Helen to help her from the car. 'I thought so,' she said with a snort. 'They always use this hotel for conferences.'

"'It looks fine to me,' I ventured.

"'Oh, it is not bad. You will especially enjoy the choice of cold or cold water, and the factory food.' Helen was paying the driver from a selection of large silver and copper coins.

"'I thought Hungarian food was wonderful,' I said consolingly. 'I'm sure I've heard that somewhere. Goulash and paprika, and so on.'

"Helen rolled her eyes. 'Everyone always mentions goulash if you say *Hungary*. Just as everyone mentions Dracula if you say *Transylvania*.' She laughed. 'But you can ignore the hotel food. Wait until we eat at my aunt's house, or my mother's, and then we will discuss Hungarian cooking.'

"'I thought your mother and aunt were Romanian,' I objected, and was immediately sorry; her face froze.

"'You may think whatever you like, Yankee,' she told me peremptorily, and picked up her own suitcase before I could take it for her.

"The hotel lobby was quiet and cool, lined with marble and gilt from a more prosperous age. I found it pleasant and saw nothing for Helen to be ashamed of in it. A moment later I realized that I was in my first communist country — on the wall behind the front desk were photographs of government officials, and the dark blue uniform of all the hotel personnel had something self-consciously proletarian about it. Helen checked us in and handed me my room key. 'My aunt has arranged things very well,' she said with satisfaction. 'And there is a telephone message from her to say that she will meet us here at seven o'clock this evening to take us out to dinner. We will go to register at the conference first, and attend a reception there at five o'clock.'

"I was disappointed by the news that the aunt would not be taking us home for her own Hungarian food and a glimpse of the life of the bureaucratic elite, but I reminded myself hurriedly that I was, after all, an American and should not expect every door to fly open to me here. I might be a risk, a liability, or at the least an embarrassment. In fact, I thought, I would do well to keep a low profile and make as little trouble as possible for my hosts. I was lucky to be here at all, and the last thing I wanted was any problem for Helen or her family.

"My room upstairs was plain and clean, with incongruous touches of former grandeur in the fat bodies of gilded cherubs in the upper corners and a marble basin in the shape of a great mollusk shell. As I washed my hands there and combed my hair in the mirror above it, I looked from the simpering *putti* to the narrow, tightly made bed, which could have been an army cot, and grinned. My room was on a different floor from Helen's this time — the aunt's foresight? — but at least I would have those outdated cherubs and their Austro-Hungarian wreaths for company.

"Helen was waiting for me in the lobby, and

she led me silently through the grand doors of the hotel into the grand street. She was wearing her pale blue blouse again — in the course of our travels, I had gradually become rather rumpled while she managed still to look washed and ironed, which I took for some kind of East European talent — and she had pinned her hair up in a soft roll in the back. She was lost in thought as we strolled toward the university. I didn't dare ask what she was thinking, but after a while she told me of her own volition. 'It is so odd to come back here very suddenly like this,' she said, glancing at me.

"'And with a strange American?'

"'And with a strange American,' she murmured, which didn't sound like a compliment.

"The university was made up of impressive buildings, some of them echoes of the fine library we'd seen earlier, and I began to feel some trepidation when Helen gestured toward our destination, a large classical hall bordered around the second story with statues. I stopped to crane up at them and was able to read some of their names, spelled in their Magyar versions: Plato, Descartes, Dante, all of them crowned with laurels and draped in classical robes. The other figures were less familiar to me: Szent István, Mátyás Corvinus, János Hunyadi. They brandished scepters or bore mighty crowns aloft.

"'Who are they?' I asked Helen.

"'I'll tell you tomorrow,' she said. 'Come on — it's after five now.'

"We entered the hall with several animated young people I took to be students and made our way to a huge room on the second floor. My stomach lurched a little; the place was full of professors in black or gray or tweed suits and crooked ties — they had to be professors — eating from little plates of red peppers and white cheese and drinking something that smelled like a strong medication. They were all historians, I thought with a groan, and although I was supposed to be one of them, my heart was sinking fast. Helen was immediately surrounded by a knot of colleagues, and I caught a glimpse of her shaking hands in a comradely way with a man whose white pompadour reminded me of some kind of dog. I had almost decided to go pretend to look out the window at the magnificent church facade opposite when Helen's hand grasped my elbow for a split second — was that wise of her? — and steered me into the crowd.

"'This is Professor Sándor, the chairman of the history department at the University of Budapest and our greatest medievalist,' she told me, indicating the white dog, and I hurried to introduce myself. My hand was crushed in a grip of iron, and Professor Sándor expressed his great honor at having me join the conference. I wondered briefly if he was the friend of the mysterious aunt. To my surprise, he spoke a clear, if slow, English. 'The pleasure is all ours,' he told me warmly. 'We expect happily your lecture tomorrow.'

"I expressed my reciprocal feeling of honor at being allowed to address the conference and was very careful not to catch Helen's eye as I spoke.

"'Excellent,' Professor Sándor boomed. 'We have a big respect for the universities of your country. May our two countries live in peace and friendship for every year.' He saluted me with his glass of the medicinal clear stuff I'd been smelling, and I hastened to return the salute, since a glass of it had magically appeared in my hand. 'And now, if there is something we can do to make your stay in our beloved Budapest more happier, you must say it.' His great dark eyes, bright in an aging face and contrasting weirdly with his white mane, reminded me for a moment of Helen's, and I took a sudden liking to him.

"'Thank you, Professor,' I told him sincerely, and he slapped my back with a big paw.

"'Please, come, eat, drink, and we will talk.' Right after this, however, he vanished to other duties, and I found myself in the midst of eager questions from the other members of the faculty and visiting scholars, some of whom looked even younger than I. They clustered around me and Helen, and gradually I heard among their voices a babble of French and German, and some other language that might have been Russian. It was a lively group, a charming group, actually, and I began to forget my nervousness. Helen introduced me with a distant graciousness that struck me as just the right note for the occasion, explaining smoothly the nature of our work together and the article we would soon be publishing in an American journal. The eager faces crowded around her, too, with quick questions in Magyar, and a little flush came to her face as she shook hands and even kissed the cheeks of a few of her old acquaintances. They had not forgotten her, clearly — but then how could they? I thought. I noticed that she was one of several women in the room, some older than she and a few quite young, but she eclipsed all of them. She was taller, more vivid, more poised, with her broad shoulders, her beautifully shaped head and heavy curls, her look of animated irony. I turned to one of the Hungarian faculty members so that I would not stare at her; the fiery drink was starting to course through my veins.

"'Is this a typical gathering at a conference here?' I wasn't sure what I meant, but it was something to say while I took my eyes off Helen.

"'Yes,' said my companion proudly. He was a short man of about sixty in a gray jacket and gray tie. 'We have many international gatherings at the university, especially now.'

"I wanted to ask what he meant by *especially now,* but Professor Sándor had materialized again and was guiding me toward a handsome man who seemed very eager to meet me. 'This is Professor Géza József,' he told me. 'He would like to make your acquaintance.' Helen turned at the same moment, and to my utter surprise I saw a look of displeasure — was it even disgust? — flash over her face. She made her way toward us immediately, as if to intervene.

"'How are you, Géza?' She was shaking hands with him, formally and a little coldly, before I'd even had time to greet the man.

"'How good to see you, Elena,' Professor József said, bowing a little to her, and I caught something strange in his voice, too, which could have been mockery but could have been some other emotion. I wondered if they were speaking English only for my benefit.

"'And you,' she said flatly. 'Allow me to introduce my colleague with whom I have been working in America —'

"'What a pleasure to meet you,' he said, giving me a smile that illuminated his fine features. He was taller than I, with thick brown hair and the confident posture of a man who loves his own virility — he would have been magnificent on horseback, riding across the plains with herds of sheep, I thought. His handshake was warm, and he gave me a welcoming cudgel on the shoulder with his other hand. I failed to see why Helen would find him repulsive, although I couldn't shake the impression that she did. 'And you will honor us with a lecture tomorrow? That is splendid,' he said. Then he paused for a second. 'But my English is not so good. Would you prefer we speak in French? German?'

"'Your English is far better than either my French or German, I'm sure,' I responded promptly.

"'You are very kind.' His smile was a meadow of flowers. 'I understand your field is the Ottoman domination of the Carpathians?'

"News certainly traveled fast here, I thought; it was just like home. 'Ah, yes,' I concurred. 'Although I am sure I will have much to learn from your faculty on that subject.'

"'Surely no,' he murmured kindly. 'But I have done a little research on it myself and would be pleased to discuss it with you.'

"'Professor József has a great range of interests,' Helen put in. Her tone would have frozen hot water. This was all very puzzling, but I reminded myself that every academic department suffers from civil unrest, if not outright war, and that this one was probably no exception. Before I could think of anything conciliatory to say, Helen turned to me abruptly. 'Professor, we must go to our next meeting,' she said. For a second, I didn't know whom she was addressing, but she put her hand firmly under my arm.

"'Oh, I see you are very busy.' Professor József was all regret. 'Perhaps we can discuss the Ottoman question another time? I would be pleased to show you a little of our city, Professor, or take you for lunch —'

"'The professor will be fully engaged through-out the conference,' Helen told him. I shook hands with the man as warmly as her icy gaze would permit, and then he took her free hand in his.

"'It is a delight to see you back in your home-land,' he told her, and bowing over her hand, he kissed it. Helen snatched it away, but a strange look crossed her face. She was somehow moved by the gesture, I decided, and for the first time I disliked the charming Hungarian historian. Helen steered me back to Professor Sándor, where we made our apologies and expressed our ea-gerness to hear the next day's lectures.

"'And we will expect your lecture with all the pleasure.' He pressed my hand in both of his. Hungarians were tremendously warm people, I thought with a glow that was only partly the ef-fect of the drink in my bloodstream. As long as I postponed all real thought of that lecture my-self, I felt adrift in satisfaction. Helen took my arm, and I thought she searched the room with a quick glance before we made our exit.

"'What was that all about?' The evening air was refreshingly cool, and I felt more aglow than

529

ever. 'Your compatriots are the most cordial people I think I've ever met, but I had the impression you were ready to behead Professor József.'

"'I was,' she said shortly. 'He is unsufferable.'

"'Insufferable, more likely,' I pointed out. 'What makes you treat him like that? He greeted you as an old friend.'

"'Oh, there's nothing wrong with him, really, except that he is a flesh-eating vulture. A vampire, actually.' She stopped short and stared at me, her eyes large. 'I didn't mean —'

"'Of course you didn't,' I said. 'I checked his canines.'

"'You are unsufferable, too,' she said, taking her arm from mine.

"I looked regretfully at her. 'I don't mind your holding my arm,' I said lightly, 'but is that a good idea in front of your entire university?'

"She stood gazing at me, and I couldn't decipher the darkness in her eyes. 'Don't worry. There was not anyone present from anthropology.'

"'But you knew many of the historians, and people talk,' I persisted.

"'Oh, not here.' She gave her dry snort of laughter. 'We are all workers-in-arms together here. No gossip or conflict — only comradely dialectic. You will see tomorrow. It is really quite a little utopia.'

"'Helen,' I groaned. 'Would you be serious, for once? I'm simply worried about your reputation here — your political reputation. After all, you must come back here someday and face all these people.'

"'Must I?' She took my arm again, and we walked on. I made no move to pull away; there was little I could have valued more at that moment than the brush of her black jacket against my elbow. 'Anyway, it was worth it. I did it only to make Géza gnash his teeth. His fangs, that is.'

"'Well, thank you,' I muttered, but I didn't trust myself to say anything more. If she had intended to make anyone jealous, it had certainly worked with me. I suddenly saw her in Géza's strong arms. Had they been involved before Helen had left Budapest? They would have been a striking match, I thought — both were so handsomely confident, so tall and graceful, so dark haired and broad shouldered. I felt, suddenly, puny and Anglo, no match for the horsemen of the steppe. Helen's face prohibited further questions, however, and I had to content myself with the silent weight of her arm.

"All too soon, we turned in at the gilded doors of the hotel and were in the hushed lobby. As soon as we entered, a lone figure stood up among the black upholstered chairs and potted palms, waiting quietly for us to approach. Helen gave a little cry and ran forward, her hands outstretched. 'Éva!'"

Chapter 39

"SINCE MY MEETING with her — I saw her only three times — I have often thought of Helen's aunt Éva. There are people who stick in one's memory much more clearly after a brief acquaintance than others whom one sees day after day over a long period. Aunt Éva was certainly one of those vivid people, someone my memory and imagination have conspired to preserve in living color for twenty years. I have sometimes used Aunt Éva to fill the shoes of characters in books, or figures in history; for example, she stepped in automatically when I encountered Madame Merle, the personable schemer in Henry James's *Portrait of a Lady.*

"In fact, Aunt Éva has stood in for such a number of formidable, fine, subtle women, in my musings, that it is a little difficult for me to reach back now to her real self as I encountered her on an early summer evening in Budapest in 1954. I do remember that Helen flew into her arms with uncharacteristic affection, and that Aunt Éva herself did not fly, but stood calm and dignified, embracing her niece and kissing her

533

soundly on each cheek. When Helen turned, flushed, to introduce us, I saw tears shining in the eyes of both women. 'Éva, this is my American colleague, whom I told you about. Paul, this is my aunt, Éva Orbán.'

"I shook hands, trying not to stare. Mrs. Orbán was a tall, handsome woman of perhaps fifty-five. What hypnotized me about her was her stunning resemblance to Helen. They might have been an older and much younger sister, or twins, one of whom had aged through hard experience while the other had stayed magically young and fresh. In fact, Aunt Éva was only a shade shorter than Helen and had Helen's strong, graceful posture. Her face might once have been even lovelier than Helen's, and it was still very beautiful, with the same straight, rather long nose, pronounced cheekbones, and brooding dark eyes. Her hair color puzzled me until I realized that it could never have had its origins in nature; it was a weird purplish red, with some white growing out at the roots. During our subsequent days in Budapest, I saw this dyed hair on many women, but that first glimpse of it startled me. She wore small gold earrings and a dark suit that was the sister of Helen's, with a red blouse underneath.

"As we shook hands, Aunt Éva looked into my face very seriously, almost earnestly. Maybe she was scanning me for any weakness of character to warn her niece about, I thought, and then chided myself; why should she even consider me a potential suitor? I could see a web of fine lines around her eyes and at the corners of her lips, the record of a transcendent smile. That smile appeared after a moment, as if she could not suppress it for long. No wonder this woman could arrange additions to conferences and stamps in visas at the drop of a hat, I thought; the intelligence she radiated was matched only by her smile. Like Helen's, too, her teeth were beautifully white and straight, something I was beginning to realize was not a given among Hungarians.

"'I am very glad to meet you,' I said to her. 'Thank you for arranging the honor of my attending the conference.'

"Aunt Éva laughed and pressed my hand. If I had thought her calm and reserved the moment before, I had been fooled; she broke out now in a voluble stream of Hungarian, and I wondered if I was supposed to understand any of it. Helen came to my rescue at once. 'My aunt does not speak English,' she explained, 'although she understands more than she likes to admit. The older people here studied German and Russian and sometimes French, but English was much rarer. I will translate for you. Shh —' She put a fond hand on her aunt's arm, adding some injunction in Hungarian. 'She says you are very welcome here and hopes you won't get into any trouble, as she put the whole office of the undersecretary of visa affairs into an uproar to get you in. She expects an invitation from you to your lecture — which she will not understand that well, but it is the principle of the thing — and you must also satisfy her curiosity about your university at home, how you met me, whether I behave properly in America, and what kind of food your mother cooks. She will have other questions later.'

"I looked at the pair of them in astonishment. They were both smiling at me, these two magnificent women, and I saw a remarkable likeness of Helen's irony in her aunt's face, although Helen could have benefited from a study of her aunt Éva's frequent smile. There was certainly no fooling someone as clever as Éva Orbán; after all, I reminded myself, she had risen from a village in Romania to a position of power in the Hungarian government. 'I will certainly try to satisfy your aunt's interest,' I told Helen. 'Please explain to her that my mother's specialties are meat loaf and macaroni-and-cheese.'

"'Ah, meat loaf,' Helen said. Her explanation to her aunt brought an approving smile. 'She asks you to convey her greetings and congratulations to your mother in America on her fine son.' I felt myself turning red, to my annoyance, but promised to deliver the message. 'Now she would like to take us to a restaurant you will enjoy very much, a taste of old Budapest.'

"Minutes later, the three of us were seated in the back of what I took to be Aunt Éva's private car — not a very proletarian vehicle, by the way — and Helen was pointing out the sights, prompted by her aunt. I should say that Aunt Éva never uttered a word of English to me throughout our two meetings, but I had the impression this was as much a matter of principle — an anti-Western protocol, perhaps? — as anything else; when Helen and I had any exchange, Aunt Éva often seemed to understand it at least partially even before Helen translated. It was as if Aunt Éva was making a linguistic declaration that things Western were to be treated with some distance, even a little revulsion, but an individual Westerner was quite possibly a nice person and should be shown full Hungarian hospitality. Eventually I got used to speaking with her through Helen, so much so that I sometimes had the impression of being on the brink of understanding those waves of dactyls.

"Some communications between us needed no interpreter, anyway. After another glorious ride along the river, we crossed what I later learned was Széchenyi Lánchid, the Széchenyi Chain Bridge, a miracle of nineteenth-century engineering named for one of Budapest's great beautifiers, Count István Széchenyi. As we turned onto the bridge, the full evening light, reflected off the Danube, flooded the whole scene, so that the exquisite mass of the castle and churches in Buda, where we were headed, was thrown into gold-and-brown relief. The bridge itself was an elegant monolith, guarded at each end by lions couchants and supporting two huge triumphant arches. My spontaneous gasp of admiration prompted Aunt Éva's smile, and Helen, sitting between us, smiled proudly, too. 'It is a wonderful city,' I said, and Aunt Éva squeezed my arm as if I had been one of her own grown children.

"Helen explained to me that her aunt wanted me to know about the reconstruction of the bridge. 'Budapest was very badly damaged in the war,' she said. 'One of our bridges has not even yet been fully repaired, and many buildings suffered. You can see that we are still rebuilding in every part of the city. But this bridge was repaired for its — how do you say it? — the centennial of its construction, in 1949, and we are very proud of that. And I am particularly proud because my aunt helped to organize the reconstruction.' Aunt Éva smiled and nodded, then seemed to remember that she wasn't supposed to understand any of this.

"A moment later we plunged into a tunnel that appeared to run almost under the castle itself, and Aunt Éva told us she had selected one of her favorite restaurants, a 'truly Hungarian' place on József Attila Street. I was still amazed by the names of Budapest's streets, some of them simply strange or exotic to me and some, like this one, redolent of a past I had thought lived only in books. József Attila Street turned out to be as politely grand as most of the rest of the city, not at all a muddy track lined with barbaric encampments where Hun warriors ate in their saddles. The restaurant was quiet and elegant inside, and the maître d' came hurrying forward to greet Aunt Éva by name. She seemed used to this sort of attention. In a few minutes we were settled at the best table in the room, where we could enjoy views of old trees and old buildings, strolling pedestrians in their summer finery, and glimpses of noisy little cars zooming through the city. I sat back with a sigh of pleasure.

"Aunt Éva ordered for all of us, as a matter of course, and when the first dishes came, they were accompanied by a strong liquor called *pálinka* that Helen said was distilled from apricots. 'Now we will have something very good with this,' Aunt Éva explained to me through Helen. 'We call these *hortobàgyi palacsinta*. They are a kind of pancake filled with veal, a tradition with the shepherds in the lowlands of Hungary. You will like them.' I did, and I liked all the dishes that followed — the stewed meats and vegetables, the layers of potatoes and salami and hard-boiled eggs, the heavy salads, the green beans and mutton, the wonderful golden-brown bread. I hadn't realized until then how hungry I'd been during our long day of travel. I noticed, too, that Helen and her aunt ate unabashedly, with a relish no polite American woman would have dared to show in public.

"It would be a mistake to convey the impression that we simply ate, however. As all of this tradition went down the hatch, Aunt Éva talked and Helen translated. I asked the occasional question, but for the most part, I remember, I was very busy absorbing both the food and the information. Aunt Éva seemed to have firmly in mind the fact that I was a historian; perhaps she even suspected my ignorance on the subject of Hungary's own history and wanted to be sure I didn't embarrass her at the conference, or perhaps she was prompted by the patriotism of the long-established immigrant. Whatever her motive, she talked brilliantly, and I could almost read her next sentence on her mobile, vivid face before Helen interpreted it for me.

"For example, when we'd finished toasting friendship between our countries with the *pálinka,* Aunt Éva seasoned our shepherd's pancakes with a description of Budapest's origins — it had once been a Roman garrison called Aquincum, and you could still find the odd Roman ruin lying around — and she painted a vivid picture of Attila and his Huns stealing it from the Romans in the fifth century. The Ottomans were actually mild-mannered latecomers, I thought. The stewed meats and vegetables — one dish of which Helen called *gulyás,* assuring me with a stern look that it was not goulash, which was called something else by Hungarians — gave rise to a long description of the invasion of the region by the Magyars in the ninth century. Over the layered potato-and-salami dish, which was certainly much better than meat loaf or macaroni-and-cheese, Aunt Éva described the coronation of King Stephen I — Saint István, ultimately — by the pope in 1000 AD. 'He was a heathen in animal skins,' she told me through Helen, 'but he became the first king of Hungary and converted Hungary to Christianity. You will see his name everywhere in Budapest.'

"Just when I thought I could not eat another bite, two waiters appeared with trays of pastries and tortes that would not have been out of place in an Austro-Hungarian throne room, all swirls of chocolate or whipped cream, and with cups of coffee — *'Eszpresszó,'* Aunt Éva explained. Somehow we found room for everything. 'Coffee has a tragic history in Budapest,' Helen translated for Aunt Éva. 'A long time ago — in 1541, actually — the invader Süleyman I invited one of our generals, whose name was Bálint Török, to have a delicious meal with him in his tent, and at the end of the meal, while he was drinking his coffee — he was the first Hungarian person to taste coffee, you see — Süleyman informed him that the best of the Turkish troops had been taking over Buda Castle while they were eating. You can imagine how bitter that coffee tasted.'

"Her smile was more rueful than luminous this time. The Ottomans again, I thought — how clever they were, and cruel, such a strange mixture of aesthetic refinement and barbaric tactics. In 1541 they had already held Istanbul for nearly a century; remembering this gave me a sense of their abiding strength, the firm hold from which they'd reached their tentacles across Europe, stopping only at the gates of Vienna. Vlad Dracula's fight against them, like that of many of his Christian compatriots, had been the struggle of a David against a Goliath, with far less success than David achieved. On the other hand, the efforts of minor nobility across Eastern Europe and the Balkans, not only in Wallachia but also in Hungary, Greece, and Bulgaria, to name only a few countries, had eventually routed the Ottoman occupation. All of this Helen had succeeded in transferring to my brain, and it left me, on reflection, with a certain perverse admiration for Dracula. He must have known that his defiance of the Turkish forces was doomed in the short term, and yet he had struggled for most of his life to rid his territories of the invaders.

"'That was actually the second time the Turks occupied this region.' Helen sipped her coffee and set it down with a sigh of satisfaction, as if it tasted better to her here than anywhere in the world. 'János Hunyadi overcame them at Belgrade in 1456. He is one of our great heroes, with King István and King Matthias Corvinus, who built the new castle and the library I told you about. When you hear the church bells ringing all over the city at noon tomorrow, you can remember it is for Hunyadi's victory centuries ago. They are still rung for him every day.'

"'Hunyadi,' I said thoughtfully. 'I think you mentioned him the other night. And did you say his victory was in 1456?'

"We looked at each other; any date that fell within Dracula's lifetime had become a sort of signal between us. 'He was in Wallachia at the time,' said Helen in a low voice. I knew she didn't mean Hunyadi, because we had also made a silent pact not to mention Dracula's name in public.

"Aunt Éva was too sharp to be put off by our silence, or by a mere language barrier. 'Hunyadi?' she asked, and added something in Hungarian.

"'My aunt wants to know if you have a special interest in the period when Hunyadi lived,' Helen explained.

"I wasn't sure what to say, so I answered that I found all of European history interesting. This lame remark won me a subtle look, almost a frown, from Aunt Éva, and I hastened to distract her. 'Please ask Mrs. Orbán if I could put some questions to her myself.'

"'Of course.' Helen's smile seemed to take in both my request and my motive. When she translated for her aunt, Mrs. Orbán turned to me with a gracious wariness.

"'I was wondering,' I said, 'if what we hear in the West about Hungary's current liberalism is true.'

"This time Helen's face registered wariness, too, and I thought I might get one of her famous kicks under the table, but her aunt was already nodding and beckoning her to translate. When Aunt Éva understood, she dropped an indulgent smile on me, and her answer was gentle. 'Here in Hungary, we have always valued our way of life, our independence. That is why the periods of Ottoman and Austrian rule were so difficult for us. The true government of Hungary has always progressively served the needs of its people. When our revolution brought workers out of oppression and poverty, we were asserting our own way of doing things.' Her smile deepened, and I wished I could read it better. 'The Hungarian Communist Party is always in tune with the times.'

"'So you feel Hungary is flourishing under the government of Imre Nagy?' Since I'd entered the city, I'd been wondering what changes the administration of Hungary's new and surprisingly liberal prime minister had brought to the country when he'd replaced the hard-line communist prime minister Rákosi the year before, and whether he enjoyed all the popular support we read about in newspapers at home. Helen translated a little nervously, I thought, but Aunt Éva's smile was steady.

"'I see you know your current events, young man.'

"'I've always been interested in foreign relations. It's my belief that the study of history should be our preparation for understanding the present, rather than an escape from it.'

"'Very wise. Well, then, to satisfy your curiosity — Nagy enjoys great popularity among our people and is carrying out reforms in line with our glorious history.'

"It took me a minute to realize that Aunt Éva

was carefully saying nothing, and another minute to reflect on the diplomatic strategy that had allowed her to keep her position in the government throughout the ebb and flow of Soviet-controlled policy and pro-Hungarian reforms. Whatever her personal opinion of Nagy, he now controlled the government that employed her. Perhaps it was the very openness he had created in Budapest that made it possible for her — a high-ranking government official — to take an American out to dinner. The gleam in her fine dark eyes could have been approval, though I wasn't sure, and as it later turned out, my guess was correct.

"'And now, my friend, we must allow you to get some sleep before your big lecture. I am looking forward to it and I will let you know afterward what I think of it,' Helen translated. Aunt Éva gave me a hospitable nod, and I couldn't help smiling back. The waiter appeared at her elbow as if he had heard her; I made a feeble attempt to request the check, although I had no idea what the proper etiquette was or even if I'd changed enough money at the airport to pay for all those fine dishes. If there had ever been a bill, however, it vanished before I saw it and was paid invisibly. I held Aunt Éva's jacket for her in the cloakroom, vying with the maître d' for it, and we sailed back into the waiting car.

"At the foot of that splendid bridge, Éva murmured a few words that made her chauffeur stop the car. We got out and stood looking across at the glow of Pest and down into the rippling dark water. The wind had turned a little cool, sharp against my face after the balmy air of Istanbul, and I had a sense of the vastness of Central Europe's plains just over the horizon. The scene before us was the kind of sight I had wanted all my life to see; I could hardly believe I was standing there looking over the lights of Budapest.

"Aunt Éva said something in a low voice, and Helen translated softly. 'Our city will always be a great one.' Later I remembered that line vividly. It came back to me almost two years after this, when I learned how deep Éva Orbán's commitment to the new reform government had actually been: her two grown sons were killed in a public square by Soviet tanks during the uprising of the Hungarian students in 1956, and Éva herself fled to northern Yugoslavia, where she disappeared into villages with fifteen thousand other Hungarian refugees from the Russian puppet state. Helen wrote to her many times, insist-

ing that she allow us to try to bring her to the
United States, but Éva refused even to apply for
emigration. I tried again a few years ago to find
some trace of her, without success. When I lost
Helen, I lost touch with Aunt Éva, too."

Chapter 40

"I WOKE THE NEXT MORNING to find myself staring right up at those gilt cherubs above my hard little bed, and for a moment I couldn't remember where I was. It was an unpleasant feeling; I found myself adrift, farther from home than I'd ever imagined, unable to remember if this was New York, Istanbul, Budapest, or some other city. I felt I'd had a nightmare just before waking. A pain in my heart reminded me forcibly of Rossi's absence, a feeling I often experienced first thing in the morning, and I wondered if the dream had taken me to some grim place where I might have found him if I'd stayed long enough.

"I discovered Helen breakfasting in the dining room of the hotel with a Hungarian newspaper spread out in front of her — the sight of the language in print gave me a hopeless feeling, since I couldn't extract meaning from a single word of the headlines — and she greeted me with a cheerful wave. The combination of my lost dream, those headlines, and my rapidly approaching lecture must have showed in my face, because she looked quizzically at me as I approached. 'What a sad expression. Have you been thinking about Ottoman cruelties again?'

"'No. Just about international conferences.' I sat down and helped myself to her basket of rolls and a white napkin. The hotel, for all its shabbiness, seemed to specialize in immaculate napery. The rolls, accompanied by butter and strawberry jam, were excellent, and so was the coffee that appeared a few minutes later. No bitterness there.

"'Don't worry,' Helen said soothingly. 'You are going to —'

"'Knock their socks off?' I prompted.

"She laughed. 'You are improving my English,' she told me. 'Or destroying it, maybe.'

"'I was very struck by your aunt last night.' I buttered another roll.

"'I could see that you were.'

"'Tell me, exactly how did she come here from Romania and achieve such a high position? If you don't mind my asking.'

"Helen sipped her coffee. 'It was an accident of destiny, I think. Her family was very poor — they were Transylvanians who lived off a small plot of land in a village that I have heard is not even there anymore. My grandparents had nine children and Éva was the third. They sent her to work when she was six years old because they needed the money and could not feed her. She worked in the villa of some wealthy Hungarians who owned all the land outside the village. There were many Hungarian landowners there between the wars — they were caught there by the changing borders after the Treaty of Trianon.'

"I nodded. 'That was the one that rearranged the borders after the First World War?'

"'Very good. So Éva worked for this family from the time she was quite young. She has told me they were kind to her. They let her go home on Sundays sometimes and she remained close to her own family. When she was seventeen the people she worked for decided to return to Budapest, and they took her with them. There she met a young man, a journalist and revolutionary named János Orbán. They fell in love and married, and he survived his army service in the war.' Helen sighed. 'So many young Hungarian men fought all over Europe in the First War, you know, and they are buried in mass graves in Poland, Russia . . . In any case, Orbán rose to power in the coalition government after the war, and was rewarded in our glorious revolution by a cabinet post. Then he was killed in an automobile accident, and Éva raised their sons and carried on his political career. She is an amazing woman. I have never known exactly what her personal convictions are — sometimes I have the feeling that she keeps an emotional distance from all politics, as if they are simply her profession. I think my uncle was a passionate man, a convinced follower of Leninist doctrine and an admirer of Stalin before his atrocities were known here. I cannot say if my aunt was the same, but she has built a remarkable career for herself. Her sons have had every possible privilege as a result, and she has used her power to help me, also, as I have told you.'

"I had been listening intently. 'And how did you and your mother come here?'

"Helen sighed again. 'My mother is twelve years younger than Éva,' she said. 'She was always Éva's favorite among the little children in their family, and she was only five when Éva was taken to Budapest. Then, when my mother was nineteen and unmarried, she became pregnant. She was afraid her parents and everyone else in the village would find out — in such a traditional culture, you understand, she would have been in danger of expulsion and perhaps death from starvation. She wrote to Éva and asked for her help, and my aunt and uncle arranged her travel to Budapest. My uncle met her at the border, which was heavily guarded, and took her back to the city. I once heard my aunt say he paid an enormous bribe to the border officials. Transylvanians were hated in Hungary, especially after the Treaty. My mother told me that my uncle had won her complete devotion — not only did he rescue her from a terrible situation, but he also never let her feel the difference between their national origins. She was heartbroken when he died. He was the one who brought her safely into Hungary and gave her a new life.'

"'And then you were born?' I asked quietly.

"'Then I was born, at a hospital in Budapest, and my aunt and uncle helped to raise and educate me. We lived with them until I was in high school. Éva took us into the countryside during the war and found food for all of us somehow. My mother was educated here, too, and learned Hungarian. She always refused to teach me any Romanian, although I sometimes heard her speaking it in her sleep.' She gave me a bitter glance. 'You see what your beloved Rossi reduced our lives to,' she said, her mouth twisting. 'If it had not been for my aunt and uncle, my mother might have died alone in some mountain forest and been eaten by the wolves. Both of us, actually.'

"'I'm thankful to your aunt and uncle, too,' I said, and then, fearing her sardonic glance, busied myself pouring more coffee from the metal pot at my elbow.

"Helen made no reply, and after a minute she pulled some papers from her purse. 'Shall we go over the lecture once more?'"

"The morning sunshine and cool air outside were full of menace for me; all I could think about as we walked toward the university was the moment, rapidly approaching now, when I would have to deliver my lecture. I had given only one lecture before this, a joint presentation with Rossi the previous year when he had organized a conference on Dutch colonialism. Each of us had written half of the lecture; my half had been a miserable attempt to distill into twenty minutes what I thought my dissertation was going to be about before I had written a word of it; Rossi's had been a brilliant, wide-ranging treatise on the cultural heritage of the Netherlands, the strategic might of the Dutch navy, and the nature of colonialism. Despite my general sense of inadequacy about the whole thing, I'd been flattered by his including me. I'd also been sustained throughout the experience by his compact and confident presence beside me at the podium, his friendly thump on my shoulder as I relinquished the audience to him. Today I would be on my own. The prospect was dismal, if not terrifying, and only the thought of how Rossi would have handled it steadied me a little.

"Elegant Pest lay all around us, and now, in broad daylight, I could see that its magnificence was under construction — reconstruction, rather — where it had been damaged in the war. Many houses were still missing walls or windows in their upper floors, or even the whole upper floor, for that matter, and if you looked closely, nearly every surface, whatever it was made of, was pockmarked with bullet holes. I wished we had time to walk farther, so that I could see more of Pest, but we had agreed between us that we would attend all the morning sessions of the conference that day to make our presence there as legitimate as possible. 'And there is something I want to do later, too, in the afternoon,' Helen said thoughtfully. 'We will go to the university library before it closes.'

"When we reached the large building where

the reception had been held the night before, she paused. 'Do me a favor.'

"'Certainly. What?'

"'Don't talk with Géza József about our travels or the fact that we are looking for someone.'

"'I'm not likely to do that,' I said indignantly.

"'I'm just warning you. He can be very charming.' She raised her gloved hand in a conciliatory gesture.

"'All right.' I held the great baroque door for her and we went in.

"In a lecture room on the second floor, many of the people I'd seen the night before were already seated in rows of chairs, talking with animation or shuffling through papers. 'My God,' Helen muttered. 'The anthropology department is here, too.' A moment later she was engulfed in greetings and conversation. I saw her smiling, presumably at old friends, colleagues from years of work in her own field, and a wave of loneliness broke over me. She seemed to be indicating me, trying to introduce me from a distance, but the torrent of voices and their meaningless Hungarian made an almost palpable barrier between us.

"Just then I felt a tap on my arm and the formidable Géza was before me. His handshake and smile were warm. 'How do you enjoy our city?' he asked. 'Is everything to your liking?'

"'Everything,' I said with equal warmth. I had Helen's warning firmly in mind, but it was difficult not to like the man.

"'Ah, I am delighted,' he said. 'And you will be giving your lecture this afternoon?'

"I coughed. 'Yes,' I said. 'Yes, exactly. And you? Will you be lecturing today?'

"'Oh, no, not I,' he said. 'Actually, I am researching a topic of great interest to me these days. But I am not ready to give a lecture about it.'

"'What is your topic?' I couldn't help asking, but at that moment Professor Sándor of the towering white pompadour called the session to order from a podium. The crowd settled into the seats like birds on telephone wires and grew quiet. I sat in the back next to Helen, glancing at my watch. It was only nine-thirty, so I could relax for a while. Géza József had taken a seat in the front; I could see the back of his handsome head in the first row. Looking around, I could also see several other faces familiar from last night's introductions. It was an earnest, slightly scruffy crowd, everyone gazing at Professor Sándor.

"'*Guten Morgen,*' he boomed, and the microphone screeched until a student in a blue shirt and black tie came up to fix it. 'Good morning, honored visitors. *Guten Morgen, bonjour,* welcome to the University of Budapest. We are proud to introduce you to the first European convention of historians of —' Here the microphone began to screech again, and we lost several phrases. Professor Sándor had apparently run out of English, too, for the time being, and he continued for some minutes in a mixture of Hungarian, French, and German. I gathered from the French and German that lunch would be served at twelve o'clock, and then — to my horror — that I would be the keynote speaker, the apex of the conference, the highlight of the proceedings, that I was a distinguished American scholar, a specialist not only in the history of the Netherlands but also in the economics of the Ottoman Empire and the labor movements of the United States of America (had Aunt Éva invented that one on her own?), that my book on the Dutch merchant guilds in the era of Rembrandt would be appearing the following year, and that they were deeply fortunate to have been able to add me to their program only this week.

"This was all worse than my wildest dreams, and I vowed that Helen would pay if she had had a hand in it. Many of the scholars in the audience were turning to look at me, smiling graciously, nodding, even pointing me out to one another. Helen sat regal and serious beside me, but something about the curve of her black-jacketed shoulder suggested — only to me, I hoped — the almost perfectly hidden desire to laugh. I tried to look dignified, too, and to remember that this, even all this, was for Rossi.

"When Professor Sándor had finished booming, a little bald man gave a lecture that seemed to be about the Hanseatic League. He was followed by a gray-haired woman in a blue dress whose subject concerned the history of Budapest, although I could follow none of it. The remaining speaker before lunch was a young scholar from the University of London — he looked about my own age — and to my great relief he spoke in English, while a Hungarian philology student read a translation of his lecture into German. (It was strange, I thought, to hear all this German here only a decade after the Germans had nearly destroyed Budapest, but I reminded myself that it had been the lingua franca of the Austro-Hungarian Empire.) Professor Sándor introduced the Englishman as Hugh James, a professor of East European history.

"Professor James was a solid man in brown

tweeds and an olive tie; in that setting he looked so indescribably, characteristically English that I fought back a laugh. His eyes twinkled at the audience, and he gave us a pleasant smile. 'I never expected to find myself in Budapest,' he said, gazing around at us, 'but it is very gratifying to me to be here in this greatest city of Central Europe, a gate between East and West. Now, then, I should like to take a few minutes of your time to ruminate on the question of what legacies the Ottoman Turks left in Central Europe as they withdrew from their failed siege of Vienna in 1685.'

"He paused and smiled at the philology student, who earnestly read this first sentence back to us in German. They proceeded like this, alternating languages, but Professor James must have strayed off the page more than he stayed on it, because as his talk unfolded, the student frequently shot him a look of bewilderment. 'We have all, of course, heard the story of the invention of the croissant, the tribute of a Parisian pastry chef to Vienna's victory over the Ottomans. The croissant, of course, represented the crescent moon of the Ottoman flags, a symbol the West devours with coffee to this very day.' He looked around, beaming, and then seemed to realize, as I just had, that most of these eager

Hungarian scholars had never been to Paris or Vienna. 'Yes — well, the legacy of the Ottomans can be summarized in one word, I think: aesthetics.'

"He went on to describe the architecture of half a dozen Central and East European cities, games and fashions, spices and interior design. I listened with a fascination that was only partly the relief of being able to fully understand his words; much of what we had just seen in Istanbul came rushing back to me as James discussed the Turkish baths of Budapest and the Proto-Ottoman, Austro-Hungarian buildings of Sarajevo. When he described Topkapı Palace, I found myself nodding vigorously, until I realized I should probably be more discreet.

"Tumultuous applause followed the lecture, and then Professor Sándor invited us to convene in the dining hall for lunch. In the crush of scholars and food, I managed to find Professor James just as he was sitting down at a table. 'May I join you?'

"He jumped up with a smile. 'Certainly, certainly. Hugh James. How do you do?' I introduced myself in return and we shook hands. When I'd seated myself opposite him, we looked at each other with friendly curiosity. 'Ah,' he said, 'so you're the keynote speaker? I'm very much looking forward to your talk.' Up close, he appeared older than I by ten years, and had extraordinary light brown eyes, watery and a little bulging, like a basset hound's. I had already recognized his speech as being from the north of England.

"'Thank you,' I said, trying not to cringe visibly. 'And I enjoyed every minute of yours. It really covered a remarkable spectrum. I wonder if you know my — er — mentor, Bartholomew Rossi. He's English, too.'

"'Well, of course!' Hugh James unfurled his napkin with an enthusiastic flourish. 'Professor Rossi is one of my favorite writers — I've read most of his books. You work with him? How very fortunate.'

"I had lost track of Helen, but at that moment I caught sight of her at the luncheon buffet with Géza József at her side. He was speaking earnestly almost in her ear, and after a minute she permitted him to follow her to a small table on the other side of the hall. I could see her well enough to make out the sour expression on her face, but it didn't make the scene much more palatable to me. He was leaning toward her, gazing into her face while she looked down at her food, and I felt almost crazed by my desire to know what he was saying to her.

"'In any case' — Hugh James was still talking about Rossi's work — 'I think his studies of Greek theater are marvelous. The man can do anything.'

"'Yes,' I said absently. 'He's been working on an article called "The Ghost in the Amphora," about the stage props used in the Greek tragedies.' I stopped, suddenly realizing I might be giving away Rossi's trade secrets. If I hadn't halted myself, however, Professor James's face would have brought me up short.

"'The what?' he said, clearly astonished. He set down his fork and knife, abandoning his lunch. 'Did you say "The Ghost in the Amphora"?'

"'Yes.' I'd forgotten even about Helen and Géza now. 'Why do you ask?'

"'But this is astounding! I think I must write to Professor Rossi at once. You see, I've recently been studying a most interesting document from fifteenth-century Hungary. That's what brought me to Budapest in the first place — I've been looking into that period of Hungary's history, you know, and then I tagged along at the conference with Professor Sándor's kind permission. In any case, this document was written by one of King Matthias Corvinus's scholars, and it mentions the ghost in the amphora.'

"I remembered that Helen had referred to King Matthias Corvinus the night before; hadn't he been the founder of the great library in the Buda castle? Aunt Éva had told me about him, too. 'Please,' I said urgently, 'explain.'

"'Well, I — it's rather a silly sounding thing, but I've been very interested for several years in the folk legends of Central Europe. It started as a bit of a lark, I suppose, long ago, but I've become absolutely mesmerized by the legend of the vampire.'

"I stared at him. He looked as ordinary as before, with his ruddy, jolly face and tweed jacket, but I felt I must be dreaming.

"'Oh, I know it sounds juvenile — Count Dracula and all that — but you know it really is a remarkable subject when you dig into it a bit. You see, Dracula was a real person, although of course not a vampire, and I'm interested in whether his history is in any way connected with folk legends of the vampire. A few years ago I started looking for written material on the topic, to see if there even was any, since of course the vampire existed mainly in oral legend in Central and East European villages.'

"He leaned back, drumming his fingers on the

edge of the table. 'Well, lo and behold, working in the university library here, I turned up this document that Corvinus apparently commissioned — he wanted someone to collect all knowledge of vampires from earliest times. Whoever the scholar was who got the job, he was certainly a classicist, and instead of tramping around villages as any good anthropologist would have done, he began poking through Latin and Greek texts — Corvinus had a lot of these here, you know — to find references to vampires, and he turned up this ancient Greek idea, which I haven't seen anywhere else — at least not until you mentioned it just now — of the ghost in the amphora. In ancient Greece, and in Greek tragedies, the amphora sometimes contained human ashes, you see, and the ignorant folk of Greece believed that if things didn't go quite right with the burial of the amphora, it could produce a vampire — I'm not quite sure how, yet. Perhaps Professor Rossi knows something about this, if he's writing about ghosts in amphorae. A remarkable coincidence, isn't it? Actually, there are still vampires in modern Greece, according to folklore.'

"'I know,' I said. 'The *vrykolakas*.'

"This time it was Hugh James's turn to stare.

His protuberant hazel eyes grew enormous. 'How do you know that?' he breathed. 'I mean — I beg your pardon — I'm just surprised to meet someone else who —'

"'Is interested in vampires?' I said dryly. 'Yes, that used to surprise me, too, but I'm getting used to it, these days. How did you become interested in vampires, Professor James?'

"'Hugh,' he said, slowly. 'Please call me Hugh. Well, I —' He looked hard at me for a second, and for the first time I saw that under his cheerful, bumbling exterior there glowed an intensity like a flame. 'It's dreadfully strange and I don't usually tell people about this, but —'

"I really couldn't bear the delay. 'Did you, by any chance, find an old book with a dragon in the center?' I said.

"He eyed me almost wildly, and the color drained from his healthy face. 'Yes,' he said. 'I found a book.' His hands gripped the edge of the table. 'Who are you?'

"'I found one, too.'

"We sat looking at each other for a few long seconds, and we might have sat speechless even longer, delaying all we had to discuss, if we hadn't been interrupted. Géza József's voice was at my ear before I noticed his presence; he

567

had come up behind me and was bending over our table with a genial smile. Helen came hurrying up, too, and her face was strange — almost guilty, I thought. 'Good afternoon, comrades,' he said cordially. 'What's this about finding books?'"

Chapter 41

"WHEN PROFESSOR JÓZSEF bent over our table with his friendly question, I wasn't sure for a moment what to say. I had to talk with Hugh James again as soon as possible, but in private, not in this crush of people, and certainly not with the very person Helen had warned me about — why? — breathing down my neck. At last I mustered a few words. 'We were sharing our love of antique books,' I said. 'Every scholar should be able to admit to that, don't you think?'

"By this time Helen had caught up with us and was eyeing me with what I took to be mingled alarm and approval. I rose to pull out a chair for her. In the midst of my need to dissemble before Géza József, I must have communicated some excitement to her, for she stared from me to Hugh. Géza looked genially at all of us, but I fancied I saw a slight narrowing of his handsome epicanthic eyes; so, I thought, the Huns must have squinted into the Western sun through the slits of their leather headgear. I tried not to look at him again.

"We might have remained there parrying or avoiding looks all day if Professor Sándor had not suddenly appeared. 'Very good,' he trumpeted. 'I find you enjoy your lunch. You are finished? And now, if you will be very kind to come with me, we will arrange your lecture to begin.'

"I flinched — I had actually forgotten for a few minutes the torture that awaited me — but I rose in obedience. Géza dropped respectfully behind Professor Sándor — a little too respectfully? I asked myself — and that gave me a blessed moment to look at Helen. I widened my eyes and motioned toward Hugh James, who had also risen politely to his feet at Helen's approach and was standing mutely at the table. She frowned, puzzled, and then Professor Sándor, to my great relief, clapped Géza on the shoulder and led him away. I thought I read annoyance in the young Hungarian's massive suit-jacketed back, but perhaps I had already imbibed too much of Helen's paranoia about him. In any case, it gave us an instant of freedom.

"'Hugh got a book,' I whispered, shamelessly breaking the Englishman's confidence.

"Helen stared, but without comprehension. 'Hugh?'

"I nodded quickly at our companion, and he

stared at us. Then Helen's jaw dropped. Hugh stared at her in turn. 'Did she also —?'

"'No,' I whispered. 'She's helping me. This is Miss Helen Rossi, anthropologist.'

"Hugh shook her hand with brusque warmth, still staring. But Professor Sándor had turned back and was waiting for us, and there was nothing we could do but follow him. Helen and Hugh stayed as close to my side as if we'd been a flock of sheep.

"The lecture room was already beginning to fill, and I took a place in the front row, pulling my notes from my briefcase with a hand that didn't quite tremble. Professor Sándor and his assistant were fiddling with the microphone again, and it occurred to me that perhaps the audience wouldn't be able to hear me, in which case I had little to worry about. All too soon, however, the equipment was working and the kind professor was introducing me, bobbing his white head enthusiastically over some notes. He outlined once again my remarkable credentials, described the prestige of my university in the United States, and congratulated the conference on the rare treat of hearing me, all in English this time, probably for my benefit. I realized suddenly that I had no interpreter to render my dog-eared lecture notes into German while I spoke, and this idea gave me a burst of confidence as I stood to face my trial.

"'Good afternoon, colleagues, fellow historians,' I began, and then, feeling that was pompous, put down my notes. 'Thank you for giving me the honor of speaking to you today. I would like to talk with you about the period of Ottoman incursion into Transylvania and Wallachia, two principalities that are well known to you as part of the current nation of Romania.' The sea of thoughtful faces looked fixedly at me, and I wondered if I detected a sudden tension in the room. Transylvania, for Hungarian historians, as for many other Hungarians, was touchy material. 'As you know, the Ottoman Empire held territories across Eastern Europe for more than five hundred years, administering them from a secure base after its conquest of ancient Constantinople in 1453. The Empire was successful in its invasions of a dozen countries, but there were a few areas it never managed to completely subdue, many of them mountainous pockets of Eastern Europe's backwoods, whose topography and natives both defied conquest. One of these areas was Transylvania.'

"I went on like this, partly from my notes and

partly from memory, experiencing now and then a wave of scholarly panic; I didn't know the material well yet, although Helen's lessons about it were vividly etched in my mind. After this introduction, I gave a brief overview of Ottoman trade routes in the region and then described the various princes and nobles who had attempted to repulse the Ottoman incursion. I included Vlad Dracula among them, as casually as I could, because Helen and I had agreed that to leave him out of the talk altogether might appear suspicious to any historian who knew of his importance as a destroyer of Ottoman armies. It must have cost me more than I'd thought it would to utter that name in front of a crowd of strangers, because as I began to describe his impalement of twenty thousand Turkish soldiers, my hand flew out a little too suddenly and I knocked over my glass of water.

"'Oh, I'm sorry!' I exclaimed, glancing miserably out at a mass of sympathetic faces — sympathetic with the exception of two. Helen looked pale and tense, and Géza Jószef was leaning a little forward, unsmiling, as if he took the keenest interest in my blunder. The blue-shirted student and Professor Sándor both rushed to my rescue with their handkerchiefs, and after a second I was able to proceed, which I did with all the dignity I could muster. I pointed out that although the Turks had eventually overcome Vlad Dracula and many of his comrades — I thought I should work the word in somewhere — uprisings of this sort had persisted over generations until one local revolution after another toppled the Empire. It was the local nature of these uprisings, with their ability to fade back into their own terrain after each attack, that had ultimately undermined the great Ottoman machine.

"I had meant to end more eloquently than this, but it seemed to please the crowd, and there was ringing applause. To my surprise, I had finished. Nothing terrible had occurred. Helen slumped back, visibly relieved, and Professor Sándor came beaming up to shake my hand. Looking around, I noted Éva in the back, clapping away with her lovely smile very wide. Something was amiss in the room, however, and after a minute I realized that Géza's stately form had vanished. I couldn't recall his slipping out, but perhaps the end of my lecture had been too dull for him.

"As soon as I was done, everyone stood up and began to talk in a babble of languages. Three or four of the Hungarian historians came over to shake my hand and congratulate me. Professor Sándor was radiant. 'Excellent!' he cried. 'I am full of pleasure to know you understand so well our Transylvanian history in America.' I wondered what he would have thought if he'd known I'd learned everything in my lecture from one of his colleagues, seated at a restaurant table in Istanbul.

"Éva came up and gave me her hand, too. I wasn't sure whether to kiss or shake it, but finally decided on the latter. She looked if anything taller and more imposing today in the midst of this gathering of men in shabby suits. She had on a dark green dress and heavy gold earrings, and her hair, curling under a little green hat, had changed from magenta to black overnight.

"Helen came over to talk with her, too, and I noticed how formal they were with each other in this gathering; it was hard to believe Helen had run to her arms the night before. Helen translated her aunt's congratulations for me: 'Very nice work, young man. I could see by everyone's faces that you managed to offend no one, so probably you didn't say very much. But you stand up straight at the podium and look your audience in the eye — that will take you far.' Aunt

Éva tempered these remarks with her dazzling, even-toothed smile. 'Now I must get home to do some chores there, but I will see you at dinner tomorrow night. We can dine at your hotel.' I hadn't known we were going to have dinner with her again, but I was glad to hear it. 'I am so sorry I cannot make you a really good dinner at home, as I would like to,' she told me. 'But when I explain that I am under construction like the rest of Budapest, I am sure you will understand. I could not have a visitor see my dining room in such a mess.' Her smile was thoroughly distracting, but I managed to glean two pieces of information from this speech — one, that in this city of (presumably) tiny apartments, she had a dining room; and two, that whether or not it was a mess, she was too wary to serve dinner to a strange American there. 'I must have a little conference with my niece. Helen can come to me tonight, if you can spare her.' Helen translated all this with guilty exactness.

"'Of course,' I said, returning Aunt Éva's smile. 'I am sure you have a lot to discuss after a long separation. And I think I will have dinner plans myself.' My eye was already searching out Hugh James's tweed jacket in the crowd.

"'Very well.' She offered her hand again, and this time I kissed it like a true Hungarian, the first time I had ever kissed a woman's hand, and Aunt Éva departed.

"This break was followed by a talk in French on peasant revolts in France in the early modern period, and by further performances in German and Hungarian. I listened to them seated in the back again, next to Helen, enjoying my anonymity. When the Russian researcher on the Baltic States left the podium, Helen assured me in a low voice that we had been there long enough and could leave. 'The library is open for another hour. Let's slip out now.'

"'Just a minute,' I said. 'I want to secure my dinner date.' It took little effort for me to find Hugh James again; he was clearly looking for me, too. We agreed to meet at seven in the lobby of the university hotel. Helen was going to take the bus to her aunt's house, and I saw in her face that she would be wondering the whole time what Hugh James had to tell us.

"The walls of the university library, when we reached it, glowed an unblemished ocher, and I found myself marveling again at the rapidity with which the Hungarian nation was rebuilding itself after the catastrophe of war. Even the most tyrannical of governments could not be wholly wicked if it could restore so much beauty for its citizenry in such a short time. That effort had probably been fueled just as much by Hungarian nationalism, I speculated, remembering Aunt Éva's noncommittal remarks, as by communist fervor. 'What are you thinking?' Helen asked me. She had pulled on her gloves and had her purse firmly over her arm.

"'I'm thinking about your aunt.'

"'If you like my aunt so much, perhaps my mother will not be your style,' she said with a provoking laugh. 'But we shall see, tomorrow. Now, let's take a look for something in here.'

"'What? Stop being so mysterious.'

"She ignored me, and we entered the library together through heavy carved doors. 'Renaissance?' I whispered to Helen, but she shook her head.

"'It's a nineteenth-century imitation. The original collection here wasn't even in Pest until the eighteenth century, I think — it was in Buda, like the original university. I remember one of the librarians told me once that many of the oldest books in this collection were given to the library by families who were running away from

Ottoman invaders in the sixteenth century. You see, we owe the Turks for some things. Who knows where all those books would be now, otherwise?'

"It was good to walk into a library again; it smelled like home. This one was a neoclassical treasure house, all dark-carved wood, balconies, galleries, frescoes. But what drew my eye were the rows of books, hundreds of thousands of them lining the rooms, floor to ceiling, their red and brown and gilt bindings in neat rows, their marbled covers and endpapers smooth under the hand, the bumpy vertebrae of their spines brown as old bones. I wondered where they had been hidden during the war, and how long it had taken to range them again on all these re-constructed shelves.

"A few students were still turning through volumes at the long tables, and a young man was sorting stacks of them behind a big desk. Helen stopped to speak with him and he nodded, beckoning us toward a great reading room I'd already glimpsed through an open door. There he located a large folio for us, placed it on a table, and left us alone. Helen sat down and drew off her gloves. 'Yes,' she said softly. 'I think this is what I remember. I looked at this volume just before I left Budapest last year, but I did not think then that it had any great significance.' She opened it to the title page, and I saw it was in a language I didn't know. The words looked strangely familiar to me, and yet I could not read a single one of them.

"'What is this?' I put a finger on what I took to be the title. The page was a fine thick paper, printed in brown ink.

"'This is Romanian,' Helen told me.

"'Can you read it?'

"'Certainly.' She put her hand on the page, close to mine. I saw that our hands were nearly the same size, although hers had finer bones and narrow square-tipped fingers. 'Here,' she said. "'Did you study French?'

"'Yes,' I admitted. Then I saw what she meant and began to decipher the title. '*Ballads of the Carpathians*, 1790.'

"'Good,' she said. 'Very good.'

"'I thought you couldn't speak Romanian,' I said.

"'I speak poorly, but I can read it, more or less. I studied Latin for ten years in school, and my aunt taught me to read and write a great deal of Romanian. Against my mother's wishes, of course. My mother is very stubborn. She seldom talks about Transylvania, but she has never abandoned it, either, in her heart.'

"'And what is this book?'

"She turned the first leaf over, gently. I saw a long column of text, none of which I could understand at a glance; in addition to the unfamiliarity of the words, many of the Latin letters in which it was written were ornamented with crosses, tails, circumflexes, and other symbols. It looked more like witchcraft to me than like a Romance language. 'I found this book when I did the last wave of my research before leaving for England. There's not so much material about him in this library, actually. I did find a few documents about vampires, because Mátyás Corvinus, our bibliophile king, was curious about them.'

"'Hugh said as much,' I muttered.

"'What?'

"'I'll explain later. Go on.'

"'Well, I didn't want to leave any stone unturned here, so I read through a huge mass of material on the history of Wallachia and Transylvania. It took me several months. I made myself read even what was in Romanian. Of course, a lot of documents and histories about Transylvania are in Hungarian, from Hungary's centuries of domination, but there are some Romanian sources as well. This is a collection of texts of folk songs from Transylvania and Wallachia, published by an anonymous collector. Some of them are much more than folk songs — they are epic poems.'

"I felt a little disappointed; I had been expecting some kind of rare historical document, something about Dracula. 'Do any of them mention our friend?'

"'No, I'm afraid not. But there was one song in here that stayed in my mind, and I thought of it again when you told me about what Selim Aksoy wanted us to see in the archive in Istanbul — you know, that passage about the monks from the Carpathians entering the city of Istanbul with their wagon and mules, remember? I wish now that we had asked Turgut to write down a translation for us.' She began to turn through the folio very carefully. Some of the long texts were illustrated at the top with woodcuts, mostly ornaments with a look of folk embroideries, but also a few crude trees, houses, and animals. The type was neatly printed, but the book itself had a rough, homemade quality. Helen ran her finger along the first lines of the poems, her lips moving slowly, and shook her head. 'Some of these are so sad,' she said. 'You know, we Romanians are different, at heart, from Hungarians.'

"'How is that?'

"'Well, there is a Hungarian proverb that says, "The Magyar takes his pleasures sadly." And it is true — Hungary is full of sad songs, too, and the villages are full of violence, drinking, suicide. But Romanians are even sadder, even sadder. We are sad not from life but by nature, I think.' She bent her head over the old book, her eyelashes heavy on her cheek. 'Listen to this — this is typical of these songs.' She translated haltingly, and the result was something like this, although this particular song is a different one and comes from a little volume of nineteenth-century translations that is now in my personal library:

The child that is dead was ever sweet and fair.
Now younger sister the same smile doth wear.
She saith to their mother: "Oh, Mother, dear,
My good dead sister told me not to fear.
The life she might not live she gives to me,
That I might bring fresh happiness to thee."
But, nay, the mother could not raise her head,
And sat a-weeping for the one now dead.

"'Good God,' I said with a shudder. 'It's easy to see how a culture that could create a song like that believed in vampires — produced them, even.'

"'Yes,' Helen said, shaking her head, but she was already searching further through the volume. 'Wait.' She paused suddenly. 'This could have been it.' She was pointing to a short verse with an ornate woodcut above it that seemed to depict buildings and animals enmeshed in a prickly forest.

"I sat in suspense for a few long minutes while Helen read in silence, and at last she looked up. There was a spark of excitement in her face; her eyes shone. 'Listen to this — as well as I can translate.' And here, I reproduce for you an exact translation, which I have kept these twenty years in my papers:

They rode to the gates, up to the great city.
They rode to the great city from the land
of death.
"We are men of God, men from the
Carpathians.
We are monks and holy men, but we bring
only evil news.
We bring news of a plague to the great city.
Serving our master, we come weeping for
his death."
They rode up to the gates and the city wept
with them
When they came in.

"A shudder went through me at this weird verse, but I had to object. 'This is very general. The Carpathians are mentioned, but they must show up in dozens or even hundreds of old texts. And "the great city" could mean anything. Maybe it means the City of God, the kingdom of heaven.'

"Helen shook her head. 'I don't think so,' she said. 'For the people of the Balkans and Central Europe — Christian and Muslim — the great city has always been Constantinople, unless you count the people who made pilgrimages to Jerusalem or Mecca over the centuries. And the mention of a plague and monks — it seems to me somehow connected to the story in Selim Aksoy's passage. Couldn't the master they mentioned be Vlad Ţepeş himself?'

"'I suppose,' I said doubtfully, 'but I wish we had more to go on. How old do you think this song is?'

"'That's always very hard to judge in the case of folk lyrics.' Helen looked thoughtful. 'This volume was printed in 1790, as you can see, but there is no publisher's name or place-name in it. Folk songs can survive two or three or four hundred years easily, so these could be centuries older than the book. The song could date back to the late fifteenth century, or it could be even older, which would defeat our purposes.'

585

"'The woodcut is curious,' I said, looking more closely.

"'This book is full of them,' Helen murmured. 'I remember being struck by them when I first looked through it. This one seems to have nothing to do with the poem — you'd think it would have been illustrated by a praying monk or a high-walled city, something like that.'

"'Yes,' I said slowly, 'but look at it up close.' We bent over the tiny illustration, our heads nearly touching above it. 'I wish we had a magnifying glass,' I said. 'Doesn't it look to you as if this forest — or thicket, whatever it is — has things hidden in it? There's no great city, but if you look carefully here you can see a building like a church, with a cross on top of a dome, and next to it —'

"'Some little animal.' She narrowed her eyes. Then, 'My God,' she said. 'It's a dragon.'

"I nodded, and we hung over it, hardly breathing. The tiny rough shape was dreadfully familiar — outspread wings, tail curling in a minute loop. I didn't need to get out for comparison the book stored in my briefcase. 'What does this mean?' The sight of it, even in miniature, made my heart pound uncomfortably.

"'Wait.' Helen was peering at the woodcut, her face an inch from the page. 'Oh, dear,' she said. 'I can hardly see it, but there is a word here, I think, spaced out among the trees, one letter at a time. They're very small, but I'm sure these are letters.'

"'Drakulya?' I said, as quietly as I could.

"She shook her head. 'No. It could be a name, though — Ivi — Ivireanu. I don't know what that is. It is not a word I have ever seen, but "u" is a common ending for Romanian names. What on earth is this about?'

"I sighed. 'I don't know, but I think your instinct is right — this page has some connection with Dracula, otherwise the dragon wouldn't be there. Not that dragon, anyway.'

"We glanced helplessly at each other. The room, so pleasant and inviting half an hour before, looked dismal to me now, a mausoleum of forgotten knowledge.

"'The librarians know nothing about this book,' Helen said. 'I remember asking them about it, because it is such a rarity.'

"'Well, we can't solve this either, then,' I said at last. 'Let's at least take a translation with us, so we know what we've seen.' I took down her dictation on a sheet of notebook paper and made a hasty sketch of the woodcut. Helen was looking at her watch.

"'I must return to the hotel,' she said.

"'Me, too, or I'll miss Hugh James.' We gathered our belongings and replaced the book on its shelf with all the reverence due a relic.

"Perhaps it was the turmoil of imagination into which the poem and its illustration had thrown me, or perhaps I was more tired than I'd realized from travel, staying up late at Aunt Éva's restaurant, and lecturing to a crowd of strangers. When I entered my room, it took me a long moment to register what I saw there, and a longer one to conclude that Helen might be seeing the same sight in her own quarters two floors above. Then I suddenly feared for her safety and took flight for the stairs without stopping to examine anything. My room had been searched, nook and cranny, drawer and closet and bedclothes, and every article I possessed had been tossed about, damaged, even torn by hands not merely hasty but malicious."

Chapter 42

"BUT CAN'T YOU get the police to help? This place is overflowing with them, it seems.' Hugh James broke a piece of bread in half and took a hearty bite. 'What a dreadful thing to have happen in a foreign hotel.'

"'We've called the police,' I assured him. 'At least I think we have, because the hotel clerk did it for us. He said no one could come until late tonight or early tomorrow morning, and not to touch anything. He's put us in new rooms.'

"'What? Do you mean Miss Rossi's room was ransacked, too?' Hugh's great eyes grew rounder. 'Was anyone else in the hotel hit?'

"'I doubt it,' I said grimly.

"We were seated at an outdoor restaurant in Buda, not far from Castle Hill, where we could look out over the Danube toward the Parliament House on the Pest side. It was still very light and the evening sky had set up a blue-and-rose shimmer on the water. Hugh had picked out the spot — it was one of his favorites, he said. Budapestians of all ages strolled the street in front of us, many of them pausing at the balustrades above the river to look at the lovely scene, as if they, too, could never get enough of it. Hugh had ordered several national dishes for me to try, and we had just settled in with the ubiquitous golden-crusted bread and a bottle of Tokay, a famous wine from the northeastern corner of Hungary, as he explained. We'd already dispensed with the preliminaries — our universities, my erstwhile dissertation (he chuckled when I told him the scope of Professor Sándor's misconceptions about my work), Hugh's research on Balkan history and his forthcoming book on Ottoman cities in Europe.

"'Was anything stolen?' Hugh filled my glass.

"'Nothing,' I said glumly. 'Of course, I hadn't left my money there, or any of my — valuables — and the passports are at the front desk, or maybe at the police station, for all I know.'

"'What were they looking for, then?' Hugh toasted me briefly and took a sip.

"'It's a very, very long story.' I sighed. 'But it fits in pretty nicely with some other things we need to talk about.'

"He nodded. 'All right. Unto the breach, then.'

"'If you'll take your turn, as well.'

"'Of course.'

"I drank half my glass for fortification and began at the beginning. I wouldn't have needed the wine to erase any doubts about telling Hugh James all of Rossi's story; if I didn't tell him everything, I might not learn everything he knew himself. He listened in silence, with obvious absorption, except when I mentioned Rossi's decision to conduct research in Istanbul, when he jumped. 'By Jove,' he said. 'I'd thought of going there myself. Going back, I mean — I've been there twice, but never to look for Dracula.'

"'Let me save you some trouble.' I refilled his glass this time and told him about Rossi's adventures in Istanbul and then about his disappearance, at which Hugh's eyes bulged, although he said nothing. Finally I described my meeting with Helen, leaving out nothing about her claim to Rossi, and all of our travels and research to date, including our encounters with Turgut. 'You see,' I concluded, 'at this point it hardly surprises me to have my hotel room turned upside down.'

"'Yes, exactly.' He seemed to brood for a moment. We had made our way through a multitude of stews and pickles by this time, and he put his fork down rather sadly, as if regretting to see the last of them. 'It's most remarkable, our meeting like this. But I'm distressed to hear about Professor Rossi's disappearance — very distressed. That's dreadfully strange. I wouldn't have sworn before hearing your story that there was more involved in researching Dracula than the usual stuff. Except that I have had an odd feeling, you know, about my own book, this whole time. One doesn't want to go just on odd feelings, but there it is.'

"'I can see I haven't stretched your credulity as much as I feared I might.'

"'And these books,' he mused. 'I count four of them — mine, yours, Professor Rossi's, and the one belonging to that professor in Istanbul. It's damned strange that there should be four such alike.'

"'Have you ever met Turgut Bora?' I asked. 'You said you've been to Istanbul a few times.'

"He shook his head. 'No, I've never even heard the name. But then he's in literature, and I wouldn't have come across him in the history department there, or at any conferences. I'd appreciate your helping me get in touch with him someday, if you would. I've never been to the archive you describe, but I read about it in England and was thinking of giving it a try. You've saved me the trouble, though, as you say. You know, I'd never thought of the thing as a map —

the dragon in my book. That's an extraordinary idea.'

"'Yes, and possibly a matter of life or death for Rossi,' I said. 'But now it's your turn. How did you come across your book?'

"He looked grave. 'As you've described in your case — and the other two — I didn't so much come across my book as receive it, although from where or from whom I couldn't tell you. Perhaps I should give you a little background.' He was silent a moment, and I had the sense that this was a difficult subject for him. 'You see, I took my degree at Oxford nine years ago, and then went to teach at the University of London. My family lives in Cumbria, in the Lake District, and they are not wealthy. They struggled — and I did, too — so that I could have the best of educations. I always felt a bit on the outside, you know, particularly at my public school — my uncle helped put me through there. I suppose I studied harder than most, trying to excel. History was my great love, from the beginning.'

"Hugh patted his lips with his napkin and shook his head, as if remembering youthful folly. 'I knew by the end of my second year of university that I was going to do rather well, and this goaded me further. Then the war came and interrupted everything. I'd finished almost three years at Oxford. I first heard of Rossi there, by the way, although I never met him. He must have left for America several years before I came to the university.'

"He stroked his chin with a large, rather chapped hand. 'I couldn't have loved my studies more, but I loved my country, too, and I enlisted right away, in the navy. I was shipped out to Italy and then home again a year later with wounds in my arms and legs.'

"He touched his white cotton shirtsleeve gingerly, just above the cuff, as if feeling the surprise of blood there again. 'I recovered rather quickly and wanted to go back out, but they wouldn't take me — one eye had been affected when the ship blew up. So I returned to Oxford and tried to ignore the sirens, and I finished my degree just after the war ended. The last weeks I was there were some of the happiest of my life, I think, in spite of all the shortages — this terrible curse had been lifted from the world, I was almost done with my delayed studies, and a girl back home I'd loved most of my life had finally agreed to marry me. I had no money, and there was no food anyway, but I ate sardines in my room and wrote love letters home — I guess you don't mind my telling you all this — and I studied like a demon for my examinations. I got myself into a great state of fatigue, of course.'

"He picked up the bottle of Tokay, which was empty, and set it down again with a sigh. 'I was nearly done with the whole ordeal, and we'd set a wedding date for the end of June. The night before my last examination, I stayed up until the wee hours looking over my notes. I knew I'd covered everything I needed to already, but I simply couldn't stop myself. I was working in a corner of the library in my college, sort of tucked away behind some bookshelves where I didn't have to watch the other few madmen in there looking through their own notes.

"'There are some awfully nice books in those little libraries, and I let myself get distracted for a moment or two by a volume of Dryden's sonnets just a hand's reach away. Then I made myself put it back, thinking I'd better go out and have a cigarette and try to concentrate again afterward. I tucked the book back into the shelf and went to the courtyard. It was a lovely spring night, and I stood there thinking about Elspeth and the cottage she was fixing up for us, and about my best friend — would have been my best man — who'd died over the Ploieşti oil fields with the Americans, and then I went back up to the library. To my surprise, Dryden was lying there on my desk as if I'd never put it away, and I thought I must be getting pretty noddle-headed with all the work. So I turned to put it up, but I saw there was no space for it. It had been right next to Dante, I was sure, but now there was a different book there, a book that had a very old-looking spine with a little creature engraved on it. I pulled it out and it fell open in my hands to — well, you know.'

"His friendly face was pale now, and he searched first his shirt and then his pants pockets until he found a package of cigarettes. 'You don't smoke?' He lit one and drew heavily on it. 'I was caught by the appearance of the book, its apparent age, the menacing look of the dragon — everything that struck you, too, about yours. There were no librarians there at three in the morning, so I went down to the catalog and dug around a bit by myself, but I learned only Vlad Ţepeş's name and lineage. Since there was no library stamp in the book, I took it home with me.

"'I slept poorly and couldn't concentrate in the least on my examination the next morning; all I could think of was getting to the other libraries and perhaps to London to see what I could find out. But I didn't have time, and when I went up for my wedding, I took the little book and kept looking at it at odd moments. Elspeth caught me with it, and when I explained she didn't like it, not a bit. That was five days to our wedding and yet I couldn't stop thinking about the book, and talking to her about it, too, until she told me not to.

"'Then one morning — it was two days to the wedding — I had a sudden inspiration. You see, there's a great house not too far from my parents' village, a Jacobean pile people come to see on bus tours. I'd always thought it sort of a bore on our school trips, but I remembered that the nobleman who'd built it had been a book collector and had things from all over the world. Since I couldn't go to London until after the wedding, I thought I'd get myself into the house library, which is famous, and poke around, perhaps even find something on Transylvania. I told my parents I was going for a walk, and I knew they'd assume I was going to see Elsie.

"'It was a rainy morning — foggy, too, and cold. The housekeeper at the great house said they weren't open for tours that day, but she let me come in to look at the library. She'd heard about the wedding in the village, knew my grandmother, and brewed me a cup of tea. By the time I had my mackintosh off and had found twenty shelves of books from that old Jacobean's Grand Tour, which had reached rather farther east than most, I'd forgotten everything else.

"'I turned through all these wonders, and others he had collected in England, perhaps after his tour, until I came across a history of Hungary and Transylvania, and in it I found a mention of Vlad Ţepeş, and then another, and finally, to my joy and astonishment, I came across an account of Vlad's burial at Lake Snagov, before the altar of a church he had refurbished there. This account was a legend taken down by an English adventurer to the region — he called himself simply "A Traveller" on the title page, and he was a contemporary of the Jacobean collector. This would have been about 130 years after Vlad's death, you see.

"'"A Traveller" had visited the monastery in Snagov in 1605. He had talked a good deal with the monks there, and they had told him that according to legend a great book, a treasure of the monastery, had been placed on the altar during Vlad's funeral, and the monks present at the ceremony had signed their names in it, and those who could not write had drawn a dragon in honor of the Order of the Dragon. No mention, unfortunately, of what had happened to the book after that. But I found this most remarkable. Then the Traveller said that he asked to look at the tomb, and the monks showed him a flat stone in the floor before the altar. It had a portrait of Vlad Drakulya painted on it, and Latin words across it — perhaps painted also, since the Traveller didn't mention engraving and was struck by the lack of the usual cross to mark the gravestone. The epitaph, which I copied down with care — out of what instinct I didn't know — was in Latin.' Hugh dropped his voice, glanced behind him, and stubbed out his cigarette in the ashtray on our table.

"'After I'd written it down and struggled with it a while, I read my translation aloud: "Reader, unbury him with a —" You know how it goes. The rain was still coming down hard outside, and a window that had got loose somewhere in the library slammed open and shut, so I felt a breath of damp air nearby. I must have been jumpy, because I knocked over my teacup and a drop of tea spilled on the book. While I was wiping this up and feeling dreadful about my clumsiness, I noticed my watch — it was already one o'clock and I knew I ought to get home to dinner. There didn't seem to be anything else relevant to look at there, so I put away the books, thanked the housekeeper, and went back down the lanes between all those June roses.

"'When I got to my parents' house, expecting to see them and perhaps Elsie gathering at the table, I found things in an uproar. Several friends and neighbors were there, and my mother was weeping. My father looked very upset.' Here Hugh lit another cigarette, and the match shook in the gathering darkness. 'He put a hand on my shoulder and told me there had been an automobile accident on the main road as Elsie was driving a borrowed car back from some shopping in a nearby town. It had been raining hard, and they thought she'd seen something and swerved. She was not dead, thank the Lord, but badly injured. Her parents had gone at once to the hospital and mine had been waiting at home for me, to tell me.

"'I found a car and drove there so fast I almost had an accident myself. You don't want to hear all this, I'm sure, but — she was lying with her head bandaged and her eyes wide-open. That's how she looked. She lives at a sort of home now, where she's very well treated, but she doesn't speak or understand much, or feed herself. The awful thing about this is . . .' His voice began to tremble. 'The awful thing is, I've always assumed it was an accident, really an accident, and now that I've heard your stories — Rossi's friend Hedges, and your — your cat — I don't know what to think.' He smoked hard.

"I let out a deep breath. 'I'm very, very sorry. I wish I knew what to say. What a terrible thing for you.'

"'Thank you.' He seemed to be trying to recover some of his usual demeanor. 'It's been some years now, you know, and time helps. It's simply that —'

"I didn't know then, as I know now, what hung at the other end of that sentence, which he did not finish — the futile words, the unspeakable litany of loss. As we sat there, the past suspended between us, a waiter came out with a candle in a glass lantern and set it on our table. The café was filling with people, and I could hear shouts of laughter from inside.

"'I'm stunned by what you just told me about Snagov,' I said after a while. 'You know, I'd never heard any of that about the tomb — the inscription, I mean, and the painted face and the lack of a cross. The correspondence of the inscription with the words Rossi found on the maps in the Istanbul archive is extremely important, I think — it's proof that Snagov was at least the original site of Dracula's tomb.' I pressed my fingers to my temples. 'Why, then, why does the map — the dragon map in the books and in the archive — not correspond to the topography of Snagov — the lake, the island?'

"'I wish I knew.'

"'Did you continue your research about Dracula after that?'

"'Not for several years.' Hugh stubbed out his cigarette. 'I didn't have the heart to. About two years ago, though, I found myself thinking about him again, and when I started working on my current book, my Hungarian book, I kept an eye out for him.'

"It had grown quite dark now, and the Danube glowed with reflected lights from the bridge and the buildings of Pest. A waiter came to offer *eszpresszó,* and we accepted gratefully. Hugh took a sip and set his cup down. 'Would you like to see the book?' he asked.

"'The one you're researching?' I was puzzled for a moment.

"'No — my dragon book.'

"I started. 'You have it here?'

"'I always carry it on me,' he said sternly. 'Well, almost always. Actually, I left it at my hotel during the lectures today, because I thought it might be safer there while I was lecturing. When I think it might have been stolen —' He stopped. 'Yours was not in your room, was it?'

"'No.' I had to smile. 'I carry mine around, too.'

"He pushed our coffee cups carefully aside and opened his briefcase. From it he took a polished wooden box, and from that a parcel wrapped in cloth, which he placed on the table. Inside it was a book smaller than mine but bound in the same worn vellum. The pages were browner and more brittle than those in my book, but the dragon in the center was the same, filling the pages to their very edges and glowering up at us. Silently, I opened my briefcase and took out my own book, setting its central image next to Hugh's dragon. They were identical, I thought, bending close to each.

"'Look at this smudge over here — even that's the same. They were printed from the same block,' Hugh said in a low voice.

"He was right, I saw. 'You know, this reminds me of something else, which I forgot to tell you just now. Miss Rossi and I stopped by the university library this afternoon before going back to the hotel, because she wanted to look up something she saw there a while back.' I described the volume of Romanian folk songs and the weird lyrics about monks entering a great city. 'She thought this might have something to do with the story in the Istanbul manuscript I told you about. The lyrics were very general, but there was an interesting woodcut at the top of the page, a sort of thicket of woods with a tiny church and dragon among them, and a word.'

"'Drakulya?' Hugh guessed, as I had in the library.

"'No, Ivireanu.' I looked it up in my notebook and showed him the spelling.

"His eyes widened. 'But that's remarkable!' he cried.

"'What? Tell me quickly.'

"'Well, it's just that I saw that name in the library yesterday.'

"'In the same library? Where? In the same book?' I was too impatient to wait politely for the answer.

"'Yes, in the university library, but not in the same book. I've been poking around there all week for material for my project, and since I always have our friend in the back of my mind, I keep finding the odd reference to his world. You know, Dracula and Hunyadi were bitter enemies, and Dracula and Matthias Corvinus after that, so you run into Dracula now and then. I mentioned to you at lunch that I'd found a manuscript commissioned by Corvinus, the document that mentions the ghost in the amphora.'

"'Oh, yes,' I said eagerly. 'Is that also where you saw the word *Ivireanu?*'

"'Actually, no. The Corvinus manuscript is very interesting, but for different reasons. The manuscript says — well, I have copied a little here. The original is in Latin.'

"He got out his notebook and read me a few lines. '"In the year of Our Lord 1463, the king's humble servant offers him these words from great writings, all to give His Majesty information on the curse of the vampire, may he perish in hell. This information is for His Majesty's royal collection. May it assist him in curing this evil in our city, in ending the presence of vampires, and in keeping the plague from our dwellings." And so on. Then the good scribe, whoever he was, goes on to list the references he's found in various classical works, including tales of the ghost in the amphora. As you can tell, the date of the

605

manuscript is the year after Dracula's arrest and his first imprisonment near Buda. You know, your description of that same concern on the part of the Turkish sultan, which you detected in those documents in Istanbul, prompts me to think Dracula made trouble wherever he went. Both mention the plague, and both are concerned with the presence of vampirism. It's quite similar, isn't it?'

"He paused thoughtfully. 'Actually, that connection with plague is not so far-fetched, in a way — I read in an Italian document at the British Museum Library that Dracula used germ warfare against the Turks. He must have been one of the first Europeans to use it, in fact. He liked to send any of his own people who'd contracted infectious diseases into the Turkish camps, dressed like Ottomans.' In the lantern light, Hugh's eyes were narrow now, his face shining with an intense concentration. It rushed over me that in Hugh James we had found an ally of the keenest intelligence.

"'This is all fascinating,' I said. 'But what about the mention of the word *Ivireanu?*'

"'Oh, I'm so sorry.' Hugh smiled. 'I'm a bit off track. Yes, I did see that word in the library here. I came across it three or four days ago, I think, in a seventeenth-century New Testament in Romanian. I was looking through it because I thought the cover showed an unusual influence of Ottoman design. The title page had the word *Ivireanu* across the bottom — I'm sure it was the same word. I didn't think much about it at the time — to be frank, I'm always running across Romanian words that mystify me, because I know so little of the language. It caught my attention because of the typeface, actually, which was sort of elegant. I assumed it was a place-name or something of the sort.'

"I groaned. 'And that was all? You've never seen it anywhere else?'

"'I'm afraid not.' Hugh was attending to his deserted cup of coffee. 'If I run across it again, I'll be sure to let you know.'

"'Well, it may have little to do with Dracula, after all,' I said, to comfort myself. 'I just wish we had more time to examine this library. We have to fly back to Istanbul on Monday, unfortunately — I don't have permission to stay beyond the duration of the conference. If you do find anything of interest —'

"'Of course,' Hugh said. 'I'll be around for another six days. If I find something, shall I write to you at your department?'

"This gave me a turn; it had been days since I'd thought seriously about home, and I had no idea when I would next be checking my mail in my departmental box there. 'No, no,' I said hastily. 'At least, not yet. If you find something you really think might help us, please call Professor Bora. Just explain to him that we talked. If I speak with him myself, I'll let him know you might get in touch with him.' I took out Turgut's card and wrote the number down for Hugh.

"'Very good.' He tucked it into his breast pocket. 'And here's my card for you. I do hope we'll be running into each other again.' We sat there in silence for a few seconds, his gaze lowered to the table with its empty cups and plates and flickering candle flame. 'Look here,' he said finally. 'If all you've said is true — or all Rossi said, anyway — and there is a Count Dracula, or a Vlad the Impaler — extant — in some awful sense, then I'd like to help you —'

"'Eradicate him?' I finished quietly. 'I'll remember that.'

"There seemed to be nothing left for us to say just now, although I hoped we would talk again someday. We found a taxi to take us back to Pest, and he insisted on walking me into the hotel. We were saying a cordial good-bye at the front desk when the clerk I'd talked with earlier suddenly came out of his cubicle and grasped my arm. 'Herr Paul!' he said urgently.

"'What is it?' Hugh and I both turned to stare at the man. He was a tall, drooping man in a blue worker's jacket, with mustaches that would have suited a Hun warrior. He pulled me close to speak in a low voice, and I managed to signal to Hugh not to leave us. There was no one else in sight, and I didn't especially want to be alone with any new crisis.

"'Herr Paul, I know who was in your *zimmer* this afternoon.'

"'What? Who?' I said.

"'Hmm, hmm.' The clerk began almost to hum to himself and to glance around, searching his jacket pocket in what would have been a meaningful way if only I'd understood his meaning. I wondered if the man was some sort of idiot.

"'He wants a bribe,' Hugh translated in an undertone.

"'Oh, for heaven's sake,' I said in exasperation, but the man's eyes seemed to glaze over, brightening only when I fished out two large Hungarian bills. He took them secretively and hid them in his pocket, but said nothing to acknowledge my capitulation.

"'Herr American,' he whispered. 'I know it was not only *ein* man from this afternoon. It is two men. One comes in first, very important man. Then the other. I see him when I go up with a suitcase to another *zimmer*. Then I see them. They talk. They walk out together.'

"'Didn't anyone stop them?' I snapped. 'Who were they? Were they Hungarian?' The man was glancing all around him again, and I suppressed the urge to throttle him. This atmosphere of censorship was taking a toll on my nerves. I must have looked angry, because Hugh put a restraining hand on my arm.

"'Important man Hungarian. Other man not Hungarian.'

"'How do you know?'

"He lowered his voice. 'One man Hungarian, but they speaks *Anglisch* together.' That was all he would say, despite my increasingly threatening questions. Since he had apparently decided he'd given me enough information for the number of forints I'd handed over, I might never have heard another word from him had it not been for something that seemed suddenly to catch his attention. He was looking past me, and after a second I turned, too, to follow his gaze through the great window by the hotel door. Through it, for a split second, I saw a hungry, hollow-eyed countenance I'd come to know much too well, a face that belonged in a grave, not on the street. The clerk was spluttering, clinging to my arm. 'There he is, with his devil face — the *Anglischer* man!'

"With what must have been a howl, I shook off the clerk and ran for the door; Hugh, with great presence of mind (I later realized), plucked an umbrella from the stand by the desk and bolted after me. Even in my alarm, I kept a tight grip on my briefcase, and that slowed me down as I ran. We turned this way and that, dashed up the street and back, but it was no use. I hadn't even heard the man's footsteps, so I couldn't tell which way he'd fled.

"Finally, I stopped to lean against the side of a building, trying to catch my breath. Hugh was panting hard. 'What was it?' he gasped.

"'The librarian,' I said when I could manage a few words. 'The one who followed us to Istanbul. I'm sure it was him.'

"'Good Lord.' Hugh wiped his forehead with his sleeve. 'What's he doing here?'

"'Trying to get the rest of my notes,' I wheezed.

'He's a vampire, if you can believe that, and now we've led him to this beautiful city.' Actually, I said more than that, and Hugh must have recognized from our common language all the American variants of infuriation. The thought of the curse I was trailing almost brought tears to my eyes.

"'Come, now,' Hugh said soothingly. 'They've had vampires here before, as we know.' But his face was white and he stared around him, gripping the umbrella.

"'Blast it!' I beat the side of the building with my fist.

"'You've got to keep a close eye out,' Hugh said soberly. 'Is Miss Rossi back?'

"'Helen!' I hadn't thought of her at once, and Hugh seemed on the verge of a smile at my exclamation. 'I'll go back now and check. I'm going to call Professor Bora, too. Look, Hugh — you keep a close eye out, too. Be careful, all right? He saw you with me, and that doesn't seem to be good luck for anyone these days.'

"'Don't worry about me.' Hugh was looking thoughtfully at the umbrella in his hand. 'How much did you pay that clerk?'

"I laughed in spite of my breathlessness. 'Yes, keep it on you.' We shook hands heartily, and Hugh vanished up the street in the direction of his hotel, which wasn't far. I didn't like his going on his own, but there were people in the street now, strolling and talking. In any case, I knew he'd always go his own way; he was that sort of man.

"Back in the hotel lobby, there was no sign of the terrified clerk. Perhaps it was only that his shift had ended, for a clean-shaven young man had taken his place behind the counter. He showed me that the key to Helen's new room was on its hook, so I knew she must still be with her aunt. The young man let me use the phone, after a careful arrangement for the cost, and then it took me a couple of tries to make Turgut's number ring. It galled me to call from the hotel phone, which I knew could be bugged, but it was the only possibility at this hour. I would have to hope our conversation would be too peculiar to be understood. At last I heard a clicking on the line, and then Turgut's voice, far away but jovial, answering in Turkish.

"'Professor Bora!' I shouted. 'Turgut, it's Paul, calling from Budapest.'

"'Paul, my dear man!' I thought I'd never heard anything sweeter than that rumbling, distant voice. 'There's some problem on the line — give me your number there in case we are cut asunder.'

"I got it from the hotel clerk and shouted it to

him. He shouted back. 'How are you? Have you found him?'

"'No!' I shouted. 'We are fine, and I've learned a little more, but something awful has happened.'

"'What is that?' I could hear his consternation, faintly, over the line. 'Have you been hurt? Miss Rossi?'

"'No — we're fine, but the librarian has followed us here.' I heard a swell of words that could have been some Shakespearean curse but was impossible to distinguish from the static. 'What do you think we should do?'

"'I don't know yet.' Turgut's voice was a little clearer now. 'Do you carry all the time the kit I gave you?'

"'Yes,' I said. 'But I can't get close enough to this ghoul to do anything with it. I think he searched my room today while we were at the conference, and apparently someone helped him.' Perhaps the police were listening in at this very moment. Who knew what they would make of all this anyway?

"'Be very careful, Professor.' Turgut sounded worried. 'I do not have any wise advice for you, but I shall have some news soon, maybe even before you return to Istanbul. I am glad you called tonight. Mr. Aksoy and I have found a new document, one neither one of us has ever seen before. He found it in the archive of Mehmed. This document was written by a monk of the Eastern Orthodox Church in 1477, and it must be translated.'

"There was static on the line again, and I had to shout. 'Did you say 1477? What language is it in?'

"'I cannot hear you, dear boy!' Turgut bellowed, far away. 'There was a rainstorm here. I will call you tomorrow night.' A Babel of voices — I couldn't tell whether they were Hungarian or Turkish — broke in on us and swallowed his next words. More clicking followed, and then the line went dead. I hung up slowly, wondering if I should call back, but the clerk was already taking the phone from me with a worried expression and adding up my bill on a scrap of paper. I paid glumly and stood there for a moment, not liking to go up to my bare new room, to which I'd been allowed to take only my shaving instruments and a clean shirt. My spirits were sinking rapidly — it had already been a very long day, after all, and the clock in the lobby said nearly eleven.

"They would have sunk lower still if a taxi hadn't pulled up at that moment. Helen got out and paid the driver, then came through the great door. She hadn't noticed me by the desk yet, and her face was grave and reticent, with the melancholy intensity I'd sometimes noticed in it. She had wrapped herself in a shawl of downy black-and-red wool that I had never seen before, perhaps a gift from her aunt. It muted the harsh lines of her suit and shoulders and made her skin glow white and luminous even under the crude lighting of the lobby. She looked like a princess, and I stared unabashedly at her for a moment before she saw me. It was not only her beauty, thrown into relief by the soft wool and the regal angle of her chin, that kept me riveted. I was remembering again, with an uneasy quiver inside, the portrait in Turgut's room — the proud head, the long straight nose, the great dark eyes with their heavy, hooded lids above and below. Perhaps I was just very tired, I told myself, and when Helen saw me and smiled, the image vanished again from my inner sight."

Chapter 43

IF I HADN'T shaken Barley awake, or if he had been alone, he would have passed in slumber across the border into Spain, I think, to be rudely awakened by the Spanish customs officers. As it was, he stumbled onto the platform at Perpignan half asleep, so that I was the one who asked the way to the bus station. The blue-coated conductor frowned, as if he thought we should be at home in the nursery by this hour, but he was kind enough to find our orphaned bags behind the station counter. Where were we going? I told him we wanted a bus to Les Bains, and he shook his head. For that we would have to wait till morning — didn't I know it was almost midnight? There was a clean hotel up the street where I and my — "Brother," I supplied quickly — could find a room. The conductor looked us over, observing my darkness and extreme youth, I supposed, and Barley's lanky blondness, but he only made a clicking sound with his tongue and walked on.

"The next morning dawned even fairer and more beautiful than the one before, and when I

617

met Helen in the hotel dining room for breakfast, my forebodings of the previous night were already a distant dream. Sun came through the dusty windows and lit the white tablecloths and heavy coffee cups. Helen was making some notes in a little notebook at the table. 'Good morning,' she said affably as I sat down and poured myself coffee. 'Are you ready to meet my mother?'

"'I haven't thought about anything else since we reached Budapest,' I confessed. 'How are we going to get there?'

"'Her village is on a bus route that is north of the city. There is only one bus there on Sunday mornings, so we must be sure we do not miss it. The ride is about an hour through very boring suburbs.'

"I doubted anything about this excursion could bore me, but I held my peace. One thing still troubled me, however. 'Helen, are you sure you want me to come along? You could go talk with her alone. Maybe that would be less embarrassing to her than your showing up with a total stranger — an American, to boot. And what if my presence got her in trouble?'

"'It is exactly your presence that will make it easier for her to talk,' Helen said firmly. 'She is very reserved around me, you know. You will charm her.'

"'Well, I've certainly never been accused of being charming before.' I helped myself to three slices of bread and a plate of butter.

"'Don't worry — you are not.' Helen gave me her most sardonic smile, but I thought I saw a glint of affection in her eyes. 'It is just that my mother is easy to charm.'

"She did not add, *Rossi charmed her, so why not you?* I thought it better to leave the subject there.

"'I hope you let her know we're coming.' I wondered, looking at her across the table, if she would tell her mother about the librarian's attack on her. The little scarf was wound firmly around her neck, and I tried hard not to glance at it.

"'Aunt Éva sent a message to her last night,' Helen said calmly, and passed me the preserves.

"The bus, when we caught it at the northern edge of the city, wound slowly in and out of suburbs, as Helen had predicted — first old outlying neighborhoods much damaged by the war, and then a host of newer buildings, rising high and white like tombstones for giants. This was the communist progress that was often elaborated upon with hostility in the Western press, I thought — the herding of millions of people all over Eastern Europe into sterile high-rise apartments. The bus stopped at several of these complexes, and I found myself wondering how sterile they really were; around the base of each lay homely gardens full of vegetables and herbs, bright flowers and butterflies. On a bench outside one building, close to the bus stop, two old men in white shirts and dark vests were playing a board game — what, I couldn't make out at a distance. Several women got on the bus in brightly embroidered blouses — a Sunday costume? — and one carried a cage with a live hen inside it. The driver waved the hen in with everyone else, and her owner settled in the back of the bus with some knitting.

"When we had left the suburbs behind, the bus lumbered out onto a country road, and here I saw fertile fields and wide, dusty roads. Sometimes we passed a horse-drawn wagon — the wagon made like a simple basket of wooden boughs — driven by a farmer in a black fedora and vest. Now and then we caught up with an automobile that would have been in a museum in the United States. The land was beautifully green and fresh, and yellow-leaved willows hung over the little streams that wound through it. From time to time we rode into a village; sometimes I could pick out the onion cupolas of an Orthodox church among the other church towers. Helen leaned across me for a view, too. 'If we kept on this road, we'd reach Esztergom, the first capital of the Hungarian kings. That's certainly worth seeing, if only we had the time.'

"'Next time,' I lied. 'Why did your mother choose to live out here?'

"'Oh, she moved here when I was still in high school, to be close to the mountains. I did not want to go with her — I stayed in Budapest with Éva. She has never liked the city, and she said the Börzsöny Mountains, north of here, remind her of Transylvania. She goes there with a hiking club every Sunday, except when the snows are heavy.'

"This added another little piece to the mosaic portrait of Helen's mother that I was constructing in my mind. 'Why didn't she move to the mountains themselves?'

"'There is no work there — it is mostly a national park. Besides, my aunt would have forbidden it, and she can be very stern. She thinks my mother has isolated herself too much already.'

"'Where does your mother work?' I peered out at a village bus stop; the only person standing there was an old woman dressed completely in black, with a black kerchief on her head and a bunch of red and pink flowers in one hand. She didn't get on the bus when we pulled up, nor did she greet anyone who got off. As we drove away I could see her staring after us, holding up her nosegay.

"'She works at the village cultural center, filing papers and typing a little and making coffee for the mayors of the bigger towns when they drop by. I have told her it is degrading work for someone of her intelligence, but she always shrugs and goes on doing it. My mother has made a career of remaining simple.' There was a note of bitterness in Helen's voice, and I wondered if she thought this simplicity had harmed not only the mother's career but also the daughter's opportunities. Those had been provided abundantly by Aunt Éva, I reflected. Helen was smiling her upside-down smile, a chilling one. 'You will see for yourself.'

"Helen's mother's village was identified by a sign on the outskirts, and in a few minutes our bus pulled into a square surrounded by dusty sycamores, with a boarded-up church at one side. An old woman, twin of that black-garbed grandmother I'd seen in the last village, waited alone under the bus shelter. I looked a question at Helen, but she shook her head, and, sure enough, the old lady embraced a soldier who got off ahead of us.

"Helen seemed to take our lonely arrival for granted, and she led me briskly down side streets past the quiet houses with flowers in their window boxes and shutters drawn against the bright sunlight. An elderly man sitting on a wooden chair outside one house nodded and touched his hat. Near the end of the street a gray horse was tied to a post, drinking water greedily from a bucket. Two women in housedresses and slippers talked outside a café, which seemed to be closed. From across the fields I could hear church bells, and closer by, the songs of birds in the linden trees. Everywhere there was a drowsy humming in the air; nature was only a step away, if you knew which direction to step.

"Then the street ended abruptly in a weedy field, and Helen knocked at the door of the last house. It was very small, a yellow stucco cottage with a red-tiled roof, and looked freshly painted outside. The roof overhung the front, making a natural porch, and the front door was dark wood with a big rusted handle. The house stood slightly apart from its neighbors, and with no colorful kitchen garden or newly laid sidewalk leading to it, as many of the other houses on the street had. Because of a heavy shadow from the eaves, for a minute I could not see the face of the woman who answered Helen's summons. Then I saw her clearly, and a moment later she was embracing Helen and kissing her cheek, calmly and almost formally, and turning to shake my hand.

"I don't know exactly what I had expected; perhaps the story of Rossi's desertion and Helen's birth had led me to imagine a sad-eyed, aging beauty, wistful or even helpless. The real woman before me had Helen's upright carriage, although she was shorter and heavier than her daughter, and a firm, cheerful countenance, round cheeked and dark eyed. Her plain dark hair was drawn back in a knot. She had on a striped cotton dress and a flowered apron. Unlike Aunt Éva, she wore no makeup or jewelry, and her clothing was similar to that of the housewives I'd seen in the street outside. She had been doing some kind of housework, in fact, for her sleeves were rolled to the elbow. She shook my hand with a friendly grip, saying nothing but looking right into my eyes. Then, for just a moment, I saw the shy girl she must have been more than two decades before, hidden in the depths of those dark eyes with the crow's-feet around them.

"She ushered us in and gestured for us to sit at the table, where she had set three chipped cups and a plate of rolls. I could smell coffee brewing. She had been cutting up vegetables, too, and a sharp aroma of raw onions and potatoes hung in the room.

"It was her only room, I now saw, trying not to look around too conspicuously — it served as her kitchen, bedroom, and sitting area. It was immaculately clean, the narrow bed in one corner made up with a white quilt and ornamented with several white pillows embroidered in bright colors. Next to the bed stood a table that held a book, a lamp with a glass chimney, and a pair of eyeglasses, and beside that a small chair. At the foot of the bed was a wooden chest, painted with flowers. The kitchen area, where we sat, consisted of a simple cookstove and a table and chairs. There was no electricity, nor was there a bathroom (I learned about the outhouse in the back garden only later in the visit). On one wall hung a calendar with a photograph of workers in a factory, and on another wall hung a piece of embroidery in red and white. There were flowers in a jar and white curtains at the windows. A tiny woodstove stood near the kitchen table, with sticks of wood piled next to it.

"Helen's mother smiled at me, still a little shyly, and then I saw for the first time her resemblance to Aunt Éva, and perhaps also some of what might have attracted Rossi. She had a smile of exceptional warmth, which began slowly and then dawned on its recipient with complete openness, almost radiance. It faded only slowly, too, as she sat down to cut more vegetables. She glanced up at me again and said something in Hungarian to Helen.

"'She wants me to give you your coffee.' Helen busied herself at the stove and served up a cup, stirring in sugar from a tin. Helen's mother put down her knife to push the plate of rolls toward me. I took one politely and thanked her in my awkward two words of Hungarian. That radiant, slow smile began to flicker again, and she looked from me to Helen, again telling her something I could not understand. Helen reddened and turned back to the coffee.

"'What is it?'

"'Nothing. Just my mother's village ideas, that is all.' She came to seat herself at the table, setting coffee before her mother and pouring some for herself. 'Now, Paul, if you will excuse us, I'll ask her for news of herself and what is happening in the village.'

"While they talked, Helen in her quick alto and her mother in murmured responses, I let my gaze wander over the room again. This woman lived not only in remarkable simplicity — perhaps her neighbors here did, too — but also in great solitude. There were only two or three books in sight, no animals, not even a potted plant. It was like the cell of a nun.

"Glancing back at her, I saw how young she was, far younger than my own mother. Her hair held a few gray threads where it was parted on top, and her face was lined with years, but there was something remarkably sound and healthy about her, an attractiveness completely apart from fashion or age. She could have married many times over, I reflected, and yet she chose to live in this conventual silence. She was smiling at me again and I smiled back; her face was so warm that I had to resist an urge to stretch out my hand and hold one of hers where it gently whittled a potato.

"'My mother would like to know all about you,' Helen told me, and with her help I answered every question as fully as I could, each put to me in quiet Hungarian, with a searching look from the interlocutor, as if she could make me understand by the power of her gaze. Where in America was I from? Why had I come here? Who were my parents? Did they mind my traveling far away? How had I met Helen? Here she inserted several other questions that Helen seemed disinclined to translate, one of them accompanied by a motherly hand smoothing Helen's cheek. Helen looked indignant, and I didn't press her to explain. Instead, we went on to my studies, my plans, my favorite foods.

"When Helen's mother was satisfied, she got up and began putting vegetables and pieces of meat in a big dish, which she spiced with something red from a jar over the stove and slid into the oven. She wiped her hands on her apron and sat down again, looking from one of us to the other without speaking, as if we had all the time in the world. At last Helen stirred, and I guessed from the way she cleared her throat that she meant to broach the purpose of our visit. Her mother watched her quietly, with no change of expression until Helen gestured at me on the word *Rossi*. It took all my nerve, sitting at a village table far from everything familiar to me, to fix my eyes on that tranquil face without flinching. Helen's mother blinked, once, almost as if someone had threatened to strike her, and for a second her eyes flew to my face. Then she nodded thoughtfully and posed some question to Helen. 'She asks how long you have known Professor Rossi.'

"'For three years,' I said.

"'Now,' Helen said, 'I will explain to her about his disappearance.' Gently and deliberately, not so much as if talking to a child but as if urging herself on against her own will, Helen spoke to her mother, sometimes gesturing at me and sometimes forming a picture in the air with her hands. At last I caught the word *Dracula,* and at that sound I saw Helen's mother blanch and catch the edge of the table. Helen and I both jumped to our feet, and Helen quickly poured a cup of water from the pitcher on the stove. Her mother said something quick and harsh. Helen turned to me. 'She says she always knew this would happen.'

"I stood by helplessly, but when Helen's mother had taken a few sips of water, she seemed partly recovered. She looked up, and then, to my surprise, took my hand as I had wanted to take hers a few minutes before and drew me back down to my chair. She held my hand fondly, simply, caressing it as if soothing a child. I couldn't imagine any woman in my own culture doing this on first meeting a man, and yet nothing could have seemed more natural to me. I understood then what Helen had meant when she'd said that of the two older women in her family, her mother was the one I would like best.

"'My mother wants to know if you honestly believe that Professor Rossi was taken by Dracula.'

"I inhaled deeply. 'I do.'

"'And she wishes to know if you love Professor Rossi.' Helen's voice was faintly disdainful, but her face was earnest. If I could safely have taken her hand in my free one, I would have.

"'I would die for him,' I said.

"She repeated this to her mother, who suddenly squeezed my fingers in a grip of iron; I realized later that hers was a hand strengthened by endless work. I could feel the roughness of her fingers, the calluses on her palms, the swollen knuckles. Looking down at that powerful small hand, I saw that it was years older than the woman it belonged to.

"After a moment, Helen's mother released me and went to the chest at the foot of her bed. She opened it slowly, moved several items inside, and took out what I immediately saw was a packet of letters. Helen's eyes widened and she spoke a sharp question; her mother said nothing, only returning in silence to the table and putting the package into my hand.

"The letters were in envelopes, without stamps, yellowing with age and bound together by a frayed red cord. As she gave them to me, Helen's mother closed my fingers over the cord with both her hands, as if urging me to cherish them. It took me only a second's glance at the handwriting on the first envelope to see that it was Rossi's, and to read the name to which they were addressed. That name I already knew, in the recesses of my memory, and the address was Trinity College, Oxford University, England."

Chapter 44

"I WAS DEEPLY MOVED when I held Rossi's letters in my hands, but before I could think about them, I had an obligation to fulfill. 'Helen,' I said, turning to her, 'I know you have sometimes felt I didn't believe the story of your birth. I did doubt it, at moments. Please forgive me.'

"'I am as surprised as you are,' Helen responded in a low voice. 'My mother never told me she had any of Rossi's letters. But they were not written to her, were they? At least, not this one on top.'

"'No,' I said. 'But I recognize this name. He was a great English literary historian — he wrote about the eighteenth century. I read one of his books in college, and Rossi described him in the letters he gave me.'

"Helen looked puzzled. 'What does this have to do with Rossi and my mother?'

"'Everything, maybe. Don't you see? He must have been Rossi's friend Hedges — that was the name Rossi used for him, remember? Rossi must have written to him from Romania, although that doesn't explain why these letters are in your mother's possession.'

"Helen's mother sat with folded hands, looking from one of us to the other with an expression of great patience, but I thought I detected a flush of excitement in her face. Then she spoke, and Helen translated for me. 'She says she will tell you her whole story.' Helen's voice was choked, and I caught my breath.

"It was a halting business, the older woman speaking slowly and Helen acting as her interpreter and occasionally pausing to express to me her own surprise. Apparently, Helen herself had heard only the outlines of this tale before, and it shocked her. When I got back to the hotel that night, I wrote it down from memory, to the very best of my ability; it took me much of the night, I remember. By then many other strange things had happened, and I should have been tired, but I can still recall that I recorded it with a kind of elated meticulousness.

"'When I was a girl, I lived in the tiny village of P— in Transylvania, very close to the Argeş River. I had many brothers and sisters, most of whom still live in that region. My father always said that we were descended from old and noble families, but my ancestors had fallen on hard times, and I grew up without shoes or warm blankets. It was a poor region, and the only people there who lived well were a few Hungarian families, in their big villas downriver. My father was terribly strict and we all feared his whip. My mother was often sick. I worked in our field outside the village from the time I was small. Sometimes the priest brought us food or supplies, but usually we had to manage as well as we could alone.

"'When I was about eighteen, an old woman came to our village from a village higher up in the mountains, above the river. She was a *vracă*, a healer, and one with special powers to look into the future. She told my father she had a present for him and his children, that she had heard about our family and wanted to give him something magical that was rightfully his. My father was an impatient man, with no time for superstitious old women, although he himself always rubbed all the openings of our cottage with garlic — the chimney and door frame, the keyhole and the windows — to keep out vampires. He sent the old woman rudely away, saying he had no money to give her for whatever she was peddling. Later, when I went to the village well for water, I saw her standing there and I gave her a drink and some bread. She blessed me and told me I was kinder than my father and that she would reward my generosity. Then she took from a bag at her waist a tiny coin, and she put it in my hand, telling me to hide it and keep it safe because it belonged to our family. She said also that it came from a castle above the Argeş.

"'I knew I should show the coin to my father, but I did not, because I thought he would be angry at my talking with the old witch. Instead, I hid it under my corner of the bed I shared with my sisters and I told no one about it. Sometimes I would get it out when I thought nobody was looking. I would hold it in my hand and wonder what the old woman had meant by giving it to me. On one side of the coin was a strange creature with a looped tail, and on the other a bird and a tiny cross.

"'A couple of years passed and I continued to work my father's land and help my mother in the house. My father was in despair about having several daughters. He said we would never get married because he was too poor to give anything for a dowry, and that we would always be a trouble to him. But my mother told us that everyone in the village said we were so beautiful that someone would marry us anyway. I tried to keep my clothes clean and my hair combed and neatly braided, so that I might be chosen someday. I did not like any of the young men who asked me to dance at the holidays, but I knew I would soon have to marry one of them so that I would not be a burden to my parents. My sister Éva had long since gone to Budapest with the Hungarian family she worked for, and sometimes she sent us a little money. She even sent me some good shoes once, a pair of leather city shoes of which I was very proud.

"'This was my situation in life when I met Professor Rossi. It was unusual for strangers to come to our village, especially anyone from far away, but one day everyone was passing around the news that a man from Bucharest had come to the tavern, and with him a man from another country. They were asking questions about the villages along the river and about the ruined castle in the mountains upriver, a day's walk above our village. The neighbor who stopped by to tell us about this also whispered something to my father as he sat on his bench outside our door. My father crossed himself and spat in the dust. "Rubbish and nonsense," he said. "No one should be asking such questions. It is an invitation to the Devil."

"'But I was curious. I went out to get water so that I could hear more about it, and when I entered the village square, I saw the strangers sitting at one of the two tables outside our tavern, talking with an old man who was always there. One of the strangers was large and dark, like a Gypsy but in city clothes. The other wore a brown jacket in a style I had never seen before, and wide trousers tucked into walking boots, and a broad brown hat on his head. I stayed on the other side of the square, near the well, and from there I could not see the foreigner's face. Two of my friends wanted a closer look and whispered to me to come with them. I went reluctantly, knowing my father would disapprove.

"'As we walked past the tavern, the foreign man glanced up, and I saw to my surprise that he was young and handsome, with a golden beard and bright blue eyes like the people in the German villages of our country. He was smoking a pipe and talking quietly with his companion. A worn canvas bag with straps for the arms sat on the ground next to him, and he was writing something in a cardboard book. He had a look on his face that I liked immediately — it was absentminded, gentle, and very alert all at the same time. He touched his hat to us and looked quickly away, and the ugly man touched his hat, too, and stared at us, and then they went back to talking with old Ivan and writing things down. The large man seemed to be talking to Ivan in Romanian, and then he would turn to the younger one and say something in a language I could not understand. I walked quickly on with my friends, not wanting the handsome stranger to think I was more forward than they were.

"'The next morning it was said in the village that the strangers had given money to a young man in the tavern to show them the way up to the ruined castle called Poenari, high above the Argeş. They would be gone overnight. I heard my father tell one of his friends that they were looking for the castle of Prince Vlad — he remembered when the fool with the Gypsy's face had been there once before, looking for it. "A fool never learns," my father said angrily. I had not heard this name — Prince Vlad — before. People in our village usually called the castle Poenari or Arefu. My father said the man who had taken the strangers there was crazed for a little money. He swore no payment would ever make him, my father, spend the night there because the ruins were full of evil spirits. He said that probably the stranger was looking for treasure, which was foolish because all the treasure of the prince who had lived there was deeply buried and had a wicked spell on it. My father said if anyone found it, and if it were exorcised, he should have had some of it himself, some of it belonged by rights to him. Then he saw me and my sisters listening, and he closed his mouth tightly.

"'What my father had said reminded me of the little coin the old woman had given me, and I thought guiltily that I had something I should have given to my father. But a rebellion rose up inside me, and I decided to try to give my coin to the handsome stranger, since he was looking for treasure at the castle. When I had the chance, I took the coin from its hiding place and knotted it in the corner of a kerchief, which I tied to my apron.

"'The stranger did not appear again for two days, and then I saw him sitting by himself at the same table, looking very tired, his clothes dirty and torn. My friends said that the city Gypsy had left that day and the stranger was alone. No one knew why he wanted to stay longer. He had taken the hat off his head and I could see his rumpled light brown hair. Some other men were with him, and they were having a drink. I did not dare come close or speak to the stranger because those men were with him, so I stopped to talk with a friend for a while. While we were talking, the stranger got up and went into the tavern.

"'I felt very sad and I thought it would be impossible for me to give my coin to him. But luck was with me that evening. Just as I was leaving my father's field, where I had stayed to work while my brothers and sisters were doing other chores, I saw the stranger walking by himself at the edge of the woods. He was walking along the path to the river, walking with his head bent and his hands clasped behind him. He was completely alone, and now that I had the chance to speak with him, I felt frightened. To give myself courage, I grasped the knot in my kerchief where the coin was hidden. I walked toward him and then stood in the path, waiting for his approach.

"'It seemed to take a long time, while I stood there waiting. He must not have noticed me until we were almost face-to-face. Then he suddenly glanced up from the path, looking very surprised. He took off his hat and stepped aside, as if to let me pass him, but I stayed very still, gathering my courage, and said hello to him. He bowed a little and smiled, and we stood staring at each other for a moment. There was nothing in his face or manner to make me feel afraid, but I was almost overcome by shyness.

"'Before I could lose all my courage, I untied the kerchief from my belt and unwrapped the coin. I handed it to him, silently, and he took it from my hand and turned it over, looking at it with care. Suddenly a light flashed over his face, and he glanced at me again, very sharply, as if he could look through my heart. He had the brightest, bluest eyes you can imagine. I felt a trembling all over. "*De unde?* — from where?" He gestured to show me his question. I was surprised that he seemed to know a few words of our language. He tapped the ground, and I understood. Had I gotten it out of the earth? I shook my head. *"De unde?"*

"'I tried to show him an old woman, kerchief on her head, bending over her stick — I showed her handing me the coin. He nodded, frowned. He made the signs of the old woman, then pointed along the path toward our village. "From there?" No — I shook my head again and pointed upriver and into the sky, to where I thought the castle was, and the old woman's village. I pointed to him and showed feet walking — up there! The light came into his face again, and he closed his hand on the coin. Then he handed it back to me, but I refused it, pointing to him and feeling myself turn red. He smiled, for the first time, and bowed to me, and I felt as if heaven had opened up to my eyes for a moment. *"Multumesc,"* he said. "Thank you."

"'Then I wanted to hurry away, before my father missed me at the supper table, but the stranger stopped me with a quick motion. He pointed to himself. *"Ma numesc Bartolomeo Rossi,"* he said. He repeated it, then wrote it for me in the earth at our feet. It made me laugh to try to pronounce it after him. Then he pointed at me. *"Voi?"* he said. "What is your name?" I told him and he repeated it, smiling again. *"Familia?"* He seemed to be groping for words.

"'"My family name is Getzi," I told him.

"'Surprise seemed to fill his face. He pointed in the direction of the river, then at me, and said something again and again, followed by the word *Drakulya,* which I understood to mean *of the dragon.* I could not gather his meaning. Finally, shaking his head and sighing, he said, "Tomorrow." He pointed at me, at himself, at the spot where we stood, and at the sun in the sky. I understood that he was asking me to meet him there at the same time the next evening. I knew my father would be very angry if he found out about this. I pointed to the ground under our feet, then put my finger to my lips. I didn't know another way to tell him not to talk about this to anyone in the village. He looked startled, but then he put his finger to his lips, too, and smiled at me. I had still felt somewhat afraid of him until that minute, but his smile was kind and his blue eyes sparkled. He tried again to return the coin to me, and when I again refused to take it, he bowed, put on his hat, and went back into the woods in the direction he had come from. I understood that he was letting me return to the village alone, and I set out quickly, without letting myself look back at him.

"'All that evening, at my father's table, and washing and drying the dishes with my mother, I thought about the stranger. I thought about his foreign clothes, his polite bow, his expression that was absentminded and alert at the same time, his beautifully bright eyes. I thought about him all the next day as I spun and wove with my sisters, made our dinner, drew water, and worked in the fields. Several times my mother scolded me for not paying attention to what I was doing. At evening, I stayed behind to finish my weeding alone, and I felt relieved when my brothers and father disappeared toward the village.

"'As soon as they were gone, I hurried to the edge of the wood. The stranger was sitting there against a tree, and when he saw me he jumped up and offered me a seat on a log near the path. But I was afraid someone from the village might pass by, and I led him deeper into the woods, my heart beating hard. There we sat on two rocks. The woods were full of the evening sounds of the birds — it was early summer and very green and warm.

"'The stranger took the coin I had given him out of his pocket and set it carefully on the ground. Then he pulled a couple of books from his knapsack and began to turn through them. I understood later that these were dictionaries in Romanian and some language he could understand. Very slowly, looking often at his books, he asked me if I had seen any other coins like the one I had given him. I said I had not. He said the creature on the coin was a dragon, and he asked me if I had ever seen this dragon anywhere else, on a building or a book. I said I had one on my shoulder.

"'At first, he could not understand what I was saying at all. I was proud of the fact that I could write our alphabet and read a little — we had a village school for a while when I was a child, and a priest had come to teach us there. The stranger's dictionary was very confusing to me, but together we found the word *shoulder.* He looked puzzled and asked again, *"Drakul?"* He held up the coin. I touched the shoulder of my blouse and nodded. He looked at the ground, his face reddening, and suddenly I felt that I was the brave one. I opened my wool vest and took it off, then untied the neck of my blouse. My heart was pounding, but something had come over me and I could not stop myself. He looked away, but I pulled my blouse off my shoulder and pointed.

"'I could not remember a time when I had not had a small dark green dragon imprinted on my skin there. My mother said it was put on one child in every generation of my father's family and that he had chosen me because he thought I might grow up to be the ugliest. He said that his grandfather had told him this was necessary to keep evil spirits away from our family. I heard about it only once or twice, because usually my father did not like to talk about it, and I did not even know which relative of his generation had the mark, whether it was on his own body somewhere or on one of his brothers or sisters. My dragon looked very different from the little dragon on the coin, so that until the stranger had asked me if I owned anything else with a dragon on it, I had never connected the two.

"'The stranger looked carefully at the dragon on my skin, holding the coin up next to it, but without touching me or even leaning closer. The red flush stayed in his face and he seemed relieved when I tied my blouse again and put on my vest. He looked through his dictionaries and asked me who had put the dragon there. When I said my father had done it, with the help of an old woman in the village, a healer, he asked if he could talk with my father about this. I shook my head so hard that he blushed deeply again. Then he told me, with great difficulty, that my family came from the line of an evil prince who had built the castle above the river. This prince had been called "the son of the dragon," and he had killed many people. He said the prince had become a *pricolic,* a vampire. I crossed myself and asked Mary for her protection. He asked me if I knew this story and I said I did not. He asked me how old I was and if I had brothers and sisters, and if there were other people in the village with our name.

"'At last I pointed to the sun, which had nearly

set, to show him that I had to go home, and he stood up quickly, looking serious. Then he gave me his hand and helped me to my feet. When I grasped his hand, my heart leaped into my fingers. I was confused and I turned away quickly. But suddenly I thought to myself that he was too much interested in evil spirits and might put himself in danger. Perhaps I could give him something that would protect him. I pointed to the ground and the sun. "Come tomorrow," I said. He hesitated for a moment, and finally he smiled. He put his hat on and touched the brim. Then he disappeared into the woods.

"'The next morning when I went to the well, he was sitting at the tavern with the old men, again writing something. I thought I saw his gaze on me, but he showed no sign of recognizing me. I was very happy inside, because I understood that he had kept our secret. In the afternoon, when my father and mother and brothers and sisters were out of the house, I did a wicked thing. I opened my parents' wooden chest and I took from it a little silver dagger I had seen there several times before. My mother had once said it was for killing vampires if they came to trouble the people or the herds. I also took a handful of garlic flowers from my mother's garden. I hid these items in my kerchief when I went to the fields.

"'This time, my brothers worked a long time beside me and I could not shake them off, but finally they said they would go back to the village, and they told me to come with them. I said I would gather some herbs from the wood and come in a few minutes. I was very nervous by the time I reached the stranger, whom I found deep in the woods on our ledge of rocks. He was smoking his pipe, but when I came toward him he put it down and jumped to his feet. I sat down with him and showed him what I had brought. He looked startled when he saw the knife, and very interested when I explained to him that he could use it to kill *pricolici*. He wanted to refuse it, but I begged him so earnestly to take it that he stopped smiling and put it thoughtfully into his knapsack, wrapping it first in my kerchief. Then I gave him the garlic flowers and showed him that he should keep some in his jacket pocket.

"'I asked him how long he would be staying in our village, and he showed me five fingers — five more days. He made me understand that he would travel to several villages nearby, walking to each from our village, to talk with people about the castle. I asked him where he would go when he left our village at the end of five days. He said that he was going to a country called Greece, which I had heard of before, and then back to his own village in his own country. Drawing in the forest earth, he showed me that his country, called England, was an island far away from our country. He showed me where his university was — I did not know what he meant — and wrote the name of it in the dirt. I still remember those letters: OXFORD. Afterward I wrote them down sometimes, to look at them again. It was the strangest word I had ever seen.

"'Suddenly, I understood that he would leave soon and that I would never see him again, or anyone like him, and my eyes filled with tears. I had not meant to cry — I never cried over the annoying young men in the village — but my tears would not obey me and they ran down my cheeks. He looked very distressed and pulled a white handkerchief out of his jacket pocket and gave it to me. What was the problem? I shook my head. He rose slowly and gave me his hand to help me up, as he had the night before. While I was getting up, I stumbled and fell against him without meaning to, and when he caught me we kissed each other. Then I turned and ran through the woods. At the path, I looked back. He was standing there, as still as a tree, looking after me. I ran all the way to the village and lay awake during the night with his handkerchief hidden in my hand.

"'The next evening he was there in the same place, as if he had never moved from the spot where I had left him. I ran to him and he opened his arms to me and caught me. When we could not kiss each other anymore, he spread his jacket on the ground and we lay down together. In that hour, I learned about love, one moment at a time. Up close, his eyes were as blue as the sky. He put flowers in my braids and kissed my fingers. I was surprised by many things he did, and things I did, and I knew it was wrong, a sin, but I felt the joy of heaven opening around us.

"'After that there were three nights until he left. We met earlier each evening. I told my mother and father any excuse I could think of, and I always came home with herbs from the woods as if I had gone there to gather them. Every night Bartolomeo told me he loved me and begged me to come with him when he left the village. I wanted to, but I was afraid of the large world he came from, and I could not imagine how I would escape my father. Every night I asked him why he couldn't stay with me in the village, and he shook his head and said he had to return to his home and his work.

"'On the last night before he left the village, I began to cry as soon as we touched each other. He held me and kissed my hair. I had never met any man so gentle and kind. When I had stopped crying, he drew from his finger a little silver ring with a seal on it. I don't know for certain, but I think now it was the seal of his university. He wore it on the smallest finger of his left hand. He took it off and put it on my ring finger. Then he asked me to marry him. He must have been studying his dictionary, because I understood him right away.

"'At first it seemed so impossible an idea that I simply began to cry again — I was very young — but then I agreed. He made me understand that he would return for me in four weeks. He would go to Greece to take care of something there — what, I could not understand. Then he would come back for me and would give my father some money to make him happy. I tried to explain that I had no dowry, but he would not listen. Smiling, he showed me the dagger and coin I had given him, and then made a circle of his hands around my face and kissed me.

"'I should have felt happy, but I had a sense that evil spirits were present, and I was afraid something might happen to keep him from returning. Every moment we spent together that evening was very sweet, because I thought each was the last. He was so confident, so sure that we would see each other again soon. I could not say good-bye until it was almost dark in the woods, but I began to fear my father's anger and at last I kissed Bartolomeo one more time, made sure the garlic flowers were in his pocket, and left him. I turned back again and again. Each time I looked back, I saw him standing in the woods, holding his hat in his hand. He looked very lonely.

"'I cried as I walked along, and I took the little ring off my finger, kissing it, and knotted it in my kerchief. When I reached home my father was angry and wanted to know where I had been after dark without permission. I told him that my friend Maria had lost a goat and I had been helping her search for it. I went to bed with a heavy heart, feeling sometimes hopeful and then sad again.

"'The next morning I heard that Bartolomeo had left the village, traveling with a farmer in his cart toward Târgoviste. The day was very long and sad for me, and in the evening I went to our meeting place in the woods, to be alone there. Seeing it made me weep again. I sat on our rocks and finally lay down where we had lain every evening. I put my face against the earth and sobbed. Then I felt my hand brush against something among the ferns, and to my surprise I found there a package of letters in envelopes. I could not read the handwriting on them, where they were addressed to someone, but on the flap of each his beautiful name was printed, as in a book. I opened some of them and kissed his writing, although I could see that they were not addressed to me. I wondered for a moment if they could have been written to another woman, but I put this thought out of my mind as soon as it came. I realized the letters must have fallen out of his knapsack when he had opened it to show me he had the dagger and coin I'd given him.

"'I thought of trying to mail them to Oxford in the island of England, but I could not think of any way to send them unnoticed. Also, I didn't know how I could pay to send something. It would cost money to mail a package to his far-away island, and I had never owned any money apart from the little coin I had given to Bartolomeo. I decided to save the letters to give him when he returned for me.

"'Four weeks passed very, very slowly. I made notches on a tree near our secret place, so that I could keep track of the days. I worked in the field, helped my mother, spun and wove for our next winter's clothing, went to church, and listened wherever I could for news of Bartolomeo. At first the old men talked about him a little, and shook their heads over his interest in vampires. "No good can come of that," one of them would say, and the rest would agree. It gave me a terrible mixture of happiness and pain to hear this. I was glad to listen to someone else talking about him, since I could never speak a word to anyone, but it also sent a chill through me to think that he might be attracting the attention of *pricolici*.

"'I wondered constantly what would happen when he came back. Would he walk up to my father's door, knock on it, and ask my father for my hand in marriage? I imagined how surprised my family would be. They would all gather at the door and stare while Bartolomeo gave them gifts and I kissed them good-bye. Then he would lead me away to a waiting wagon, maybe even to an automobile. We would ride out of the village and across lands I could not imagine, beyond the mountains, beyond the great city where my sister Éva lived. I hoped we would stop to see Éva, because I had always loved her best. Bartolomeo would love her, too, because she was strong and brave, a traveler like him.

"'I passed four weeks in this way, and by end of the fourth week I was tired and could not eat or sleep very much. When I had cut almost four weeks of notches in my tree, I began to wait and watch for a sign of his return. Whenever a wagon came into the village, the sound of its wheels made my heart jump. I went for water three times a day, watching and listening for news. I told myself that he probably would not come after exactly four weeks, and that I should wait a week more. After the fifth week, I felt ill and I was certain that the prince of the *pricolici* had killed him. Once I even had the thought that my beloved might return to me in the form of a vampire himself. I ran to the church in the middle of the day and prayed in front of the icon of the blessed Virgin to take away this horrible idea.

"'In the sixth and seventh weeks I began to give up hope. In the eighth week I knew suddenly by many signs I had heard about among the married women that I would have a child. Then I cried silently in my sisters' bed at night and I felt the whole world, even God and the Holy Mother, had forgotten about me. I did not know what had happened to Bartolomeo, but I believed it must have been something terrible, because I knew he had truly loved me. In secret I gathered the herbs and roots that were said to prevent a child from coming into the world, but it was no use. My child was strong inside me, stronger than I was, and I began to love that strength in spite of myself. When I secretly placed my hand on my belly, I felt Bartolomeo's love and I believed he could not have forgotten about me.

"'I knew I had to leave the village before I brought shame on my family and my father's anger on myself. I thought of trying to find the old woman who had given me the coin. Perhaps she would take me in and let me cook and clean for her. She had come from one of the villages above the Argeş, near the castle of the *pricolic,* but I did not know which village, or whether she was still alive. There were bears and wolves in the mountains, and many evil spirits, and I did not dare wander through the forest all alone.

"'At last I decided to write my sister Éva, something I had done once or twice before. I took some paper and an envelope from the house of the priest, where I worked in the kitchen sometimes. In the letter, I told her my situation and begged her to come for me. It took another five weeks for her answer to arrive. Thank the Lord, the farmer who brought it in with some supplies gave it to me and not to my father, and I read it in secret, in the woods. The middle of my body was growing round already, so that it felt strange when I sat down on a log, although I could still hide my roundness with my apron.

"'There was some money in the letter, Romanian money, more than I had ever seen, and Éva's note was short and practical. She said I should leave the village on foot, walk to the next village, about five kilometers away, and then get a ride in a wagon or truck to Târgoviste. From there I could find a ride to Bucharest, and from Bucharest I could travel by train to the Hungarian border. Her husband would meet me at the border office in T— on September 20 — I still remember the date. She said I should plan my travel as well as I could to arrive there on that day. Enclosed in her letter I would find a stamped invitation from the government of Hungary, which would help me enter the country. She sent me love, told me to be very careful, and wished me a safe journey. When I came to the end of the letter, I kissed her signature and blessed her with all my heart.

"'I packed my few belongings in a little bag, including my good shoes to save for the train journey, the letters Bartolomeo had lost, and his silver ring. One morning as I was leaving our cottage, I hugged and kissed my mother, who was getting old and sicker. I wanted her to know later that I had said good-bye to her in some way. I think she was surprised, but she didn't ask me any questions. Instead of going to the fields that morning, I set out through the woods, avoiding the road. I stopped to say good-bye to the secret place in the woods where I had lain with Bartolomeo. The four weeks of notches on the tree were already fading. At that spot I put his ring on my finger and tied a kerchief over my head, like a married woman. I could feel winter coming in the yellowing leaves and cool air. I stood there for a few moments, and then I set out along the path to the next village.

"'I don't remember all of that trip, only that I was very tired and sometimes very hungry. One night I slept in the house of an old woman who gave me a good soup and told me my husband should not let me travel alone. Another time I had to sleep in a barn. At last I found a ride to Târgoviste, and then another to Bucharest. When I could I bought bread, but I did not know how much money I would need for the train, so I was very careful. Bucharest was very large and beautiful, but it frightened me because there were so many people, all in fine clothes, and men who looked boldly at me on the street. I had to sleep in the train station. The train was frightening, too, a huge black monster. Once I was sitting inside, next to a window, I felt my heart lifting a little bit. We rode past many wonderful sights — mountains and rivers and open fields, very different from our Transylvanian forests.

"'At the border station, I learned that it was September 19, and I slept on a bench until one of the guards let me come into his booth and gave me some hot coffee. He asked me where my husband was, and I said I was going to Hungary to see him. The next morning a man in a black suit and hat came looking for me. He had a very kind face and he kissed me on both cheeks and called me "sister." I loved my brother-in-law from that moment until the day he died, and I love him still. He was more my brother than any brother in my own family. He took care of everything, buying me a hot dinner on the train, which we ate at a table with a tablecloth. We could eat and look out the train window at everything passing by.

"'At the Budapest station, Éva was waiting for us. She wore a suit and a beautiful hat, and I thought she looked like a queen. She hugged and kissed me many times. My baby was born at the best hospital in Budapest. I wanted to name her Éva, but Éva said she would rather name her herself, and she called her Elena. She was a lovely baby, with big dark eyes, and she smiled very early, when she was only five days old. People said they had never seen a baby smile so young. I had hoped she would have Bartolomeo's blue eyes, but she looked only like my family.

"'I waited to write to him until after the baby was born, because I wanted to tell him about a real baby, not to tell him only about my pregnancy. When Elena was one month old, I asked my brother-in-law to help me find an address for Bartolomeo's university, Oxford, and I wrote the strange words myself on the envelope. My brother-in-law penned the letter for me in German, and I signed it with my own hand. In the letter I told Bartolomeo that I had waited for him for three months and then had left the village because I knew I would have his child. I told him about my travels and about my sister's home in Budapest. I told him about our Elena, how sweet she was, how happy. I told him I loved him and was frightened that something terrible had happened to prevent his returning. I asked him when I would see him, and whether he could come to Budapest to get me and Elena. I told him that no matter what had happened, I would love him to the end of my life.

"'Then I waited again, this time a long, long time, and when Elena was already taking her first steps, a letter came from Bartolomeo. It was from America, not from England, and it was written in German. My brother-in-law translated it for me in a very gentle voice, but I saw that he was too honest to change anything it said. In his letter Bartolomeo said he had received a letter from me that had gone first to his former home in Oxford. He told me politely that he had never heard of me or seen my name before, and that he had never been to Romania, so that the child I described could not be his. He was sorry to hear such a sad story and he wished me better fortunes. It was a short letter and very kind, not harsh, and in it there was no sign that he knew me.

"'I cried for a long time. I was young and I did not understand that people can change, that their minds and feelings can change. When I had been in Hungary for several years, I began to understand that you can be one person at home and a different person when you are in a different country. I realized that something like this had happened to Bartolomeo. In the end, my only wish was that he had not lied, had not said he didn't know me at all. I wished that because I had felt when we were together that he was an honorable person, a truthful person, and I did not want to think badly of him.

"'I raised Elena with the help of my relatives, and she became a beautiful and brilliant girl. I know this is because she has Bartolomeo's blood in her. I told her about her father — I never lied to her. Maybe I didn't tell her enough, but she was too young to understand that love makes people blind and foolish. She went to the university and I was very proud of her, and she told me that she had heard her father was a great scholar in America. I hoped someday she might meet him. But I did not know he was at the university you went to there,' Helen's mother added, turning almost reproachfully to her daughter, and in this abrupt way she finished her story.

"Helen murmured something that could have

been either apology or self-defense, and shook her head. She looked as stunned as I felt. Throughout the story she had sat quiet, translating as if barely breathing, murmuring something else only when her mother described the dragon on her shoulder. Helen told me much later that her mother had never undressed in front of her, never taken her to the public baths as Éva had.

"At first we sat in silence at the table, the three of us, but after a moment Helen turned to me, gesturing helplessly toward the package of letters that lay before us on the table. I understood; I'd been thinking the same thing. 'Why didn't she send some of these to Rossi to prove he had been with her in Romania?'

"She looked at her mother — with a profound hesitation in her eyes, I thought — and then apparently put this question to her. Her mother's answer, when she translated it for me, brought a lump to my throat, a pain that was partly for her and partly for my perfidious mentor. 'I thought about doing that, but from his letter I understood that he had changed his mind completely. I decided it would make no difference for me to send him these letters, except to bring me more pain, and then I would have lost some of the few pieces of him that I could keep.' She extended her hand as if to touch his handwriting, then withdrew it. 'I only regretted not returning to him what was really his. But he had kept so much of me — perhaps it was not wrong for me to keep these for myself?' She glanced from Helen to me, her eyes suddenly a little less tranquil. It was not defiance I saw there, I thought, but the flare of some old, old devotion. I looked away.

"Helen was defiant, even if her mother was not. 'Then why didn't she at least give these letters to me long ago?' Her question was fierce, and she turned it on her mother the next second. The older woman shook her head. 'She says,' Helen reported, her face hardening, 'that she knew I hated my father and she was waiting for someone who loved him.' As she still does herself, I could have added, for my own heart was so full that it seemed to give me an extra perception of the love buried for years in this bare little house.

"My feelings were not for Rossi alone. Sitting there at the table, I took Helen's hand in one of mine, and her mother's work-worn hand in the other, and held them tightly. At that moment, the world in which I had grown up, its reserve and silences, its mores and manners, the world in which I had studied and achieved and occasionally attempted to love, seemed as far off as the Milky Way. I couldn't have spoken if I'd wanted to, but if my throat had cleared I might have found some way to tell these two women, with their so different but equally intense attachments to Rossi, that I felt his presence among us.

"After a moment Helen quietly withdrew her hand from my grasp, but her mother held on to me as she had before, asking something in her gentle voice. 'She wants to know how she can help you find Rossi.'

"'Tell her she has helped me already, and that I will read these letters as soon as we leave to see if they can guide us further. Tell her we will let her know when we find him.'

"Helen's mother inclined her head humbly at this, and rose to check the stew in the oven. A wonderful smell drifted from it and even Helen smiled, as if this return to a home not her own had its compensations. The peace of the moment emboldened me. 'Please ask her if she knows anything about vampires that might help us in our search.'

"When Helen translated this, I saw I had shattered our fragile calm. Her mother looked away and crossed herself, but after a moment she seemed to muster her forces to speak. Helen listened intently and nodded. 'She says you must remember that the vampire can change his shape. He can come to you in many forms.'

"I wanted to know what this meant exactly, but Helen's mother had already begun to dish up our meal with a hand that trembled. The warmth of the oven and the smell of meat and bread filled the small house, and we all ate heartily, if in silence. Now and then Helen's mother gave me more bread, patting my arm, or poured out fresh tea for me. The food was simple but delicious and abundant, and sunlight came in the front windows to ornament our meal.

"When it was done Helen went outside with a cigarette, and her mother beckoned to me to follow her around the side of the house. In the back there was a shed with a few chickens scratching around it, and a hutch with two long-eared rabbits. Helen's mother took one of the rabbits out, and we stood together in a companionable dumb show, scratching its soft head while it blinked and struggled a little. I could hear Helen through one of the windows now, washing up the dishes inside. The sun was warm on my head, and beyond the house the green fields hummed and wavered with an inexhaustible optimism.

"Then it was time for us to leave, to walk back to the bus, and I put Rossi's letters into my briefcase. As we went out again, Helen's mother stopped in the doorway; she seemed to have no thought of walking through the village to see us onto the bus. She took both my hands in hers and shook them warmly, looking into my face. 'She says she wishes only safe journeys for you, and that you will find what you are longing for,' Helen explained. I looked into the darkness in the older woman's eyes and thanked her with all my heart. She embraced Helen, holding her face sadly between her hands for a moment, and then let us go.

"At the edge of the road, I turned back to see her again. She was standing in the doorway, one hand against the frame, as if our visit had weakened her. I put my briefcase down in the dust and went back to her so quickly that I didn't know for a moment I had moved at all. Then, remembering Rossi, I took her in my arms and kissed her soft, lined cheek. She clung to me, a head shorter than I, and buried her face in my shoulder. Suddenly she pulled away and vanished into the house. I thought she wanted to be alone with her emotions and I turned away, too, but in a second she was back. To my astonishment, she grasped my hand and closed it over something small and hard.

"When I opened my fingers I saw a silver ring with a tiny coat of arms on it. I understood at once that it was Rossi's, which she was returning to him through me. Her face shone above it; her eyes glowed lustrously dark. I bent and kissed her again, but this time on the mouth. Her lips were warm and sweet. As I released her, turning swiftly back to my briefcase and to Helen, I saw on the older woman's face the gleam of a single tear. I've read there is no such thing as a single tear, that old poetic trope. And perhaps there isn't, since hers was simply companion to my own.

"As soon as we were settled in the bus, I got out Rossi's letters and carefully opened the first one. In recording it here, I will honor Rossi's desire to protect his friend's privacy with a nom de plume — a nom de guerre, he'd called it. It was very strange to see Rossi's handwriting again —

that same younger, less cramped version of it —
on the yellowing pages.

"'You're going to read them here?' Helen, leaning almost against my shoulder, looked startled.

"'What, can you wait?'

"'No,' she said."

Chapter 45

June 20, 1930

My dear friend,

I haven't a soul in the world to talk to at this moment, and I find myself with pen in hand wishing for your company, in particular — you would be full of your usual mild amazement at the scene I'm enjoying just now. I've been in a state of disbelief myself today — as you would be if you could see where I am — on a train, although that's hardly a clue in itself. But the train is puffing towards Bucarest. Good God, man, I hear you say through its whistle. But it is true. I hadn't planned to come here, but something quite remarkable has brought me. I was in Istanbul until just a few days ago, on a bit of research I've been keeping under my hat, and I found something there that made me want to come here. Not want to, actually; it would be more accurate to say I'm terrified to, and yet feel compelled. You are such an old rationalist — you aren't going to care for all this a bit, but I wish like the devil I had your brains along on my jaunt; I'm going to need every scrap of mine and more to find what I'm looking for.

We're slowing for a town, with a chance to buy breakfast — I'll desist for the moment and come back to this later.

Afternoon — Bucarest
I'm down for what would be a siesta if my mind weren't in such a state of unrest and excitement. It's accursedly hot here — I thought this would be a land of cool mountains, but if it is I haven't reached any yet. Nice hotel, Bucarest is a sort of tiny Paris of the East, grand and small and a little faded, all at the same time. It must have been dashing in the Eighties and Nineties. It took me forever to find a cab, and then a hotel, but my rooms are fairly comfortable and I can rest and wash and think about what to do. I'm half inclined not to set down here what I'm about, but you'll be so very perplexed by my ravings if I don't that I think I must. To make it short and shocking, I'm on a quest of sorts, an historian's hunt for Dracula — not Count Dracula of the romantic stage, but a real Dracula — Drakulya — Vlad III, a fifteenth-century tyrant who lived in Transylvania and Wallachia and dedicated

himself to keeping the Ottoman Empire out of his lands as long as possible. I stopped in Istanbul the better part of a week to see an archive there that contains some documents about him collected by the Turks, and while there I found a most remarkable set of maps that I believe to be clues to the whereabouts of his tomb. I'll explain to you at greater length when I'm home what sent me on this chase, and I simply have to beg your indulgence in the meantime. You can chalk it up to youth, you old sage, my setting out on this chase at all.

In any case, my stay in Istanbul turned dark at the end and has rather frightened me, although that will surely sound foolish at a distance. But I'm not easily put off a quest once I've begun, as you know, and I couldn't help coming on here with copies I've made of those maps, to look for more information about Drakulya's tomb. I should explain to you, at the very least, that he is supposed to have been buried in an island monastery in Lake Snagov, in western Roumania — Wallachia, the region is called. The maps I found in Istanbul, with his tomb clearly marked on them, show no island, no lake, and nothing that looks like western Roumania, as far as I can tell. It always seems to me a good idea to check the obvious first, since the obvious is sometimes the right answer. I've resolved, therefore — but here I'm sure you're shaking your head over what you will call foolish stubbornness — to make my way to Lake Snagov with the maps and ascertain for myself that the tomb is not there. How I will go about that, I don't yet know, but I can't begin to be satisfied hunting elsewhere until I have ruled out this possibility. And, perhaps, after all, my maps are some kind of ancient hoax and I will find ample proof that the tyrant sleeps there and always has.

I must be in Greece by the fifth, so I have precious little time for this whole excursion. I only want to know if my maps fit anything at the site of the tomb. Why I need to know this, I cannot tell even you, dear man — I wish I knew, myself. I intend to conclude my Roumanian journey by visiting as much as I can of Wallachia and Transylvania. What comes to your mind when you think of the word Transylvania, if you ponder it at all? Yes, as I thought — wisely, you don't. But what comes to my mind are mountains of savage beauty, ancient castles, werewolves, and witches — a land of mag-

ical obscurity. How, in short, am I to believe I will still be in Europe, on entering such a realm? I shall let you know if it's Europe or fairyland when I get there. First, Snagov — I set out tomorrow.

Your devoted friend,
Bartholomew Rossi

June 22
Lake Snagov

My dear friend,

I haven't yet seen any place to post my first letter — to post it with the confidence, that is, that it will ever reach your hands — but I'll go hopefully on here despite that, since a great deal has happened. I spent all day yesterday in Bucarest trying to locate good maps — I now have at least some road maps of Wallachia and Transylvania — and talking with everyone I could find at the university who might have some interest in the history of Vlad Ţepeş. No one here seems to want to discuss the subject, and I have the sense of their inwardly, if not outwardly, crossing themselves when I mention Dracula's name. After my experiences in

Istanbul, this makes me a little nervous, I confess, but I will press on for now.

In any case, yesterday I found a young professor of archaeology at the university who was kind enough to inform me that one of his colleagues, a Mr. Georgescu, has made a speciality of the history of Snagov and is digging out there this summer. Of course, I was tremendously excited to learn this and have decided to put myself, maps and bags and all, into the hands of a driver who can take me out there today; it is only some hours' drive from Bucarest, he says, and we leave at one o'clock. I must go now to lunch somewhere — the little restaurants here are uncommonly nice, with glimpses of an Oriental luxury in their cuisine — before we depart.

Evening

My dear friend,

I can't help continuing this spurious correspondence of ours — may it unfold itself under your eyes eventually — because it's been such a remarkable day that I simply must talk with someone. I left Bucarest in a neat little taxicab of sorts, driven by an equally neat little man with whom I could barely exchange two words (Snagov being one of them). After a brief session with my road maps, and many reassuring pats on the shoulder (my shoulder, that is), we set off. It took us all of the afternoon. We puttered along roads mainly paved but very dusty, and through a lovely landscape mainly agrarian but occasionally forested, to reach Lake Snagov.

My first intimation of the place was the driver's waving an excited hand, on which I looked out and saw only forest. This was just an introduction, however. I don't quite know what I'd expected; I suppose I'd been so wrapped up in my historian's curiosity that I hadn't stopped to expect anything in particular. I was jolted out of my obsession by the first sight of the lake. It is an exceptionally lovely place, my friend, bucolic and otherworldly. Imagine, if you will, a sparkling long water, which you catch glimpses of from the road between dense groves of trees. Nestled here and there in the woods are fine villas — often you can see only an elegant chimney, or a curving wall — many of which appear to date from early in the last century, or earlier.

When you get to an opening in the forest — we parked near a little restaurant of sorts with three boats drawn up behind it — you look out across the lake to the island where the monastery lies, and there — there at last — you get a panorama that has surely changed little over centuries. The island is a short boat ride from shore and is wooded like the banks of the lake. Above its trees rise the splendid Byzantine cupolas of the monastery church, and across the water comes the sound of bells — struck (I later learned) by a monk's wooden mallet. That sound of bells floating across the water made my heart turn over; it seemed to me exactly one of those messages from the past that cry out to be read, even if one cannot be sure what they say. My driver and I, standing there in the late-afternoon light reflected off the water, might have been spies for the Turkish army, peering out at this bastion of an alien faith, instead of two rather dusty modern men leaning against an automobile.

I could have stood looking and listening far longer without growing restless, but my determination to find the archaeologist before nightfall sent me into the restaurant. I used a little sign language and my best pidgin Latin to get us a boat to the island. Yes, yes, there was a man from Bucarest digging with a shovel over there, the owner managed to convey to me — and twenty minutes later we were disembarking on the shore of the island. The monastery was even lovelier up close, and rather forbidding, with its ancient walls and high cupolas, each crowned with an ornate seven-pointed cross. The boatman led us up steep steps to it, and I would have entered the great wooden doors at once, but the fellow pointed us around the back.

Skirting those beautiful old walls, I realized suddenly that for the first time I was actually walking in Dracula's footsteps. Until then, I had been following his trail through a maze of documents, but now I stood on ground that his feet — in what sort of shoes? Leather boots, with a cruel spur buckled to them? — had probably trodden. If I had been one for crossing myself, I would have done it at that moment; as it was, I had the sudden urge to tap the boatman on his rough woollen shoulder and ask him to row us safely to shore again. But I didn't, as you can imagine, and I hope I shall not ultimately regret having stayed my hand.

Behind the church, in the midst of a large ruin, we did indeed find a man with a shovel. He was a hearty-looking, middle-aged man with curly black hair, his white shirt untucked, sleeves rolled to the elbow. Two boys worked beside him, turning carefully through the soil by hand, and from time to time he set down his shovel and did the same. They were concentrated around a very small area, as if they had found something of interest there, and only when our boatman shouted a greeting did they all look up.

The man in the white shirt came forwards, scanning all of us with very sharp dark eyes, and the boatman made some sort of introduction, helped along by the driver. I held out my hand and tried one of my few Roumanian phrases before lapsing into English:"Ma numesc Bartolomeo Rossi. Nu va suparati . . ." I learned this delightful phrase, with which one interrupts strangers with a request for information, from the concierge at my hotel in Bucarest. It means, literally, "Don't be angry" — can you imagine an everyday utterance more redolent of history? "Don't pull out your dagger, friend — I'm simply lost in this wood and need directions out of it." I don't know whether it was my use of the phrase, or my probably atrocious accent, but the archaeologist burst into laughter as he gripped my hand.

Up close, he was a sturdy, deeply tanned fellow with a network of lines around his eyes and mouth. Two top teeth were missing from his smile, and most of the remaining ones glinted with gold. His hand was prodigiously strong, dry and rough as a farmer's. "Bartolomeo Rossi," he said in a rich voice, still laughing. "Ma numesc Velior Georgescu. How doo you doo? How can I help you?" For a moment I was transported to our walking trip last year; he might have been any one of those weatherbeaten highlanders of whom we were constantly asking directions, only with dark hair instead of sandy.

"You speak English?" I puzzled stupidly.

"A wee bit," said Mr. Georgescu. "It has been a long time since I have had the chance to practice, but it will come back to my toongue yet." His speech was fluent and rich, with the burr of a rolled "r."

"I beg your pardon," I said hastily. "I understand you have a special interest in Vlad III and I would very much like to talk with you. I'm an historian from Oxford University."

He nodded. "I'm glad to hear of your interest. Have you coome so far just to see his grave?"

"Well, I had hoped —"

"Ah, you hooped, you hooped," said Mr. Georgescu, clapping me on the shoulder not unkindly. "But I shall have to bring down your hoopes a bit, my lad." My heart leapt — was it possible that this man, too, thought Vlad was not buried here? But I decided to bide my time and listen carefully before asking any more questions. He was studying me quizzically, and now he smiled again. "Coome, I'll take you for the walking toour." He gave his assistants a few quick instructions, which appeared to be an invitation to stop working, for they brushed off their hands and flopped down under a tree. Leaning his shovel against a half-excavated wall, he beckoned to me. In my turn, I let the driver and boatman know I was taken care of and crossed the boatman's palm with silver. He touched his hat and disappeared, and the driver sat down against the ruin and took out a pocket flask.

"Very good. We will go around the outside first." Mr. Georgescu waved a broad hand about him. "You know the history of this island? A little? There was a church here in the fourteenth century, and the monastery was built a wee bit later, also in that century. The first church was wooden, and the second was stoone, but

681

the stoone church sank right into the lake in 1453. Remarkable, doon't you think? Dracula came to power in Wallachia for the second time in 1462, and he had his own ideas. I believe he liked this monastery because an island is easy to protect — he was always looking for places he could fortify against the Turks. This is a good one, doon't you think?"

I agreed, trying not to stare at him. The man's English was so fascinating that I was finding it hard to concentrate on what he said, but his last point had sunk in. It took only a glance around to picture even a few monks defending this stronghold from invaders. Velior Georgescu was gazing about us with approval, too. "Therefoore, Vlad made a fortress of the existing monastery. He built fortified walls around it, and a prison and a toorture chamber. Also an escape tunnel and a bridge to the shore. He was a canny lad, Vlad was. The bridge is long gone, of course, and I am excavating the rest. This, where we are digging now, was the prison. We have found several skeletons in it already." He smiled broadly and his gold teeth gleamed in the sun.

"And this is Vlad's church, then?" I pointed at the lovely building nearby, with its soaring

cupolas and the dark trees rustling around its walls.

"Noo, I'm afraid not," said Georgescu. "The monastery was partly burned by the Turks in 1462, when Vlad's brother Radu, an Ottoman puppet, was on the throne of Wallachia. And just after Vlad was buried here, a terrible storm blew his church into the lake." Was Vlad buried here? I longed to ask it, but I kept my mouth firmly closed. "The peasants must have thought it was God's punishment for his sins. The church was rebuilt in 1517 — it took three years, and you see here the results. The outside walls of the monastery are a restoration, only about thirty years auld."

We had strolled to the edge of the church, and he patted the mellowed masonry as if slapping the rump of a favorite horse. As we stood there, a man suddenly rounded the corner of the church and came towards us — a white-bearded, bent old man in black robes and black pillbox hat with long flaps that descended to his shoulders. He walked with the aid of a stick, and his robe was tied with a narrow rope from which hung a ring of keys. Around his neck on a chain dangled a very fine old cross of the type I'd seen on the church cupolas.

I was so astonished by this apparition that I nearly fell over; I can't describe the effect it had on me, except to say that it was very much as if Georgescu had successfully conjured a ghost. But my new acquaintance went forwards, smiling at the monk and bowing over his gnarled hand, on which sparkled a gold ring that Georgescu respectfully kissed. The old man seemed fond of him, too, for he placed his fingers on the archaeologist's head for a moment and smiled, a wan, sere smile that involved even fewer teeth than Georgescu's. I caught my name in the introductions and bowed to the monk as gracefully as I could, though I couldn't bring myself to kiss his ring.

"This is the abboot," Georgescu explained to me. "He is the last one here and he has only three other monks living with him now. He has been here since he was a yooung man and he knows the island much better than I ever will. He welcomes you and gives you his blessing. If you have any questions for him, he says, he will try to answer them." I bowed my thanks, and the old man moved slowly on. A few minutes later I saw him sitting quietly on the edge of the ruined wall behind us, like a crow resting in the afternoon sunlight.

"*Do they live here year-round?*" *I asked Georgescu.*

"*Oh, yes. They are here in the moost difficult winters.*" *My guide nodded.* "*You will hear them chanting the mass if you dinna leave too airly.*" *I assured him that I wouldn't want to miss such an experience.* "*Now, let us go in the church.*" *We went around to the front doors, great carved wooden ones, and there I entered a world I had never known before, quite a different one from our Anglican chapels.*

It was cold inside, and before I could see anything in the penetrating darkness of the interior, I could smell a smoky spice on the air and feel a clammy draft from the stones, as if they were breathing. When my eyes adjusted to the gloom, it was only to catch faint gleams of brass and candle flame. The daylight filtered in dimly, through heavy, dark colored glass. There were no pews or chairs, apart from some tall wooden seats built along one of the walls. Near the entrance burned a stand of candles, dripping thickly and giving off a smell of scorching wax; some of them were stuck in a brass crown at the top and some placed in a pot of sand around the base. "*The monks light these every day, and now and then there are other* visitors who do, as well," Georgescu explained. "The ones around the top are for the living, and the ones around the bottom are for the soouls of the dead. They bairn until they go out by themselves."

At the center of the church he pointed upwards, and I saw a dim, floating face above us, at the peak of the dome. "Are you familiar with our Byzantine churches?" Georgescu asked. "Christ is always in the center, looking doon. This candelabrum" — a great crown hung from the center of Christ's chest, filling the main space of the church, but the candles in it had burned out — "is typical, too."

We proceeded to the altar. I felt suddenly like an invader, but there was no sign of the monks and Georgescu strode ahead with proprietary cheerfulness. The altar was hung with embroidered cloths, and in front of it lay a mass of woven wool rugs and mats in folk motifs that I would have called Turkish if I hadn't known better. The top of the altar was adorned with several richly decorated objects, among them an enamelled crucifix and a gold-framed icon of the Virgin and Child. Behind it rose a wall of sad-eyed saints and even sadder angels, and in their midst was a pair of beaten-gold doors

*backed by purple velvet curtains, leading some-
where completely hidden and mysterious.*

*All this I made out with difficulty, through
the dusk, but the gloomy beauty of the scene
moved me. I turned to Georgescu. "Did Vlad
worship here? In the previous church, I mean?"*

*"Oh, cairtainly." The archaeologist chuckled.
"He was a pious auld murtherer. He built
many churches and other monasteries, to be
sure that plenty of people were praying for his
salvation. This was one of his favorite places and
he was very cloose to the monks here. I doon't
know what they thought of his bad deeds, but
they loved his support of the monastery. Besides, he protected them from the Turks. But
the treasures you see here were brought from
other churches — peasants stole everything
valuable in the last century, when the church
was closed. Look here — this is what I wanted
to show you." He squatted down and turned
back the rugs in front of the altar. Directly before it I saw a long rectangular stone, smooth
and undecorated but clearly a grave marker.
My heart began to thud.*

"Vlad's tomb?"

*"Yes, according to legend. Some of my col-
leagues and I excavated here a few years ago*

and found an empty hole — it contained only a few animal boones."

I caught my breath. "He wasn't in it?"

"Absolutely not." Georgescu's teeth glinted like the brass and gold all around us. "The written records say that he was buried here, in front of the altar, and that the new church was built on the same foundations as the auld, so his toomb was not disturbed. You can imagine how disappointed we were not to find him."

Disappointed? *I thought. I found the idea of the empty hole below more frightening than disappointing.*

"In any case, we decided to pooke around a little more, and over here" — he led me back down the nave to a spot near the front entrance and moved another rug — "over here we found a second stoone just the same as the first." I stared down at it. This one was indeed the same size and shape as the first and also undecorated. "So we doog this up, too," Georgescu explained, patting it.

"And you found —?"

"Oh, a very nice skeleton." He reported this with obvious satisfaction. "In a casket that had part of the shroud still over it — amazing, after five centuries. The shroud was royal purple *with gold embroidery and the skeleton inside was in good condition. Beautifully dressed, too, in purple broocade with dark red sleeves. The most wonderful thing was that sewn to one of the sleeves we found a little ring. The ring is rather plain, but one of my colleagues believes it was part of a larger oornament that showed the symbol of the Oorder of the Dragon."*

My heart had lost a beat or two, by this point, I confess. "The symbol?"

"Yes, a dragon with long claws and a looped tail. Those who were invested in the Oorder wore this image somewhere on their person at all times, usually as a brooch or clasp for the cloak. Our friend Vlad was no doubt invested in it, probably by his father, when he reached manhood." Georgescu smiled up at me. "But I have the feeling you knew that already, Professor."

I was struggling with warring emotions of regret and relief. "So this was his grave, and the legends just had the exact spot wrong."

"Oh, I doon't think so." He smoothed the rug back over the stone. "Not all my colleagues would agree with me, but I think the evidence is clairly against it."

I couldn't help staring at him in surprise. "But what about the regal clothing and the little ring?"

Georgescu shook his head. "This fellow was probably a member of the Oorder, too — a high-ranking nobleman — and perhaps he was dressed up in Dracula's best clothes for the occasion. Perhaps he was even invited to die so that there would be a body to fill the toomb — who knows exactly when."

"Did you rebury the skeleton?" I had to ask it; the stone lay so very close to our feet.

"Oh, noo — we packed him off to the history museum in Bucarest, but you can't go see him there — they locked him up in storage with all his nice clothes. It was a shame." Georgescu did not look terribly sorry, as if the skeleton had been appealing but unimportant, at least compared with his true quarry.

"I don't understand," I said, staring at him. "With so much evidence, exactly why don't you think he was Vlad Dracula?"

"It's very simple," Georgescu countered cheerfully, patting the rug. "This fellow had his head on. Dracula's was cut off and taken to Istanbul by the Turks as a troophy. All the sources are in agreement about that. So now I'm digging in

the old prison for another toomb. I think the body was removed from its burial site in front of the altar to outwit grave robbers, or perhaps to protect it from later Turkish invasions. He's on this island somewhere, the auld bugger."

I was transfixed by all the questions I wanted to ask Georgescu, but he stood and stretched. "Wouldn't you like to go across to the restaurant for supper? I'm hungry enough to devour a sheep whoole. But we can hear the beginning of the service first, if you'd like. Where are you staying?"

I confessed that I had no idea yet and that I needed also to provide lodgings for my driver. "There's a great deal I should like to talk with you about," I added.

"And I with you," he agreed. "We can doo that during our supper."

I needed to speak to my driver, so we made our way back to the ruined prison. It devolved that the archaeologist kept a little boat below the church and could row us over, and that he would prevail upon the owner of the restaurant to find local rooms for us. Georgescu stowed away his gear and dismissed the assistants, and we returned to the church in time to see the abbot and his three monks, equally black garbed, processing into the church through the doors of the sanctuary. Two of the monks were elderly, but one was still brown of beard and stood firmly upright. They walked slowly around to face the altar, the abbot leading with a cross and orb in his hands. His bent shoulders carried a purple-and-gold mantle that caught the glow of the candle flames.

At the altar they bowed, the monks prostrating themselves full-length for a moment on the stone floor — just over the empty tomb, I noticed. For a moment, I had the horrifying sense that they were bowing not to the altar but to the grave of the Impaler.

Suddenly an eerie sound rose up; it seemed to come from the church itself, to curl out of the walls and dome like mist. They were chanting. The abbot went through the little doors behind the altar — I tried not to crane for a glimpse of the inner sanctum — and brought out a great book with an enamelled cover, tracing his blessing over it in the air. He laid it on the altar. One of the monks handed him a censer on a long chain; this he swung above the book, dusting it with an aromatic smoke. All around us, above and behind and below, rose the dissonant sacred music with its buzzing drone and wavering heights. My skin crawled, for I realized that at that moment I was closer to the heart of Byzantium than I'd ever been in Istanbul. The ancient music and the rite that accompanied it had probably changed little since they were performed for the emperor in Constantinople.

"The service is very long," Georgescu whispered to me. "They woon't mind if we slip away." He took a candle from his pockets, lit it from a burning wick in the stand near the entrance, and set it in the sand below.

In the restaurant on the shore, a dingy little place, we ate heartily of stews and salads served up by a timid girl in village dress. There was a whole chicken and a bottle of heavy red wine, which Georgescu poured liberally. My driver had apparently made friends in the kitchen, so that we found ourselves utterly alone in the panelled room with its fading views of lake and island.

Once we had warded off the worst of our hunger, I asked the archaeologist about his wonderful command of English. He laughed with his mouth full. "I owe that to my mither and father, God rest their souls," he said. "He was a Scottish archaeologist, a mediaevalist, and she was a Scottish Gypsy. I was raised from a bairn in Fort William and worked with my father until he died. Then some of my mother's relatives asked her to travel with them to Roumania, where they came from. She'd been boorn and bred in a village in western Scotland, but when my father was gone she wanted only to leave. My father's family hadn't been kind about her, you see. So she brought me here, when I was just fifteen, and I've been here since. When we came here I took her family name. To blend in a bit better."

This story left me speechless for a moment, and he grinned. "It's an odd tale, I know. What's yours?"

I told him, briefly, about my life and studies, and about the mysterious book that had come into my possession. He listened with brows knit together, and when I was done he nodded slowly. "A strange story, no doubt about it."

I took the book from my bag and handed it to him. He looked through it carefully, pausing to gaze for long minutes at the woodcut in the center. "Yes," he told me thoughtfully. "This is very much like many images associated with the Oorder. I've seen a similar dragon on pieces of jewellery — that little ring, for example. But

I've never seen a book like this one before. No idea where it came from, then?"

"None," I admitted. "I hope to have it examined by a specialist one day, perhaps in London."

"It's a remarkable piece of work." Georgescu handed it gently back to me. "And now that you've seen Snagov, where do you intend to go? Back to Istanbul?"

"No." I shuddered, but I didn't want to tell him why. "I've got to return to Greece to attend a dig, actually, in a couple of weeks, but I thought I'd go for a glimpse of Târgoviste, since that was Vlad's main capital. Have you been there?"

"Ah, yes, of coourse." Georgescu scraped his plate clean like a hungry boy. "That's an interesting place for any pursuer of Dracula. But the really interesting thing is his castle."

"His castle? Does he really have a castle? I mean, does it still exist?"

"Well, it's a ruin, but a rather nice one. A ruined fortress. It's a few miles up the River Argeş from Târgoviste, and you can get there rather easily by road, with a climb on foot to the very top. Dracula favored any place that could be easily defended from the Turks, and this one is *a love of a site. I'll tell you what —" He was fishing in his pockets and now he found a little clay pipe and began to fill it with fragrant tobacco. I passed him a light. "Thank you, lad. I'll tell you what — I'll go along with you. I can stay only a couple of days, but I could help you find the fortress. It's a great deal easier if you have a guide. I haven't been there in a wandering moon, and I'd like to see it again myself."*

I thanked him sincerely; the idea of striking out into the heart of Roumania without an interpreter had made me uneasy, I admit. We agreed to start tomorrow, if my driver will take us as far as Târgoviste. Georgescu knows a village near the Argeş where we can stay for a few shillings; it isn't the nearest to the fortress, but he doesn't like going to that village anymore as he was once almost chased out of it. We parted with a hearty good night, and now, my friend, I must blow out my light to sleep for the next adventure, of which I shall keep you apprised.

Yours most affectionately,
Bartholomew

Chapter 46

My dear friend,

My driver was indeed able to take us north to Târgoviste today, after which he returned to his family in Bucarest, and we have settled for the night in an old inn. Georgescu is an excellent travelling companion; along the way he regaled me with the history of the countryside we were passing through. His knowledge is very broad and his interests extend to local architecture and botany, so that I was able to learn a tremendous amount today.

Târgoviste is a beautiful town, mediaeval still in character and containing at least this one good inn where a traveller can wash his face in clean water. We are now in the heart of Wallachia, in a hilly country between mountains and plain. Vlad Dracula ruled Wallachia several times during the 1450s and '60s; Târgoviste was his capital, and this afternoon we walked around the substantial ruins of his palace here, Georgescu pointing out to me the different chambers and describing their probable uses. Dracula was not born here but in

Transylvania, in a town called Sighisoara. I won't have time to see it, but Georgescu has been there several times, and he told me that the house in which Dracula's father lived — Vlad's birthplace — still stands.

The most remarkable of many remarkable sights we saw here today, as we prowled the old streets and ruins, was Dracula's watchtower, or rather a handsome restoration of it done in the nineteenth century. Georgescu, like a good archaeologist, turns up his Scotch-Romany nose at restorations, explaining that in this case the crenellations around the top aren't quite right; but what can you expect, he asked me tartly, when historians begin using their imaginations? Whether or not the restoration is quite accurate, what Georgescu told me about that tower gave me a shiver. It was used by Vlad Dracula not only as a lookout in that era of frequent Turkish invasions but also as a vantage point from which to view the impalements that were carried out in the court below.

We took our evening meal in a little pub near the center of town. From there we could see the outer walls of the ruined palace, and as we ate our bread and stew, Georgescu told me that Târ-

goviste is a most apt place from which to travel to Dracula's mountain fortress. "The second time he captured the Wallachian throne, in 1456," he explained, "he decided to build a castle above the Argeş to which he could escape invasions from the plain. The mountains between Târgoviste and Transylvania — and the wilds of Transylvania itself — have always been a place of escape for the Wallachians."

He broke a piece of bread for himself and mopped up his stew with it, smiling. "Dracula knew there were already a couple of ruined fortresses, dating at least as far back as the eleventh century, above the river. He decided to rebuild one of them, the ancient Castle Argeş. He needed cheap labour — don't these things always come doon to having good help? So in his usual kindhairted way he invited all his boyars — his lairds, you know, to a little Easter celebration. They came in their best clothes to that big courtyard right here in Târgoviste, and he gave them a great deal of food and drink. Then he killed off the ones he found most inconvenient, and marched the rest of them — and their wives and little ones — fifty kilometers up into the mountains to rebuild Castle Argeş."

Georgescu hunted around the table, apparently for another piece of bread. "Well, it's moore complicated than that, actually — Roumanian history always is. Dracula's older brother Mircea had been murthered years before by their political enemies in Târgoviste. When Dracula came to power he had his brother's coffin doog up and found that the pooor man had been buried alive. That was when he sent out his Easter invitation, and the results gave him revenge for his brother as well as cheap labour to build his castle in the mountains. He had brick kilns built up near the original fortress, and anyone who'd survived the journey was forced to work night and day, carrying bricks and building the walls and towers. The auld songs from this region say that the boyars' fine clothes fell off them in rags before they were done." Georgescu scraped at his bowl. "I've noticed Dracula was often as practical a fellow as he was a nasty one."

So tomorrow, my friend, we will set out on the trail of those unfortunate nobles, but by wagon, where they toiled into the mountains on foot.

It is remarkable to see the peasants walking around in their native costumes among the more modern dress of the townspeople. The men wear white shirts with dark vests and tremendous leather slippers laced up to the knee with leather thongs, for all the world like Roman shepherds come back to life. The women, who are mainly dark like the men and often quite handsome, wear heavy skirts and blouses with a vest tightly fastened over everything, and their clothing is embroidered with rich designs. They seem a lively folk, laughing and shouting over the business of bargaining in the marketplace, which I visited yesterday morning when I first arrived.

Less than ever do I have a way to mail this, so for now I shall keep it tucked safely in my bag.

Yours truly,
Bartholomew

My dear friend,

We have, to my delight, succeeded in making the trek to a village on the Argeş, a day's ride through mythically steep mountains in the wagon of the farmer whose palm I crossed liberally with silver. As a result I'm sore to the bones today, but elated. This village is a place of wonder for me, something from Grimm, not

701

real life, and I wish you could see it for just an hour, to feel its immense distance from the whole West European world. The little houses, some of them poor and shabby but most with a rather cheerful air, have long low eaves and large chimneys, topped with the gigantic nests of the storks who summer here.

I walked all around with Georgescu this afternoon and discovered that a square in the center of the village provides their gathering place, with a well for the inhabitants and a great trough for the livestock, which are driven right through town twice a day. Under a ramshackle tree is the tavern, a noisy place where I have had to buy one round after another of unholy firewater for the local drinkers — think of this as you sit at the Golden Wolf with your tame pint of stout! There are one or two men among them with whom I can actually communicate a bit.

Some of these men, too, remember Georgescu from his last visit here six years ago and they greeted him with great thumps on the back when we first went in this afternoon, although others seem to avoid him. Georgescu says it is a day's ride up to the fortress and back, and no one is yet willing to take us there. They talk of wolves, and bears, and of course vampires — pricolici, *they call them in their language. I'm getting the feel for a few words of Roumanian, and my French, Italian, and Latin are all of the greatest service while I try to puzzle things out. As we interviewed some of the white-haired drinkers this evening, most of the town turned out to gawk not very discreetly at us — housewives, farmers, crowds of barefoot small children, and the young maidens, who are on the whole dark-eyed beauties. At one point, I was so surrounded by villagers pretending to draw water or sweep front steps or consult with the tavern keeper that I had to laugh aloud, which made them all stare.*

More tomorrow. How I could use a good hour's talk with you, and in my — our — own language!

Yours with devotion,
Rossi

My dear friend,
We have been, to my solemn awe, up to Vlad's fortress and back. I know now why I wanted to see it; it made real for me, a little, in life the frightening figure I seek in his death —

or will soon be seeking, somehow, somewhere, if my maps are of any help. I shall try to describe our excursion for you, as I wish you to be able to imagine the scene and as I want a record of it myself.

We set out around dawn in the wagon of a young farmer here, who seems to be a prosperous fellow and is the son of one of the old-timers at the tavern. He had apparently received orders from his sire to take us, and didn't much like the appointment. When we first mounted the wagon, in the earliest light of the town square, he pointed up to the mountains a few times, shaking his head and saying, "Poenari? Poenari?" Finally, he seemed to resign himself to the task and gave rein to his horses, two big brown machines pulled from the fields for the day.

The man himself was a formidable-looking character, tall and hugely broad-shouldered under his blouse and wool vest, and with his hat on he towered a good two heads above us. This made his timidity about the excursion a little comic for me, although I certainly shouldn't laugh about the fears of these peasants after what I saw in Istanbul (which, as I said before, I shall tell you in person). Georgescu tried to engage him during our drive into the deep forest, but the poor man sat holding his reins in silent despair (I thought), like a prisoner being led away to the block. Now and then his hand crept inside his shirt as if he wore some kind of protective amulet there — I guessed this from the leather thong around his neck and had to resist the temptation to request a look at it. I felt pity for the man and what we were putting him through, against all the proscriptions of his culture, and resolved to give him a little extra remuneration at the end of the trip.

We intended to stay the night, to give ourselves ample time to examine everything and to try to talk with any peasants we might encounter who live close to the site, and to this end the man's father had provided us with rugs and blankets, and his mother had given us a store of bread, cheese, and apples tied up in a bundle in the back of the wagon. As we entered the forest, I felt a distinctly unscholarly thrill. I remembered Bram Stoker's hero setting off into the Transylvanian forests — a fictional version of them, in any case — by stagecoach, and almost wished we'd departed at evening, so that I too might have glimpses of mysterious fires in the woods, and hear wolves howling. It was a shame, I thought, that Georgescu had never read the book, and I resolved to try to send him a copy from England, if I ever got back to such a humdrum place. Then I remembered my encounter in Istanbul and it sobered me.

We rode slowly through the forest, because the road was rutted and pocked with holes and because it began almost at once to climb uphill. These forests are very deep, dim inside even at hottest noon, with the eerie coolness of a church interior. Riding through them, one is utterly surrounded by trees and by a fluttering hush; nothing is visible from the wagon track for miles at a stretch, apart from the endless tree trunks and underbrush, a dense mix of spruce and varied hardwoods. The height of many of the trees is tremendous and their crowns block the sky. It is like riding among the pillars of a vast cathedral, but a dark one, a haunted cathedral where one expects glimpses of the Black Madonna or martyred saints in every niche. I noted at least a dozen tree species, among them soaring chestnuts and a type of oak I'd never seen before.

At one point where the ground levelled out,

we rode into a nave of silvery trunks, a beech grove of the sort one still stumbles on — but rarely — in the most wooded of English manor grounds. You've seen them, no doubt. This one could have been a marriage hall for Robin Hood himself, with huge elephantine trunks supporting a roof of millions of tiny green leaves, and last year's foliage lying in a fawn-colored carpet under our wheels. Our driver did not seem to register any of this beauty — perhaps when you live your entire life among such scenes, they do not register as beauty but as the world itself — and sat hunched over in the same disapproving silence. Georgescu was busy with some notes from his work at Snagov, so I had no one with whom to share a word of the loveliness all around us.

After we'd driven nearly half the day, we came out into an open field, green and golden under the sun. We had risen quite high, I saw, from the village, and could look out over a dense vista of trees, sloping so steeply downwards from the edge of the field that to step off towards them would be to fall sharply. From there the forest plunged into a gorge and I saw the River Argeş for the first time, a vein of sil-

ver below. On its opposite bank rose enormous forested slopes, which looked unscalable. It was a region for eagles, not people, and I thought with awe of the many skirmishes fought here between Ottomans and Christians. That any empire, however daring, would try to penetrate this landscape seemed to me the height of folly. I understood more fully why Vlad Dracula had chosen this region for his stronghold; it hardly needed a fortress to make it less pregnable.

Our guide jumped down and unpacked our midday meal, and we ate it on the grass under scattered oaks and alders. Then he stretched out under a tree and put his hat over his face, and Georgescu stretched out under another, as if this were a matter of course, and they slept for an hour while I rambled about the meadow. It was wonderfully quiet apart from the moan of the wind in those boundless forests. The sky rose bright blue above everything. Walking to the other side of the field, I could see a similar clearing rather far below, presided over by a shepherd in white garments and a broad brownish hat. His flock — sheep, apparently — drifted around him like clouds, and I reflected that he could have been standing there in just that way, leaning on his staff, since the days of Trajan. I felt a great peace come over me. The macabre nature of our errand faded from my mind, and I thought I could have stayed up there in that fragrant meadow for an aeon or two, like the shepherd.

In the afternoon our way led up on steeper and steeper roads, and finally into a village that Georgescu said was the nearest to the fortress; here we sat a while at the local tavern with glasses of that very fortifying brandy, which they call pălincă. *Our driver made it clear that he intended to stay with the horses while we went on foot to the fortress; under no circumstances would he climb up there, much less spend the night with us in the ruins. When we pressed him, he growled, "Pentru nimica în lime," and put his hand on the leather thong around his neck. Georgescu told me this meant "Absolutely not." So obstinate was the man about all this that finally Georgescu chuckled and said the walk was a reasonable one and the last part had to be done on foot anyway. I wondered a little at Georgescu's wanting to sleep out in the open, instead of returning to the village, and to be honest I didn't quite rel-*

ish the idea of an overnight there myself, although I didn't say so.

Eventually we left the fellow to his brandy and the horses to their water and went on our way with the bundles of food and blankets on our backs. As we were walking along the main street, I remembered again the story of the boyars of Târgoviste, limping upwards towards the original ruined fortress, and then I thought of what I had seen — or believed I had seen — in Istanbul, and I felt again a pang of uneasiness.

The track soon narrowed to a small wagon road, and after this to a footpath through the forest, which sloped upwards before us. Only the last stretch gave us a steep climb, and this we negotiated with ease. Suddenly, we were on a windy ridge, a stony spine that broke out of the forest. At the very top of this spine, on a vertebra higher than all the rest, clung two ruined towers and a litter of walls, all that remained of Castle Dracula. The view was breathtaking, with the River Argeş barely twinkling in the gorge below and villages scattered here and there at a stone's drop along it. Far to the south, I saw low hills that Georgescu said were the plains of Wallachia, and to the north tow-

ering mountains, some capped with snow. We had made our way to the perch of an eagle.

Georgescu led the climb over tumbled rocks and we stood at last in the midst of the ruin. The fortress had been a small one, I saw at once, and had long since been abandoned to the elements; wildflowers of every description, lichens, moss, fungus, and stunted, windblown trees had made their ancient home in it. The two towers that still stood were bony silhouettes against the sky. Georgescu explained that it originally had five towers, from which Dracula's minions could watch for Turkish incursions. The courtyard in which we stood had once had a deep well, for sieges, and also — according to legend — a secret passageway that led to a cave far below on the Argeş. Through this Dracula had escaped the Turks in 1462 after using the fortress intermittently for about five years. Apparently he had never returned to it. Georgescu believed he had identified the castle chapel at one end of the courtyard, where we peered into a crumbling vault. Birds flew in and out of the tower walls, snakes and small animals rustled out of sight ahead of us, and I had the sense that nature would soon take the rest of this citadel for her own.

By the time our archaeological lesson was over, the sun hung just above the western hills and the shadows of rock, tree, and tower had lengthened around us. "We could walk back to the last village," Georgescu said thoughtfully. "But then we'll have to hike back up if we want to look around again in the morning. I'd still rather camp here, wouldn't you?"

By then I felt that I had much rather not, but Georgescu looked so matter-of-fact, so scientific, beaming up at me with his sketchbook in hand, that I didn't want to say so. He set about gathering dead wood from the area, and I helped him, and soon we had a fire crackling away on the stones of the ancient courtyard, carefully scraped clean of moss for the purpose. Georgescu seemed to enjoy the fire immensely, whistling over it, adjusting loose sticks, and setting up a primitive rig for the cook pot he produced from his rucksack. Soon he was making stew and cutting bread, smiling at the flames, and I remembered that he was, after all, as much Gypsy as Scottish.

The sun set before our supper was quite ready, and when it dropped behind the mountains, the ruins were plunged into darkness, towers stark against a perfect twilight. Some-

thing — owls? bats? — fluttered in and out of the empty window sockets, from which arrows had flown towards the Turkish troops so long ago. I got my rug and pulled it as close to the fire as I safely could. Georgescu was dishing up a miraculously good meal, and as we ate it he talked again about the history of the place. "One of the saddest tales about Dracula legend comes from this place. You have heard about Dracula's first wife?"

I shook my head.

"The peasants who live around here tell a story about her that I think is probably true. We know that in the fall of 1462, Dracula was chased from this fortress by the Turks, and he did not return to the place when he reigned Wallachia again in 1476, just before he was killed. The songs from these villages up here say that the night the Turkish army reached the opposite cliff there" — he pointed into the dark velvet of the forest — "they camped at the auld fortress of Poenari, and tried to bring Dracula's castle down by firing their cannons across the river. They were not successful, so their commander gave oorders for a grand assault on the castle the next morning."

Georgescu paused to poke the fire into a

brighter blaze; the light danced on his swarthy face and gold teeth, and his dark curls took on a look of horns. "During the night, a slave in the Turkish camp who was a relative of Dracula secretly shot an arrow into the opening in the tower of this castle where he knew Dracula's private rooms lay. Bound to the arrow was a warning to the Draculas to flee the castle before he and his family were taken prisoner. The slave could see the figure of Dracula's wife reading the message by candlelight. The peasants say in their auld songs that she told her husband she would be eaten by the fish of the Argeş before she would be a slave to the Turks. The Turks weren't very nice to their prisoners, you know.' Georgescu smiled devilishly at me over his stew. "Then she ran up the steps of the tower — probably that one there — and threw herself off the top. And Dracula, of course, went on to escape through the secret passageway." He nodded matter-of-factly. "This part of the Argeş is still called Riul Doamnei, which means the Princess's River."

I shivered, as you can imagine — I had looked that afternoon over the precipice. The drop to the river below is almost unimaginably far.

"Did Dracula have children by this wife?"

"Oh, yes." Georgescu scooped up a little more stew for me. "Their son was Mihnea the Bad, who ruled Wallachia at the beginning of the sixteenth century. Another charming fellow. His line led to a whole series of Mihneas and Minceas, all unpleasant. And Dracula married again, the second time to a Hungarian woman who was a relative of Matthias Corvinus, the king of Hungary. They produced a lot of Draculas."

"Are there still any in Wallachia or Transylvania?"

"I doon't think so. I would have found them if there were." He tore off a chunk of bread and handed it to me. "That second line had land in the Szekler region and they were all mixed up with Hungarians. The last of them married into the nooble Getzi family and they vanished, too."

I wrote all this down in my notebook, between mouthfuls, although I didn't believe it would lead me to any tomb. This made me think of a last question, which I didn't quite like to ask in that enormous and deepening darkness.

"Isn't it possible that Dracula was buried

here, or that his body was moved here from Snagov, for safekeeping?"

Georgescu chuckled. "Still hoopeful, are you? No, the auld fellow's in Snagov somewhere, mark my words. Of course, that chapel over there had a crypt — there's a sunken area, with a couple of steps down. I doog it up years ago, when I first came here." He gave me a broad grin. "The villagers wouldn't speak to me for weeks. But it was empty. Not even a few boones."

Soon after this he began to yawn enormously. We pulled our supplies close to the fire, rolled up in our sleeping rugs, and lay quiet. The night was chilly and I was glad I'd worn my warmest clothing. I looked up at the stars for a time — they seemed wonderfully close to that dark precipice — and listened to Georgescu's snores.

Eventually I must have slept, too, because when I woke the fire was low and a wisp of cloud covered the mountaintop. I shivered and was about to get up to throw more wood on the fire when a rustling close by made my blood freeze. We were not alone in the ruin, and whatever shared that dark uneven hall with us was very near. I got slowly to my feet, thinking to rouse Georgescu if I needed to and wondering if he carried any weapons in his Gypsy bag with the cook pots. Dead silence had fallen, but after a few seconds the suspense was too much for me. I pushed a branch from our pile of kindling into the fire, and when it caught I had a torch, which I held cautiously aloft.

Suddenly, in the depths of the overgrown area of the chapel, my torchlight caught the red gleam of eyes. I would be lying, my friend, if I said my hair didn't all stand on end. The eyes moved a little nearer and I couldn't tell how close to the ground they were. For a long moment they regarded me, and I felt, irrationally, that they were full of a kind of recognition, that they knew who I was and were taking my measure. Then, with a scuffling in the underbrush, a great beast came half into view, turned its gaze this way and that, and trotted away into the darkness. It was a wolf of startling size; in the dim light I could see its shaggy fur and massive head for just a second before it slipped out of the ruin and vanished.

I lay down again, unwilling to wake Georgescu now that the danger seemed past, but I could not sleep. Again and again — in my mind, at least — I saw those keen, know-

ing eyes. I suppose I would have dozed off eventually, but as I lay there I became aware of a distant sound, which seemed to drift up to us out of the darkness of the forest. At last I felt too uneasy to stay in my blankets, and I rose again and crept across the brushy courtyard to look over the wall. The sheerest drop over the precipice was to the Argeş, as I've described, but there was to my left an area where the forests sloped more gently, and from down there I heard a murmur of many voices and saw a glimmering that might have been campfires. I wondered if Gypsies camped in these woods; I'd have to ask Georgescu about that in the morning. As if this thought had conjured him, my new friend suddenly appeared, shadowy, at my side, shuffling with sleep.

"Soomething amiss?" He peered over the wall.

I pointed. "Could it be a Gypsy camp?"

He laughed. "Noo, not so far from civilization." He followed this with a yawn, but his eyes in the glow of our dying fire showed bright and alert. "It's peculiar, though. Let's go have a look."

I didn't like this idea in the least, but a few minutes later we had our boots on and were creeping quietly down the path towards the sound. It grew steadily louder, a rising and falling, an eerie cadence — not wolves, I thought, but men's voices. I tried not to step on any branches. Once I observed Georgescu reach into his jacket — he did have a gun, I thought with satisfaction. Soon we could see firelight flickering through the trees, and he motioned to me to creep low, and then to squat next to him in the underbrush.

We had reached a clearing in the woods, and it was, astoundingly, full of men. They stood two rings deep around a bright bonfire, facing it and chanting. One, apparently their leader, stood near the fire, and whenever their chant rose to a crescendo each of them lifted a stiff arm in a salute, putting his other hand on the shoulder of the next man. Their faces, weirdly orange in the firelight, were stiff and unsmiling, and their eyes glittered. They wore a uniform of some sort, dark jackets over green shirts and black ties. "What is this?" I murmured to Georgescu. "What are they saying?"

"All for the Fatherland!" he hissed in my ear. "Stay very quiet or we are dead. I think this is the Legion of the Archangel Michael."

"What is that?" I tried to just move my lips. It

would have been difficult to imagine anything less angelic than those stony faces and rigid out-stretched arms. Georgescu beckoned me away and we crept back into the woods. But before we turned I noticed a movement on the other side of the clearing, and to my increasing astonish-ment I saw a tall man in a cloak, his dark hair and sallow face caught for a second by the light from the fire. He stood outside the rings of uniformed men, his face joyful; in fact, he seemed to be laughing. After a second I couldn't see him anymore and thought he must have slipped into the trees, and then Georgescu pulled me along up the slope.

"When we were safely back at the ruin — weirdly, it did feel safe now, by contrast — Georgescu sat down by the fire and lit his pipe, as if for relief. "Good God, man," he breathed. "That could have been the end of us."

"Who are they?"

He tossed his match into the fire. "Criminals," he said shortly. "They are also called the Iron Guard. They are sweeping through the villages in this part of the country, picking up young men and converting them to hatred. They hate the Jews, in particular, and want to rid the warld of them." He drew fiercely on his pipe.

"We Gypsies know that where Jews are killed, Gypsies are always murthered, too. And then a lot of other people, usually."

I described the strange figure I'd seen outside the circle.

"Oh, to be sure," Georgescu muttered. "They attract all kinds of strange admirers. It won't be long till every shepherd in the mountains is deciding to join them."

It took us some time to settle to sleep again, but Georgescu assured me the Legion was unlikely to scale the mountain once they'd begun their rituals. I managed only an uncomfortable doze and was relieved to see that dawn came early to that eagle's eyrie. It was quiet now, still rather foggy, and no wind moved the trees around us. As soon as the light was strong enough, I went cautiously to the crumbling vaults of the chapel and examined the wolf's tracks. They could be clearly seen on the near side of the chapel, large and heavy, in the earth. The strange thing was that there was only one set of them, which led away from the chapel area, directly out of the sunken beds of the crypt, with no sign of how the wolf had made its way in there in the first place — or perhaps I simply couldn't read its trail well enough in the undergrowth behind the chapel. I puzzled over this long after we had break-fasted, made some more sketches, and set off down the mountain.

Again, I must stop for the present, but my warmest regards go out to you from a faraway land —

Rossi

Chapter 47

My dear friend,

I can't imagine what you'll think of this weird and one-sided correspondence when it finally reaches you, but I'm compelled to continue, if only to make notes for myself. We returned yesterday afternoon to the village on the Argeş from which we began our journey to Dracula's fortress, and Georgescu has set off for Snagov, with a hearty embrace and a squeeze to my shoulders and the wish that we may be in touch again someday. He has been a most genial guide and I shall certainly miss him. At the last moment I felt a pang of guilt at not having told him everything I'd observed in Istanbul, and yet I couldn't bring myself to breach my own silence. He wouldn't have believed it anyway, and so I should not have been sparing him any mishaps by trying to persuade him of it. I could imagine all too well his hearty laugh, his scientific shake of the head, his dismissal of my fantastic imagination.

He urged me to travel back with him as far as Târgoviste, but I had already resolved to stay a few more days in this area to visit some of the local churches and monasteries, and to learn, perhaps, a little of the region that surrounded Vlad's stronghold. This was the reason I gave to myself and Georgescu, in any case, and he recommended several sites Dracula would undoubtedly have visited in his lifetime. I think I had another motivation, my friend, which is the sense that I may never again come to such a place, so remote, so far from my usual researches, and so piercingly beautiful. Having resolved to use my last free days here rather than hurry to Greece ahead of schedule, I've been relaxing a bit at the tavern, trying to improve my bits of Roumanian by attempting with poor success to talk with the elders about the legends of the region. Today I walked the woodlands near the village, coming upon a shrine that stood alone beneath a tree. It was built of ancient stones with a roof of thatch, and I thought its original part might have been there long before Dracula's troops galloped these roads. The fresh flowers inside had just wilted, and candle wax had pooled below the crucifix.

As I was returning towards the village, I met with an equally startling sight — a young vil-

lage girl who stood motionless in my path in her peasant dress, for all the world like a figure of history. As she showed no sign of moving, I stopped to speak with her, and to my amazement she presented me with a coin. It was clearly very old — mediaeval — and showed on one side the figure of a dragon. I felt sure, although without proof, that it must have been coined for the Order of the Dragon. The girl of course spoke only Roumanian, but I managed to learn from her that she was given it by an old woman who came down to this village at some point from the river cliffs near Vlad's castle. The girl also told me that her family name is Getzi, although she seemed to have no inkling of its significance. You can imagine my excitement at this: I was in all likelihood standing face-to-face with a descendant of Vlad Dracula. The thought was both astonishing and unnerving (although the girl's purity of face and graceful demeanor were as far as possible from anything monstrous or cruel). When I tried to return the coin she seemed to insist I keep it, which I've done for now, though I shall certainly try again to give it back. We arranged to talk further tomorrow, and I must desist now to make a sketch of the coin, and to study my dictionary in the hope of being able to ask her more about her family and their origins.

My dear friend,

Last night I made a little further headway in speaking with the young woman I told you about — her name is indeed Getzi, and she spelled it for me with the same spelling Georgescu gave me for my notes. I was astonished by the quickness of her understanding, as we tried to converse, and found that in addition to great natural gifts of perception she can read and write and was able to help me look up words in my dictionary. I enjoyed watching her mobile face and bright, dark eyes fill with each new comprehension. She has never learned another language, of course, but I have no doubt she could do so with ease, had she the right instruction.

This struck me as a remarkable phenomenon, to find such intelligence in this remote and simple place; perhaps it is further proof that she is descended from noble, educated, clever people. Her father's family came here so long ago that no one remembers it, but some of them were Hungarian, as far as I could make out. She said her father believes himself heir to the prince of the Castle Argeş and that there is treasure buried there, something all the peasants here apparently think. With difficulty, I made out that they believe that on certain saints' days a supernatural light illuminates the site of the buried treasure, but everyone in the villages is too much afraid to go looking for it. The girl's gifts, so clearly superior to her surroundings, kept reminding me of those of Hardy's beautiful Tess of the d'Urbervilles, the noble milkmaid. I know you don't venture past 1800, my friend, but I reread the book last year and I recommend it to you as a detour from your usual strolls. I doubt there is any treasure, by the way, or Georgescu would have found it already.

She also explained to me the startling fact that one member of each generation of her family is stamped on the skin with a tiny dragon. This, as much as her name, and her father's story about it, has convinced me that she is part of a living branch of the Order of the Dragon. I would like to talk with her father, but when I proposed this, she looked so distressed that I would have been a cad to pursue it. This culture is a traditional one, to an extreme, and I am wary of jeopardizing her rep-

utation with her people — I'm certain she's taken a risk even in speaking alone with me and am all the more grateful for her interest and assistance.

I'm off now to walk in the woods a bit; I have so much to think about here that I feel I need to clear my head a bit.

My dear friend, my only confidant,

Two days have passed, and I hardly know how to write to you about them, or if I shall ever show this to anyone. These two days have made for me the difference of a lifetime. They have filled me with equal portions of hope and fear. I feel that in their course I have stepped across a line into a new life. What it will mean, ultimately, I cannot tell. I am both the happiest man in creation and the most anxious.

Two nights ago, after I last wrote to you, I met again the angelic young woman I have been describing, and our conversations this time led to a sudden change — a kiss, in fact — before she fled. I was sleepless all night, and when the morning came I left my room in the village and wandered into the woodland. There I walked awhile, sitting down now and then on a rock or stump in the shifting, delicate *green of the early morning, seeing her face among the trees or in the light itself. I wondered many times if I should leave the village immediately, as I might already have offended her.*

The whole day passed in this way, as I walked here and there, returning to the village only for a midday meal, where I was afraid I would encounter her any second and yet hoped I would. But there was no sign of her, and in the evening I made my way back to our meeting place, thinking that if she came there again I would tell her as well as I could manage that I owed her an apology and would trouble her no more. Just as I was giving up the hope of seeing her, and was deciding that I had offended her deeply and should leave the village the next morning, she appeared among the trees. I saw her for a second in her heavy skirts and black vest, her bare head dark as polished wood, her braid hanging over her shoulder. Her eyes were dark, too, and frightened, but the radiant intelligence of her face leapt out at me.

I opened my mouth to speak to her, and at that moment she flew across the gap that separated us and threw herself into my arms. To my astonishment, she seemed to have given herself completely to me, and our feelings soon brought us to a full intimacy as tender and pure as it was unplanned. I found we could speak to each other freely — in which of our languages I am no longer sure — and I could read the world and perhaps all my own future in the darkness of her eyes, with their thick lashes and the delicate Asiatic fold at the inner corner.

When she had gone, and I was left alone with my trembling emotion, I tried to consider what I had done, what we had done, but my sense of completion and happiness interfered at every mental turn. Today I will go to wait for her again, because I cannot help it, because my whole being seems now to be bound up in the being of one so different from myself and yet so exquisitely familiar that I can scarcely understand what has happened.

My dear friend (if it is still you to whom I write),

I have lived four days in paradise now, and my love for the angel who presides over it seems to be exactly that — love. Never before have I felt for any woman what I feel now, in this alien place. With only a few more days to think, I have, of course, been considering this from every angle. The idea of leaving her and never seeing her again seems to me as impossible as that I should never see my home again. On the other hand, I have struggled with what bringing her with me would mean — how, in the first place, I could cruelly detach her from her own home and family, and what the consequences would be were she to come with me to Oxford. This last thought is complicated in the extreme, but the starkness of the situation is clear to me: if I departed without her it would break both our hearts, and it would also be an act of cowardice and villainy, after what I have taken from her.

I have now resolved to make her my wife as soon as possible. Our lives will no doubt be a strange path, but I am certain her natural grace and acuity of mind will carry her through whatever we encounter together. I cannot leave her here and wonder all my life what might have been, nor can I desert her in such a situation. I have all but decided that I will ask her tonight to marry me a month from now. I think I shall return first to Greece, where I can borrow from my colleagues — or have wired —

*enough money to present her father with com-
pensation for taking her away; I have little left
here, and I don't dare undertake this otherwise. In addition, I feel I must attend the dig to
which I've been invited there — a nobleman's
grave near Knossos. My future work may rest
with these colleagues, and with it I shall support her and myself in the life we build together.*

*After this I will come back for her — and how
long four weeks of separation will be! It is my
wish to see if the priests at Snagov might marry
us there, so that Georgescu could be our witness. Of course, if her parents insist that we
marry before leaving the village, I am willing
to do that instead. She shall travel with me as
my wife, in any case. I shall send a telegram to
my parents from Greece, I think, and then take
her to them for a stay when we reach England.
And you, dear friend, if you are reading this
already, could you look a little into the matter
of rooms outside the college — very discreetly —
cost, of course, being of importance? I would
also like for her to study English as soon as
possible; I am certain she will excel in it. Perhaps autumn will find you at our fireside, my*

friend, and then you, too, will see the reason in my madness. Until then, you are the only one to whom I feel free to turn in this matter, as soon as I can send this to you, and I pray you will judge kindly of me, out of the largeness of your heart.

Yours in joy and anxiety,
Rossi

Chapter 48

"THAT WAS THE LAST of Rossi's letters, probably the last he had written his friend. Sitting beside Helen on the bus back to Budapest, I refolded the pages with care and took her hand for just a second. 'Helen,' I said hesitantly, because I felt one of us, at least, must say it aloud. 'You are descended from Vlad Dracula.' She looked at me, and then out the bus window, and I thought I saw on her face that she herself did not know how to feel about this, but that it made all the blood in her veins suddenly writhe and coil."

"When Helen and I stepped off the bus in Budapest, it was nearly evening already, but I realized with a feeling of shock that we had left this bus station the same day, that very morning. I felt I had lived a couple of years since that moment. Rossi's letters rested safely in my briefcase and their contents filled my head with poignant images; I could see a reflection of them in Helen's eyes, too. She kept one hand tucked around my arm, as if the revelations of the day had shaken her confidence. I wanted to put my whole arm around her, to embrace and kiss her in the street, to tell her I would never leave her and that Rossi never should have — never should have left her mother, that is. I contented myself with pressing her hand firmly to my side, and letting her guide us back to the hotel.

"At the moment we reached the lobby, I had again the feeling that we'd been away a long time — how strange it was that these unfamiliar places were starting to seem familiar to me within a couple of days, I thought. There was a note for Helen from her aunt, which she read eagerly. 'I thought so. She wants us to have dinner with her this evening, here in the hotel. She will tell us her good-byes then, I suppose.'

"'Will you tell her?'

"'About the letters? Probably. I always tell Éva everything, sooner or later.' I wondered if she had told her anything about me that I did not know, and suppressed the idea.

"We had scant time to wash and dress in our rooms before supper — I changed into the cleaner of two dirty shirts and shaved over the elaborate basin — and when I came downstairs again Éva was already there, although Helen was not. Éva stood at the front window, her back to me, her face toward the street and the fading evening light. Seen this way she had less of the formidable alertness and intensity of her public demeanor; her back in its dark green jacket was relaxed, even a little stooped. Turning suddenly, she saved me the trouble of deciding whether or not to call out to her, and I saw worry in her face before her wonderful smile dawned in my direction. She hurried forward to shake my hand, I to kiss hers. We did not exchange a word, but for all that we could have been old friends meeting after a separation of months or years.

"A moment later Helen appeared, to my relief, and she translated us into the dining room, with its glossy white cloths and ugly china. Aunt Éva ordered for all of us, as before, and I sat back, tired, while they spoke together for a few minutes. They seemed at first to be exchanging affectionate jokes, but soon Éva's face clouded and I saw her pick up her fork and twirl it somberly between thumb and forefinger. Then she whispered something to Helen that made Helen's brow knit, too.

"'What's wrong?' I asked uneasily. I had already had my fill of secrets and mysteries.

"'My aunt has made a discovery.' Helen lowered her voice, although few of the diners around us could have known English. 'Something that may be unpleasant for us.'

"'What?'

"Éva nodded and spoke again, again very quietly, and Helen's brow furrowed deep. 'This is bad,' she said in a whisper. 'My aunt has been questioned about you — about us. She told me she received a visit this afternoon from a police detective whom she has known for a long time. He apologized and said it was only their routine, but he interrogated her about your presence in Hungary, your interests, and our — our relationship. My aunt is very clever in these matters, and when she questioned him in return, he managed to reveal that he had been — how do you say? — put on the case by Géza József.' Her voice dropped to an almost inaudible murmur.

"'Géza!' I stared at her.

"'I told you he is a nuisance. He tried to question me at the conference, too, but I ignored him. Apparently that made him angrier than I had guessed.' She paused. 'My aunt says he is a member of the secret police and can be quite dangerous to us. They do not like the liberal reforms of the government and are trying to keep the old ways.'

"Something in her tone made me ask, 'Did you already know this? What his position is?'

"She nodded guiltily. 'I'll tell you about it later.'

"I wasn't sure how much I wanted to know, but the idea of our being pursued by the handsome giant was certainly distasteful to me. 'What does he want?'

"'He apparently feels you are involved in more than historical research. He believes you have come here looking for something else.'

"'He's right,' I pointed out in a low voice.

"'He is determined to find out what it is. I am sure he knows where we went today — I hope he will not question my mother, too. My aunt turned the detective away from the — the scent as well as she could, but now she is worried.'

"'Does your aunt know what — whom — I'm looking for?'

"Helen was silent for a moment, and when she raised her eyes there was something like a plea in them.

"'Yes. I thought she might be able to help us somehow.'

"'Does she have any advice?'

"'She only says it's a good thing we are leaving Hungary tomorrow. She warned us not to talk with any strangers as we depart.'

"'Of course,' I said angrily. 'Maybe József would like to study Dracula documents with us at the airport.'

"'Please.' Her voice was a bare whisper. 'Don't joke about this, Paul. It can be very serious. If I ever want to return here —'

"I subsided into a shamed silence. I hadn't meant it as a joke, only as an expression of exasperation. The waiter was bringing dessert — pastries and coffee that Aunt Éva urged on us with motherly concern, as if by fattening us a little she could guard us from the world's evils. While we ate, Helen told her aunt about Rossi's letters, and Éva nodded slowly, attentive, but said nothing. When our cups were empty, she turned deliberately to me, and Helen translated with downcast eyes.

"'My dear young man,' Éva said, pressing my hand just as her sister had done earlier in the day. 'I do not know if we will ever see each other again, but it is my hope that we will. In the meantime, look after my beloved niece, or at least let her look after you' — she gave Helen a sly glance, which Helen apparently pretended not to see — 'and be certain that you both return safely to your studies. Helen has told me about your mission, and it is a worthy one, but if you do not accomplish it soon, you must return home with the knowledge that you did everything that you could. Then you must go on with your life, my friend, because you are young and it is in front of you.' She patted her lips with her napkin and rose. At the door to the hotel she silently embraced Helen and leaned forward to kiss me on each cheek. She was grave, and no tears glistened in her eyes, but I saw on her face a deep, still sorrow. The elegant car was waiting. My last glimpse of her was her sober wave from its back window.

"For a few seconds, Helen seemed unable to speak. She turned toward me, turned away. Then she rallied and looked at me decisively. 'Come, Paul. This is our final hour of freedom in Budapest. Tomorrow we will have to hurry to the airport. I want to go for a walk.'

"'A walk?' I said. 'What about the secret police and their interest in me?'

"'They want to know what you know, not to stab you in a dark alley. And don't be vain,' she said, smiling. 'They are just as interested in me as in you. We will stay in well-lit places, along the main street, but I wish you to see the city one more time.'

"I was glad enough to do this, knowing it

might be my last view of it in a lifetime, and we went out again into the balmy night. We wandered toward the river, staying, as Helen had promised, on the main thoroughfares. At the great bridge we paused, and then she strolled onto it, running one hand thoughtfully along the railings. Above the vast water we paused again, looking back and forth at the two sides of Budapest, and I felt again its majesty and the explosion of war that had nearly destroyed it. The lights of the city shone everywhere, quivering in the black surface of the water. Helen stood for a while at the railing, then turned, as if reluctantly, to walk back toward Pest. She had taken off her jacket, and when she turned I saw a jagged shape on the back of her blouse. Leaning closer, I suddenly realized it was an enormous spider. It had spun a web all the way across her back; I could clearly see the glinting filaments. I remembered then that I'd seen cobwebs all along the bridge railing, where she'd been running her hand. 'Helen,' I said softly. 'Don't get upset — there's something on your back.'

"'What?' She froze.

"'I'm going to brush it off,' I said gently. 'It's just a spider.'

"A shudder went through her, but she stood

obediently motionless while I flicked the creature off her back. I admit that it gave me a shudder, too, because the spider was the largest I'd ever seen, almost half the width of my hand. It hit the railing next to us with an audible thwack and Helen screamed. I'd never heard her express fear before, and that little scream made me suddenly want to grab her and shake her, even hit her. 'It's all right,' I said quickly, taking her by the arm, trying to stay calm. To my surprise, she gave a sob or two before she could steady herself. It astonished me that a woman who could shoot at vampires was so shaken by a spider, but this had been a long day and a strained one. She surprised me again by turning to look at the river and saying in a low voice, 'I promised I would tell you about Géza.'

"'You don't have to tell me anything.' I hoped I didn't sound irritable.

"'I don't want to lie by silence.' She walked a few feet away, as if to leave the spider completely behind, although it had vanished, probably into the Danube. 'When I was a university student, I was in love with him for a little while, or thought I was, and in return he helped my aunt to get me my fellowship and passport to leave Hungary.'

"I recoiled, staring at her.

"'Oh, it wasn't so crude,' she said. 'He did not say, "You sleep with me and then you can go to England." He is actually rather subtle. He did not get everything he wanted from me, either. But by the time I was no longer charmed with him, I had my passport in my hand. That was how it happened, and when I realized it, I already had a ticket to freedom, to the West, and I was not willing to give it up. And I thought it was worth it to find my father. So I played along with Géza until I could escape to London, and then I left him a letter breaking my ties with him. I wanted to be honest about that, at least. He must have been very angry, but he never wrote me.'

"'And how did you know he was with the secret police?'

"She laughed. 'He was too vain to keep it to himself. He wanted to impress me. I did not tell him that I was more frightened than impressed, and more disgusted than frightened. He told me about people he had sent to jail, or had sent to be tortured, and implied that there was worse. It is impossible not to hate such a person, ultimately.'

"'I'm not glad to hear this, since he's interested in my movements,' I said. 'But I'm glad to know that's how you feel about him.'

743

"'What did you think?' she demanded. 'I've been trying to stay away from him from the minute we got here.'

"'But I sensed some complicated feeling in you when you saw him at the conference,' I admitted. 'I couldn't help thinking that perhaps you had loved him, or still loved him, something like that.'

"'No.' She shook her head, looking down at the dark current. 'I could not love an interrogator — a torturer — probably a murderer. And if I did not reject him for all this — in the past and even more now — there would be other things for which I would reject him.' She turned slightly in my direction, but without meeting my gaze. 'They are smaller things, but still very important. He is not kind. He does not know when to say something comforting and when to be silent. He does not really care about history. He does not have soft gray eyes or bushy eyebrows, or roll his sleeves up to the elbow.' I stared at her, and now she looked me full in the face with a kind of determined courage. 'In short, the biggest problem with him is that he is not you.'

"Her gaze was almost unreadable, but after a moment she began to smile, as if in spite of herself, as if fighting herself, and it was the beautiful smile of all the women in her family. I stared, an unbeliever still, and then I took her into my arms and kissed her passionately. 'What did you think?' she murmured, as soon as I could let her go for a second. 'What did you think?'

"We stood there for long minutes — it might have been an hour — and then she suddenly drew back with a groan and put her hand to her neck. 'What is it?' I asked quickly.

"She hesitated for a moment. 'My wound,' she said slowly. 'It has healed, but sometimes it hurts me for a moment. And just now I thought — what if I should not have touched you?'

"We stared at each other. 'Let me see it,' I said. 'Helen, let me see it.'

"Silently, she untied her scarf and lifted her chin in the light of the streetlamp. On the skin of her strong throat I saw two purple marks, nearly closed over. My fears receded a little; she had clearly not been bitten since the first attack. I leaned over and touched my lips to the spot.

"'Oh, Paul, don't!' she cried, starting back.

"'I don't care,' I said. 'I will heal it myself.' I searched her face, then. 'Or did that make it hurt?'

"'No, it was soothing,' she admitted, but she put her hand over the spot, almost protectively, and after a minute tied her scarf on again. I knew then that even if her contamination had been slight, I must watch her more carefully than ever. I fished in my pocket. 'We should have done this long ago. I want you to wear this.' It was one of the little crucifixes we'd brought from Saint Mary's Church at home. I fastened it around her neck, so that it hung discreetly below the scarf. She seemed to breathe a sigh of relief, touching it with her finger.

"'I am not a believer, you know, and I felt I was too much the scholar to —'

"'I know. But what about that time in Saint Mary's Church?'

"'Saint Mary's?' She frowned.

"'At home, near the university. When you came in to read Rossi's letters with me, you put some holy water on your forehead.'

She thought a minute. 'Yes, I did. But that was not belief. It was from a feeling of homesickness.'

"We walked slowly back over the bridge and along the dark streets without touching each other. I could still feel her arms twined around me.

"'Let me come to your room with you,' I whispered as we came in sight of the hotel.

"'Not here.' I thought her lips quivered. 'We are being watched.'

"I didn't repeat my request, and was glad for the distraction that awaited us at the front desk of the hotel. When I asked for my key, the clerk handed it over with a scrap of paper scrawled in German: Turgut had called and wanted me to call him back. Helen waited while I went through the ritual of begging for the phone and giving the guard a little incentive to help me — I had stooped low, in these last days here — and then I dialed hopelessly for a while until it rang far away. Turgut answered with a rumble and a quick switch to English. 'Paul, dear man! Thank the gods you have called. I have news for you — important news!'

"My heart leaped into my throat. 'Did you find —' A map? The tomb? Rossi?

"'No, my friend, nothing so miraculous. But the letter Selim found has been translated and it is an astounding document. It was written by a monk of the Orthodox faith, in Istanbul, in 1477. Can you hear me?'

"'Yes, yes!' I shouted, so that the clerk glared at me and Helen looked anxious. 'Go on.'

"'In 1477. There is much more. I think it is important that you follow the information of this letter. I will show it to you when you get back tomorrow. Yes?'

"'Yes!' I shouted. 'But does the letter say they buried — him — in Istanbul?' Helen was shaking her head, and I could read her thoughts — the line might be bugged.

"'I cannot tell, from the letter,' Turgut rumbled. 'I am still uncertain where he is buried, but it is not very likely that the tomb is here. I think you must prepare yourself for a new trip. You will probably need succor from the good aunt again, also.' Despite the static, I could hear a grim note in his voice.

"'A new trip? But where?'

"'To Bulgaria!' shouted Turgut, far away.

"I stared at Helen, the receiver slipping in my hand. 'Bulgaria?'"

Part Three

There was one great tomb more lordly than all the rest; huge it was, and nobly proportioned. On it was but one word,

DRACULA.

— Bram Stoker, *Dracula*, 1897

Chapter 49

SOME YEARS AGO I found among my father's papers a note that would have no place in this history except that it is the only memento of his love for Helen that has ever come into my hands, apart from his letters to me. He kept no journals as such, and his occasional notes to himself were almost entirely concerned with his work — musings on diplomatic problems, or on history, especially as it pertained to some international conflict. These reflections, and the lectures and articles that grew from them, now reside in the library of his foundation, and I am left, after all, with only one piece of writing he did entirely for himself — for Helen. I knew my father as a man devoted to fact and ideal, but not to poetry, which makes this document all the more important to me. Because this is no children's book, and because I would like it to be as full a record as possible, I have included it here despite some of my own scruples. Quite possibly he wrote other letters like it, but it would have been characteristic of him to destroy them — perhaps to burn them in the tiny garden behind our house in Amsterdam, where as a young girl I sometimes found charred and unreadable scraps of paper in the little stone grill — and this one may have survived by accident. The letter is undated, so I have also hesitated about where to place it in this chronology. I give it at this point because it refers to the earliest days of their love, although the anguish in it leads me to believe that he wrote this letter when it could no longer have been delivered to her.

Oh my love, I wanted to tell you how I have thought about you. My memory belongs entirely to you, because it reverts constantly these days to our first moments alone together. I have asked myself many times why other affections can't replace your presence, and I always return to the illusion that we are still together, and then — unwillingly — to the knowledge that you have made a hostage of my memory. When I least expect it, I am overwhelmed by your words in recollection. I feel the weight of your hand over mine, both our hands hidden under the edge of my jacket, my jacket folded on the seat between us, the exquisite lightness of your fingers, your profile turned away from me, your exclamation when we entered Bulgaria together, when we first flew over the Bulgarian mountains.

Since we were young, my dear, there has been a revolution about sex, a bacchanalia of mythic proportions that you have not lived to see — now, in the Western world, at least, young people apparently encounter each other without preliminaries. But I remember our restrictions with almost as much longing as I remember their legal consummation, much later. This is the kind of memory I can share with no one: the intimacy we had with each other's clothing, in a situation in which we had to delay fulfillments, the way the removal of any garment was a burning question between us, so that I recall with agonizing clarity — and when I least want to — both the delicate base of your neck and the delicate collar of your blouse, that blouse whose outline I knew by heart before my fingers ever brushed its texture or touched its pearly buttons. I remember the scent of train travel and harsh soap in the shoulder of your black jacket, the slight roughness of your black straw hat, as fully as I do the softness of your hair, which was almost exactly the same shade. When we dared to spend half an hour together in my hotel room in Sofia before appearing for another grim meal, I felt that my longing would destroy me. When you hung your jacket on a chair, and laid your blouse over it, slowly and deliberately, when you turned to face me with eyes that never wavered from mine, I was paralyzed by fire. When you put my hands on your waist and they had to choose between the heavy polish of your skirt and the finer polish of your skin, I could have wept.

Perhaps it was then that I found your single blemish — the one place, perhaps, I never kissed — the tiny curling dragon on the wing of your shoulder blade. My hands must have crossed it before I saw it. I remember my intake of breath — and yours — when I found it and stroked it with a reluctantly curious finger. In time it became for me part of the geography of your smooth back, but at that first moment it fueled the awe in my desire. Whether or not this happened in our hotel in Sofia, I must have learned it around the time when I was memorizing the edge of your lower teeth

The Historian

and their fine serration, and the skin around your eyes, with its first signs of age like cobwebs —

Here my father's note breaks off, and I can only revert to his more guarded letters to me.

Chapter 50

"TURGUT BORA and Selim Aksoy were waiting for us at the airport in Istanbul. 'Paul!' Turgut embraced and kissed me and beat me on the shoulders. 'Madam Professor!' He shook Helen's hand in both of his. 'Thank goodness you are safe and sound. Welcome to your triumphal return!'

"'Well, I wouldn't call it triumphal,' I said, laughing in spite of myself.

"'We will converse, we will converse!' Turgut cried, slapping me soundly across the back. Selim Aksoy followed all this with a quieter greeting. Within an hour we found ourselves at the door of Turgut's apartment, where Mrs. Bora was clearly delighted by our reappearance. Helen and I both exclaimed aloud when we saw her: today she was dressed in very pale blue, like a small spring flower. She looked quizzically at us. 'We like your dress!' Helen exclaimed, taking Mrs. Bora's little hand in her long one.

"Mrs. Bora laughed. 'Thank you,' she said. 'I sue all my clothes for me.' Then she and Selim Aksoy served us coffee and something she explained was *börek,* a roll of pastry with salty cheese inside, as well as a dinner of five or six other dishes.

"'Now, my friends, tell us what you have learned.'

"This was a tall order, but together we filled him in on our experiences at the conference in Budapest, my meeting with Hugh James, Helen's mother's story, Rossi's letters. Turgut listened with wide eyes as we described Hugh James's discovery of his dragon book. Recounting all this, I felt we had indeed learned a lot. Unfortunately, none of it pointed to Rossi's whereabouts.

"Turgut told us in his turn that they had had serious troubles during our absence from Istanbul; two nights before, his kind friend the archivist had been attacked a second time in the apartment where he was now resting. The first man they'd had watching him had fallen asleep on duty and had seen nothing. They had a new guard now, whom they hoped would be more careful. They were taking every precaution, but poor Mr. Erozan was very unwell.

"They had another kind of news, too. Turgut gulped down his second cup of coffee and hurried to retrieve something from his grisly study next door. (I was relieved not to be invited into it today.) He emerged carrying a notebook and sat down again next to Selim Aksoy. They looked gravely at us. 'I told you on the phone that we found a letter in your absence,' Turgut said. 'The original letter is in Slavonic, the old language of the Christian churches. As I told you, it was written by a monk from the Carpathians and it concerns his travels to Istanbul. My friend Selim is surprised that it is not in Latin, but perhaps this monk was a Slav. Shall I read it in no time?'

"'Of course,' I said, but Helen held up her hand.

"'Just one minute, please. How and where did you find it?'

"Turgut nodded approvingly. 'Mr. Aksoy found it in the archive, actually — the one you visited with us. He has spent three days looking at all manuscripts from the fifteenth century that are in that archive. This he found with a small collection of documents from the infidel churches — that is to say, Christian churches that were allowed to remain open in Istanbul during the rule of the Conqueror and his successors. There are not many such in the archive because they were usually kept by the monasteries, and especially by the patriarchate of Constantinople. But some church documents came into the hands of the sultan, particularly if they concerned new agreements for the churches under the Empire — such an agreement was called a *firman*. Sometimes the sultan received letters of — how do you say? — petition, in some church matter, and there are those in the archive, too.'

"He translated quickly for Aksoy, who wanted him to explain something else. 'Yes — my friend gives us a good information about this. He reminds me that soon after the Conqueror took the city, he appointed a new patriarch for the Christians, Patriarch Gennadius.' Aksoy, listening, nodded vigorously. 'And the sultan and Gennadius had a very civil friendship — I told you that the Conqueror was tolerant of Christians in his empire once he had conquered them. Sultan Mehmed asked Gennadius to write for him an explanation of the Orthodox faith and then had it translated for his personal library. There is a copy of this translation in the archive. Also, there are copies of some of the churches' charters, which they had to submit to the Conqueror, and these are there, too. Mr. Aksoy was looking through one of the church charters, from a church in Anatolia, and between two of its leaves he found this letter.'

"'Thank you.' Helen sat back on the cushions.

"'Alack, I cannot show you the original, but of course we could not take it out of the archives. You may go yourselves to see it while you are here, if you wish. It is written out in a beautiful hand, on a small sheet of parchment, with one edge torn. Now I shall read our translation to you, which we have made in English. Please to remember that this is the translation of a translation, and some points may be lost along that path.'

"And he read us the following:

Your Excellency, Lord Abbot Maxim Eupraxius:
A humble sinner begs your ear. As I have described, there was great controversy in this company since our mission failed yesterday. The city is not a safe place for us, and yet we believed we could not leave it without knowing what has become of the treasure we seek. This morning, by the grace of the Almighty, a new way opened, which I must record for you here. The abbot of Panachrantos, hearing from the abbot our host, his good friend, about our sore and private distress, came to us at Saint Irine in person. He is a gracious and holy man of fifty years old, who lived his long life first in the Great Lavra at Athos and now for many

years as monk and abbot at Panachrantos. Upon coming to us, he held council alone with our host, and then they spoke with us in our host's chambers, with complete secrecy, all novices and servants being dismissed from the chambers first. He told us he had not heard before this morning of our presence here, and upon hearing it had come to his friend to give him news which he had not shared earlier, wishing never to endanger him or his monks. In brief, he revealed to us that what we seek has been transported already out of the city and into a haven in the occupied lands of the Bulgarians. He has given us the most secret instructions for our safety in traveling thither, and has named for us the sanctuary which we must find. We would fain wait here a while, to send word to you and receive your orders in this matter, but these abbots told us also that some Janissaries of the sultan's court have come already to the patriarch to question him about the disappearance of that which we seek. It is most dangerous now for us to linger even a day and we shall be safer even in our progress through the infidel lands than we are here. Excellency, forgive our willfulness in setting out without being able to send for instructions from you, and may God's blessing and yours be upon us in this our decision. If it is necessary, I shall destroy even this record before it can reach your hands, and shall come to tell you with my own tongue, if it be not cut out first, of our search.

The humble sinner Br. Kiril
April, the Year of Our Lord 6985

"There was a deep silence when Turgut had finished. Selim and Mrs. Bora sat quietly, and Turgut rubbed his silver mane with a restless hand. Helen and I looked at each other.

"'The Year of Our Lord 6985?' I said finally. 'What does that mean?'

"'Medieval documents were dated from a calculation of the date of the Creation in Genesis,' Helen explained.

"'Yes.' Turgut nodded. 'The year 6985, by modern reckoning, is 1477.'

"I couldn't help sighing. 'It's a remarkably vivid letter, and obviously full of great concern about something. But I'm out of my league here,' I said ruefully. 'The date certainly makes me suspect some connection with the excerpt that Mr. Aksoy found earlier. But what proof do we have that the monk who wrote this new letter came from the Carpathians? And why do you think this is connected with Vlad Dracula?'

"Turgut smiled. 'Excellent questions, as usual, my young doubter. Let me try to answer them. As I told you, Selim knows the city very well, and when he found this letter and understood enough of it to see that it might be useful, he took it to a friend of his who is the keeper of the ancient monastery library at Saint Irine, which still exists. This friend translated it for him into Turkish and was very much interested in the letter because it mentioned his monastery. However, he could find in his library no record of such a visit in 1477 — either it was not recorded or any documents about it disappeared long ago.'

"'If the mission they describe was a secret and dangerous one,' Helen pointed out, 'they would not have been likely to record it.'

"'Very true, dear madam.' Turgut nodded at her. 'In any case, Selim's monastic friend helped us in one important matter — he searched the oldest church histories which he has there and discovered that the abbot to whom this letter is addressed, this Maxim Eupraxius, was late in his life a great abbot on Mount Athos. But in 1477, when this letter was written to him, he was the abbot of the monastery at Lake Snagov.' Turgut uttered these last words with a triumphant emphasis.

"We sat in excited silence for a few moments. Finally Helen broke it. '"We are men of God, men from the Carpathians,"' she murmured.

"'I beg your pardon?' Turgut gazed at her with interest.

"'Yes!' I took up Helen's line. '"Men from the Carpathians." It's from a song, a Romanian folk song Helen found in Budapest.' I described to them the hour we'd spent turning through the old book of songs at the University of Budapest library, the fine woodcut at the top of the page of a dragon and a church hiding among trees. Turgut's eyebrows rose almost to his shaggy hair when I mentioned this, and I rummaged quickly in my papers. 'Where is that thing?' A moment later, I'd found my handwritten translation among the folders in my briefcase — God, I thought, if I ever lose this briefcase! — and I read it aloud to them, leaving silences for Turgut to translate for Selim and Mrs. Bora:

They rode to the gates, up to the great city.
They rode to the great city from the land of
death.

The Historian

"We are men of God, men from the
Carpathians.
We are monks and holy men, but we bring
only evil news.
We bring news of a plague to the great city.
Serving our master, we come weeping for his
death."
They rode up to the gates and the city wept
with them
When they came in.

"'Ye gods, how peculiar and frightening,'
Turgut said. 'Are all your native songs like this,
madam?'

"'Yes, most of them,' Helen said, laughing. I realized that in my excitement I'd actually forgotten for two minutes that she was sitting next to
me. With difficulty I forced myself not to reach a
hand out to grasp hers, not to stare at her smile
or the wisp of dark hair against her cheek.

"'And our dragon at the top, hidden among
trees — there must be a connection.'

"'I wish I could have seen it.' Turgut sighed.
Then he slapped the edge of the brass table so
suddenly that all our cups rattled. His wife
put a gentle hand on his arm, and he patted it

reassuringly. 'No — look — the plague!' He turned to Selim and they exchanged a rapid fire of Turkish.

"'What?' Helen's eyes were narrow with concentration. 'The plague in the song?'

"'Yes, my dear.' Turgut combed his hair back with his hand. 'Besides the letter, we found one other fact about Istanbul in this exact period — something my friend Aksoy already knew, actually. In the late summer of 1477, in the hottest weather, there was what our historians call a Little Plague. It took many lives in the old Pera quarter of the city — what we call Galata, now. The bodies were impaled through the heart before they were burned. This is rather unusual, he says, because normally the bodies of the unlucky ones were simply burned outside the city gates to prevent further infection. But it was a short plague and did not take so many people.'

"'You think these monks, if they were the same ones, brought plague to the city?'

"'Of course, we do not know,' Turgut admitted. 'But if your song describes the same group of monks —'

"'I have been thinking of something.' Helen

set her cup down. 'I cannot remember, Paul, if I told you about this, but Vlad Dracula was one of the first military strategists in history to use — how do you say? — illnesses in war.'

"'Germ warfare,' I supplied. 'Hugh James told me.'

"'Yes.' She tucked her feet under her. 'During the sultan's invasions of Wallachia, Dracula liked to send people who were sick with plague or smallpox into the Ottoman camps disguised as Turks. They would infect as many people as possible before dying there.'

"If it hadn't been so gruesome, I would have smiled. The Wallachian prince was formidably creative as well as destructive, an enemy clever in the extreme. A second later I realized that I'd just thought of him in present tense.

"'I see.' Turgut nodded. 'You mean that perhaps this group of monks, if they were indeed the same monks, brought the plague with them from Wallachia.'

"'It does not explain one thing, however.' Helen frowned. 'If some of them were sick with the plague, why did the abbot of Saint Irine let them stay there?'

"'Madam, that is true,' Turgut admitted. 'Although if it was not the plague, but another kind of contamination — but there is no way to know.' We sat frustrated, contemplating this.

"'Many Orthodox monks came through Constantinople on pilgrimage even after the conquest,' Helen said finally. 'Maybe this was simply a group of pilgrims.'

"'But they were looking for something they apparently didn't find on their pilgrimage, at least in Constantinople,' I pointed out. 'And Brother Kiril says they are going to go into Bulgaria disguised as pilgrims, as if they weren't actually pilgrims — at least, that's what he seems to be saying.'

"Turgut scratched his head. 'Mr. Aksoy has thought about this,' he said. 'He explains to me that most of the great Christian relics in the churches of Constantinople were destroyed or stolen during the invasion — icons, crosses, the bones of saints. Of course, there weren't so many treasures here in 1453 as there had been when Byzantium was a great power, because the most beautiful ancient things were stolen by the Latin Crusade of 1204 — you no doubt know about this — and taken back to Rome and Venice and other cities in the West.' Turgut spread his hands before him in a gesture of deprecation. 'My father told me about the wonderful horses on the Basilica of San Marco in Venice, stolen from Byzantium by crusaders. The Christian invaders were just as bad as the Ottoman ones, you see. In any case, my fellows, during the invasion of 1453 some of the church treasures were hidden, and some were even taken out of the city before Sultan Mehmed's siege and concealed in monasteries outside the walls, or carried in secret to other lands. If our monks were pilgrims, perhaps they came to the city in the hope of visiting a holy object and then found it missing. Perhaps what the abbot of the second monastery told them was the story of a great icon that had been taken safely to Bulgaria. But we have no method of knowing, from this letter.'

"'I see now why you want us to go to Bulgaria.' I resisted again the urge to take Helen's hand. 'Although I can't imagine how we'd find out more about this story when we got there, let alone how we'd get in. And are you certain there is no other place we should search in Istanbul?'

"Turgut shook his head somberly and picked up his neglected coffee cup. 'I have used every channel I could think of, including some — I am sorry to say — that I cannot tell you about. Mr.

Aksoy has looked everywhere, in his own books, in his friends' libraries, in the university archives. I have talked with every historian I could find, including one who studies the graveyards of Istanbul — you have seen our beautiful graveyards. We cannot find any mention of an unusual burial of a foreigner here in that period. Mayhap we have missed something, but I do not know where else to look in a quick time.' He gazed earnestly at us. 'I know it would be very difficult for you to go to Bulgaria. I would do it myself, except that it would be even more difficult for me, my friends. As a Turk, I could not even attend one of their academic conferences. No one hates the descendants of the Ottoman Empire the way the Bulgarians do.'

"'Oh, the Romanians try their very best,' Helen assured him, but her words were tempered by a smile that made him chuckle in return.

"'But — my God.' I sat back against the cushions of the divan, feeling awash in one of those waves of unreality that had been breaking over me with increasing frequency. 'I don't see how we can do this.'

"Turgut leaned forward and set before me the English translation of the monk's letter. 'He did not know either.'

"'Who?' I groaned.

"'Brother Kiril. Listen, my friend, when did Rossi disappear?'

"'More than two weeks ago,' I admitted.

"'You do not have any time to lose. We know Dracula is not in his grave in Snagov. We think he was not buried in Istanbul. But' — he tapped the paper — 'here is one piece of evidence. Of what, we do not know, but in 1477 someone from Snagov Monastery went to Bulgaria — or tried to. It is worth learning about. If you find nothing, you have tried your best. Then you can go home and mourn your teacher with a clear heart, and we, your friends, will honor forever your valor. But if you do not try, you will always wonder and grieve without relief.'

"He picked up the translation again and ran a finger over it, then read aloud, '"It is most dangerous now for us to linger even a day and we shall be safer even in our progress through the infidel lands than we are here." Here, my friend. Put this in your bag. This copy is for you, the English one. With it here is a copy in the Slavonic, which Mr. Aksoy's monastic friend has written out.'

"Turgut leaned forward. 'Furthermore, I have learned that there is a scholar in Bulgaria whom you can seek for help. His name is Anton Stoichev. My friend Aksoy greatly admires his work, which is published in many languages.' Selim Aksoy nodded at the name. 'Stoichev knows more about the medieval Balkans than anyone else alive, especially about Bulgaria. He lives near Sofia — you must ask about him.'

"Helen took my hand suddenly, openly, surprising me; I'd thought we would keep our relationship secret even here, among friends. I saw Turgut's glance fall on the little motion. The warm lines around his eyes and mouth deepened, and Mrs. Bora smiled frankly at us, clasping her girlish hands around her knees. Clearly, she approved of our union, and I felt a sudden blessing of it by these kindhearted people.

"'Then I will call my aunt,' Helen said firmly, squeezing my fingers.

"'Éva? What can she do?'

"'As you know, she can do anything.' Helen smiled at me. 'No, I do not know exactly what she can or will do. But she has friends as well as enemies in the secret police of our country' — she dropped her voice, as if in spite of herself — 'and they have friends everywhere in Eastern Europe. And enemies, of course — they all spy on each other. It may put her in some danger — that is the only thing I regret. And we will need a big, big bribe.'

"'*Bakshish.*' Turgut nodded. 'Of course. Selim Aksoy and I have thought about this. We have found twenty thousand liras you may use. And although I cannot go with you, my fellows, I will give you whatever help I can, and so will Mr. Aksoy.'

"I was looking hard at him now, and at Aksoy — they sat upright across from us, their coffee forgotten, very straight and serious. Something in their faces — Turgut's large and ruddy, Aksoy's delicate, both keen-eyed, both calmly but almost fiercely alert — was suddenly familiar to me. A sensation I couldn't name went over me; for a second it stayed the question in my mouth. Then I gripped Helen's hand more tightly in mine — that strong, hard, already beloved hand — and looked into Turgut's dark gaze.

"'Who are you?' I said.

"Turgut and Selim glanced at each other and something appeared to pass silently between them. Then Turgut spoke in a low, clear voice. 'We work for the sultan.'"

Chapter 51

"HELEN AND I DREW BACK as one. For a second I thought Turgut and Selim must be aligned with some dark power, and I struggled with the temptation to grab my briefcase and Helen's arm and flee the apartment. How except through occult means could these two men, whom I'd thought of as my friends, work for a sultan long dead? Actually, all the sultans were long dead, so whichever one Turgut was referring to could not be of this world anymore. And had they been lying to us about a host of other issues?

"My confusion was cut short by Helen's voice. She leaned forward, pale, her eyes large, but her question was a calm one, and eminently practical, in the situation — so practical at first that it took me a moment to understand it. 'Professor Bora,' she said slowly, 'how old are you?'

"He smiled at her. 'Ah, my dear madam, if you are asking whether I am five hundred years old, the answer is — fortunately — no. I work for the Majestic and Splendid Refuge of the World, Sultan Mehmed II, but I never had the incomparable honor of meeting him.'

"'Then what on earth are you trying to tell us?' I burst out.

"Turgut smiled again and Selim nodded kindly at me. 'I had not intended to tell you this at all,' Turgut said. 'However, you have given to us your trust in many things, and because you ask this so perceptive question, my friend, we will explain. I was born in the normal way in 1911 and I hope to die in the normal way in my bed in — oh, about 1985.' He chuckled. 'However, my family members always live a long, long time, so I shall be cursed with sitting on this divan when I am too old to be respectable.' He put an arm around Mrs. Bora's shoulders. 'Mr. Aksoy is also of the age you see him here. There is nothing so strange about us. What we will tell you, which is the deepest secret I could entrust to anyone, and which you must keep secret no matter what may happen, is that we are part of the Crescent Guard of the Sultan.'

"'I don't think I have ever heard of them,' Helen said, frowning.

"'No, Madam Professor, you have not.' Turgut glanced at Selim, who sat listening patiently, obviously trying to follow our conversation, his green eyes quiet as a pond. 'We believe that no one has heard of us except our members. We were formed as a secret guard from among the most elite corps of the Janissaries.'

"I remembered, suddenly, those stony, bright-eyed young faces I'd seen in the paintings from the Topkapı Saray, their solid ranks grouped near the sultan's throne, near enough to spring on a potential assassin — or on anyone, for that matter, who suddenly fell from the sultan's favor.

"Turgut seemed to read my thoughts, for he nodded. 'You have heard of the Janissaries, I see. Well, my fellows, in 1477, Mehmed the Magnificent and Glorious called to him twenty officers who were the most trustworthy and the best educated of all his corps, and conferred on them in secret the new symbol of the Crescent Guard. They were given one purpose, which they were to fulfill — at the cost of their lives, if necessary. That purpose was to keep the Order of the Dragon from bringing any more torment to our great empire, and to hunt down and kill its members wherever they could be found.'

"Helen and I both inhaled, but for once I got there before she did. 'The Crescent Guard was formed in 1477 — the year the monks came to Istanbul!' I tried to puzzle it out as I spoke. 'But the Order of the Dragon was founded long before that — by the Emperor Sigismund in 1400, right?'

"'It was 1408, to be exact, my friend. Of course. By 1477 the Sultans had already had quite a problem with the Order of the Dragon and its wars on the Empire. But in 1477, His Gloriousness the Refuge of the World decided that there might be even worse raids from the Order of the Dragon in the future.'

"'What do you mean?' Helen's hand was motionless in mine, and cold.

"'Even our charter does not say this directly,' Turgut admitted, 'but I am certain it is no coincidence that the sultan founded the Guard only months after the death of Vlad Ţepeş.' He put his hands together, as if in prayer — although, I remembered, his ancestors would have prayed prostrate, on their faces. 'The charter says that His Magnificence founded the Crescent Guard to pursue the Order of the Dragon, most despised enemies of his majestic empire, through all time and space, over land and sea and even across death.'

"Turgut leaned forward, his eyes glowing and his silver mane springing up wildly. 'It is my theory that His Gloriousness had a sense, or even knowledge, of the danger Vlad Dracula might deliver to the Empire after his — Dracula's — death.' He raked his hair back. 'As we have seen, the sultan also founded at that time his collection of documents about the Order of the Dragon — the archive was not a secret, but it was used in secret by our members and still is. And now, this marvelous letter Selim has found, and your folk song, madam — these are further proof that His Gloriousness had a good reason to worry.'

"My brain was still seething with questions. 'But how did you — and Mr. Aksoy — come to be part of this Guard?'

"'The membership is handed down from fathers to eldest sons. Each son receives his — how is it in English? — his induction at the age of nineteen. If a father has only unworthy sons, or none, he lets the secret die with him.' Turgut retrieved, finally, his deserted coffee cup, and Mrs. Bora moved to fill it for him. 'The Crescent Guard was kept so well a secret that even the other Janissaries did not know that some of their ranks belonged to such a group. Our beloved *fatih* died in 1481, but his Guard continued. The Janissaries rose to great power sometimes, under weaker sultans, but we kept our secret. When the Empire finally vanished even from Istanbul, no one knew about us and we remained. Our charter was kept safe by Selim Aksoy's father during the first Great War, and by Selim during the last one. He retains it now, in a secret place that is our tradition.' Turgut drew a breath and took a grateful gulp of his coffee.

"'I thought,' Helen put in a little suspiciously, 'that you said your father was Italian. How did he come to be in the Crescent Guard?'

"'Yes, madam.' Turgut nodded over his cup. 'My maternal grandfather, actually, was a very active member of the Guard and he could not endure for the line to die with him, but he had only a daughter. When he saw that the Empire would end forever in his lifetime —'

"'Your mother!' Helen exclaimed.

"'Yes, my dear.' Turgut's smile was wistful. 'You are not the only one here who can claim a remarkable mother. As I think I told you, she was one of the best-educated women of her time in our country — one of the only splendidly educated ones, actually — and my grandfather spared nothing to pour into her all his knowledge and ambition, and to prepare her for service in the Guard. She became interested in engineering when that was still a new science here, and after her induction to the Guard, he allowed her to go to Rome to study — he had friends there. She was proficient in very advanced mathematics and could read in four languages, including Greek and Arabic.' He said something in Turkish to his wife and Selim, and they both nodded agreement. "She could ride as well as any cavalryman of the sultans' and — although very few people knew this — shoot like one, also.' He almost winked at Helen, and I remembered her little gun — where did she keep it, anyway? 'She learned from my grandfather a great deal about the lore of the vampire and how to protect the living from his evil strategies. Her picture is there, if you would like to see her.'

"He got up and brought it to us from a carved table in the corner, putting it very gently into Helen's hand. It was a striking image, with that marvelous delicate clarity of photographic portraits from early in the century. The lady sitting for her lengthy exposure in an Istanbul studio looked patient and composed, but her photographer, under his great black cloth, had captured something like amusement in her eyes. The sepia of her skin was flawless above her dark dress. Her face was Turgut's, but fine of nose and chin where his was heavy, opening like a crisp flower on the stem of her slender throat — the visage of an Ottoman princess. Her hair, under an elaborate plumed hat, was piled up in dark clouds. Her eyes met mine with that glint of humor, and I regretted suddenly the years that separated us.

"Turgut took the little frame fondly into his own hand again. 'My grandfather chose with wisdom when he broke the tradition and made her a member of the Guard. It was she who found some scattered pieces of our archive in other libraries and brought them back to the collection. When I was five she killed a wolf at our summer cottage, and when I was eleven she taught me to ride and shoot. My father was devoted to her, although she frightened him with her fearlessness — he always said he had followed her back to Turkey from Rome to talk her out of too much bravery. Like the most trustworthy wives of the members of our Guard, my father knew about her membership and he worried constantly about her safety. He is over there —' He pointed to a portrait in oils that I had noticed earlier, where it hung by the windows. The man looking out of it was a solid, comfortable, quaint person in a dark suit, with black eyes and hair and a soft expression; Turgut had told us that his father had been a historian of the Italian Renaissance, but I could easily imagine the man in the portrait playing marbles with his young son while his wife tended to the boy's more serious education.

"Helen stirred beside me, stretching her legs discreetly. 'You said your grandfather was an active member of the Crescent Guard. What does that mean? What are your activities?'

"Turgut shook his head regretfully. 'That, madam fellow, I cannot tell even you two in detail. Some things must remain secret. We have told you this much because you asked — you almost guessed — and because we would like you to have complete faith in our assistance. It is very much to the benefit of the Guard that you should go into Bulgaria, and go as soon as possible. Today the Guard is small — there are only a few of us left.' He sighed. 'I, for one, alas, have no son — or daughter — to whom to pass my trust, although Mr. Aksoy is raising his nephew in our traditions. But you may believe that all the power of Ottoman determination will go with you, in one way or another.'

"I resisted the urge to groan aloud again. I could have argued with Helen, perhaps, but arguing with the secret might of the Ottoman Empire was beyond me. Turgut raised a finger. 'I must give you one warning, and a very serious one, my friends. We have put into your hands a secret that has been kept with care — and with success, we believe — for five hundred years. We have no reason to think that our ancient foe knows it, although he surely hates and fears our city as he did in his lifetime. In the charter of the Guard, His Magnificence laid down his rule. Anyone who betrays the secret of the Guard to our enemies will be punished by immediate execution. This has never occurred, to my knowledge. But I ask you to be careful, for your own sakes as well as ours.'

"There was no hint of malice or threat in his voice, only a grave depth, and I heard in it the implacable loyalty that had made his sultan conqueror of the Great City, the previously impregnable, arrogant city of the Byzantines. When he had said, 'We work for the sultan,' he had meant exactly that, even if he himself had been born half a millennium after Mehmed's death. The sun was sinking lower outside the parlor windows, and a rosy light reached Turgut's big face, suddenly ennobling it. I thought for a moment how fascinated Rossi would have been by Turgut, how he would have seen in him living history, and I wondered what questions — questions I could not even begin to formulate myself — Rossi might have asked him.

"It was Helen, however, who said the right thing. Rising to her feet so that we all rose with her, she gave her hand to Turgut. 'We are honored by what you have told us,' she said, looking proudly into his face. 'We will guard your secret and the wishes of the sultan with our lives.' Turgut kissed her hand, clearly moved, and Selim Aksoy bowed to her. There seemed no need for me to add anything; setting aside for the moment her people's traditional hatred of their Ottoman oppressors, she had spoken for both of us.

"'We might have stood that way all day, looking wordlessly at one another as the twilight fell, if Turgut's telephone had not suddenly given a screech. He bowed his excuses and went across the room to answer it, and Mrs. Bora began to load the remains of our meal onto a brass tray. Turgut listened to his caller for a few minutes, spoke in some agitation, and then replaced the receiver abruptly. He turned to Selim and addressed him in rapid Turkish, and Selim quickly put on his shabby jacket.

"'Has something happened?' I asked.

"'Yes, alas.' Turgut smote his chest with a punishing hand. 'It is the librarian, Mr. Erozan. The man I left to watch him went out for a moment, and he called now to say that my friend has been attacked again. Erozan is unconscious and the man is going for a doctor. This is very serious. It is the third attack, and just at sunset.'

"Shocked, I reached for my jacket, too, and Helen slipped on her shoes, although Mrs. Bora put a pleading hand on her arm. Turgut kissed his wife, and as we hurried out, I turned once to see her standing pale and frightened at the door to the apartment."

Chapter 52

"WHERE CAN WE SLEEP?" Barley said doubtfully. We were in our hotel room in Perpignan, a double room we'd gotten by telling the elderly clerk, too, that we were brother and sister. He'd given it to us without a murmur, although he'd looked dubiously from one of us to the other. We couldn't afford separate rooms, and we both knew it. "Well?" Barley said, a little impatiently. We looked at the bed. There was no other place, not even a rug on the bare and polished floor. Finally Barley made a decision — for himself, at least. While I stood frozen to the spot, he went into the bathroom with some clothes and a toothbrush, emerging a few minutes later in cotton pajamas as pale as his hair.

Something about this picture, and his failure at nonchalance, made me laugh aloud, even while my cheeks burned, and then he began to laugh, too. We both laughed until the tears rent our faces — Barley bent double, crossing his arms over his skinny middle, and I clutching the depressing old armoire. In hysterical laughter, we relinquished all the tension of the trip, my fears,

Barley's disapproval, my father's anguished letters, our arguments. Years later, I learned the term *fou rire* — a crazy fit of laughter — and that was my first one, there in that French hotel. My first *fou rire* was followed by other firsts, as we stumbled toward each other. Barley grabbed my shoulders with as little elegance as I had held onto the armoire a moment before, but his kiss was angelically graceful, his youthful experience pressing softly into my utter lack of it. Like our laughter, it left me winded.

All my previous knowledge of lovemaking was drawn from polite movies and confusing books, and I was mostly unable to proceed. Barley, however, proceeded for me, and I followed gratefully, if clumsily. By the time we found ourselves lying on the stale, neat bed, I had already learned something of the negotiation between lovers and their clothing. Each garment seemed to me a momentous decision, Barley's pajama shirt first of all; its removal revealed an alabaster torso and surprisingly muscled shoulders. The shedding of my blouse and ugly white brassiere was as much my decision as his. He told me that he loved the color of my skin, because it was completely different from his, and it was true that my arm had never looked so olive as when it lay against the snow of Barley's. He drew the flat of his hand across me, and across my remaining clothes, and for the first time I did the same to him, discovering the alien contours of the male body; I seemed to be feeling my way shyly over the craters of the moon. My heart knocked inside me with such force that I worried he would be able to feel it striking his breast.

In fact, there was so much to do, to take care of, that we didn't remove any more clothing, and a great deal of time seemed to pass before Barley curled himself around me with a strangled sigh, murmuring, "You're just a kid," and put one arm possessively over my shoulders and neck.

When he said this, I suddenly knew that he, too, was just a kid — an honorable kid. I think I loved him more in that moment than at any other.

Chapter 53

"THE BORROWED APARTMENT where Turgut had left Mr. Erozan was perhaps a ten-minute walk from his own—or a ten-minute run, because we all but ran, even Helen in her heeled pumps hurrying along with us. Turgut muttered (and swore, I guessed) under his breath. He had brought with him a little black bag, which I thought might contain medical supplies in case the doctor did not come, or didn't come in time. At last we found ourselves climbing the wooden stairway in an old house. We tore up the stairs after Turgut and he threw open a door at the top.

"The house had apparently been divided into dingy little apartments; in this one a bed, chairs, and a table furnished the main room, and a single lamp lit it. Turgut's friend lay on the floor with a blanket over him, and from beside him a stammering man of about thirty rose to greet us. The man was almost hysterical with fright and contrition; he kept wringing his hands and telling Turgut something over and over. Turgut pushed him aside and he and Selim knelt by Mr. Erozan.

789

The poor victim's face was ashen, his eyes were closed, and his breath came in rattling gasps. There was an ugly tear in his neck, larger than when we'd last seen it, but the more horrible because it was strangely clean, if ragged, with only a fringe of blood at the edges. It occurred to me that such a deep wound ought to bleed copiously, and the realization sent a thrill of nausea to my stomach. I put my arm around Helen and we stood staring, unable to look away.

"Turgut was examining the wound without touching it and now he glanced up at us. 'A few minutes ago, this damnable man went for a strange doctor without consulting me, but the doctor was out. That, at least, is fortunate, because we do not want a doctor here now. But he left Erozan alone just at sunset.' He spoke with Aksoy, who got up suddenly and — with a force I would not have predicted — struck the hapless watchman and sent him from the room. The man backed away and then we heard his terrified descent down the stairwell. Selim locked the door behind him and looked out the window to the street, as if to satisfy himself that the fellow wouldn't be returning. Then he knelt by Turgut and they conferred in low voices.

"After a moment, Turgut reached into the bag

he had brought with him. I saw him draw from it an object already familiar to me: it was a vampire-hunting kit similar to the one he had given me in his study more than a week earlier, except that this one was in a finer box, ornamented with Arabic writing and what looked like mother-of-pearl inlay. He opened it and took stock of the instruments inside. Then he looked up at us again. 'Professors,' he said quietly, 'my friend has been bitten by the vampire at least three times, and he is dying. If he dies naturally in this condition, he will soon become undead.' He wiped his forehead with a big hand. 'This is a terrible moment now, and I must ask you to leave the room. Madam, you must not see this.'

"'Please, let us do whatever will help you,' I began hesitantly, but Helen stepped forward.

"'Let me stay,' she told Turgut in a low voice. 'I want to know how it is done.' For a moment, I wondered why she craved this knowledge and found myself remembering — surreal thought — that she was, after all, an anthropologist. He glared at her, then seemed to acquiesce without words, and bent again to his friend. I hoped, still, that what I had already guessed was wrong, but Turgut was murmuring something in his friend's ear. He took Mr. Erozan's hand and stroked it.

"Then — and this was perhaps the worst of all the awful things that followed — Turgut pressed his friend's hand to his own heart and broke out in a keening wail, words that seemed to come to us from the depths of a history not only too ancient but too alien for me to distinguish their syllables, a howl of grief akin to the muezzin's call to prayer, which we had heard from the minarets in the city — except that Turgut's wail sounded more like a summons to hell — a string of horror-stricken notes that seemed to arise from the memory of a thousand Ottoman camps, a million Turkish soldiers. I saw the fluttering banners, the splashes of blood on the legs of their horses, the spear and the crescent, the glitter of sunlight on scimitars and chain mail, the beautiful and mutilated young heads, faces, bodies; heard the screams of men crossing into the hand of Allah and the cries of their faraway mothers and fathers; smelled the reek of burning houses and fresh gore, the sulfur of cannon fire, the conflagrations of tent and bridge and horseflesh.

"Most strangely, I heard in the midst of this roar a cry I could understand at will: '*Kaziklu Bey!* The Impaler!' In the heart of the chaos I seemed to see a figure different from the rest, a dark-clad, cloaked man on horseback wheeling among the bright colors, his face drawn up in a snarl of concentration and his sword harvesting Ottoman heads, which rolled heavily in their pointed helmets.

"Turgut's voice fell back and I found I was standing near him now, looking down at the dying man. Helen was blessedly real next to me — I opened my mouth to ask her a question and saw that she had heard the same horror in Turgut's chant. I remembered without wanting to that the blood of the Impaler ran in her veins. She turned to me for a second, her face shocked but steady; it came to me just in time that Rossi's heritage — mild, patrician, Tuscan, and Anglo — also ran through her, and I saw Rossi's incomparable kindness in her eyes. In that moment, I think — not later, not at home in my parents' stodgy brown church, not in front of any minister — I married her, I wed her in my heart, I cleaved to her for life.

"Turgut, silent now, had placed the string of prayer beads on his friend's throat, which made the body quiver a little, and selected from the stained satin in the box a tool longer than my hand and made of bright silver. 'I have never had to do this before, God save me, in my life,' he said quietly. He opened Mr. Erozan's shirt and I saw the aging skin, the curling chest hair gray as ashes, rising and falling unevenly. Selim searched the room with silent efficiency and brought Turgut a brick that had apparently been used as a door prop, and this homely object Turgut took in his hand, weighing it for a second. He put the sharp end of the stake on the left side of the man's chest and began a low chant, in which I caught words I remembered from somewhere — book, movie, conversation? — '*Allahu akbar, Allahu akbar:* Allah is great.' I couldn't, I knew, force Helen to leave the room any more than I could leave it myself, but I pulled her back a step as the brick descended. Turgut's hand was large and steady. Selim held the stake upright for him and with a splintering, sucking thud it went into the body. Sluggish blood welled around the point and smeared the pale skin. Mr. Erozan's face convulsed horribly for a second and his lips drew back from his yellowing teeth like a dog's. Helen stared and I did not dare look away; I didn't want her to watch anything I couldn't see with her. The librarian's body quivered, the stake suddenly went down to its hilt, and Turgut sat back, as if waiting. His lips trembled and sweat had sprung out all over his face.

"After a moment the body relaxed and then the face; the lips drooped peacefully over Mr. Erozan's mouth, a sigh came up out of his chest; his feet in their pathetically worn socks twitched and were still. I kept a firm hold on Helen, and felt her shiver next to me, but she stood quiet. Turgut raised his friend's limp hand and kissed it. I saw tears running down his ruddy face, dripping into his mustache, and he covered his eyes with one hand. Selim touched the dead librarian's brow, then rose and pressed Turgut's shoulder.

"After a moment, Turgut recovered himself enough to stand and blow his nose into a handkerchief. 'He was a very good man,' he said to us, his voice unsteady. 'A generous, kind man. Now he rests in Muhammad's peace instead of joining the legions of hell.' He turned away to wipe his eyes. 'My fellows, we must get this body away from here. There is a doctor at one of the hospitals who — he will help us. Selim will remain here with the door locked while I call, and the doctor will come with the ambulance and sign the necessary certificates.' Turgut took from his pocket several cloves of garlic and placed them gently in the dead man's mouth. Selim removed the stake and washed it at the sink in the corner, putting it carefully away in the beautiful box. Turgut cleaned up every trace of blood, bandaged the man's chest with a dishcloth and rebuttoned his shirt, then took from the bed a sheet, which he let me help him spread over the body, covering its now-quiet face.

"'Now, my dear friends, I ask of you this favor. You have seen what the undead can do, and we know they are here. You must protect yourselves every minute. And you must go to Bulgaria — as soon as possible — in the next few days, if you can arrange this. Call me at my apartment when you have made your plans.' He looked hard at me. 'If we do not see each other in person before you go, I wish you all the best possible good fortune and safety. I will think of you every moment. Please call me as soon as you come back to Istanbul, if you come back here.'

"I hoped he meant *If that's how you route your travel* and not *If you survive Bulgaria.* He shook hands warmly with us, and so did Selim, who followed this up by kissing Helen's hand very shyly.

"'We will go now,' Helen said simply, taking my arm, and we walked out of that sad room and down the stairs to the street."

Chapter 54

"MY FIRST IMPRESSION of Bulgaria — and my memory of it ever after — was of mountains seen from the air, mountains high and deep, darkly verdant and mainly untouched by roads, although here and there a brown ribbon ran among villages or along sudden sheer cliffs. Helen sat quietly next to me, her eyes fixed on the small porthole of the airplane window, her hand resting in mine under cover of my folded jacket. I could feel her warm palm, her slightly chilled, fine fingers, the absence of rings. We could occasionally see glinting veins in the crevasses of the mountains, which must, I thought, be rivers, and I strained without hope for some configuration of winding dragon tail that might be the answer to our puzzle. Nothing, of course, fit the outlines I already knew with my eyes closed.

"And nothing was likely to, I reminded myself, if only to quell the hope that rose uncontrollably in me again at the sight of those ancient mountains. Their very obscurity, their look of having been untouched by modern history, their mysterious lack of cities or towns or industrialization made me hopeful. I felt somehow that the more perfectly hidden the past was in this country, the more likely it was to have been preserved. The monks, whose lost trail we now soared above, had made their way through mountains like these — perhaps these very peaks, although we didn't know their route. I mentioned this to Helen, wanting to hear myself voice my hopes aloud. She shook her head. 'We don't know for a fact that they reached Bulgaria or even actually set out for it,' she reminded me, but she softened the flat scholarship of her tone with a caress of my hand under the jacket.

"'I don't know anything about Bulgarian history, you know,' I said. 'I'm going to be lost here.'

"Helen smiled. 'I am not an expert myself, but I can tell you that Slavs migrated to this area from the north in the sixth and seventh centuries, and a Turkic tribe called the Bulgars came here in the seventh, I think. They united against the Byzantine Empire — wisely — and their first ruler was a Bulgar named Asparuh. Tsar Boris I made Christianity the official religion in the ninth century. He is a great hero here, apparently, in spite of that. The Byzantines ruled from the eleventh to the beginning of the thirteenth, and then Bulgaria became very powerful until the Ottomans crushed them in 1393.'

"'When were the Ottomans driven out?' I asked with interest. We seemed to be meeting them everywhere.

"'Not until 1878,' Helen admitted. 'Russia helped Bulgaria to expel them.'

"'And then Bulgaria sided with the Axis in both wars.'

"'Yes, and the Soviet army brought a glorious revolution just after the war. What would we do without the Soviet army?' Helen gave me her most brilliant and bitter smile, but I squeezed her hand.

"'Keep your voice down,' I said. 'If you won't be careful, I'll have to be careful for both of us.'"

"The airport in Sofia was a tiny place; I'd expected a palace of modern communism, but we descended to a modest area of tarmac and strolled across it with the other travelers. Nearly all of them were Bulgarian, I decided, trying to catch something of their conversations. They were handsome people, some of them strikingly so, and their faces varied from the dark-eyed pale Slav to a Middle-Eastern bronze, a kaleidoscope of rich hues and shaggy black eyebrows, noses long and flaring, or aquiline, or deeply hooked, young women with curly black hair and noble foreheads, and energetic old men with few teeth. They smiled or laughed and talked eagerly with one another; one tall man gesticulated to his companion with a folded newspaper. Their clothes were distinctly not Western, although I would have been hard put to say what it was about the cuts of suits and skirts, the heavy shoes and dark hats, that was unfamiliar to me.

"I also had the impression of a barely concealed happiness among these people as their feet touched Bulgarian soil — or asphalt — and this disturbed the picture I'd carried there with me of a nation grimly allied with the Soviets, Stalin's right-hand ally even now, a year after his death — a joyless country in the grip of delusions from which they might never awake. The difficulties of obtaining a Bulgarian visa in Istanbul — a passage oiled in great part by Turgut's sultanic funding and by calls from Aunt Éva's Bulgarian counterpart in Sofia — had only increased my trepidations about this country, and the cheerless bureaucrats who had finally, grudgingly stamped their approval in our passports in

Budapest had seemed to me already embalmed in oppression. Helen had confided to me that the very fact that the Bulgarian embassy had granted us visas at all made her uneasy.

"Real Bulgarians, however, appeared to be a different race altogether. On going into the airport building, we found ourselves in customs lines, and here the din of laughter and talk was even louder, and we could see relatives waving over the barriers and shouting greetings. Around us people were declaring small bits of money and souvenirs from Istanbul and previous destinations, and when our turn came we did the same.

"The eyebrows of the young customs officer disappeared into his cap at the sight of our passports, and he took the passports aside for a few minutes to consult with another officer. 'Not a good omen,' Helen said under her breath. Several uniformed men gathered around us, and the oldest and most pompous-looking began to question us in German, then in French, and finally in broken English. As Aunt Éva had instructed, I calmly pulled out our makeshift letter from the University of Budapest, which implored the Bulgarian government to let us in on important academic business, and the other letter Aunt Éva had obtained for us from a friend in the Bulgarian embassy.

"I don't know what the officer made of the academic letter and its extravagant mix of English, Hungarian, and French, but the embassy letter was in Bulgarian and bore the embassy seal. The officer read it in silence, his huge dark eyebrows knit over the bridge of his nose, and then his face took on a surprised, even an astonished expression, and he looked at us in something like amazement. This made me even more nervous than his earlier hostility had, and it occurred to me that Éva had been rather vague with us about the contents of the embassy letter. I certainly couldn't ask now what it said, and I felt miserably at sea when the officer broke into a smile and actually clapped me on the shoulder. He made his way to a telephone in one of the little customs booths and after considerable effort seemed to have reached someone. I didn't like the way he smiled into the receiver and glanced across at us every few seconds. Helen shifted uneasily next to me and I knew she must be reading even more into all this than I was.

"The officer finally hung up with a flourish, helped reunite us with our dusty suitcases, and led us to a bar inside the airport, where he bought us little shots of a head-emptying brandy called *rakiya,* partaking thoroughly himself. He asked us in his several broken languages how long we'd been committed to the revolution, when we had joined the Party, and so on, none of which made me feel any more comfortable. It all set me to pondering more than ever the possible inaccuracies of our letter of introduction, but I followed Helen's lead and merely smiled, or made neutral remarks. He toasted friendship among the workers of every nation, refilling our glasses and his own. If one of us said something — some platitude about visiting his beautiful country, for example — he shook his head with a broad smile, as if contradicting our statements. I was unnerved by this until Helen whispered to me that she'd read about this cultural idiosyncrasy: Bulgarians shook their heads in agreement and nodded in disagreement.

"When we'd had exactly as much *rakiya* as I could tolerate with impunity, we were saved by the appearance of a dour-faced man in a dark suit and hat. He looked only a little older than I was and would have been handsome if any expression of pleasure had ever flitted across his countenance. As it was, his dark mustache barely hid disapprovingly pursed lips, and the fall of black hair over his forehead concealed none of his frown. The officer greeted him with deference and introduced him as our assigned guide to Bulgaria, explaining that we were privileged in this, because Krassimir Ranov was highly respected in the Bulgarian government, associated with the University of Sofia, and knew as well as anyone the interesting sights of their ancient and glorious country.

"Through a haze of brandy I shook the man's fish-cold hand and wished to heaven we could see Bulgaria without a guide. Helen seemed less surprised by all this and greeted him, I thought, with just the right mixture of boredom and disdain. Mr. Ranov still hadn't uttered a word to us, but he appeared to take a hearty dislike to Helen even before the officer reported too loudly that she was Hungarian and was studying in the United States. This explanation made his mustache twitch over a grim smile. 'Professor, madam,' he said — his first words — and turned his back on us. The customs officer beamed, shook our hands, pounded me on the shoulders as if we were old friends already, and then indicated with a gesture that we must follow Ranov.

"Outside the airport, Ranov hailed a cab, which

had the most antiquated interior I'd ever seen in a vehicle, black fabric stuffed with something that could have been horsehair, and told us from the front seat that hotel rooms had been arranged for us at a hotel of the best reputation. 'I believe you will find it comfortable, and it has an excellent restaurant. Tomorrow we shall meet for breakfast there, and you may explain to me the nature of your research and how I can help you make arrangements to complete it. You will no doubt wish to meet with your colleagues at the University of Sofia and with the appropriate ministries. Then we shall arrange for you a short tour of some of Bulgaria's historic places.' He smiled sourly and I stared at him in growing horror. His English was too good; despite his marked accent, it had the tonelessly correct sound of one of those records from which you can learn a language in thirty days.

"His face had something familiar in it, too. I'd certainly never seen him before, but it made me think of someone I knew, with the accompanying frustration of my not being able to remember who on earth it was. This feeling persisted for me during that first day in Sofia, dogging me on our all-too-guided tour of the city. Sofia was strangely beautiful, however — a blend of nineteenth-century elegance, medieval splendor, and shining new monuments in the socialist style. At the city's center, we toured a grim mausoleum that held the embalmed body of the Stalinist dictator Georgi Dimitrov, who'd died five years before. Ranov took off his hat before entering the building and ushered me and Helen ahead of him. We joined a line of silent Bulgarians filing past Dimitrov's open coffin. The dictator's face was waxen, with a heavy dark mustache like Ranov's. I thought of Stalin, whose body had reportedly joined Lenin's the year before, in a similar shrine on Red Square. These atheist cultures were certainly diligent in preserving the relics of their saints.

"My sense of foreboding about our guide increased when I asked him if he could put us in touch with an Anton Stoichev and saw him recoil. 'Mr. Stoichev is an enemy of the people,' he assured us in his irritable voice. 'Why do you wish to see him?' And then, strangely, 'Of course, if you desire it, I can arrange this. He does not teach at the university anymore — with his religious views he could not be trusted with our youth. But he is famous and perhaps you would like to see him for that reason?'"

•   •   •

" 'Ranov has been told to give us whatever we want,' Helen remarked quietly when we had a moment alone, outside the hotel. 'Why is that? Why does someone think that is a good idea?' We looked fearfully at each other.

" 'I wish I knew,' I said.

" 'We are going to have to be very careful here.' Helen's face was grave, her voice low, and I didn't dare to kiss her in public. 'Let us have an agreement from this moment that we will never reveal anything but our scholarly interests, and those as little as possible, if we have to discuss our work in front of him.'

" 'Agreed.' "

Chapter 55

"IN THESE LAST YEARS, I've found myself remembering over and over my first sight of Anton Stoichev's house. Perhaps it made such a deep impression on me because of the contrast between urban Sofia and his haven just outside it, or perhaps I remember it so often because of Stoichev himself — the particular and subtle nature of his presence. I think, however, that I feel a keen, almost breathless anticipation when I recall the sight of Stoichev's front gate because our meeting with him was the turning point in our search for Rossi.

"Much later, when I read aloud about the monasteries that lay outside the walls of Byzantine Constantinople, sanctuaries where their inhabitants sometimes escaped citywide edicts about one point of church ritual or another, where they were not protected by the great walls of the city but were a degree removed from the state's tyrannical reach, I thought of Stoichev — his garden, its leaning apple and cherry trees starred with white, the house settled into a deep yard, its new leaves and blue beehives, the old double wooden gate with the portal above it that kept us out, the air of quiet over the place, the air of devotion, of deliberate retreat.

"We stood before that gate while the dust settled around Ranov's car. Helen was the first to press the handle of one of the old latches; Ranov hung sullenly back as if he hated being seen there, even by us, and I felt strangely rooted to the ground. For a moment I was hypnotized by the midmorning vibration of leaves and bees, and by an unexpected, sickening feeling of dread. Stoichev, I thought, might well prove no help, a final dead end, in which case we would return home having walked a long path to nowhere. I'd imagined it a hundred times already: the silent flight back to New York from Sofia or Istanbul — I would like to see Turgut one more time, I thought — and the reorganization of my life at home without Rossi, the questions about where I had been, the problems with the department over my long absence, the resumption of my writing about those Dutch merchants — placid, prosaic people — under the guidance of some vastly inferior new adviser, and the closed door to Rossi's office. Above all, I dreaded that closed door, and the ongoing investigation, the inadequate questioning of the police — 'So — Mr. —

er — Paul, is it? You took a trip two days after your adviser disappeared?' — the small and puzzled gathering at a memorial service of sorts, eventually the question of Rossi's works, his copyrights, his estate.

"Returning with my hand intertwined with Helen's would be a great consolation, of course. I intended to ask her, when this horror was somehow over, to marry me; I would have to save a little money first, if I could, and take her to Boston to meet my parents. Yes, I would return with her hand in mine, but there would be no father from whom to request it in marriage. I watched through a shimmer of grief as Helen opened the gate.

"Inside, Stoichev's house was sinking softly into an uneven ground — part yard and part orchard. The foundation of the house was built from a brownish-gray stone held together with white stucco; I later learned that this stone was a kind of granite, out of which most of Bulgaria's old buildings have sprung. Above the foundation the walls were brick, but brick of the softest, mellowest red-gold, as if they had been soaking in sunlight for generations. The roof was of fluted red ceramic tiles. Roof and walls were a little dilapidated. The whole house looked as if it had grown slowly out of the earth and was now slowly returning to it, and as if the trees had grown above it simply to shade this process. The first floor had put out a rambling wing on one side, and on the other stretched a trellis, which was covered with the tendrils of grapevines above and walled with pale roses below. Under the trellis sat a wooden table and four rough chairs, and I imagined how the shadow of the grape leaves would deepen there as summer progressed. Beyond this, and beneath the most venerable of the apple trees, hovered two ghostly beehives; near them, in full sun, lay a little garden where someone had already coaxed up translucent greens in neat rows. I could smell herbs and perhaps lavender, fresh grass and frying onions. Someone tended this old place with care, and I half expected to get a glimpse of Stoichev in monk's habit, kneeling with his trowel in the garden.

"Then a voice began to sing inside, perhaps in the vicinity of the crumbling chimney and first-floor windows. It was not the baritone chant of the hermit, but a sweet, strong feminine voice, an energetic melody that made even Ranov, sulking next to me with his cigarette, look interested. *'Izvinete!'* he called. *'Dobar den!'* The singing stopped abruptly and was followed by a clatter and a thump. Stoichev's front door opened and the young woman who stood there stared hard at us, as if the last thing she'd imagined in her yard was people.

"I would have stepped forward, but Ranov cut me off, removing his hat, nodding, bowing, greeting her in a flow of Bulgarian. The young woman had put her hand to her cheek, regarding Ranov with a curiosity that seemed to me mingled with wariness. At second glance, she was not quite as young as I'd thought, but there was an energy and vigor about her that made me think she might be the author of the resplendent little garden and the good smells from the kitchen. Her hair was brushed back from a round face; she had a dark mole on her forehead. Her eyes, mouth, and chin looked like a pretty child's. She had an apron over her white blouse and blue skirt. She surveyed us with a sharp glance that had nothing to do with the innocence of her eyes, and I saw that under her quick interrogations Ranov even opened his wallet and showed her a card. Whether she was Stoichev's daughter or his housekeeper — did retired professors have housekeepers, in a communist country? — she was no fool. Ranov seemed to be making an uncharacteristic effort at charm; he turned, smiling, to introduce us to her. 'This is Irina Hristova,' he explained as we shook hands. 'She is the ness of Professor Stoichev.'

"'The nest?' I said, thinking for a second that this was some elaborate metaphor.

"'The daughter of his sister,' Ranov said. He lit another cigarette and offered one to Irina Hristova, who refused with a decided nod. When he explained that we were from America, her eyes widened and she looked us over very carefully. Then she laughed, although I never knew what that meant. Ranov scowled again — I don't think he was capable of looking pleasant for more than a few minutes at a time — and she turned and led us in.

"Again the house took me by surprise; it might be a sweet old farm outside, but inside, in a dusk that contrasted strongly with the sunlight of the front walk, it was a museum. The door opened directly onto a large room with a fireplace, where sunlight fell across the stones in place of fire. The furniture — dark, intricately carved bureaus set with mirrors, princely chairs and benches — would have been arresting in itself, but what drew my eye and Helen's murmur of admiration was the rare mix of folk textiles and primitive paintings — icons, mainly, of a quality that in many cases seemed to me to surpass what we'd seen in the churches in Sofia. There were luminous-eyed Madonnas and thin-lipped, sad saints, large and small, highlighted with gilt paint or encased in beaten silver, apostles standing in boats, and martyrs patiently undergoing their martyrdoms. The rich, smoke-tinted, ancient colors were echoed on all sides by rugs and aprons woven in geometrical patterns, and even an embroidered vest and a couple of scarves trimmed with tiny coins. Helen pointed to the vest, which had strips of horizontal pockets sewn down each side. 'For bullets,' she said, simply.

"Next to the vest hung a pair of daggers. I wanted to ask who'd worn it, who'd caught those bullets, who'd carried those daggers. Someone had filled a ceramic jug on a table below them with roses and fronds of green, which looked supernaturally alive among all those fading treasures. The floor was highly polished. I could see another, similar room beyond.

"Ranov was looking around, too, and now he snorted. 'In my opinion, Professor Stoichev is permitted to keep too many national possessions. These should be sold for the benefit of the people.'

"Either Irina understood no English or she didn't deign to respond to this; she turned away and led us out of the room and up a narrow flight of stairs. I don't know what I expected to see at the top. Perhaps we would find a littered den, a cave where the old professor hibernated, or perhaps, I thought — with that now-familiar twinge of misery — we might find a neat, orderly office of the sort that had masked Professor Rossi's tumultuous and splendid mind. I had all but put this vision behind me when the door at the top of the stairs opened, and a white-haired man, small but erect, came out on the landing. Irina hurried to him, grasping his arm with both hands and addressing him in quick Bulgarian mixed with some excited laughter.

"The old man turned to us, calm, quiet, his face deeply withdrawn, so that I had for a minute the sense that he was gazing down at the floor, although he looked directly at us. I stepped forward then and offered my hand. He shook it gravely and turned to Helen and shook hers as well. He was polite, he was formal, he had the kind of deference that is not really deference but dignity, and his large, dark eyes went from one of us to the other, and then took in Ranov, who hung back watching the scene. At this Ranov came up and shook hands with him, too — patronizingly, I thought, disliking our guide more every minute. I wished with all my heart that he would leave, so that we could speak alone with Professor Stoichev. I wondered how on earth we were going to accomplish any kind of honest discussion, learn anything from Stoichev at all, with Ranov hovering behind us like a fly.

"Professor Stoichev turned slowly and ushered us into the room. This room, as it turned out, was one of several on the top floor of the house. It was never clear to me, during our two visits there, where its inhabitants slept. As far as I could see, the upper story of the house contained only the long, narrow sitting room that we were entering, and several smaller rooms opening off it. The doors to the other rooms stood ajar, and sunlight filtered into them through the green trees in the windows opposite and caressed the bindings of innumerable books, books that lined the walls and sat in wooden crates on the floor, or lay heaped on tables. Among them were shelved loose documents of all shapes and sizes, many of them clearly of great antiquity. No, this was not Rossi's neat study but rather a sort of cluttered laboratory, the upper story of a collector's mind. Everywhere I saw sunlight touching old vellum, old leather, tooled bindings, hints of gilt, crumbling page corners, knobby bindings — red and brown and bone-colored wonderful books — books and scrolls and manuscripts in a working disarray. Nothing was dusty, nothing heavy was heaped on anything fragile, and yet these books, these manuscripts were absolutely everywhere in Stoichev's rooms, and I had a sense of being surrounded by them in a way one is not even in a museum, where such precious objects would have been more sparsely, methodically displayed.

"On one wall of the sitting room hung a primitive map, painted, to my amazement, on leather. I couldn't help stepping toward it, and Stoichev smiled. 'Do you like that?' he asked. 'It is the Byzantine Empire in about 1150.' It was the first time he had spoken, and he used a quiet, correct English.

"'While Bulgaria was still among its territories,' Helen mused.

"Stoichev glanced at her, clearly pleased. 'Yes, exactly. I think this map was made in Venice or Genoa and brought to Constantinople, perhaps as a gift to the emperor or someone in his court. This is a copy which a friend has made for me.'

"Helen smiled, touching her chin in thought. Then she almost winked at him. 'The emperor Manuel I Comnenus, perhaps?'

"I was stunned and Stoichev looked astonished, too. Helen laughed. 'Byzantium used to be quite a hobby with me,' she said. The old historian smiled, then, and bowed to her, suddenly courtly. He gestured to the chairs around a table in the middle of the sitting room, and we all sat down. From where I sat I could see the yard behind the house, sloping gradually to the edge of a wood, and the fruit trees, some of them already forming small green fruits. The windows were open, and that same hum of bees and rustle of leaves came to us. I thought how pleasant it must be for Stoichev, even in exile, to sit up here among his manuscripts and read or write and listen to that sound, which no heavy-handed state could muffle, or which no bureaucrat had yet chosen to send him away from. It was a fortunate imprisonment, as such things went, and perhaps more voluntary than we had any way of ascertaining.

"Stoichev said nothing else for a while, although he looked intently at us, and I wondered what he thought of our appearing there, and whether he planned to find out who we were. After a few minutes, thinking he might never address us, I spoke to him. 'Professor Stoichev,' I said, 'please forgive this invasion of your solitude. We are very grateful to you and to your niece for letting us visit you.'

"He looked at his hands on the table — they were fine and freckled with age spots — and then at me. His eyes, as I've said, were hugely dark, and they were the eyes of a young man, although his clean-shaven olive face was old. His ears were unusually large and stuck out from the sides of his head in the midst of neatly clipped white hair; they actually caught some of the light from the windows, so that they looked translucent, pinkish around the edges like a rabbit's. Those eyes, with their combined mildness and wariness, had something of the animal in them, too. His teeth were yellow and crooked, and one of them, in the front, was covered in gold. But they were all there, and his face was startling when he smiled, as if a wild animal had suddenly formed a human expression. It was a wonderful face, a face that in its youth must have had an unusual radiance, a great visible enthusiasm — it must have been an irresistible face.

"Stoichev smiled now, with such force that it

made Helen and me smile, too. Irina dimpled at us. She had settled herself in a chair under an icon of someone — I assumed it was Saint George — putting his spear with vigor through an undernourished dragon. 'I am very glad that you have come to see me,' Stoichev said. 'We don't get so many visitors, and visitors who speak English are even more rare. I am very glad to be able to practice my English with you, although it is not as good as it was, I am afraid.'

"'Your English is excellent,' I said. 'Where did you learn it, if you don't mind my asking?'

"'Oh, I do not mind,' said Professor Stoichev. 'I had the good fortune to study abroad when I was young, and some of my studies were conducted in London. Is there anything with which I can help you, or did you only wish to visit my library?' He said this so simply that it took me by surprise.

"'Both,' I said. 'We wished to visit it, and we wished to ask you some questions for our research.' I paused to hunt for words. 'Miss Rossi and I are very much interested in the history of your country in the Middle Ages, although I know far less about it than I ought to, and we have been writing some — ah — ' I began to falter, because it swept over me that despite Helen's brief lecture on the plane I actually knew nothing about Bulgarian history, or so little that it could only sound absurd to this erudite man who was the guardian of his country's past; and also because what we had to discuss was highly personal, terribly improbable, and not at all something that I wanted to broach with Ranov sneering down at the table.

"'So you are interested in the medieval Bulgaria?' said Stoichev, and it seemed to me that he, too, glanced in Ranov's direction.

"'Yes,' said Helen, coming quickly to my rescue. 'We are interested in the monastic life of medieval Bulgaria, and we have been researching it as well as we can for some articles we would like to produce. Specifically, we would like to know about life in the monasteries of Bulgaria in the late medieval period, and about some of the routes that brought pilgrims to Bulgaria, and also routes by which pilgrims from Bulgaria traveled to other lands.'

"Stoichev lit up, shaking his head with apparent pleasure so that his large delicate ears caught the light. 'That is a very good topic,' he said. He looked beyond us, and I thought he must be gazing into a past so deep that it was really the well of time, and seeing more clearly than perhaps anyone else in the world the period to which we had alluded. 'Is there something in particular you will write about? I have many manuscripts here that might be useful to you, and I would be happy to permit you to look at them, if you would like.'

"Ranov shifted in his chair, and I thought again how much I disliked his watching us. Fortunately, most of his attention seemed to be focused on Irina's pretty profile, across the room. 'Well,' I said. 'We'd like to learn more about the fifteenth century — the late fifteenth century, and Miss Rossi here has done quite a bit of work on that period in her family's native country — that is — '

"'Romania,' Helen put in. 'But I was raised and educated in Hungary.'

"'Ah, yes — you are our neighbor.' Professor Stoichev turned to Helen and gave her the gentlest of smiles. 'And you are from the University of Budapest?'

"'Yes,' said Helen.

"'Perhaps you know my friend there — his name is Professor Sándor.'

"'Oh, yes. He is the head of our history department. He is quite a friend of mine.'

"'That is very nice — very nice,' Professor Stoichev said. 'Please give him my warmest greetings if you have the chance.'

"'I will.' Helen smiled at him.

"'And who else? I do not think I know anyone else who is there now. But your name, Professor, is very interesting. I know this name. There is in the United States' — he turned to me again, and back to Helen; to my discomfort I saw Ranov's gaze narrowing on us — 'a famous historian named Rossi. He is perhaps a relative?'

"Helen, to my surprise, flushed pink. I thought maybe she didn't yet relish admitting this in public, or felt some lingering doubt about doing so, or that perhaps she had noticed Ranov's sudden attention to the conversation. 'Yes,' she said shortly. 'He is my father, Bartholomew Rossi.'

"I thought Stoichev might very naturally wonder why an English historian's daughter claimed she was Romanian and had been raised in Hungary, but if he had any such questions he kept them to himself. 'Yes, that is the name. He has written very fine books — and on such a range of topics!' He slapped his forehead. 'When I read some of his early articles, I thought he would make a fine Balkan historian, but I see that he has abandoned that area and gone into many others.'

"I was relieved to hear that Stoichev knew Rossi's work and thought well of it; this might give us some credentials, in his eyes, and might also make it easier to enlist his sympathies. 'Yes, indeed,' I said. 'In fact, Professor Rossi is not only Helen's father but also my adviser — I'm working with him on my dissertation.'

"'How fortunate.' Stoichev folded one veined hand over the other. 'And what is your dissertation about?'

"'Well,' I began, and this time it was my turn to flush. I hoped Ranov wasn't watching these changes of color too closely. 'It's about Dutch merchants in the seventeenth century.'

"'Remarkable,' said Stoichev. 'That is quite an interesting topic. Then what brings you to Bulgaria?'

"'It's a long story,' I said. 'Miss Rossi and I became interested in doing some research on connections between Bulgaria and the Orthodox community in Istanbul after the Ottoman conquest of the city. Even though this is a departure from the topic of my dissertation, we have been writing some articles about it. In fact, I've also just given a lecture at the University of Budapest on the history of — parts of Romania under the Turks.' I immediately saw this was a mistake; perhaps Ranov hadn't known we'd been in Budapest as well as Istanbul. Helen was composed, however, and I took my cue from her. 'We would like very much to finish our research here in Bulgaria, and we thought you might well be able to help us.'

"'Of course,' Stoichev said patiently. 'Perhaps you could tell me exactly what interests you most about the history of our medieval monasteries and the routes of pilgrimages, and about the fifteenth century in particular. It is a fascinating century in Bulgarian history. You know that after 1393 most of our country was under the Ottoman yoke, although some parts of Bulgaria were not conquered until well into the fifteenth century. Our native intellectual culture was preserved from that time on very much by the monasteries. I am glad you are interested in the monasteries because they are one of the richest sources of our heritage in Bulgaria.' He paused and refolded his hands, as if waiting to see how familiar this information was to us.

"'Yes,' I said. There was no help for it. We would have to talk about some aspect of our search with Ranov sitting right there. After all, if I asked him to leave, he would immediately become suspicious about our purpose here. Our only hope was to make our questions sound as scholarly and impersonal as possible. 'We believe there are some interesting connections between the Orthodox community in fifteenth-century Istanbul and the monasteries of Bulgaria.'

"'Yes, of course that is true,' said Stoichev, 'especially since the Bulgarian church was placed by Mehmed the Conqueror under the jurisdiction of the patriarch of Constantinople. Before that, of course, our church was independent, with its own patriarch in Veliko Trnovo.'

"I felt a wave of gratitude toward this man with his erudition and wonderful ears. My comments had been close to inane, and yet he was answering them with circumspect — not to mention informative — politeness.

"'Exactly,' I said. 'And we're especially interested — we found a letter — that is, we were recently in Istanbul ourselves' — I was careful not to glance at Ranov — 'and we found a letter that has to do with Bulgaria — with a group of monks who traveled from Constantinople to a monastery in Bulgaria. We're interested for the purposes of one of our articles in tracing their route through Bulgaria. Perhaps they were on pilgrimage — we're not quite sure.'

"'I see,' said Stoichev. His eyes were warier and more luminous than ever. 'Is there any date on this letter? Can you tell me a little about its contents or who wrote it, if you know that, and where you found it? To whom it was addressed, and so on, if you know these things?'

"'Certainly,' I said. 'In fact, we have a copy of it here. The original letter is in Slavonic, and a monk in Istanbul wrote it out for us. The original resides in the state archive of Mehmed II. Perhaps you would like to read the letter for yourself.' I opened my briefcase and got the copy out, handing it to him, hoping Ranov would not ask for it next.

"Stoichev took the letter and I saw his eyes flash over the opening lines. 'Interesting,' he said, and to my disappointment he set it down on the table. Perhaps he was not going to help us after all, or even read the letter. 'My dear,' he said, turning to his niece, 'I don't think we can look at old letters without offering these guests something to eat and drink. Would you bring us *rakiya* and a little lunch?' He nodded with particular politeness toward Ranov.

"Irina rose promptly, smiling. 'Certainly, Uncle,' she said, in beautiful English. There was no

827

end, I thought, to the surprises in this household. 'But I would like some help to bring it up the stairs.' She gave Ranov the slightest glance from her clear eyes and he got up, smoothing his hair.

"'I will be glad to help the young lady,' he said, and they went downstairs together, Ranov thumping noisily on the steps and Irina chattering to him in Bulgarian.

"As soon as the door closed behind them, Stoichev leaned forward and read the letter with greedy concentration. When he was done, he looked up at us. His face had lost ten years, but it was tense, too. 'This is remarkable,' he said in a low voice. We rose out of the same instinct and came to sit close to him at his end of the long table. 'I am astonished to see this letter.'

"'Yes — what?' I said eagerly. 'Do you have any sense of what it might mean?'

"'A little.' Stoichev's eyes were enormous and he looked intently at me. 'You see,' he added, 'I, too, have one of Brother Kiril's letters.'"

Chapter 56

I REMEMBERED ALL TOO WELL the bus station in Perpignan, where I had stood with my father the year before, waiting for a dusty bus to the villages. The bus pulled up again now, and Barley and I boarded it. Our ride to Les Bains, along broad rural roads, was also familiar to me. The towns we passed were girded with square, shorn plane trees. Trees, houses, fields, and old cars all seemed made of the same dust, a café-au-lait cloud that covered everything.

The hotel in Les Bains was much as I remembered it, too, with its four stories of stucco, its iron window grills and boxes of rosy flowers. I found myself longing for my father, breathless with the thought that we'd see him soon, perhaps in a few minutes. For once I led Barley, pushing the heavy door open and putting my bag down in front of the marble-topped desk inside. But then that desk seemed so extremely high and dignified that I felt shy again and had to force myself to tell the sleek old man behind it that I thought my father might be staying here. I didn't remember the old man from our visit here, but he was patient, and after a minute he said there was indeed a foreign monsieur by that name staying there, but *la clé* — his key — was not in, and therefore he himself must be out. He showed us the empty hook. My heart leaped, and leaped again a moment later when a man I did remember opened the door behind the counter. It was the maître d' from the little restaurant, poised and graceful and in a hurry. The old man arrested him with a question and he turned to me *étonné,* as he said at once that the young lady was here, and how she had grown, how grown-up and lovely. And her — friend?

"*Cousin,*" Barley said.

But monsieur had not mentioned that his daughter and nephew would be joining him, what a nice surprise. We must all dine there that evening. I asked where my father was, if anybody knew, but no one did. He had left early, the older man contributed, perhaps to take a morning walk. The maître d' said they were still full, but if we needed other rooms he could see to that. Why didn't we go up to my father's room and leave our bags, at least? My father had taken a suite with a nice view and a little parlor to sit in. He — the maître d' — would give us *l'autre clé* and make us some coffee. My father would be back soon, probably. We agreed gratefully to all these suggestions. The creaking elevator took us up so slowly that I wondered if the maître d' was pulling the chain himself down in the cellar.

My father's room, when we got the door open, was spacious and pleasant, and I would have enjoyed every nook of it if I hadn't felt, uncomfortably, that I was invading his sanctuary for the third time in a week. Worse was the sudden sight of my father's suitcase, his familiar clothes around the room, his battered leather shaving kit and good shoes. I'd seen these objects only a few days ago, in his room at Master James's house in Oxford, and their familiarity hit me hard.

But even this was eclipsed by another shock. My father was by nature an orderly man; any room or office he inhabited, however briefly, was a model of neatness and discretion. Unlike many of the bachelors, widowers, divorcés whom I later met, my father never sank into that state that makes solo men drop the contents of their pockets in piles on tables and bureaus, or store their clothes in piles over the backs of chairs. Never before had I seen my father's possessions in rank disorder. His suitcase sat half unpacked by the bed. He had apparently rummaged through it and pulled out one or two items, leaving a trail of socks and undershirts on the floor. His light canvas coat sprawled across the bed. In fact, he had changed clothes, also in a great hurry, and deposited his suit in a heap by the suitcase. It occurred to me that perhaps this was not my father's doing, that his room had been searched while he was not in it. But that pile of his suit, shed like a snake's skin onto the floor, made me think otherwise. His walking shoes were not in their usual place in the suitcase and the cedar shoe trees he kept in them had been flung aside. He had clearly been in the greatest hurry of his life.

Chapter 57

"WHEN STOICHEV TOLD US he had one of Brother Kiril's letters, Helen and I looked at each other in amazement. 'What do you mean?' she said finally.

"Stoichev tapped Turgut's copy with excited fingers. 'I have a manuscript that was given to me in 1924 by my friend Atanas Angelov. It describes a different part of the same journey, I am certain. I did not know that any other documents from these travels were in existence. In fact, my friend died suddenly just after he gave them to me, poor fellow. Wait —' He rose, swaying in his haste, so that both Helen and I leaped up to catch him in case he fell. He righted himself without assistance, however, and went into one of the smaller rooms, gesturing for us to follow and to avoid tripping on the piles of books that lined it. There he scanned the shelves and then reached for a box, which I helped him take down. From it he pulled a cardboard file tied with fraying cord. He brought this back to the table and opened it under our eager eyes, drawing out a document so fragile that I shuddered to watch him handling it. He stood looking at it for a long minute, as if paralyzed, and then sighed. 'This is the original, as you can see. The signature —'

We bent over it, and there, with a rush of gooseflesh over my arms and neck, I saw an exquisitely penned Cyrillic name that even I could read — Kiril — and the year: 6985. I looked at Helen, and she bit her lip. The faded name of this monk was terribly real. So was the fact that he had once been as alive as we were, had set a quill to this parchment with a warm, living hand.

"Stoichev looked almost as awed as I felt, although the sight of such an old manuscript must have been his daily fare. 'I have translated it into Bulgarian,' he said, after a moment, and drew out another sheet, this one typed onionskin. We sat down. 'I will try to read it to you.' He cleared his throat and gave us a rough but competent version of a letter that has since been widely translated.

Your Excellency, Lord Abbot Eupraxius:
I take my pen in hand to fulfill the task you have in your wisdom put upon me, and to tell you the particulars of our mission as we come to them. May I do justice to them and to your wishes, with God's assistance. We sleep this night

near Virbius, two days' journey from you, at the monastery of Saint Vladimir, where the holy brothers have welcomed us in your name. As you have instructed, I went alone to the lord abbot and told him our mission in the greatest secrecy, with not even a novice or servant present. He has commanded our wagon to remain under lock in the stables within the courtyard, with two guards from among his monks and two from among our number. I hope we may meet often with such understanding and safe-keeping, at least until we cross into the infidel lands. As you have instructed, I placed one book in the lord abbot's hands, with your injunctions, and saw that he hid it forthwith, not even opening it before me.

The horses are tired after our climb through the mountains and we will sleep here yet another night after this one. We ourselves are now well refreshed by the services of their church here, in which two icons of the most pure Virgin have performed miracles as recently as eighty years ago. One of them still shows the miraculous tears she wept for a sinner, which are now turned to rare pearls. We have offered earnest prayers to her for protection in our mission, that we may safely reach the great city and even in the capital of the enemy find a haven from which to attempt our task.

I am yours most humbly in the name of the Father, the Son, and the Holy Spirit,

Br. Kiril
April, the Year of Our Lord 6985

"I think Helen and I hardly breathed as Stoichev read this aloud. He translated slowly and methodically, and with no small skill. I was just about to exclaim aloud over the indubitable connection between the two letters when a thud of feet on the wooden stairs below made us all look up. 'They are coming back,' Stoichev said quietly. He put the letter away, and I placed ours with it for the time being, in his safekeeping. 'Mr. Ranov — he was assigned to you as your guide?'

"'Yes,' I said quickly. 'And he seems far too interested in our work here. There is a lot more we must tell you about our research, but it's rather private and also —' I paused.

"'Dangerous?' inquired Stoichev, turning his wonderful old face toward us.

"'How did you guess?' I couldn't hide my amazement. Nothing we had said so far implied danger.

"'Ah.' He shook his head, and I heard in his sigh a depth of experience and regret I couldn't begin to fathom. 'There are some things I should tell you, also. I never expected to see another of these letters. Talk to Mr. Ranov as little as possible.'

"'Don't worry.' Helen shook her head and they regarded each other for a second with a smile.

"'Quiet,' Stoichev said softly. 'I will take care that we can talk again.'

"Irina and Ranov came into the sitting room with a clash of plates, and Irina began setting out glasses and a bottle of amber liquid. Ranov came behind her bearing a loaf of bread and a dish of white beans. He was smiling and he looked almost domesticated. I wished I could thank Stoichev's niece. She settled her uncle comfortably in his chair and made us sit down, and I realized that the morning's excursion had left me terribly hungry.

"'Please, honored guests, make yourselves welcome.' Stoichev waved a hand over the table as if it belonged to the emperor of Constantinople. Irina poured glasses of brandy — the smell alone could have killed a small animal — and he toasted us gallantly, his yellow-toothed smile wide and genuine. 'I drink to friendship among scholars everywhere.'

"We all returned this toast with enthusiasm except for Ranov, who raised his glass ironically and looked around at us.

"'May your scholarship advance the knowledge of the Party and the people,' he said, giving me a little bow. This almost took the edge off my appetite; was he speaking generally, or did he want to advance the Party's knowledge through something particular we knew? But I returned the bow and downed my *rakiya*. I decided there was no way to drink it except quickly, and the third-degree burn I received on the back of my throat was soon replaced by a pleasant glow. Enough of this beverage, I thought, and I might be in danger of liking Ranov slightly.

"'I am glad to have the chance to talk with anyone who is interested in our medieval history,' Stoichev said to me. 'Perhaps it would be interesting for you and Miss Rossi to see a holiday that celebrates two of our great medieval figures. Tomorrow is the day of Kiril and Methodii, creators of the great Slavonic alphabet. In English you would say Cyril and Methodius — you call it Cyrillic, do you not? We say *kirilitsa*, for Kiril, the monk who invented it.'

"For a moment I was confused, thinking of our Brother Kiril, but when Stoichev spoke again

I saw what he had in mind, and how resourceful he was.

"'I am very busy with my writing this afternoon,' he said, 'but if you would like to come back tomorrow, some of my former students will be here to celebrate the day, and I can tell you more about Kiril then.'

"'That is extremely kind of you,' Helen said. 'We do not want to use too much of your time, but we would be honored to join you. Can that be arranged, Comrade Ranov?'

"The *comrade* did not seem to be lost on Ranov, who scowled at her over his second glass of brandy. 'Certainly,' he said. 'If that is how you would like to accomplish your research, I am happy to be of assistance.'

"'Very good,' Stoichev said. 'We will gather here at about one-thirty, and Irina will have something nice for our lunch. It is always a pleasant group. You may meet some scholars whose work you will find interesting.'

"We thanked him profusely and obeyed Irina's urging to eat, although I noticed that Helen, too, avoided the rest of the *rakiya*. When we had finished the simple meal, Helen rose at once and we all followed suit. 'We will not tire you further, Professor,' she said, taking his hand.

"'Not at all, my dear.' Stoichev shook her hands warmly, but I thought he did look weary. 'I shall look forward to our meeting tomorrow.'

"Irina showed us to the gate again, through the green yard and gardens. 'Until tomorrow,' she said, smiling at us, and added something pert in Bulgarian that made Ranov smooth his hair down before putting his hat on again. 'She is a very pretty girl,' he remarked complacently as we walked to his car, and Helen rolled her eyes at me behind his back.

"It wasn't until evening that we had a few minutes alone together. Ranov had taken his departure after an interminable dinner in the bleak hotel dining room. Helen and I walked upstairs together — the elevator was broken again — and then lingered in the hall near my room, moments of sweetness filched from our peculiar situation. Once we thought that Ranov must be gone, we went back downstairs, strolled out to a café on a side street nearby, and sat there under the trees.

"'Someone is watching us here, also,' Helen said quietly, as we seated ourselves at a metal table. I laid my briefcase carefully across my lap; I'd stopped even setting it under café tables.

Helen smiled. 'But at least this is not bugged, like my room. And yours.' She looked up into the green branches above us. 'Linden trees,' she said. 'In a couple of months they will be covered with flowers. People make tea out of them at home — probably here, too.' When you sit at a table outside like this, you must clean off the table first because the blossoms and the pollen fall everywhere. They smell like honey, very sweet and fresh.' She made a quick motion, as if brushing aside thousands of pale green flowers.

"I took her hand then, and turned it over so that I could see her palm with its graceful lines. I hoped they meant she would have a long life and good fortune, both shared by me. 'What do you make of Stoichev's having that letter?'

"'It might be a stroke of luck for us,' she mused. 'At first I thought it was only a piece of a historical puzzle — a wonderful piece, but how was it going to help us? But when Stoichev guessed our letter was dangerous, then I felt a great deal of hope that he knows something important.'

"'I hoped so, too,' I admitted. 'But I also thought he might mean simply that it was politically sensitive material, like so much of his work — because it involves the history of the church.'

"'I know.' Helen sighed. 'It might mean only that.'

"'And that would be enough to make him wary of discussing it in front of Ranov.'

"'Yes. We will have to wait until tomorrow to find out what he meant.' She laced her fingers through mine. 'It is agonizing for you to wait every day, isn't it?'

"I nodded slowly. 'If you knew Rossi,' I said, and stopped.

"Her eyes were fixed on mine and she slowly brushed back a lock of hair that had slipped out of its pins. The gesture was so sad that it gave full weight to her next words. 'I do begin to know him, through you.'

"At that moment, a waitress in a white blouse came out to us and asked something. Helen turned to me. 'What to drink?' The waitress looked curiously at us, creatures who spoke a foreign language.

"'What do you know how to order?' I teased Helen.

"'*Chai*,' she said, pointing at herself and me. 'Tea, please. *Molya*.'

"'You're learning fast,' I said, when the waitress had gone back inside.

"She shrugged. 'I've studied some Russian. Bulgarian is very close.'

"When the waitress had returned with our tea, Helen stirred it with a somber face. 'It is such a relief to get away from Ranov that I can hardly bear to think about seeing him again tomorrow. I don't see how we are going to do any serious research with him at our backs.'

"'If I knew whether he actually suspects anything about our search, I'd feel better,' I confessed. 'The strange thing is, he reminds me of someone I've met before, but I seem to have amnesia about who that is.' I glanced at Helen's serious, lovely face, and in that second I felt my brain groping for something, fluttering on the edge of some puzzle, and it wasn't the question of Ranov's possible twin. It had to do with Helen's face in the twilight, and the act of lifting my tea to drink, and the odd word I had chosen. My mind had fluttered there before, but this time the thought broke through in a rush.

"'Amnesia,' I said. 'Helen — Helen, amnesia.'

"'What?' She frowned at my intensity, puzzled.

"'Rossi's letters!' I almost shouted. I pulled open my briefcase so hastily that our tea slopped onto the table. 'His letter, his trip to Greece!'

"It took me several minutes to find the damn thing among my papers, and then to trace the passage, and then to read it aloud to Helen, whose eyes widened slowly to a shocked darkness. 'You remember the letter about how he went back to Greece — to Crete — after having his map taken away from him in Istanbul, and how his luck changed to bad and everything went wrong?' I rattled the page in front of her. 'Listen to this: "The old men in Crete's *tavernas* seemed much more inclined to tell me their two hundred and ten vampire stories than they were to explain where I might find other shards of pottery like that one, or what ancient shipwrecks their grandfathers had dived into and plundered. One evening I let a stranger buy me a round of a local speciality called, whimsically, amnesia, with the result that I was sick all the next day."'

"'Oh, my God,' Helen said softly.

"'I let a stranger buy me a drink called amnesia,' I paraphrased, trying to keep my voice down. 'Who the hell do you think that stranger was? And that's why Rossi forgot — '

"'He forgot — ' Helen seemed hypnotized by the word. 'He forgot Romania — '

"'— that he had been there at all. His letters to Hedges said he was going back to Greece from

Romania, to get some money and attend an archaeological dig —'

"'And he forgot my mother,' Helen finished, almost inaudibly.

"'Your mother,' I echoed, with a sudden image of Helen's mother standing in her doorway, watching us leave. 'He never meant not to go back. He suddenly forgot everything. And that's — that's why he told me he couldn't always remember his research clearly.'

"Helen's face was white now, her jaw clenched, her eyes harsh and filling with tears. 'I hate him,' she said in a low voice, and I knew she did not mean her father."

Chapter 58

"WE ARRIVED AT STOICHEV'S GATE the next morning promptly at one-thirty. Helen squeezed my hand, ignoring Ranov's presence, and even Ranov seemed in a festive mood; he frowned less than usual and had put on a heavy brown suit. From behind the gate, we could hear the sounds of conversation and laughter and smell wood smoke and some delicious meat cooking. If I put all thought of Rossi firmly out of my mind, I could feel festive, too. I felt that today, of all days, something would happen to help me find him, and I resolved to celebrate the feast of Kiril and Methodius as wholeheartedly as possible.

"Inside the yard, we could see groups of men and a few women gathered under the trellis. Irina flitted here and there behind the table, re-filling people's plates and pouring glasses full of that powerful amber liquid. When she saw us, she hurried forward, arms outstretched as if we were already old friends. She shook hands with me and Ranov and kissed Helen on the cheeks. 'I am very happy that you came. Thank you,' she said. 'My uncle has not been able to sleep at all,

or to eat anything, since you were here yesterday. I hope you will tell him that he must eat.'
Her pretty face was puckered.

"'Please don't worry,' said Helen. 'We will do
our best to persuade him.'

"We found Stoichev holding court under the
apple trees. Someone had set a ring of wooden
chairs there, and he sat in the largest with several younger men around him. 'Oh, hello!' he exclaimed, struggling to his feet. The other men rose
quickly to give him a hand, and waited to greet
us. 'Welcome, my friends. Please to meet my
other friends.' With a frail wave, he indicated the
faces around him. 'These are some of my students from before the war, and they are so kind
to come back and see me.' Many of these men,
with their white shirts and shabby dark suits,
were youthful only in comparison with Ranov;
most of them were in their fifties, at least. They
smiled and shook our hands warmly, one of them
bending to kiss Helen's with formal courtesy. I
liked their alert, dark eyes, their quiet smiles
glinting with gold teeth.

"Irina came up behind us; she seemed to be
urging everyone to eat once again, for after a
minute we found ourselves carried along by a
wave of guests to the tables under the trellis.

There we found a groaning board indeed, and also the source of the wonderful smell, which turned out to be a whole sheep roasting over an open pit in the yard near the house. The table was laden with earthenware dishes of sliced potatoes, tomato and cucumber salad, crumbling white cheese, loaves of golden bread, pans of the same flaky cheese pastry we had eaten in Istanbul. There were meat stews, chilled bowls of yogurt, grilled eggplants and onions. Irina left us no peace until our plates were almost too heavy to carry, and she followed us back into the little orchard bearing glasses of *rakiya.*

"In the meantime, Stoichev's students had clearly been vying with one another to see who could bring him the most food, and now they filled his glass to the brim, and he slowly rose to his feet. All over the yard people shouted for quiet, and then he toasted them with a short speech, in which I caught the names of Kiril and Methodius, as well as mine and Helen's. When he was done, a cheer went up from the whole company. *'Stoichev! Za zdraveto na Profesor Stoichev! Nazdrave!'* Cheers rang all around us. Everyone's face was lit up for Stoichev; everyone turned to him with a smile and a raised glass, and some had tears in their eyes. I remembered Rossi, how he'd listened so modestly to the cheers and speeches with which we had marked his twentieth anniversary at the university. I turned away with a lump in my throat. Ranov, I noted, was drifting around under the trellis, a glass in his hand.

"When the company settled again to eating and talking, Helen and I found ourselves in places of honor next to Stoichev. He smiled and nodded to us. 'How pleasant for me that you could come to join us today. You know, this is my favorite holiday. We have many saints' days in the church calendar, but this one is dear to all those who teach and learn, because it is when we honor the Slavonic heritage of alphabet and literature, and the teaching and learning of many centuries that have grown from Kiril and Methodii and their great invention. Besides, on this day all my favorite students and colleagues come back to interrupt their ancient professor at his work. And I am very grateful to them for the interruption.' He looked around with that affectionate smile and clapped the nearest of his colleagues on the shoulder. I saw with a twinge of sorrow how fragile his hand was, thin and almost translucent.

"After a while Stoichev's students began to drift away, either to the table, where the spitted sheep had just been carved, or to wander in the garden in twos and threes. As soon as they were gone, Stoichev turned to us with an urgent face. 'Come,' he said. 'Let us talk while we are able to. My niece has promised to keep Mr. Ranov busy as long as she can. I have a few things to tell you, and I understand you have much to tell me, as well.'

"'Certainly.' I pulled my chair closer to his, and Helen did the same.

"'First of all, my friends,' Stoichev said, 'I read again carefully the letter you left with me yesterday. Here is your copy of it.' He took it from his breast pocket. 'I will give it to you now, to keep it safe. I read it many times, and I believe that it was written by the same hand that wrote the letter I possess — Brother Kiril, whoever he was, wrote both of them. I do not have your original to look at, of course, but if this is an accurate copy, the style of composition is the same, and the names and dates certainly agree. I think we can have little doubt that these letters were part of the same correspondence, and that they were either delivered separately or separated from each other by circumstances we will never know. Now, I have some other thoughts for you, but first you must tell me more about your research. I have the impression that you did not come to Bulgaria to learn only about our monasteries. How did you find this letter?'

"I told him that we'd begun our research for reasons that would be difficult for me to describe, because they did not sound very rational. 'You said you had read the work of Professor Bartholomew Rossi, Helen's father. He recently disappeared under very strange circumstances.'

"As quickly and clearly as I could, I sketched for Stoichev my discovery of the dragon book, Rossi's disappearance, the contents of the letters and the copies of the strange maps we carried with us, and our research in Istanbul and Budapest, including the folk song and the woodcut with the word *Ivireanu* in it, which we'd seen in the university library in Budapest. I left out only the secret of the Crescent Guard. I didn't dare pull any documents from my briefcase with so many other people in sight, but I described for him the three maps and the similarity of the third to the dragon in the books. He listened with the utmost patience and interest, his brow furrowed under his fine white hair and his dark eyes wide. Only once did he interrupt, to ask urgently for a more exact description of each of the dragon books — mine, Rossi's, Hugh James's,

Turgut's. I saw that because of his knowledge of manuscripts and early publishing, the books must hold peculiar interest for him. 'I have mine here,' I added, touching the briefcase in my lap.

"He started, staring at me. 'I would like to see this book when that is possible,' he said.

"But the point that seemed to pique his interest even more was Turgut and Selim's discovery that the abbot to whom Brother Kiril's letters were addressed had presided over the monastery at Snagov in Wallachia. 'Snagov,' he said in a whisper. His old face had flushed crimson and I wondered for a moment if he was going to faint. 'I should have known this. And I have had that letter in my library for thirty years!'

"I hoped I would have the chance to ask him, too, where he'd found his letter. 'You see, there is fairly good evidence that the monks of Brother Kiril's party traveled from Wallachia to Constantinople before coming to Bulgaria,' I said.

"'Yes.' He shook his head. 'I have always thought it described a journey of monks from Constantinople, on pilgrimage in Bulgaria. I never realized — Maxim Eupraxius — the abbot of Snagov —' He seemed almost overcome with swift ruminations, which flashed across his mobile old face

like a windstorm and made him blink his eyes
rapidly. 'And this word *Ivireanu* that you found,
and also Mr. Hugh James, in Budapest —'

"'Do you know what it means?' I asked eagerly.

"'Yes, yes, my son.' Stoichev seemed to be
looking through me without seeing. 'It is the
name of Antim Ivireanu, a scholar and printer at
Snagov at the end of the seventeenth century —
long after Vlad Ţepeş. I have read about Ivireanu's work. He made a great name among the
scholars of his time and he attracted many illus-
trious visitors to Snagov. He printed the holy
gospels in Romanian and Arabic, and his press
was the first one in Romania, in all probability.
But — my God — perhaps it was not the first, if
the dragon books are much older. There is a
great deal I must show you!' He shook his head,
wide-eyed. 'Let us go into my rooms, quickly.'

"Helen and I glanced around. 'Ranov is busy
with Irina,' I said in a low voice.

"'Yes.' Stoichev got to his feet. 'We will go in
this door at the side of the house. Hurry, please.'

"We needed no urging. The look on his face
alone would have been enough to make me follow him up a cliff. He struggled up the stairs and
we went slowly after him. At the big table he sat

down to rest. I noticed it was scattered with books and manuscripts that hadn't been there the day before. 'I have never had very much information about that letter, or the others,' Stoichev said when he'd caught his breath.

"'The others?' Helen sat down beside him.

"'Yes. There are two more letters from Brother Kiril — with mine and the one in Istanbul, that is four. We must go to Rila Monastery immediately to see the others. This is an incredible discovery, to reunite them. But that is not what I must show you. I never made any connection —' Again he seemed too stunned to speak for long.

"After a moment, he went into one of the other rooms and came back carrying a paper-covered volume, which proved to be an old scholarly journal printed in German. 'I had a friend —' he stopped. 'If only he had lived to see this day! I told you — his name was Atanas Angelov — yes, he was a Bulgarian historian and one of my first teachers. In 1923 he was doing some researches in the library at Rila, which is one of our great treasure-houses of medieval documents. He found there a manuscript from the fifteenth century — it was hidden inside the wooden cover of an eighteenth-century folio.

This manuscript he wanted to publish — it is the chronicle of a journey from Wallachia to Bulgaria. He died while he was making notes on it, and I finished them and published it. The manuscript is still at Rila — and I never knew —' He smote his head with his frail hand. 'Here, quickly. It is published in Bulgarian, but we will look through it and I will tell you the most important points.'

"He opened the faded journal with a hand that trembled, and his voice trembled, too, as he picked out for us an outline of Angelov's discovery. The article that he had written from Angelov's notes, and the document itself, have since been published in English, with many updates and with endless footnotes. But even now I can't look at the published version without seeing Stoichev's aging face, the wispy hair falling over protuberant ears, the great eyes bent to the page with burning concentration, and above all his halting voice."

Chapter 59

THE "CHRONICLE" OF ZACHARIAS
OF ZOGRAPHOU
By Atanas Angelov and Anton Stoichev

INTRODUCTION

Zacharias's "Chronicle" as a Historical Document

Despite its famously frustrating incompleteness, the Zacharias "Chronicle," with the embedded "Tale of Stefan the Wanderer," is an important source of confirmation of Christian pilgrimage routes in the fifteenth-century Balkans, as well as information about the fate of the body of Vlad III "Ţepeş" of Wallachia, long believed to have been buried at the monastery on Lake Snagov (in present-day Romania). It also provides us with a rare account of Wallachian neomartyrs (although we cannot know for certain the national origins of the monks from Snagov, with the exception of Stefan, the subject of the "Chronicle"). Only seven other neomartyrs of Wallachian origin are recorded, and none of these is known to have been martyred in Bulgaria.

856

The untitled "Chronicle," as it has come to be called, was written in Slavonic in 1479 or 1480 by a monk named Zacharias at the Bulgarian monastery on Mount Athos, Zographou. Zographou, "the monastery of the painter," originally founded in the tenth century and acquired by the Bulgarian church in the 1220s, is located near the center of the Athonite peninsula. As with the Serbian monastery Hilandar, and the Russian Panteleimon, the population of Zographou was not limited to its sponsoring nationality; this and the lack of any other information about Zacharias make it impossible to determine his origins: he could have been Bulgarian, Serbian, Russian, or perhaps Greek, although the fact that he wrote in Slavonic argues for a Slavic origin. The "Chronicle" tells us only that he was born sometime in the fifteenth century and that his skills were held in esteem by Zographou's abbot, since the abbot chose him to hear the confession of Stefan the Wanderer in person and record it for an important bureaucratic and perhaps theological purpose.

The travel routes mentioned by Stefan in his tale correspond to several well-known pilgrimage routes. Constantinople was the ultimate destination for Wallachian pilgrims, as it was for all of the eastern Christian world. Wallachia, and particularly the monastery of Snagov, was also a pilgrimage site, and it was not unknown for the route of a pilgrim to touch both Snagov and Athos at its extremes. That the monks passed through Haskovo on their way to the Bachkovo region indicates that they probably took a land route from Constantinople, traveling through Edirne (present-day Turkey) into southeastern Bulgaria; the usual ports on the Black Sea coast would have put them too far north for a stop in Haskovo.

The appearance of traditional pilgrimage destinations in Zacharias's "Chronicle" raises the question of whether Stefan's tale is a pilgrimage document. However, the two purported reasons for Stefan's wanderings — exile from the fallen city of Constantinople after 1453 and the transport of relics and search for a "treasure" in Bulgaria after 1476 — make this at least a variation on the classic pilgrim's chronicle. Furthermore, only Stefan's departure from Constantinople as a young monk seems to have been motivated primarily by the desire to seek out holy sites abroad.

A second topic on which the "Chronicle" sheds light is the final days of Vlad III of Wallachia (1428?–76), popularly known as Vlad

Ţepeş — the Impaler — or Dracula. Although several historians who were his contemporaries give descriptions of his campaigns against the Ottomans and his struggles to capture and retain the Wallachian throne, none address in detail the matter of his death and burial. Vlad III made generous contributions to the monastery at Snagov, as Stefan's tale asserts, rebuilding its church. It is likely that he also requested burial there, in keeping with the tradition of founders of and major donors to foundations throughout the Orthodox world.

The "Chronicle" has Stefan asserting that Vlad visited the monastery in 1476, the last year of his life, perhaps a few months before his death. In 1476, Vlad III's throne was under tremendous pressure from the Ottoman sultan Mehmed II, with whom Vlad had been at war intermittently since around 1460. At the same time, his hold on the Wallachian throne was threatened by a contingent of his boyars that was prepared to side with Mehmed should he stage a new invasion of Wallachia.

If Zacharias's "Chronicle" is accurate, Vlad III paid a visit to Snagov that is otherwise unrecorded and must have been extremely dangerous to him personally. The "Chronicle" reports

Vlad's bringing treasure to the monastery; that he did so at great personal risk indicates the importance to him of his tie with Snagov. He must have been well aware of the constant threats to his life, both from the Ottomans and from his primary Wallachian rival during that period, Basarab Laiota, who held the Wallachian throne briefly after Vlad's death. Since little political gain could come from his visiting Snagov, it seems reasonable to speculate that Snagov was important to Vlad III for spiritual or personal reasons, perhaps because he planned to make it his last resting place. In any case, Zacharias's "Chronicle" confirms that he gave Snagov particular attention near the end of his life.

The circumstances of Vlad III's death are very unclear, and have been further clouded by conflicting folk legends and shoddy scholarship. In late December 1476 or early January 1477, he was ambushed, probably by part of the Turkish army in Wallachia, and killed in the skirmish that followed. Some traditions have held that he was actually killed by his own men, who mistook him for a Turkish officer when he climbed a hill to get a better view of an ongoing battle. A variant of this legend asserts that some of his men had been looking for a chance to assassinate him, in punishment for his infamous cruelty. Most sources that discuss his death agree that Vlad's corpse was decapitated and his head taken to Sultan Mehmed in Constantinople as proof that a great enemy had fallen.

In either case, according to Stefan's tale, some of Vlad III's men must still have been loyal to him, since they risked bringing his corpse to Snagov. The headless corpse was long believed to have been buried in the Snagov church, in front of the altar.

If the tale of Stefan the Wanderer is to be trusted, Vlad III's corpse was secretly transported from Snagov to Constantinople, and from there to a monastery called Sveti Georgi, in Bulgaria. The purpose of this deportation, and what the "treasure" was that the monks were seeking first in Constantinople and then in Bulgaria, is unclear. Stefan's tale asserts that the treasure would "hasten the salvation of the soul of this prince," which indicates that the abbot must have thought this theologically necessary. Possibly they sought some holy Constantinopolitan relic spared by both the Latin and Ottoman conquests. He might also not have wanted to take on the responsibility for destroying the corpse at Snagov, or mutilating it in accordance with beliefs about vampire prevention, or to take the risk that this might be carried out by local villagers. This would have been a natural reluctance, given Vlad's status and the fact that members of the Orthodox clergy were discouraged from participating in corpse mutilation.

Unfortunately, no likely burial site for Vlad III's remains has ever been found in Bulgaria, and even the location of the foundation called Sveti Georgi, like that of the Bulgarian monastery Paroria, is unknown; it was probably abandoned or destroyed during the Ottoman era, and the "Chronicle" is the only document that sheds light on even a general location. The "Chronicle" claims that they traveled only a short distance — "not much farther" — from the monastery at Bachkovo, located about thirty-five kilometers south of Asenovgrad on the Chepelarska River. Clearly, Sveti Georgi was situated somewhere in south central Bulgaria. This area, which includes much of the Rhodope Mountains, was among the last Bulgarian regions to be conquered by the Ottomans; some particularly rugged terrain in the area was never brought under full Ottoman domination. If Sveti Georgi was located in the mountains, this might have accounted in part for its selection as a relatively safe resting place for the remains of Vlad III.

Despite the claim of the "Chronicle" that it became a pilgrimage site after the Snagov monks settled there, Sveti Georgi does not appear in other primary sources of the period, or in any later sources, which could indicate that it vanished or was deserted relatively soon after Stefan's departure from it. We do know something of the founding of Sveti Georgi, however, from a single copy of its *typikon* preserved in the library at Bachkovo Monastery. According to this document, Sveti Georgi was founded by Georgios Komnenos, a distant cousin of the Byzantine emperor Alexios I Komnenos, in 1101. Zacharias's "Chronicle" asserts that the monks there were "old and few" when the group from Snagov arrived; presumably those few monks had preserved the regime outlined by the *typikon* and were joined in it by the Wallachian monks.

It is worth noting that the "Chronicle" emphasizes the journey of the Wallachians through Bulgaria in two different ways: by describing the martyrdom of two of them at the hands of Ottoman officials in some detail and by recording the attention given by the Bulgarian population to their progress through the country. There is no way to know what provoked the Ottomans in Bulgaria, with their general toleration of Christian religious activities, to see the Wallachian monks as a threat. Stefan reports through Zacharias that his friends were "interrogated" in the town of Haskovo before being tortured and killed, which suggests that Ottoman authorities believed they possessed politically sensitive information of some sort. Haskovo is located in southeast Bulgaria, a region that was securely under Ottoman command by the fifteenth century. Strangely, the martyred monks were given the traditional Ottoman punishments for stealing (amputation of the hands) and for running away (amputation of the feet). Most neomartyrs under the Ottomans were tortured and killed through other methods. These forms of punishment, as well as the search of the monks' wagon described by Stefan in his tale, make clear the Haskovo officials' accusation of thievery, although they were apparently unable to prove the charge.

Stefan reports widespread attention from the Bulgarian people along the route, which could have accounted for Ottoman curiosity. However, only eight years earlier, in 1469, the relics of Sveti Ivan Rilski, the hermit founder of Rila Monastery, had been translated from Veliko Trnovo to a chapel at Rila, a procession witnessed and described by Vladislav Gramatik in his "Narrative of the Transportation of the Remains of Sveti Ivan." During this translation, Ottoman officials tolerated the attention given by local Bulgarians to the relics, and the journey served as an important unifying event and symbol for Bulgarian Christians. Both Zacharias and Stefan would probably have been aware of the famous journey of Ivan Rilski's bones, and some written account of it may have been available to Zacharias at Zographou by 1479.

This earlier — and very recent — toleration of a similar religious procession through Bulgaria makes Ottoman concern about the journey of the Wallachian monks particularly significant. The search of their wagon — probably carried out by officers of the guard of a local pasha — indicates that some knowledge of the purpose of their journey had perhaps reached Ottoman officials in Bulgaria. Certainly the Ottoman authorities would not have been eager to house in Bulgaria the remains of one of their greatest political enemies, or to tolerate the veneration of those remains. More puzzling, however, is the fact that on searching the wagon they must have found nothing, since Stefan's tale later mentions the interment of the body at Sveti Georgi. We can only speculate on how they would have hidden an entire (if headless) corpse, if they were indeed carrying one.

Finally, a point of interest for both historians and anthropologists is the reference in the "Chronicle" to the beliefs of the monks at Snagov vis-à-vis their visions in the church there. They could not agree about what had transpired with Vlad III's corpse during their vigil for him, and they named several of the methods traditionally cited as the basis for the transformation of a corpse into the living dead — a vampire — indicating a general belief among them that he was at risk of such an outcome. Some of them believed they had seen an animal jumping over the corpse and others that a supernatural force in the form of fog or wind had entered the church and caused the body to sit up. The case of an animal is widely documented in Balkan folklore about vampire genesis, as is the belief that vampires can turn into fog or mist. Vlad III's notorious bloodletting, and his conversion to Catholicism in the household of the Hungarian king Mátyás Corvinus, would probably have been known to the monks, the former since it was common knowledge in Wallachia and the latter because it must have been a concern in the Orthodox community there (and particularly in Vlad's favored monastery, where the abbot was probably his confessor).

The Manuscripts

The "Chronicle" of Zacharias is known through two manuscripts, *Athos 1480* and *R. VII. 132;* the latter is also referred to as the "Patriarchal Version." *Athos 1480,* a quarto manuscript in a single semiuncial hand, is housed in the library at Rila Monastery in Bulgaria, where it was discovered in 1923. This, the earlier of the two versions of the "Chronicle," was almost certainly penned by Zacharias himself at Zographou, probably from notes made at Stefan's deathbed. Despite his claim that he "took down every word," Zacharias must have made this copy after considerable composition; it reflects a polish he could not have achieved on the spot, and contains only one correction. This original manuscript was probably housed in the Zographou library until at least 1814, since it is mentioned by title in a bibliography of fifteenth- and sixteenth-century manuscripts at Zographou dating from that year. It resurfaced in Bulgaria in 1923, when the Bulgarian historian Atanas Angelov discovered it hidden in the cover of an eighteenth-century folio treatise on the life of Saint George *(Georgi 1364.21)* in the library at Rila Monastery. Angelov ascertained in 1924 that no copy was extant at Zographou. It is unclear exactly when or how this original made its way from Athos to Rila, although the threat of pirate raids on Athos during the eighteenth and nineteenth centuries may have played a part in its removal (and that of numerous other precious documents and artifacts) from the Holy Mountain.

The second and only other known copy or version of the Zacharias "Chronicle" — *R. VII.132* or the "Patriarchal Version" — is housed at the library of the Oecumenical Patriarchate in Constantinople and has been paleographically dated to the mid- or late sixteenth century. It is probably a later version of a copy sent to the patriarch by the abbot of Zographou in Zacharias's time. The original of this version presumably accompanied a letter from the abbot to the patriarch, alerting the patriarch to the possibility of a heresy in the Bulgarian monastery Sveti Georgi. The letter is no longer extant, but it is probable that for reasons of efficiency and discretion the abbot of Zographou requested Zacharias to recopy his

chronicle for delivery to Constantinople, keeping the original for the Zographou library. Between fifty and a hundred years after its receipt,
the "Chronicle" was still considered important
enough to the patriarchal library to be preserved
by recopying.

The "Patriarchal Version," in addition to being a
probable later copy of a missive from Zographou,
differs from *Athos 1480* in another important
way: it eliminates part of the story of what the
monks in the vigil at the church of Snagov
claimed to have witnessed there, namely from the
line "One monk saw an animal" to the line "the
headless body of the prince stirred and tried to
rise." This passage may have been eliminated in
the later copy in an attempt to keep users of the
patriarchal library from unnecessary exposure to
information about the heresy described by Stefan, or perhaps to minimize their exposure to superstitions about the origins of the walking dead,
a set of beliefs the church administration generally opposed. The "Patriarchal Version" is difficult
to date, although it is almost certainly the copy
listed in a Patriarchal library catalog from 1605.

A final similarity — a striking and perplexing
one — exists between the two extant manuscripts of the "Chronicle." Both were torn off by

hand at more or less the same point in the story. *Athos 1480* ends with "I learned," while the "Patriarchal Version" continues "that it was no ordinary plague, but instead," each having been neatly sundered after a complete line, presumably removing the part of Stefan's tale that gave evidence of a possible heresy or other evil at the monastery of Sveti Georgi.

A clue to the dating of this damage may be found in the library catalog mentioned above, which lists the "Patriarchal Version" as "incomplete." We can therefore assume that the end of this version was torn off before 1605. There is no way to know, however, whether the two acts of vandalism occurred during the same period, or whether one inspired the other in a much later reader, or how similar the two endings of the document actually were. The fidelity of the "Patriarchal Version" to the Zographou manuscript, with the exception of the vigil passage noted above, indicates that the story probably ended identically or at least very similarly in the two versions. Furthermore, the fact that the "Patriarchal Version" was torn off despite its elimination of the passage about the supernatural events in the church at Snagov supports the idea that it still concluded with a description of heresy or evil at Sveti

Georgi. There is to date no other example, among medieval Balkan manuscripts, of systematic tampering with two copies of the same document hundreds of miles distant from each other.

Editions and Translations

The "Chronicle" of Zacharias of Zographou has been published twice before. The first edition of it was a Greek translation with limited commentary included in Xanthos Constantinos's *History of the Byzantine Churches*, 1849. In 1931 the Oecumenical Patriarchate printed a pamphlet of it in the original Slavonic. Atanas Angelov, who discovered the Zographou version in 1923, planned to publish it with extensive commentary but was prevented from fulfilling this project by his death in 1924. Some of his notes were published posthumously in *Balkanski istoricheski pregled* in 1927.

THE "CHRONICLE" OF ZACHARIAS OF ZOGRAPHOU

This tale was told to me, Zacharias the penitent, by my Brother in Christ, Stefan the Wanderer from *Tsarigrad*. He came to our monastery of Zographou in the year 6987 [1479]. Here he related to us the strange and wonderful events of his life. Stefan the Wanderer was fifty-three years of age when he arrived among us, a wise and pious man who had seen many countries. Thanks be to the Holy Mother who guided him to us from Bulgaria, whence he had wandered with a company of monks from Wallachia and endured many sufferings at the hands of the infidel Turk and seen two of his friends martyred in the town of Haskovo. He and his brothers carried with them through the infidel lands some relics of marvelous power. With these relics they made a procession deep into the country of the Bulgarians and were famous throughout the countryside, so that Christian men and women came out along all the roadsides as the procession passed them, to bow to them or kiss the sides of the wagon. And these holy relics were taken thus to the monastery called Sveti Georgi and there enshrined. So that although the monastery was a small and quiet place many pilgrims came to it thereafter on their way from the monasteries at Rila and Bachkovo or from holy Athos. But Stefan the Wanderer was the first we knew here who had been in Sveti Georgi.

When he had lived with us some months, it was remarked that he did not speak freely of this monastery of Sveti Georgi, although he told many tales of the other blessed places he had visited, sharing them with us from his pious nature that we who had lived always in one country might gain some knowledge of the wonders of Christ's church in different lands. Thus he told us once about an island chapel in the Bay of Maria, in the sea of the Venetians, on an isle so small that the waves lap each of its four walls and about the island monastery of Sveti Stefan two days' journey south of it along the coast, where he took the name of its patron and gave up his own. This much he told us, and many other things besides, including the sighting of fearsome monsters in the Marble Sea.

And he told us most frequently about the churches and monasteries of the city of Constantinople before the infidel troops of the sultan desecrated them. He described to us with reverence their priceless, miracle-working icons, such as the image of the Virgin in the great church of Saint Sophia, and her veiled icon in the sanctuary at Blachernae. He had seen the tomb of Saint John Chrysostom and of the emperors, and the head of the blessed Saint Basil in the church of the Panachrantos, as well as numerous other holy relics. How fortunate for him and for us, the recipients of his tales, that when he was still young he had left the city to wander again, so that he was far distant from it when the devil Muhammad built near it a diabolically strong fortress for the purposes of attacking the city, and soon after broke down the great walls of Constantinople and killed or enslaved its noble people. Then, when Stefan was far away and heard this news, he wept with the rest of Christendom for the martyred city.

And he brought with him to our monastery rare and wonderful books in his horse's pack, which he had collected and from which he drew divine inspiration, as he himself was a master of the Greek, Latin, and Slavic languages and probably others besides. He told us these many things and put his books into our library to bring glory to it forever, which, although most of us could read in only one language and some not all, they did. He gave these gifts saying that he too had ended his travels and would remain forever, like his books, at Zographou.

Only I and one other brother remarked that Stefan spoke not of his sojourn in Wallachia, except to say that he had been a novice there, and neither did he speak much of the Bulgarian monastery called Sveti Georgi, until the end of his life. For when he came to us, he was already sick, and suffered much from fevers in his limbs, and after less than a year he told us he hoped soon to bow before the throne of the Savior, if enough of his sins could be overlooked by the One who forgives all true penitents. When he lay in his last illness he asked to make a confession to our abbot, because he had witnessed evils that he must not die in the possession of, and the abbot, being very struck by his confession, asked me to require it of him again and write down all he said, because he, the abbot, wished to send a letter about it to Constantinople. This I did with all speed and without error, sitting by Stefan's bedside and listening with a heart full of terror to the tale he patiently told me, after which he was given holy communion and died in his sleep and was buried at our monastery.

The Tale of Stefan of Snagov, Faithfully Transcribed by Zacharias the Sinner

I, Stefan, after years of wandering and also after the loss of the beloved and holy city of my birth, Constantinople, went in search of rest north of the great river that divides the Bulgarians from Dacia. I wandered into the plain and then the mountains, and at length I found my way to the monastery that sits on the island in Lake Snagov, a most beautifully secluded and defensible place. There the good abbot welcomed me and I took my seat at table with monks as humble and dedicated to prayer as any I had met in all my journeys. They called me their brother and shared freely with me the food and drink of their meal, and I felt more at peace in the midst of their devout silence than I had in many months. As I worked hard, and followed humbly every direction of the abbot, he soon granted me permission to stay among them. Their church was not large but was of surpassing beauty, with famed bells whose sound rang across the water.

This church and the monastery had received the utmost assistance and fortification from the prince of that region, Vlad son of Vlad Dracul, who was twice chased from his throne by the sultan and other enemies. He was also once long imprisoned by Matthias Corvinus, king of the Magyars. This prince Dracula was very brave, and in reckless battle he plundered or took back from the infidels many of the lands they stole, and of his battle spoils he gave to the monastery, and was constantly desirous that we should pray for him and his family and their safety, which we did. Some of the monks whispered that he had sinned through exceeding cruelty and also had, while prisoner of the Magyar king, allowed himself to be converted to the Latin faith. But the abbot would hear no ill word of him from anyone and had more than once concealed him and his men in the sanctuary of the church when other nobles wished to find and kill him.

In the last year of his life, Dracula came to the monastery, as he had been wont to do more often in earlier times. I did not see him then, because the abbot had sent me and one other monk on an errand to another church, where he had some business. When I returned, I heard that the lord Drakulya had been there and had left new treasures. One brother, who traded for our supplies with the peasants in that region and heard many stories in the countryside, whispered that Dracula was as likely to present a bag of ears and noses as a sack of treasure, but when the abbot heard about this remark he punished the speaker very soundly. Thus I never saw Vlad Dracula in life, but I did see him in death, which I shall report soon enough.

Perhaps four months later there came word that he had been surrounded in a battle and there caught and slain by the infidel soldiers, first killing more than forty of them with his great sword. Upon his death, the sultan's soldiers cut off his head and took it away with them to show their master.

All this was known by the men of Prince Dracula's camp, and although many hid away after his death, some of them brought this news and also his body to the monastery of Snagov, after which they also fled. The abbot wept when he saw the body lifted from the boat and prayed aloud both for the Lord Dracula's soul and for the protection of God, because the crescent of the infidel was now coming very near. He caused the body to be laid in state in the church.

It was one of the most dreadful sights I have seen, this headless corpse robed in red and purple and surrounded by many flickering candle flames. We sat in watches in the church, keeping the holy vigil, for another three days and nights. I sat in the first vigil, and all was peaceful in the church apart from the sight of the mutilated body. In the second vigil all was peaceful again — so said the brothers who watched that night. But on the third night some of the tired brothers dozed, and something occurred to strike terror into the hearts of the others. What it was they could not later agree, each having seen something different. One monk saw an animal leap from the shadows of the stalls and over the coffin, but could not ascertain what shape the animal had. Others felt a gust of wind or saw a thick fog enter the church, which guttered many of the candles, and they swore by the saints and angels and especially the archangels Mikhail and Gabriel that in the dark the headless body of the prince stirred and tried to rise. There was a great shrieking among the brothers in the church, who lifted their voices in terror, and by this the whole community was roused. These monks, running out, related their visions with bitter disagreement among them.

Then the abbot came forward and I saw in the light of the torch he held that he grew very pale and awed at the stories they related, crossing himself many times. He reminded all who were present that the soul of this nobleman was in our hands and that we must act accordingly. He led us into the church, relighting the candles there, and we saw that the body lay quietly as before in its coffin. The abbot caused the church to be searched, but no animal nor any demon was found in any corner. Then he bid us to compose ourselves and go to our cells, and when the hour for the first service came it was held as usual and all was calm.

But the next evening he called eight monks together, honoring me by inclusion among them, and said that we would only make a pretense of burying the prince's body in the church, but that it must instead be conveyed at once from this place. He said that he would tell only one of us, in secret, where we were to take it and why, that the others might be protected as long as possible by our ignorance, and this he did, selecting a monk who had been with him there for many years but telling the rest [of us] only to follow obediently and ask no questions.

In this way I, who had thought never to wander again, became a traveler once more and crossed a long distance, entering with my companions the city of my birth, which had become the seat of the infidels' kingdom, and I found much that was changed there. The great church of Saint Sophia was taken for a mosque and we could not enter it. Many churches had been destroyed or allowed to fall into ruins, and others turned into houses of worship for the Turks, even the Panachrantos. And there I learned that we were looking for a treasure that might hasten the salvation of the soul of this prince, and that this treasure had already been procured at terrible risk by two holy and brave monks from the monastery of Saint Saviour and taken secretly out of the city. But some of the sultan's Janissaries had become suspicious, and because of this we were placed in danger and forced to wander once more to find it, this time traveling into the old kingdom of the Bulgars.

As we passed through the country, it seemed that some of the Bulgarians knew already of this mission, for more and more of them came out along the roads, bowing silently to our procession, and some followed for many miles, touching our wagon with their hands or kissing the side of it. During this journey a most terrible thing occurred. While we were passing through the town of Haskovo, some of the guards of the town rode out to us and stopped us with force and harsh words. They searched our wagon, declaring they would find whatever we carried, and discovering two bundles, they seized them and opened them. When these proved to be food, the infidels threw them in the road with wrath and arrested two of our number. These good monks, protesting that they knew nothing and thus angering the evil ones, had their hands and feet cut off, salt being put in their wounds before they died. They let the rest of us live but dispatched us with curses and whippings. We were afterward able to secure the bodies and limbs of our dear friends and reunite them for Christian burial in the monastery of Bachkovo, whose monks prayed many days and nights for their devout souls.

After this event, we were very much saddened and terrified, but we traveled on, not much farther and without incident, to the monastery of Sveti Georgi. There the monks, although they were old and few, welcomed us and told us that indeed the treasure we sought had been brought to them by two pilgrims some months previous to this, and all was well. We could not think of returning to Dacia soon through so many dangers, and thus we settled there. The relics we had conveyed thither were secretly enshrined at Sveti Georgi and their fame among Christians brought many to worship there, and they also kept silence. For some time we lived in peace at this place and the monastery was built up greatly by our labors. Soon, however, a plague broke out in the villages near us, although at first it did not infect the monastery. I learned [that it was no ordinary plague, but instead]

[At this point the manuscript is cut or torn off.]

Chapter 60

"WHEN STOICHEV had finished, Helen and I sat mute for a couple of minutes. Stoichev himself shook his head now and then, drawing one hand over his face as if to wake himself from a dream. At last Helen spoke. 'It is the same journey — it must be the same journey.'

"Stoichev turned to her. 'I believe it is. And surely Brother Kiril's monks were transporting the remains of Vlad Ţepeş.'

"'And this means that — except for the two who were murdered by the Ottomans — they reached a Bulgarian monastery safely. Sveti Georgi — where is it?'

"It was the question I had most wanted to ask out of all the puzzles that pressed on me. Stoichev put his hand to his brow. 'If only I knew,' he muttered. 'No one knows. There is no monastery called Sveti Georgi in the Bachkovo region, and no evidence that there ever was one there. Sveti Georgi is one of several medieval monasteries in Bulgaria that we know existed but which vanished during the early centuries of the Ottoman yoke. It was probably burned, and the stones scattered or used for other buildings.' He looked sadly at us. 'If the Ottomans had some reason to hate or fear this monastery it was probably completely destroyed. Certainly they did not permit it to be rebuilt, as Rila Monastery was. I was very interested, at one time, in finding the location of Sveti Georgi.' He fell silent for a minute. 'After my friend Angelov died, I tried for a while to continue his research. I went to *Bachkovski manastir,* and I talked with the monks and asked many people in the region, but no one knew of a monastery called Sveti Georgi. I never found it on any of the old maps I examined, either. I have wondered if perhaps Stefan gave Zacharias a false name for it. I thought that there would be a legend among the people of the region, at least, if the relics of such an important figure as Vlad Dracula had been buried there. I wanted to go to Snagov, before the war, to see what I could learn there —'

"'If you had, you might have met Rossi, or at least that archaeologist — Georgescu,' I exclaimed.

"'Perhaps.' He smiled strangely. 'If Rossi and I had indeed met there, perhaps we could have joined our knowledge then, before it was too late.'

"I wondered if he meant, *Before the revolution in Bulgaria, before I was exiled here;* I didn't want to ask. A second later, however, he explained. 'You see, I stopped my research rather suddenly. The day when I returned from the Bachkovo region, with my mind full of a plan to go to Romania, I came back to my apartment in Sofia to find an awful scene.'

"He paused again and closed his eyes. 'I try not to think about that day. I must tell you first that I had a little apartment near *Rimskaya stena* — the Roman wall in Sofia, a very ancient site — and I loved it for the history of the city all around it. I had gone out to buy groceries and left my papers and books about Bachkovo and other monasteries open on my desk. When I returned I saw that someone had gone through all my things, pulled books off the shelves, and searched my closet. On the desk, all over my papers, was a small trail of blood. You know how ink — stains — a page —' He broke off, looking piercingly at us now. 'In the middle of the desk there lay a book I had never seen before —' Suddenly he rose and shuffled into the other room again, and we heard him moving around, shifting books. I should have gotten up to help him, but

I sat instead staring helplessly at Helen, who seemed frozen, too.

"After a moment Stoichev returned with a large folio in his arms. It was bound in worn leather. He laid it in front of us and we watched as he opened it with his reluctant old hands and showed us, wordlessly, the many blank pages, the great image in the center. The dragon looked smaller here, because the larger pages of the folio left considerable empty space around it, but it was certainly the same woodcut, down to the smudge I'd noticed in Hugh James's. There was another smudge, too, in the yellowing border near the dragon's claws. Stoichev pointed to it, but he seemed so overcome with some emotion — distaste, fear — that he apparently forgot for a moment to address us in English. '*Kr'v*,' he said. 'Blood.' I bent close. The brown smear was clearly a fingerprint.

"'My God.' I was remembering my poor cat, and Rossi's friend Hedges. 'Was there someone or something else in the room? What did you do, when you saw this?'

"'There was no one in the room,' he said in a low voice. 'The door had been locked, and it was still locked when I returned and went in and saw this terrible scene. I called the police, and they looked everywhere and finally they — how do you say? — they analyzed a sample of the fresh blood and did some comparisons. They discovered easily whose blood type it was, at least.'

"'Whose?' Helen leaned forward.

"Stoichev's voice dropped even lower, so that I too leaned forward to catch the words. Sweat stood out on his wrinkled face. 'It was mine,' he said.

"'But —'

"'No, of course not. I had not been there. But the police thought I had prepared the entire scene myself. The one thing that did not match was this fingerprint. They said they had never seen a human print like it — it had too few lines. They gave me back the book and my papers and caused me to pay some money for playing tricks with the law. And I almost lost my teaching position.'

"'And you dropped your research?' I guessed.

"Stoichev lifted his thin shoulders helplessly. 'It is the only project I have not continued. I might have gone on, even then, except for this.' He turned slowly to the second leaf of the folio. 'This,' he repeated, and there on the page we saw a single word written in a beautiful and archaic hand in ancient, mellowed ink. I knew just enough by now of Kiril's famous alphabet to puzzle it out, although the first letter stumped me for a second. Helen read it aloud. 'STOICHEV,' she whispered. 'Oh, you found your own name in it. How terrible.'

"'Yes, my own name, and in a handwriting and an ink that were clearly medieval. I have always regretted that I was a coward about this project, but I was afraid. I thought that something might happen to me — like what happened to your father, madam.'

"'You feared with good reason,' I told the old scholar. 'But we hope it's not too late for Professor Rossi.'

"He straightened in his chair. 'Yes. If we can somehow find Sveti Georgi. First, we must go to Rila and look at the other letters by Brother Kiril. As I said, I never before connected them with the "Chronicle" of Zacharias. I do not have copies of them here, and the authorities at Rila have not allowed them to be published, although several historians — including myself — have requested permission. And there is someone at Rila with whom I would like you to talk. He may not be of any assistance, however.'

"Stoichev looked as if he had something else

to say, but at that moment we heard vigorous footsteps on the stairs. He tried to rise, then shot me a pleading look. I snatched up the dragon folio and plunged into the next room with it, where I hid it as well as I could behind a box. I rejoined Stoichev and Helen in time to see Ranov open the door to the library.

"'Ah,' he said. 'A conference of historians. You are missing your own party, Professor.' He browsed unabashedly through the books and papers on the table and at last picked up the old journal from which Stoichev had read us parts of the 'Chronicle' of Zacharias. 'This is the object of your attention?' He almost smiled at us. 'Perhaps I should read it, too, to educate myself. There is much I still do not know about the medieval Bulgaria. And your so-distracting niece is not as interested in me as I thought. I have given her a serious invitation at the most beautiful end of your garden, and she is rather resistant.'

"Stoichev flushed angrily and seemed on the verge of speaking, but to my surprise Helen saved him. 'Keep your dirty bureaucratic hands off that girl,' she said, looking Ranov in the eye. 'You are here to bother us, not her.' I touched her arm, hoping she would not enrage the man somehow; the last thing we needed was a political disaster. But she and Ranov simply gave each other a long, measured glare, and then each turned away.

"In the meantime, Stoichev had recovered himself. 'It would be most helpful for the research of these visitors if you would arrange for them to travel to Rila,' he told Ranov calmly. 'I would like to travel with them also, and it will be an honor for me to show them the library of Rila myself.'

"'Rila?' Ranov weighed the journal in his hand. 'Very well. We will make that our next excursion. It may be possible the day after tomorrow. I will send a message to you, Professor, to let you know when you can meet us there.'

"'Couldn't we go tomorrow?' I tried to sound casual.

"'So you are in a hurry?' Ranov raised his eyebrows. 'It takes time to arrange such a large request.'

"Stoichev nodded. 'We will wait patiently, and the professors can enjoy the sights of Sofia until then. Now, my friends, this has been a pleasant exchange of ideas, but Kiril and Methodii will not mind if we also eat, drink, and be merry, as they say. Come, Miss Rossi —' He extended his fragile hand to Helen, who helped him up. 'Give me your arm and we will go to celebrate a day of teaching and learning.'

"The other guests had begun to gather under the trellis, and we soon saw why: three of the younger men were taking musical instruments out of their bags and setting up near the tables. A lanky fellow with a shock of dark hair was testing the keys of a black-and-silver accordion. Another man had a clarinet. He played a few notes while the third musician got out a large skin drum and a long stick with a padded tip. They sat down in three chairs close together and grinned at one another, played a warble or two, adjusted their seats. The clarinet player removed his jacket.

"Then they exchanged glances and were off, spinning out of nowhere the liveliest music I had ever heard. Stoichev beamed from his throne behind the roast lamb, and Helen, sitting next to me, squeezed my arm. It was a tune that whirled up into the air like a cyclone, then jolted along in a rhythm unfamiliar to me but irresistible once my toe had caught it. The accordion panted in and out and notes soared from the accordionist's fingers. I was astounded by the speed and energy with which they all played. The sound brought whoops of joy and encouragement from the crowd.

"After only a few minutes, some of the men listening jumped up, grabbing one another's belts behind the waist, and began a dance as lively as the tune. Their highly polished shoes lifted and stamped on the grass. They were soon joined by several women in sober dresses, who danced with their upper bodies erect and still, their feet a blur. The dancers' faces were radiant; they all smiled as if they couldn't help it, and the teeth of the accordionist flashed in response. The man at the front of the line had produced a white pocket handkerchief and he held it high to lead them, whirling it around and around. Helen's eyes were very bright, and she tapped her hand on the table as if she couldn't stay still. The musicians played on and on, while the rest of us cheered and toasted them and drank, and the dancers showed no sign of stopping. At last the tune ended and the line fell apart, each dancer wiping off copious sweat and laughing aloud. The men came to refill their glasses, and the women searched for handkerchiefs and touched up their hair, chuckling together.

"Then the accordionist began to play again, but this time it was a slow series of trills, long drawn-out notes in a wailing key. He threw back his shaggy head, showing his teeth in a song. It was half song, actually, and half howl, a baritone melody so wrenching that I found my heart constricting with loss, with all the losses of my life. 'What is he singing?' I asked Stoichev, to cover my emotion.

"'It is an old song, very old — I think at least three or four hundred years. It tells the story of a beautiful Bulgarian maiden who is chased by the Turkish invaders. They want her for the harem of the local pasha, and she refuses. She runs up a high mountain near her village and they gallop after her on their horses. At the top of the mountain is a cliff. There she cries out that she would rather die than become the mistress of an infidel, and she throws herself off the cliff. Later a spring rises up at the foot of the mountain, and it is the purest, sweetest water in that valley.'

"Helen nodded. 'We have songs with a similar theme in Romania.'

"'They exist wherever the Ottoman yoke fell over the Balkan peoples, I think,' Stoichev said gravely. 'We have in Bulgarian folklore thousands of such songs, with various themes — all are a cry of protest against the enslavement of our people.'

"The accordionist seemed to feel he had wrung our hearts sufficiently, for at the end of the song he gave a wicked smile and burst into dance music once more. This time most of the guests rose to join the line, which snaked around the terrace. One of the men urged us to come along, and after a second Helen followed, although I stayed firm in my chair next to Stoichev. I enjoyed watching her, though. She caught the dance step after a short demonstration. Some kind of dance must have been in her blood; she held herself with natural dignity, her feet moving surely to the jagged beat. Following her lithe form in the pale blouse and black skirt, her glowing face with the dark curls escaping around it, I found myself almost praying that nothing would ever harm her, and wondering, too, if she would let me keep her safe."

Chapter 61

"IF MY FIRST glimpse of Stoichev's house had filled me with sudden hopelessness, my first glimpse of Rila Monastery filled me with awe. The monastery sat in a dramatically deep valley — almost filling it, at that point — and above its walls and domes rose the Rila Mountains, which are very steep and forested with tall spruces. Ranov had parked his car in the shade outside the main gate, and we made our way in with several clumps of other tourists. It was a hot, dry day; the Balkan summer seemed to be closing in, and dust from the bare ground swirled around our ankles. The great wooden doors of the gate were open, and we went through them into a sight I can never forget. Around us loomed the striped walls of the monastery fortress, with their alternating patterns of black and red on white plaster, hung with long wooden galleries. Filling a third of the enormous courtyard was a church of exquisite proportions, its porch heavily frescoed, its pale green domes alight in the midday sun. Beside it stood a muscular, square tower of gray stone, visibly older than everything else in sight. Stoichev told us that this was Hrelyo's Tower, built by a medieval nobleman as a haven from his political enemies. It was the only remaining part of the earliest monastery on the site, which had been burned by the Turks and rebuilt centuries later in this striped splendor. As we stood there, the church bells began to toll, frightening a flock of birds into the sky. They soared upward, startled, and, following them with my gaze, I saw again the unimaginably high peaks above us — a day's climb, at least. I caught my breath; was Rossi here somewhere, in this ancient place?

"Helen, standing next to me with a thin scarf tied over her hair, put her arm through mine, and I remembered the moment in Hagia Sophia, that evening in Istanbul that seemed history already but had actually been only days before, when she had grasped my hand so hard. The Ottomans had conquered this land long before they had taken Constantinople; by rights, we should have begun our trip here, not in Hagia Sophia. On the other hand, even before that, the doctrines of the Byzantines, their elegant arts and architecture, had reached out from Constantinople to flavor Bulgarian culture. Now Saint Sophia was a museum among mosques, while this dramatically secluded valley brimmed with Byzantine culture.

"Stoichev, beside us, was clearly enjoying our astonishment. Irina, in a broad-brimmed hat, held his arm tightly. Only Ranov stood alone, scowling at the beautiful scene, turning his head suspiciously when a group of black-cowled monks passed us on their way into the church. It had been a struggle for us to persuade him to pick up Stoichev and Irina in his car and bring them along; he wanted Stoichev to have the honor of showing us Rila, he said, but there was no reason Stoichev couldn't take the bus like the rest of the Bulgarian people. I'd restrained myself from pointing out that he, Ranov, didn't seem to take the bus much himself. We had finally prevailed, although this didn't prevent Ranov from grumbling about the old professor most of the way from Sofia to Stoichev's house. Stoichev had used his fame to promote superstition and antipatriotic ideas; everyone knew that he had refused to drop his very unscientific allegiance to the Orthodox church; he had a son studying in East Germany who was almost as bad as he was. But we had won the battle, Stoichev could ride with us, and Irina whispered gratefully during our stop for lunch at a mountain tavern that she would have tried to prevent her uncle from going at all if they'd had to take the bus; he couldn't stand such a hard trip in this heat.

"'This is the wing where the monks still live,' Stoichev said. 'And over there, along that side, is the hostel where we will sleep. You will see how peaceful it is here at night, in spite of all the visitors in the day. This is one of our greatest national treasures, and many people come to see it, especially in the summer. But at night it becomes very quiet again. Come,' he added, 'we will go in to see the abbot. I called him yesterday and he is expecting us.' He led the way with surprising vigor, looking eagerly around, as if the place gave him new life.

"The abbot's audience chambers, when we reached them, were on the first floor of the monastic wing. A black-gowned monk with a long brown beard held the door for us and we went in, Stoichev removing his hat and entering first. The abbot rose from a bench near the wall and came forward to meet us. He and Stoichev greeted each other very cordially, Stoichev kissing his hand and the abbot blessing the old man. The abbot was a lean, upright man of perhaps sixty, his beard streaked with gray and his blue eyes — I was rather surprised to realize there were blue-eyed Bulgarians — tranquil. He shook hands with us in a very modern way, and with Ranov, who greeted him with obvious disdain. Then he gestured for us all to sit down, and a monk brought in a tray of glasses — not full of *rakiya,* in this place, but of cool water, accompanied by small dishes of that rose-flavored paste we had encountered in Istanbul. I noticed that Ranov did not drink his, as if he suspected poison.

"The abbot was clearly delighted to see Stoichev there, and I imagined the visit must be a particular pleasure to both of them. He asked us through Stoichev where we were from in America, whether we had visited other monasteries in Bulgaria, what he could do to help us, how long we would be able to stay. Stoichev spoke with him at length, translating obligingly so that we could answer the abbot's questions. We could use the library as much as we liked, the abbot said; we could sleep in the hostel; we should attend the services in the church; we were welcome anywhere except the monks' quarters — this with a gentle nod at Helen and Irina — and they would not hear of Professor Stoichev's friends paying for their lodging. We thanked him gratefully and Stoichev got to his feet. 'Now,' he said, 'since we have these kind permissions, we will go to the library.' He was already making his way cautiously to the door, kissing the abbot's hand, bowing.

"'My uncle is very excited,' Irina whispered to us. 'He says to me that your letter is a great discovery for Bulgarian history.' I wondered if she knew how much was actually riding on this research, what shadows lay across our path, but it was impossible for me to read anything more in her expression. She helped her uncle through the door and we followed him along the tremendous wooden galleries that lined the courtyard, Ranov trailing us with a cigarette in his hand.

"The library was a long gallery on the first floor, nearly opposite the abbot's rooms. At the entrance, a black-bearded monk ushered us in; he was a tall, gaunt-faced man and it seemed to me that he looked hard at Stoichev for a moment before nodding to us. 'This is Brother Rumen,' Stoichev told us. 'He is the librarian monk at present. He will show us what we need to see.'

"A few books and manuscripts had been put into glass-fronted display cases and labeled for the tourists; I would have liked to look at these, but we were on our way to a deeper recess, which opened out of the back of the room. It was miraculously cool in the depths of the monastery, and even the few raw electric bulbs could not completely chase away the profound darkness in the corners. In this inner sanctum, wooden cabinets and shelves were laden with boxes and trays of books. In the corner a little shrine held an icon of the Virgin and her stiff, precocious baby flanked by two red-winged angels, with a jeweled gold lamp hanging before them. The old, old walls were whitewashed stucco and the smell that engulfed us was a familiar odor of slowly decaying parchment, vellum, velvet. I was glad to see that Ranov had at least had the grace to put out his smoke before following us into this treasure-house.

"Stoichev tapped his foot on the stone floor as if summoning spirits. 'Here,' he said, 'you are looking at the heart of the Bulgarian people — this is where for hundreds of years the monks preserved our heritage, often in secret. Generations of faithful monks copied these manuscripts, or hid them when the monastery was attacked by the infidel. This is a small percentage of the legacy of our people — much of it was destroyed, of course. But we are grateful for these remains.'

"He spoke with the librarian, who began to look carefully through labeled boxes on the shelves. After a few minutes he brought down a wooden box and took from it several volumes. The top one was decorated with a startling painting of Christ — at least I took it to be Christ — an orb in one hand and a scepter in the other, his face clouded with Byzantine melancholy. To my disappointment, Brother Kiril's letters were not housed in this glorious binding, but in a plainer one beneath it, which had the look of old bone. The librarian carried it to a table and Stoichev sat eagerly down to it, opening it with relish. Helen and I drew out our notebooks and Ranov strolled around the library shelves as if too bored to stay in one place.

"'As I remember,' Stoichev said, 'there are two letters here, and it is unclear whether there were more — whether Brother Kiril wrote others that have not survived.' He pointed to the first page. It was covered in a close, rounded, calligraphic hand, and the parchment was deeply aged, almost brown. He turned to the librarian with a question. 'Yes,' he told us, pleased. 'They have typed these in Bulgarian, and some of the other rare documents from this period, as well.' The librarian set a folder in front of him, and Stoichev sat silent a while, examining the typed pages and turning back to the ancient calligraphy. 'They have done quite a good job,' he said at last. 'I will read you the best translation I can, for your notes.' And he read to us a halting version of these two letters.

Your Excellency, Lord Abbot Eupraxius:
We are now three days upon the high road journeying out of Laota toward Vin. One night we slept in the stable of a good farmer, and one night at the hermitage of Saint Mikhail, where no monks now live but which gave us at least the dry shelter of a cave. The last night we were forced for the first time to make our camp in the forest, spreading rugs on the rustic floor and placing our bodies within a circle of the horses and wagon. Wolves came close enough in the night for us to hear their howling, whereupon the horses tried in terror to bolt. With great difficulty we subdued them. Now I am heartily glad for the presence of Brothers Ivan and Theodosius, with their height and strength, and I bless your wisdom in placing them among us.

Tonight we are made welcome in the house of a shepherd of some wealth and also of piety; he has three thousand sheep in this region, he tells us, and we are bid sleep on his soft sheepskins and mattresses, although I for one have elected the floor as more fitting to our devotions. We are out of the forest here, among open hills that roll on every side, where we may walk with equal blessing in rain and sunshine. The good man of the house tells us they have twice suffered the raids of the infidel from across the river, which is now a few days' walk only, if Brother Angelus can mend himself and keep to our pace. I think to let him ride one of the horses, although the sacred weight they pull is great enough already on them. Fortunately, we have seen no signs of infidel soldiers on the road.

> Your most humble servant in Christ,
> Br. Kiril
> April, the Year of Our Lord 6985

Your Excellency, Lord Abbot Eupraxius:
  We have left the city some weeks behind us and are now riding openly in the territory of the infidels. I dare not write our location, in case we should be captured. Perhaps we should have chosen the sea route after all, but God will be our Protector along the way we have chosen. We have seen the burned remains of two monasteries and one church. The church

was smoking as yet. Five monks were hung there for conspiring to a rebellion, and their surviving brothers are scattered to other monasteries already. This is the only news we have learned, as we cannot talk long with the people who come out to our wagon. There is no reason to think one of these monasteries is the one we seek, however. The sign will be clear there, the monster equal to the saint. If this missive can be delivered to you, my lord, it shall be as soon as possible.

Your most humble servant in Christ,
Br. Kiril
June, the Year of Our Lord 6985

"When Stoichev had finished, we sat in silence. Helen was scribbling notes still, her face intent over her work, Irina sat with her hands folded, Ranov stood negligently against a cabinet, scratching under his collar. For myself, I had given up trying to write down the events described in the letter; Helen would catch everything anyway. There was no clear evidence here of a particular destination, no mention of a tomb, no scene of burial — the disappointment I felt was choking.

"But Stoichev seemed far from downcast. 'Interesting,' he said, after long minutes. 'Interesting. You see, your letter from Istanbul must lie between these two letters here, chronologically. In the first and second letters, they are traveling through Wallachia toward the Danube — that is clear from the place-names. Then comes your letter, which Brother Kiril wrote in Constantinople, perhaps hoping to send it and the previous letters from there. But he was unable or afraid to send them — unless these are just copies — we have no way to know. And the last letter is dated June. They took a land route like the one that is described by the Zacharias "Chronicle." In fact, it must have been the same route, from Constantinople through Edirne and Haskovo, because that was the major road from *Tsarigrad* into Bulgaria.'

"Helen looked up. 'But can we be sure this last letter describes Bulgaria?'

"'We cannot be absolutely certain,' Stoichev admitted. 'However, I believe it is very probable. If they traveled from *Tsarigrad* — Constantinople — into a country where monasteries and churches were being burned in the late fifteenth century, it is very likely that this was Bulgaria. Also, your letter from Istanbul states that they intend to go to Bulgaria.'

"I couldn't help voicing my frustration. 'But there's no further information about the location of the monastery they were looking for. Assuming it even was Sveti Georgi.' Ranov had settled at the table with us and was looking at his thumbs; I wondered if I should hide my interest in Sveti Georgi from him, but how else were we going to ask Stoichev about it?

"'No.' Stoichev nodded. 'Brother Kiril would certainly not have written the name of their destination in his letters, just as he did not write the name of Snagov with Eupraxius's titles. If they had been caught, these monasteries might have suffered extra persecution, eventually, or at least might have been searched.'

"'There is an interesting line in here.' Helen had finished her notes. 'Could you read that again — that the sign in the monastery they sought was a monster equal to a saint? What do you think this meant?'

"I looked quickly at Stoichev; this line had struck me, too. He sighed. 'It might refer to a fresco or an icon that was in the monastery — in Sveti Georgi, if that was indeed their destination. It is difficult to imagine what such an image might have been. And even if we could find Sveti Georgi itself, there is little hope that an icon that was there in the fifteenth century would still be there, especially since the monastery was probably burned at least once. I do not know what this means. Perhaps it is even a theological reference that the abbot would have understood but that we cannot, or perhaps it referred to some secret agreement between them. We must keep it in our minds, however, since Brother Kiril names it as the sign that will tell them they have come to the right place.'

"I was still wrestling with my disappointment; I realized now that I had expected these letters in their faded binding to hold the final key to our search, or at least to shed some light on the maps I still hoped to use.

"'There is a larger issue that is very strange.' Stoichev ran a hand over his chin. 'The letter from Istanbul says that the treasure they seek — perhaps a holy relic from *Tsarigrad* — is in a particular monastery in Bulgaria, and that is why they must go there. Please read me that passage again, Professor, if you will be so kind.'

"I had taken out the text of the Istanbul letter, to have beside me while we studied Brother

Kiril's other missives. 'It says, " . . . what we seek
has been transported already out of the city and
into a haven in the occupied lands of the Bulgarians.'

"'That is the passage,' Stoichev said. 'The question is' — he tapped a long forefinger on the
table in front of him — 'why would a holy relic,
for example, have been smuggled out of Constantinople in 1477? The city had been Ottoman
since 1453 and most of its relics were destroyed
in the invasion. Why did the monastery of
Panachrantos send a remaining relic into Bulgaria twenty-four years later, and why was that
the particular relic these monks had gone to
Constantinople to find?'

"'Well,' I reminded him, 'we know from the
letter that the Janissaries were looking for the
same relic, so it had some value for the sultan
also.'

"Stoichev considered. 'True, but the Janissaries looked for it after it was taken safely out
of the monastery.'

"'It must have been a holy object with political power for the Ottomans, as well as a spiritual
treasure for the monks of Snagov.' Helen was
frowning, tapping her cheek with her pen. 'A
book, perhaps?'

"'Yes,' I said, excited now. 'What if it was a book that contained some information the Ottomans wanted and the monks needed?' Ranov, across the table, suddenly gave me a hard look.

"Stoichev nodded slowly, but I remembered after a second that this meant disagreement. 'Books of that period did not usually contain political information — they were religious texts, copied many times for use in the monasteries or for the Islamic religious schools and mosques, if they were Ottoman. It is not likely that the monks would make such a dangerous journey even for a copy of the holy gospels. And they would already have had such books at Snagov.'

"'Just a minute.' Helen's eyes were wide with thought. 'Wait. It must have been something connected with Snagov's needs, or the Order of the Dragon, or maybe the wake for Vlad Dracula — remember the "Chronicle"? The abbot wanted Dracula buried somewhere else.'

"'True,' Stoichev mused. 'He wanted to send Dracula's body to *Tsarigrad* even at the risk of the lives of his monks.'

"'Yes,' I said. I think I was about to say something else, to meander down some other path of inquiry, but suddenly Helen turned to me and shook my arm.

"'What?' I said, but by then she had recovered herself.

"'Nothing,' she said softly, without looking at either me or Ranov. I wished to God he would get up and go outside to smoke, or get tired of the conversation, so that Helen could speak up freely. Stoichev glanced at her keenly, and after a moment he began to explain in a droning voice how medieval manuscripts were made and copied — sometimes by monks who were actually illiterate and encoded generations of small errors in them — and how their different hand-writings were codified by modern scholars. I was puzzled about why he was going on at such length, although what he said held considerable interest for me. Fortunately, I stayed quiet during his disquisition, for after a while Ranov actually began to yawn. Finally, he stood up and made his way out of the library, pulling a pack of ciga-rettes from his jacket pocket. As soon as he was gone Helen seized my arm again. Stoichev watched her intently.

"'Paul,' she said, and her face was so strange that I caught her around the shoulders, thinking she might faint. 'His head! Don't you see? Drac-ula went back to Constantinople to get his head!'

"Stoichev made a little choked sound, but too

late. At that moment, glancing around, I saw Brother Rumen's angular face around the edge of a bookshelf. He had come silently back into the room, and although his back was to us while he put something away, it was a listening back. After a moment, he went quietly out again, and we all sat silent. Helen and I glanced helplessly at each other and I got up to check the depths of the room. The man was gone, but it would probably be a matter of a short time before someone else — Ranov, for example — heard about Helen's exclamation. And what use might Ranov make of that information?"

Chapter 62

"FEW MOMENTS in my years of research, writing, and thought have prompted for me such a sudden access of clarity as that moment when Helen spoke her guess aloud in the library at Rila. Vlad Dracula had returned to Constantinople for his head — or, rather, the abbot of Snagov had sent his body there to be reunited with it. Had Dracula requested this ahead of time, knowing the bounty placed on his famous head in his lifetime, knowing the sultan's penchant for displaying the heads of his enemies to the populace? Or had the abbot taken this mission upon himself, not wanting the headless body of his possibly heretical — or dangerous — sponsor to remain at Snagov? Surely, a vampire without a head couldn't pose much of a threat — the picture was almost comical — but the disturbances among his monks might have been enough to persuade the abbot to give Dracula a proper Christian burial elsewhere. Probably the abbot couldn't have taken upon himself the destruction of his prince's body. And who knew what promises the abbot had made Dracula ahead of time?

"A singular image drifted back to me: Topkapı Palace in Istanbul, where I'd strolled that recent sunny morning, and the gates where the Ottoman executioners had displayed the heads of the sultan's enemies. Dracula's head would have warranted one of the highest spikes, I thought — the Impaler finally impaled. How many people would have gone to see it, this proof of the sultan's triumph? Helen had told me once that even the inhabitants of Istanbul had feared Dracula and worried that he might fight his way into their very city. No Turkish encampment would have to tremble again at his approach; the sultan had finally gotten control of that troublesome region and could set an Ottoman vassal on the Wallachian throne, as he'd wanted to years before. All that was left of the Impaler was a gruesome trophy, with its shriveled eyes and tangled, blood-caked hair and mustache.

"Our companion seemed to be musing over a similar picture. As soon as we were certain Brother Rumen had left, Stoichev said in a low voice, 'Yes, it is quite possible. But how could the monks of Panachrantos have gotten Dracula's head from the sultan's palace? It was indeed a treasure, as Stefan named it in his tale.'

"'How did we get visas to enter Bulgaria?'

Helen asked, raising her eyebrows. '*Bakshish* — a lot of it. The monasteries were quite poor after the conquest, but some of them might have had hidden stores — gold coin, jewels — something to tempt even the guards of the sultan.'

"I pondered this. 'Our guidebook for Istanbul said that the heads of the sultan's enemies were thrown into the Bosphorus after they had been displayed for a while. Maybe someone from Panachrantos intercepted that process — that might have been less dangerous than trying to get it from the palace gates.'

"'We simply cannot know the truth about this,' Stoichev said, 'but I think Miss Rossi's guess is a very good one. His head was the most likely object they could have sought in *Tsarigrad*. There is a good theological reason, too, for their having done so. Our Orthodox beliefs state that as far as possible the body must be whole in death — we do not practice cremation, for example — because on the Day of Judgment we will be resurrected in our bodies.'

"'What about the saints and all their relics, scattered everywhere?' I asked doubtfully. 'How are they going to be resurrected whole? Not to mention that I saw five of Saint Francis's hands in Italy a few years ago.'

"Stoichev laughed. 'The saints have special privileges,' he said. 'But Vlad Dracula, although he was an excellent Turk-killer, was certainly not a saint. In fact, Eupraxius was quite worried about his immortal soul, at least according to Stefan's tale.'

"'Or about his immortal body,' Helen pointed out.

"'So,' I said, 'maybe the monks of Panachrantos took his head to give it proper burial, at the risk of their lives, and the Janissaries noticed the theft and began searching, so the abbot sent it out of Istanbul rather than bury it there. Maybe there were pilgrims going to Bulgaria from time to time' — I glanced at Stoichev for confirmation — 'and they sent it for burial at — well, at Sveti Georgi, or some other Bulgarian monastery where they had connections. And then the monks from Snagov arrived, but too late to reunite the body with the head. The abbot of Panachrantos heard about it and spoke with them, and the Snagov monks decided to complete their mission by following with the body. Besides, they had to get the hell out of there before the Janissaries got interested in them, too.'

"'Very good, for a speculation.' Stoichev gave me his wonderful smile. 'As I said, we cannot know for certain, because these are events at which our documents only hint. But you have made a convincing picture of them. We will get you away from the Dutch merchants, eventually.' I felt myself flush, partly from pleasure and partly from chagrin, but his smile was genial.

"'And then the Ottoman network was put on guard by the presence and departure of the Snagov monks' — Helen picked up the possible story — 'and maybe they searched the monasteries and discovered that the monks had stayed at Saint Irine, and they sent news of the monks' journey to the officials along their route, perhaps to Edirne and then to Haskovo. Haskovo was the first large Bulgarian town the monks entered, and that is where they were — what is the term? — detained.'

"'Yes,' Stoichev finished. 'The Ottoman officials tortured two of them for information, but those two brave monks said nothing. And the officials searched the wagon and found only food. But this leaves a question — why did the Ottoman soldiers not find the body?'

"I hesitated. 'Maybe they weren't looking for a body. Maybe they were still looking for the head. If the Janissaries had learned very little in Istanbul about the whole thing, they might have thought that the Snagov monks were the trans-porters of the head. The "Chronicle" of Zacharias said that the Ottomans were angry when they opened some bundles and found only food. The body could have been hidden in the woods nearby, if the monks had some warning of the search.'

"'Or perhaps they constructed the wagon so that there was a special place to hide it,' pondered Helen.

"'But a corpse would have stunk,' I reminded her bluntly.

"'That depends on what you believe.' She gave me her quizzical, charming smile.

"'What I believe?'

"'Yes. You see, a body that is at risk for becoming undead, or is already undead, does not decay, or it decomposes more slowly. Traditionally, if villagers in Eastern Europe suspected vampirism, they would dig up corpses to check for decomposition, and ritually destroy those that were not decaying properly. It is still done sometimes, even now.'

"Stoichev shuddered. 'A peculiar activity. I have heard of it even in Bulgaria, although of course it is illegal now. The Church has always discouraged the desecration of graves, and now

our government discourages all superstitions —
as well as it can.'

"Helen almost shrugged. 'Is it any stranger than
hoping for bodily resurrection?' she asked, but
she smiled at Stoichev, and he too was charmed.

"'Madam,' he said, 'we have very different in-
terpretations of our heritage, but I salute your
quickness of mind. And now, my friends, I would
like some time to study your maps — it has occurred to me that there are materials in this library that may be of assistance in reading them.
Give me an hour — what I do now will be dull
for you, and slow for me to explain.'

"Ranov had just come in again, restlessly, and
stood looking around the library. I hoped he
hadn't caught the mention of our maps.

"Stoichev cleared his throat. 'Perhaps you will
like to go into the church and see its beauty.' He
glanced very slightly toward Ranov. Helen immediately got up and went to Ranov to engage him in
some slight complication, while I fished discreetly
in my briefcase and pulled out my file of copies of
the maps. When I saw the eagerness with which
Stoichev took them, my heart leaped with hope.

"Unfortunately, Ranov seemed more interested
in hovering over Stoichev's work and conferring
with the librarian than in following us, although

I devoutly wished we could draw him off. 'Would you help us find some dinner?' I asked him. The librarian stood silent, studying me closely.

"Ranov smiled. 'Are you hungry? It is not yet time for the meal here, which is supper at six o'clock. We will wait for that. We will have to eat with the monks, unfortunately.' He turned his back on us and began to study a shelf of leather-bound volumes, and that was that.

"Helen followed me to the door and squeezed my hand. 'Shall we go for a walk?' she said, once we were outside.

"'I don't know whether I know how to do anything without Ranov, at this point,' I said grimly. 'What will we talk about without him?'

"She laughed, but I could see she was worried, too. 'Should I go back and try again to distract him?'

"'No,' I said. 'Better not. The more we do that the more he'll wonder what Stoichev is looking at. We can't get rid of him any more than we could a fly.'

"'He would make a good fly.' Helen took my arm. The sun was still brilliant in the courtyard, and hot when we left the shadow of the immense monastery walls and galleries. Looking up, I could see the forested slopes around the monastery, and the vertical rock peaks above them. Far overhead, an eagle banked and wheeled. Monks in their heavy, belted black gowns, tall black hats, and long black beards came and went between the church and the first floor of the monastery, or swept the wooden gallery floors, or sat in a triangle of shade near the porch of the church. I wondered how they endured the summer heat in those garments. The interior of the church gave me some insight; it was as cool as a springhouse, lit only by twinkling candles and the glimmer of gold, brass, jewels. The inner walls were ornately gilded and painted with images of saints and prophets — 'Nineteenth-century work,' Helen said confidently — and I paused before an especially sober image, a saint with a long white beard and neatly parted white hair gazing straight out at us. Helen sounded out the letters near his halo. 'Ivan Rilski.'

"'The one whose bones were brought here eight years before our Wallachian friend entered Bulgaria? The "Chronicle" mentioned him.'

"'Yes.' Helen brooded over the image, as if she thought it might speak to us if she stood there long enough.

"The endless waiting was starting to tell on my nerves. 'Helen,' I said, 'let's go for a walk. We can climb up the mountain there and get a view.' If I didn't exert myself a little, the thought of Rossi was going to drive me crazy.

"'All right,' Helen agreed, and she gave me a hard look, as if reading my impatience. 'If it is not too far. Ranov will never let us go far.'

"The path up the mountain wound through dense forest that shielded us from the afternoon heat almost as well as the church had. It was so good to be free of Ranov that for a few minutes I simply swung Helen's hand back and forth as we walked. 'Do you think it was hard for him to choose between us and Stoichev?'

"'Oh, no,' Helen said flatly. 'He certainly has someone else following us. We will encounter whoever it is after a while, especially if we are gone more than half an hour. He can't possibly keep up with us alone, and he has to tend to Stoichev carefully, to find out what our research will lead to.'

"'You sound so matter-of-fact,' I told her, glancing at her profile as she strode along the dirt track. She had pushed her hat back on her head, and her face was a little flushed. 'I can't imagine having grown up knowing all these cynical things, being under surveillance.'

"Helen shrugged. 'It did not seem so terrible because I did not know anything different.'

"'And yet you wanted to leave your country and go to the West.'

"'Yes,' she said, looking sideways at me. 'I wanted to leave my country.'

"We stopped to rest for a few minutes on a fallen tree near the road. 'I've been thinking about why they let us come into Bulgaria,' I told Helen. Even here, out in the woods, I was lowering my voice.

"'And why they are letting us wander around by ourselves at all.' She nodded. 'Have you thought about that?'

"'It seems to me,' I told her slowly, 'that if they aren't stopping us from finding whatever we're looking for — which they could do so easily — it's because they *want* us to find it.'

"'Good, Sherlock.' Helen fanned my face with her hand. 'You are learning a great deal.'

"'So, let's say they actually know or suspect what we're looking for. Why would they think it was valuable or even possible that Vlad Dracula is undead?' It cost me an effort to say this aloud, although I'd dropped my voice to a whisper. 'You've told me many times yourself that communist governments hold peasant superstition in contempt. Why would they encourage us like this, by not preventing us? Do they think they're going to get some kind of supernatural power over the Bulgarian people if we find his tomb here?'

"Helen shook her head. 'That would not be it. Their interest is certainly based in power, but it is always scientific in approach. Besides, if there is to be a discovery of anything interesting, they do not want an American to have the credit for it.' She mused a little. 'Think — what would be more powerful to science than the discovery that the dead can be brought to life, or to un-death, in any case? Especially for the East Bloc, with its great leaders embalmed in their own tombs?"

"A vision of Georgi Dimitrov's yellow face, in the mausoleum in Sofia, flashed on me. 'Then we have all the more reason to destroy Dracula,' I said, but I could feel the perspiration break out on my forehead.

"'And I wonder,' Helen added somberly, 'if destroying him would make that much difference in the future. Think of what Stalin did to his people, and Hitler. They did not need to live five hundred years to accomplish these horrors.'

"'I know,' I said. 'I've thought about that, too.'

"Helen nodded. 'The strange thing, you know, is that Stalin openly admired Ivan the Terrible. Two leaders who were willing to crush and kill their own people — to do anything necessary — in order to consolidate their power. And whom do you think Ivan the Terrible admired?'

"I felt the blood draining from my heart. 'You told me there were many Russian tales about Dracula.'

"'Yes. Exactly.'

"I stared at her.

"'Can you imagine a world in which Stalin could live for five hundred years?' She was scraping a soft place on the log with her fingernail. 'Or perhaps forever?'

"I found myself clenching my fists. 'Do you think we can find a medieval grave without leading anyone else to it?'

"'It will be very difficult, perhaps impossible. I am certain they have people watching us everywhere.'

"At this moment a man came around the bend in the path. I was so startled by his sudden appearance that I almost swore aloud. But he was a simple-looking person, roughly dressed and with a bundle of branches on his shoulder, and he waved a hand to us in greeting and passed on. I looked at Helen.

"'You see?' she said quietly."

"Partway up the mountain we found a steep outcropping of rock. 'Look,' Helen said. 'Let's sit here for a few minutes.'

"The steep, wooded valley lay directly below us, almost filled by the walls and red roofs of the monastery. I could see clearly now the enormous size of the complex. It formed an angular shell around the church, whose domes glowed in the afternoon light, and Hrelyo's Tower rose in its midst. 'You can tell from up here how well-fortified the place was. Imagine how often enemies must have looked down on it like this.'

"'Or pilgrims,' Helen reminded me. 'For them it would have been a spiritual destination, not a military challenge.' She leaned back against a tree trunk, smoothing her skirt. She had dropped her handbag, taken off her hat, and rolled up the sleeves of her pale blouse for relief from the heat. Fine perspiration stood out on her forehead and cheeks. Her face wore the expression I loved best — she was lost in thought, gazing inward and outward at the same time, her eyes wide and intent, her jaw firm; for some reason I valued this look even more than the ones she turned directly on me. She wore her scarf around her neck, although the librarian's mark had faded to a bruise, and the little crucifix glinted below it. Her harsh beauty sent a pang through me, not of mere physical longing but of something akin to awe at her completeness. She was untouchable, mine but lost to me.

"'Helen,' I said, without taking her hand. I hadn't meant to speak, but I couldn't stop myself. 'I'd like to ask you something.'

"She nodded, her eyes and thoughts still on the tremendous sanctuary below us.

"'Helen, will you marry me?'

"She turned slowly in my direction, and I wondered if I was seeing astonishment, amusement, or pleasure on her face. 'Paul,' she said sternly. 'How long have we known each other?'

"'Twenty-three days,' I admitted. I realized now that I hadn't thought carefully about what I would do if she said no, but it was too late to retract the question, to save it for another moment. And if she said no I couldn't throw myself off a mountain in the middle of my search for Rossi, although I might be tempted to.

"'Do you think you know me?'

"'Not at all,' I countered staunchly.

"'Do you think I know you?'

"'I'm not sure.'

"'We have so little experience of each other. We come from completely different worlds.' She smiled this time, as if to take some of the sting out of her words. 'Besides, I have always thought I would not get married. I am not the sort who marries. And what about this?' She touched the scarf on her neck. 'Would you marry a woman who has been marked by hell?'

"'I would protect you from any hell that could ever come near you.'

"'Would that not be a burden? And how could we have children' — her look was hard and direct — 'knowing they might be affected somehow by this contamination?'

"It was hard for me to speak through the burning in my throat. 'Then is your answer no, or shall I just ask you again another time?'

"Her hand — I couldn't imagine doing without that hand, with its square-tipped fingernails and soft skin over hard bone — closed over mine, and I thought fleetingly that I didn't have a ring to put on it.

"Helen glanced gravely at me. 'The answer is that of course I will marry you.'

"After weeks of futile search for the other person I loved best, I was too stunned by the ease of this discovery to speak or even to kiss her. We sat close together in silence, looking down at the red and gold and gray of the vast monastery."

Chapter 63

BARLEY STOOD BESIDE ME in my father's hotel room, contemplating the mess, but he was quicker to see what I had missed — the papers and books on the bed. We found a tattered copy of Bram Stoker's *Dracula*, a new history of medieval heresies in southern France, and a very old-looking volume on European vampire lore.

Among the books lay papers, including notes in his own hand, and among these a scattering of postcards in a hand completely unfamiliar to me, a fine dark ink, neat and minute. Barley and I began of one accord — again, how glad I was not to be alone — to search through everything, and my first instinct was to gather up the postcards. They were ornamented with stamps from a rainbow of countries: Portugal, France, Italy, Monaco, Finland, Austria. The stamps were pristine, without postmarks. Sometimes the message on a card ran over onto four or five more, neatly numbered. Most astonishingly, each was signed "Helen Rossi." And each was addressed to me.

Barley, looking over my shoulder, took in my astonishment, and we sat down together on the edge of the bed. The first was from Rome — a black-and-white photograph of the skeletal remains of the Forum.

May 1962

My beloved daughter:
 In what language should I write to you, the child of my heart and my body, whom I have not seen in more than five years? We should have been speaking together all this time, a no-language of small sounds and kisses, glances, murmuring. It is so difficult for me to think about, to remember what I have missed, that I have to stop writing today, when I have only started trying.

Your loving mother,
Helen Rossi

The second was a color postcard, already fading, of flowers and urns — *"Jardins de Boboli —* The Gardens of Boboli — Boboli."

May 1962

My beloved daughter:
 I will tell you a secret: I hate this English. English is an exercise in grammar, or a class in

literature. In my heart, I feel I could speak best with you in my own language, Hungarian, or even in the language that flows inside my Hungarian — Romanian. Romanian is the language of the fiend I am seeking, but even that has not spoiled it for me. If you were sitting on my lap this morning, looking out at these gardens, I would teach you a first lesson: "Ma numesc . . ." And then we would whisper your name over and over in the soft tongue that is your mother tongue, too. I would explain to you that Romanian is the language of brave, kind, sad people, shepherds and farmers, and of your grandmother, whose life he ruined from a distance. I would tell you the beautiful things she told me, the stars at night above her village, the lanterns on the river. "Ma numesc . . ." Telling you about that would be unbearable happiness for one day.

> *Your loving mother,*
> *Helen Rossi*

Barley and I looked at each other, and he put his arm softly around my neck.

Chapter 64

"WE FOUND STOICHEV in a state of excitement at the library table. Ranov sat across from him, drumming his fingers and occasionally glancing at a document as the old scholar set it aside. He looked as irritated as I'd seen him yet, which suggested that Stoichev hadn't been answering his questions. When we came in, Stoichev looked up eagerly. 'I think I've got it,' he said in a whisper. Helen sat down next to him and I leaned over the manuscripts he was examining. They were similar to Brother Kiril's letters in design and execution, written in a beautifully close, neat hand on leaves that were faded and crumbling at the edges. I recognized the Slavonic script from the letters. Next to them he had laid out our maps. I found myself hardly breathing, hoping against hope that he would tell us something of real import. Perhaps the tomb was even here at Rila, I thought suddenly — perhaps that's why Stoichev insisted on coming here, because he suspected as much. I was surprised and uneasy, though, that he wanted to make any announcement in front of Ranov.

"Stoichev looked around, glanced at Ranov, rubbed his wrinkled forehead with his hand, and said in a low voice, 'I believe the tomb is not in Bulgaria.'

"I felt the blood drain out of my head. 'What?' Helen was looking fixedly at Stoichev, and Ranov turned away from us, drumming his fingers on the table as if only half listening.

"'I am sorry to disappoint you, my friends, but it is clear to me from this manuscript, which I had not examined in many years, that a group of pilgrims traveled back to Wallachia from Sveti Georgi about 1478. This manuscript is a customs document — it gave them permission to take some kind of Christian relics of Wallachian origin back to Wallachia. I am sorry. Perhaps you will be able to travel there one day to examine further this issue. If you would like to continue your research on the routes of pilgrims in Bulgaria, however, I will be happy to assist you.'

"I stared at him, speechless. We could not possibly get into Romania after all this, I thought. It had been a miracle that we had gotten this far.

"'I recommend that you acquire permission to see some other monasteries and the routes on which they are located, particularly the Bachkovo Monastery. It is a beautiful example of our Bulgarian Byzantinism and the buildings are much older than those of Rila. Also, they have some very rare manuscripts that monks on pilgrimage brought to the monastery as gifts. It will be interesting for you, and you can gather in that way some material for your articles.'

"To my amazement, Helen seemed completely acquiescent with this plan. 'Could this be arranged, Mr. Ranov?' she asked. 'Perhaps Professor Stoichev would like to accompany us, as well.'

"'Oh, I am afraid I must return to my home,' Stoichev said regretfully. 'I have much work to do. I wish I could be there to help you at Bachkovo, but I can send a letter of introduction with you for the abbot. Mr. Ranov can be your interpreter, and the abbot will help you with any translations of manuscripts you wish to make. He is a fine scholar of the history of the monastery.'

"'Very well.' Ranov looked pleased to hear that Stoichev would be leaving us. There was nothing we could say about this terrible situation, I thought; we had to simply go through with a pretense at research at another monastery, and decide along the way what to do next. Romania? The image of Rossi's door at the university rose up before me once more: it was closed, locked.

Rossi would never open it again. I followed numbly as Stoichev put the manuscripts back in their box and shut the lid. Helen carried it to a shelf for him and helped him out the door. Ranov trailed us in silence — a silence I took to contain some gloating. Whatever we'd actually come to find was beyond us now, and we would be left alone with our guide again. Then he could get us to finish up our research and leave Bulgaria as soon as possible.

"Irina had apparently been in the church; she drifted toward us across the hot courtyard as we emerged, and at the sight of her Ranov turned aside to smoke in one of the galleries, then strolled toward the main gate and disappeared through it. I thought I saw him walk a little faster as he reached the gate; perhaps he needed a break from us, too. Stoichev sat heavily down on a wooden bench near the gate, with Irina's protective hand on his shoulder. 'Look here,' he said very quietly, smiling up at us as if we were just chatting. 'We must talk quickly while our friend cannot hear us. I did not mean to frighten you. There is no document about a pilgrimage back to Wallachia with some relics. I am sorry to say that I was lying. Vlad Dracula is certainly buried at Sveti Georgi, wherever that is, and I have found something very important. In the "Chron-icle," Stefan said Sveti Georgi was close to Bachkovo. I could not see any relationship be-tween the Bachkovo area and the maps you have, but there is a letter here from the abbot of Bachkovo to the abbot of Rila, from the early six-teenth century. I did not dare to show it to you in front of our companion. This letter states that the abbot of Bachkovo no longer needs assis-tance from the abbot of Rila or any other clerics in suppressing the heresy at Sveti Georgi, be-cause the monastery has been burned and its monks scattered. He warns the abbot of Rila to keep a close watch for any monks from there, or any monks who might spread the idea that the dragon has slain Sveti Georgi — Saint George — because this is the sign of their heresy.'

"'The dragon has slain — wait,' I said. 'You mean that line about the monster and the saint? Kiril said they were looking for a monastery with a sign that the saint and the monster were equal.'

"'Saint George is one of our most important figures in Bulgarian iconography,' Stoichev said quietly. 'It would be a strange reversal indeed for the dragon to overcome Saint George. But you re-member that the Wallachian monks were looking for a monastery that already had that sign, because that would be the correct place to bring Dracula's body to reunite it with his head. Now I am beginning to wonder if there was a larger heresy we do not know about — one that might have been known in Constantinople, or Wallachia, or even by Dracula himself. Did the Order of the Dragon have its own spiritual beliefs, outside the order of the Church? Could it have created a heresy somehow? I have never thought of such a possibility before today.' He shook his head. 'You must go to Bachkovo and ask the abbot there if he knows anything about this equality or reversal of monster and saint. You must ask him in secret. My letter to him — which your guide will take from you and read — will imply only that you wish to do research about pilgrimage routes, but you must find a way to talk with him in secret. Also, there is a monk there who used to be a scholar, a noted investigator of the history of Sveti Georgi. He worked with Atanas Angelov and was the second person to see the "Chronicle" of Zacharias. His name was Pondev when I knew him, but I do not know what it is now that he is a monk. The abbot can help you identify him. There is something else. I do not have here a map of the area near Bachkovo, but I believe that to the northeast of the monastery somewhere there is a long, winding valley that probably once contained a river. I remember seeing this once and speaking with the monks about it when I visited the region, although I do not remember now what they called it. Could this be our dragon's tail? But what, then, would be the wings of the dragon? Perhaps the mountains? You must look for them, also.'

"I wanted to kneel before Stoichev and kiss his foot. 'But won't you come with us?'

"'I would defy even my niece to do that,' he replied, smiling up at her, 'but I fear it would only raise more suspicion. If your guide thinks that I am still interested in this research, he will be even more attentive. Come to see me as soon as you return to Sofia, if you can. I will think of you all the time and wish for your safe journey and the discovery of what you seek. Here — you must take this.' He put into Helen's hand a little object, but she closed her fingers quickly over it, and I didn't see what it was or where she'd put it.

"'Mr. Ranov has been gone a long time, for him,' she observed softly.

"I looked quickly at her. 'Shall I go check on him?' I had learned to trust Helen's instincts, and

I walked to the main gate without waiting for an answer.

"Just outside the great complex, I saw Ranov standing with another man near a long blue car. The other fellow was tall and graceful in his summer suit and hat, and something about him made me stop short in the shadow of the gate. They were in the middle of an earnest discussion, which broke off suddenly. The handsome man gave Ranov a slap on the back and swung into the seat of the car. I felt the jolt of that friendly cuff, myself — I knew that gesture — it had landed on my own shoulder once. Surely, incredible as it seemed, the man now driving swiftly out of the dusty parking area was Géza József. I shrank back into the courtyard and returned to Helen and Stoichev as quickly as I could. Helen eyed me keenly; perhaps she was learning to trust my instincts, too. I drew her aside for a moment, and Stoichev, although he looked puzzled, was too polite to question me. 'I think József is here,' I whispered quickly. 'I didn't see his face, but someone who looked like him was talking with Ranov just now.'

"'Shit,' Helen said softly. I think that was the first and last time I ever heard her swear.

"A moment later, Ranov came hurrying up. 'It is time for supper,' he said flatly, and I wondered if he was regretting having left us alone with Stoichev for a few minutes. I felt sure from his tone that he hadn't seen me outside. 'Come with me. We will eat.'

"The silent monastery supper was delicious, a homemade meal served by two monks. A handful of tourists was apparently staying in the hostel with us, and I noted that some of them spoke languages other than Bulgarian. The German-speakers must be on vacation from East Germany, I thought, and perhaps that other sound was Czech. We ate greedily, sitting at a long wooden table, with the monks lined up at another table nearby, and I anticipated with pleasure the narrow cots that awaited us. Helen and I had no moment alone, but I knew she must be thinking about József's presence. What did he want with Ranov? Or, rather, what did he want from us? I remembered Helen's warning that we were being followed. Who had told him where we were?

It had been an exhausting day, but I was so anxious to get to Bachkovo that I would gladly have set out on foot if that could have gotten me there faster. Instead we would sleep, to prepare for the next day's travel. Mingled with the snores from East Berlin and Prague, I would hear Rossi's voice musing over some controversial point in our work, and Helen saying, half amused at my lack of perspicacity, 'Of course I will marry you.'"

Chapter 65

June 1962

My beloved daughter:
We are wealthy, you know, because of some terrible things that happened to me and your father. I left most of that money with your father, for your care, but I have enough to last me through a long search, a siege. I exchanged some of it in Zurich almost two years ago, and opened a bank account there under a name I will never tell anyone. My bank account is deep. I draw from that money once a month, to pay for the rented rooms, the archival fees, the meals in restaurants. I spend as little as possible so that one day I can give to you everything that remains, my little one, when you are a woman.

Your loving mother,
Helen Rossi

ELIZABETH KOSTOVA

June 1962

My beloved daughter:

Today was one of the bad days. (I will never send this card. If I ever send any of them, it will not be this one.) Today was one of the days when I cannot remember if I am seeking this devil or simply running from him. I stand before the mirror, an old mirror in my room at the Hotel d'Este; the glass has spots like moss, creeping up its curved surface. I pull off my scarf, I stand here and finger the scar on my neck, a redness that never fully heals. I wonder if you will find me before I can find him. I wonder if he will find me before I can find him. I wonder why he has not found me already. I wonder if I will ever see you again.

Your loving mother,
Helen Rossi

August 1962

My beloved daughter:

When you were born, your hair was black and stuck to your slimy head in curls. After they washed and dried you, it became a soft down around your face, dark hair like mine, but also coppery like your father's. I lay in a

The Historian

*pool of morphine, and held you and watched
the lights in your newborn hair change from
Gypsy dark to bright, and then back to dark.
Everything about you was polished and shone;
I had shaped and polished you inside me without knowing what I was doing. Your fingers
were golden, your cheek was rose, your eyelashes and eyebrows were the feathers of the
baby crow. My happiness overflowed even the
morphine.*

Your loving mother,
Helen Rossi

Chapter 66

"I WOKE EARLY in my cot in the men's dormitory at Rila; sunshine was just beginning to come through the small windows, which looked out on the courtyard, and some of the other tourists were still sound asleep on the other cots. I'd heard the earliest call of the church bell, in the dark, and now that bell was tolling again. My first thought on waking this time was that Helen had said she would marry me. I wanted to see her again, to see her as soon as possible, to find a moment to ask her if yesterday had been a dream. The sunshine that filled the courtyard outside was an echo of my sudden happiness, and the morning air seemed to me unbelievably fresh, full of centuries of freshness.

"But Helen was not at breakfast. Ranov was there, sullen as ever, smoking, until a monk asked him gently to go outside with his cigarette. As soon as the meal was over, I went along the corridor to the women's row, where Helen and I had parted the night before, and found the door standing open. The other women, the Czechs and Germans, had gone, leaving their beds neatly made. Helen was still asleep, apparently; I could see her form in the cot nearest the window. She was turned toward the wall, and I stepped in, silently, reasoning that she was my fiancée now, and I had the right to kiss her good morning, even in a monastery. I closed the door behind me, hoping no monks would happen by.

"Helen lay with her back to the room, on a cot near the window. When I drew closer, she rolled slightly in my direction, as if sensing my presence. Her head was tipped back, her eyes closed, her dark curls spread over the pillow. She was deeply asleep and an audible, almost stertorous breathing came from her lips. I thought she must have been tired after our travels and our walk of the day before, but something about the very abandon of her attitude made me step closer, uneasy. I bent over her, thinking I would kiss her even before she awoke, and then in a single terrible moment I saw the greenish pallor of her face and the fresh blood on her throat. Where the nearly healed wound had been, in the deepest part of her neck, two small gashes oozed, red and open. There was a little blood on the edge of the white sheet, too, and more on the sleeve of her cheap-looking white gown, where she'd thrown one arm back in her sleep.

The front of her gown was pulled askance and slightly torn, and one of her breasts was bare almost to the dark nipple. I saw all this in a frozen instant, and my heart seemed to stop beating inside me. Then I reached down and drew the sheet gently over her nakedness, as if covering a child for sleep. I couldn't think of any other motion, at that moment. A thick sob filled my throat, a rage I didn't yet quite feel.

"'Helen!' I shook her shoulder gently, but her face did not change. I saw now how haggard she looked, as if she were in pain even in her sleep. Where was the crucifix? I remembered it suddenly, and looked all around. I found it by my foot; the narrow chain was broken. Had someone torn it off, or had she broken it herself in sleep? I shook her again. 'Helen, wake up!'

"This time she stirred, but fretfully, and I wondered if I might somehow harm her by bringing her to consciousness too quickly. After a second, however, she opened her eyes, frowning. Her movements were very feeble. How much blood had she lost during this night, this night when I'd been sleeping soundly in the next corridor? Why had I left her alone, then or on any night?

"'Paul,' she said, as if puzzled. 'What are you doing here?' Then she seemed to struggle to sit up and discovered the disarray of her gown. She put her hand to her throat, while I watched in a speechless anguish, and drew it slowly away. There was sticky, drying blood on her fingers. She stared at them, and at me. 'Oh, God,' she said. She sat upright and I felt a first hint of relief, despite the horror in her face; if she'd lost a lot of blood, she would've been too weak for even that much action. 'Oh, Paul,' she whispered. I sat down on the edge of the bed and took her other hand in mine and gripped it hard.

"'Are you completely awake?' I said.

"She nodded.

"'And you know where you are?'

"'Yes,' she said, but then she put her head down over her bloody hand and broke into harsh low sobs, a horrifying sound. I had never before heard her cry out loud. The sound went through my body like a wave of bitter cold.

"'I'm here.' I kissed her clean hand.

"She squeezed my fingers, weeping, then tried to gather herself. 'We must think what — is that my crucifix?'

"'Yes.' I held it up, watching her carefully, but to my infinite relief there was no sign of recoil in her face. 'Did you remove it?'

"'No, of course not.' She shook her head and a

leftover tear rolled down her cheek. 'And I don't remember breaking it. I don't think they — he — would dare to, if the legend is accurate.' She was wiping her face now, keeping her hand carefully clear of the wound on her throat. 'I must have broken it while I slept.'

"'I think so, judging from where I found it.' I showed her the spot on the floor. 'And it doesn't make you feel — uncomfortable — to have it near you?'

"'No,' she said wonderingly. 'At least, not *yet*.' The cold little word made me catch my breath.

She reached out and touched the crucifix, at first hesitantly, and then took it in her hand. I let out my breath. Helen sighed, too. 'I fell asleep thinking about my mother, and about an article I would like to write on the figures in Transylvanian embroidery — they are famous, you know — and then I didn't wake until now.' She frowned. 'I had a bad dream, but my mother was mixed all through it, and she was — shooing away a great black bird. When she had frightened it away, she bent over and kissed my forehead, as she used to when I was a little girl going to sleep, and I saw the mark' — she paused, as if thinking pained her a little — 'I saw the mark of the dragon on her bare shoulder, but it seemed to me just a part of her, not something terrible. And when I received her kiss on my forehead, I was not so afraid.'

"I felt the prickle of a strange awe, remembering the night I had apparently kept my cat's destroyer at bay in my apartment by reading through midnight about the lives of the Dutch merchants I had come to love. Something had protected Helen, too, at least to some degree; she had been cruelly injured but not drained of blood. We looked silently at each other.

"'This could have been much worse,' she said.

"I put my arms around her and felt the trembling of her usually firm shoulders. I was shaking, myself. 'Yes,' I whispered. 'But we must guard you from anything else.'

"She shook her head, suddenly, as if in wonder. 'And this is a monastery! I can't understand it. The undead abhor such a place.' She pointed to the cross over the door, the icon and holy lamp hanging in the corner. 'Here in the sight of the Virgin?'

"'I don't understand it, either,' I said slowly, turning her hand over in mine. 'But we know that monks traveled with Dracula's remains, and that he was probably buried in a monastery. There is something strange in that already. Helen' — I squeezed her hand — 'I've been thinking about something else. The librarian from home — he found us in Istanbul and then in Budapest. Couldn't he have followed us here, too? Could he have attacked you last night?'

"She winced. 'I know. He bit me once in the library, so he might want me again, might he not? But I felt strongly in my dream it was something else — someone much more powerful. But how could one of them get in, even if he was not afraid of a monastery?'

"'That part is simple.' I pointed to the nearest window, which stood slightly ajar five feet from Helen's cot. 'Oh, God, why did I let you stay here alone?'

"'I was not alone,' she reminded me. 'There were five other people sleeping in the room with me. But you are right — he can change shape, as my mother said — a bat, a mist —'

"'Or a great black bird.' Her dream had sprung up in my mind again.

"'Now I have been bitten twice, more or less,' she said, almost dreamily.

"Helen!' I shook her. 'I will never let you be alone again, not for an hour.'

"'Never an hour to myself?' Her old smile, sarcastic and loving, returned for a moment.

"'And I want you to promise me — if you feel something I can't feel, if you feel something looking for you —'

"'I will tell you, Paul, if I feel anything like that at all.' She spoke fiercely now, and her promise seemed to rouse her to action. 'Come, please. I need food and I need some red wine or brandy, if we can find it. Bring me a towel, there, and the basin — I will wash my neck and bind it.' Her passionate practicality was contagious and I obeyed at once. 'Later we will go in the church and clean this wound with the holy water, when no one is looking. If I can tolerate that, we can hope a great deal. How strange' — I was glad to see her cynical smile again — 'I have always felt all this church ritual is nonsense, and I still do.'

"'But apparently he does not think it is nonsense,' I said soberly.

"I helped her sponge off her throat, taking care not to touch the open lesions, and watched the door while she dressed. The sight of the wound up close was so terrible to me that I thought for a minute I would have to leave the room and give way to my tears outside. But although Helen moved weakly, I could see the set determination in her face. She tied on her customary scarf and found a piece of string in her baggage with which to make a new chain for the crucifix — this one stronger, I hoped. Her sheets were hopelessly stained, but only in small spots. 'We will let the monks think — well, that there have been women in their dormitory,' Helen said in her forthright way. 'It is surely not the first time they will have washed out some blood.'"

"By the time we emerged from the church, Ranov was lounging in the courtyard. He narrowed his eyes at Helen. 'You have slept very late,' he said accusingly. I looked carefully at his eyeteeth when he spoke, but they didn't appear any sharper than usual; if anything, they were ground down and gray in his unpleasant smile."

Chapter 67

"I HAD FOUND IT exasperating that Ranov had been so reluctant to take us to Rila, but it was far more disturbing to see his enthusiasm about taking us to Bachkovo. During the car ride, he pointed out all kinds of sights, many of which were interesting in spite of his running commentary on them. Helen and I tried not to look at each other, but I was sure she felt the same miserable apprehension. Now we had József to worry about, too. The road from Plovdiv was narrow, and it curved along a rocky stream on one side and steep cliffs on the other. We were making our way gradually into mountains again — in Bulgaria, you could never be far from mountains. I remarked on this to Helen, who was gazing out the opposite window in the backseat of Ranov's car, and she nodded. '*Balkan* is a Turkish word for *mountain*.'"

"The monastery had no grand entrance — we simply pulled off the road into a dirt lot, and from there it was a short walk to the monastery gate. *Bachkovski manastir* sat among high barren hills, partly forested and partly bare rock, close to the narrow river; even in early summer, the landscape was already dry, and I could easily imagine how the monks must have valued that nearby source of water. The outer walls were the same dun-colored stone as the hills around them. The monastery roofs were fluted red ceramic tile, like that I'd seen on Stoichev's old house and on hundreds of houses and churches along the roadsides. The entrance to the monastery was a yawning archway, as perfectly dark as a hole in the ground. 'Can we simply walk in?' I asked Ranov.

"He shook his head, meaning yes, and we stepped into the cool darkness of the arch. It took us a few seconds of slow progress to make our way into the sunny courtyard, and during those moments inside the monastery's deep wall, I could hear nothing but our footsteps.

"Maybe I'd expected another grand public space, like that at Rila; the intimacy and beauty of the main courtyard at Bachkovo brought a sigh to my lips, and Helen murmured something aloud, too. The monastery church filled much of the courtyard, and its towers were red, angular, Byzantine. There were no gold domes here, only an ancient elegance — the simplest materials arranged in harmonious forms. Vines grew on the church towers; trees nestled against them; one magnificent cypress rose like a steeple. Three monks in black robes and hats stood talking outside the church. The trees threw patches of shade on the brilliant sun of the yard, and a soft breeze had come up, moving the leaves. To my surprise, chickens ran here and there, scratching the antique paving stones, and a striped kitten was chasing something into a crevice in the wall.

"As at Rila, the inside walls of the monastery were long balconied galleries, stone and wood. The stone lower wall of some of the galleries, like the portico of the church, was covered in faded frescoes. Apart from the three monks, the chickens, and the kitten, there was no one in sight. We were alone there, alone in Byzantium.

"Ranov went up to the monks and engaged them in conversation while Helen and I hung back a little. After a second he returned. 'The abbot is away, but the librarian is here and can help us.' I didn't like that *us,* but I said nothing. 'You can look in the church while I go find him.'

"'We will come with you,' Helen said firmly, and we all followed one of the monks into the galleries. The librarian was working in a room on the first floor; he rose from his desk to greet us as we entered. The space was bare, except for an iron stove and a bright rug on the floor. I wondered where the books were, the manuscripts. Apart from a couple of volumes on the wooden desk, I saw no sign of a library here.

"'This is Brother Ivan,' Ranov explained. The monk bowed to us without offering his hand; in fact, his hands were tucked out of sight in his long sleeves, crossed over his body. It occurred to me that he didn't want to touch Helen. The same thing must have occurred to Helen, because she backed away and stood almost behind me. Ranov exchanged a few words with him. 'Brother Ivan asks you to please sit down.' We sat obediently. Brother Ivan had a long, serious face above his beard, and he studied us for a few minutes. 'You may ask him some questions,' Ranov said encouragingly.

"I cleared my throat. There was no help for it; we were going to have to ask our questions in front of Ranov. I would have to try to make them sound purely scholarly. 'Would you ask Brother Ivan for us if he knows anything about pilgrims coming here from Wallachia?'

"Ranov put this question to the monk, and at the word *Wallachia*, Brother Ivan's face brightened. 'He says the monastery had an important connection with Wallachia beginning at the end of the fifteenth century.'

"My heart began to pound, although I tried to sit quietly. 'Yes? What was that?'

"They conversed a little further, Brother Ivan waving a long hand toward the door. Ranov nodded. 'He says that around that time the princes of Wallachia and Moldova began to give much support to this monastery. There are manuscripts in the library here that describe their support.'

"'Does he know why they did this?' Helen asked quietly.

"Ranov questioned the monk. 'No,' he said. 'He only knows these manuscripts show their support.'

"'Ask him,' I said, 'if he knows of any groups of pilgrims coming here from Wallachia around that time.'

"Brother Ivan actually smiled. 'Yes,' Ranov reported. 'There were many. This was an important stop on the pilgrimage routes from Wallachia. Many pilgrims went on from here to Athos or to Constantinople.'

"I could have ground my teeth. 'But a particular group of pilgrims from Wallachia, carrying a —

some kind of relic, or searching for some relic —
does he know any such story?'

"Ranov seemed to be holding back a triumphant smile. 'No,' he said. 'He has not seen
any account of such pilgrims. There were many
pilgrims during that century. *Bachkovski manastir* was very important then. The patriarch of
Bulgaria was exiled here from his office in Veliko Trnovo, the old capital, when the Ottomans
captured the country. He died here in 1404 and
was buried here. The oldest part of the monastery,
and the only part that is original, is the ossuary.'

"Helen spoke up again. 'Could you ask him,
please, if he has a monk among the brothers
here who used to be named Pondev?'

"Ranov relayed the question, and Brother Ivan
looked puzzled, then wary. 'He says that must be
old Brother Angel. He used to be named Vasil
Pondev, and he was an historian. But he is not —
right in the head — anymore. You will not learn
anything from speaking with him. The abbot is
our great scholar now, and it is a shame that he
is away while you are here.'

"'We'd still like to talk with Brother Angel,' I
told Ranov. And so it was arranged, although
with much frowning on the part of the librarian,
who led us back out into the glowing sunlight of

the courtyard and through a second arched entryway. This brought us into another courtyard, which had a very old building in the center. This second courtyard was not as well-tended as the first, and the buildings and paving stones had a crumbling, derelict look. There were weeds underfoot, and I noted a tree growing from the corner of the roof; in time, it would be large enough to destroy that end of the structure, if they let it stay. I could easily imagine that repairing this house of God was not the Bulgarian government's highest priority. They had Rila as their showcase, with its 'pure' Bulgarian history and its connections to rebellion against the Ottomans. This ancient place, beautiful as it was, had taken root under the Byzantines, invaders and occupiers like the later Ottomans, and it had been Armenian, Georgian, Greek — hadn't we just heard that it had also been independent under the Ottomans, unlike the other Bulgarian monasteries? No wonder the government let trees grow out of its roofs.

"The librarian took us into a corner room. 'The infirmary,' Ranov explained. This cooperative version of Ranov was making me more nervous by the hour. The librarian opened a rickety wooden door, and inside we saw a scene of such pathos that I don't really like to remember it. Two old monks were housed there. The room was furnished only with their cots, a single wooden chair, and an iron stove; even with that stove the place must have been bitterly cold during the mountain winters. The floor was stone, the walls bare whitewash except for a shrine in one corner: hanging lamp, elaborately carved shelf, tarnished icon of the Virgin.

"One of the old men was lying on his cot and did not look at us as we entered. I saw after a moment that his eyes were permanently closed, swollen and red, and that he turned his chin from time to time as if trying to see with it. He was mostly covered with a white sheet, and one of his hands fumbled with the edge of the cot, as if to find the limit of space, the point where he might roll off if he wasn't careful, while his other hand fumbled with the loose flesh of his own neck.

"The more functional resident of the room was upright in the only chair, a staff leaning against the wall near him as if his journey from the cot to the seat had been a long one. He was dressed in black robes, which hung unbelted over a protruding belly. His eyes were open, and hugely blue, and they turned on us with uncanny seeing as we entered. His whiskers and hair stuck out like white weeds all around him, and his head was bare. Somehow this made him look more ill and anomalous than anything else did, this uncovered head in a world in which all monks wore their tall black hats constantly. This bareheaded monk could have been an illustration for a prophet in some nineteenth-century Bible, except that his expression was anything but visionary. He wrinkled his big nose upward as if we smelled bad, and chewed the corners of his mouth, and narrowed and widened his eyes every few minutes. I couldn't have said whether he looked fearful, or sneering, or diabolically amused, because his expression shifted constantly. His body and hands reposed in the shabby chair, as if all the motions they might have made had been sucked upward into his twitching face. I looked away.

"Ranov was talking with the librarian, who gestured around the room. 'This man in the chair is Pondev,' Ranov said flatly. 'The librarian warns us that we will receive very little normal speech from him.' Ranov approached the man cautiously, as if he thought Brother Angel might bite, and looked into his face. Brother Angel — Pondev — swung his head around to look at him, the imitative gesture of an animal in a zoo cage.

Ranov seemed to be making a stab at introductions, and after a second Brother Angel's surreally blue eyes wandered to our faces. His own face wrinkled and twitched. Then he spoke, and the words came in a rush, followed by a grinding tangle, a growl. One of his hands went up into the air and made a sign that could have been half a cross or an attempt to keep us away.

"'What's he saying?' I asked Ranov in a low voice.

"'Only nonsense,' said Ranov with interest. 'I have never heard anything like it. It seems to be partly prayers — something superstitious from their liturgy — and partly about the Sofia trolley system.'

"'Can you try asking him a question? Tell him we are historians like him and we want to know if a group of pilgrims came here from Wallachia by way of Constantinople in the late fifteenth century, carrying a holy relic.'

"Ranov shrugged but made the attempt, and Brother Angel responded with a snarl of syllables, shaking his head. Did that mean yes or no? I wondered. 'More nonsense,' Ranov noted. 'This time it sounds like something about the invasion of Constantinople by the Turks, so at least he understood that much.'

"Suddenly the old man's eyes seemed to clear, as if their crystalline focus had really taken us in for the first time. In the midst of his strange flow of sounds — language, was it? — I distinctly heard the name *Atanas Angelov.*

"'Angelov!' I cried, speaking directly to the old monk. 'Did you know Atanas Angelov? Do you remember working with him?'

"Ranov listened with care. 'It is still mostly nonsense, but I will try to tell you what he is saying. Listen carefully.' He began to translate, quickly and dispassionately; much as I disliked him, I had to admire his skill. "I worked with Atanas Angelov. Years ago, maybe centuries. He was crazy. Turn off that light over there — it hurts my legs. He wanted to know everything about the past, but the past does not want you to know her. She says no no no. She springs up and injures you. I wanted to take the number eleven, but that does not go to our neighborhood anymore. In any case, Comrade Dimitrov canceled the pay we were going to receive, for the good of the people. Good people."'

"Ranov took a breath, during which he must have missed something, since Brother Angel's flow of words continued. The old monk was still motionless in his chair from the neck down, but his head wagged and his face contracted. '"Angelov found a dangerous place, he found a place called Sveti Georgi, he heard the singing. That is where they buried a saint and danced on his grave. I can offer you some coffee, but it is only ground wheat, wheat and dirt. We don't even have any bread."'

"I knelt in front of the old monk and took his hand, although Helen seemed to want to hold me back. His hand was as limp as a dead fish, white and puffy, the nails yellow and weirdly long. 'Where is Sveti Georgi?' I pleaded. I felt that in another minute I might begin to cry, in front of Ranov and Helen and these two desiccated creatures in their prison.

"Ranov crouched next to me, trying to catch the monk's wandering eyes. *'K'de e Sveti Georgi?'* But Brother Angel had followed his own gaze into a faraway world again. '"Angelov went to Athos and saw the *typikon,* he went into the mountains and found the terrible place. I took the number eleven to his apartment. He said, 'Come quickly I have found out something. I am going back there to dig in the past.' I would give you some coffee, but it is only dirt. Oh, oh, he was dead in his room, and then his body was not in the morgue."' Brother Angel broke into a smile that made me back away. He had two teeth and his gums were ragged. The breath that spilled from his mouth would have killed the devil himself. He began to sing in a high, trembling voice.

The dragon came down our valley.
He burned the crops and took the maidens.
He frightened the Turkish infidel and
protected our villages.
His breath dried up the rivers and we walked
across them.

"As Ranov finished translating, Brother Ivan, the librarian, spoke up with some animation. He still had his hands in his sleeves, but his face was bright and interested. 'What's he saying?' I asked quickly.

"Ranov shook his head. 'He says he has heard this song before. He collected it from an old woman in the village of Dimovo, Baba Yanka, who is a great singer there, where the river dried up long ago. They have several festivals there where they sing these old songs, and she is the leader of the singers. One of these will be in two days, the festival of Saint Petko, and you may wish to hear her.'

"'More folk songs,' I groaned. 'Please ask Mr.

Pondev — Brother Angel — if he knows what this song means.'

"Ranov put the question with considerable patience, but Brother Ivan sat grimacing and twitching and said nothing. After a moment, the silence drove me to the very edge of my feelings. 'Ask him if he knows anything about Vlad Dracula!' I shouted. 'Vlad Ţepeş! Is he buried in this region? Has he ever heard that name? The name *Dracula?*' Helen had seized my arm, but I was beside myself. The librarian stared at me, although he seemed to feel no alarm, and Ranov gave me what I might have called a pitying look if I'd wanted to pay closer attention.

"But the effect on Pondev was horrifying. He turned very pale and his eyes rolled back in his head like great blue marbles. Brother Ivan leaped forward and grabbed him as he slumped from the chair, and he and Ranov managed to get him onto the cot. He was a clumsy mass, swollen white feet protruding from the bedclothes, arms dangling around their necks. When they had him safely prone, the librarian fetched water from a pitcher and trickled some on the poor man's face. I stood aghast; I hadn't meant to cause such anguish, and perhaps now I'd killed one of our only remaining sources of information. After an endless moment, Brother Angel stirred and opened his eyes, but now they were wild eyes, wary as a hunted beast's, and they flickered in terror around the room as if he couldn't see us at all. The librarian patted his chest and tried to make him more comfortable on the cot, but the old monk pushed his hands away, trembling. 'Let us leave him,' Ranov said somberly. 'He is not going to die — of this, at least.' We followed the librarian out of the room, all of us silent and chastened.

"'I'm sorry,' I said, in the reassuring brightness of the courtyard.

"Helen turned to Ranov. 'Could you ask the librarian if he knows anything more about that song, or what valley it came from?'

"Ranov and the librarian conferred, the librarian glancing at us. 'He says it comes from Krasna Polyana, the valley on the other side of those mountains, to the northeast. You may come with him to the saint's festival in two days if you wish to stay here. This old singer might know something about it — she will at least be able to tell you where she learned it.'

"'Do you think that would be helpful?' I murmured to Helen.

"She gave me a sober look. 'I don't know, but it is all we have. Since it mentions a dragon, we should pursue it. In the meantime, we can explore Bachkovo thoroughly, and perhaps use the library if this librarian will help us.'

"I sat wearily down on a stone bench at the edge of the galleries. 'All right,' I said."

Chapter 68

September 1962

My beloved daughter:

Damn this English! But when I try to write to you in Hungarian, a few lines, I know at once that you are not listening. You are growing up in English. Your father, who believes that I am dead, speaks to you in English as he swings you up onto his shoulder. He speaks to you in English as he puts your shoes on — you have been wearing real shoes for years now — and in English as he holds your hand in a park. But if I speak to you in English, I feel that you cannot hear me. I didn't write to you at all for a long time, because I could not hear you listening in any language. I know your father believes I am dead, because he has never tried to find me. If he had tried to, he would have succeeded. But he cannot hear me in any language.

Your loving mother,
Helen

May 1963

My beloved daughter:

I do not know how many times I have silently explained to you that in the first few months you and I were very happy together. The sight of you waking from your nap, your hands moving before any other part of you stirred, your dark lashes fluttering next, and then your stretching, your smiling, filled me completely. Then something happened. It was not something outside of me, not an external threat to you. It was something inside me. I began to search your perfect body over and over for some sign of injury. But the injury was to me, even before this puncture on my neck, and it would not quite heal. I became afraid to touch you, my perfect angel.

Your loving mother,
Helen

July 1963

My beloved daughter:

I seem to be missing you more than ever today. I am in the university archives in Rome. I have been here six times in the last two years.

The Historian

The guards know me, the archivists know me, the waiter at the café across the street from the archive knows me and would like to know me better if I didn't turn away coldly, pretending I don't see his interest. This archive contains records of a plague in 1517, whose victims developed only one sore, a red wound on the neck. The pope ordered them to be buried with stakes through their hearts and garlic in their mouths. In 1517. I am trying to make a map through time of his movements or — since it is impossible to tell the difference — the movements of his servants. This map, really a list in my notebook, already fills many pages. But what use I can put it to I do not know yet. While I work I am waiting to discover this.

Your loving mother,
Helen

September 1963

My beloved daughter:
    I am ready, almost, to give up and return to you. Your birthday is this month. How can I miss another birthday? I would return to you immediately, but I know that if I do, the same

thing will happen. I will feel my uncleanness, as I first did six years ago — I will feel the horror of it, I will see your perfection. How can I be near you knowing that I am tainted? What right do I have to touch your smooth cheek?

Your loving mother,
Helen

October 1963

My beloved daughter:

I am in Assisi. These astounding churches and chapels, climbing their hill, fill me with a sense of despair. We might have come here, you in your little dress and hat, and I, and your father, all of us holding hands, as tourists. Instead, I am working in the dust of a monastic library, reading a document from 1603. Two monks died here in December of that year. They were found in the snow with their throats only a little mutilated. My Latin has lasted very well, and my money buys any help I might need with interpreting, translating, laundering my dresses. As it does visas, passports, train tickets, a false identity card. I never had money when I was growing up. My mother, in the vil-

The Historian

lage, barely knew what it looked like. Now I am learning that it buys everything. No, not everything. Not everything I want.

Your loving mother,
Helen

Chapter 69

"THOSE TWO DAYS at Bachkovo were some of the longest of my life. I wanted to hurry to the promised festival immediately, wanted it to occur instantly, so that we could try to follow the one word of that song — *dragon* — to its nesting place. Yet I also dreaded the moment that I thought must inevitably come, when this possible clue, too, would vanish in smoke, or turn out to be related to nothing at all. Helen had already warned me that folk songs were notoriously slippery; their origins tended to be lost over centuries, their texts changed and evolved, their singers seldom knew where they'd come from or how old they were. 'That's what makes them folk songs,' she said wistfully, smoothing my shirt collar as we sat in the courtyard our second day at the monastery. She was not given to domestic little caresses like that one, so I knew she must be worried. My eyes burned and my head ached as I looked around the sunny cobbles where the chickens scratched. It was a beautiful place, a rare and for me exotic place, and here we were seeing its life flow on as it had since the eleventh century: the chickens looked for bugs, the kitten rolled near our feet, the brilliant light pulsed on the fine red-and-white stonework all around us. I could hardly feel its beauty anymore.

"On the second morning, I woke very early. I thought perhaps I'd heard the church bells ringing but couldn't decide if that had been part of my dream. From the window of my cell, with its rough curtain, I could see four or five monks making their way into the church. I put on my clothes — God, they were dirty now, but I could not be bothered with washing clothes — and went quietly down the gallery stairs to the courtyard. It was very early indeed, dusky outside, and the moon was setting over the mountains. I thought for a moment of entering the church and lingered near the door, which was open; from inside spilled candlelight and a smell of burning wax and incense, and the interior that looked profoundly dark at midday was warm and beckoning at this hour. I could hear the monks chanting. The melancholy swell of the sound went into my heart like a dagger. They had probably been doing just this, some dim morning in 1477 when Brothers Kiril and Stefan and the other monks had left the graves of their martyred friends — in the ossuary? — and set off through the mountains, guarding the treasure in their wagon. But which direction had they gone? I faced east, then west — where the moon was dropping out of sight very fast — then south.

"A breeze had begun to stir the leaves of the lindens, and after a few minutes I saw the first light of the sun reaching far across the slopes and over the monastery wall. Then, belatedly, a rooster crowed somewhere in the confines of the monastery. It would have been a moment of exquisite pleasure, the kind of immersion in history I'd always dreamed of, if I'd had the heart for it. I found myself turning slowly, willing myself to intuit the direction Brother Kiril had traveled. Somewhere out there was a tomb — maybe — whose location had been lost so long that even the knowledge of it had vanished. It might be a day's journey on foot, or three hours, or a week. 'Not much farther and without incident,' Zacharias had said. How far was not much farther? Where had they gone? The earth was stirring now — those forested mountains with their dusty outcroppings of rock, the cobbled courtyard under my feet and the monastery meadows and farm — but it kept its secret."

• • •

"At about nine that morning we set off in Ranov's car with Brother Ivan navigating in the
front seat. We took the road along the river for
about ten kilometers, and then the river seemed
to disappear, and the road followed a long, dry
valley, which looped precipitously around among
hills. The sight of this landscape jarred something in my memory. I nudged Helen and she
frowned at me. 'Helen, the river valley.'

"Her face cleared then, and she tapped Ranov
on the shoulder. 'Ask Brother Ivan where the
river went. Did we cross it somewhere?'

"Ranov spoke to Brother Ivan without turning
and reported back to us. 'He says the river dried
up here — it is behind us now, where we crossed
the last bridge. This was the river valley a long time
ago, but there is no more water in the valley.'
Helen and I looked silently at each other. Ahead
of us, at the end of the valley, I saw two peaks rising sharply out of the hills, two lone mountains
like angular wings. And between them, still far
off, we could see the towers of a little church.
Helen suddenly grasped my hand hard.

"A few minutes later we turned up a dirt track
into broad hills, obeying a sign for a village I'll

call Dimovo. Then the road narrowed and Ranov pulled up in front of the church, although Dimovo itself was nowhere in sight.

"The Church of Sveti Petko the Martyr was very small — a weathered stucco chapel — and it sat by itself in a meadow that might have been used for haying late in the season. Two crooked oak trees made a shelter above it, and next to it huddled a graveyard of a sort I hadn't seen before — peasant graves, some of them dating back to the eighteenth century, Ranov explained proudly. 'This is traditional — there are many such places where the rural workers are buried even today.' The grave markers were stone or wood, with a triangular cap at the top, and many had small lamps set at their bases. 'Brother Ivan says the ceremony will not begin until eleventhirty,' Ranov told us as we lingered there. 'They are preparing the church now. He will take us to visit Baba Yanka first, and then we will return to observe everything.' He gave us a hard look, as if to see what interested us most.

"'What's going on there?' I pointed to a group of men working in the field next to the church. Some were dragging wood — logs and great branches — into a pile, while others set down bricks and stones around them. They had already collected a vast arsenal from the forest.

"'Brother Ivan says that is for the fire. I had not realized this, but there will be walking in the fire.'

"'Fire walking!' Helen exclaimed.

"'Yes,' Ranov said flatly. 'You know of this custom? It is rare in Bulgaria in this modern era, and even rarer in this part of the country. I have heard of fire walking only in the Black Sea region. But this is a poor and superstitious area that the Party is still working to improve. I have no doubt such things will be eliminated eventually.'

"'I have heard of this.' Helen turned earnestly to me. 'It was a pagan custom, and it became a Christian one in the Balkans as the people were converted. Usually it is not so much walking as dancing. I am very glad we will get to watch such a thing.'

"Ranov shrugged and herded us away toward the church, but not before I'd seen one of the men working around the wood suddenly lean forward and ignite the pile. It caught quickly and blazed up, then spread, then began to roar. The wood was tinder dry and the flames soon reached the top of the pile, so that every branch glowed. Even Ranov stood still. The men who'd built it stepped back a few feet, then a few more, and stood wiping their hands on their trousers. With a rush the fire leaped fully to life. The flames were nearly as high as the roof of the church nearby, although far enough from it for safety. We watched the fire eating this enormous meal until Ranov turned away again. 'They will let it burn and die for the next few hours,' he said. 'Even the most superstitious would not dance in it now.'

"As we entered the church, a young man, apparently the priest, came forward to greet us. He shook our hands with a pleasant smile, and he and Brother Ivan bowed cordially to each other. 'He says he's honored to have you here for their saint's day,' Ranov reported a little dryly.

"'Tell him we are honored to be able to see the festival. Would you ask him who Sveti Petko is?'

"The priest explained that he was a local martyr, killed by the Turks during their occupation for his refusal to give up his faith. Sveti Petko had been the priest of an earlier church on this site, which the Turks had burned, and even after his church was destroyed he had refused to accept the Muslim faith. This church had been erected later and his relics interred in the old crypt. Today, many people would come to kneel there. His special icon, and two others of great power, would be carried in procession around the church and through the fire. Here was Sveti Petko, painted on the front wall of the church — he pointed to a faded fresco behind him, which showed a bearded face not unlike his own. We should come back and take a tour of the church when he had everything ready. We were welcome to see the whole ceremony and to receive the blessing of Sveti Petko. We would not be the first pilgrims from other lands who had come to him and been relieved of sickness or pain. The priest smiled sweetly at us.

"I asked him through Ranov if he had ever heard of a monastery called Sveti Georgi. He shook his head. 'The nearest monastery is *Bachkovski,*' he said. 'Sometimes monks from other monasteries have come here on pilgrimage, too, over the years — mostly long ago.' I took this to mean that pilgrimages had probably ceased since the communist takeover, and made a mental note to ask Stoichev about this when we got back to Sofia.

"'I will ask him to find Baba Yanka for us,' Ranov said after a moment. The priest knew exactly which house was hers. He wished he could go with us, but the church had been closed up for months — he came here only on holidays — so he and his assistant still had much to do.

"The village lay in a hollow just below the meadow where the church stood, and it was the smallest community I'd seen since coming to the East Bloc: no more than fifteen houses huddled almost fearfully together, with apple trees and flourishing vegetable gardens around the outskirts, dirt paths just wide enough for a wagon to drive through the middle, an ancient well with a wooden pole and bucket hanging over it. I was struck by the utter lack of modernity and found myself reading it for signs of the twentieth century. Apparently this century was not occurring there at all. I felt almost betrayed when I saw a white plastic bucket in the side yard of one of the stone houses. These houses seemed to have grown up out of piles of gray rock, their upper stories stuccoed as an afterthought, their roofs made of smooth slate shingles. Some of them boasted beautiful old half-timbered ornamentation that would have looked at home in a Tudor village.

"As we entered Dimovo's one street, people began to come out of their houses and barns to greet us — mainly old people, many of them gnarled almost beyond belief from hard labor, the women grotesquely bowlegged, the men hunched forward as if perpetually carrying an invisible sack of something heavy. Their faces were brown-skinned, red-cheeked — they smiled and called greetings, and I saw the flash of toothless gums or glinting metal in their mouths. At least they got some dental work, I thought, although it was hard to imagine where or how. A few of them came forward to bow to Brother Ivan, and he blessed them and seemed to be making inquiries among them. We walked to Baba Yanka's house in the midst of a small crowd, the youngest members of whom might have been seventy, although Helen told me later that these peasants were probably twenty years younger than they looked to me.

"Baba Yanka's house was a very small one, barely a cottage, and it leaned heavily against a little barn. She herself had made her way to her front door to see what was going on; my first glimpse of her was the bright spot of her red-flowered head scarf, then her striped bodice and apron. She peered out, looking at us, and some of the other villagers shouted her name, which made her nod her head rapidly. The skin of her face was mahogany, her nose and chin sharp, her eyes — as we came nearer and nearer — apparently brown but lost in folds of wrinkles.

"Ranov called out something to her — I could only hope it wasn't anything commanding or disrespectful — and after staring at us for a few minutes, she shut the wooden door. We waited quietly outside, and when it opened again I saw she was not as tiny as I'd imagined; she came solidly up to Helen's shoulder and her eyes were merry in a cautious face. She kissed Brother Ivan's hand and we shook hands with her, which seemed at first to confuse her. Then she shooed us into the house as if we'd been a pack of runaway chickens.

"Her house was very poor inside, but clean, and I noticed with a twinge of sympathy that she'd ornamented it with a vase of fresh wildflowers, which sat on the scratched, scrubbed table. Helen's mother's house had been a mansion compared to this neat, broken-down room with a ladder to the second floor nailed against one wall. I wondered how long Baba Yanka would be able to navigate the ladder, but she was moving around the room with so much energy that it slowly dawned on me that she was not actually old. I whispered this to Helen and Helen nodded. 'Fifty, perhaps,' she whispered back.

"This hit me with fresh force. My own mother, in Boston, was fifty-two, and she could have been this woman's granddaughter. Baba Yanka's hands were as gnarled as her feet were light; I watched her bring out cloth-covered dishes and set glasses before us and wondered what she'd done with those hands all her life to make them look like that. Felled trees, perhaps, chopped firewood, harvested crops, worked in cold and heat. She stole a glance or two at us as she worked, each glance accompanied by a quick smile, and finally poured us a beverage — something white and thick — which Ranov downed at once, nodding to her and wiping off his mouth with his handkerchief. I followed suit, but it almost killed me; the stuff was lukewarm and tasted distinctly of barnyard floor. I tried not to gag visibly while Baba Yanka twinkled at me. Helen drank hers with dignity and Baba Yanka patted her hand. 'Sheep's milk blended with water,' Helen told me. 'Think of it as a milk shake.'

"'I will ask her now if she will sing,' Ranov told us. 'That is what you want, is it not?' He conferred for a moment with Brother Ivan, who turned on Baba Yanka. The woman shrank back, nodding desperately. No, she would not sing; clearly, she didn't want to. She gestured at us and put her hands under her apron. But Brother Ivan was persistent.

"'We will ask her to sing whatever she wants to sing first,' Ranov explained. 'Then you may ask her about the song that interests you.'

"Baba Yanka appeared to have resigned herself, and I wondered if her whole protest had been a ritual of modesty, because she was already smiling again. She sighed, then drew her shoulders up under her worn, red-flowered blouse. She looked at us without guile and opened her mouth. The sound that came out was astonishing; first of all it was astonishingly loud, so that the glasses all but rattled on the table and the people outside the open door — half the village seemed to have gathered — stuck their heads in. It vibrated from the walls and under our feet and made her strings of onions and peppers sway above the battered stove. I took Helen's hand, secretly. First one note shook us, and then another, each long and slow, each a wail of deprivation and hopelessness. I remembered the maiden who leaped from a high cliff rather than be taken into the pasha's harem and wondered if this was a similar text. But strangely enough, Baba Yanka smiled with every note, breathing in huge sections of air, beaming at us. We listened in stunned silence until she suddenly ceased; the last note seemed to go on and on in the tiny house.

"'Please ask her to tell us the words,' Helen said.

"With some apparent struggle — which didn't diminish her smile — Baba Yanka recited the words of the song, and Ranov translated.

The hero lay dying at the top of the green mountain.
The hero lay dying with nine wounds in his side.
O, you falcon, fly to him and tell him his men are safe,
Safe in the mountains, all his men.
The hero had nine wounds in his side,
But it was the tenth that killed him.

"Baba Yanka clarified some point with Ranov when she was done, beaming still and shaking a finger at him. I had the feeling she would spank him and send him to bed without supper if he did anything wrong in her house. 'Ask her how old the song is,' Helen prompted him, 'and where she learned it.'

"Ranov put the question and Baba Yanka burst into peals of laughter, gesturing over her shoulder, waving her hands. Ranov actually grinned. 'She says it is as old as the mountains and not even her great-grandmother knew how old that was. She learned it from her great-grandmother, who lived to be ninety-three.'

"Next Baba Yanka had questions for us. When she fixed her eyes on us, I saw that they were wonderful eyes, almond shaped under the weathering of sun and wind, and golden brown, almost amber, made brighter by the red of her kerchief. She nodded, apparently in disbelief, when we told her we were from America.

"'*Amerika?*' She appeared to ponder this. 'That must be beyond the mountain.'

"'She's a very ignorant old woman,' Ranov amended. 'The government is doing its best to raise the standard of education here. It is an important priority.'

"Helen had gotten out a piece of paper and now she took the old woman's hand. 'Ask her if she knows a song like this — you will have to translate it for her. "The dragon came down our valley. He burned the crops and took the maidens."' Ranov passed this on to Baba Yanka. She listened attentively for a moment, and suddenly her face contracted with fear and displeasure;

she drew back in her wooden chair and crossed herself quickly. *'Ne!'* she said vehemently, withdrawing her hand from Helen's. *'Ne, ne.'*

"Ranov shrugged. 'You understand. She doesn't know it.'

"'Clearly she does,' I said quietly. 'Ask her why she is afraid to tell us about it.'

"This time the old woman looked stern. 'She won't talk about it,' Ranov said.

"'Tell her we will give her a reward.' Ranov's eyebrows went up again, but he put the offer to Baba Yanka. 'She says we must shut the door.' He got up and quietly closed the doors and wooden shutters, blocking out the spectators in the street. 'Now she will sing.'

"There couldn't have been a greater contrast between Baba Yanka's performance of the first song and her performance of this one. She seemed to shrink in her chair, huddling down in the seat and looking at the floor. Her jolly smile was gone, and her amber eyes fixed on our feet. The melody that came out of her was certainly a melancholy one, although the last line of the verse seemed to me to end on a defiant note. Ranov translated carefully. Why, I wondered again, was he being so helpful?

The dragon came down our valley.
He burned the crops and took the maidens.
He frightened the Turkish infidel and
protected our villages.
His breath dried up the rivers and we walked
across them.
Now we must defend ourselves.
The dragon was our protector,
But now we defend ourselves against him.

"'Well,' Ranov said. 'Is that what you wanted to hear?'

"'Yes.' Helen patted Baba Yanka's hand and the old woman broke out in a scolding voice. 'Ask her where this one is from and why she fears it,' Helen requested.

"Ranov needed a few minutes to sort through Baba Yanka's reproaches. 'She learned this song in secret from her great-grandmother, who told her never to sing it after dark. The song is an un-lucky song. It sounds lucky but it is unlucky. They do not sing it here except on Saint George's Day. That is the only day you can sing it safely, without bringing bad luck. She hopes you have not made her cow die in this way, or worse.'

"Helen smiled. 'Tell her I have a reward for her, a gift that takes away all bad luck and puts good luck in its place.' She opened Baba Yanka's worn hand and put a silver medallion in it. 'This belongs to a very devout and wise man and he sends it to you for your protection. It shows Sveti Ivan Rilski, a great Bulgarian saint.' I realized that this must be the little object Stoichev had put into Helen's hand. Baba Yanka looked at it for a moment, turning it on her rough palm, then raised it to her lips and kissed it. She tucked it into some secret compartment in her apron. *'Blagodarya,'* she said. She kissed Helen's hand, too, and sat fondling it as if she had found a long-lost daughter. Helen turned to Ranov again. 'Please just ask her if she knows what the song means and where it came from. And why do they sing it on Saint George's Day?'

"Baba Yanka shrugged at this. 'The song means nothing. It is just an unlucky old song. My great-grandmother told me that some people believed it came from a monastery. But that is not possible, because monks do not sing such songs — they sing the praises of God. We sing it on Saint George's Day because it invites Sveti Georgi to kill the dragon and end his torture of the people.'

"'What monastery?' I cried. 'Ask her if she knows of a monastery called Sveti Georgi, one that disappeared a long time ago.'

"But Baba Yanka only nodded — no — and clicked her tongue. 'There is no monastery here. The monastery is at Bachkovo. We have only the church, where I will sing with my sister this afternoon.'

"I groaned and made Ranov try one more time. This time he clicked his tongue too. 'She says she knows of no monastery. There has never been a monastery here.'

"'When is Saint George's Day?' I asked.

"'On May sixth.' Ranov stared me down. 'You have missed it by several weeks.'

"I was silent, but in the meantime Baba Yanka had cheered up again. She shook our hands and kissed Helen and made us promise to hear her singing that afternoon — 'It is much better with my sister. She sings the second voice.'

"We told her we would be there. She insisted on giving us some lunch, which she had been preparing when we came in; it was potatoes and a kind of gruel, and more of the sheep's milk, which I thought I might be able to get used to if I stayed a few months. We ate as gratefully as we could, praising her cooking, until Ranov told us we should go back to the church if we wanted to see the beginning of the service. Baba Yanka parted from us reluctantly, squeezing our hands and arms and patting Helen's cheeks.

"The fire next to the church had almost burned down now, although a few logs still flamed on top of the coals, pale in the bright afternoon sun. The villagers were already beginning to gather near the church, even before its bells began to ring. The bells rang and rang in the small stone tower at its peak, and then the young priest came to the door. He was dressed in red and gold now, with a long embroidered cape over his robes and a black shawl draped over his hat. He carried a smoking censer on a gold chain, which he swung in three directions outside the church door.

"The people gathered there — women dressed like Baba Yanka in stripes and flowers or in black from head to toe, and men in rough brown woolen vests and trousers, with white shirts tied or buttoned at their necks — fell back as the priest emerged. He came out among them, blessing them with the sign of the cross, and some of them bowed their heads or bent over in front of him. Behind him came an older man, dressed like a monk in plain black, whom I took to be his assistant. This man held an icon in his arms, which was draped with purple silk. I got a quick glimpse of it — a stiff, pale, dark-eyed visage. This must be Sveti Petko, I thought. The villagers followed the icon silently around the edge of the church in a streaming mass, many of them walking with canes or leaning on the arms of the younger ones. Baba Yanka found us and took my arm proudly, as if to show her neighbors what good connections she had. Everyone stared at us; it occurred to me that we were getting at least as much attention as the icon.

"The two priests led us in silence around the back of the church and along the other side, where we could see the fire ring at a short distance and smell the smoke that rose from it. The flames were dying down, unattended, the last great logs and branches already a deep orange, all of it settling into a mass of coals. We made this procession three times around the church, and then the priest halted again at the church porch and began to chant. Sometimes his elderly assistant answered him, and sometimes the congregation murmured a response, crossing themselves or bowing. Baba Yanka had let go of my arm, but she stayed close to us. Helen was watching everything with a keen interest, I saw, and so was Ranov.

"At the end of this outdoor ceremony, we followed the congregation into the church, which was dark as a tomb after the brilliance of the fields and groves. It was a small church, but the interior had a kind of exquisite scale the bigger churches we'd seen couldn't boast. The young priest had put the icon of Sveti Petko in a place of honor near the front, propped on a carved podium. I noticed Brother Ivan bowing before the altar. As usual, there were no pews; the people stood or knelt on the cold stone floor, and a few old women prostrated themselves in the center of the church. The side walls contained niches that were frescoed or housed icons, and in one of them yawned a dark opening that I thought must go down to the crypt. It was easy to imagine centuries of peasant worship here and in the older church that had stood here before this one.

"After what seemed like an eternity, the chanting ceased. The people bowed once more and began to drift out of the church, some of them stopping here and there to kiss icons or to light candles, which they placed in the iron candelabra near the entrance. The church bells began to ring and we followed the villagers outdoors again, where the sun and breeze and brilliant fields smote us without warning. A long table had been set out under some trees, and women were already uncovering dishes there and pouring something from ceramic pitchers. Then I saw there was a second fire pit on this side of the church, a small one, where a spitted lamb hung. Two men were cranking it around and around over the coals and the smell brought a primitive watering to my mouth. Baba Yanka filled our plates for us herself and took us to a blanket away from the crowd. There we met her sister, who looked just like her except taller and thinner, and we all gorged on the good food. Even Ranov, folding his legs in their city suit carefully on the woven blanket, seemed almost content. Other villagers stopped by to greet us and to ask Baba Yanka and her sister when they would be singing, an attention they waved away with the dignity of opera stars.

"When the lamb had been completely devoured and the women were scraping the dishes over a wooden bucket, I noticed that three men had brought out musical instruments and were preparing to play. One of them had the oddest instrument I had ever seen up close — a bag made of cleaned white animal skin with wooden pipes sticking out of it. It was clearly a kind of bagpipe, and Ranov told us that it was an ancient instrument in Bulgaria, the *gaida,* made of the skin of a goat. The old man who cradled it in his arms gradually blew it up like a great balloon; this process took a good ten minutes and he was bright red before he'd finished. He nestled it under his arm and puffed into one of the pipes and everyone cheered and applauded. It had the sound of an animal, too, a loud bleat, a shriek or squawk, and Helen laughed. 'You know,' she told me, 'there is a bagpipe in every herding culture in the world.'

"Then the old man began to play, and after a moment his friends joined him, one on a long wooden flute, whose voice swirled around us in a fluid ribbon, and the other beating a soft skin drum with a padded stick. Some of the women jumped up and formed a line, and a man with a white handkerchief, as we'd seen at Stoichev's, led them around the meadow. The people too old and infirm to dance sat smiling with their terrible teeth and empty gums, or patted the ground beside them, or tapped their canes.

"Baba Yanka and her sister stayed quietly where they were, as if their moment had not come. They waited until the flute player began to call for them, gesturing and smiling, and then until their audience joined the call, and then they feigned some reluctance, and finally they got up and went, hand in hand, to stand next to the musicians. Everyone fell quiet, and the *gaida* played a little introduction. The two old women began to sing, their arms twined around each other's waists now, and the sound they made — a stomach-churning harmony, harsh and beautiful — seemed to come from one body. The sound of the *gaida* grew up around it, and then the three voices, the voices of the two women and the goat, rose together and spread over us like the groaning of the earth itself. Helen's eyes were suddenly suffused with tears, which was so unlike her that I put my arm around her in front of everyone.

"After the women had sung five or six songs, with cheers in between from the crowd, everyone rose — at what signal, I couldn't tell, until I saw the priest approaching again. He carried the icon of Sveti Petko, now draped in red velvet, and behind him came two boys, each dressed in a dark robe and each carrying an icon completely covered in white silk. This procession made its way around to the other side of the church, the musicians walking behind it playing a somber melody, and halted between the church and the great fire ring. The fire had burned down completely now; only a circle of coals remained, infernally red and deep. Wisps of smoke rose up from it now and then as if something underneath were alive and breathing. The priest and his helpers stood by the church wall, holding their treasures in front of them.

"At last the musicians struck up a new tune — lively but somber at the same time, I thought — and one by one the villagers who could dance, or at least walk, fell into a long snaking line that made its way slowly around the fire. As the line wound around in front of the church, Baba Yanka and another woman — not her sister, this time, but an even more weather-beaten woman whose clouded eyes looked nearly blind — came forward and bowed to the priest and to the icons. They took their shoes and socks off and set them carefully by the church steps, kissed Sveti Petko's forbidding face, and received the priest's blessing. The priest's young helpers gave an icon to each woman, pulling off the silk covers. The music surged higher; the *gaida* player was sweating profusely, his face scarlet, his cheeks enormous.

"Next Baba Yanka and the woman with the clouded eyes danced forward, never losing their step, and then, while I held myself very still, watching, they danced barefoot into the fire. Each woman held her icon up in front of her as she entered the ring; each held her head high, staring with dignity into another world. Helen's hand tightened on mine until my fingers ached. Their feet rose and fell in the coals, brushing up living sparks; once I saw Baba Yanka's striped skirt smolder at the hem. They danced through embers to that mysterious rhythm of drum and bagpipe, and each went a different direction inside the circle of the fire.

"I hadn't been able to see the icons as they'd entered the ring, but now I noted that one, in the hands of the blind woman, showed the Virgin Mary, her child on her knee, her head tilted under a heavy crown. I couldn't see the icon Baba Yanka carried until she came around the circle again. Baba Yanka's face was startling, her eyes enormous and fixed, her lips slack, her weathered skin glowing from the terrible heat. The icon she carried in her arms must have been very old, like that of the Virgin, but through its smoke stains and the wavering heat I could make out an image quite distinctly: it showed two figures facing each other in a sort of dance of their own, two creatures equally dramatic and forbidding. One was a knight in armor and red cape, and the other was a dragon with a long, looping tail."

Chapter 70

December 1963

My beloved daughter:

I am in Naples now. This year, I am trying to be more systematic about my search. Naples is warm in December, and I am grateful because I have a bad cold. I never knew what it meant to be lonely before I left you, because I had never been loved as your father loved me — and you, too, I think. Now I am a woman alone in a library, wiping my nose and making notes. I wonder if anyone has ever been so alone as I am there, and in my hotel room. In public I wear my scarf or a high-necked blouse. As I cut up my lunch, and eat it alone, someone smiles at me and I smile back. Then I look away. You are not the only person with whom I am not fit to associate.

Your loving mother,
Helen

ELIZABETH KOSTOVA

February 1964

My beloved daughter:

Athens is dirty and noisy, and it is difficult for me to get access to the documents I need at the Institute for Medieval Greece, which seems to be as medieval as its contents. But this morning, as I sit on the Acropolis, I can almost imagine that one day our separation will be over, and we will sit — you a grown woman, perhaps — on these fallen stones and look out over the city. Let's see: you will be tall, like me, like your father, with cloudy dark hair — very short or in a thick braid? — and wear sunglasses and walking shoes, perhaps a scarf over your head if the wind is as rough as it is today. And I will be aging, wrinkled, proud only of you. The waiters at the cafés will stare at you, not at me, and I will laugh proudly, and your father will glare at them over his newspaper.

Your loving mother,
Helen

March 1964

My beloved daughter:

My fantasy about the Acropolis was so strong yesterday that I went there again this morning, just to write to you. But once I was sitting up there, gazing out over the city, the wound on my neck began to throb, and I thought that a presence close by was catching up with me, so that I could only look around and around trying to see among the crowds of tourists anyone suspicious. I cannot understand why this fiend has not come down the centuries to find me yet. I am his for the taking already, polluted already, longing slightly for him. Why does he not make his move and put me out of this misery? But as soon as I think this, I realize that I must continue to resist him, to surround and guard myself with every charm against him, and to find his many haunts in the hope of catching him in one of them, catching him so completely unaware that I can perhaps make history by destroying him. You, my lost angel, are the fire behind this desperate ambition.

Your loving mother,
Helen

Chapter 71

"WHEN WE SAW the icon that Baba Yanka carried, I don't know who gasped first, me or Helen, but each of us suppressed the reaction at once. Ranov was leaning against a tree not ten feet away, and to my relief I perceived that he was looking out over the valley, bored and contemptuous, busy with his cigarette, and had apparently not noticed the icon. A few seconds later Baba Yanka had turned away from us, and then she and the other old woman danced with the same lively, dignified step out of the fire and toward the priest. They returned the icons to the two boys, who covered them again at once. I kept my eye on Ranov. The priest was blessing the old women now, and they were led away by Brother Ivan, who gave them a drink of water. Baba Yanka cast us a proud glance as she went by, flushed, smiling and almost winking, and Helen and I bowed to her, out of a single awe. I looked carefully at her feet as she passed; her worn, bare feet appeared completely undamaged, as did the other woman's. Only their faces showed the heat of the fire, like a sunburn.

"'The dragon,' Helen murmured to me as we watched them.

"'Yes,' I said. 'We have to find out where they keep this icon and how old it is. Come on. The priest promised us a tour of the church.'

"'What about Ranov?' Helen didn't look around.

"'We'll just have to pray he doesn't decide to follow us,' I said. 'I don't think he saw the icon.'

"The priest was returning to the church, and the people had started to drift away. We followed him slowly, and found him setting the icon of Sveti Petko back on its podium. The other two icons were nowhere to be seen. I bowed my thanks and told him in English how beautiful the ceremony had been, waving my hands and pointing outside. He seemed pleased. Then I gestured around the church and raised my eyebrows. 'May we take a tour?'

"'Tour?' He frowned for a second, and then smiled again. Wait — he needed only to disrobe. When he returned in his everyday black garb, he took us carefully into every niche, pointing out *'ikoni'* and *'Hristos'* and some other things we more or less understood. He seemed to know a great deal about the place and its history, if only we'd been able to understand him. At last I asked him where the other icons were, and he pointed to the yawning hole I'd noticed earlier in one of the side chapels. They had apparently already been returned to the crypt, where they were kept. He fetched his lantern, obligingly, and led us down.

"The stone steps were steep, and the breath of cold that reached us from below made the church itself seem warm. I gripped Helen's hand tightly as we picked our way down after the priest's lantern, which illuminated the old stones around us. The small room below was not completely dark, however; two stands of candles blazed next to an altar, and after a moment we could see, if dimly, that it was not an altar but an elaborate brass reliquary, partly covered with richly embroidered red damask. On it stood the two icons in silver frames, the Virgin and — I took a step forward — the dragon and the knight. 'Sveti Petko,' the priest said cheerfully, touching the casket.

"I pointed to the Virgin, and he told us something that had to do with *Bachkovski manastir,* although we couldn't understand more than that. Then I pointed to the other icon, and the priest beamed. 'Sveti Georgi,' he said, indicating the knight. He pointed to the dragon. *'Drakula.'*

"'That probably just means dragon,' Helen warned me.

"I nodded. 'How can we ask him how old he thinks it is?'

"'*Star? Staro?*' Helen guessed.

"The priest shook his head in agreement. *'Mnogo star,'* he said solemnly. We stared at him. I held up my hand and counted fingers. Three? Four? Five? He smiled. Five. Five fingers — about five hundred years.

"'He thinks it's fifteenth century,' Helen said. 'God, how are we going to ask him where it's from?' I pointed to the icon, gestured around at the crypt, pointed up to the church above us. But when he understood he gave the universal gesture of ignorance; his shoulders and eyebrows rose and fell together. He didn't know. He seemed to try to tell us that the icon had been here at Sveti Petko for hundreds of years — beyond that, he didn't know.

"At last he turned, smiling, and we prepared to follow him and his lantern back up the steep steps. And we would have left that place forever, and in complete hopelessness, if Helen had not suddenly caught the narrow heel of her pump between two of the stones underfoot. She gasped with annoyance — I knew she did not have another pair of shoes with her — and I bent quickly to free her. The priest was nearly out of sight, but the candles blazing next to the reliquary afforded me enough light to see what was engraved on the vertical of the bottom step, right next to Helen's foot. It was a small dragon, crude but unmistakable, and unmistakably the same design as the one in my book. I dropped to my knees on the stones and traced it with one hand. It was so familiar to me that I could have carved it there myself. Helen crouched next to me, her shoe forgotten. 'My God,' she said. 'What is this place?'

"'Sveti Georgi,' I said slowly. 'This must be Sveti Georgi.'

"She peered at me in the dim light, her hair falling into her eyes. 'But the church is eighteenth century,' she objected. Then her face cleared. 'You think that —'

"'Lots of churches have much older foundations, right? And we know this one was rebuilt after the Turks burned the original. Couldn't it have been a monastery church, for a monastery everyone forgot long ago?' I was whispering in my excitement. 'It could have been rebuilt decades or centuries later, and renamed for the martyr they did remember.'

"'Helen turned in horror and stared at the brass reliquary behind us. 'Do you also think —'

"'I don't know,' I said slowly. 'It seems unlikely to me they could have confused one set of relics with another, but how recently do you think that box has been opened?'

"'It does not look big enough,' she said. She seemed unable to say more.

"'It doesn't,' I agreed, 'but we have got to try it. At least, I've got to. I want you to stay out of this, Helen.'

"She gave me a quizzical look, as if puzzled by the idea that I would even try to send her away. 'It is very serious to break into a church and desecrate the grave of a saint.'

"'I know,' I said. 'But what if this isn't the grave of a saint?'

"There were two names neither of us could have managed to utter in that dark, cold place with its flickering lights and smell of beeswax and earth. One of those names was Rossi.

"'Right now? Ranov will be looking for us,' Helen said.

"When we emerged from the church, the shadows of the trees around it were lengthening, and Ranov was looking for us, his face impatient. Brother Ivan stood by, although I noticed they hardly spoke to each other. 'Did you have a good nap?' Helen asked politely.

"'It is time for us to go back to Bachkovo.' Ranov's voice was curt again; I wondered if he was disappointed that we had apparently found nothing here. 'We will leave for Sofia in the morning. I have business to take care of there. I hope you are satisfied with your research.'

"'Almost,' I said. 'I would like to visit Baba Yanka one more time and thank her for her help.'

"'Very well.' Ranov looked annoyed, but he led the way back down into the village, Brother Ivan walking silently behind us. The street was quiet in the golden evening light, and everywhere there was a smell of cooking. I saw an old man come out to the central water pump and fill a bucket. At the far end of Baba Yanka's little street, a herd of goats and sheep was being led in; we could hear their plaintive voices and see them crowding one another between the houses before a boy whisked them around the corner.

"Baba Yanka was delighted to see us. We congratulated her, through Ranov, on her wonderful singing and on the fire dance. Brother Ivan blessed her with a silent gesture. 'How is it that you don't get burned?' Helen asked her.

"'Oh, that is the power of God,' she said softly. 'I do not remember later how it happened. Sometimes my feet feel hot afterward, but I never burn them. It is the most beautiful day of the year for me, even though I do not remember much of it. For months I am as peaceful as a lake.'

"She took an unlabeled bottle from her cupboard and poured us glasses of a clear brown liquor. The bottle had long weeds floating in it, which Ranov explained were herbs, for flavor. Brother Ivan declined, but Ranov accepted a glass. After a few sips he began to question Brother Ivan about something in a voice as friendly as nettles. They were soon deep in a debate we could not follow, although I frequently caught the word *politicheski*.

"When we had sat listening for a while, I interrupted for a moment to get Ranov's help in asking Baba Yanka if I could use her bathroom. He laughed unpleasantly. He was certainly back in his old humor, I thought. 'I am afraid it is not so nice here,' he said. Baba Yanka laughed, too, and pointed to the back door. Helen said she would follow me and wait her turn. The outhouse in Baba Yanka's backyard was even more dilapidated than her cottage, but wide enough to hide our quiet flight among the trees and beehives and through the back gate. There was no one in sight, but we strolled when we reached the road, went quietly into the bushes, and scrambled up the hill. Mercifully, there was no one around the church, either, which already lay in deep shadow. The fire pit glowed faintly red under the trees.

"We didn't bother to try the front door, where we could be seen from the road; instead we hurried around the back. There was a low window there, covered on the inside with purple curtains. 'That will lead into the sanctuary,' Helen said. But the wooden frame was only latched, not bolted shut, and with a little splintering we got it open and crawled in between the curtains, closing everything carefully behind us. Inside, I saw that Helen was right; we were behind the iconostasis. 'Women are not allowed here,' she said in a low voice, but she was looking around her with a scholar's curiosity as she spoke.

"The room behind the iconostasis was dominated by a tall altar covered in fine cloths and candles. Two ancient books stood on a brass stand nearby, and hooks along the walls held the gorgeous vestments we had seen the priest wearing earlier. Everything was terribly still, terribly quiet. I found the holy gate through which the priest appeared to his congregation, and we pushed our way guiltily into the dark church. There was a little illumination from the narrow windows, but all the candles had been extinguished, probably from fear of fire, and it took me a while to locate a box of matches on a shelf. I selected a candle for each of us from one of the candelabra and lit them. Then we made our way with great caution down the stairs. 'I hate this,' I heard Helen murmur behind me, but I knew she didn't mean she would stop, under any circumstances. 'How soon do you think Ranov will miss us?'

"The crypt was the darkest place I'd ever been, all its candles firmly extinguished, and I was grateful for the two spots of light we carried. I lit the extinguished candles from the one I held. They blazed up, catching a sparkle of gold embroidery on the reliquary. My hands had begun to shake pretty badly, but I managed to take Turgut's little dagger in its sheath out of my jacket pocket, where I had been keeping it since we'd left Sofia. I set it on the floor near the reliquary, and Helen and I gently lifted the two icons from their places — I found myself averting my eyes from the dragon and Saint George — and propped them against one wall. We removed the heavy cloth and Helen folded it out of the way. All this time I was listening with every fiber of my body for any sound, here or in the church above, so that the silence itself began to thrum and whine in my ears. Once Helen caught my sleeve, and we listened together, but nothing stirred.

"When the reliquary lay bare, we looked down on it, trembling. The top was beautifully molded with bas-relief — a long-haired saint with one hand raised to bless us, presumably a portrait of the martyr whose bones we might find inside. I caught myself hoping that we would indeed find just a few holy shards of bone, and then close the whole thing up. But then there was the emptiness that would follow — the lack of Rossi, the lack of revenge, the loss. The reliquary lid seemed nailed down, or bolted, and I couldn't for the life of me pry it open. We tipped it a little in the process, and something shifted inside, gruesomely, and seemed to tap against the interior. It was indeed too small for anything but a child's body, or some odd parts, but it was very heavy. It occurred to me for a horrible moment that perhaps only Vlad's head had ended up here after all, although that would leave a lot of other matters unexplained. I began to sweat and to wonder if I should go back up and hunt for some tool in the church above, although I wasn't very hopeful of finding anything.

"'Let's try to put it on the floor,' I said through gritted teeth, and together we somehow slid the box safely down. There I might be able to get a better look at the hasps and hinges of the top, I thought, or even brace myself to yank it open.

"I was about to attempt this when Helen gave a little cry. 'Paul, look!' I turned quickly and saw that the dusty marble on which the reliquary had rested was not a solid block; the top had shifted a little with our struggle to move the reliquary off it. I don't believe I was breathing anymore, but together, without words, we managed to remove the marble slab. It was not thick, but it weighed a fortune, and we were both panting by the time it was leaning against the back wall. Underneath lay a long slab of rock, the same rock as the floor and walls, a stone the length of a man. The portrait on it was crude in the extreme, chiseled directly into the hard surface — not the face of a saint but of a real man, a hard-faced man with staring almond eyes, a long nose, a long mustache — a cruel face topped with a triangular hat that managed to look jaunty even in this rough outline.

"Helen drew back, white lipped in the candle-light, and I fought the urge to take her arm and run up the steps. 'Helen,' I began softly, but there was nothing else to say. I picked up the dagger and Helen slipped a hand into some part of her clothing — I never did see where — and drew out the tiny pistol, which she put an arm's-length away, near the wall. Then we reached under the edge of the gravestone and lifted. The stone slid halfway off, a marvelous construction. We were both shaking visibly, so that the stone all but slipped out of our grasp. When it was off we looked down at the body inside, the heavily closed eyes, the sallow skin, the unnaturally red lips, the shallow, soundless breathing. It was Professor Rossi."

Chapter 72

"I WISH I COULD SAY that I did something brave, or useful, or caught Helen in my arms to make sure she wouldn't faint, but I didn't. There is almost nothing worse than a much-loved face transformed by death, or physical decay, or horrifying illness. Those faces are monsters of the most frightening kind — the unbearable beloved. 'Oh, Ross,' I said, and the tears welled up and ran down my cheeks so suddenly that I couldn't even feel them coming.

"Helen took a step closer and looked down at him. I saw now that he was wearing the clothes he'd had on the night I'd last talked with him, nearly a month ago; they were torn and dirty, as if he'd been in an accident. His tie was gone. An ooze of blood filled the lines of one side of his neck and made a scarlet estuary on his soiled collar. His mouth was slack and swollen around that faint breath, and apart from the rise and fall of his shirt, he was still. Helen put out her hand. 'Don't touch him,' I said sharply, which only increased my own horror.

"But Helen seemed as much in a trance as he was, and after a second, her lips trembling, she brushed his cheek with her fingers. I don't know whether it was worse yet that he opened his eyes, but he did. They were still very blue, even in that murky candlelight, but the whites were bloodshot and the lids swollen. Those eyes were horribly alive, too, and puzzled, and they moved here and there as if trying to take in our faces, while his body stayed deathly still. Then his gaze seemed to settle on Helen, bending over him, and the blue of his eyes cleared with tremendous force, opening as if to take her in whole. 'Oh, my love,' he said very softly. His lips were cracked and thick, but his voice was the voice I loved, the crisp accent.

"'No — my mother,' Helen said as if groping for speech. She put her hand against his cheek. 'Father, it's Helen — Elena. I'm your daughter.'

"He lifted one hand then, as if he controlled it only waveringly, and took hers. His hand was bruised and the nails overgrown and yellowing. I wanted to tell him that we'd have him out of there in no time, that we were going home, but I knew already how desperately wounded he was. 'Ross,' I said, bending nearer. 'It's Paul. I'm here.'

"His eyes turned in bewilderment from me to Helen and back again, and then he closed them with a sigh that went all through his swollen frame. 'Oh, Paul,' he said. 'You came for me. You shouldn't have done it.' He looked at Helen again, his eyes clouding over, and seemed to want to say something else. 'I remember you,' he murmured, after a moment.

"I fumbled for my inside jacket pocket and took out the ring Helen's mother had given me. I held it close to his eyes, but not too close, and then he dropped Helen's hand and touched the face of the ring clumsily. 'For you,' he said to Helen. Helen took it and put it on her finger.

"'My mother,' she said, her mouth trembling openly now. 'Do you remember? You met her in Romania.'

"He looked at her with something like his old keenness and smiled, his face crooked. 'Yes,' he whispered at last. 'I loved her. Where did she go?'

"'She is safe in Hungary,' Helen said.

"'You are her daughter?' There was a kind of wonder in his voice now.

"'I am your daughter.'

"The tears came slowly up to the surface of his eyes, as if they did not flow with ease anymore, and ran down the lines at their corners.

The trails they left glistened in the candlelight. 'Please take care of her, Paul,' he said faintly.

"'I'm going to marry her,' I told him. I put my hand on his chest. There was a kind of inhuman wheezing inside it, but I made myself hold him there.

"'That's — good,' he said finally. 'Is her mother alive and well?'

"'Yes, Father.' Helen's face quivered. 'She is safe in Hungary.'

"'Yes, you said that.' He closed his eyes again.

"'She still loves you, Rossi.' I stroked his shirt-front with an unsteady hand. 'She sent you this ring and — a kiss.'

"'I tried so many times to remember where she was, but something —'

"'She knows you tried. Rest for a moment.' His breathing had become alarmingly hoarse.

"Suddenly, his eyes flew open and he struggled to rise. The effort was awful to watch, especially since it produced almost no result. 'Children, you must leave at once,' he panted. 'It is very dangerous for you here. He will come back and kill you.' His eyes darted from side to side.

"'Dracula?' I asked softly.

"His face went wild for a moment at the name. 'Yes. He is in the library.'

"'Library?' I said, looking around in astonishment despite the horror of Rossi's face before us. 'What library?'

"'His library is in there —' He tried to point to a wall.

"'Ross,' I said urgently. 'Tell us what happened and what we should do.'

"He seemed to struggle with his eyesight for a moment, focusing on me and blinking rapidly. The dried blood on his neck moved with his struggle to breathe. 'He came for me suddenly, to my office, and took me on a long journey. I was not — conscious for some of it, so I do not know what place this is.'

"'Bulgaria,' Helen said, keeping his swollen hand tenderly.

"His eyes flickered again with an old interest, a spark of curiosity. 'Bulgaria? So that's why —' He tried to moisten his lips.

"'What did he do to you?'

"'He brought me here to look after his — diabolical library. I have resisted in every way I could think of. It was my fault, Paul. I had started doing some research again, for an article —' He struggled for breath. 'I wanted to show him as part of a — greater tradition. Beginning with the Greeks. I — I heard there was a new scholar at the university writing on him, although I couldn't find out the man's name.'

"At this, I heard Helen draw her breath in sharply. Rossi's eyes flickered toward her. 'It seemed to me that I should finally publish —' He was wheezing now and he closed his eyes for a moment. Helen, holding his hand, had begun to tremble against me; I kept a tight grip on her waist.

"'It's all right,' I said. 'Just rest.' But Rossi seemed determined to finish.

"'Not all right,' he choked, his eyes still closed. 'He gave you the book. I knew then he would come for me, and he did. I fought him, but he has almost made me — like him — ' He seemed unable to raise his other hand and he turned his neck and head, clumsily, so that we could suddenly see a deep puncture wound in the side of his throat. It was still open, and when he moved it gaped and oozed. Our gaze on it seemed to make him wild again, and he looked beseechingly at me. 'Paul, is it getting dark outside?'

"A wave of horror and despair went through

me, shooting through my hands. 'Can you feel it, Ross?'

"'Yes, I know when the dark is coming, and I become — hungry. Please. He will hear you soon. Hurry — leave.'

"'Tell us how to find him,' I said desperately. 'We'll kill him now.'

"'Yes, kill him, if you can do it without endangering yourself. Kill him for me,' he whispered, and for the first time I saw that he could still feel anger. 'Listen, Paul. There is a book in there. A life of Saint George.' He began to struggle with his breathing again. 'Very old, with a Byzantine cover — no one has ever seen such a book. He has many great books, but this one is —' He seemed for a moment to faint, and Helen pressed his hand between hers, beginning to weep in spite of herself. When he came to, he whispered, 'I hid it behind the first cabinet to the left. Take it with you if you can. I have written something — I have put something inside it. Hurry, Paul. He is waking up. I am waking up with him.'

"'Oh, Jesus.' I looked around for some kind of help — what, I didn't know. 'Ross, please — I can't let him have you. We'll kill him and you'll get well. Where is he?' But now Helen was calmer and she picked up the dagger and showed it to him.

"He seemed to let out a long breath, and it was mingled with a smile. I saw then how his teeth had lengthened, like a dog's, and how the corner of his lip was already chewed raw. Tears ran freely from his eyes and trickled down his bruised cheekbones. 'Paul, my friend —'

"'Where is he? Where is the library?' I made the question even more urgent, but Rossi could not speak again.

"Helen made a quick gesture, and I understood, and dug a rock quickly from the edge of the floor. It took me a long moment to loosen it, and in that moment I feared I could hear some movement in the church above us. Helen unbuttoned his shirt and opened it gently, and she set the tip of Turgut's dagger over his heart.

"He kept his eyes on us for a moment, trustingly, so that they looked blue as a child's, and then shut them. As soon as they closed I gathered all my strength and brought down onto the hilt of the dagger that ancient stone, a stone set in place by the hands of an anonymous monk or hired peasant, some vanished denizen of the twelfth or thirteenth century. Probably that stone had lain quiet as centuries of monks trod on it, bringing bones to their ossuary, or wine to their cellar. That stone had not moved when the corpse of a foreign Turk-killer was carried secretly over it and hidden in a fresh grave in the floor nearby, or when Wallachian monks celebrated a heretical new mass above it, or when the Ottoman police came searching in vain for the corpse, or when Ottoman horsemen rode into the church with their torches, or when a new church rose overhead, or when the bones of Sveti Petko were brought in their reliquary to sit close to it, or when pilgrims knelt on it to receive the neomartyr's blessing. It had rested there those many centuries, until I dug it roughly from its place and gave it a new use, and that is all I can write about it."

Chapter 73

May 1954

I have no one to whom to write this, and no hope that it will ever be found, but it seems to me a crime not to attempt to record my knowledge while I am still able to, and God only knows how long that will be.

I was taken from my university office some days ago — I am not sure how many, but I surmise that this is still the month of May. On that night I said good-bye to my beloved student and friend, who had shown me his copy of the demonic book I had tried for years to forget. I saw him walk away with all the help I could possibly give him. Then I shut my office door and sat for a few moments in great regret and fear. I knew that I was culpable. I had renewed in secret my research into the history of vampires and I fully intended to come around by degrees to an expansion of my knowledge of the legend of Dracula, and perhaps even to solve at last the mystery of the whereabouts of his tomb. I had let time, rationality, and pride lull me into believing there would be no con-

sequences to renewing my research. I admitted my guilt to myself even in that first moment of solitude.

It had cost me a terrible pang to give Paul my research notes and the letters I'd written about my experiences, not because I wanted them for myself any longer — all desire to continue my research had vanished in me the second he had shown me his book. I simply, deeply regretted having to put this gruesome knowledge into his hand, although I was sure that the more he understood the better he would be able to protect himself. I could only hope that if any punishment followed, I would be the sufferer and not Paul, with his youthful optimism, his light step, his untried brilliance. Paul cannot be more than twenty-seven; I have had decades of life and much undeserved happiness. This was my first thought. My next thoughts were practical. Even if I wished to protect myself, I had no way to do so immediately, except my own faith in the rational. I had kept my notes but not any traditional means of warding off evil — no crucifixes or silver bullets, no braids of garlic. I had never resorted to those, even at the height of my research, but now I began to regret that I had ad-

vised Paul to use only the resources of his own mind.

These thoughts required the space of a minute or two, and as it turned out, I had only a minute or two at my disposal. Then, with a sudden rush of foul, cold air, an immense presence was upon me, so that I could hardly see, and my entire body seemed to rise out of its chair with fear. I was enveloped, blinded in an instant, and I felt I must be dying, though from what I couldn't tell. In the midst of it I had the strangest vision of youth and loveliness, a feeling more than a vision, a sense of myself much younger and full of love for something or someone. Perhaps that is the way one dies. If so, when my time comes — and it will come soon, whatever terrible form it takes — I hope this vision will be with me again in the last moment.

After this I remember nothing, but a nothing that lasted for a period I could not and still cannot measure. When I came slowly to myself again, I was amazed to find myself alive. I could not see or hear, in the first seconds. It was like emerging from a brutal surgery, and my awakening was immediately followed by a comprehension that I was in pain, that my whole body was terribly weak and ached profoundly, that there was a burning in my right leg and in my throat and head. The air was cold and dank, and whatever I lay on was cold, so that I felt chilled all over. This sensation was followed by light — a dim light but enough to convince me that I was not blind and that my eyes were open. This light, and the pain, more than anything else, confirmed to me that I was alive. I began to remember what I thought at first must have been the evening before — Paul coming to my office with his shocking discovery. Then I understood with a sudden plunging of my heart that I must be in the custody of evil; that was why my body had been brutalized and why I seemed surrounded by the very smell of evil.

I moved my limbs as cautiously as I could and managed through my great weakness to turn my head, and then to lift it. My sight was blocked by a dim wall not four inches away, but the feeble light I'd already perceived came in from above it. I sighed and heard my own sigh; this made me believe I could still hear, as well, and that I was simply in so silent a place that it had given me the illusion of deafness. I listened harder than ever, and, hearing noth-

ing, I raised myself cautiously to a sitting position. The action sent miserable pain and weakness through all my limbs, and I felt my head throbbing. In the sitting position I regained more of my tactile sense and found I was lying on stone, and the low wall on each side of me helped me prop myself up. There was a terrible buzzing in my head, which seemed to fill the space all around me. It was a dim space, as I've said, silent and dwindling to darkness in the corners. I felt around with my hands. I was sitting up in an open sarcophagus.

This discovery sent a wave of nausea through me, but at the same moment I noted that I still wore the garments I'd had on in the office, although my shirt and jacket were torn in one sleeve and my tie was gone. The fact that I had my own clothes, however, gave me some reassurance; this was not death, not mere insanity, and I had not awakened in another era, unless I'd transported my clothes there with me. I felt my clothes and found my wallet in the front pocket of my pants. It was a shock to feel this familiar item under my hands. My watch, I found to my sorrow, was gone from my wrist, and my good pen from my inside jacket pocket.

Then I brought my hand up to my throat and face. My face seemed unchanged, apart from a very tender bruise on the forehead, but in the muscle of my throat I found a wicked puncture, sticky under my fingers. When I moved my head too far or swallowed hard, the wound made a sucking sound, appalling to me beyond all rationality. The punctured area was swollen, too, and throbbed with pain under my touch. I felt I might faint again from horror and hopelessness, and then I recalled that I had the strength to sit upright. Perhaps I had not lost as much blood as I'd at first feared, and perhaps that meant I had been bitten only once. I felt like myself, not like a demon; I felt no longing for blood, no wickedness of heart. Then a great misery swept over me. What did it matter whether I felt no bloodthirst yet? Wherever I was, it would surely be only a matter of time before I was fully corrupted. Unless, of course, I could escape.

I moved my head slowly, looking around, trying to make my eyes clear, and then I was able to discern the source of the light. It was a reddish glow far away in the darkness — but how far I could not tell — and between me and that glow loomed dark heavy shapes. I ran my hands down the outside of my house of stone. The sarcophagus seemed to be close to the ground, or to a stone floor, and I felt around until I'd determined that I could climb out into the dimness without falling any great distance. It was a long step out onto the floor, and my legs shook terribly, so that I stumbled to my knees as soon as I'd got out of the sarcophagus. Now I could see a little better, too. I made my way towards the source of soft reddish light with my hands in front of me, in the process bumping into what seemed to be another sarcophagus, which I found empty, and into a piece of wooden furniture. When I collided with the wood I heard something soft fall, but couldn't see what it was.

This groping in the dimness was terrifying, and I expected at any second to be pounced on by the Thing that had brought me there. I wondered again if I might not actually be dead — if this was some terrible version of death, which I had momentarily mistaken for a continuation of life. But nothing pounced on me, the pain in my legs was convincing enough, and I was getting closer to the light, which danced and flickered at one end of the long chamber. Before this glow, I could see now, loomed a mo-

tionless dark bulk. When I was within a few yards of it I saw a fire on a hearth, burning low and red. It was framed by an arched stone fireplace, and it gave enough light to play off several massive old pieces of furniture — a great desk littered with papers, a carved chest, a tall angular chair or two. In one of the chairs, which had its back to me and its front to the fire, someone was sitting very still — I saw a dark shape just above the chair back. I wished now that I had felt my way in the opposite direction, away from the light and towards some possible escape, but I was terribly drawn by my glimpse of that dark shape and the regal chair below it, and by the soft red of the fire. On the one hand, it took all my willpower to walk towards it, and on the other I could not have turned away if I had tried.

I came slowly into the firelight on my bruised legs, and as I rounded the great chair a figure slowly rose and turned to me. Because his back was now to the fire, and because there was so little light around us, I could not see his face, although I thought in the first second that I caught a glimpse of bone-white cheek and glittering eye. He had long, curling, dark hair, which fell around his shoulders in a short mantle. There was something about his movement that was indescribably different from that of a living man, but whether it was swifter or slower I couldn't have said. He was only a little taller than I, but gave a sense of height and bulk, and I could see the spread of his broad shoulders against the firelight. Then he reached for something, bending to the fire. I wondered if he was about to kill me and I stayed very quiet, hoping to die with some dignity, however it happened. But he was merely touching a long taper to the fire, and when it caught he lit other tapers in a candelabrum near his chair and turned again to face me.

Now I could see him better, although his face was still in shadow. He wore a peaked cap of gold and green with a heavy jewelled brooch pinned above his brow, and a massive-shouldered tunic of gold velvet with a green collar laced high under his large chin. The jewel on his brow and the gold threads in his collar glittered in the firelight. A cape of white fur was drawn around his shoulders and pinned with the silver symbol of a dragon. His clothing was extraordinary; I felt almost as frightened of it as I did of his strange undead presence. It was real clothing, living, fresh *clothing, not the faded pieces of a museum exhibition. He wore it with extraordinary richness and grace, too, standing silently before me, so that the cape fell down around him like the swirl of snow. The candlelight revealed a blunt-fingered, scarred hand on a dagger hilt, and farther down a powerful leg in green hose and a booted foot. He shifted a little, turning in the light, but still silent. I could see his face better now, and the cruel strength of it made me shrink back — the great dark eyes under knitted brows, the long straight nose, the broad bonelike cheeks. His mouth, I saw now, was closed in a hard smile, ruby and curving under his wiry, dark mustache. At one corner of his lips I saw a stain of drying blood — oh, God, how that made me recoil. The sight of it was terrible enough, but the immediate realization that it was probably mine, my own blood, made my head swim.*

He drew himself up even more proudly and looked me full in the face across the dimness that separated us. "I am Dracula," he said. The words came out cold and clear. I had the sense that they were in a language I did not know, although I understood them perfectly. I was unable to speak and stood staring at him in a horrified paralysis. His body was only ten feet from me, and it was undeniably real and powerful, whether it was actually dead or alive. "Come," he said in that same cold, pure tone. "You are tired and hungry after our journey. I have set out a supper for you." His gesture was graceful, even courtly, with a flash of jewels on his big white fingers.

I saw a table near the fire, laden with covered dishes. I could smell food now, too — good, real, human food — and the aroma made me feel faint. Dracula moved quietly to the table and poured out a glass of something red from a decanter there, something I thought for a moment must be blood. "Come," he said again, more softly. He moved away and sat down in his chair, as if he thought I might be more likely to approach if he stayed at a little distance. I went haltingly towards the empty chair by the table, my legs trembling under me from sheer weakness as well as fear. I sat down among the dark cushions there, a collapse, and looked at the dishes. Why, I wondered, did I long to eat when I might die any moment? It was a mystery only my body understood. Dracula was gazing into the fire now; I could see the ferocious profile, the long nose and strong chin, the dark curl of hair over his shoulder. He had pressed his hands thoughtfully together, so that his mantle and embroidered sleeves fell away, showing wrists of green velvet and a great scar across the back of his near hand. His attitude was quiet and pensive; I began to feel I was dreaming rather than menaced, and I dared to lift the lids of some of the dishes.

Suddenly I was so hungry that I could hardly restrain myself from eating wildly with both hands, but I managed to lift the metal fork and bone knife on the table and carve up first a roasted chicken and then a piece of some gamey dark meat. There were ceramic bowls of potatoes and gruel, a hard bread, a hot soup full of greens. I ate ravenously, trying to slow myself enough to keep my stomach from cramping. The silver goblet at my elbow was brimming with strong red wine, not blood, and I drank it all. Dracula did not stir during my meal, although I couldn't help glancing at him every few seconds. When I was done I felt almost ready to die, content for a long minute. So this was why a person about to be executed was given a last meal, I thought. It was my first clear thought since I had awakened in the sarcophagus. I slowly covered the empty dishes, trying to make as little noise as possible, and sat back, waiting.

After a long while, my companion turned in his chair. "You have finished your dinner," he said quietly. "Then perhaps we can converse a little, and I will tell you why I have brought you here." His voice was clear and cold again, but this time I noticed a faint rattle in its depths, as if the mechanism that produced it was infinitely old and worn. He sat looking thoughtfully at me, and I felt myself shrinking under his gaze. "Do you have any idea where you are?"

I had hoped not to have to speak to him, but I felt that there was little point in my keeping silent, which might enrage him, although he seemed calm enough at the moment. It had also suddenly occurred to me that by answering, by engaging him somehow, I might buy a little time in which to test my surroundings for possible escape, or for some means to destroy him, if I could work up the nerve, or both. This must be night, or he would not be awake, if the legend was accurate. Eventually morning must come, and if I was alive to see it he would have to sleep while I stayed awake.

"Do you have any idea where you are?" he repeated, almost patiently.

"Yes," I said. I could not bring myself to address him by any title. "At least, I think so. This is your tomb."

"One of them." He smiled. "My favorite one, in any case."

"Are we in Wallachia?" I could not help asking it.

He shook his head so that the firelight moved in his dark hair and over his bright eyes. There was something inhuman about the gesture that made my stomach twist inside me. He did not move like a living person, and yet — again — I couldn't have said exactly what the difference was. "Wallachia became too dangerous. I should have been allowed to rest there forever, but there was no possibility of that. Imagine — after fighting so hard for my throne, for our freedom, I could not even lay my bones there."

"Where are we, then?" I tried, again in vain, to feel this was an ordinary conversation. Then I realized that I didn't simply want to make the night pass swiftly or safely, if there was any chance of that. I wanted, too, to learn something about Dracula. Whatever he was, this creature, he had lived five hundred years. His answers would die with me, of course, but this fact did not prevent me from feeling a twinge of curiosity.

"Ah, where are we," Dracula repeated. "It does not matter, I think. We are not in Wallachia, which is still ruled by fools."

I stared at him. "Do you — do you know about the modern world?"

He looked at me with a surprised amusement that set his terrible face curling. For the first time I saw the long teeth, the receding gums, which gave him the look of an old dog when he smiled. The vision was gone as quickly as it had come — no, his mouth was normal, apart from that small stain of my blood — or someone's — below the dark mustache. "Yes," he said, and I was afraid for a second that I would have to hear him laugh. "I know the modern world. It is my prize, my favorite work."

I felt that some kind of frontal attack might be in my interest, if it engaged him. "Then what do you want with me? I have avoided the modern for many years — unlike you, I live in the past."

The Historian

"Oh, the past." He put his fingertips together again in the firelight. "The past is very useful, but only for what it can teach us about the present. The present is the rich thing. But I am very fond of the past. Come. Why not show you now, since you have eaten and rested?" He rose, again with that movement that seemed determined by some force other than the limbs of his body, and I rose quickly with him, afraid that this might be a trick, that he might lunge for me now. But he turned slowly and lifted a candle out of the stand near his chair and held it up. "Take a light with you," he said, moving away from the hearth and into the dark of the great chamber. I took a second candle and followed him, staying clear of his strange clothing and chilling movements. I hoped he was not going to lead me back to my sarcophagus.

By the sparse light of our candles I began to see things I had not been able to see before — wonderful things. I could now make out long tables before me, tables of an ancient solidity. And on these lay piles and piles of books — crumbling leather-bound volumes and gilt covers that picked up the glimmer of my candle flame. There were other objects, too — never had I seen such an inkstand, or such strange quills and pens. There was a stack of parchment, glimmering in the candlelight, and an old typewriter supplied with thin paper. I saw the gleam of jewelled bindings and boxes, the curl of manuscripts in brass trays. There were great folios and quartos bound in smooth leather, and rows of more modern volumes on long shelves. In fact, we were surrounded; every wall seemed to be lined with books. Holding up my candle, I began to make out titles here and there, sometimes an elegant bloom of Arabic in the center of a red-leather binding, sometimes a Western language I could read. Most of the volumes were too old to have titles, however. It was a storehouse beyond compare, and I began to itch in spite of myself to open some of those books, to touch the manuscripts in their wooden trays.

Dracula turned, holding his candle aloft, and the light picked out the glow of jewels on his cap — topaz, emerald, pearl. His eyes were very bright. "What do you think of my library?"

"It looks like a — a remarkable collection. A treasure-house," I said.

A kind of pleasure went over his terrible face. "You are correct," he said softly. "This li-

brary is the finest of its kind in the world. It is the result of centuries of careful selection. But you will have plenty of time to explore the wonders I have assembled here. Now let me show you something else."

He led the way towards a wall we had not yet approached, and there I saw a very old printing press, such as one comes across in late-mediaeval illustrations — a heavy contraption of black metal and dark wood with a great screw on top. The round plate was obsidian with the polish of ink; it picked up our light like a demonic mirror. There was a sheet of thick paper lying on the shelf of the press. Leaning closer I saw that it was partly printed, a discarded attempt, and that it was in English. "The Ghost in the Amphora," ran the title. "Vampires from Greek Tragedy to Modern Tragedy." And the byline: "Bartholomew Rossi."

Dracula must have been waiting for my gasp of astonishment, and I did not disappoint him. "You see, I keep up with the finest modern research — up to the minute, as they say. When I cannot get a published work, or I want it at once, I sometimes print it myself. But here is something that will interest you easily as much."

He pointed at a table behind the press. It held a row of woodcuts. The largest of them, propped up to view, was the dragon of our books — mine and Paul's — in reverse, of course. With difficulty, I kept myself from exclaiming aloud. "You are surprised," Dracula said, holding his light near the dragon. Its lines were so familiar to me that I could have cut them with my own hand. "You know this image very well, I think."

"Yes." I held my candle tightly. "Did you print the books yourself? And how many of them are there?"

"My monks printed some of them, and I have continued their work," he said quietly, looking down at the woodcut. "I have nearly fulfilled my ambition of printing fourteen hundred and fifty three of them, but slowly, so that I have time to distribute them as I work. Does that number mean anything to you?"

"Yes," I said after a moment. "It is the year of the fall of Constantinople."

"I thought you would see it," he said with his bitter smile. "It is the worst date in history."

"It seems to me there are many contenders for that honor," I said, but he was shaking his great head above his great shoulders.

"No," he said. He lifted his candle high and in its light I saw his eyes blaze up, red in their depths like a wolf's, and full of hatred. It was like seeing a dead gaze suddenly rustle to life; I had thought his eyes bright before, but now they were savage with light. I could not speak; I could not look away. After a second he turned and contemplated the dragon again. "He has been a good messenger," he said thoughtfully.

"Did you leave mine for me? My book?"

"Let us say that I arranged it." He reached his battle-scarred fingers out to touch the carved block. "I am very careful about how they are distributed. They go only to the most promising scholars, and to those I think may be persistent enough to follow the dragon to his lair. And you are the first who has actually done it. I congratulate you. My other assistants I leave out in the world, to do my research."

"I did not follow you," I ventured to say. "You brought me here."

"Ah —" Again that curve of the ruby lips, the twitch of the long mustache. "You would not be here if you had not wanted to come. No one else has ever disregarded my warning twice in a lifetime. You have brought yourself."

ELIZABETH KOSTOVA

I looked at the old, old press and the woodcut of the dragon. "Why do you want me here?" I did not wish to rouse his anger with my questions; tomorrow night he could kill me, if he liked, if I'd found no escape during the daytime hours. But I could not help asking him this.

"I have been waiting a long time for someone to catalogue my library," he said simply. "Tomorrow you shall look at all of it in freedom. Tonight we shall talk." He led the way back to our chairs with his powerful, slow step. His words gave me a great deal of hope — apparently he really did not mean to kill me tonight, and besides, my curiosity was rising high in me. I was not dreaming, it seemed; I was speaking with one who had lived through more history than any historian can presume to study in even a rudimentary way in a single career. I followed him, at a careful distance, and we sat down before the fire again. As I settled myself, I noticed that the table with my empty supper dishes was gone, and in its place was a comfortable ottoman, on which I cautiously propped my feet. Dracula sat magnificently upright in his great chair. Although his chair was tall, wooden, and mediaeval, mine was comfortably upholstered, like my ottoman,

as if he had thought to provide his guest with something suited to modern weakness.

We sat in silence for long minutes, and I'd just begun to wonder if he meant us to sit this way all night when he began to speak again. "In life, I loved books," he said. He turned to me a little, so that I could see the glint of his eyes and the lustre of his shaggy hair. "Perhaps you do not know that I was something of a scholar. This seems not widely known." He spoke dispassionately. "You do know that the books of my day were very limited in scope. In my mortal life, I saw mainly those texts that the church sanctioned — the gospels and the Orthodox commentary on them, for example. These works were of no use to me, in the end. And by the time I first took my rightful throne, the great libraries of Constantinople had been destroyed. What remained of them, in the monasteries, I could never enter to see with my own eyes." He was looking deeply into the fire. "But I had other resources. Merchants brought me strange and wonderful books from many places — Egypt and the Holy Land, and the great monasteries of the West. From these I learned about the ancient occult. As I knew I could not attain a heavenly paradise" — *again that dis-*

passionate tone — "I became an historian in order to preserve my own history forever."

He fell silent for some time, and I was afraid to ask more. At last, he seemed to rouse himself, tapping his great hand on the arm of his chair. "That was the beginning of my library."

I was too curious to keep silent, although I found the question bitterly hard to frame. "But after your — death, you continued to collect these books?"

"Oh, yes." He turned to look at me now, perhaps because I had asked this of my own volition, and smiled grimly. His eyes, hooded in the firelight, were terrible to meet. "I have told you, I am a scholar at heart, as well as a warrior, and these books have kept me company through my long years. There is much of a practical nature to be learned from books, also — statesmanship, for example, and the battle tactics of great generals. But I have many kinds of books. You shall see tomorrow."

"And what is it you wish me to do for your library?"

"As I said, to catalogue it. I have never made a full record of my holdings, of their origins and condition. This will be your first task, and you will accomplish it more swiftly and bril-

liantly than anyone else would be able to, with your many languages and the breadth of your knowledge. In the course of this task, you will handle some of the most beautiful books — and the most powerful — ever produced. Many of them do not exist anywhere else anymore. Perhaps you know, Professor, that only about one one-thousandth of the literature ever published is still in existence? I have set myself the task of raising that fraction, over the centuries." As he spoke, I noticed again the peculiar clarity and coldness of his voice, and that rattling in the depths of it — like the rattle of the snake, or cold water running over stones.

"Your second task will be much larger. In fact, it will last forever. When you know my library and its purposes as intimately as I do, you will go out into the world, under my command, and search for new acquisitions — and old ones, too, for I shall never stop collecting from the works of the past. I will put many archivists at your disposal — the finest of them — and you shall bring more under our power."

The dimensions of this vision, and his full meaning, if I was comprehending it correctly, broke over me like a cold sweat. I found my

voice, but unsteadily. "Why will you not con-
tinue to do this yourself?"

He smiled into the fire, and again I saw that
flash of a different face — the dog, the wolf. "I
shall have other things to attend to now. The
world is changing and I intend to change with
it. Perhaps soon I will not need this form" —
he indicated with a slow hand his mediaeval
finery, the great dead power of his limbs — "in
order to accomplish my ambitions. But the li-
brary is precious to me and I would like to see
it grow. Besides, I have felt for some time that it
is less and less secure here. Several historians
have come close to finding it, and you would
have found it yourself if I had left you long
enough to your own devices. But I needed you
here at once. I smell a danger approaching,
and the library must be catalogued before it is
moved."

It helped me, for a moment, to pretend
again that I was dreaming. "Where will you
move it?" And me with it? I might have added.

"To an ancient spot, older even than this
one, that has many fine memories for me. A re-
mote place, but one closer to the great modern
cities, where I can easily come and go. We shall
set the library down there and you shall in-

crease it vastly." He looked at me with a sort of confidence that might have been fondness, on a human face. Then he stood up with his vigorous, strange movement. "We have conversed enough for one night — I see that you are tired. Let us use these hours to read a while, as I usually do, and then I shall go out. When morning comes, you must take the paper and pens you will find near the press and begin your catalogue. My books are already sorted by category, rather than by century or decade. You will see. There is a typewriter also, which I have provided for you. You may wish to compile the catalogue in Latin, but I leave this to your discretion. And, of course, you are free now and at any time to read whatever you would like to."

With this he rose from his chair and selected a book from the table, then sat down again with it. I was afraid not to follow suit, and took up the first volume that came to hand. It turned out to be an early edition of Machiavelli: The Prince, accompanied by a series of discourses on morality I'd never before seen or even heard of. I could not begin to decipher any of it, in my present state of mind, but sat staring at the type, or turned a page at random. *Dracula seemed deeply engrossed in his book. I wondered, stealing a glance at him, how he had accustomed himself to this nocturnal, underground existence, the life of a scholar, after a lifetime of battle and action.*

At last he rose and set his volume quietly aside. Without a word, he stepped into the darkness of the great hall, so that I could no longer make out his form. Then I heard a dry scratching sound, as of an animal in crumbling earth, or the striking of a match, although no light appeared, and I felt myself vastly alone. I strained my ears, but I couldn't tell which direction he had gone. He was not going to feast on me tonight, at least. I wondered fearfully what he was saving me for, when he might have made me his minion that much more swiftly and slaked his thirst at the same time. I sat in my chair some hours, rising now and then to stretch my sore body. I dared not sleep as long as it was night, but I must have dozed a little in spite of myself just before dawn, because I woke suddenly to feel a change in the air, although no new light entered that dark chamber, and to see Dracula's cloaked form approaching the fireside. "Good day," he said quietly, and turned away towards the dark wall where my sarcophagus lay. I had risen to my feet, compelled by his presence. Then, once again, I could not see him and a deep silence shrouded my ears.

After a long while I took my candle up and relit the candelabrum and also some candles I found in sconces along the walls. On many of the tables I discovered ceramic lamps or small iron lanterns, and I lit several of these as well. The increased illumination was a relief to me, but I wondered if I would ever see daylight again, or if I had already begun an eternity of darkness and flickering candle flame — this in itself stretched before me as a version of hell. At least I could see a little more of the chamber now; it was very deep in every direction and the walls were lined with great cabinets and shelves. Everywhere I saw books, boxes, scrolls, manuscripts, the piles and rows of Dracula's vast collection. Along one wall stood the dim shapes of three sarcophagi. I went closer with my light. The two smaller ones were empty — one of these must have been the one in which I'd found myself.

Then I saw the largest sarcophagus of all, a great tomb more lordly than all the rest, huge in the candlelight, nobly proportioned. Along the side ran one word, cut in Latin letters: DRACULA. *I raised my candle and looked in, almost against my own will. The great body lay there, inert. For the first time I could see his closed, cruel face clearly, and I stood staring at it in spite of my revulsion. His brow was knitted tightly as if from a disturbing dream, the eyes open and staring, so that he looked more dead than asleep, his skin waxen yellow, his long dark lashes unmoving, his strong, almost handsome features translucent. A tumble of long dark hair fell around his shoulders, filling the sides of the sarcophagus. The most terrible thing to me was the richness of the color in his cheeks and lips, and the full look his face and form had not had in the firelight. He had spared me for a time, it was true, but out in the night somewhere he had drunk his fill. The little spot of my blood was gone from his lips; now they bloomed ruby beneath his dark mustache. He looked so full of an artificial life and health that it made my own blood run cold to see that he did not breathe — his chest never rose and fell in the slightest degree. Strange, too: he was wearing a different suit of clothes, these as rich and fine as the ones I'd seen already, a tunic and boots of deep red, a mantle and cap of purple velvet. The mantle was a little shabby over the shoulders, and the cap sported a brown feather. His collar shone with gems.*

I stood there gazing until the strangeness of the sight made me feel faint, and then I fell back a pace to try to gather my thoughts. It was early in the day, still — I had hours until sunset. I would look first for an escape, and then for a means to destroy the creature while he slept, so that whether I succeeded or failed in vanquishing him I might immediately flee. I took my light firmly in hand. Suffice it to say that I searched the great stone chamber for upwards of two hours without finding any exit. At one end, opposite the hearth, was a great wooden door with an iron lock, and this I pushed and pulled and tried until I was weary and sore. It did not budge a crack; in fact, I believe it had not been opened in many years — perhaps centuries. There was no other means of egress — no other door, no tunnel or loose stone or opening of any sort. Certainly there were no windows, and I felt sure we were quite deep underground. The only niche in the walls was the one where the three sarcophagi lay, and there, too, the stones were immovable. It was a torment to me to feel along that wall in sight of Dracula's still face with its hugely open eyes; even if the eyes never moved I felt they must have some secret power to watch and curse.

I sat down by the fire again to recover my fading strength. The fire never burned lower, I noticed, holding my hands above it, although it was consuming real branches and logs and gave off a palpable, comforting heat. I realized for the first time, too, that it was smokeless; had it been burning so all night? I drew a hand over my face, warning myself. I needed every ounce of my sanity. In fact — in this moment I made my resolution — I would make it my task to keep my mind and moral fibre intact to my last moment. That would be my sustenance, the final one left to me.

When I had collected myself, I began my search again, systematically, looking for any possible way to destroy my monstrous host. If I managed to do so, of course, I would still die alone here, without escape, but he would never again leave this chamber to prey upon the outside world. I thought fleetingly and not for the first time of the comfort of suicide — but that I could not allow myself. I was already at *risk for becoming like Dracula, and legend as-serted that any suicide might become undead without the added contamination I had re-ceived — a cruel legend, but still I had to heed it. That way was closed to me. I went through every nook and cranny of the chamber, open-ing drawers and boxes, checking shelves, hold-ing my candle aloft. It was unlikely that the clever prince had left me any weapon that might be used against him, but I had to search. I found nothing, not even an old piece of wood that I might somehow have sharp-ened into a stake. When I tried to pull a log from the fireplace, the flames blazed up sud-denly, burning my hand. I tried this several times, but with the same demonic result each time.*

At last I returned to the great central sar-cophagus, dreading the last resort that lay there: the dagger that Dracula himself wore at his belt. His scarred hand was closed over its hilt. The dagger might well be made of silver, in which case I could plunge it into his heart, if I could bring myself to take it from his body. I sat down for a while to gather courage for this endeavor, and to overcome my revulsion. Then I stood and put my hand cautiously near the dagger, holding up my candle with the other hand. My careful touch did not prompt any flicker of life in the rigid face, I saw, although the cruelty of the expression, the deep pinched look of the nose, seemed to grow sharper. But I found to my terror that the great hand was closed on the dagger hilt for a reason. I would have to pry it off myself to reach the dagger. I put my hand on Dracula's and the feel of it was a horror I do not wish to put down here, even for nobody but myself. His hand was closed like a stone over the dagger's hilt. I could not pry it off or even move it; I might as well have tried to remove a marble dagger from the hand of a statue. The dead eyes seemed to kindle with hatred. Would he remember this later, when he awoke? I fell back, exhausted and repelled beyond strength, and sat on the floor again for some time with my candle.

At last, seeing no possible success to my schemes, I resolved on a new course of action. First, I would make myself sleep a short time, while it was still around midday, at the latest, so that I might awake long before Dracula without his waking first and finding me asleep. This I managed for the space of an hour or two, I think — I must find some better way to sense or measure time in this vacuum — by lying down before the hearth with my jacket folded under my head. Nothing could have persuaded me to climb back into that sarcophagus, but I managed some comfort from the warmth of the hearthstones under my aching limbs.

When I awoke, I listened carefully for any sound, but the chamber was deathly still. I found the table near my chair supplied again with a savory meal, although Dracula lay in the same state of paralysis in his tomb. Then I went in search of the typewriter I had seen earlier. Here I have been writing since then, as swiftly as I can, to record everything I have observed. In this way I have found some measure of time again, too, since I know my own typing pace and the number of pages I can cover in an hour. I am writing these last lines now by the light of one candle; I've extinguished the others to save them. I am famished now, and miserably cold, in the dankness away from the fire. Now I will hide these pages, eat something, and engage myself in the work Dracula has set for me, so that he will find me at it when he wakes. Tomorrow I will try to write further, if I am still alive and enough myself to do so.

ELIZABETH KOSTOVA

Second Day

After I wrote my first entry above, I folded the pages I'd written and inserted them behind a nearby cabinet, where I could reach them again but where they were not visible from any angle. Then I took a fresh candle and made my way slowly among the tables. There were tens of thousands of books in the great room, I estimated — perhaps hundreds of thousands counting all the scrolls and other manuscripts. They lay not only on the tables but in piles inside the heavy old cabinets and along the walls on rough shelves. Mediaeval books seemed to be mixed with fine Renaissance folios and modern printing. I found an early Shakespeare quarto — histories — next to a volume of Thomas Aquinas. There were massive works on alchemy from the sixteenth century next to an entire cabinet of illuminated Arabic scrolls — Ottoman, I surmised. There were Puritan sermons on witchcraft and small volumes of nineteenth-century poetry and long works of philosophy and criminology from our own century. No, there was no pattern in time, but I saw another pattern emerging clearly enough.

Arranging the books as they would have been stored in the history collection of a nor-

mal library would take weeks or months, but since Dracula considered them sorted, according to his own interests, I would leave them as they were and merely try to distinguish one type of collection here from another. I thought the first collection began at the wall of the chamber near the immovable door and ranged through three cabinets and across two large tables: statesmanship and military strategy, I might call it.

Here I found more Machiavelli, in exquisite folios from Padua and Florence. I found a biography of Hannibal by an eighteenth-century Englishman and a curling Greek manuscript, dating back perhaps to the library of Alexandria: Herodotus on the Athenian wars. I began to feel a new chill as I turned through book after manuscript, each one more startling than the last. There was a dog-eared first edition of Mein Kampf *and a diary in French —* handwritten, spotted here and there with brown mould — that appeared from its opening dates and accounts to chronicle the Reign of Terror from the point of view of a government official. I would have to look at it more closely later — the diarist seemed not to have named himself anywhere. I found a large volume on the tactics of Napoleon's first military campaigns, printed while he was on Elba, I calculated. In a box on one of the tables I found a yellowing typescript in the Cyrillic alphabet; my Russian is rudimentary, but I was certain from the headings that it was an internal memo from Stalin to someone in the Russian military. I couldn't read much of it, but it contained a long list of Russian and Polish names.

These were some of the items I could identify at all; there were also many books and manuscripts whose authors or subjects were completely new to me. I had just begun a list of everything I could identify, dividing it roughly by century, when I felt a deepened cold, like a breeze where there was no breeze, and I looked up to see that strange figure standing ten feet away, on the other side of one of the tables.

He was dressed in the red-and-violet finery I'd seen in the sarcophagus, and he was larger and more solid than I seemed to remember from the night before. I waited, speechless, to see if he would attack me at once — did he remember my attempt to take his dagger? But he inclined his head slightly, as if in greeting. "I see you have begun your work. You will, no doubt, have questions for me. First, let us *breakfast, and then we will talk of my collections." I saw a glint in his face, through the dimness of the hall, perhaps a flash of gleaming eye. He led the way with that inhuman but imperious stride back to our fireside, and there I found hot food and drink again, including a steaming tea that brought some relief to my chilled limbs. Dracula sat watching the smokeless fire, his head erect on his great shoulders. Without wishing to, I thought about the decapitation of his corpse — on that point, all the accounts of his death agreed. How did he retain his head now, or was this all illusion? The collar of his fine tunic rose high under his chin, and his dark curls tumbled around it and fell to his shoulders.*

"Now," he said, "let us take a brief tour." He lit all the candles again, and I followed him from table to table while he lit the lanterns there. "We shall have something to read by." I did not like the way the light played on his face as he bent over each new flame, and I tried to look instead at more of the book titles. He came to my side as I stood before the rows of scrolls and books in Arabic I'd noticed before. To my relief, he was still five feet away, but an acrid smell rose from his presence and I fought off a little

faintness. I must keep my wits about me, I thought; there was no telling what this night would bring. "I see you have found one of my prizes," he was saying. There was a rumble of satisfaction in his cold voice. "These are my Ottoman holdings. Some of them are very old, from the first days of their diabolical empire, and this shelf here contains volumes from their last decade." He smiled in the flickering light. "You cannot imagine what a satisfaction it was for me to see their civilization die. Their faith is not dead, of course, but their sultans are gone forever, and I have outlived them." I thought for a moment that he might laugh, but his next words were grave. "Here are great books made for the sultan about his many lands. Here" — he touched the edge of a scroll — "is the history of Mehmed, may he rot in hell, by a Christian historian turned flatterer. May he rot in hell also. I tried to find him myself, that historian, but he died before I could reach him. Here are the accounts of Mehmed's campaigns, by his own flatterers, and of the fall of the Great City. You do not read Arabic?"

"Very little," I confessed.

"Ah." He seemed amused. "I had the opportunity to learn their language and their writing *while I was their prisoner. You know that I was in bondage to them?"*

I nodded, trying not to look at him.

"Yes, my own father left me to the father of Mehmed, as a pledge that we would not wage war against the Empire. Imagine, Dracula a pawn in the hands of the infidel. I wasted no time there — I learned everything I could about them, so that I might surpass them all. That was when I vowed to make history, not to be its victim." His voice was so fierce that I glanced at him in spite of myself and saw the terrible blaze in his face, the hatred, the sharp upwards curl of the mouth under its long mustache. Then he did laugh, and the sound was equally horrifying. "I have triumphed and they are gone." He put his hand on a finely tooled leather binding. "The sultan was so much afraid of me that he founded an order of their knights to pursue me. There are still a few of them, somewhere in Tsarigrad — a nuisance. But they are fewer and fewer, their ranks are dwindling to nothing, while my servants multiply around the globe." He straightened his powerful body. "Come. I will show you my other treasures, and you must tell me how you propose to catalogue them all."

He led me from one section to another, pointing out particular rarities, and I saw that my surmise about the patterns of his collecting were correct. Here was a large cabinet full of manuals of torture, some of them dating to the ancient world. They ranged through the prisons of mediaeval England, to the torture chambers of the Inquisition, to the experiments of the Third Reich. Some of the Renaissance volumes contained woodcuts of implements of torture, others diagrams of the human body. Another section of the room chronicled the church heresies for which many of those manuals of torture had been employed. Another corner was dedicated to alchemy, another to witchcraft, another to philosophy of the most disturbing sort.

Dracula paused in front of a great bookshelf and laid his hand on it affectionately. "This is of special interest to me, and will be to you, as well, I think. These works are biographies of me." Each volume there was connected in some way to his life. There were works by Byzantine and Ottoman historians — some of them very rare originals — and their many reprints through the ages. There were pamphlets from mediaeval Germany, Russia, Hungary, Con-

stantinople, all documenting his crimes. Many of them I'd neither seen nor heard of in my research, and I felt an unreasonable flare of curiosity before I remembered that I had no reason, now, to complete that research. There were also numerous volumes of folklore, from the seventeenth century on, ranging over the legend of the vampire — it struck me as strange and terrible that he included these so frankly among his own biographies. He brought his great hand to rest on an early edition of Bram Stoker's novel and smiled, but said nothing. Then he moved quietly away into another section.

"This is of special interest to you as well," he said. "These are works of history about your century, the twentieth. A fine century — I look forward to the rest of it. In my day, a prince was able to eliminate troublesome elements only one person at a time. You do this with an infinitely greater sweep. Think, for example, of the improvement from the accursed cannon that broke the walls of Constantinople to the divine fire your adoptive country dropped onto the Japanese cities some years ago." He gave me the trace of a bow, courtly, congratulatory. "You will have read many of these

works already, Professor, but perhaps you will glance through them with a new perspective."

At last he bade me settle by the fire again, and I found more of the steaming tea waiting at my elbow. When we were both resting in our chairs, he turned to me. "Soon, I must take my own refreshment," he said quietly. "But first, I will ask you a question." My hands began to tremble in spite of myself. I had tried until now to speak to him as little as possible without incurring his rage. "You have enjoyed my hospitality, such as I can offer here, and my boundless faith in your gifts. You shall enjoy the eternal life that only a few beings can claim. You have the free run of what is certainly the finest archive of its kind on the face of the earth. Rare works are open to you that, indeed, cannot now be seen anywhere else. All this is yours." He stirred in his chair, as if it was difficult for him to keep his great, undead body completely still for long. "Furthermore, you are a man of unparalleled sense and imagination, of keen accuracy and profound judgment. I have much to learn from your methods of research, your synthesis of sources, your imagination. For all these qualities, as well as

The Historian

the great scholarship they feed, I have brought you here, to my treasure-house."

Again he paused. I watched his face, unable to look away. He gazed at the fire. "With your unflinching honesty, you can see the lesson of history," he said. "History has taught us that the nature of man is evil, sublimely so. Good is not perfectible, but evil is. Why should you not use your great mind in service of what is perfectible? I ask you, my friend, to join me of your own accord in my research. If you do so, you will save yourself great anguish, and you will save me considerable trouble. Together we will advance the historian's work beyond anything the world has ever seen. There is no purity like the purity of the sufferings of history. You will have what every historian wants: history will be reality to you. We will wash our minds clean with blood."

He turned the full flood of his gaze on me then, the eyes with their ancient knowledge blazing up and the red lips parted. It would have been a face of the most exquisite intelligence, I suddenly thought, if it had not been shaped by so much hatred. I struggled not to faint, not to go to him on the instant and throw myself on my knees before him, not to put myself under his hand. He was a leader, a prince. He brooked no trespasses. I summoned my love of all I had had in my life, and I formed the word as firmly as I could. "Never."

His face kindled, pale, the nostrils and lips twitching. "You will certainly die here, Professor Rossi," he said, as if trying to control his voice. "You will never leave these chambers alive, although you will go out from them in a new life. Why not have some choice in the matter?"

"No," I said as softly as I could.

He stood, menacingly, and smiled. "Then you shall work for me against your will," he said. A darkness began to pool before my eyes, and I held internally to my small reserve of — what? My skin began to tingle and stars came out in front of me, against the dim walls of the chamber. When he stepped closer I saw his face unmasked, a sight so terrible that I cannot remember it now — I have tried. Then I did not know anything else for a long time.

I woke in my sarcophagus, in the dark, and I thought it was once again the first day, my first awakening there, until I realized that I'd known immediately where I was. I was very weak, much weaker this time, and the wound in my neck oozed and throbbed. I had lost blood, but not so much as to incapacitate me completely. After some time I managed to move around, to climb trembling out of my imprisonment. I remembered the moment I had lost consciousness. I saw by the glow of the remaining candles that Dracula slept again in his great tomb. His eyes were open, glassy, his lips red, his hand closed over his dagger — I turned away in the deepest horror of body and soul and went to crouch by the fire and to try to eat the meal I found there.

Apparently he means to destroy me gradually, perhaps to leave open to me until the last minute the choice he presented last night, so that I might still bring him all the power of a willing mind. I have only one purpose now — no, two: to die with as much of myself intact as I can, in the hope that it may later be some small restraint on the terrible deeds I will do once I am undead, and to stay alive long enough to write all I can in this record, although it will probably crumble to dust unread. These ambitions are my only sustenance now. It is a fate beyond anything I could weep for.

Third Day
I am no longer completely certain of the day; I begin to feel that some other days may have passed, or that I have dreamed several weeks, or that my abduction occurred a month ago. In any case, this is my third writing. I spent the day examining the library, not in order to fulfill Dracula's wishes that I catalogue it for him but to learn whatever I could from it that might be of benefit to anyone — but it is hopeless. I shall just record that I discovered today that Napoleon had two of his own generals assassinated during his first year as emperor, deaths I have never seen chronicled elsewhere. I also examined a brief work by Anna Comnena, the Byzantine historian, entitled "The Torture Commissioned by the Emperor for the Good of the People" — if my Greek serves me. I found a fabulously illustrated volume of cabala, perhaps from Persia, in the section on alchemy. Among the shelves of the collection on heresies, I came across a Byzantine Saint John, but there is something wrong with the beginning of the text — it is about dark, not light. I will have to look carefully at it. I also found an English volume from 1521 — it is dated — called Philosophie of the Aweful, *a work about*

*the Carpathians I have read about but be-
lieved existed no longer.*

*I am too tired and battered to study these
texts as I might — as I should — but wherever
I see something new and strange I pick it up
with an urgency out of proportion to my complete helplessness here. Now I must sleep again,
a little, while Dracula does, so that I can face
my next ordeal somewhat rested, whatever
happens.*

Fourth Day?

*My mind itself begins to crumble, I feel; try
as I may, I can't keep proper track of time or of
my efforts to look through the library. I do not
simply feel weak but ill, and today I had a sensation that sent fresh misery through what remains of my heart. I was looking at a work in
Dracula's unparalleled archive on torture, and
I saw in a fine French quarto there the design
for a new machine that would cleave heads in-
stantaneously from their bodies. There was an
engraving to illustrate this — the parts of the
machine, the man in elegant dress whose theoretical head had just been separated from its
theoretical body. As I looked at this design, I felt
not only disgust at its purpose, not only won-*

der at the wonderful condition of the book, but also a sudden longing to see the real scene, to hear the shouts of the crowd and see the spurt of blood over that lace jabot and velvet jacket. Every historian knows the thirst to see the reality of the past, but this was something new, a different sort of hunger. I flung the book aside, put my throbbing head down on the table, and wept for the first time since my imprisonment began. I had not wept in years, in fact, not since my mother's funeral. The salt of my own tears comforted me a little — it was so ordinary.

Day

The monster sleeps, but he did not speak to me all of yesterday, except to ask me how the catalogue is coming along, and to examine my work on it for a few minutes. I am too tired to continue the task just now, or even to type much. I will sit in front of the fire and try to collect a little of my old self there.

Day

Last night he sat me before the fire again, as if we were still holding civilized discourse, and told me that he will move the library soon, sooner than he had originally intended, because some threat to it is drawing closer. "This will be your last night, and then I will leave you here a little," he said, "but you will come to me when I call for you. Then you may resume your work in a new and safer place. Later we shall see about sending you out into the world. Think all you can about whom you will bring to me, to help us in our task. For now, I shall leave you where you will not be found, in any case." He smiled, which made my vision blur, and I tried to watch the fire instead. "You have been most obstinate. Perhaps we will disguise you as a holy relic." I had no desire to ask him what he meant by this.

So it is only a matter of a short time before he finishes my mortal life. Now all my energy goes to strengthening myself for the last moments. I am careful not to think of the people I have loved, in the hope that I will be less likely to think of them in my next, damned state. I will hide this record in the most beautiful book I have found here — one of the few works in the library that does not now give me a horrified pleasure — and then I will hide that book as well, so that it will cease to belong to this archive. If only I could consign myself to dust with it. I feel sunset approaching, somewhere out in the world where light and dark still exist, and I will use all my waning energy to remain myself to the last moment. If there is any good in life, in history, in my own past, I invoke it now. I invoke it with all the passion with which I have lived.

Chapter 74

"HELEN TOUCHED HER FATHER'S forehead with two fingers, as if conferring a blessing. She was fighting sobs now. 'How can we move him out of here? I want to bury him.'

"'There's no time,' I said bitterly. 'He'd rather we got out alive, I'm sure.'

"I took my jacket off and spread it gently over him, covering his face. The stone lid was too heavy to put back on. Helen picked up her little pistol, carefully checking it even in the midst of her emotion. 'The library,' she whispered. 'We must find it immediately. And did you hear something a moment ago?'

"I nodded. 'I think I did, but I couldn't tell where it was coming from.' We stood listening hard. The silence hung unbroken above us. Helen was trying the walls now, feeling along them with her pistol in one hand. The candlelight was frustratingly dim. We went around and around, pressing and tapping. There were no niches, no oddly protruding rocks, no possible openings, nothing that looked suspicious.

"'It must be almost dark outside,' Helen muttered.

"'I know,' I said. 'We've probably got ten minutes and then we shouldn't be here, I'm sure of that.' We went around the little room again, checking every inch. The air was chill, especially now that I wasn't wearing my jacket, but sweat began to trail down my back. 'Maybe the library is in another part of the church, or in the foundation.'

"'It has to be completely hidden, probably underground,' Helen whispered. 'Otherwise someone would have known of it long ago. Also, if my father is in this grave — ' She didn't finish, but it was the question that had tormented me even in the first moment of shock, seeing Rossi there: where was Dracula?

"'Isn't there anything unusual here?' Helen was looking at the low, vaulted ceiling now, trying to reach it with her fingertips.

"'I don't see anything.' Then a sudden thought made me snatch a candle from the stand and crouch down. Helen followed me swiftly.

"'Yes,' she breathed. I was touching the carved dragon on the vertical of the lowest step. I had stroked it with my finger during our first visit to the crypt; now I pushed it hard, put my weight into it. It was firm in the wall. But Helen's sensitive hands were already feeling the stones around it, and she suddenly found a loose one; it simply came out in her hand, like a tooth, from where it was embedded next to the dragon carving. A small dark hole gaped where it had been; I put my hand in and waved it around, but encountered only space. Helen slipped hers in, however, and brought it back toward the dragon, behind the carving. 'Paul!' she cried softly.

"I followed her grasp into the dark. There was certainly a handle there, a large handle of cold iron, and when I pushed on it the dragon lifted easily out of its space under the step without disturbing any of the other stones around it or the step above it. It was a finely chiseled piece of work, we saw now, with an iron handle in the shape of a horned beast drilled into it, presumably so you could pull it shut behind you when you went down the narrow stone steps opening before us. Helen took a second candle and I grabbed the matches. We entered on hands and knees — I remembered suddenly Rossi's bruised and scraped appearance, his torn clothes, and wondered if he'd been dragged more than once through this opening — but we were soon able to stand upright on the steps.

"The air that came up to meet us was cold and dank in the extreme, and I fought to control a trembling deep inside and to keep a firm hold on Helen, who was also trembling, during the steep descent. At the bottom of fifteen steps was a passage, infernally dark, although our candle-light showed iron sconces pinned high on the walls, as if it had once been illuminated. At the end of the passageway — again, it seemed to me about fifteen steps forward, and I was careful to count them — was a door of heavy and clearly very old wood, wearing into splinters near the bottom, and again that eerie door handle, a long-horned creature wrought in iron. I felt more than saw Helen raise her pistol. The door was wedged firm, but on examining it closely I found it bolted from the side we were on. I put all my weight under the heavy latch, and then I pulled the door open with a slow fear that nearly melted my bones.

"Inside, the light of our candles, feeble as it was, fell on a great chamber. There were tables near the door, long tables of an ancient solidity, and empty bookshelves. The air of the room was surprisingly dry after the chill of the passage, as if it had some secret ventilation or was dug into a protected depth of earth. We stood clinging to each other, and listened hard, but there was no sound in the room. I wished devoutly that we could see beyond the darkness. The next thing our light picked up was a branching candelabrum filled with half-burned candles, and this I lit all over. It illuminated high cabinets now, and I looked cautiously inside one of them. It was empty. 'Is this the library?' I said. 'There's nothing here.'

"We stood still again, listening, and Helen's pistol glinted in the increased light. I thought that I should have offered to carry it, to use it if necessary, but I had never handled a gun, and she, I knew very well, was a crack shot. 'Look, Paul.' She pointed with her free hand, and I saw what had caught her gaze.

"'Helen,' I said, but she was moving forward. After a second my light reached a table that had not been illuminated before, a great stone table. It was not a table, I saw an instant later, but an altar — no, not an altar, but a sarcophagus. There was another nearby — had this been a continuation of the monastery's crypt, a place where its abbots could rest in peace, away from Byzantine torches and Ottoman catapults? Then we saw beyond them the largest sarcophagus of all. Along the side ran one word, cut into the stone:

DRACULA. Helen raised her gun, and I gripped my stake. She took a step forward and I kept close to her.

"At that moment we heard a commotion behind us, at a distance, and the crash of footsteps and scrambling bodies, which almost obscured the faint sound in the darkness beyond the tomb, a trickling of dry earth. We leaped forward like one being and looked in — the largest sarcophagus had no covering slab and it was empty, as were the other two. And that sound: somewhere in the darkness, some small creature was making its way up through the tree roots.

"Helen fired into the dark and there was a crashing of earth and pebbles; I ran forward with my light. The end of the library was a dead end, with a few roots hanging down from the vaulted ceiling. In the niche on the back wall where an icon might once have stood, I saw a trickle of black slime on the bare stones — blood? An infiltration of moisture from the earth?

"The door behind us burst open and we swung around, my hand on Helen's free arm. Into our candlelight came a strong lantern, flashlights, hurrying forms, a shout. It was Ranov, and with him a tall figure whose shadow leaped forward to engulf us: Géza József, and at his heels a terrified

Brother Ivan. He was followed by a wiry little bureaucrat in dark suit and hat, with a heavy dark mustache. There was another figure, too, one who moved haltingly, and whose slow progress, I realized now, must have hampered them at every step: Stoichev. His face was a strange mixture of fear, regret, and curiosity, and there was a bruise on his cheek. His old eyes met ours for a long sorrowful moment, and then he moved his lips, as if thanking his God to find us alive.

"Géza and Ranov were on us in a fraction of a second. Ranov had a gun trained on me and Géza on Helen, while the monk stood openmouthed and Stoichev waited, quiet and wary, behind them. The dark-suited bureaucrat stood just out of the light. 'Drop your gun,' Ranov told Helen, and she let it fall obediently to the floor. I put my arm around her, but slowly. In the gloomy candlelight their faces looked more than sinister, except for Stoichev's. I saw that he would have hazarded a smile at us if he had not been so frightened.

"'What the hell are you doing here?' Helen said to Géza before I could stop her.

"'What the hell are you doing here, my dear?' was his only answer. He looked taller than ever, dressed in a pale shirt and pants and heavy walking boots. I hadn't realized at the conference that I actually hated his guts.

"'Where is he?' Ranov growled. He looked from me to Helen.

"'He's dead,' I said. 'You came through the crypt. You must have seen him.'

"Ranov frowned. 'What are you talking about?'

"Something, some instinct I owed to Helen, perhaps, stopped me from saying more.

"'Whom do you mean?' Helen said coldly.

"Géza trained his gun a little more exactly on her. 'You know what I mean, Elena Rossi. Where is Dracula?'

"This was easier to answer, and I let Helen go first. 'He is not here, evidently,' she said in her nastiest voice. 'You may examine the tomb.' At this the little bureaucrat took a step forward and seemed about to speak.

"'Stay with them,' Ranov said to Géza. Ranov moved carefully forward among the tables, glancing around at everything; it was clear to me that he'd never been here before. The dark-suited bureaucrat followed him without a word. When they reached the sarcophagus, Ranov held up his lantern and his gun and looked cautiously inside. 'It is empty,' he threw back to Géza. He turned to the other two, smaller sarcophagi.

'What is this? Come here, help me.' The bureaucrat and the monk stepped obediently forward. Stoichev followed more slowly and I thought I saw a light in his face as he looked around him at the empty tables, the cabinets. I could only guess what he made of this place.

"Ranov was already peering into the sarcophagi. 'Empty,' he said heavily. 'He is not here. Search the room.' Géza was already striding among the tables, holding his light up to every wall, opening cabinets. 'Did you see him or hear him?'

"'No,' I said, more or less truthfully. I told myself that if only they didn't injure Helen, if they let her go, I would consider this expedition a success. I would never ask life for anything else. I also thought, with fleeting gratitude, of Rossi's delivery from this whole situation.

"Géza said something that must have been a curse in Hungarian, because Helen nearly smiled, despite the gun aimed at her heart. 'It is useless,' he said, after a moment. 'The tomb in the crypt is empty, and this one is also. And he will never return to this place, since we have found it.' It took me a moment to digest this. The tomb in the crypt was empty? Then where was Rossi's body, which we'd just left there?

Ranov turned to Stoichev. 'Tell us about what is here.' They had lowered their guns at last and I drew Helen to me, which made Géza give me one sour look, although he said nothing.

"Stoichev held his lantern up as if he had been waiting for this moment. He went to the nearest table and tapped it. 'These are oak, I think,' he said slowly, 'and they could be medieval in their design.' He looked under the table at a leg joint, tapped a cabinet. 'But I do not know much about furniture.' We waited, silently.

"Géza kicked the leg of one of the ancient tables. 'What am I going to say to the Minister of Culture? That Wallachian belonged to us. He was a Hungarian prisoner and his country was our territory.'

"'Why don't we quarrel about that when we find him?' Ranov growled. I realized suddenly that their only common language was English, and that they loathed each other. At that moment I knew whom Ranov reminded me of. With his heavyset face and thick dark mustache, he looked like the photographs I'd seen of the young Stalin. People like Ranov and Géza did minimal damage only because they had minimal power.

"'Tell your aunt to be more careful with her phone calls.' Géza gave Helen a baleful look and I felt her stiffen against me. 'Now leave this damned monk to guard the place,' he added to Ranov, and Ranov issued a command that made poor Brother Ivan tremble. At that moment, the light from Ranov's lantern suddenly fell in a new direction. He had been raising it here and there, examining the tables. Now his light slanted across the face of the dark-suited, severely hatted little bureaucrat, who was standing silently by Dracula's empty sarcophagus. Perhaps I wouldn't have noticed his face at all if it hadn't been for the strange expression it wore — a look of private grief suddenly illuminated by the lantern. I could see plainly the bone-thin face under the awkward mustache, and the familiar glitter of the eyes. 'Helen!' I shouted. 'Look!' She stared, too.

"'What?' Géza turned on her in an instant.

"'This man — ' Helen was aghast. 'That man there — he is — '

"'He's a vampire,' I said flatly. 'He followed us from our university in the United States.' I had barely begun to speak before the creature was in flight. He had to come straight toward us to get out, barreling into Géza, who tried to seize him, and pushing past Ranov. Ranov was quicker on his feet; he grabbed the librarian, they collided hard, and then Ranov leaped back from him with a cry and the librarian was in flight again. Ranov turned and shot the hurtling figure before it was many feet away. It didn't falter for a second — Ranov might have been shooting into air. Then the evil librarian was gone, so suddenly that I wasn't sure whether he'd actually reached the passage or vanished before our eyes. Ranov ran after him, through the doorway, but returned almost immediately. We all stood staring at him; his face was white, and where he grasped the torn cloth of his jacket, a little blood was already trickling between his fingers. After a long minute Ranov spoke. 'What the hell is this about?' His voice trembled.

"Géza shook his head. 'My God,' he said. 'He bit you.' He took a step back from Ranov. 'And I was alone with that little man several times. He said he could tell me where we could find the Americans, but he never told me he was — '

"'Of course he never told you,' Helen said contemptuously, although I tried to keep her quiet. 'He wanted to find his master, to follow us to him, not to kill you. You were more useful to him this way. Did he give you our notes?'

"'Shut up.' Géza looked inclined to strike her, but I heard the fear and awe in his voice, and I quietly drew her away.

"'Come.' Ranov was herding us with his gun again, one hand on his wounded shoulder. 'You have been of very little assistance. I want you back in Sofia and on a plane as soon as possible. You are lucky we don't have permission to make you disappear — it would be too inconvenient.' I thought he was going to kick us as Géza had done to the table leg, but he turned instead and ushered us brusquely out of the library. He made Stoichev walk ahead; I guessed with a pang what the old man must have been through, in the course of this coercive chase. Clearly, Stoichev hadn't intended for us to be followed; I'd believed that from my first glimpse of the misery in his face. Had he made it back to Sofia before they forced him to turn around and follow us? I hoped Stoichev's international reputation would protect him from further abuse, as it had in the past. But Ranov — that was the worst of it. Ranov would probably return, infected, to his duties with the secret police. I wondered if Géza would try to do anything about this, but the Hungarian's face looked so forbidding that I didn't dare to address him.

"I looked back once, from the doorway, at the princely sarcophagus that had lain here for nearly five hundred years. Its occupant might be anywhere now, or on his way to anywhere. At the top of the steps we crawled one by one through the opening — I prayed none of those guns would go off — and there I saw something very strange. The reliquary of Saint Petko sat open on its pedestal. They must have had some tools, to open it where we had failed. The marble slab underneath was back in place and covered with its embroidered cloth, undisturbed. Helen shot me a blank look. Glancing into the reliquary as we passed it, I saw a few pieces of bone, a polished skull — all that remained of the local martyr.

"Outside the church, in the heavy night, there was a confusion of cars and people — Géza had apparently arrived with an entourage, two of whom were guarding the church doors. Dracula certainly hadn't escaped that way, I thought. The mountains loomed around us, darker than the dark sky. Some of the villagers had gotten wind of the arrivals and come up with lighted torches; they fell back at Ranov's approach, staring at his torn and bloody jacket, their faces strained in the uneven light. Stoichev caught my arm; his face bobbed near my ear. 'We closed it,' he whispered.

"'What?' I bent to listen to him.

"'The monk and I went down first, into the crypt, while those — those thugs searched the church and the woods for you. We saw the man in the grave — not Dracula — and I knew you had been there. So we closed it up and when they came down they opened the reliquary only. They were so angry then that I thought they would throw out the poor saint's bones.' Brother Ivan looked sturdy enough, I thought, but Professor Stoichev's frailty must conceal a rare strength. Stoichev looked sharply at me. 'But who was that in the grave underneath, if it was not — ?'

"'It was Professor Rossi,' I whispered. Ranov was opening car doors, ordering us in.

"Stoichev gave me a quick, eloquent look. 'I am so sorry.'"

"That is how we left my dearest friend resting in Bulgaria, may he sleep there in peace until the end of the world."

Chapter 75

"AFTER OUR ADVENTURE IN A CRYPT, the Boras' front parlor looked like heaven on earth. It was an exquisite relief to be there again, with cups of hot tea in our hands — the weather had taken a rare cool turn that week, although it was June already — and Turgut smiling at us from the cushions of the divan. Helen had slipped off her shoes at the door to the apartment and put on some tasseled red slippers Mrs. Bora brought her. Selim Aksoy was there, too, sitting quietly in the corner, and Turgut made sure that he and Mrs. Bora got a fair translation of everything.

"'Are you certain that the tomb was empty?' Turgut had asked it once already, but seemed unable to refrain from asking again.

"'Quite sure.' I glanced at Helen. 'What we don't know is whether the noise we heard was the sound of Dracula escaping somehow as we came in. It was probably dark outside by then, and easy for him to move around.'

"'And he could have changed shape, of course, if the legend is correct.' Turgut sighed. 'Damn his eyes! You were very close to catching him, my friends, closer than the Crescent Guard has come in five centuries. I am passing glad you were not killed, but terribly sorry also that you were not able to destroy him.'

"'Where do you think he went?' Helen leaned forward, her eyes intensely dark.

"Turgut stroked his big chin. 'Well, my dear, I cannot guess. He can travel far and fast, but I do not know how far he would go. To another ancient site, I am sure, some hiding place that has been undisturbed for centuries. It must have been a blow for him to leave Sveti Georgi, but he would understand that this site will be guarded now for a long time to come. I would give my right hand to know whether he has remained somewhere in Bulgaria or left the country altogether. Borders and politics do not mean very much to him, I am certain.' Turgut's frown was harsh on his kind face.

"'You do not think he would follow us?' Helen asked simply, but something in the angle of her shoulders made me think that the very simplicity with which she asked this question cost her an effort.

"Turgut shook his head. 'I hope not, Madam

Professor. I should think he would be a little afraid of you two by now, since you found him when no one else could.'

"Helen was silent, and I didn't like the doubt in her face. Selim Aksoy and Mrs. Bora watched her with a particular tenderness, too, I thought; maybe they were wondering how I could have allowed her to go into such a dangerous situation in the first place, even if we'd managed to return whole.

"Turgut turned to me. 'And I am deeply sorry about your friend Rossi. I would have liked to meet him.'

"'And I know you would have enjoyed each other's company,' I said sincerely, taking Helen's hand. Her eyes filled whenever Rossi's name came up, and now she looked away, as if for privacy.

"'I wish I could have met Professor Stoichev, also.' Turgut sighed again and set his cup down on the brass table before us.

"'That would have been magnificent,' I said, smiling at the picture of the two scholars comparing notes. 'You and Stoichev could have explained the Ottoman Empire and the medieval Balkans to each other. Maybe you will meet someday.'

"Turgut shook his head. 'I do not think so,' he said. 'The barriers between us are as high and — prickly — as they were between any *tsar* and pasha. But if you ever speak with him again, or write to him, by all means give him my regards.'

"It was an easy promise to make.

"Selim Aksoy wanted Turgut to put a question to us, and Turgut listened to him gravely. 'We are wondering,' he told us, 'if in the midst of all that danger and chaos you saw the book that Professor Rossi described — a life of Saint George, was it not? Did the Bulgarians take it to the university in Sofia?'

"Helen's laugh could be surprisingly girlish when she was really delighted, and I refrained from kissing her soundly in front of all of them. She had barely smiled since we'd left Rossi's grave. 'It is in my briefcase,' I said. 'For the moment.'

"Turgut stared, astounded, and it took him a long minute to recollect his duties as interpreter. 'And how did it find a home there?'

"Helen was mute, smiling, so I explained. 'I didn't think of it again myself until we were back in Sofia, at the hotel.' No, I couldn't tell them the whole truth, so I gave them a polite version.

"The whole truth was that when we had finally been alone together for ten minutes in Helen's hotel room, I took her into my arms and kissed her smoky dark hair, pulled her against my shoulder, fitting her to me through our soiled travel clothes like the other part of myself — Plato's missing half, I thought — and then I felt not only the relief of our having survived together to embrace there, and the beauty of her long bones, her breath against my neck, but also something inexplicably wrong about her body, something lumpy and hard. I drew back and looked at her, fearful, and saw her wry smile. She laid her finger to her lips. It was merely a reminder; we both knew the room was probably bugged.

"After a second she put my hands on the buttons of her blouse, which was now shabby and dirty from our adventures. I unbuttoned it without letting myself dare to think, and drew it off. I've said that women's undergarments were more complicated in those days, with secret wires and hooks and strange compartments — an inner armor. Wrapped in a handkerchief and warmed against Helen's skin was a book — not the great folio I'd imagined when Rossi had told us about its existence, but a volume small enough to fit in my hand. Its casing was elaborately patterned gold over painted wood and leather. The gold was set with emeralds, rubies, sapphires, lapis, fine pearls — a little firmament of jewels, all to honor the face of the saint at the center. His delicate Byzantine features looked as if they'd been painted a few days earlier, rather than centuries, and his wide, sad, dragon-forgiving eyes seemed to follow mine. His eyebrows rose in fine arches above them, the nose was long and straight, his mouth sadly severe. The portrait had a roundness, a fullness, a realism I hadn't seen in Byzantine art before, a look of Roman ancestry. If I had not been in love already, I would have said this was the most beautiful face I'd ever seen, human but also celestial, or celestial but also human. Across the neck of his robe I saw finely inked words. 'Greek,' Helen said. Her voice was less than a whisper, hovering at my ear. 'Saint George.'

"Inside were small sheets of parchment in breathtakingly good condition, each covered in a fine medieval hand, also Greek. Here and there I saw exquisite pages of illustration: Saint George driving his spear into the maw of a writhing dragon while a crowd of nobles looked on; Saint George receiving a tiny gilded crown from Christ, who reached down with it from his heavenly throne; Saint George on his deathbed, mourned by red-winged angels. Each was filled with astounding, miniature detail. Helen nodded and drew my ear close to her mouth again, barely breathing. 'I am no expert on this,' she whispered, 'but I think it might have been made for the emperor of Constantinople — exactly which one remains to be seen. This is the seal of the later emperors.' Sure enough, on the inside front cover was painted a double-headed eagle, the bird that looked backward into Byzantium's august past and forward into its limitless future; it hadn't been sharp-eyed enough to see ahead to the toppling of the Empire by an upstart infidel.

"'That means it dates at least from the first half of the fifteenth century,' I breathed. 'Before the conquest.'

"'Oh, I think it is much older than that,' Helen whispered, gently touching the seal. 'My father — my father said it was very old. And you see the insignia here indicates Constantine Porphyrogenitus. He reigned in' — she searched an inner file — 'the first half of the tenth century. He was in power before *Bachkovski manastir* was founded. The eagle must have been added later.'

"I scarcely breathed the words. 'You mean that

this is more than a thousand years old?' Holding the book carefully in both hands, I sat down on the edge of the bed next to Helen. Neither of us made a sound; we were speaking more or less with our eyes. 'It's in nearly perfect condition. And you intend to smuggle such a treasure out of Bulgaria? Helen,' I told her with a glance, 'you are out of your mind. And what about the fact that it belongs to the Bulgarian people?'

"She kissed me, took the book out of my hands, and opened it to the front. 'It was a gift from my father,' she whispered. The inside front cover had a deep flap of leather over it, and she reached carefully inside this. 'I have waited to look at this until we could open it together.' She drew out a packet of thin paper covered with dense typing. Then we read together, in silence, Rossi's agonized journal. When we were done, neither of us spoke, although we were both weeping. At last Helen wrapped the book in the handkerchief again and put it carefully back in its hiding place against her skin.

"Turgut smiled as I finished a diluted version of this story. 'But there is more I have to tell you, and it is very important,' I said. I described Rossi's terrible imprisonment in the library. They listened with still, grave faces, and when I came to the fact that Dracula knew of the continued existence of a guard formed by the sultan to pursue him, Turgut drew a sharp breath. 'I am sorry,' I said.

"He translated quickly for Selim, who bowed his head and then said something in a soft voice. Turgut nodded. 'He says the thing I most feel. This terrible news only means we must be the more diligent in pursuing the Impaler, and in keeping his influence from our city. His Gloriousness the Refuge of the World would command us in just this way, if he were alive. This is true. And what will you do with this book when you go home?'

"'I know someone who has a connection with an auction house,' I said. 'We will be very careful, of course, and we'll wait a while before we do anything. I expect some museum will get it, sooner or later.'

"'And the money?' Turgut shook his head. 'What will you do with so much?'

"'We're thinking it over,' I said. 'Something in the service of good. We don't yet know what.'

"Our plane to New York left at five, and Turgut began looking at his watch as soon as we'd finished our last enormous lunch on the divans. He had an evening class to teach, alas, alack, but Mr.

Aksoy would ride with us to the airport in a taxi-cab. When we stood to go, Mrs. Bora brought out a scarf of the finest cream-colored silk, embroidered with silver, and put it around Helen's neck. It hid the shabbiness of her black jacket and soiled collar and we all gasped — at least I did, and I can't have been alone. Her face above the scarf was the countenance of an empress. 'For your marriage day,' Mrs. Bora said, standing on tiptoe to kiss her.

"Turgut kissed Helen's hand. 'It belonged to my mother,' he said simply, and Helen could not speak. I spoke for both of us, shaking their hands. We would write, we would think of them. Life being long, we would see one another again."

Chapter 76

"THE LAST PART OF MY STORY is perhaps the hardest for me to tell, since it begins with so much happiness, in spite of everything. We returned quietly to the university and took up our work again. I was questioned by the police once more, but they seemed satisfied that my trip abroad had been connected with research, and not with Rossi's vanishing. The newspapers had seized upon his disappearance by then and made a local mystery of it, which the university did its best to ignore. My chairman questioned me, too, of course, and of course I told him nothing, except to say that I grieved as much as anyone for Rossi. Helen and I were married in my parents' church in Boston that autumn — even in the midst of the ceremony I couldn't help noticing how bare and plain it was, how devoid of incense.

"My parents were a little stunned by all this, of course, but they could not help liking Helen, ultimately. None of her native harshness showed around them, and when we visited them in Boston I often found Helen laughing in the kitchen with my mother, teaching her to cook Hungarian specialties, or discussing anthropology with my father in his cramped study. For myself, although I felt the pain of Rossi's death and the frequent melancholy it seemed to cause in Helen, I found that first year full of a brimming joy. I finished my dissertation under a second adviser, whose face remained a blur to me throughout the process. It was not that I cared about Dutch merchants anymore; I only wanted to complete my education so that I could settle us comfortably somewhere. Helen published a long article on Wallachian village superstitions, which was well-received, and began a dissertation on the remnants of Transylvanian customs in Hungary.

"We wrote something else, too, as soon as we returned to the States: a note to Helen's mother, care of Aunt Éva. Helen didn't dare to put much information into it, but she told her mother in a few brief lines that Rossi had died remembering and loving her. Helen sealed the letter with a look of despair on her face. 'I will tell her everything someday,' she said, 'when I can whisper it into her ear.' We never knew for certain whether this letter reached its destination because neither Aunt Éva nor Helen's mother wrote back, and within a year Soviet troops had invaded Hungary.

"I fully intended to live happily ever after, and I mentioned to Helen soon after we married that I hoped we would have children. At first she shook her head, touching the scar on her neck with gentle fingers. I knew what she meant. But her exposure had been minimal, I pointed out; she was well and strong and healthy. As time went by she seemed lulled by her own complete recovery, and I saw her looking with wistful eyes into the baby carriages we passed on the street.

"Helen received her doctorate in anthropology the spring after we were married. The speed with which she wrote her dissertation shamed me; I would often wake during that year to find that it was five in the morning and she had already left our bed for her desk. She looked pale and tired, and the day after she defended her dissertation I woke to blood on the sheets, and Helen lying next to me faint and wracked with pain: a miscarriage. She had been waiting to surprise me with good news. She was ill for several weeks afterward, and very quiet. Her dissertation received the highest honors, but she never spoke of that.

"When I got my first teaching job, in New York City, she urged me to take it, and we moved. We settled in Brooklyn Heights, in a pleasantly run-down brownstone. We took walks along the promenade to watch the tugboats navigating the port and the great passenger liners — the last of their race — pulling out for Europe. Helen taught at a university as good as mine and her students adored her; there was a magnificent balance to our lives, and we were making a living doing what we liked best.

"Now and then we took out the *Life of Saint George* and looked slowly through it, and the day came when we went to a discreet auction house with it, and the Englishman who opened it nearly fainted. It was sold privately, and eventually made its way to the Cloisters, in upper Manhattan, and a great deal of money made its way into a bank account we had set up for the purpose. Helen disliked elaborate living as much as I did, and apart from the attempt to send small amounts to her relatives in Hungary, we left the money alone, for the time being.

"Helen's second miscarriage was more dramatic than the first, and more dangerous; I came home one day to a pattern of bloody footsteps on the parquet floor in the hall. She had managed to call the ambulance herself and was nearly out of danger by the time I reached the hospital. Afterward, the memory of those footprints woke me over and over in the middle of the night. I began to fear we would never have a healthy child and to wonder how this would affect Helen's life, in particular. Then she became pregnant again, and month after cautious month passed without incident. Helen grew as softeyed as a Madonna, her form round under her blue wool dress, her walk a little unsteady. She was always smiling; this one, she said, was the one we would keep.

"You were born in a hospital overlooking the Hudson. When I saw that you were dark and fine-browed like your mother, and as perfect as a new coin, and that Helen's eyes were overflowing with tears of pleasure and pain, I held you up in your tight cocoon to give you a glimpse of the ships below. That was partly to hide my own tears. We named you for Helen's mother.

"Helen was enthralled by you; I would like you to know that fact more than almost anything else about our lives. She had left her teaching during the pregnancy and seemed content to spend hours at home playing with your fingers and feet, which she said with a wicked smile were completely Transylvanian, or rocking you in the big chair I bought her. You smiled early and your eyes followed us everywhere. I left my office on impulse sometimes to come home and make sure the two of you — my dark-haired women — were still lying drowsily on the sofa together.

"One day, I arrived home early, at four, bringing some little boxes of Chinese food and some flowers for you to stare at. No one was in the living room, and I found Helen leaning over your crib while you took a nap. Your face was exquisitely tranquil in sleep, but Helen's was smeared with tears, and for a second she didn't seem to register my presence. I took her into my arms and felt, with a chill, that something in her returned only slowly to my embrace. She would not tell me what had been troubling her, and after a few futile rounds I didn't dare question her further. That evening she was playful over the carried-in food and the carnations, but the next week I found her in tears again, silent again, looking through one of Rossi's books, which he had signed for me when we'd first begun our work together. It was his huge volume on the Minoan civilization, and it lay across her lap, open to one of Rossi's own photographs of a sacrificial altar on Crete. 'Where's the baby?' I said.

"She raised her head slowly and stared at me, as if reminding herself what year it was. 'She's asleep.'

"I found myself, strangely, resisting the urge to go into the bedroom and check on you. 'Darling, what's the matter?' I put the book away and held her, but she shook her head and said nothing. When I finally went in to see you, you were just waking in your crib, with your lovely smile, flipping over on your stomach, pushing yourself up to look at me.

"Soon Helen was silent almost every morning and cried for no apparent reason every evening. Since she wouldn't talk to me, I insisted she see a doctor, and then a psychoanalyst. The doctor said he could find nothing wrong with her, that women were sometimes blue during the first months of motherhood, that she would be fine once she got used to it. I discovered too late, when a friend of ours ran into Helen at the New York Public Library, that she had not been going to the analyst at all. When I confronted her with this, she said she'd decided that some research would cheer her up more, and had been using the babysitter's time for that instead. But her mood was so low some evenings that I concluded she desperately needed a change of scene. I took a little money from our hoard and bought airline tickets to France for early spring.

"Helen had never been to France, although she'd read about it all her life and spoke an excellent schoolgirl French. She looked cheerful on Montmartre, commenting with some of her old wryness that *le Sacré Coeur* was even more monumentally ugly than she'd ever dreamed. She liked pushing your carriage in the flower markets, and along the Seine, where we lingered, turning through the wares of the booksellers while you sat looking at the water in your soft red hood. You were an excellent traveler at nine months and Helen told you it was only the beginning.

"The concierge at our pension turned out to be the grandmother of many, and we left you sleeping under her care while we toasted each other at a brass-railed bar or drank coffee outside with our gloves on. Above all, Helen — and you, with your bright eyes — loved the echoing vault of Notre Dame, and eventually we wandered farther south to see other cavernous beauties — Chartres and its radiant glass; Albi with its peculiar red fortress-church, home of heresies; the halls of Carcassone.

"Helen wanted to visit the ancient monastery of Saint-Matthieu-des-Pyrénées-Orientales, and we decided to go there for a day or two before returning for Paris and the flight home. I thought her face had brightened considerably on the trip, and I liked the way she lay sprawled across our hotel bed in Perpignan, flipping through a history of French architecture that I'd bought in Paris. The monastery had been built in the year 1000, she told me, although she knew I'd already read that whole section. It was the oldest surviving example of Romanesque architecture in Europe. 'Almost as old as the *Life of Saint George*,' I mused, but at this she closed the book and her face and lay staring at you hungrily where you played on the bed beside her.

"Helen insisted that we approach the monastery on foot, like pilgrims. We climbed the road from Les Bains on a cool spring morning, our sweaters tied around our waists as we grew warmer. Helen carried you in a corduroy pack on her chest, and when she got tired I carried you in my arms. The road was empty at this season, except for one silent, dark-haired peasant who passed us on his horse, going up. I told Helen we should have asked him for a ride, but she didn't answer; her low mood had returned this morning, and I noted with anxiety and frustration that her eyes filled with tears from time to time. I knew already that if I asked her what was wrong she would shake her head, shake me off, so I tried to content myself with holding you tenderly as we climbed, pointing out the views to you when we turned a bend in the road, long vistas of dusty fields and villages below. At the summit of the mountain the road broke into a wide estuary of dust, with an old car or two parked there, and the peasant's horse — apparently — tied to a tree, although the man himself was nowhere in sight. The monastery rose above this area, heavy stone walls climbing the very summit, and we went up through the entrance and into the care of the monks.

"In those days, Saint-Matthieu was much more a working monastery than it is now, and it must have had a community of twelve or thirteen, leading the lives their predecessors had for a thousand years, with the exception of the fact that they gave the occasional tour to visitors and kept an automobile parked for their own use outside the gates. Two monks showed us around the exquisite cloisters — I remember how surprised I was when I went to the open end of the courtyard and saw that sheer drop over outcroppings of rock, the vertical cliff, the plains below. The mountains around the monastery are even higher than the summit where it perches, and on their distant flanks we could see veils of white that I realized after a moment were waterfalls.

"We sat a while on a bench near this precipice, with you balanced between us, looking out at the enormous noon sky and listening to the bubbling water in the monastery cistern at the center, carved of red marble — heaven only knew how they'd hauled that up here, centuries before. Helen seemed more cheerful again, and I noted with pleasure the peace in her face. Even if she was still sad at times, this trip had been well worthwhile.

"Eventually Helen said she wanted to see more of the place. We put you back in your sack and went around to the kitchens and the long refectory where the monks still ate, and the hostel where pilgrims could still sleep on cots, and the scriptorium, one of the oldest parts of the complex, where so many great manuscripts had been copied and illuminated. There was a sample of one under glass there, a Matthew open to a page bordered with tiny demons goading one another downward. Helen actually smiled over it. The chapel was next — it was small, like everything else in the monastery, but its proportions were melody in stone; I'd never seen the Romanesque like this, so intimate and lovely. Our guidebook claimed that the rounding outward of the apse was the first moment of the Romanesque, a sudden gesture that brought in light across the altar. There was some fourteenth-century glass in the narrow windows, and the altar itself was perfectly arrayed for mass in red and white, with golden candlesticks. We left quietly.

"At last the young monk who was our guide said we'd seen everything but the crypt, and we followed him down there. It was a small dank hole off the cloisters, architecturally interesting for an early Romanesque vault held up by a few squat columns, and for a grimly ornamented stone sarcophagus dating from the earliest century of the monastery's existence — the resting place of their first abbot, said our guide. Next to the sarcophagus sat an elderly monk lost in his meditations; he looked up, kind and confused, when we entered, and bowed to us without rising from his chair. 'We have had a tradition here for centuries that one of us sits with the abbot,' explained our guide. 'Usually it is an older monk who has held this honor for his lifetime.'

"'How unusual,' I said, but something about the place, perhaps the chill, made you whimper and struggle on Helen's chest, and seeing that she was tired I offered to take you up to the fresh air. I stepped out of that dank hole with a sense of relief myself and went to show you the fountain in the cloisters.

"I'd expected Helen to follow me at once, but she lingered underground, and when she came up again her face was so changed that I felt a rush of alarm. She looked animated — yes, more lively than I'd seen her in months — but also pale and wide-eyed, intent on something I couldn't see. I moved toward her as casually as I could; I asked her if there'd been anything else of interest down there. 'Maybe,' she said, but as if she couldn't quite hear me for the roar of thoughts inside. Then she turned to you, suddenly, and took you from me, hugging you and kissing your head and cheeks. 'Is she all right? Was she frightened?'

"'She's fine,' I said. 'A little hungry, maybe.' Helen sat down on a bench, fished out a jar of baby food, and began to feed you, singing you one of those little songs I couldn't understand — Hungarian or Romanian — while you ate. 'This is a beautiful place,' she said after a minute. 'Let's stay for a couple of days.'

"'We have to get back to Paris by Thursday night,' I objected.

"'Well, there is not much difference between staying here for a night and staying in Les Bains,' she said calmly. 'We can walk down tomorrow and catch the bus, if you think we need to go so soon.'

"I agreed, because she seemed so strange, but I felt some reluctance even as I went to discuss this with the tour-guide monk. He applied to his superior, who said that the hostel was empty and we were welcome. Between the simple lunch and simpler supper they gave us in a room off the kitchen, we wandered the rose gardens, walked in the steep orchard outside the walls, and sat in the back of the chapel to hear the monks sing mass while you slept on Helen's lap. A monk made up our cots with clean, coarse sheets. After you fell asleep on one of them, with ours pushed up close on either side so that you couldn't roll out, I lay reading and pretending not to watch Helen. She sat in her black cotton dress on the edge of her cot, looking out toward the night. I was thankful the curtains were closed, but eventually she got up and lifted them and stood gazing out. 'It must be dark,' I said, 'with no town near.'

"She nodded. 'It is very dark, but that is the way it has always been here, don't you think?'

"'Why don't you come to bed?' I reached over you and patted her cot.

"'All right,' she said, without any sign of protest. In fact, she smiled at me and bent over to kiss me before she lay down. I caught her in my arms for a moment, feeling the strength in her shoulders, the smooth skin of her neck. Then she stretched out and covered herself, and appeared to drift off long before I'd finished my chapter and blown out the lantern.

"I woke at dawn, feeling a sort of breeze go through the room. It was very quiet; you breathed next to me under your wool baby blanket, but Helen's cot was empty. I got up soundlessly and put on my shoes and jacket. The cloisters outside were dim, the courtyard gray, the fountain a shadowy mass. It occurred to me that it would take some time for the sun to reach this place, since it first had to climb above those huge eastern peaks. I looked all around for Helen without calling out, because I knew she liked to rise early and might be sitting deep in thought on one of the benches, waiting for dawn. There was no sign of her, however, and as the sky lightened a little I began to search more rapidly, going once to the bench where we'd sat the day before and once into the motionless chapel, with its ghostly smell of smoke.

"At last I began to call her name, quietly, and then louder, and then in alarm. After a few minutes, one of the monks came out of the refectory, where they must have been eating the first silent meal of the day, and asked if he could help me, if I needed something. I explained that my wife was missing, and he began to search with me. 'Perhaps madame went for a walk?' But there was no sign of her in the orchard or the parking area or the dark crypt. We looked everywhere as the sun came over the peaks, and then he went for some other monks, and one of them said he would take the car down to Les Bains to make inquiries. I asked him, on impulse, to bring the police back with him. Then I heard you crying in the hostel; I hurried to you, afraid you'd rolled off the cots, but you were just waking. I fed you quickly and kept you in my arms while we looked in the same places again.

"Finally I asked that all the monks be gathered and questioned. The abbot gave his consent readily and brought them into the cloisters. No one had seen Helen after we'd left the kitchens for the hostel the night before. Everyone was worried — 'La pauvre,' said one old monk, which sent a wave of irritation through me. I asked if anyone had spoken with her the day before, or noticed anything strange. 'We do not speak with women, as a general rule,' the abbot told me gently.

"But one monk stepped forward, and I recognized at once the old man whose job it was to sit in the crypt. His face was as tranquil and kind as it had been by lantern light in the crypt the day before, with that mild confusion I had noted then. 'Madame stopped to speak to me,' he said. 'I did not like to break our rule, but she was such a quiet, polite lady that I answered her questions.'

"'What did she ask you?' My heart had already been pounding, but now it began to race painfully.

"'She asked me who was buried there, and I explained that it was one of our first abbots, and that we revere his memory. Then she asked what great things he had done and I explained that we have a legend' — here he glanced at the abbot, who nodded for him to continue — 'we have a legend that he had a saintly life but was the unfortunate recipient of a curse in death, so that he rose from his coffin to do harm to the monks, and his body had to be purified. When it was purified, a white rose grew out of his heart to signify the Holy Mother's forgiveness.'

"'And this is why someone sits guard on him?' I asked wildly.

"The abbot shrugged. 'That is simply our tradition, to honor his memory.'

"I turned to the old monk, stifling a desire to throttle him and see his gentle face turn blue. 'Is this the story you told my wife?'

"'She asked me about our history, monsieur. I did not see anything wrong with answering her questions.'

"'And what did she say to you in response?'

"He smiled. 'She thanked me in her sweet voice and asked me my name, and I told her, Frère Kiril.' He folded his hands over his waist.

"It took me a moment to make sense of these sounds, the name made unfamiliar by a Francophone stress on the second syllable, by that innocent *frère*. Then I tightened my arms around you so I wouldn't drop you. 'Did you say your name is Kiril? Is that what you said? Spell it.'

"The astonished monk obliged.

"'Where did this name come from?' I demanded. I couldn't keep my voice from shaking. 'Is it your real name? Who are you?'

"The abbot stepped in, perhaps because the old man seemed genuinely perplexed. 'It is not his given name,' he explained. 'We all take names when we take our vows. There has always been a Kiril — someone always has this name — and a Frère Michel — this one, here —'

"'Do you mean to tell me,' I said, holding you fast, 'that there was a Brother Kiril before this one, and one before him?'

"'Oh, yes,' said the abbot, clearly puzzled now by my fierce questioning. 'As long in our history as anyone knows. We are proud of our traditions here — we do not like the new ways.'

"'Where did this tradition come from?' I was nearly shouting now.

"'We don't know that, monsieur,' the abbot said patiently. 'It has always been our way here.'

"I stepped close to him and put my nose almost against his. 'I want you to open the sarcophagus in the crypt,' I said.

"He stepped back, aghast. 'What are you saying? We can't do that.'

"'Come with me. Here —' I gave you quickly to the young monk who'd shown us around the day before. 'Please hold my daughter.' He took you, not as awkwardly as one might have expected, and held you in his arms. You began to cry. 'Come,' I said to the abbot. I drew him toward the crypt and he gestured for the other monks to stay behind. We went quickly down the steps. In the chill hole, where Brother Kiril had left two candles burning, I turned to the abbot. 'You don't have to tell anyone about this, but I must see inside that sarcophagus.' I paused for emphasis. 'If you don't help me I will bring the whole weight of the law down on your monastery.'

"He flashed me a look — fear? resentment? pity? — and went without speaking to one end of the sarcophagus. Together, we slid aside the heavy cover, just far enough to see inside. I held up one of the candles. The sarcophagus was empty. The abbot's eyes were huge, and he slid the lid back with a mighty shove. We regarded each other. He had a fine, shrewd, Gallic face that I might have liked immensely in another situation. 'Please do not tell the brothers about this,' he said in a low voice, and then he turned and climbed out of the crypt.

"I followed him, struggling to think what I should do next. I would take you and go back to Les Bains immediately, I decided, and make sure the police had actually been alerted. Maybe Helen had decided to return to Paris ahead of us —

why, I couldn't imagine — or even to fly home. I could feel a terrible pounding in my ears, my heart in my throat, blood rising in my mouth.

"By the time I stepped into the cloisters again, where the sun was now flooding the fountain and the birds were singing and lighting on the ancient paving, I knew what had happened. I had tried hard for an hour not to think it, but now I almost didn't need the news, the sight of two monks running toward the abbot, calling out. I remembered that these two had been dispatched to search outside the monastery walls, in the orchard, the vegetable gardens, the groves of dry trees, the outcroppings of rock. They had just come from the steep side — one of them pointed to the edge of the cloister where Helen and I had sat with you between us on a bench the day before, looking down into that measureless chasm. 'Lord Abbot!' one of them cried, as if he could not even begin to address me directly. 'Lord Abbot, there is blood on the rocks! Down there, below!'

"There are no words for such moments. I ran to the edge of the cloisters, clinging to you, feeling your petal-smooth cheek against my neck. The first of my tears was welling in my eyes, and it was hot and bitter beyond anything I'd ever known. I looked over the low wall. On an out-cropping of rock fifteen feet below, there was a scarlet splash — not large, but distinct in the morning sun. Below that the gulf yawned, the mists rose, the eagles hunted, the mountains fell to their very roots. I ran for the main gate, stumbled around the outer walls. The precipice was so steep that even if I hadn't been holding you I could not have climbed down safely to that first outcropping. I stood watching a wave of loss come through the celestial air toward me, through that beautiful morning. Then my grief reached me, an unspeakable fire."

Chapter 77

"I STAYED THERE THREE WEEKS, at Les Bains and the monastery, searching the cliffs and forests with the local police and with a team called in from Paris. My mother and father flew to France and spent hours playing with you, feeding you, pushing your carriage around the town — I think that was what they were doing. I filled out forms in slow little offices. I made useless phone calls, searching for French words to express the urgency of my loss. Day after day I scoured the woods at the foot of the cliff, sometimes in the company of a cold-faced detective and his team, sometimes alone with my tears.

"At first I wanted only to see Helen alive, walking toward me with her customary dry smile, but eventually I was reduced to a bitter half longing for her broken form, hoping to stumble on it somewhere in the rocks and brush. If I could take her body home — or to Hungary, I sometimes thought, although how I would get into Soviet-controlled Hungary was a conundrum — I would have something of her to honor, to bury, some way to finish this and be alone with my grief. I almost couldn't admit to myself that I wanted her body for another purpose, as well — to ascertain whether her death had been completely natural, or if she needed me to fulfill the bitter duty I had carried out for Rossi. Why could I not find her body? Sometimes, especially in the mornings, I felt she had simply fallen, that she would never have left us on purpose. I could believe then that she had an innocent, elemental grave somewhere in the woods, even if I would never find it. But by afternoon I was remembering only her depressions, her strange moods.

"I knew that I would grieve for the rest of my life, but this utter lack of even her body tormented me. The local doctor gave me a sedative, which I took at night so that I could sleep and build up strength to search the woods again the next day. When the police grew busy with other matters, I searched alone. Sometimes I turned up other relics in the underbrush: stones, crumbling chimneys, and once part of a shattered gargoyle — had it fallen as far as Helen? There were few gargoyles on the monastery walls now.

"At last my mother and father persuaded me

that I could not do this forever, that I should take you back to New York for a while, that I could always come back and look again. Police all over Europe had been alerted, through the French network; if Helen were alive — they said it soothingly — someone would find her. In the end, I gave up not because of these reassurances but because of the forest itself, the meteoric steepness of the cliffs, the denseness of the undergrowth, which tore my trousers and jacket as I pushed through it, the terrible size and height of the trees, the silence that surrounded me there whenever I stopped moving and groping and stood still for a few minutes.

"Before we left, I asked the abbot to say a blessing for Helen at the far end of the cloister, where she'd jumped. He made a service of it, gathering the monks around him, holding up to the vast air one ritual object after another — it didn't matter to me what they actually were — and chanting to an enormity that swallowed his voice at once. My father and mother stood with me, my mother wiping her eyes rapidly, and you squirmed in my arms. I held you fast; I had almost forgotten, in these weeks, how soft your dark hair was, how strong your protesting legs. Above all, you were alive; you breathed against my chin and your small arm went around my neck, companionably. When a sob shook me, you grabbed my hair, pulled my ear. Holding you, I vowed that I would try to recover some life, a life of some sort."

Chapter 78

BARLEY AND I SAT LOOKING at each other across my mother's postcards. Like my father's letters, they broke off without giving me much understanding of the present. The main thing, the thing that was burned into my brain, was their dates. She had written them after her death.

"He's gone to the monastery," I said.

"Yes," said Barley. I swept up the cards and put them on the marble top of the dressing table.

"Let's go," I said. I looked through my purse, took out the little silver knife in its sheath, and put it carefully in my pocket.

Barley leaned over and kissed my cheek. It surprised me. "Let's go," he said.

The road to Saint-Matthieu was longer than I'd remembered, dusty and hot even in late afternoon. There were no cabs in Les Bains — at least none in sight — so we set out on foot, walking swiftly through rolling farmland until we reached the edge of the forest. From there the road began to climb the peak. Entering the woods, with their mix of olive and pine, their towering oaks, was like entering a cathedral; it was dim and cool and we dropped our voices, although we hadn't been saying much. I was hungry, in the midst of my anxiety; we hadn't even waited for the maître d's coffee. Barley took off the cotton cap he was wearing and wiped his forehead.

"She wouldn't have survived such a fall," I said once through the constriction in my throat.

"No."

"My father never wondered — at least not in his letters — if she was pushed by someone."

"That's true," Barley said, replacing his cap.

I was silent for a while. Our feet on the uneven pavement — the road was still paved, at this point — made the only sound. I didn't want to say these things, but they welled up in me anyway. "Professor Rossi wrote that suicide puts a person at risk for becoming a — becoming —"

"I remember that," said Barley simply. I wished I hadn't spoken. The road wound high now. "Maybe someone will come by in a car," he added.

But no car appeared and we walked faster and faster, so that after a while we panted instead of speaking. The walls of the monastery took me by surprise when we came out of the woods around the last bend; I hadn't remembered that bend, or the sudden opening at the peak of the mountain, the huge evening all around us. I barely remembered the flat dusty area below the front gate, where today there were no cars parked. Where were the tourists? I wondered. A moment later we were close enough to read the sign — repairs, no visitors this month. It was not enough to slow our footsteps. "Come on," Barley said. He took my hand and I was deeply glad for it; my own had begun to tremble.

The front walls around the gate were ornamented with scaffolding now. A portable cement mixer — cement? here? — stood in our path. The wooden doors under the portal were firmly shut but not locked, we discovered, trying the iron ring with cautious hands. I didn't like breaking in; I didn't like the fact that there was no sign of my father. Maybe he was still down in Les Bains, or someplace else. Could he be searching the foot of the cliff as he had years ago, hundreds of feet below, out of our range of vision? I began to regret our impulse to come straight to the monastery. In addition, although true sunset was perhaps an hour away, the sun was dropping swiftly behind the Pyrénées to the west, slipping visibly behind the highest peaks. The woods we'd just come out of were already in deep gloom, and soon the last color of the day would drain from the monastery's walls.

We stepped inside, cautiously, and went up into the courtyard and cloisters. The red marble fountain bubbled audibly in the center. There were the delicate corkscrewed columns I remembered, the long cloisters, the rose garden at the end. The golden light was gone, replaced by shadows of a deep umber. Nobody was in sight. "Do you think we should go back to Les Bains?" I whispered to Barley.

He seemed about to answer when we caught a sound — chanting, from the church on the other side of the cloister. Its doors were shut, but we could hear distinctly the progress of a service inside, with intervals of silence. "They're all in there," Barley said. "Maybe your father is, too."

But I doubted this. "If he's here, he's probably gone down —" I paused and looked around the courtyard. It had been almost two years since my visit here with my father — my second visit, I now knew — and I couldn't remember for a moment where the entrance to the crypt was. Suddenly I saw the doorway, as if it had opened in the nearby wall of the cloisters without my noticing. I remembered now the peculiar beasts carved in stone around it: griffins and lions, drag-

ons and birds, strange animals I couldn't identify, hybrids of good and evil.

Barley and I both looked at the church, but
the doors stayed firmly shut, and we crept across
the courtyard to the crypt doorway. Standing
there a moment under the gaze of those frozen
beasts, I could see only the shadow into which
we would have to descend, and my heart shrank
inside me. Then I remembered that my father
might be down there — might, in fact, be in
some kind of terrible trouble. And Barley was
holding my hand still, lanky and defiant next to
me. I almost expected him to mutter something
about the odd things my family got into, but he
was taut beside me, poised as I was for anything.
"We don't have a light," he whispered.

"Well, we can't go into the church for one," I
pointed out unnecessarily.

"I've got my lighter." Barley took it out of his
pocket. I hadn't known he smoked. He flicked it
on for a second, held it above the steps, and we
descended together into darkness.

At first it was dark indeed, and we were feeling our way down the steepness of the ancient
steps, and then I saw a light flickering in the
depths of the vault — not Barley's lighter, which
he relit every few seconds — and I was terribly

afraid. That shadowy light was somehow worse than darkness. Barley gripped my hand until I felt the life draining out of it. The stairwell curved at the bottom and when we came around the last turn I remembered what my father had told me, that this had been the nave of the earliest church here. There was the abbot's great stone sarcophagus. There was the shadowy cross carved in the ancient apse, the low vaulting above us, one of the earliest surviving gestures of the Romanesque in all of Europe.

I took this in peripherally, however, because just then a shadow on the other side of the sarcophagus detached itself from deeper shadows and straightened up: a man holding a lantern. It was my father. His face looked ravaged in the shifting light. He saw us in the instant we saw him, I think, and he swore — "Jesus Christ!" We stared at each other. "What are you doing here?" he demanded in a low voice, looking from me to Barley, holding up the lantern in front of our faces. His tone was ferocious — full of anger, fear, love. I dropped Barley's hand and ran to my father, around the sarcophagus, and he caught me in his arms. "Jesus," he said, stroking my hair for a second. "This is the last place you should be."

"We read the chapter in the archive at Oxford," I whispered. "I was afraid you were —" I couldn't finish. Now that we had found him, and he was alive, and looked like himself, I was shaking all over.

"Get out of here," he said, and then caught me closer. "No. It's too late — I don't want you out there alone. We have a few more minutes before the sun sets. Here" — he thrust the light at me — "hold this, and you" — to Barley — "help me with the lid." Barley stepped forward at once, although I thought I saw his knees shaking, too, and he helped my father slide the lid slowly off the big sarcophagus. I saw then that my father had propped a long stake against the wall nearby. He must have been prepared for the sight of some long-sought horror in that stone coffin, but not for what he actually saw. I lifted the lantern for him, wanting but not wanting to look, and we all gazed down into the empty space, dust. "Oh, God," he said. It was a note I had never heard in his voice before, a sound of absolute despair, and I remembered that he had looked into this emptiness once before. He stumbled forward, and I heard the stake clatter on the stone. I thought he was going to cry, or tear his hair, bent over that empty grave, but he was motionless in his grief. "God," he said again, almost whispering. "I thought I had the right place, the right date, finally — I thought —"

He did not finish, because then there stepped from the shadows of the ancient transept, where no light pierced, a figure completely unlike anything any of us had ever seen. It was so strange a presence that I couldn't have screamed even if my throat hadn't immediately closed. My lantern illuminated its feet and legs, one arm and shoulder, but not the shadowed face, and I was too terrified to raise the light higher. I shrank closer to my father and so did Barley, so that we were all more or less behind the barrier of the empty sarcophagus.

The figure drew a little nearer and stopped, its face still shadowed. I could see by then that it had the form of a man, but he did not move like a human being. His feet were clad in narrow black boots indescribably different from any boots I'd ever seen, and they made a quiet padding sound on the stones when he stepped forward. Around them fell a cloak, or perhaps just a larger shadow, and he had powerful legs clothed in dark velvet. He was not as tall as my father, but his shoulders under the heavy cloak were broad, and something about his dim outline gave the impression of much greater height. The cloak must have had a hood, because his face was all shadow. After the first appalling second I could see his hands, white as bone against his dark clothing, with a jeweled ring on one finger.

He was so real, so close to us that I could not breathe; in fact, I began to feel that if I could only force myself to go nearer to him I would be able to breathe again, and then I began to long to go a little closer. I could feel the silver knife in my pocket, but nothing could have persuaded me to reach for it. Something glinted where his face must have been — reddish eyes? teeth, a smile? — and then, with a gush of language, he spoke. I call it a gush because I have never heard such a sound, a guttural rush of words that might have been many languages together or one strange language I had never heard. After a moment it resolved itself into words I could understand, and I had the sense that they were words I knew with my blood, not my ears.

Good evening. I congratulate you.

At this my father seemed to come to life again. I don't know how he found the strength to speak. "Where is she?" he cried. His voice trembled with fear and fury.

You are a remarkable scholar.

I don't know why, but at that moment, my

body seemed to move toward him slightly of its own volition. My father put his hand up at almost the same second and gripped my arm very hard, so that the lantern swayed and terrible shadows and lights danced around us. In that second of illumination, I saw something of Dracula's face, just a curve of drooping dark mustache, a cheekbone that could have been actual bone.

You have been the most determined of them all. Come with me and I will give you knowledge for ten thousand lifetimes.

I didn't know, still, how I could understand him, but I thought he was calling out to my father. "No!" I cried. I was so terrified at having actually spoken to that figure that I felt my consciousness sway inside me for a moment. I had the sense that the presence before us might be smiling, although his face was in darkness again.

Come with me, or let your daughter come.

"What?" my father asked me, almost inaudibly. It was at this moment that I knew he could not understand Dracula's words, and perhaps could not even hear Dracula. My father was answering my cry.

The figure appeared to think for a while in silence. He shifted his strange boots on the stone. There was something about his shape under the ancient clothes that was not only gruesome but also graceful, an old habit of power.

I have waited a long time for a scholar of your gifts.

The voice was soft now and infinitely dangerous. We stood in a darkness that seemed to flood us from that dark figure.

Come with me of your own volition.

Now my father seemed to lean toward him a little, his grip still on my arm. What he couldn't understand he could apparently feel. Dracula's shoulder twitched; he shifted his terrible weight from one leg to another. The presence of his body was like the actual presence of death, and yet he was alive and moving.

Do not keep me waiting. If you will not come I will come for you.

Now my father seemed to gather all of his strength. "Where is she?" he shouted. "Where is Helen?"

The figure rose up and I saw an angry gleam of teeth, bone, eye, the shadow of the hood swinging over his face again, his inhuman hand clenching at the margin of the light. I had the terrible sense of an animal crouched to pounce, of a leaping toward us, even before he moved, and then there was a footfall on the shadowy stairs behind him, and a flash of motion that we felt in the air because we could not see it. I raised the lantern with a scream that seemed to me to come from outside myself, and I saw Dracula's face — which I can never forget — and then, to my utter astonishment, I saw another figure, standing just behind him. This second person had apparently just come down the stairs, a dark and inchoate form like his, but bulkier, the outline of a living man. The man was moving rapidly, and he had something bright in his raised hand. But Dracula had sensed his presence already, and turned with his arm out, and pushed the man away. Dracula's strength must have been prodigious, because suddenly the powerful human figure collided with the crypt wall. We heard a silent thud, then a groan. Dracula was turning this way and that in a kind of horrible distraction, first for us, and then toward the groaning man.

Suddenly there was again the sound of footsteps on the stairs — light ones, this time, accompanied by the beam of a strong flashlight. Dracula had been caught off balance — he turned too late, a blur of darkness. Someone searched the scene swiftly with the light, raised an arm, and fired once.

Dracula did not move as I'd expected a moment earlier, hurtling over the sarcophagus toward us; instead he was falling, first backward, so that his chiseled, pale face surfaced again for a moment, and then forward and forward, until there was a thud on the stone, a breaking sound like flung bone. He lay convulsed for a second and at last was still. Then his body seemed to be turning to dust, to nothing, even his ancient clothes decaying around him, sere in the confusing light.

My father dropped my arm and ran toward the flashlight's beam, skirting the mass on the floor. "Helen," he called — or maybe he wept her name, or whispered it.

But Barley was pushing forward, too, and he had caught up my father's lantern. A large man lay on the flagstones, his dagger beside him. "Oh, Elsie," said a broken English voice. His head oozed a little dark blood, and even as we watched in paralyzing horror, his eyes grew still.

Barley threw himself into the dust next to that shattered form. He seemed to be actually strangling with surprise and grief. "Master James?"

Chapter 79

THE HOTEL IN LES BAINS boasted a high-ceilinged parlor with a fireplace, and the maître d' had lit a fire there and stubbornly closed the parlor doors against other guests. "Your trip to the monastery has tired you" was all he had said, setting a bottle of cognac near my father, and glasses — five glasses, I noted, as if our missing companion were still there to drink with us — but I saw from the look that my father exchanged with him that much more than that had passed between them.

The maître d' had been on the phone all evening, and he had somehow made things right with the police, who had questioned us only in the hotel and released us under his benevolent eye. I suspected he'd also taken care of calling a morgue or a funeral parlor, whatever one used in a French village. Now that everyone official was gone, I sat on the uncomfortable damask sofa with Helen, who reached over to stroke my hair every few minutes, and tried not to imagine Master James's kind face and solid form inert under a sheet. My father sat in a deep chair by the fire and gazed at her, at us. Barley had put his long legs up on an ottoman and was trying, I thought, not to stare at the cognac, until my father recollected himself and poured us each a glass. Barley's eyes were red with silent weeping, but he seemed to want to be left alone. When I looked at him, my own eyes filled with tears for a moment, uncontrollably.

My father looked across at Barley, and I thought for a moment that he was going to cry, too. "He was very brave," my father said quietly. "You know that his attack made it possible for Helen to shoot as she did. She would not have been able to shoot through the heart like that if the monster had not been distracted. I think James must have known in the last moments what a difference he had made. And he avenged the person he had loved best — and many others." Barley nodded, still unable to speak, and there was a little silence among us.

"I promised I would tell you everything when we could sit quietly," Helen said at last, setting down her glass.

"You're sure you wouldn't like me to leave you alone?" Barley spoke reluctantly.

Helen laughed, and I was surprised by the melody of her laugh, so different from her speaking voice. Even in that room half full of grief, her laugh did not seem out of place. "No, no, my dear," she said to Barley. "We can't do without you." I loved her accent, that harsh yet sweet English of hers that I thought I already knew from so long ago I couldn't remember the time. She was a tall, spare woman in a black dress, an outdated sort of dress, with a coil of graying hair around her head. Her face was striking — lined, worn, her eyes youthful. The sight of her shocked me every time I turned my head — not only because she was there, real, but because I had always imagined only the young Helen. I had never included in my imagination all her years away from us.

"Telling will take a long, long time," she said softly, "but I can say a few things now, at least. First, that I am sorry. I have caused you such pain, Paul, I know." She looked at my father across the firelight. Barley stirred, embarrassed, but she stopped him with a firm gesture. "I caused myself an even greater pain. Second, I should have told you this already, but now our daughter" — her smile was sweet and tears gleamed in her eyes — "our daughter and our friends can be my witnesses. I am alive, not undead. He never reached me a third time."

I wanted to look at my father, but I couldn't bring myself even to turn my head. It was his private moment. I heard, though, that he did not sob aloud.

She stopped and seemed to draw a breath. "Paul, when we visited Saint-Matthieu and I learned about their traditions — the abbot who had risen from the dead and Brother Kiril, who guarded him — I was filled with despair, and also with a terrible curiosity. I felt that it could not be coincidence that I had wanted to see the place, had longed for it. Before we went to France, I had been doing more research in New York — without telling you, Paul — hoping to find Dracula's second hiding place and to avenge my father's death. But I had never seen anything about Saint-Matthieu. My longing to go there began only when I read about it in your guidebook. It was just a longing, with no scholarly basis."

She looked around at us, her beautiful profile drooping. "I had taken up my research again in New York because I felt that I had been the cause of my father's death — through my desire to outshine him, to reveal his betrayal of my mother — and I could not bear the thought. Then I began to feel that it was my evil blood — Dracula's blood — that had caused me to do this, and I realized that I had passed this blood to my baby, even if I seemed to have healed from the touch of the undead myself."

She paused to stroke my cheek and to take my hand in hers. I quivered under her touch, the closeness of this strange, familiar woman leaning against my shoulder on the divan. "I felt more and more unworthy, and when I heard Brother Kiril's explanation of the legend at Saint-Matthieu, I felt that I would never be able to rest until I knew more. I believed that if I could find Dracula and exterminate him I might be completely well again, a good mother, a person with a new life.

"After you fell asleep, Paul, I went out to the cloisters. I had considered going into the crypt again with my gun, trying to open the sarcophagus, but I thought I could not do it alone. While I was trying to decide whether or not to wake you, to beg you to help me, I sat on the cloister bench, looking over the cliff. I knew I should not be there alone, but I was drawn to the place. There was beautiful moonlight, and mist creeping along the walls of the mountains."

Helen's eyes had grown strangely wide. "As I sat there, I felt the crawling of the skin on my back, as if something stood just behind me. I turned quickly, and on the other side of the cloister, where the moonlight could not fall, I seemed to see a dark figure. His face was in shadow, but I could feel, rather than see, burning eyes upon me. It was only the work of a moment more before he would spread his wings and reach me, and I was completely alone on the parapet. Suddenly I seemed to hear voices, agonizing voices in my own head that told me I could never overcome Dracula, that this was his world, not mine. They told me to jump while I was still myself, and I stood up like a person in a dream and jumped."

She sat very straight now, looking into the fire, and my father drew his hand over his face. "I wanted to fall free, like Lucifer, like an angel, but I had not seen those rocks. I fell on them instead and cut my head and arms, but there was a large cushion of grass there, too, and the fall did not kill me or break my bones. After some hours, I think, I woke to the cold night, and felt blood seeping around my face and neck, and saw the moon setting and the drop below. My God, if I had rolled instead of fainting —" She paused. "I knew I could not explain to you what I had tried to do, and the shame of it came over me like a kind of madness. I felt I could never be worthy, after that, of you or our daughter. When I could stand, I got up, and I found that I had not bled so much. And although I was very sore, I had not broken anything and I could feel that he had not swooped down upon me — he must have given me up for lost, too, when I jumped. I was terribly weak and it was hard for me to walk, but I went around the monastery walls and down the road, in the dark."

I thought my father might weep again, but he was quiet, his eyes never leaving hers.

"I went out into the world. It was not so hard to do. I had brought my purse with me — out of habit, I suppose, and because I had my gun and my silver bullets in it. I remember almost laughing when I found the purse still on my arm, on the precipice. I had money in it, too, a lot of money in the lining, and I used it carefully. My mother always carried all her money, too. I suppose it was the way the peasants in her village did things. She never trusted banks. Much later, when I needed more, I drew from our account in New York and put some in a Swiss bank. Then I left Switzerland as quickly as I could, in case you should try to trace me, Paul. Ah, forgive me!" she cried out suddenly, tightening her grip on my fingers, and I knew she meant her absence, not the money.

My father clenched his hands together. "That withdrawal gave me hope for a few months, or at least put a question into my mind, but my bank could not trace it. I got the money back." But not you, he could have added, and didn't. His face shone, weary and glad.

Helen dropped her eyes. "In any case, I found a place to stay for a few days, away from Les Bains, until my cuts could heal. I hid myself until I could go out into the world."

Her fingers strayed to her throat and I saw the small white scar I had already noticed many times. "I knew in my bones that Dracula had not forgotten about me, and that he might search for me again. I filled my pockets with garlic and my mind with strength. I kept my gun with me, my dagger, my crucifix. Everywhere I went I stopped in the village churches and asked for a blessing, although sometimes even entering their doors made my old wound throb. I was careful to keep my neck covered. Eventually I cut my hair short and colored it, changed my clothes, wore dark glasses. For a long time I stayed away from cities, and then I began little by little to go to the archives where I had always wanted to do my research.

"I was thorough. I found him everywhere I

went — in Rome in the 1620s, in Florence under the Medici, in Madrid, in Paris during the Revolution. Sometimes it was the report of a strange plague, sometimes an outbreak of vampirism in a great cemetery — Père Lachaise, for example. He seemed always to have liked scribes, archivists, librarians, historians — anyone who handled the past through books. I tried to deduce from his movements where his new tomb was, where he had hidden himself after we opened his tomb at Sveti Georgi, but I couldn't discover any pattern. I thought that once I found him, once I killed him, I would come back and tell you how safe the world had become. I would earn you. I lived in fear that he would find me before I could find him. And everywhere I went I missed you — oh, I was so lonely."

She picked up my hand again and caressed it like a fortune-teller, and I felt, in spite of myself, a surge of anger — all those years without her. "Finally I thought that even if I was not worthy, I wanted to have just a glimpse of you. Both of you. I had read about your foundation in the papers, Paul, and I knew you were in Amsterdam. It was not hard to find you, or to sit in a café near your office, or to follow you on a trip or two — very carefully — very, very carefully. I never let myself see either of you face-to-face, for fear you would see me. I came and went. If my research was going well, I allowed myself a visit to Amsterdam and followed you from there. Then one day — in Italy, at Monteperduto — I saw him on the piazza. He was following you, too, watching you. That was when I realized he had become strong enough to go out in broad daylight sometimes. I knew that you were in danger, but I thought that if I went to you, to warn you, I might bring the danger closer. After all, he might be looking for me, not you, or he might be trying to make me lead him to you. It was an agony. I knew that you must be doing some kind of research again — that you must be interested in him again, Paul — to attract his notice. I could not decide what to do."

"It was me — my fault," I murmured, squeezing her plain, lined hand. "I found the book."

She looked at me for a moment, her head to one side. "You are a historian," she said after a moment. It wasn't a question. Then she sighed. "For several years, I had been writing postcards to you, my daughter — without sending them, of course. One day, I thought that I could communicate with the two of you from a distance, to let you know I was alive without letting anyone else see me. I sent them to Amsterdam, to your house, in a package addressed to Paul."

This time I turned to my father in amazement and anger. "Yes," he told me sadly. "I felt I could not show them to you, could not upset you without being able to find your mother for you. You can imagine what that period was like for me." I could. I remembered suddenly his terrible fatigue in Athens, the evening I'd seen him looking half dead at the desk in his room. But he smiled at us, and I realized that he might now smile every day.

"Ah." She smiled too. There were deep lines around her mouth, I saw, and the corners of her eyes were creased.

"And I began looking for you — and for him." His smile grew grave.

She was gazing at him. "And then I saw I must give up my research and simply follow him following you. I saw you sometimes, and saw you doing your own research again — watched you going into libraries, Paul, or coming out of them, and how I wished I could tell you all I had learned myself. Then you went to Oxford. I hadn't been to Oxford before in the course of my search, although I'd read that they had an outbreak of vampirism there in the late medieval period. And in Oxford you left a book open —"

"He shut it when he saw me," I put in.

"And me," said Barley with his lightning grin. It was the first time he'd spoken, and I was relieved to see that he could still look cheerful.

"Well, the first time he looked at it, he forgot to close it." Helen almost winked at us.

"You're right," said my father. "Come to think of it, I did forget."

Helen turned to him with her lovely smile. "Do you know I had never seen that book before? *Vampires du Moyen Age?*"

"A classic," my father said. "But a very rare one."

"I think Master James must have seen it, too," Barley put in slowly. "You know, I saw him in there just after we surprised you at your research, sir." My father looked perplexed. "Yes," Barley said. "I'd left my mackintosh on the main floor of the library, and I went back for it less than an hour later. And I saw Master James coming out of the niche in the balcony, but he didn't see me. I thought he looked awfully worried, sort of cross and distracted. I thought about that when I decided to call him, too."

"You called Master James?" I was surprised, but past feeling indignant. "When? Why did you do that?"

"I called him from Paris because I remembered something," Barley said simply, stretching his legs. I wanted to go over and twine my arm around his neck, but not in front of my parents. He looked at me. "I told you I was trying to remember something, on the train, something about Master James, and when we got to Paris I remembered it. I'd seen a letter on his desk once when he was putting away some papers — an envelope, actually, and I liked the stamp on it, so I looked a little more closely.

"It was from Turkey, and it was old — that's what made me look at the stamp — well, it was postmarked twenty years ago, from a Professor Bora, and I thought to myself that I wanted to have a big desk someday, and get letters from all over the world. The name *Bora* stuck with me, even at the time — it sounded so exotic. I didn't open it or read the letter, of course," Barley added hastily. "I wouldn't have done that."

"Of course not." My father snorted softly, but I thought his eyes shone with affection.

"Well, as we were getting off the train in Paris, I saw an old man on the platform, a Muslim, I guess, in a dark red hat with a long tassel, and a long robe, like an Ottoman pasha, and I suddenly remembered that letter. Then your father's story hit me again — you know, the name of the Turkish professor" — he gave me a somber look — "and I went to the phone. I realized Master James must still be in on this hunt, in some way."

"Where was I?" I asked jealously.

"In the bathroom, I suppose. Girls are always in the bathroom." He might as well have blown me a kiss, but not in front of the others. "Master James was livid with me on the phone, but when I told him what was going on, he said I was in his good graces forever." Barley's red lips trembled a little. "I didn't dare ask him what he meant to do, but now we know."

"Yes, we do," my father echoed sadly. "He must have done the calculation from that old book, too, and figured out that it was sixteen years to the week since Dracula's last visit to Saint-Matthieu. Then he'd certainly have realized where I was going. In fact, he was probably checking up on me when he went up to the rare-book niche — he was after me several times in Oxford to tell him what was wrong, worried about my health and spirits. I didn't want to drag him into it, knowing what a risk was involved."

Helen nodded. "Yes. I think I must have been there just before he was. I found the open book and did the calculation for myself, and then I heard someone on the stairs and slipped out in the other direction. Like our friend, I saw that you would go to Saint-Matthieu, Paul, to try to find me and to find that fiend, and I traveled as fast as I could. But I didn't know which train you would take, and I certainly didn't know our daughter would try to follow you, too."

"I saw you," I said in wonder. She gazed at me, and we let it drop for the moment. There would be so much time to talk. I could see she was tired, that we were all tired to the bone, that we could not even begin to say to one another tonight what a triumph this had been. Was the world safer because we were all together, or because he was finally gone from it? I looked into a future I had never known about before. Helen would live with us and blow out the candles in the dining room. She would come to my graduation from high school and my first day at university and help me dress for my wedding, if I ever married. She would read aloud to us in the front room after dinner, she would rejoin the world and teach again, she would take me to buy shoes and blouses, she would walk with her arm around my waist.

I could not know then that she would also drift from us at times, not speaking for hours, fingering her neck, or that a wasting illness would take her away for good nine years later — long before we had gotten used to having her back, although we might never have gotten used to that, might never have tired of the reprieve of her presence. I couldn't foresee that our last gift would be knowing that she rested in peace, when it could have been otherwise, and that this certainty would be both heartbreaking and curative for us. If I had been able to foresee these things at all, I might have known that my father would disappear for a day after her funeral, and that the little dagger in our parlor cabinet would go with him, and that I would never, never ask him about it.

But at that fireside in Les Bains, the years we would have with her stretched ahead of us in endless benediction. They began a few minutes later when my father rose and kissed me, shook Barley's hand with momentary fervor, and drew Helen from the divan. "Come," he said, and she leaned on him, her story spent for now, her face weary, joyful. He was gathering her hands in his. "Come up to bed."

Epilogue

A COUPLE OF YEARS AGO, a strange opportunity presented itself to me while I was in Philadelphia for a conference, an international gathering of medieval historians. I had never been to Philadelphia before and I was intrigued by the contrast between our meetings, which delved into a feudal and monastic past, and the lively metropolis around us, with its more recent history of Enlightenment republicanism and revolution. The view from my fourteenth-floor hotel room downtown showed an odd mix of skyscrapers and blocks of seventeenth- or eighteenth-century houses, which looked like miniatures next to them.

During our few hours of leisure, I slipped away from the endless talk of Byzantine artifacts to see some real ones in the magnificent art museum. There I picked up a pamphlet for a small literary museum and library downtown, whose name I'd heard years before from my father, and whose collection I had reason to know about. It was as important a site for Dracula scholars — whose numbers, of course, have swelled consid-

1159

erably since my father's first investigations — as many archives in Europe. There, I recalled, a researcher might see Bram Stoker's notes for *Dracula,* culled from sources at the British Museum Library, and an important medieval pamphlet, as well. The opportunity was irresistible. My father had always wanted to visit this collection; I would spend an hour there for his sake. He had been killed by a land mine in Sarajevo more than ten years before, working to mediate Europe's worst conflagration in decades. I hadn't known for nearly a week; the news, when it found me, had left me marooned in silence for a year. I still missed him every day, sometimes every hour.

That was how I came to find myself in a small, climate-controlled room in one of the city's nineteenth-century brownstones, handling documents that breathed not only a distant past but also the urgency of my father's researches. The windows looked out on a couple of feathery street trees and across to more brownstones, their elegant facades unsullied by any modern additions. There was only one other scholar in the small library that morning, an Italian woman who whispered into her cell phone for a few minutes before opening someone's handwritten diaries — I tried not to crane at them — and beginning to read. When I had settled myself with a notebook and a light sweater against the air-conditioning, the librarian brought me first Stoker's papers and then a small cardboard box bound with ribbon.

Stoker's notes were a pleasant diversion, a study in chaotic note taking. Some were written in a cramped hand, some typed on ancient onionskin. Among them lay newspaper clippings about mysterious events and leaves from his personal calendar. I thought how my father would have enjoyed this, how he would have smiled over Stoker's innocent dabbling in the occult. But after half an hour I put them carefully aside and turned to the other box. It held one slim volume, bound in a neat, probably nineteenth-century cover — forty pages printed on nearly unblemished fifteenth-century parchment, a medieval treasure, a miracle of movable type. The frontispiece was a woodcut, a face I knew from my long travail, its great eyes, wide and yet somehow sly, looking piercingly out at me, the heavy mustache drooping over a square jaw, the long nose fine and yet menacing, the sensual lips just visible.

It was a pamphlet from Nuremberg, printed

in 1491, and it told of Dracole Waida's crimes, his cruelty, his bloodthirsty feasts. I could make out, from their familiarity to me, the first lines of the medieval German: "In the Year of Our Lord 1456, Drakula did many terrible and curious things." The library had provided a translation sheet, in fact, and there I reread with a shudder some of Dracula's crimes against humanity. He had had people roasted alive, he had flayed them, he had buried them up to their necks, he had impaled infants on their mothers' breasts. My father had examined other such pamphlets, of course, but he would have valued this one for its astounding freshness, the crispness of its parchment, its nearly perfect condition. After five centuries, it looked newly printed. Its very purity unnerved me, and after a while I was glad to put it away and tie the ribbon again, wondering a little why I'd wanted to see the thing in person. That arrogant stare fixed me until I shut the book on it.

I collected my belongings, then, with a feeling of pilgrimage completed, and thanked the kind librarian. She seemed pleased by my visit; this pamphlet was one of her favorite items among their holdings; she had written an article on it herself. We parted with cordial words and a handshake and I went downstairs to the gift shop, and from there out to the warm street, with its smells of car exhaust and lunch to be had somewhere nearby. The very contrast between the purified air inside the museum and the bustle of the city outside made the oak door behind me look forbiddingly sealed, so that it startled me all the more to see the librarian hurrying out of it. "I think you forgot these," she said. "Glad I caught you." She gave me the self-conscious smile of one who returns to you a treasure — wouldn't want to lose this — your wallet, your keys, a fine bracelet.

I thanked her and took the book and notebook she handed me, startled again, nodding my acquiescence, and she disappeared into the old building as quickly as she'd descended on me. The notebook was mine, certainly, although I thought I'd packed it safely in my briefcase before leaving. The book was — I can't say now what I actually thought it was, in that first moment, only that the cover was a rubbed old velvet, very, very old, and that it was both familiar and unfamiliar under my hand. The parchment inside had none of the freshness of the pamphlet I'd examined in the library — despite the emptiness of its pages, it reeked of centuries of handling. The ferocious single image at the center was open in my hand before I could stop myself, closed again before I could look at it long.

I stood perfectly still on the street, while a feeling of unreality broke over me; the cars, passing, were just as solid as before, a car horn honked somewhere, a man with a dog on a leash was trying to get around me, between me and the ginkgo tree. I looked quickly up at the museum windows, thinking of the librarian, but they reflected only the houses opposite. No lace curtain moved there, either, and no door closed quietly as I looked around. Nothing was wrong on this street.

In my hotel room, I set my book on the glass-topped table and washed my face and hands. Then I went to the windows and stood looking out over the city. Down the block I could see the patrician ugliness of Philadelphia City Hall, with its statue of peace-loving William Penn balanced on top. From here the parks were green squares of treetops. Light glanced off the bank towers. Far to my left I could see the federal building that had been bombed the month before, the red-and-yellow cranes grappling with the debris in its center, and could hear the roar of rebuilding.

But it was not this scene that filled my gaze. I

was thinking, in spite of myself, of another one, which I seemed to have watched before. I leaned against the window, feeling the summer sun, feeling oddly safe despite my great height from the ground, as if unsafety lay for me in a completely different realm.

I was imagining a clear autumn morning in 1476, a morning just cool enough to make mist rise from the surface of the lake. A boat runs aground at the edge of the island, below the walls and domes with their iron crosses. There is the gentle scraping of a wooden bow on rocks, and two monks hurry out from beneath the trees to pull it ashore. The man who steps out of it is alone, and the feet he sets on the stone embankment are clad in finely made boots of red leather, each with a sharp spur clamped to it. He is shorter than both of the young monks but seems to tower over them. He is dressed in purple and red damask under a long black velvet cloak, which is pinned across his broad chest with an elaborate brooch. His hat is a pointed cone, black with red feathers fastened to the front. His hand, heavily scarred across the back, fiddles with the short sword at his belt. His eyes are green, preternaturally large and wide-set, his mouth and nose cruel, and his black hair and mustache show coarser white strands.

The abbot has been notified already and hurries to meet him under the trees. "We are honored, my lord," he says, extending his hand. Dracula kisses his ring and the abbot makes the sign of the cross over him. "Bless you, my son," he adds, as if in spontaneous thanksgiving. He knows that the prince's appearance is just short of miraculous; Dracula has probably crossed Turkish holdings to get here. This is not the first time the abbot's patron has appeared as if by divine transport. The abbot has heard that the metropolitan at Curtea de Argeş will soon reinvest Dracula as ruler of Wallachia, and then, no doubt, the Dragon will at last wrest all Wallachia from the Turks. The abbot's fingers touch his prince's broad forehead in benediction. "We thought the worst when you did not come in the spring. God be praised."

Dracula smiles but says nothing, giving the abbot a long look. They have argued about death before, the abbot recalls; Dracula has asked the abbot several times in confession whether he, the holy man, thinks every sinner will be admitted to paradise if he truly repents. The abbot is particularly concerned that his patron be given the last rites, when the moment comes, although he is afraid to tell him so. At the abbot's gentle insistence, however, Dracula has had himself rebaptized in the true faith to show his repentance for his temporary conversion to the heretical Western church. The abbot has forgiven him everything, privately — everything. Has not Dracula devoted his life to holding back the infidels, the monstrous sultan who is battering down all the walls of Christendom? But he wonders just as privately what the Almighty will mete out to this strange man. He hopes Dracula will not bring up the subject of paradise and is relieved when the prince asks to see what progress they have made in his absence. They walk together around the edge of the monastery courtyard, the chickens scattering before them. Dracula surveys the newly completed buildings and the lustily sprouting vegetable gardens with a look of satisfaction, and the abbot hastens to show him the walkways they have built since his last visit.

In the abbot's chamber they drink tea and then Dracula sets a velvet bag before the abbot. "Open it," he says, smoothing his mustache. His muscular legs are braced far apart in his chair;

the ever-present sword still hangs at his side. The abbot wishes Dracula would give his gifts with more humility, but he quietly opens the sack. "Turkish treasure," Dracula says, his smile broadening. One of his lower teeth is missing, but the rest are strong and white. Inside the bag the abbot finds jewels of infinite beauty, large clusters of emeralds and rubies, heavy gold rings and brooches of an Ottoman make, and among them other items, including a fine cross of chased gold with dark sapphires. The abbot doesn't want to know where these have come from. "We will furnish the sacristy and put in a new baptismal font," Dracula says. "I want you to order artisans from wherever you want. This will easily pay for it, with enough left over for my grave."

"Your grave, my lord?" The abbot looks respectfully at the floor.

"Yes, Eminence." His hand goes to his sword hilt again. "I have been thinking about it and I would like to be placed before the altar, with a marble stone above. You will give me the finest sung services, of course. Bring in a second choir for that." The abbot bows, but he is unnerved by the man's face, the glint of calculation in the green eyes. "In addition, I have some requests, which you will remember carefully. I want my portrait painted on the gravestone, but no cross."

The abbot looks up, startled. "No cross, my lord?"

"No cross," the prince says firmly. He looks the abbot full in the face, and for a moment the abbot does not dare to ask more. But he is this man's spiritual adviser, and after another moment he speaks up. "Every grave is marked with the suffering of our Savior, and yours must have the same honor."

Dracula's face darkens. "I do not plan to subject myself long to death," he says in a low voice.

"There is only one way in which to escape death," the abbot says bravely, "and that is through the Redeemer, if He grants us His grace."

Dracula stares at him for a few minutes and the abbot tries not to look away. "Perhaps," he says finally. "But recently I met a man, a merchant who has traveled to a monastery in the West. He said there is a place in Gaul, the oldest church in their part of the world, where some of the Latin monks have outwitted death by secret means. He offered to sell me their secrets, which he has inscribed in a book."

The abbot shudders. "God preserve us from

such heresies," he says hastily. "I am certain, my son, that you refused this temptation."

Dracula smiles. "You know I am fond of books."

"There is only one true Book, and that is the one we must love with all our hearts and all our souls," the abbot says, but at the same moment he is unable to take his eyes off the prince's scarred hand and the inlaid hilt with which it plays. Dracula wears a ring on his little finger; the abbot well knows, without looking closer, the ferociously curling symbol on it.

"Come." To the abbot's relief, Dracula has apparently tired of this debate, and he stands up suddenly, vigorously. "I want to see your scribes. I will have a special job for them soon."

They go together into the tiny scriptorium, where three of the monks sit copying manuscripts, according to the old way, and one carves letters to print a page of the life of Saint Anthony. The press itself stands in one corner. It is the first printing press in Wallachia, and Dracula runs a proud hand over it, a heavy, square hand. The oldest of the scriptorium monks stands at a table near the press, chiseling a block of wood. Dracula leans over it. "And what will this be, Father?"

"Saint Mikhail slaying the dragon, Excellency,"

the old monk murmurs. The eyes he raises are cloudy, occluded by sagging white brows.

"Rather have the Dragon slaying the infidel," Dracula says, chuckling.

The monk nods, but the abbot shudders inwardly, again.

"I have a special commission for you," Dracula tells him. "I shall leave a sketch for it with the lord abbot."

In the sunshine of the courtyard, he pauses. "I will stay for the service, and take communion with you." He turns a smile on the abbot. "Do you have a bed for me in one of the cells tonight?"

"As always, my lord. This house of God is your home."

"And now let us go up in my tower." The abbot knows well this practice of his patron; Dracula always likes to survey the lake and surrounding shores from the highest point in the church, as if to check for enemies. He has good reason, thinks the abbot. The Ottomans seek his head from year to year, the king of Hungary bears him no small malice, his own boyars hate and fear him. Is there anyone who is not his enemy, apart from the residents of this island? The abbot follows him slowly up the winding stair, bracing himself for the ringing of the bells, which will soon begin, and which sounds very loud up here.

The dome of the tower has long openings on every side. When the abbot reaches the top, Dracula is already standing at his favorite post, staring across the water, his hands clasped behind him in a characteristic gesture of thought, of planning. The abbot has seen him stand this way in front of his warriors, directing the strategy for the next day's raid. He looks not at all like a man in constant peril — a leader whose death could occur at any hour, who should be pondering every moment the question of his salvation. He looks instead, the abbot thinks, as if all the world is before him.

About the Author

Elizabeth Kostova graduated from Yale and holds an MFA from the University of Michigan, where she won the Hopwood Award for the Novel-in-Progress.